THE COUNT OF MONTE CRISTO

THE COUNT
OF
MONTE CRISTO

By
ALEXANDRE DUMAS

Author of
"The Three Musketeers," etc.

WARD, LOCK & CO., LIMITED
LONDON AND MELBOURNE

MADE IN ENGLAND
Printed in Great Britain by Butler & Tanner Ltd., Frome and London

CONTENTS

CONTENTS

CONTENTS

7

CHAP.		PAGE
LXVII	The Office of the Procureur du Roi	484
LXVIII	A Summer Ball	489
LXIX	The Inquiry	492
LXX	The Ball	497
LXXI	Bread and Salt	501
LXXII	Madame de Saint Méran	503
LXXIII	The Promise	509
LXXIV	The Villefort Family Vault	521
LXXV	Procès-verbal	525
LXXVI	Progress of M. Cavalcanti the Younger	530
LXXVII	Haïdée	534
LXXVIII	Janina	545
LXXIX	The Lemonade	555
LXXX	The Accusation	562
LXXXI	The Room of the Retired Baker	565
LXXXII	The Burglary	573
LXXXIII	The Hand of God	580
LXXXIV	Beauchamp	583
LXXXV	The Journey	586
LXXXVI	The Trial	590
LXXXVII	The Challenge	596
LXXXVIII	The Insult	600
LXXXIX	The Night	605
XC	The Meeting	609
XCI	The Mother and Son	615
XCII	The Suicide	619
XCIII	Valentine	623
XCIV	The Confession	626
XCV	The Father and Daughter	631
XCVI	The Contract	635
XCVII	The Departure for Belgium	640
XCVIII	The Hotel of the Bell and Bottle	644
XCIX	The Law	650
C	The Apparition	654
CI	The Serpent	658
CII	Valentine	660
CIII	Maximilian	663
CIV	Danglars' Signature	667

8   CONTENTS

....

THE COUNT OF MONTE CRISTO

CHAPTER I

MARSEILLES—THE ARRIVAL

ON the 24th of February, 1815, the watch-tower of Notre Dame
de la Garde signalled the three-masted ship *Pharaon*, coming
from Smyrna, Trieste, and Naples.

One of the pilots of the coast at once set out from the port,
skirted the Château d'If, and finally boarded the ship between
Cape Morgion and the Isle of Rion.

Immediately the platform of Fort Saint-Jean was covered
with gazers; for the arrival of a ship is always an important
affair at Marseilles, particularly when the vessel, as in the case
of the *Pharaon*, has been built, rigged, and laden in the dock-
yards of old Phocée, and belongs to a shipowner of the city.

In the meantime the ship made way; it had safely passed
the strait between the Isle of Calasareigne and the Isle of Jaros;
it had doubled Pomègue, and it now approached the harbour
under topsails, jib, and foresail, but so slowly and solemnly that
the spectators began asking each other what accident could
have occurred on board. Experts in navigation could, however,
see at a glance that, if any mishap had arisen, it was not connected with the ship herself, for as she bore down she appeared
to be in perfect condition, with anchor ready to be dropped,
and bowsprit shrouds hung loose, while near the pilot stood a
young man, who superintended every movement of the vessel,
and repeated all the pilot's orders. The vague uneasiness which
hung over the spectators had so much affected one of their
number that he jumped into a small boat and was rowed off
to meet the *Pharaon*, which he reached opposite the creek of La
Réserve.

The young sailor left his post by the side of the pilot, as soon
as he saw the approach of the man in the boat, and advanced

to the side of the vessel, hat in hand. He was a young fellow of from eighteen to twenty years of age—tall, slender, and with fine dark eyes and ebony locks, and the resolute expression of one inured to danger from infancy.

" Ah ! is that you, Dantès ? " cried the man in the boat. " What can be the matter ? and why is there this air of melancholy on board ? "

" A great misfortune, Monsieur Morrel ! " answered the young man, " and for me particularly. We lost our gallant captain, Leclère, off Civita Vecchia."

" And the cargo ? " demanded the shipowner quickly.

" Has arrived safely, Monsieur Morrel. I think you may rest satisfied on that score ; but our poor captain——"

" How did it come about ? " inquired the shipowner, his manner visibly relieved ; " what happened to the brave captain? "

" He died of brain fever, in terrible suffering." Then turning to the men on deck, he called, " Holla there ! all hands to moor ship ! "

The young seaman cast a glance to see that his orders were being executed, and then turned again to his interlocutor.

" And what caused this unfortunate affair ? " continued the shipowner, taking up the thread of the conversation where it had been interrupted.

" Mon Dieu ! monsieur, it came about in the most unexpected manner. Captain Leclère had a long conversation with the commander of the port before leaving Naples, and afterwards appeared greatly agitated. At the end of twenty-four hours he was seized with fever, and in three days he was dead. He now rests beneath the waves, decently enveloped in a hammock, just off the island of El Giglio, with a couple of thirty-six pound shot at his head and his heels. We are bringing his cross of honour and his sword to his widow. To think," added the young man, with a melancholy smile, " that after making war on the English for ten years, he should at last die in his bed like anybody else ! "

" Well, well, Monsieur Edmond, we are all mortal, and in due course the old must make way for the young, or there would be no promotion ; and since you assure me that the cargo——"

" Is in good condition, Monsieur Morrel. I answer for it ; and I advise you not to take £1,000 for the profits of the voyage. If you will come on board, your supercargo, M. Danglars, will give you all the information you desire, while I look to the anchoring and put the ship in mourning."

The owner grasped the rope which Dantès threw to him, and with a dexterity which would have done him credit if he had been sailor-born, climbed up the side of the ship. The young sailor then returned to his post, whilst the person he had referred to as Danglars came up to meet the shipowner.

The new comer was a man of about twenty-five or twenty-six years of age, and not by any means prepossessing in appearance. Obsequious towards his superiors and insolent towards his subordinates, he was, on account of his overbearing disposition, as well as by reason of his holding the unpopular post of responsible agent, almost as much disliked by the crew as Edmond Dantès was beloved.

" So, Monsieur Morrel," said Danglars, " you have, I suppose, heard the bad news ? "

" Yes, yes. Poor fellow ; poor Leclère ! He was a brave, honest man."

" And a capital seaman, too, who had grown old in the service, which is very necessary for a man entrusted with the interests of such an important house as that of Morrel and Son," replied Danglars.

" Well, it hardly seems to me," said Morrel, following Dantès with his eyes as he busied himself about the anchorage, " that it is essential a seaman should be old to know his business well, Danglars. There is our friend, Edmond, who goes about his work like a man who does not need to ask counsel from anybody ! "

" Yes," said Danglars, darting a malicious glance sideways to where Dantès was standing. " Yes, he is young, and youth is confident. Scarcely was the captain dead, when he took the command, and spent a day and a half at the Island of Elba, instead of returning direct to Marseilles."

" As for taking command of the vessel," said the shipowner, " that was his duty, as mate ; but he was wrong to lose a day and a half at Elba, unless the ship had to be repaired."

" The ship was as right and well as I am, and as I hope always to see you, Monsieur Morrel ; the day and a half were wasted out of pure caprice, for the sake of a little pleasure on land."

" Dantès," said the shipowner, " come here a moment."

" Pardon, monsieur," answered Dantès, " I will be with you in an instant." Then turning to the crew, " Down anchor ! " he cried.

The anchor fell at once, and the chain ran through the porthole with a noise. Dantès remained at his post until this last manœuvre was completed, then he called out, " Lower the pennant halfmast, reverse the ensign, and slope the yards."

" Upon my word," said Danglars, " he thinks himself captain already, as you see."

" Pardon, Monsieur Morrel," said Dantès, approaching ; " now that the ship is anchored, I am quite at your service."

Danglars stepped back a little.

" I wished to ask why you delayed at Elba."

" I do not know, monsieur ; it was to fulfil a last command of Captain Leclère's, who, when he died, gave into my keeping a packet for the Grand Marshal Bertrand."

" Then you saw the Grand Marshal ? "

" Yes."

Morrel looked round quickly, and then drew Dantès aside.

" And how is the Emperor ? " he asked suddenly.

" Well, if I may judge by my eyes."

" You saw him also, then ? "

" He came to the Marshal's while I was there. He asked me questions about the ship ; when she had left Marseilles, the course she had taken, and what was her cargo. I believe if she had been clear of cargo, and I had been the owner, he would have bought her ; but I told him I was only mate, and that she belonged to the firm of Morrel and Son. ' Ah ! ' he said, ' I know them. The Morrels have been shipowners from father to son, and one Morrel served in the same regiment with me when I belonged to the garrison at Valence.' "

" Mon Dieu ! that's true ! " cried the shipowner with delight ; " it was Policar Morrel, my uncle, who afterwards became captain. Dantès, you must tell my uncle that the Emperor remembers him, and you'll see the old soldier will weep when he hears it." Then clapping the young man in a friendly manner on the shoulder, he continued, " Well, well, you were right, Dantès, to follow the instructions of Captain Leclère, though if it were known that you had delivered up a packet to the Marshal, and had conversed with the Emperor, it might compromise you."

" How could it possibly do so, monsieur ? " replied Dantès ; " I do not even know what it was I had to deliver, and the Emperor only asked me questions which he might have put to any stranger. But here are the officers of health and the customs ! " he continued. " Excuse me for a moment, monsieur."

The young man turned away, and as he did so, Danglars approached.

" So ! " said he, " he appears to have given you good reasons for dropping anchor at Porto Ferrajo ? "

" Excellent reasons, my dear Danglars. It was Captain Leclère who had ordered the putting into port."

" By the by, speaking of Captain Leclère, has he not given you a letter from him ? "

" A letter for me ? No. Had he one, then ? "

" I thought that besides the packet, Captain Leclère handed him a letter."

" What packet are you speaking of, Danglars ? "

" The one that Dantès delivered at Porto Ferrajo, to be sure."

" But how came you to know that he had a packet to leave at Porto Ferrajo ? "

Danglars coloured.

" I was passing the captain's door, which was half open, and I saw him give up this packet and letter to Dantès."

" He has said nothing about the letter," observed Morrel ; " but if there is one he will be sure to give it me."

Danglars reflected a moment.

" But, I beg, Monsieur Morrel," he said at last, " that you will not mention it to Dantès, for I may be mistaken."

At this moment the young man returned, and Danglars walked away.

" Well, my good Dantès, and have you done your business ? " began Morrel. " You have nothing further to do here ? "

" No, everything is right."

" Then you can come and dine with me ? "

" You must excuse me, if you please, Monsieur Morrel, I must first go and see my father ; but I am grateful for the honour you do me."

"Ah ! well ; you are right, Dantès. I know you are a good son."

" As far as you know, my father is well, I suppose ? " said Dantès with a little hesitation.

" Yes ; I believe so, my dear Edmond, though I scarcely ever see him."

" He keeps very much to his little room."

" That shows, at any rate, that he does not want for anything during your absence ! Well ! after you have made this visit, I shall count upon you, at any rate."

" You must excuse me, if you please, monsieur ; for after seeing my father, I have yet another visit to pay, which my heart will not let me delay."

" Oh ! so that is it, Dantès ? I forgot that some one at the Catalans must expect you as impatiently as your father. It is the fair Mercédès ? "

Dantès smiled.

' Ah ! ah ! " laughed the shipowner. " Now I am no longer surprised that she came to me three times to ask for news of the *Pharaon*. Well, my good Edmond, I must not keep you ; you have managed my affairs well enough, so I ought to give you leisure for your own. Have you need of money ? "

" No, monsieur ; I have the salary for the voyage, that is nearly three months' pay."

" You are a steady fellow, Edmond. Now away with you, and see your father. I have a son, and I should be very vexed with him, if, after a three months' voyage, he did not hasten to see me. You have nothing further to say to me ? "

" No, monsieur."

" Captain Leclère, when he was dying, did not give you any letter for me ? "

" He could not write, monsieur ; but that reminds me that I wish to ask for a fortnight's leave of absence."

" To get married, eh ? "

" Yes, monsieur, and then to go on to Paris."

" Take what time you want, Dantès ; we cannot put out to sea for three months. Only, be back in three months' time ; for the *Pharaon*," continued the shipowner, clapping the young man on the shoulder, " must not start without her captain."

" Without her captain ! " exclaimed Dantès, his eyes sparkling with pleasure. " Is it truly your intention to make me captain of the *Pharaon* ? "

" If I stood alone in the matter, I would hold out my hand, my dear Dantès, and say, ' It is settled ! ' but I have a partner. Still, half the matter is settled, at any rate, since one of the voices has spoken ; and trust to me that the other will speak in your favour, for I will do my best for you."

" Oh ! Monsieur Morrel," cried the young sailor, with tears in his eyes, as he grasped the hand of the shipowner, " I thank you, indeed, both for my father's and Mercédès' sake."

" There is a God in heaven for good men, you know. Now go to your father and Mercédès, and then come back to me. I must stay and settle my accounts with Danglars. How have you got on with him during the voyage ? "

" Well, monsieur, that is according to the meaning you attach to the question. If you mean as a comrade, not very well ;

for I think he has never liked me since the day when I was silly enough, through a little quarrel we had, to propose to him to stop ten minutes at the Island of Monte Cristo, to settle the matter—a thing I was wrong to suggest, and he was right to refuse. But as regards his duties as your supercargo, I think you will be quite satisfied with the manner in which he has done his duty."

"Now if you were to become the captain of the *Pharaon*, Dantès, should you like to go on with Danglars ? " inquired the shipowner.

"Captain, or mate, Monsieur Morrel," replied Dantès, " I should always have great consideration for all who possess the confidence of my employers."

"Bravo ! Dantès, you are a downright good fellow. Now go, I will keep you no longer, for I can see you are impatient."

"Good morning, then, Monsieur Morrel ; and a thousand thanks."

The young man jumped into the boat, and gave the word to row off towards the Canebière. The shipowner smilingly watched the little boat as it reached the shore, and saw the young sailor leap out on the quay, where he was quickly lost to view among the motley crowd, which from five in the morning till nine in the evening, throngs the celebrated street of the Canebière, of which the modern Phocéens are so proud, that they say : " If Paris had only the Canebière, it would be a second Marseilles."

Turning round, the shipowner found Danglars standing behind him, apparently waiting his orders, but in reality, watching, like himself, the departure of the sailor.

But there was a great difference in the expression of the two men's faces as they looked after the young man.

CHAPTER II

FATHER AND SON

DANTÈS walked the length of the Canebière, turned into the Rue de Noailles, and entered a small house on the left side of the Allées de Meillan. He hastily ascended the four dark flights of the staircase, then stopped before a door, a little ajar, opening into a small room. In this room Dantès' father lived.

The news of the arrival of the *Pharaon* had not yet reached the old man, who, mounted on a chair, was engaged in fastening up, with trembling hands, some nasturtiums and clematis, which grew along the lattice of his window.

Suddenly a well-known voice called out:

" My father, my dear father ! "

The old man uttered a cry and turned ; then seeing his son, he fell into his arms, pale and trembling.

" What is the matter, father ? " cried the young man anxiously ; " are you ill ? "

" No, no, my dear Edmond, my son, my child ; no, only I did not expect you, and the joy and surprise at seeing you again so suddenly—ah ; Mon Dieu ! I almost feel as though I should die ! "

" Come, come ! compose yourself, father ! I am come back, and we shall be so happy together."

" So much the better, my boy ; but how are we going to be so happy, unless you are not going to leave me again ? Come, tell me all about it."

" May God pardon me for rejoicing over any good luck which brings mourning to others ; but this good fortune has come to me, and I cannot lament over it. Our brave captain, Leclère, is dead, father, and it is probable that, through M. Morrel's influence, I shall have his place. Think of that, father ! Captain at twenty years of age ! with a salary of one hundred louis and a share of the profits ! It is more than a poor sailor like me could ever have dreamt of, is it not ? "

" Yes, my son, yes," said the old man ; " it is indeed fortunate."

" And I intend the very first money that I get, that you shall have a little house with a garden, where you can plant your clematis, and nasturtiums, and honeysuckles. But what is it, father, you look as though you were ill ? "

" Patience ! patience ! it is nothing."

But his strength failing him, the old man fell backwards, exhausted.

" See ! father, I will get you a glass of wine," cried the young man, " that will bring you round. Where do you keep your wine ? " And Dantès began to open the cupboards.

" It is no use," said the old man ; " there is no wine."

" What ! no wine ! " said Dantès, turning pale, and looking first at the white, haggard face, and then at the empty cupboard ; " how is that ? have you been in want of money, father ? "

" I want for nothing since you are come," replied the old man.

" But," stammered Dantès, " I left with you two hundred francs, when I started three months ago."

" Yes, yes, Edmond, that is true ; but you forgot when you

set out that little debt to neighbour Caderousse; he reminded me about it, and said if I did not pay it, that he would go to M. Morrel; and so, fearing that might be an injury to you I paid it myself."

"But it was a hundred and forty francs," cried Dantès, "that I owed Caderousse! You paid that out of the two hundred francs which I left you?"

The old man nodded assent.

' So that you have lived for three months on sixty francs?" murmured the young man. "It makes my heart bleed to think of it."

"Bah! you are safe back," said the old man, smiling; "and we shall forget all about it, and everything will go well."

"Yes," said the young man; "I am back at last, with a fine future, and a little money in my pocket. Stay, father, take some at once, and send out and buy some things immediately."

And he emptied his pockets on to the table, turning out about a dozen gold pieces, five or six crowns, and small coins.

"Send out at once for some provisions, and let us enjoy ourselves; there is more for to-morrow."

"Gently, gently," said the old man, smiling. "People will think if they see me buying so much at once, that I was obliged to await your return before making my purchases."

"Do as you like; but, above all things, you must have a servant, father. I do not wish you to be living alone. I have some smuggled coffee and some splendid tobacco in a little chest in the hold, which you shall have to-morrow. But hush! someone is coming."

"It is Caderousse, who has probably just heard of your arrival, and is coming to congratulate you on your return."

"Indeed!" muttered Edmond; "lips that say one thing while the heart thinks another; but no matter, he is a neighbour who has sometimes done us a service, so let him be welcome."

Just as Edmond finished speaking, the dark bearded face of Caderousse appeared in the doorway. He was a man of from five to six and twenty years of age, and advanced, holding in his hand a piece of cloth, which, in his capacity of tailor, he was making into the lining of a coat.

"Eh! So you are back home again, Edmond?" said he, with a strong Marseillaise accent, smiling, as he showed his rows of white teeth.

"Here I am, neighbour Caderousse, and at your service in

any way that you require," answered Dantès, but ill-concealing his coldness as he spoke.

"Thanks, thanks; fortunately I need no assistance of any kind; indeed, it is others who need it of me sometimes."

Dantès made a sudden movement.

"I meant nothing personal, my boy. I lent you money which has been repaid; that is like good neighbours, and we are quits."

"One is never quits towards those who have obliged us," returned Dantès, "because if one no longer owes them money, one still owes them gratitude."

"Oh! there is no good in talking about it! What is past is done with, so let us talk about your happy return, my boy. I had just gone to the quay to match some maroon cloth, when I met friend Danglars. 'What! you here!' said I. 'Just so,' said he. 'I have just returned.' 'And the young fellow, Edmond, where is he?' I asked. 'With his father, I should imagine,' he answered; so off I came at once," continued Caderousse, "to have the pleasure of shaking hands with an old friend!"

"You are a good fellow, Caderousse, and really care about us," observed the old man.

"Certainly I do; and honest folk being so rare, I esteem you all the more! Why, you appear to have become quite rich," added the tailor, casting a side glance at the handful of money that Dantès had placed on the table.

"Eh! Mon Dieu!" Dantès returned carelessly, "but this money is not mine; I was just expressing to my father some fear that he had been in want during my absence, and to reassure me, he emptied his purse upon the table. Come, father, put up your money in your money-box, that is, if neighbour Caderousse does not need to borrow in his turn, in which case, it is at his service."

"Not I, my lad," said Caderousse; "I want for nothing, and, thank God, my trade keeps me. Well! and so you are on the best of terms with M. Morrel, sly dog that you are."

"M. Morrel has always been extremely good to me," Dantès replied.

"In that case, you were wrong to refuse his dinner."

"What! refuse his dinner?" broke in old Dantès. "He invited you to dine with him, did he? And why did you refuse, my son?"

"That I might come to you the sooner, father, for I was anxious to see you."

"It must have annoyed good M. Morrel," remarked Caderousse. "And when one is looking forward to becoming captain, it is necessary to flatter one's patrons a little."

"I hope to be captain without doing that," replied Dantès.

"So much the better! so much the better! And all your old friends will be glad of it, and I think I know of someone else living behind the citadel of Saint Nicholas who will not be sorry to hear of it."

"Mercédès?" inquired the old man.

"Yes, father," rejoined Dantès; "and now that I have seen you and am satisfied that you are well, I want you to let me pay a visit to the Catalans."

"Go, my son," said old Dantès, "and may God bless you in your wife as He has blessed me in my son!"

"His wife!" exclaimed Caderousse. "How you run on, father Dantès! She is not that at present, at any rate; but you do well to be as quick as you can about it, my lad. Mercédès is a pretty girl, and pretty girls always have plenty of lovers; and this fair maid is followed by a dozen."

"Indeed," remarked Edmond with a smile, in which was a shade of uneasiness.

"Oh! yes," said Caderousse; "and some are very eligible indeed; but still you are going to be captain, so, you understand, you are safe not to be refused."

"Now, come!" exclaimed the young man, "I have a better opinion of women in general, and of Mercédès in particular, and I am convinced whether I were captain or not, she would remain faithful to me."

"So much the better," returned Caderousse; "but nevertheless, my lad, take my advice—make known your arrival to her, and inform her of your hopes."

"I will," said Edmond; then embracing his father, and with a nod to Caderousse, he left the room.

The tailor remained but a few moments longer; then taking leave of the old man, he descended the stairs, and went out to rejoin Danglars, who was waiting for him at the corner of the Rue Senac.

"Well!" said Danglars; "and have you seen him?"

"I have just left him."

"And did he speak at all of his desire of becoming captain?"

"He talks as though he were captain already. It seems the thing has been promised him by M. Morrel."

" Bah ! " exclaimed Danglars, " he has not got it yet, at any rate."

" *Ma foi !* it would be a good thing if he did not have it at all," returned Caderousse, " for there will be no speaking to him."

" In fact, we should be as well pleased," observed Danglars, " if he remained as he is, or even if he got a little lower. And so he is still in love with the fair Catalan ? "

" Madly in love. He is just gone to see her ; but if I am not much mistaken, he will get a little discouragement in that quarter."

" Explain yourself ; tell me what you know about the Catalan girl. Come, speak out."

" Well, then ; every time that Mercédès comes into the town, she is accompanied by a tall fellow, a Catalan, with dark eyes and brown complexion, who appears very ardent, and whom she calls ' my cousin.' "

" Oh ! indeed ! And so you think this cousin is paying her attention ? "

" I imagine so. What the devil does a smart fellow of one and twenty want else with a pretty girl of seventeen ? "

" And you say Dantès is just gone to the Catalans now ? "

" He started out just before me."

" If we keep on this side, we can stop at La Réserve, and whilst we are drinking a glass of La Malgue we shall see Dantès on his way back, and can tell by his face what has happened."

" Come along, then," said Caderousse.

They set off at a quick step towards the inn, and ordered a bottle of wine and a couple of glasses. The landlord, Pamphile, had seen Dantès pass about ten minutes ago, he said. Satisfied that Dantès must be at the Catalans, the two men seated themselves under the spreading foliage of the planes and sycamores.

CHAPTER III

THE CATALANS

ABOUT a hundred paces from the spot where the two friends sat sipping the sparkling La Malgue wine, stood the village of the Catalans.

Once on a time, a mysterious band of colonists had arrived from Spain, and established themselves on the neck of land, which they continue to occupy to this day. No one knew exactly whence they came, and their dialect was strange. One of their leaders who understood Provençal, petitioned the Council of Marseilles for the right to settle on the bleak and barren promontory, on which they had moored their boats. The request was granted, and by the time three months had elapsed, a small village had sprung up near the spot where these Bohemians of the sea had landed. The village was constructed in a picturesque fashion, half Moorish, half Spanish, and exists to this day, inhabited by descendants of the old founders, who still speak the language of their forefathers. For three or four centuries they have remained faithful to the little promontory, never mingling or intermarrying with the Marseillaise folk, and preserving the manners and costume of their mother country, as they have also preserved the language.

We must now introduce our readers to the only street of the little village, and enter one of the small houses, on which the sun has stamped that beautiful dead-leaf colour, peculiar to the buildings of the country, and which is only embellished within with a coating of white limewash, the usual wall covering of Spanish *posadas*.

A beautiful girl, with jet black hair and eyes as soft as a gazelle, stood leaning against the wainscot, rubbing in her slender fingers a bunch of heather blossoms, which she was picking off and strewing on the floor, whilst her bare arms, which might have been modelled from those of the Venus of Arles, shook with a little feverish impatience, as she tapped the ground with her supple and well-formed foot, so that one caught a glimpse of a finely-turned ankle enclosed in a red stocking. About three steps from her, seated on a chair which he rocked backwards and forwards as he leant his shoulder against a piece of old worm-eaten furniture, was a fine grown fellow of from twenty to two and twenty years of age, who regarded her with an expression of mingled uneasiness and vexation ; his eyes looked questioningly into hers, but the calm and decided look of the young girl seemed to overawe her companion.

" Why, Easter will be here soon, Mercédès ! " remarked the young man ; " and that is the time for weddings. Come, answer me ! "

" I have answered you a hundred times, Fernando, and indeed you must be your own enemy to keep asking me again and again ! "

" Well, then ! tell me yet once more, I beg of you ; tell me until I begin to believe it. Ah ! Mon Dieu ! to have dreamt for ten years of the happiness of becoming your husband, Mercédès, and then to lose that hope which was the sole aim of my life ! "

" At any rate, I never encouraged you in the hope, Fernando," replied Mercédès. " I have always told you I love you as a brother, but do not ask me for anything beyond sisterly regard, for my heart is given to another. Have I not always said so, Fernando ? "

" Yes, I know it, Mercédès," answered the young man ; " yes, you have always exhibited towards me the cruel merit of frankness ; but do you forget that among the Catalans it is a sacred law that they should marry only between themselves ? "

" You are wrong, Fernando : it is not a law, it is a custom, that is all ; do not invoke this custom in your favour. You have been drawn for a recruit, Fernando, and at any moment you may be called to serve under the flag. Once a soldier, what would you do with me, a poor forlorn orphan girl, without fortune, and possessing only a tumbledown cottage, with a few worn-out nets, the miserable inheritance which my father left to my mother, and my mother to me."

" Well, and what does it matter, Mercédès, if you are poor and solitary ? You suit me far better so than the daughter of the proudest shipowner or the richest banker of Marseilles ! I wish to wed an honest woman and a good manager, and where can I meet your match in those respects ? "

" But, Fernando," said Mercédès, bending her head, " one may become a bad manager, and a woman may not continue honest if she loves another man than her husband. Go on with your fishing, and do not indulge in dreams which will only make the reality seem more painful to you, and rest contented with my friendship since I can offer you nothing else."

" Well, well, you are right, Mercédès. I will be a sailor, and instead of the costume of our fathers which you despise, I shall have a shiny hat, a striped shirt, and a blue jacket with anchors on the buttons. That is how one must be dressed to please you, eh ? "

" What do you mean ? " asked Mercédès, darting an imperious look at him.

" I mean, Mercédès, that you are hard and cruel to me because you are expecting some one dressed up in that fashion. And, perhaps, after all, he whom you look for is inconstant, or if *he* is not, very likely the sea is for him ! "

" Fernando," cried Mercédès ; " I thought you were good, but I have been deceived in you ! You must have a wicked

heart to call down the wrath of God to the aid of your jealousy!
And, listen, I will conceal nothing. I *do* love, and am looking
for the one of whom you speak, and if he were not to return,
instead of accusing him of the inconstancy which you suggest,
I should declare that he had died loving me."

The young Catalan made an angry gesture.

" I understand you, Fernando; you blame him because I do
not love you, and you would like to cross his dagger with your
knife. But what good would that do you? As you cannot have
me as a wife, be content for me to be a friend and sister to you;
and, besides," she added, her anxious eyes filling with tears,
"think, Fernando, as you said just now, the sea is perfidious,
and it is already three months since he left, and how I have
counted the storms during all that time!"

Fernando took a turn up and down the cottage, then stopped
in front of Mercédès, his eyes gloomy, and fists clenched.

" Now, Mercédès," he said, " tell me for the last time, have
you fully made up your mind?"

" I love Edmond Dantès," said the young girl coldly, " and
none other than he shall be my husband!"

Fernando bent his head as though completely discouraged,
and a sigh almost like a groan escaped him; then looking up
quickly, with set teeth, and inflated nostrils, he asked:

" But if he is dead?"

" If he is dead, I shall die."

" And if he has forgotten you?"

" Mercédès!" called a joyful voice outside the house. " Mercédès!"

" Ah!" cried the young girl, colouring with delight, and
bounding forward, " you see he has not forgotten me, for here
he is." And she darted towards the door and opened it, crying:
" Oh! Edmond, you are come at last!"

Fernando, pale and trembling, fell backwards into a chair.
Edmond and Mercédès remained folded in each other's arms.
An overpowering happiness isolated them from the world, and
they spoke in barely articulate words, which were the expressions
of a joy so keen, that they almost seemed to indicate suffering.
Suddenly Edmond perceived the dark visage of Fernando, as,
with a sudden movement of which he was hardly conscious,
the young Catalan placed his hand on the knife in his belt.

" Ah! pardon," said Dantès, frowning a little; " I had not
remarked that there were three of us here." Then turning to
Mercédès, " Who is this gentleman?" he inquired.

" He must be your best friend, Dantès," she replied, " for he is my friend, my cousin, my brother : it is Fernando, whom, after you, Edmond, I love better than anyone else in the world ; do you not recognize him ? "

" Ah ! yes," said Edmond ; and without loosing Mercédès, whose hand he kept in one of his, he extended the other cordially towards the young Catalan. But Fernando, far from responding to this friendly overture, remained mute and motionless as a statue. Edmond gazed first at Mercédès, agitated and trembling, then at Fernando, dark and menacing. In a glance he learnt all. He flushed angrily.

" I did not think, when I hastened to you so quickly, that I should find an enemy here, Mercédès ! "

" An enemy ! " cried the girl, with an impatient look in the direction of her cousin ; " an enemy under my roof, Edmond ! If I thought so I would take your arm and start off to Marseilles, and would leave the house for ever. And if any harm happened to you, dear Edmond," she continued, with an immovable composure, which showed Fernando that she had read his secret feelings, " I should climb up Cape Morgion, and throw myself over, head first on to the rocks."

Fernando turned pale.

" But you are mistaken, Edmond," she went on, " you have no enemy here ; there is only Fernando, who is a brother to me, and who is waiting to give you a hearty shake of the hand." And with these words the young girl turned a commanding look on the Catalan, who, as though fascinated by her expression, slowly approached Edmond, and extended his hand.

But scarcely had he touched the hand of his rival, than he felt that he had reached the limits of endurance, and rushed out of the house, and along the road.

" Oh ! " he cried, tearing at his hair like a madman, " oh ! who will deliver me from this fellow ? Woe is me ! woe is me ! "

" Oh ! the Catalan ! Fernando there ! where are you off to ? " called a voice.

The young man stopped short and, looking round, perceived Caderousse and Danglars sitting at a table under the green canopy of the trees.

Fernando regarded the two men with a stupefied air, and answered nothing.

" He seems dazed," said Danglars, giving Caderousse a nudge with his knees. " Who knows ! but we may have been deceived, and Dantès will get the best of it ? "

"Indeed! we will see about that," rejoined Caderousse; then he added, turning towards the young man: "Come, now, my young Catalan, pull yourself together."

Fernando wiped the streaming perspiration from his brow, and slowly stepped into the arbour, where the shade and coolness seemed to calm his senses.

"Good-day!" said he; "you called to me, did you not?" and he fell, rather than seated himself, on one of the seats near the table.

"I called you because you were running like a madman, and I really was afraid you were going to throw yourself into the sea," said Caderousse laughing, "and, devil take me, when one has friends, one should not only be ready to offer them a glass of wine, but endeavour to prevent them from drinking three or four pints of water."

Fernando gave a groan, which sounded almost like a sob, and dropping his head on his hands, leaned forwards on the table.

"Now! shall I tell you what I think, Fernando?" went on Caderousse, "you have just the air of a disappointed lover! Listen how he sighs! Come, come, Fernando, tell us all about it; it is not polite to give no answer when friends ask about your health."

"I am well enough," said Fernando, clenching his fists, and without lifting his head.

"Ah! you see how it is, Danglars," said Caderousse, winking across at his friend, "this is how the matter stands: Fernando here, a good, honest Catalan, and one of the best fishers in Marseilles, is in love with a pretty girl, called Mercédès, but unfortunately, it seems this pretty girl, on her side, is in love with the mate of the *Pharaon*—and as the *Pharaon* has just come into port to-day poor Fernando has been sent about his business."

"And what then?" said Fernando, raising his head and looking at Caderousse as though anxious to find someone on whom to vent his wrath; "Mercédès is independent and free, is she not, to choose whom she will?"

"Ah! well, if you take it in that manner," said Caderousse, 'it is another thing, of course! I thought myself that you were a true Catalan, and I have always heard that the Catalans were not the men to allow themselves to be supplanted by a rival, and that Fernando in particular was terrible in his vengeance."

Fernando smiled with compassion.

"A lover is never terrible," said he.

"Ah! *ma foi!* but at all events," observed Caderousse, on

whom the foaming La Malgue wine began to take effect, " at all events, Fernando is not the only one to whom Dantès' return has given annoyance ; eh, Danglars ? "

" No, you speak truly, and I should say it may cause him some trouble."

" Oh ! no matter ! " Caderousse went on, pouring out a glass of wine for Fernando, and refilling his own for the eighth or tenth time, though Danglars had barely tasted his ; " no matter, he will now marry the fair Mercédès."

All this time, Danglars had fastened a scrutinizing glance on the young man, who felt the words of Caderousse fall on his heart like molten lead.

" And when will the wedding take place ? " he asked.

" Oh ! it is not yet settled," muttered Fernando.

" No ; but it soon will be," said Caderousse, " as certainly as that Dantès will be captain of the *Pharaon* ; eh, Danglars ? "

Danglars started at this unexpected attack, and turned on Caderousse to see if the blow were premeditated ; but he could read nothing but envy on his face, already half stupefied with drunkenness.

" Well, then ! " said he, filling the glasses, " let us drink to the health of Captain Edmond Dantès, the husband of the fair Catalan ! "

Caderousse raised his glass to his lips and drained it at a draught.

Fernando took his and dashed it to the ground.

" Eh ! eh ! " cried Caderousse, " what do I see over there, on that rising ground, in the Catalans' quarter ? Look you, Fernando, you have better sight than I ; and I fancy mine is rather dim, for you know wine is a traitor. I should say it is a pair of lovers walking together, hand in hand. God forgive me ! they do not fancy they are being watched ; see them embracing ! "

None of the anguish which distorted the face of Fernando as he witnessed this spectacle, was lost on Danglars.

" Who are they, pray, Monsieur Fernando ? " he inquired.

" It is M. Edmond," replied Fernando, in a hollow voice, " and Mademoiselle Mercédès."

" Oh ! oh ! " cried Caderousse ; " and I could not recognize them ! Halloo, there ! Dantès ! Halloo ! My pretty maid ! Come this way a little, and tell us when the wedding is to be ; for M. Fernando, here, is so obstinate, he will say nothing "

" Will you be silent ? " said Danglars, pretending to pull Caderousse back, who was stretching forward out of the arbour with all the tenacity of drunkenness; "sit up, and be quiet, and leave the lovers in peace. See, look at M. Fernando there, and follow his example; he is calm and reasonable."

Perhaps Fernando, almost beside himself, and goaded by Danglars, would have darted forth on his rival, had not Mercédès, erect and smiling, raised her pretty head, as they approached, and looked brightly round; then Fernando recollected the threat she had uttered, that if any harm came to Edmond, she would kill herself; and he fell back on his seat, discouraged.

Danglars looked from one to the other of his companions—the one stupefied with drink, the other maddened with love.

"I shall get nothing from these simpletons," he murmured to himself; "and I do not care to be sitting here between a drunkard and a poltroon. Edmond's destiny is in the ascendant. He will marry the pretty girl; he will be captain, and laugh at us all; at least," he continued, a livid smile gathering round his lips—"at least, if I do not interfere."

"Halloo, there!" continued Caderousse, still shouting, and half standing as he held on to the table; "halloo, Edmond! do you not see there are friends here, or are you too proud to speak?"

"No, my dear Caderousse," said Dantès, as the pair approached, "I am not too proud, but I am so happy, and happiness is blinder than pride, I think."

"Well and good! that is a fine excuse," returned he. "Ah! good day to you, Madame Dantès."

Mercédès bowed gravely.

"That is not my title yet," said she, "and among my people it is considered to bring ill-luck if maidens are called by their lover's name before they are wedded: so pray call me Mercédès!"

"So," said Danglars, after bowing to the young pair, "the marriage will take place shortly, I suppose, Monsieur Dantès?"

"As soon as possible, Monsieur Danglars; to-day we shall make all the arrangements with my father, and to-morrow, or the day after at latest, shall have our wedding feast here at the Réserve. And I hope all our friends will join us; that is to say, you must consider yourself invited, Monsieur Danglars, and you too, Caderousse."

"And Fernando," said Caderousse, with a chuckle, "is he to come too?"

"My wife's brother is my brother also," said Edmond, "and we should both indeed regret if he were not with us at such a time."

"To-day the arrangements, to-morrow or the day after the betrothal—the devil! you are in a hurry, captain!"

"Danglars," returned Dantès, smiling, "I must say to you as Mercédès said just now to Caderousse, do not give me a title which does not yet belong to me, it may bring me ill-luck."

"I beg pardon," said Danglars. "I merely remarked that you seemed in a great hurry. Why, there is time enough; the *Pharaon* will not be starting again for three months."

"One is always in a hurry to grasp one's happiness, Monsieur Danglars, and when one has waited a long time, it is difficult to realize the happiness; but it is not only my own personal feelings I have to go to Paris."

"Ah! indeed, to Paris! You have business there?"

"Not on my own account; it is to fulfil a last commission of our poor captain, Leclère; you understand, Danglars, it is a sacred matter."

"Yes, yes, I understand," said Danglars, and then muttered to himself, "to Paris to deliver, doubtless, the letter which the Grand Marshal gave him. *Pardieu!* I have an idea, a capital idea! Ah! Dantès, my friend, you are not yet written down on the register of the *Pharaon* as Number 1." Then turning and nodding to Edmond as he moved away, he called, "A pleasant journey to you."

"Thanks," said Edmond, looking back and waving his hand. The two lovers then continued their walk peacefully and happily, like two of the elect entering the portals of heaven.

CHAPTER IV

THE PLOT

DANGLARS sat with his eyes fixed on the receding forms of the two lovers until they disappeared round one of the corners of Fort Saint Nicholas; then looking round at Fernando, he perceived that he had again fallen on the seat, whilst Caderousse was stuttering the words of a drinking song.

"Ah! well, my dear fellow," said Danglars, accosting Fernando, "this seems to be a marriage which does not bring happiness to everybody."

"It makes me mad," said Fernando.

"You love Mercédès, then?"

"I have adored her ever since we have known each other."

"And yet, there you sit tearing your hair, instead of seeking some remedy in the matter. I did not think that was the way your people acted."

" I should like to poniard the fellow, but she declares that if anything happens to him, she will kill herself."

" Imbecile ! " muttered Danglars to himself. " Whether she kills herself or not, what does it matter, provided Dantès is not made captain ? "

" And rather than Mercédès should die," Fernando continued with an accent of steadfast resolution, " I would die myself."

" See," said Danglars, " you seem to me a good youth, and I wish, I am sure, that I could pull you out of the difficulty ; but—— "

" Yes," said Caderousse, " let us see."

" My dear creature," rejoined Danglars, " you are at least three parts drunk ; finish the bottle, and then you will be quite settled ; drink away, and do not interfere with us, for what we are considering requires a little head."

" I, drunk ? " said Caderousse, " come then ! I could drink four more of your bottles. Why, they are no bigger than bottles of eau de Cologne ! Father Pamphile, more wine !" and to add emphasis to the request, Caderousse struck the table with his glass.

" You were saying, monsieur ? " began Fernando, eagerly awaiting the continuance of the interrupted remark.

" I was saying—really I have quite forgotten. This tipsy fellow has made me lose the thread of my thoughts."

" You were saying, monsieur," Fernando began again, " that you would willingly get me out of this trouble ; but you added—— "

" Yes, but I added—to get you out of this difficulty, Dantès must, of course, not be allowed to marry the girl whom you love ; and the marriage can very well be prevented, it seems to me, without Dantès' death."

" Death alone would sever them," said Fernando, emphatically.

" You reason like a noodle, my friend," said Caderousse, " and here is Danglars, who is a wideawake, clever fellow, who will now prove that you are wrong. Tell him there is no reason why Dantès should die ; besides, it would be a very sad thing. He is a good fellow is Dantès, and I am fond of him. Your health, Dantès ! "

Fernando rose with impatience.

" Never mind what he says," said Danglars, detaining the young man ; " besides, though he is drunk, he is not so very far wrong. Absence alienates as well as death. Suppose the walls of a prison were interposed between Edmond and Mercédès ? "

" Yes, but one can get out of prison," remarked Caderousse, who still grappled with the conversation, " and when one gets out, and is in Edmond Dantès' place, one would revenge one-self. Besides, why should Dantès be put in prison ? He has not been stealing, or killing, or stabbing."

" Hold your tongue," said Danglars.

" I will not hold my tongue," returned Caderousse ; " and I wish to know why Dantès should be put in prison. I am v ry fond of Dantès. Your health, Dantès ! " And he swallowed another glass of wine.

Danglars observed the increasing stupefaction in the vacant eyes of the tailor, and then addressing himself to Fernando, said :

" Well ! do you see that there is no necessity to make away with him ? "

" Certainly, if there were any means of getting him arrested, as you said just now. But how can that be done ? "

" By seeking well, we shall find a way," said Danglars. " But why the devil should I mix myself up in the matter, whe1 it does not concern me ? "

" You have some reason for personal hatred against Dan,ès ; he who himself hates, cannot well be deceived as to the s nti-ments of others."

' I ! reason for hatred against Dantès ? None, on my honour. I saw you unhappy, and was touched by your distress, that was all ; but if you imagine I am acting on my own account, why adieu, my dear friend, and get out of the mess as well as you can." Danglars half rose as though to go.

" No, no," said Fernando, holding him back, " stay a mom nt. It matters little enough to me, after all, whether you have a grudge or not against Dantès ; I hate him ; I avow it openly Find the means, and I will carry out the plan, provided Dantès is not made away with, for Mercédès would certainly kill herself if anything happened to him."

Caderousse, who was leaning with his head on the table, here looked up, and regarding his companions with a dull, fuddled air, remarked :

" Kill Dantès ! who talks of injuring Dantès ? I do not wish him to be killed. He is my friend ; he offered this morning to lend me money, as I have at other times shared mine with him ; and I will not have Dantès killed."

" And who talks of killing him, imbecile ? " retorted Danglars ; " it was simply a joke ; and now drink his health," he added, filling Caderousse's glass ; " and leave us alone."

" Yes, yes, Dantès' good health ! " said Caderousse, emptying his glass.

" But the means—the means," reiterated Fernando. " You undertook to do it."

" True," answered Danglars, " the French have this superiority over the Spaniards—that they invent, while the Spaniards ruminate."

" Invent, then," said Fernando, impatiently.

" Waiter ! " Danglars cried, " a pen, ink, and paper."

The required articles were brought, and deposited on the table in the arbour.

" To think," said Caderousse, letting his hand fall on the paper, " that this may cause a man to be more effectually done for, than if one waited at the corner of a wood to assassinate him ! I have always had more fear of a pen, a bottle of ink, and a sheet of paper, than of either sword or pistol."

" The rogue is not as drunk as he seems," said Danglars ; " pour him out another glass, Fernando."

Fernando filled up Caderousse's glass, and the latter, like a true drunkard, at once let go the paper and raised the glass to his lips. The young Catalan watched him, until almost overcome by this last libation, he placed, or rather dropped, his glass upon the table.

" Well, then ! I should say, for example," returned Danglars, " that after this voyage of Dantès, and as he landed at Naples, and the island of Elba, if some one were to denounce him to the king's advocate as a Bonapartist agent—— "

" Ah ! I will denounce him ! " said the young man quickly.

" Yes ; only you must sign your declaration, and they will confront you with the accused ; I can furnish you with something to sustain your accusation, right enough ; but Dantès cannot remain in prison for ever : some day he will get out again, and then, bad luck to him who caused him to be put there ! "

" Oh ! I only ask one thing," said Fernando, " and that is that he should seek a quarrel with me ! "

" No, no," Danglars went on, " if we decide on anything, it will be much better to take this pen, as I am doing, dip it in the ink, and write with the left hand, so that the writing is not recognized, a little denunciation in these terms."

Danglars began writing backwards with his left hand, the following lines, which bore little resemblance to his usual style of handwriting, and then passed the paper to Fernando, who read it half aloud :—" Monsieur the Procureur du Roi is warned by a friend to the throne and religion, that one Edmond Dantès, mate of the ship *Pharaon*, which arrived in port this morning from Smyrna, after having touched at Naples and Porto Ferrajo, has been commissioned by Murat with a letter for the Usurper, and by the Usurper with a letter for the Bonapartist Committee at Paris. Proof of this crime will be obtained on arresting him, for the letter will be found either on his person, or in his father's house, or in his cabin on board the *Pharaon*."

" Very good," said Danglars; " now your vengeance has a little common sense, for it cannot be brought home to you, and the matter will work itself out; and there only remains to fold up the letter in this way, and direct it to ' Monsieur le Procureur Royal,' and it is done."

" Yes, it is done," cried Caderousse, who, with a strenuous mental effort, was taking in the conversation, and instinctively comprehended all the mischief that was involved in the indictment; " yes, it is done; only it is an infamous thing! " And he stretched out his arm to clutch the letter.

" Exactly," said Danglars, pushing it out of his reach, " and I am only saying and doing it for a joke, for I should be the first to regret any harm coming to our good Dantès. There, see here! " and he took the letter, crumpled it, and tossed it into the corner of the arbour.

" That is right," said Caderousse; " Dantès is my friend, and I do not wish him to be ill-used."

" And who thinks of ill-using him! Neither Fernando nor I, certainly! " said Danglars, rising, and glancing at the young man, who sat quietly, his eyes fixed on the paper which had been flung into the corner.

" In that case," said Caderousse, " let us have some more wine, for I wish to drink the health of Edmond, and the fair Mercédès."

" You have already drunk too much, you tippler," said Danglars. " Now, it is time to be off; come, give me your arm, and let us go! "

" Oh! we will go; but I have no need of your arm. Come, Fernando, won't you walk back with us to Marseilles? "

" No," said Fernando, " I shall go back to the Catalans. I have no need to go to Marseilles."

" What, you will not, my fine fellow? Well, let everyone please himself! Come, Danglars, let us leave the young gentleman to go back to the Catalans, if he pleases."

Danglars took advantage of his companion's willingness, and led him towards Marseilles; but in order to leave the coast clear

for Fernando, he returned by the Porte Saint Victor, instead of
by the quay of Rive Neuve.

After they had gone a few yards, Danglars looked back, holding
Caderousse by the arm, and saw Fernando dart on the piece of
paper, and put it in his pocket ; then hurrying out of the arbour,
he started off towards Pillon.

" Eh ! there ; what is he doing ? " cried Caderousse ; " he told
us a lie ; he said he was going back to the Catalans, and there he
is off to the town ! Halloo ! Fernando ! "

" Oh ! it is you who cannot see straight," said Danglars ; " he
is gone towards the Vieilles Infirmeries."

" Indeed ! Well, I could have declared he turned to the right.
How wine deceives one, to be sure ! "

CHAPTER V

THE BETROTHAL FEAST

THE morning broke brilliantly. The sun rose clear and resplendent, and with its first rays the little specks on the foaming
waves became touched with a rich reddish tint, as of rubies. The
feast had been made ready at the inn of La Réserve. It was laid
out in a large room, lighted by five or six windows ; and a wooden
balcony, beneath these windows, extended the entire length of
the house. Although the repast had been fixed for mid-day,
the balcony had been covered with impatient guests since eleven
in the morning. They were principally sailors belonging to the
crew of the *Pharaon*, and a few young soldiers, friends of Dantès,
who, dressed in holiday attire, came to do honour to the occasion.
A rumour had been circulating among the company that the
owners of the ship *Pharaon* intended to honour the feast with
their presence, but this appeared such an overwhelming compliment to Dantès that it was discredited, until M. Morrel entered
the room to be received with an enthusiastic round of applause
by the sailors. The presence of the shipowner appeared to them
confirmation of the report that Dantès was to be made captain,
and as he was beloved by the crew, they testified by their cheering
their approbation of the owner's choice.

On M. Morrel's appearance, Danglars and Caderousse were
despatched to fetch the bridegroom, and make known to him the
arrival of the honoured guest. The messengers set off at full
speed ; but before they had gone a hundred yards, they perceived the little procession approaching, composed of Mercédès

B

leaning on the arm of Dantès, followed by a group of four young
Catalan maidens. Old Dantès walked on one side of the bride,
and behind them all came Fernando with a sinister smile. Danglars and Caderousse at once stated their errand, and having
exchanged with Edmond a friendly shake of the hand, they
started off, Danglars walking by Fernando, and Caderousse
accompanying Father Dantès, who was the object of general
attention. The old man was attired in a fine coat of silk taffeta,
with large cut-steel buttons ; his slender, wiry legs were encased
in superbly embroidered clocked stockings ; and his three-cornered hat was adorned with a knot of blue and white ribbons.
As he passed, supporting himself on a curious stick, twisted at the
top end like the ancient shepherd's crook, he might have been
taken for one of the spruce dandies who, in 1796, used to parade
up and down in the gardens recently re-opened at the Luxembourg
and Tuileries. By his side crept Caderousse, who, at the prospect
of a good dinner, had speedily made friends with Dantès, and
in whose mind still lingered an indistinct recollection of what
had taken place the preceding day.

As Danglars joined Fernando, he cast a scrutinizing glance at
the discomfited lover, who walked slowly behind the young
couple, his very existence forgotten by Mercédès, who had only
eyes for her beloved Edmond. From time to time the young
Catalan glanced in the direction of Marseilles, and an involuntary
nervous trembling seized him as he seemed momentarily to expect
some important development. Dantès was simply dressed, as became his position in the merchant service, and his handsome face
was illumined with pride and happiness as he gazed at his bride
elect. Mercédès, with her dark eyes and coral lips, boasted the
beauty of the fair Greeks of Cyprus and Chios, and walked with the
free, bold step peculiar to Arlesians and Andalusians.

As soon as the bridal party came in sight of La Réserve, M.
Morrel went out to meet it, followed by some soldiers and young
sailors of the company, to whom he had renewed the promise
already made to Dantès, that he should have the post of captain.
On his appearance, Edmond loosed the arm of his betrothed, and
placed it within that of M. Morrel, who, with the fair maiden,
led the way to the room where the banquet was spread.

" My father," said Mercédès, standing at the centre of the
table, " you must be on my right, please ; and, on my left, I must
place him who has been like a brother to me," she added, with
a sweetness which penetrated Fernando's heart like a dagger
thrust.

His lips turned pale, and even under the dusky hue of his complexion, he showed a deadly pallor which bore witness to the violence with which the blood rushed to his heart.   Dantès, meanwhile, had taken up his position, with M. Morrel on his right, and Danglars on his left, and with a wave of the hand, had signed to the general company to seat themselves as they would.   Then commenced a mighty onslaught on the viands, consisting of savoury Arles sausages, bright red lobsters, prawns with their coloured shells, the echinus with its prickly exterior, and the clovis, considered by the epicures of the south, a greater dainty than even the oyster, besides many other delicacies designated by grateful fishermen under the generic title of " sea-fruits."

" Dear me !   What silence reigns ! " exclaimed the old man, sipping a glass of wine, sparkling as the topaz, which father Pamphile had just placed in front of Mercédès ; " who would think that there were about thirty persons here come together for nothing in the world but to laugh and be merry ? "

' Ah ! but a husband does not always feel so very lively," remarked Caderousse.

" The fact is," said Dantès, " that I am too happy to be gay ; and if that is what you mean, neighbour, you are right.   Joy sometimes almost overwhelms like sorrow."

Danglars glanced at Fernando, whose impressionable nature absorbed and reflected every passing emotion.   " What, then ! are you in dread of anything ?   Your affairs are most flourishing ! "

" Ah ! that is just what makes me tremble," returned Dantès ; " it seems to me that mortal man was never intended to reach happiness so easily.   One must fight with fortune to conquer it, and in truth, I hardly know how or why I have merited the happiness of becoming the husband of Mercédès."

" Husband, indeed ! " cried Caderousse, laughing ; " not just yet, my fine captain ; take on yourself any marital airs, and you would soon see how you would be received ! "

Mercédès blushed.

Fernando moved uneasily on his chair, started at the smallest sound, and from time to time, wiped away the perspiration which streamed down his brow.

" Ah ! ah ! neighbour Caderousse," said Dantès.   " Come, it is hardly worth while to contradict me for so little.   Mercédès is not yet my wife, true ; but (pulling out his watch) in an hour and a half she will be ! "

Everyone uttered a cry of surprise, with the exception of father Dantès, who laughed till he showed his white teeth.   Mercédès smiled quietly, while Fernando convulsively clutched the handle of his knife.

" In an hour ? " said Danglars, turning pale. " How is that, pray ? "

" Yes, my friends," said Dantès ; " thanks to M. Morrel, to whom, next to my father, I owe more than to anyone else in the world, every difficulty has been smoothed away. We have procured the licence, and at half-past two the mayor awaits us at the Hôtel de Ville ; now it has just struck a quarter past one, so that I am not very far wrong in saying that within an hour and thirty minutes, Mercédès will have taken on herself the title of Madame Dantès."

" That is something like setting about business ! " cried father Dantès ; " you cannot say that any time has been lost, eh ? Only landed yesterday, and married to-day at three o'clock ! Ah ! give me a sailor for hitting the nail on the head at once ! "

" But the other formalities," ventured Danglars, shyly, " the contract, and all the arrangements ? "

" The contract," said Dantès, laughing. " The contract is soon settled ; Mercédès has nothing, neither have I ! We shall be married under the administration of the Commune, and it is all settled. It has not taken long to write, and there will not be much to pay."

" So, in point of fact, what we imagined was a feast of betrothal, is really the marriage feast ? " said Danglars.

" Oh ! no ; you will not be the losers. Listen—to-morrow morning I shall start for Paris ; four days for going and four days for returning, with one day for conscientiously fulfilling the commission with which I am charged ; thus I shall return within ten days and, on the following day thereafter, we shall have the genuine marriage feast."

The prospect of another joyful gathering roused the tokens of hilarity to such a pitch, that old Dantès made ineffectual efforts among the din of voices to propose the health and prosperity of the young couple.

Edmond, divining his father's meaning, responded with an affectionate smile, while Mercédès glanced at the little wooden timepiece. The guests were waxing more and more hilarious as the repast drew to a conclusion. They freely left their places to chat with their different neighbours, and as every one was talking at once, the buzz of conversation was considerable.

Danglars had begun to look as pale and anxious as Fernando himself.

As for the young Catalan, he was given up to the most burning torture, and was now pacing up and down, vainly trying to shut out from his ears the singing and the jingling of glasses. Caderousse at length approached him at the same time that Danglars, whom he seemed to avoid, also joined him in a corner of the room.

" Truly," began Caderousse, in whom Dantès' pleasant manners, coupled with the good wine, had obliterated the last spark of animosity against the young sailor, " truly, Dantès is a downright good fellow, and when I look at him sitting there by his lady-love, I think it would have been a shame to play him the wicked trick you were scheming yesterday."

" But you know very well that it had no result ; poor Fernando, here, was so completely cast down, that I felt great compassion for him at first, but as soon as he made up his mind to be best man at the wedding of his rival, I thought there was nothing more to be said."

" Shall we start now ? " said Mercédès, " it is striking two, and we are expected at a quarter past."

" Yes, yes ; we will go," said Dantès, rising quickly

" Off we go," cried the chorus of guests.

At the same moment, Danglars, who was watching Fernando balancing himself on the window sill, observed the latter open wide his haggard eyes, start up with a convulsive movement, and then fall back heavily against the casement.

Immediately a rumbling noise was heard, and the sound of heavy footsteps on the staircase and a confused sound of voices mingled with the clanking of bayonets, drowned the eager exclamations of the guests, who subsided into anxious silence as the commotion increased, and three loud knocks resounded at the door.

" In the name of the law ! " called a voice.

No one replied, and the door then opened, and a commissary of police, in official garb, entered the room, followed by four armed soldiers and a corporal.

" What is your business ? " demanded the shipowner, advancing to meet the commissary, whom he slightly knew. " Certainly, monsieur, there must be some mistake ! "

" If there is any mistake, M. Morrel," replied the commissary, " believe me, it will be soon rectified. In the meantime, I bear a warrant of arrest, and although it gives me pain to do so, I must fulfil my mission. Which of you is Edmond Dantès, gentlemen ?"

" I am he, monsieur ; what do you desire ? "

" Edmond Dantès, I arrest you in the name of the law ! "

" You arrest me ! But why ? " said Edmond, turning slightly pale.

" I cannot tell you, monsieur ; you will learn that on your examination."

M. Morrel saw at once that resistance was entirely out of the question ; a commissary, clad in his official garb, is no longer a man, he is the representative of the law, cold, deaf, and mute. Old Dantès, however, felt nothing of this, in the first shock to his paternal feelings. He darted towards the officer, praying and imploring, but his tears and supplications availed nothing.

" Monsieur," said he, " calm yourself ; perhaps your son has neglected some formality connected with the custom-house, and in all probability, when they have obtained from him the requisite information, he will be set at liberty."

" Now, what does all this mean ? " asked Caderousse.

He looked round for Fernando, but he had disappeared. The whole scene of the preceding evening at once flashed across the tailor's mind with a terrible clearness, for the suddenness of the catastrophe seemed to tear away the cloud of mystification caused by his condition on the previous night. " Oh ! oh ! " said he, in a hoarse voice, " and is this the result of that joke you were contemplating yesterday, Danglars ? If so, shame to him who has done it, for it is a cruel thing ! "

" Nothing of the sort," cried Danglars ; " you know very well that I tore up that piece of paper."

" You did not tear it up," retorted Caderousse ; " you threw it in the corner, that was all ! Where is Fernando ? "

" How can I tell ? " Danglars answered, " about his own affairs, probably. But instead of talking like this, let us go and console these poor creatures."

During this conversation, Dantès had smilingly shaken hands with all his friends, and surrendered himself, saying, " Never mind ; the matter will be cleared up, and probably I shall not even be sent to prison."

" No, no ; I will answer for it," said Danglars, who joined the group.

Dantès descended the stairs, preceded by the commissary, and surrounded by the soldiers. A carriage waited at the door, in which he seated himself, followed by the officer and two of the soldiers, and it then started along the road to Marseilles.

" Adieu, Dantès ! adieu, dear Edmond ! " cried Mercédès, darting to the balcony.

The prisoner heard the cry, coming like a sob from the heart of his betrothed, and putting his head out of the window, called, " Good-bye, Mercédès ! " The carriage disappeared round the corner of Fort Saint Nicholas.

" Wait for me here," said the shipowner ; " I will take the first conveyance I meet, and hasten to Marseilles and bring you the news."

A terrible stupor now fell on the remaining company. The old man and Mercédès stood apart, both overwhelmed in their own grief ; at last their eyes met, and feeling they were both victims of the same cruel blow, they fell into each other's arms.

At this moment, Fernando entered and, hastily drinking a glass of water, seated himself on a chair.

" It was he," said Caderousse to Danglars, with a glance towards the young man.

" I do not think it," said Danglars, " he is too foolish ; however, may the blow recoil on the perpetrator, whoever he may be ! "

" Ah ! you say nothing about the evil counsellor," said Caderousse.

In the meantime, the assembled company were commenting in their different ways on Dantès' arrest.

" And you, Danglars," said one, " what do you think of the matter ? "

" I think it is very probable that he has brought over some bales of contraband merchandise."

" But if that were so, you would probably have known of it," Danglars being the responsible agent.

" Yes, but the agent only knows of the packages that are delivered over to him. I only know that the vessel was laden with cotton which we had from Pestret at Alexandria, and from Pascal at Smyrna ; so ask me no more about it."

" Oh ! now I recollect," murmured the poor old man, " he told me yesterday that he had brought me a chest of coffee and some tobacco."

" There, you see," said Danglars, " that is it ; and during our absence the customs' officers have visited the *Pharaon* and discovered the secret."

Mercédès, however, could not believe this, and now burst forth into sobs.

" Come, come ; we must hope for the best ! " said father Dantès, hardly knowing what he said.

Fernando was about to utter some word of encouragement, but the effort choked him ; his lips moved, but he could not articulate.

" Hurrah ! " shouted one of the guests, " here is a carriage, and it is M. Morrel.   Cheer up ! he, no doubt, brings us good tidings."

Mercédès and the old man hastened to the door to meet the shipowner, who entered, looking extremely pale.

" Well, my friends," said Morrel, shaking his head, " the affair is more serious than we thought ; he is accused of being an agent of the Bonapartists."

Those of my readers who were living at the period to which this story relates, can realize the terrible nature of the accusation referred to by M. Morrel.

Mercédès uttered a piteous cry, and the old man fell into a chair.

" Ah ! " muttered Caderousse, " you have deceived me, Danglars, and the game has been played ; but I will not let this old man and young girl be overwhelmed with sorrow, and I will tell them all about it."

" Hold your tongue, you miserable fellow ! " cried Danglars, seizing his hand, " or I will not answer for your own safety. How do you know that Dantès is not guilty ?   The vessel waited at the Island of Elba, and he was a whole day at Porto Ferrajo ; if any letter is found on him which compromises him, those who uphold him will be regarded as accomplices."

Caderousse, with the rapid instinct of selfishness, felt the full weight of this argument.   " Then we will wait," he murmured.

" Yes, we will wait," Danglars repeated ; " if he is innocent he will be set at liberty ; if he is guilty, it is useless to compromise oneself for a conspirator."

The company began to separate.   Fernando, constituting himself the mainstay of the young girl, took her by the hand, and led her back towards the Catalans, while Dantès' friends collected round the poor old father, and conducted him to the Allées de Meillan.

The report that Dantès had just been arrested as a Bonapartist agent soon spread throughout the town.

" Now, could you have believed it, my dear Danglars ? " said Morrel, joining the supercargo and Caderousse on his way to the town again to obtain some direct news of Edmond from M. de Villefort, the deputy of the Procureur du Roi ; " could you have believed it possible ? "

" Indeed, monsieur, as I told you," replied Danglars, " Dantès, for no apparent reason, cast anchor at the Island of Elba, and as I said, it appeared to me suspicious."

" And have you imparted your suspicions to anyone besides myself ? "

" I have been very guarded, monsieur," said Danglars, almost in a whisper, " for you know, on account of your uncle, M. Policar Morrel, having served under the Bonapartists, and not troubling to conceal his opinions, you might be suspected of regretting Napoleon, and I should be afraid of injuring both you and Edmond."

" Right, Danglars ! you are a good fellow, and I have thought of your interests, when considering the matter of Dantès becoming captain of the *Pharaon*. I questioned Dantès as to how he got on with you, and if he had any repugnance to your continuing your post, for I hardly know why, but I had remarked a coldness between you ; and he said he believed he had not behaved rightly towards you, in one instance, but that everyone who had the confidence of his owner, would have his."

" The hypocrite ! " muttered Danglars.

" Poor Dantès ! " said Caderousse, " he was indeed a good fellow ! "

" Yes, but in the meantime," said M. Morrel, " there is the *Pharaon* without a captain."

" Well, we must hope," said Danglars, " that as we cannot start again for three months, Dantès will be at liberty again by that time."

" Exactly ; but until then ? "

" Well, I am at your service, Monsieur Morrel ; you know that I understand the management of a ship as well as a captain of experience ; and, perhaps, it would answer your purpose to make use of me, and then when Edmond gets out of prison, you will have to thank nobody ; he will take his place and I shall take mine again."

" Thanks, Danglars," said the owner, " that will arrange matters. I authorize you to take the command, and you must superintend the unloading of the goods. Whatever misfortunes occur business must not suffer."

" Be easy on that score, monsieur ; but is it possible to see our friend, Edmond ? "

" I will let you know immediately, Danglars ; I shall try to obtain an interview with M. de Villefort, and intercede with him on the prisoner's behalf. Go on board, and I will join you there." He left the two friends and turned off towards the Palais de Justice.

" You see," said Danglars to Caderousse, " the turn matters have taken ; have you still any desire to go and assist Dantès ? "

"Indeed, no ; but it is a terrible thing that a joke should have such consequences."

"You know that I tossed the paper into a corner ; I even believe I tore it up."

"No, no," said Caderousse ; "as to that, I am positive. I can see it now in the corner of the arbour all crumpled up into a ball, and I wish to goodness it was there now !"

"Well, depend upon it, Fernando picked it up, and either copied it, or got it copied, though, perhaps, he did not even take the trouble ; and now I think of it—— Good heavens ! Perhaps he has sent my own letter ! What a fortunate thing I disguised the writing !"

"Then did you really know that Dantès had been conspiring ?"

"I ? I knew nothing at all. As I said, I thought to make a joke, and nothing else ; and it seems that, like Harlequin, I spoke what was true in jest."

"However it is," said Caderousse, "you will see it will bring us ill-luck."

"If it brings ill-luck to anyone, it will be to the culprit, Fernando, and not to us. How can it get us into trouble ? We have only to keep quiet, and the storm will blow over."

"So be it," returned Caderousse ; and nodding farewell to his companion, he turned his steps towards the Allées de Meillan, shaking his head and talking to himself in a preoccupied manner.

"Good," said Danglars to himself ; "matters have taken just the course that I anticipated. I am now captain for the interim, and if that imbecile, Caderousse, will only hold his tongue, captain for good and all. The only difficulty will be if the law should release Dantès ! Ah ! but I think I may trust it for that. The law is the law !" and so saying, he jumped into a small boat, ordering the boatman to make for the *Pharaon*.

CHAPTER VI

THE DEPUTY PROCUREUR DU ROI

At the same hour that the events just narrated were taking place, a bridal feast was also being celebrated in the Rue du Grand Cours, only in this case the principal actors were amongst the most distinguished members of Marseilles society. There were present, old magistrates, who had resigned their posts under the Usurper, old officers who had left the service to pass into the army of Condé, and young men imbued by their families with sentiments of hatred towards the man of whom five years of Exile would have made a martyr and fifteeen of Restoration a demigod.

The buzz of conversation waxed fast and furious, and the keen passions of the period, always so terrible and implacable in Southern temperaments, had lively play. The Emperor, now sovereign of the Island of Elba after having been ruler over a large portion of the world, was spoken of as lost for ever, both to France and the throne. The magistrates discussed his political blunders; the military men spoke of Moscow and Leipzig; and the ladies of his divorce from Josephine. The whole of this Royalist assembly seemed rejoicing and triumphant over the annihilation of the Bonapartist cause; and life seemed to begin afresh for them, as though they had recovered from a painful dream. An old man, decorated with the cross of Saint Louis, rose and proposed to the company the health of King Louis XVIII. It was the Marquis of Saint Méran. At this toast there was great applause; glasses were jingled in the English fashion, and the ladies unfastened their bouquets, and strewed the flowers on the tablecloth.

" Ah ! " said the Marchioness de Saint Méran, a woman with cold eyes and thin lips, aristocratic, and still elegant-looking, in spite of her fifty years, " if those Revolutionists who drove us away, were here to see this, they would admit that real devotion was on our side, since we remained faithful to the falling monarchy, whilst they, on the contrary, saluted the rising sun, and made their fortunes while we lost ours. They would acknowledge that our king is indeed Louis, our well beloved, while the Usurper is Napoleon, the accursed; eh, De Villefort ? "

" Ah ! madame, but at any rate, they have fanaticism. Napoleon is the Mahomet of the West; and is regarded by his commonplace, but ambitious followers, not only as a legislator and ruler, but a type—the type of equality."

" Equality ! " cried the Marchioness ; " Napoleon the type of equality ! And what do you say then to M. de Robespierre ? It seems to me you oust him from his place to give it to the Corsican, which is something like a usurpation."

" No, madame ; I leave each one on his pedestal. Robespierre on his scaffold in the Place Louis XV., and Napoleon on his column in the Place Vendôme—the one originated an equality which lowered, and the other an equality which raised; the first brought kings to the level of the guillotine, and the latter has raised the people to the level of the throne. I do not mean to say," added Villefort, laughing, " that both were not infamous revolutionists, and that the 9th Thermidor, and the 4th April, 1814, were not both happy days for France, and equally worthy to be celebrated by the friends of order and the monarchy; and that is the reason why, irrevocably fallen as he is, I hope, for ever, Napoleon has still preserved a train of satellites. For, what would you have ? Cromwell, who was not to be compared with Napoleon, had his partisans."

" Do you know that what you are saying, Villefort, savours of revolution ? But I forgive you; one cannot be the son of a Girondist without preserving a small spice of the old leaven."

" My father was a Girondist, madame, it is true," said he, " but my father did not vote for the death of the King; my father was proscribed by the Terror, which proscribed you also, and nearly lost his head on the same scaffold on which your father fell."

" Yes," said the Marchioness, " only it was for principles diametrically opposite that they were persecuted, which is proved by the fact that all my family remained devoted to the exiled princes, while your father rallied to the new government, and after citizen Noirtier had been a Girondist, Count Noirtier became a Senator."

" Madame," said Villefort, " of what use is it to quarrel over things in which the will of heaven, even, is powerless ? For heaven may alter the future, but cannot modify the past. As far as I am concerned, I have given up not only the opinions, but the name of my father. He was, and perhaps still is, a Bonapartist, and his name is Noirtier. I am a Royalist, and call myself de Villefort. I pray you, leave the revolutionary sap to die out with the old tree, and regard only the young shoot which has started up near its root, having neither the power nor the wish to separate itself from the stock from which it sprang."

" Bravo, Villefort !" said the Marquis; " well said ! I am always beseeching the Marchioness to forget the past, but without avail. You, I hope, will be more successful."

" Well, so be it," said the Marchioness. " I am willing, I am sure, to forget the past; but nevertheless, Villefort, be inflexible for the future. If a conspirator should fall into your hands, remember that you are the more closely watched, because it is known that you belong to a family which, perhaps, is conniving at conspiracies."

" Alas ! madame, my profession and the times in which we live, compel me to be severe. and I will be so. I have already several political accusations to bring forward, and I have evidence with regard to them. Unfortunately, we have not seen the end of the matter. Napoleon is very near France, at the Island of Elba, and the consciousness of his proximity, almost in view of our shores, keeps up the spirits of his partisans. Marseilles is full of officers on half-pay, who are always seeking a quarrel with the Royalists, on some frivolous pretext, consequently, duels among the upper classes, and assassinations among the lower orders, occur."

" Yes," said the Count de Salvieux, an old friend of Saint Méran, and chamberlain of the Count d'Artois, " yes, but you know the Holy Alliance intend to remove him to Saint Helena."

" To Saint Helena ! And where is that ? " inquired the Marchioness.

" An island, about two thousand leagues off, on the other side of the equator," replied the Count.

" Unfortunately," said Villefort, " we have the treaties of 1814' and we cannot touch Napoleon without breaking the treaties.',

" Well ! let them be broken," said M. de Salvieux. " He did not regard them much when he wanted to shoot the Duke d'Enghien."

" Yes," said the Marchioness, " it is settled ; the Holy Alliance will get rid of Napoleon from Europe, and Villefort will get rid of his partisans from Marseilles. The King reigns, or does not reign ; if he reigns, his government should be strong, and his agents inflexible ; it is the only way to prevent misfortune."

" Unfortunately, madame," said Villefort, smiling, " a procureur's deputy always arrives when the harm is done."

" Oh ! Monsieur de Villefort," exclaimed a lovely young girl, the daughter of the Count de Salvieux, and a friend of Mademoiselle de Saint Méran, " do try to have a grand trial while we are at Marseilles. I have never been in a law-court, and they say it is very interesting."

" Very interesting, indeed, mademoiselle," replied the deputy. " It is a real tragedy, instead of an imaginary one, with real anguish, instead of mimic woes. For persons of an excitable temperament, who like to have their feelings roused, there is nothing, perhaps, to equal such a spectacle. So rest contented, mademoiselle, and if an occasion presents itself, you shall be gratified."

" It makes one shudder," interposed Renée de Saint Méran, looking pale, " and yet you see he jokes about it."

" And why not ? I look upon it as a duel. Already, I have

procured sentence of death five or six times against political offenders and others, and who knows how many daggers are not being secretly sharpened for my benefit?"

"Oh! heavens!" cried Renée, looking more and more alarmed, "are you speaking seriously, monsieur?"

"I could not speak more seriously," rejoined the young magistrate, with a smile, "and but for these grand law-suits, which mademoiselle desires to see, to satisfy her curiosity, and I desire, to satisfy my ambition, the situation would be unpleasant enough. Do you think that any soldiers of Napoleon would be likely to think more of killing a man whom they believed to be their personal enemy, than of killing a Russian, an Austrian, or a Hungarian, whom they had never seen before? Besides, it is necessary; without it, our profession would come to an end. For myself, when I see the fierce flash of rage in the eyes of the criminal, I feel encouraged, it spurs me on; it is not a law-suit, it is a struggle. I wrestle with him, he makes a thrust, I return it, and the fight ends, either in defeat or victory. That is pleading, you see!—It is danger which brings out eloquence. A criminal, who smiles at my retort, makes me think that I have spoken ill, that what I have said is weak, flat, and insufficient. Think, then, of the sensation of pride which a procureur experiences, when, convinced of the guilt of the accused, he sees the culprit turn pale, and bow before the weight of evidence, and the thunders of his eloquence! His head droops, it will soon fall——"

Renée uttered a cry.

"Ah!" said one of the guests; "you were magnificent in your last case, Villefort; you recollect that man who had assassinated his father; well, literally, you almost killed him before the executioner had touched him."

"Oh! for parricides, it does not matter," said Renée. "No suffering can be bad enough for such men; but for unfortunate political criminals!"

"But they are still worse, Renée; for the king is the father of the nation, and to wish to overthrow or kill the king, is to desire to kill the father of thirty-two millions of men."

"Well, only you must promise me to act with indulgence towards any whom I may recommend to you," said Renée.

"Certainly," said Villefort, with his most charming smile; "we will consult on the verdicts together."

"My dear," said the Marchioness, "you had better attend to your singing-birds, your lap dogs, and your toilettes, and

leave your future husband to manage his own affairs. In these
days, weapons of war are put aside, and the long gown is on
its trial."

" I think I should be better pleased if you were a doctor,"
remarked Renée. " An exterminating angel, though he is an
angel, has always seemed to me very terrible."

" Good Renée," murmured Villefort, eyeing the maiden with
an affectionate glance.

" My child," said the Marquis, " M. de Villefort will be the
moral and political doctor of this province; believe me, it is
a noble part to play."

" And it will be a means of causing the part which his father
played to fall out of remembrance," remarked the incorrigible
Marchioness.

" Madame," returned Villefort, with a melancholy smile, " I
have already had the honour to inform you that my father has
—at least, I hope so—abjured the errors of his past life and is
now become a true upholder of religion and order, and perhaps
a better Royalist than even I am, for with him it is a matter
of repentance, while in my case, it is but a question of choice
and sympathy."

" Yes, my dear Villefort," remarked the Count de Salvieux,
" that is just what I observed the other day at the Tuileries,
when conversing with the Minister of the Royal Household, who
asked the reason of the singular alliance between the son of a
Girondist and the daughter of an officer in the army of Condé;
and he seemed clearly to understand that this method of fusion
is part of the King's policy. It happened that his Majesty
overheard our remarks, though we were not aware of it till he
interrupted us, saying : ' Villefort ' (notice, he did not say Noirtier, but on the contrary, emphasized Villefort), ' Villefort,'
said he, ' will make his way well; he already shows judgment
and discrimination. I am glad to hear that the Marquis and
Marchioness de Saint Méran have accepted him as a son-in-law,
and I should have suggested such an alliance, if they had not
come, in the first instance, to request permission to contract
it.' "

" The King really said that ? " cried Villefort, delighted.
" What do I not owe to this noble prince ? and what would I
not do to serve him ? "

" That is right," said the Marchioness; " I like to hear you
say it. Now, if only a conspirator were to appear at this moment,
he would be welcome."

At this moment, as though Chance had awaited the expression of the wish, a valet entered, and whispered a few words in the deputy's ear.

Villefort begged to be excused, and quitted the room at once, returning after a few moments, his face lit up with a pleasant smile.

Renée gazed at him affectionately ; and certainly, with his fine features and bright expression, it was natural he should excite the innocent admiration of the fair maiden.

" Ah ! mademoiselle," said Villefort, " you were wishing just now you were going to marry a doctor ; well, I certainly have this in common with the disciples of Æsculapius, that I can never call an hour my own ; they come to disturb me even when at your side, and at our betrothal festival."

" And why were you called away ? " asked the young girl, with a little uneasiness.

" Alas ! for a malady of a desperate kind, if one believes what they tell me ; this time, the case is a grave one, almost involving the scaffold."

" Indeed ! " cried all the company together.

" It seems that they have just discovered a little Bonapartist conspiracy. This is the letter of accusation," continued Villefort, and read as follows : " ' Monsieur the Procureur du Roi is warned by a friend to the throne and religion, that one Edmond Dantès, mate of the ship *Pharaon*, which arrived in port this morning from Smyrna, after having touched at Naples and Porto Ferrajo, has been commissioned by Murat with a letter for the Usurper, and by the Usurper with a letter for the Bonapartist Committee at Paris. Proof of his crime will be obtained on arresting him, for the letter will be found either upon his person, or in his father's house, or in his cabin on board the *Pharaon*.' "

" But," said Renée, " this letter, which is after all anonymous, is addressed to the King's procureur, and not to you."

" Yes, but the procureur is absent, and in his absence the epistle is delivered to his secretary, who is empowered to open his letters ; he opened this, then sent for me, but not finding me, has given orders for the arrest."

" So the criminal has been arrested ? " said the Marchioness.

" The accused, that is to say," remarked Renée. " Where is the poor creature ? "

" At my house."

" Come, my friend," said the Marquis, " do not neglect your

duties by remaining here, when the service of the King calls you elsewhere ; go where duty summons you."

" Oh ! Monsieur de Villefort," said Renée, clasping her hands, " be merciful ; recollect it is the day of our betrothal ! "

Villefort approached the young girl, and resting his hand on the back of her chair, said, " To save you uneasiness, my dear Renée, I will do all that I can ; but if the information is trust-worthy, and the accusation true, this Bonapartist weed must be cut down."

" Bah ! " said the Marchioness, " do not listen to that child, Villefort, she will soon get over these things," and she ex-tended to the young man her thin hand, which he kissed, with a glance towards Renée, saying, with his eyes : " It is your hand that I kiss, or rather that I would kiss at this moment, beloved."

" Pardon the weak Royalist, madame," said Villefort, " and I promise to fulfil my duty as deputy of the procureur, conscien-tiously, that is to say, to be horribly severe."

But at the same time that the young magistrate uttered these words, he stole a furtive glance at his fiancée, which said as plainly as words, " Be easy, Renée ; for the sake of your love, I will be indulgent."

CHAPTER VII

THE EXAMINATION

SCARCELY had Villefort quitted the banqueting-room when his joyous expression gave place to the aspect of a man called to exercise the grave function of pronouncing on the life of his fellow-man. On this occasion, however, notwithstanding the natural mobility of his physiognomy, he experienced more diffi-culty in knitting his brows and schooling his expression. For Gérard de Villefort was, at that moment, as happy as it is possible for human being to be. Already possessed of a good fortune, he occupied at the age of twenty-seven, an elevated official post, and was about to marry a young and beautiful girl, whom he loved, not, perhaps, passionately, but reasonably, as befitting a deputy of the Procureur du Roi. Mademoiselle de Saint Méran belonged to a family holding a distinguished and influen-tial position, and their political influence would now be exerted in his own behalf ; moreover, his bride would bring him a fortune of six thousand pounds, which, on her father's death, would increase to twenty thousand. All these different consider-ations induced in Villefort a state of dazzling felicity.

At the door he met the commissary of police, who awaited him. The sight of this individual at once caused the young man to return from flights in the seventh heaven to mother earth again ; he composed his features, and approaching the officer of justice, said :

" Here I am, monsieur ; I have read the letter, and you did well to arrest the man. Now, as we walk along, give me all the particulars about him, and about the conspiracy, that you have been able to gather."

" Of the conspiracy, monsieur, we know nothing at present. All the papers found about him have been made up into a sealed bundle, and deposited on your writing-table. As to the prisoner, as you have seen by the letter, he is named Edmond Dantès, and is mate of the three-masted ship, *Pharaon*, trading in cotton to Alexandria and Smyrna, and belonging to the firm of Morrel and Son, of Marseilles."

" Had he served in the military service, before entering the mercantile marine ? "

" Oh, no ! monsieur ; he is quite a young man. About nineteen or twenty."

At this moment, as Villefort, making his way along the Grande Rue, arrived at the corner of the Rue des Conseils a man who appeared to be awaiting his coming, accosted him. It was M. Morrel.

" Ah ! Monsieur de Villefort," he cried, " I am indeed fortunate to meet you. Do you know they have just been making the most unheard-of mistake, in arresting the mate of my ship, Edmond Dantès ? "

" I am aware of it, monsieur," said Villefort ; " and am just going to examine him."

" Oh ! Monsieur Villefort ! " cried Morrel, carried away by his sincere regard for the young man, " you do not know him whom you accuse, and I know him well. He is the best and most upright fellow in the world, and I can commend him most heartily and sincerely."

Now Villefort, as we have seen, belonged to the aristocratic party, whereas Morrel belonged to the plebeian class ; therefore, speaking coldly, and with a disdainful glance, Villefort replied :

" You know, monsieur, that a man may be good in his private life, honest in his commercial relations, and capable and clever in his work, and be none the less a criminal, politically speaking ; you are aware of that, are you not, monsieur ? "

Morrel coloured, for he did not feel his conscience quite pure with regard to political opinions ; and, moreover, the confidence which Dantès had reposed in him, concerning his interview with the Grand Marshal, and the few words the Emperor had addressed to him, somewhat troubled the mind of the worthy shipowner. He added, however, with an accent of profound feeling :

" I beg of you, monsieur, be just and generous as you always are, and give the poor fellow, Dantès, up to us at once ! "

The terms in which the request was couched, sounded somewhat revolutionary to the ears of the deputy Procureur du Roi. " Give up to *us*," he repeated to himself. " This Dantès, then, is probably connected with some sect of the Carbonari. The commissary said, I believe, that he was arrested at a tavern, surrounded by companions ; it is some secret society." Then he replied, " Monsieur, if the prisoner is innocent, you will not have made a useless appeal to my justice ; but if, on the contrary, he is guilty, I shall be compelled to do my duty."

As he said these words, he reached his own house at the back of the Palais de Justice, and entered it in a dignified manner, saluting, with icy politeness, the unfortunate shipowner.

The antechamber was full of officers and police agents, and in the midst of them, closely guarded, and gazed at by those around him with fierce and searching glances, stood the prisoner, calm and motionless. Villefort crossed the hall, casting a side-long look on Dantès, and having received a bundle of papers, delivered to him by a police agent, disappeared into an adjoining room, saying, " Let the prisoner be brought in."

Rapid as had been his inspection, Villefort had noted the intelligence of the broad, open brow, the courage of the steady eye, and knitted eyebrows, and the truthfulness of the full, half-opened lips, which disclosed a double row of teeth as white as ivory. The first impression was certainly favourable to Dantès, but Villefort had so often heard it propounded that one should distrust one's first impulses, that he stifled the good instincts which might have softened his heart, and with a grave and forbidding aspect, seated himself at his desk. An instant later, Dantès entered. The young man was still pale, but calm and smiling. He saluted his judge with an easy politeness, then looked towards a chair, as he might have done in M. Morrel's drawing-room. It was then he first met the fixed expression of Villefort's eye, a look peculiar to people in office, who do not wish their thoughts to be read, but desire to penetrate those of others.

"Who are you ? and what is your name ? " demanded Ville-fort, turning over the papers the police agent had put in his hand.

"My name is Edmond Dantès, monsieur," replied the young man, "and I am mate on board the *Pharaon*, which belongs to M. Morrel and Son."

"What were you doing at the time you were arrested ? "

"I was taking part in my own betrothal festival, monsieur," said Dantès, in a slightly moved voice, so painful was the con-trast of those happy moments with the gloomy ceremony at present on hand. "I was about to marry a woman whom I have loved truly for three years."

Impassive as Villefort was ordinarily, he was nevertheless struck with this coincidence, and the trembling voice of Dantès, who had been surprised in the midst of his greatest happiness, struck a sympathetic chord in his own soul ; *he* also was about to be married, he had been happy by the side of her he loved, when they came to fetch him away, that he might contribute to destroy the joy of a man, who, like himself, had just reached the goal of all his hopes.

Turning again to Dantès, Villefort said : "Well, continue your information. Did you ever serve under the Usurper ? "

"I was about to enter the navy, when he fell from power."

"It is said your political opinions are very pronounced," said Villefort, who had not heard a whisper of anything of the kind, but was, nevertheless, not indisposed to put the question in the form of an accusation.

"My political opinions, monsieur ? alas ! I am almost ashamed to say I hardly think I have what would be called an opinion at all ; I am scarcely nineteen. I am very ignorant. Political feelings, I have none ; and all my private sentiments are included in these : I love my father, I respect M. Morrel, and I adore Mercédès. There, monsieur, that is all I have to say, and it is not particularly interesting."

While Dantès spoke, Villefort continued to regard his open, honest countenance. His experience, with regard to criminals, told him at every word that Dantès uttered, that the man before him was innocent.

"*Pardieu !* " he said mentally, "he is a nice fellow, and I shall have but little trouble, I hope, in pleasing Renée, by fulfil-ling the first request she has made of me, and shall be repaid by a gentle pressure of the hand before the public gaze, and a charming kiss in the corner."

And at this pleasant prospect, Villefort's face softened, and Dantès smiled as he saw the gentler expression.

" Are you aware if you have any enemies ? " demanded Villefort ; " or if not enemies, somebody who is jealous of you ? You are about to be made captain at nineteen years of age, which is an elevated post for you, and you are going to marry a pretty woman who loves you, which is a rare happiness in any earthly career ; these two lucky numbers in the lottery of fate may have made some people envious."

" Well, you may be right, monsieur ; but if anyone is jealous of me, I declare to you I would rather not know it, that I should not be obliged to hate him."

" Ah ! you are wrong there," returned Villefort ; " it is always best to see one's way as clearly as possible ; and, in fact, you appear to me such a worthy fellow, I am going to depart from the ordinary regulations of the law, and aid you in throwing some light on the matter, by showing you the communication which caused you to be brought before me. This is the indictment ; do you recognize the writing ? " Villefort drew the letter from his pocket, and handed it to Dantès.

The young man looked through it, a shade passing over his face. He then said :

" No, monsieur, I do not know the writing ; it is disguised, but, nevertheless, very clear, and the work of a practised hand. I am, indeed, fortunate," he went on, regarding Villefort with gratitude, " to fall into the hands of a man like you, for this fellow is indeed an enemy ! " And the young man's eyes flashed as he spoke, while Villefort noted the signs of vehement feeling underlying his quiet exterior.

" Now, listen to me," said the magistrate, " and answer frankly, as a man in a false position speaks to another who is interested in his behalf. Is there any truth whatever in this anonymous accusation ? " and with an expression of disgust, he tossed the letter back on the table.

" There is, and there is not, monsieur ; and that is the fact of the matter, on my honour as a sailor, and on my love for Mercédès."

" Speak on," said Villefort ; adding to himself, " if Renée could see me now, I think she would be pleased with me, and would no longer call me an exterminator."

" This, monsieur, was the fact of the matter," began Dantès : " After leaving Naples, Captain Leclère fell ill of brain fever ; his malady continued to increase until the end of the third day, when, feeling he should not last much longer, he called me to him. ' My dear Dantès,' said he, ' swear to me, on your honour, to carry out what I am going to charge you with, for great interests are concerned.' ' I swear it, captain,' I replied. ' Well, after my death, you will take the post of captain, make for the Island of Elba, and land at Porto Ferrajo ; then obtain an interview with the Grand Marshal, and deliver to him this letter. Another letter will then, probably, be given you, which you will be commissioned to deliver.' ' I will do it,' I replied, ' but perhaps it will not be as easy as you imagine, to obtain access to the Grand Marshal.' ' Here,' he said, ' is a ring which will remove every difficulty ; ' and so saying, he delivered to me a ring. It was only just in time ; two hours later he was seized with delirium, and the next day he was dead."

" And what did you do then ? "

" What I felt was my duty, monsieur, and what any other would have done in my place ; with sailors, the last requests of their superior are commands which they are bound to carry out. I made for the Island of Elba, and went ashore alone. As I had foreseen, there were some difficulties in getting an interview with the Grand Marshal, but I sent him the ring, and every door opened before me. He received me, questioned me as to the last moments of Captain Leclère, and gave me a letter which he charged me to convey to someone in Paris. On landing at Marseilles, I rapidly made my arrangements, and hastened to see my betrothed. Thanks to M. Morrel, we got over every ecclesiastical difficulty, and I was taking part in my betrothal feast, was to be married in an hour, and intended to start to-morrow for Paris, when this accusation, which you appear to despise as much as I do, caused my arrest."

" Yes, yes," murmured Villefort, " all this appears likely enough, and if you were guilty of anything, it was but an imprudence, and an imprudence authorized by your captain's orders. Give me this letter which was given you at Elba, give me your word to appear at the first inquiry, and go and join your friends."

" It must be there before you, monsieur, for they took it from me with all my other papers, which I recognize in that bundle."

" Ah ! wait then," said Villefort, as Dantès was about to take his hat, and depart ; " wait a moment. To whom is it addressed ? "

" *To Monsieur Noirtier, No. 13, Rue Coq-Héron, Paris.*"

If Villefort had been struck with a thunderbolt, the blow could not have been more overwhelming ; he sank into his chair, and then stretched forward to reach the papers, turning them over with precipitation, until he found the fatal letter, on which he fixed a glance of inexpressible horror.

" M. Noirtier, No. 13, Rue Coq-Héron," he murmured, turning paler and paler.

" Yes, monsieur," said Dantès ; " do you know him ? "

" No," replied Villefort, promptly ; " a faithful subject of the king does not know conspirators."

" Is there then a conspiracy ? " demanded Dantès, who, after having imagined he was set free, was now seized with a greater terror than at first. " At any rate, monsieur, I am completely ignorant of the contents of the dispatch."

" Yes," returned Villefort in a grating voice, " but you know the name of the person to whom it is addressed ! "

" I was obliged to know it, of course, monsieur, in order to deliver it."

" And you have shown this letter to no one ? " said Villefort, turning paler as he perused the letter. " And no one is aware that you were the bearer of a letter from Elba, addressed to M. Noirtier ? "

" No one, monsieur, except he who gave it to me."

The deputy, looking pale and haggard, read the letter a second time.

" And you say you do not know the contents of this letter ? " he observed.

" On my honour, monsieur, I repeat I do not. But what is the matter ? are you ill ? Shall I ring, or call someone ? "

" No," said Villefort, rising hastily, " I need nothing; it was but a passing weakness ; " then as Dantès stood waiting further examination, Villefort again dropped into his chair, and passing his cold hand over his damp brow, set himself again to read the letter. " Oh ! if he knows the contents of this letter, and if he ever learns that Noirtier is the father of Villefort, I am lost, lost for ever ! " he murmured, glancing from time to time at Edmond, as though he were longing to break down the invisible barrier which shuts in the secrets of all hearts. " Oh ! there is no doubt about it ! " he cried suddenly.

Villefort put a violent constraint upon himself, and in a voice which he endeavoured to render firm, said : " Monsieur, you are gravely compromised by these disclosures, and I am not in a position, as I hoped at first, to set you at liberty. I must, before taking such a course, consult the magistrate. I shall have to detain you as a prisoner for some time, as short a time as I am able. The principal charge against you is this letter, and you see this ? "—and Villefort approached the fireplace, tossed the paper into the fire, and waited until it was reduced to ashes. " There, you see, I have destroyed it. Now, after such an act, you feel, do you not, that you can have confidence in me ? "

" Oh ! monsieur ! order, and I will obey."

" No," said Villefort, approaching the young man, " it is not commands I wish to give you, but words of advice. I shall keep you at the Palais de Justice until evening ; you will, perhaps, be questioned by someone else. Say all that you have told me, but not a word about the letter."

" I promise, monsieur."

" You understand," said Villefort, " now that this letter is destroyed, you and I only know that it existed. It can never be brought forward against you ; therefore, if you are ever questioned, deny it, deny it boldly, and you are saved. That was the only letter you had ? "

Dantès stretched out his hand. " I swear it," he said.

Villefort rang, and the commissary of police entered, to whom the deputy whispered a few words privately

" Follow this gentleman," said Villefort to Dantès.

The latter cast a last glance of gratitude towards him, bowed, and left the room. The door had scarcely closed when Villefort's strength failed him, and he fell back, almost fainting on the chair. " Oh, my God ! " he murmured. " How have I escaped ? If the Procureur had been at Marseilles, or the magistrate had been sent for in my place, that accursed letter would have utterly ruined me ! Ah ! my father, my father, will you for ever be an obstacle to my happiness in this world, and shall I always have your past life rising against me ! " Then suddenly his expression brightened. " Let me consider," he murmured. " Yes ! now I have it ! Who knows but this letter which might have been my ruin, may not make my fortune ? Forward, Villefort ! there is work to be done ! " So saying, he started up, and having assured himself that the prisoner was no longer in the antechamber, set out for the house of his *fiancée*.

CHAPTER VIII

THE CHÂTEAU D'IF

ON reaching the antechamber, the commissary of police signed to two gendarmes, who conducted Dantès through a door communicating from the Procureur's apartment to the Palais de

Justice, and along several dark corridors to the prison, a sombre edifice fronting on to the clock-tower of Accoules.

The room in which he was placed was fairly comfortable, and its aspect somewhat appeased his uneasiness ; moreover, the words of the young deputy, uttered in a voice so full of kindly interest, recurred to his mind, like a sweet message of hope. It was about four o'clock when Dantès was left in his room ; and as it was about the beginning of March, he soon found that darkness was creeping on.

Then, as the sense of hearing grew keener, while the power of vision diminished, the slightest sound sufficed to convince him that they were coming to set him at liberty, and he would rise quickly and take a step forward towards the door ; but the noise would soon die away, or pass off in another direction, and Dantès would sink back again on his seat. At last, towards ten o'clock at night, when he was beginning to lose all hope, a key was turned in the lock, the bolts were pushed back with a grating noise, and the massive oak door opened. The dazzling light of two torches suddenly illuminated the dark cell, and Dantès beheld the shining sabres and muskets of four gendarmes. He had taken two steps forward, but remained motionless on seeing this increase of force.

" Do you come to fetch me by order of the deputy Procureur ? "

" Certainly."

" I am ready to follow you."

The knowledge that they came for him by order of M. de Ville-fort removed all fear from the mind of the unfortunate young man, and he advanced calmly and placed himself in the midst of his escort. A carriage was waiting at the street entrance, a driver on the box, and a police officer beside him.

Dantès would have asked some questions, but the door was opened, and he found himself, in another moment, seated in the carriage between two gendarmes, with the two others facing him on the opposite seat ; and the heavy conveyance at once started off. The prisoner cast a glance at the windows, they were barred ; but Dantès could see that he was being taken along the Rue Caisserie, and by the Rue Saint Laurent and Rue Taramis down to the quay. Soon he saw the lights of the barracks.

The carriage stopped, and at the same moment, a dozen soldiers came out, and placed themselves in a line, and Dantès could see their muskets shining under the lights on the quay.

" Is all this display of military force on my account ? " he asked himself.

The question was soon answered; for though the officer opened the door without making any remark, Edmond saw the soldiers arranging themselves in a double line, leaving a passage from the carriage to the quay. The two gendarmes who had been seated opposite stepped out first, then the prisoner, and the two guards who had been placed on each side of him. They then walked towards a boat which a bargeman of the customs-house kept fastened to the quay by a chain, and in a few moments, he was installed in the stern of the boat, still surrounded by the four gendarmes, whilst the police officer remained in the prow. With a violent shake the boat was loosed from its moorings, and the four sailors rowed off vigorously towards Pillon. At a shout from the crew, the chain that closes the mouth of the port was lowered, and Dantès found himself out of the harbour. The first sensation of the prisoner on reaching the open air, was a feeling of pleasure. He took a deep breath, inhaling the fresh breeze; but soon a sigh escaped him: he was passing La Réserve where he had, that same morning, been so buoyantly happy.

The boat continued its way; it had passed the Tête de Mort and was opposite the Creek of Pharo, and was now about to double the battery, which appeared to Dantès an incomprehensible manœuvre.

"But where are you taking me?" he asked of one of the gendarmes.

"We are forbidden to give any explanation."

Dantès was half a soldier himself, and he knew it was absurd to question subordinates who were forbidden to reply, so he was silent. Many strange thoughts, however, rose in his mind; he imagined that they were about to deposit him on a distant point of the coast and tell him he was free; it appeared to him a favourable sign that they had not attempted to handcuff him; besides, had not the deputy told him, that provided he never pronounced the fatal name of Noirtier, he had nothing to fear; and had he not destroyed, in his very presence, that dangerous letter, which was the only proof against him?

He waited, therefore, silently and patiently, endeavouring to penetrate the obscurity of the night. They had passed the Isle of Ratonneau, with its lighthouse, on their right, and skirting along the coast, were now just above the Catalans' creek. He strained his eyes more and more eagerly; it was there Mercédès lived, and every moment he imagined he descried on the dark shore, the indistinct and shadowy form of a woman.

A solitary light gleamed in the Catalans' quarter, and calc ing on its position, Dantès felt sure that it shone in the chamb of his beloved. Mercédès, then, was the only one watching in the little colony, and if he uttered a loud cry, she might hear him. But a false shame checked him. What would these men say, hearing him cry out like a madman? He remained mute, therefore, his eyes fixed on the light, thinking of Mercédès.

A sudden rising ground at last hid the light from view, and Dantès, turning round, found the boat standing out to sea. Notwithstanding the repugnance Dantès felt at again addressing any questions to the gendarme, he at last approached him, and taking his hand, said, "Comrade, I beseech you to have pity on me, and answer me. I am a captain, a good and loyal Frenchman, although accused of I do not know what treason; where are you taking me? Speak out, and on my honour as a sailor, I will submit and resign myself to my fate."

The gendarme scratched his ear, and looked towards his comrade, who replied with a shrug; then turning to Dantès, he said, "You are a Marseillais, and a sailor, and yet you ask me where we are going?"

"On my honour, I do not know. Tell me for pity's sake!"

"But my orders!"

"Your orders do not prevent you from telling me what, in ten minutes, half-an-hour, or an hour, perhaps, I must know. You will only be saving me an age of uncertainty. I have no intention of resisting or getting away, for it would be impossible. Where are we going?"

"Look round you."

Dantès rose and looked towards the point for which the boat was making, and about a hundred fathoms off, he saw, rising before him, the black and frowning rock, on which, like an excrescence of flint, stands the gloomy Château d'If. As this prison-fortress, which for centuries had been regarded with profound terror by the people of Marseilles, burst suddenly on Dantès' sight, he felt like a condemned criminal brought in sight of the scaffold.

"Good heavens!" he cried, "the Château d'If! You are surely not taking me there to be imprisoned; the Château d'If is a state prison for great political prisoners, and I have committed no crime. Perhaps there are magistrates and judges there?"

"There is only a governor, I imagine," returned the gendarme, "with a garrison of soldiers, jailers, and some strong walls. Come,

don't put on that air of astonishment, or you will
  you are repaying my civility by laughing at me."
  n to say that I am being taken to the Château d'If,
  soned, without any information or formality ? "
  rmalities have been gone through."

  , in spite of M. de Villefort's promise——"

  o not know what M. de Villefort promised," said the
g me ; " I only know we are going to the Château d'If. Hey !
what are you doing ? Hallo ! comrades ; help ! help ! "

With a movement, swift as lightning, but nevertheless, anticipated by the experienced officer, Dantès endeavoured to take a
leap into the sea ; but four strong hands were quickly on him, and
he was secured just as his feet were about to leave the plank. He
fell to the bottom of the boat with a cry of rage.

" Good ! " cried the gendarme, placing his knee on his chest,
" so this is how you keep your word as a sailor. Well now, my
friend, stir if you dare, and I put a ball through your head ; I
have disobeyed my first order, but will not disobey the second,
that I promise you ; " and so saying, he turned his rifle on Dantès,
who could feel the end of the muzzle resting against his temple.
For a moment the unhappy prisoner was almost tempted to make
the forbidden movement and thus end the misfortune which had
befallen him. But because the evil was so unexpected, Dantès
felt that it could not be of long duration ; the promises of M. de
Villefort, too, returned to his recollection. He therefore lay at
the bottom of the boat, clenching his hands with fury and uttering cries of rage. A moment later, a violent shock made the boat
toss to and fro.

One of the oarsmen jumped on to the rock, which the prow
had just grazed. A rope was unrolled from the pulley, and
Dantès knew they were mooring the boat. His guards now made
him rise, and conducted him on shore, holding him by the arms
and collar of his coat. He was then dragged towards some steps
leading to the entrance, the police officer following, armed with a
musket and bayonet. Dantès, however, made no further useless
resistance. He dimly perceived that there were more soldiers
stationed on the steep ascent, and he felt the flight of steps, which
obliged him to lift his feet, and noticed that he had passed through
a door which had closed behind him, but all in a mechanical
manner, as through a mist which obscured his vision. A halt
was made for a moment, during which Dantès endeavoured to
collect his scattered senses. He looked round him ; he was in a
square courtyard, formed by four high walls ; the slow, measured

tread of sentinels could be heard at intervals, and as they passed beneath the lamps projecting from the walls, the barrels of their muskets could be seen shining in the dim light. Confident that Dantès could no longer escape, the gendarmes released him and awaited orders.

" Where is the prisoner ? " inquired a voice at length.

" Here ! " answered a gendarme.

" Let him follow me to his cell."

The prisoner followed his conductor, who led the way to a subterranean cell, the bare and dripping walls of which seemed as though impregnated with tears. A small lamp, its wick swimming in grease, lit up the damp shining walls of this frightful abode. By its glimmer, Dantès scanned the countenance of his escort, a jailer of low stamp, ill-dressed, and sullen-looking.

" This is your room for the night," said he ; " it is late, and the governor is gone to bed. To-morrow, perhaps, when he has received the orders about you, you may be put somewhere else ; in the meantime, here is bread, and some water in that pitcher, and straw laid down in the corner, which is all a prisoner can want. Good-night."

And before Dantès could open his mouth to reply, the jailer had taken the light, and closing the door, left him without even the feeble glimmer which had lighted up the streaming walls of his prison. Then he found himself alone in the darkness and the silence, as mute as the gloomy vault itself, the freezing coldness of which struck on his burning brow like ice. With returning day, a few gleams of light penetrated the darkness of the solitary den, and soon the jailer came to say the prisoner was to remain there. Dantès had never once changed his position ; a hand of iron seemed to have rooted him to the spot where he was standing the previous evening, and his dark eyes were swollen with weeping. Thus he had spent the whole night, without sleeping a single instant. The jailer approached him, but Dantès appeared not to be aware of his presence.

" Have you not slept ? "

" I do not know," said Dantès.

" And are you not hungry ? " he continued.

" I do not know," said Dantès.

" Do you want anything ? "

" I want to see the governor."

The jailer shrugged his shoulders and went out.

Dantès followed him with his eyes, and stretched his hands towards the half-open door ; but it slowly closed. Then his breast seemed rent with deep-drawn sobs, and falling forward on the ground, he prayed fervently, asking himself what crime he had committed that he, so young withal, should suffer such a cruel punishment. Thus the day passed. He drank a little water, and tasted a few mouthfuls of bread. Sometimes he remained seated, absorbed in his thoughts, and then would walk round and round his prison, like a wild animal in an iron cage. One thought above all made him almost mad with rage, namely, the recollection that during his voyage to his prison, when he had been so calm and tranquil in his unsuspecting confidence, he might have thrown himself into the sea a dozen times, escaped from his keepers, gained some solitary creek, and there awaited a Genoese or Catalan vessel, on which he might have reached Italy or Spain, and thence written to Mercédès to come and join him. He might have lived happily with Mercédès and his father, for his father would have come out to join them—and now, here he was, a prisoner in the Château d'If, not knowing what had become of his father or Mercédès, and all because he had trusted in the word of De Villefort. It was enough to drive him mad, and Dantès rolled over in a fury on the fresh straw that the jailer had laid down.

The next day, at the same hour, the jailer again entered.

" Well ! " said he, " are you more reasonable to-day ? Come, cheer up, and tell me if you want anything that it is in my power to get you."

" I wish to speak to the governor."

" Eh ! " said the jailer impatiently ; " but I told you yesterday that was impossible. By the rules of the prison, a prisoner is not permitted to ask it."

" What is allowed here, then ? " demanded Dantès.

" Better food, by paying for it, and a walk, and sometimes books."

" I have no need of books, I do not care to go out, and my food is good enough ; I only want one thing, to see the governor."

" If you pester me with always repeating the same thing," said the jailer, " I will bring you no more to eat."

" Well," said Dantès, " if you bring me no more I shall die of hunger ; that is all ! "

The accent with which he uttered this showed plainly that he would be glad to die ; and as every prisoner was reckoned to bring about ten sous a day to his jailer, Dantès' keeper considered at once the deficit that would result from his death, and replied in a gentler tone :

" Listen to me ; what you ask is impossible, for such a thing was never heard of as the governor coming to see a prisoner in his cell ; but, if you behave well, they will allow you to walk out, and it is very possible that some day, when you are out, the governor will pass by ; then you can question him, and if he thinks fit, he will answer you."

" But how long must I wait," said Dantès, " before this chance meeting occurs ? "

" Oh, well ; a month, three months, six months, perhaps a year."

" That is too long," cried Dantès ; " I must see him at once ! "

" Ah ! you had better not absorb yourself in one impossible desire, or you will be mad in a fortnight. That is the way that madness always begins, and we had an example here ; it was by unceasingly offering the governor a million of money, if he would only set him at liberty, that the abbé who inhabited this very cell became distracted and was put in the dungeon."

" Listen a moment," said Dantès ; " I am not an abbé, and I am not mad ; perhaps I may become so, but unhappily for me, at the present time, I have all my senses, and I am going to make a proposal to you. I cannot offer you a million of money, for I have it not to give ; but I offer you a hundred crowns if, the first time that you go to Marseilles, you will go to the Catalans' quarter, and deliver a letter to a young girl named Mercédès ; it will hardly be a letter, a couple of lines only."

" If I were discovered, I should lose my place, which is worth a thousand francs a year, without counting the profits and food ; so you see, I should be very foolish to risk losing a thousand francs for the sake of gaining three hundred."

" Well, then," said Dantès, " bear this in mind, if you refuse to take these two lines to Mercédès, or, at any rate, to inform her that I am here, I will wait for you some day behind the door, and I will break your head with this wooden stool ! "

" Oh ! you threaten, do you ? " cried the jailer, taking a step backwards, and putting himself on the defensive ; " decidedly, your head is turned ; in three days you will be mad enough to be chained up, too ; happily, there are dungeons in the Château d'If."

Dantès seized the stool, and whirled it round his head.

" Exactly so," said the jailer ; " well, since you wish it so much, I will go and tell the governor."

" So much the better," said Dantès, placing the stool on the ground, and seating himself on it, his head hanging down, and his eyes as wild and haggard as though his senses had really deserted him. The jailer left him, and speedily returned with four soldiers and a corporal.

" By order of the governor," said he, " the prisoner here is to be taken down to the dungeon ; madmen must be put with madmen."

The soldiers took hold of Dantès, who accompanied them without resistance. The dungeon door was opened and he entered, murmuring to himself, " He is right, madmen must be put with madmen."

The door closed, and Dantès groped in front of him, with extended hands, until he came in contact with the wall ; then he seated himself in a corner, and remained motionless.

The jailer was right ; it needed but little more to render Dantès mad.

CHAPTER IX

THE EVENING OF THE BETROTHAL

VILLEFORT started out, on the termination of his interview with Dantès, along the Place du Grand Cours, on his way back to Madame de Saint Méran's. On his arrival, he found that the guests had adjourned to the drawing-room, and were taking coffee. Renée was awaiting him with an impatience that was shared by the whole company ; and as he entered the room, he was greeted with acclamation.

" Well, you decapitator ! defender of the government, and Royalist Brutus ! what is it ? tell us at once ! Are we menaced with another Reign of Terror ? Or, has the ogre of Corsica escaped from his den ? "

" Madame," said Villefort, approaching his future mother-in-law, " I must beg you to excuse me, if I am compelled to absent myself ; " and turning to the Marquis, he added, " monsieur, may I have the honour of a few words with you in private ? "

" Ah ! is the affair so grave ? "

" So grave that I am obliged to take my leave of you for a few days ; therefore," continued he, turning towards Renée, " the matter, as you may suppose, must indeed be serious."

" You are going away ! " cried Renée, unable to conceal her emotion.

" Alas ! yes, mademoiselle," replied Villefort ; " it is a matter of necessity."

" And where are you going ? " questioned the Marchioness.

" That is a state secret, madame ; however, if anyone present has commissions in Paris, I have a friend starting this evening who will undertake them with pleasure."

" You desired a moment's conversation with me ? " said the Marquis.

They left the room, the Marquis taking Villefort's arm.

" Well," said he, when they had ensconced themselves in easy-chairs, " and what is it ? speak ! "

" Certain things have occurred which necessitate my immediate departure for Paris ; and now, monsieur, excuse the apparent indiscretion of such a question, but have you any government shares ? "

" My money is all in the funds—from six to seven hundred thousand francs."

" Then sell, monsieur ; sell out at once, or you are ruined. Give me a letter for your broker, and let him sell without losing a minute, or even a second. Perhaps, after all, I shall arrive too late."

" Mon Dieu ! " cried the Marquis, " let us lose no time."

And he seated himself at the table, and wrote off a letter to his agent, ordering him to sell the shares at any price.

" Now that I have this letter," said Villefort, carefully placing it in his pocketbook, " I also need another for the King."

" But I dare not take it upon myself to address his Majesty."

" No, but I desire that you should request M. de Salvieux to do so. I require a letter by which I can gain an audience of his Majesty, without going through formalities which would waste precious time. My future is assured if I can only be the first to reach the Tuileries ; for I shall have rendered the King a service he cannot overlook."

" In that case, my dear fellow, go and get your things together, and I will fetch Salvieux, and ask him to write a letter to procure you an *entrée*."

" I must beg you to excuse me to the Marchioness, and to Mademoiselle de Saint Méran, whom I leave at such a time with profound regret."

" You had better seek them and make your own adieux."

" A thousand thanks ; and you will get me the letter ? "

The Marquis rang and a footman appeared.

" Tell the Count de Salvieux that I should be glad to speak to him."

" And now you had better go," the Marquis added, addressing Villefort.

Taking his departure, Villefort set off at full speed ; but when fairly in the street, he recollected that the sight of the procureur's deputy rushing along so precipitately would trouble the repose

C

of the whole town—he therefore resumed his usual sedate and magisterial gait. As he approached his own door, he perceived a white figure standing there, motionless. It was the beautiful Catalan maiden, who, anxious for news of her lover, had started under cover of the night, to come and learn for herself the cause of his arrest. Villefort recognized her before she named herself. The exceeding beauty and dignity of the young girl surprised him ; and when she questioned him as to what had become of her lover, he felt as if he were a criminal, and she the judge.

"The man you are speaking of," he replied roughly, "is guilty, and I can do nothing for him, mademoiselle."

A sob burst from Mercédès, and as Villefort attempted to pass her, she stopped him again.

"But at any rate, tell me where he is," she cried, "that I may learn whether he is living or dead ? "

"I do not know ; he is out of my hands now," replied Villefort ; and annoyed by the supplicating tones and gestures of the young girl, he pushed by her, entered the house, and quickly shut the door. But suffering cannot thus be shut out. Like the wound of a poisoned arrow is the bitterness of a heavy conscience. When Villefort reached his room, his limbs failed him, he uttered a sigh and fell into an arm-chair. The man he was sacrificing, the innocent lad who was paying the penalty of his own father's fault, appeared before his mental gaze, holding his bride by the hand, and arousing a spasm of agony in the young deputy's breast. The compunction he experienced was a dull, heavy pain, thrilling the heart now and again with the recollection of a past action, and inflicting a wound destined to deepen continually unto death. Then, in the soul of this man, there was a momentary hesitation. He had already, on various occasions, obtained sentence of death against several prisoners ; and these prisoners had been executed, thanks to his startling eloquence, without causing him any remorse, for they had been guilty, or at any rate, he had considered them so. But this time the case was different. He had just passed a sentence of imprisonment for life on an innocent man, at the moment of his reaching the goal of all his hopes, thereby destroying not only his liberty, but his happiness itself ; this time he was not the judge, but the executioner. As this thought weighed upon him, he was conscious of the heavy beating of his heart, and felt oppressed with a throng of vague apprehensions.

If only at that moment the gentle voice of Renée, interceding for mercy, had sounded in his ear, or if the beautiful Mercédès had again appeared to him, then doubtless he would have yielded, and with cold hands, have signed the order for Dantès' release, regardless of all risk to himself. But no voice sounded through the silence, and the door only opened to admit his valet, who came to inform him that the posthorses were harnessed.

Villefort rose like a man who has triumphed in some internal struggle. He hastened to his writing-table, and emptied some gold out of one of the drawers into his pocket, then putting on his coat with the assistance of the valet, he went out, jumped into the carriage, and ordered the driver, in a curt voice, to pull up in the Rue du Grand Cours, at M. de Saint Méran's.

Unhappy Dantès' fate was sealed!

Villefort at once obtained access to the ladies. As he entered the room, and glanced towards Renée, he trembled, for he fancied she would again adjure him to set Dantès at liberty. But the pretty young girl was now only concerned about one thing— Villefort's departure. She loved the young man truly, and he was now about to leave her, at the moment almost of becoming her husband; and Renée was inclined to be angry with the man whose crime separated her from her lover.

And what had become of Mercédès? The poor girl had found her way back to the corner of the Rue de la Loge, where Fernando awaited her. She returned to the Catalans' quarter, overwhelmed with grief and despair, and reaching her own home, threw herself on a couch, and gave way, unrestrainedly, to her grief. Fernando remained kneeling near her, pressing her cold hand, and covering it with kisses, which she endured passively, and almost unconsciously. Suffering obliterated every object from her gaze, except the figure of her beloved Edmond.

In the meantime, M. Morrel did not consider himself beaten; he had learnt that Dantès had been put in confinement; he had then hastened to all his friends, and had obtained access to several influential people of the town; but the news had already spread that the young man had been arrested as an agent of the Bonapartists, and as at this time the boldest regard any attempt of Napoleon's to get back to power as a ﬁed. dream, the shipowner everywhere met with coldness, ﬁe shut tion, or refusal of assistance, and at last went home, and endea-

Caderousse, on his part, was also restless anɖut in his present himself up in his own room, with two botᵗˡ were not sufficient to voured to drown his disquietude in drᵢᵤₛ as he was not sufficiently state of mind, he found that twoₐₙd as he was not sufficiently confuse his sense and judgmeᵗ master of himself to go forth and seek more, he remained, resting with his elbow on the rickety table, gazing into the flickering shadows thrown by the long-wicked candle.

Danglars alone was neither tormented nor uneasy; on the contrary, he rejoiced that he was revenged on an enemy, and had secured his post on board the *Pharaon*, which he had feared to lose. He therefore retired to rest at his usual hour, and slept tranquilly.

Villefort, after receiving the letter from M. de Salvieux, embraced Renée affectionately, kissed the hand of Madame de Saint Méran, and with a hearty shake of the hand from the Marquis, set off on his journey to Aix.

CHAPTER X

THE SMALL ROOM AT THE TUILERIES

THERE was in the Tuileries a small apartment with arched windows, well known as the favourite sanctum of Napoleon, of Louis XVIII, and later still, of Louis Philippe. There, at a table of walnut-wood, was seated Louis XVIII, engaged in listening carelessly enough to the remarks of a grey-haired man of about fifty years of age, of aristocratic and precise appearance, while at the same time he occupied himself with making notes on the margin of a volume of Horace, an edition by Gryphius, which, though greatly prized, was not particularly correct, and easily adapted itself to the philological remarks of his Majesty.

" You were observing, monsieur," said the King.

" That it would be impossible to feel more uneasy than I do, Sire."

" What is the trouble, my dear Blacas ? "

" Sire, I have reason to believe that a storm is rising in the south."

" Now, my dear Duke," returned the King, " I think you are ʰly informed, for I know, on the contrary, that it is extremely lov⌐ather there."

" Sire,learning though he was, Louis XVIII, nevertheless, vant, will make.

Provence and Dↄde Blacas, " if only to reassure a faithful ser- of feeling in these ᵗᵘᵗMajesty consent to send into Languedoc,

" ' *Canimus surdis*,' " ᵖʳᵒᵗome trusty men to report on the state his notes. theↄ "

ᵧ continued, still occupied with

" I am aware, Sire, that your Majesty can perfectly rely on the good feeling of the French people ; but I fear I am not altogether wrong in dreading some desperate attempt on the part of Bonaparte, or at any rate, his followers."

" My dear Blacas," returned the King, " you prevent me from working, with your false alarms."

" And you, Sire, prevent me from sleeping, with your false security."

" Now, wait, my dear fellow, wait a moment, whilst I scribble this happy thought on the ' *Pastor quum traheret* ' ; and you shall go on afterwards."

There was a moment's silence, whilst the King wrote, in small and delicate handwriting, another note on the margin of his Horace, then he said :

" Now, my dear Duke, I will listen to you."

" Sire," said Blacas, who had a momentary hope of using Villefort for his own profit, " I am compelled to inform you that they are not mere rumours, destitute of foundation, or mere idle gossipings, which make me uneasy. And, in fact," here the duke hesitated slightly, " an individual, whom I have every reason to think well of, and who was commissioned by me to keep a watch on matters in the south, has just arrived in great haste to inform me that ' great danger threatens the King,' so I at once hastened to you, Sire."

" ' *Mala ducis avi domum,* ' " continued Louis to himself, still writing.

" Does your Majesty desire that I should discontinue the subject ? "

" No, no, my dear Duke ; but put out your hand."

" Which, Sire ? "

" It does not matter ; here, to my left. Come ! I tell you the left, and you put it on the right. There now, somewhere there you will find yesterday's report of the minister of police ; but stay, here is Monsieur Dandré himself, I think. Did you not say, Monsieur Dandré ? " he added, addressing an officer who had just entered and announced the minister of police.

" Yes, Sire ; Monsieur the Baron Dandré," replied the officer.

" Ah ! exactly ; the Baron," said Louis, with a slight smile ; " let the Baron enter, and relate to the Duke all the latest news with regard to M. Bonaparte. Do not conceal anything, however grave it may be. Let me see, the Island of Elba is volcanic, and we shall soon see it bristling with bloody warfare ; ' *bella, horrida bella,* ' eh ! "

M. Dandré leant gracefully on the back of an armchair, and said :

" Does your Majesty desire to consult the report of yesterday ? "

" Yes, yes ; but address yourself to the Duke, who cannot find the report."

" Monsieur," began the Baron, turning to the Duke, " all his Majesty's subjects have reason to rejoice at the recent news which has reached us from the Island of Elba.   Bonaparte is wearied to death ; he passes whole days in watching the miners of Porto Longone at work."

" Ah ! and scratches himself by way of amusement," observed the King.   " It is a fact, my dear Duke.   Do you forget that this great man, this hero, this demigod, is afflicted with a disease of the skin ? "

" And besides that, Monsieur le Duc," interposed the minister of police, " we are inclined to think that the Usurper will go mad.   His reason grows weaker.   Sometimes he sheds burning tears, sometimes he laughs immoderately ; and occasionally he will continue for hours on the beach, throwing stones in the water ; and if he succeeds in making five or six ducks and drakes, appears as pleased as though he had gained another Marengo or Austerlitz.   You will admit, surely, that these are signs of madness ? "

" Or of wisdom, monsieur, or of wisdom," said the King, laughing ; " the great leaders of antiquity amused themselves by throwing stones into the sea ; see Plutarch's life of Scipio Africanus."

M. de Blacas remained thoughtfully standing between his careless companions.   Though Villefort had not fully enlightened him on the matter, he had nevertheless told him sufficient to cause him serious uneasiness.

" Come ! go on, Dandré," said the King, " Blacas is not yet convinced ;   describe the conversion of the Usurper to good principles ; now, Baron ! "

" These are the facts of the case, monsieur," said the minister ; " the last time that Napoleon held a review, two or three of his old soldiers, as he calls them, expressed a desire to return to France ; he granted them leave of absence, and exhorted them to serve their good king.   Those were his very words, monsieur, I know it for a fact."

" Ah ! now what do you say to that, Blacas ? " sighed the King triumphantly.

" I say, Sire, that either monsieur or I must be mistaken ; but as it is impossible that the minister of police who has the guardianship of your Majesty's safety and honour should be wrong, it is most likely I who am in error. Nevertheless, Sire, I wish, in place of your Majesty, to question the individual whom I have mentioned. Indeed, I would urge upon your Majesty to honour him by receiving him yourself."

"Willingly, Duke; under your auspices, I will receive whom you please, but it must be with arms in hand. Monsieur Dandré, have you not a more recent report than this one, which is dated the 20th February; it is now the 3rd of March?"

"No, Sire; but I expect one hourly. I left home early; possibly it may have arrived during my absence."

"Go round to the Préfecture, then, and if there should not be one, why, make one," said the King, laughing; "that is the usual plan, is it not? Remember I await you."

"In the meantime, then, Sire," said M. de Blacas, "I will bring in my messenger."

"Oh! stay one moment, just one moment," said the King. "I want to consult you on this passage: '*Molli fugiens anhelitu*'; it relates, you know, to the stag flying from the wolf. Now you are a sportsman, and a great wolf-hunter, are you not? Well, then, what do you think of '*molli anhelitu*'?"

"It is admirable, Sire; but my messenger is like the stag of which you speak, for he has just posted 220 leagues, and in less than three days!"

"That is undergoing a great deal of fatigue and trouble, my dear Duke, when there is the telegraph, which would have taken but three or four hours, and that, too, without the slightest loss of breath."

"Ah! Sire—you recompense this poor young fellow but ill, who has come such a distance, and with so much ardour to give your Majesty some useful information; if only for M. de Salvieux' sake, who recommends him, receive him graciously, I implore you."

"M. de Salvieux, my brother's chamberlain? Indeed! then he is at Marseilles? And does he also speak of this conspiracy?"

"No, but he commends M. de Villefort to me, and charges me to introduce him to your Majesty."

"M. de Villefort?" cried Louis; "and this messenger is M. de Villefort? Why did you not tell me his name at first?" returned the King, a shade of uneasiness passing over his face.

"Sire, I believed his name to be unknown to your Majesty."

"By no means; he has a keen intellect, is cultured, and, moreover, ambitious ; by the by, you know the name of his father, Noirtier ? "

" Noirtier, the Girondist, the senator, Sire ? "

" Precisely."

" And your Majesty has employed the son of such a man ? "

" Blacas, my friend, you know nothing about it. Villefort is ambitious ; to gain his end, Villefort would sacrifice everything, even his father ! "

" Then, Sire, I may bring him in ? "

" Immediately, Duke. Go at once and fetch him."

He hastened upstairs to summon De Villefort. On reaching the antechamber, however, he was obliged to invoke the authority of the King. M. de Villefort's dusty coat and careless costume excited the susceptibility of M. de Brézé, who was astounded that a young man thus attired should have the audacity to desire an audience of the King. But the Duke removed all difficulties with a single word—" the commands of his Majesty " —and Villefort was ushered in.

" Come forward, Monsieur de Villefort," said the King, " come forward."

Villefort bowed and slowly approached ; then waited for the King to question him.

" The Duke de Blacas declares, M. de Villefort," Louis began, " that you have something important to communicate to us. First and foremost, monsieur, is the danger as great, in your opinion, as they would have me believe ? "

" I believe it to be urgent, Sire, but not irreparable."

" Tell your tale then, monsieur," said the King, who began to be affected by the dismayed countenance of M. de Blacas, and the moved voice of Villefort ; " speak, and above all, begin at the beginning ; I like order in everything."

" Sire," said Villefort, " I will give your Majesty a faithful account, but I must beg to be excused, if the distress I am in throws some slight obscurity over my words."

A scrutiny of the King's countenance, after this insinuating exordium, assured Villefort of the kindly feeling of his distinguished auditor, and he continued :

" Sire, I have hastened to Paris as quickly as possible, to inform your Majesty, that in the discharge of my duties, I have discovered a veritable conspiracy, which threatens nothing less than the throne of your Majesty. Sire, the Usurper has fitted out three ships, and by this time must have left the Island of Elba, though where he is, I know not. For a certainty he will attempt a descent on Naples, or on the coast of Tuscany, or even on France. Your Majesty is not ignorant that the sovereign of the Island of Elba has kept up relations with Italy and with France."

"Yes, monsieur; I am aware of it," said the King, "and lately information has been received that Bonapartist meetings are held in the Rue Saint Jacques; but continue, I beg. How did you obtain this information?"

"Sire, it resulted from an examination of a man of Marseilles, whom I had been watching for some time, and had arrested the very day of my departure. This man, who is a turbulent sailor, and whom I suspected of Bonapartism, has been secretly to the Island of Elba; he saw there the Grand Marshal, who gave him a verbal message for a Bonapartist in Paris, whose name I cannot compel him to give up; but this message was to charge the Bonapartist to prepare the public mind for a return—so the prisoner said—a return which was close at hand."

"And where is this man?" demanded Louis.

"In prison, Sire."

"And the affair appeared to you of a grave nature?"

"So grave, Sire, that having been surprised by the occurrence in the midst of a family fête, on the very day of my betrothal, in fact, I quitted them all, my bride and friends alike, to come and lay at the feet of your Majesty, both the declaration of the fears that overwhelmed me and the assurance of my entire devotion."

"Yes, yes, but let us keep to the subject of the plot, Monsieur de Villefort."

"Sire, I fear it is something more than a plot; I am afraid that it is a conspiracy."

"A conspiracy in times like these," said Louis, with a smile, "is a matter easy to plan, but more difficult to carry out; during the last ten months my ministers have redoubled their efforts in securely guarding the coast of the Mediterranean. If Bonaparte descends on Naples, the entire coalition will have commenced marching before he reaches Piombino; if he descends on Tuscany, he will put his foot into an enemy's country; and if he descends on France, it will be with a handful of men, and we shall soon make an end of the matter, execrated as he is by the population. Be reassured, monsieur; but count none the less on our royal gratitude."

"Ah! here comes M. Dandré," cried the Duke de Blacas.

As he spoke, the minister of police appeared on the threshold, pale and trembling, and with a dazed expression, as though he had been struck by a flash of lightning. Villefort took a step backwards, as though he would retire, but a pressure of the hand from M. de Blacas detained him.

CHAPTER XI

THE CORSICAN OGRE

As Louis caught sight of the distressed countenance of his minister, he violently pushed back the table in front of him.

" What is the matter, monsieur ? " he cried ; " you appear overwhelmed : has this trouble any connection with what M. de Blacas has been saying, and which M. de Villefort has confirmed ? "

M. de Blacas also approached the Baron, but the terror of the courtier checked any exhibition of exultation on the part of the statesman—in fact, it was more advantageous to seem humiliated himself, than to humiliate the prefect of police.

" Sire," stammered the Baron.

" Well, well ; what is it ? " said Louis. " Will you speak out ? "

" Oh ! Sire, such a terrible misfortune. The Usurper left the Island of Elba on the 28th of February, and landed on the 1st of March."

" Where ? " asked the King quickly.

" In France, Sire, at a small port, near Antibes, in the Gulf Juan."

" The Usurper landed in France, near Antibes, in the Gulf Juan, about two hundred and fifty leagues from Paris, on the 1st of March, and you learn the news for the first time to-day, the 3rd of March ! eh ! monsieur ? but what you tell me is impossible ; you have been wrongly informed, or you must be mad."

" Alas ! Sire, it is only too true ! "

Louis made a gesture, expressive of anger and dismay, and rose erect, as though he had received a blow in the face, which struck him also on the heart.

" In France ! " he cried ; " the Usurper in France ! Then, they have not watched the man properly ; but, who knows ? They were, perhaps, secretly friendly to him ! "

" Oh ! Sire," cried the Duke de Blacas, " a man like M. Dandré cannot be accused of treason ! Indeed, Sire, we have all been blinded, and the minister of police has but shared in the general blindness."

" But," said Villefort—then checking himself, he drew himself back, bowing low. "Ah! pardon me, Sire, my zeal carries me away."

"Speak, monsieur, speak out boldly," said the King; "you alone have warned us of the evil, and now assist us in seeking a remedy."

"Sire," said Villefort, "the Usurper is detested in the south, and I think he is in danger there; one could easily raise Provence and Languedoc against him."

"That is true," said the minister, "only he is advancing through Gap and Sisteron."

"He is advancing?" cried Louis; "then he is marching towards Paris?"

The minister of police preserved a silence which was equivalent to an affirmative.

"And Dauphiné?" said the King to Villefort, "do you think, monsieur, that it will rise against him, like Provence?"

"Sire, I grieve to tell your Majesty the cruel truth, but the popular feeling in Dauphiné is not to be compared with that of Provence and Languedoc. The mountaineers are Bonapartists, Sire."

"Ah!" murmured Louis, "and how many men has he with him?"

"I do not know, Sire," said the minister of police. "I could obtain no information on the matter; the dispatch simply announced the landing and the route taken by the Usurper."

"And how did this dispatch reach you?" inquired the King.

The minister hung his head, and coloured deeply.

"By telegraph, Sire," he stammered.

Louis took a step forward, and crossed his arms in Napoleonic fashion.

"So," said he, pale with anger, "seven allied armies overthrew this man, and a miracle of heaven placed me on the throne of my fathers after twenty-five years of exile; and now, having reached the goal of my highest aspirations, the power which I grasp explodes and annihilates me!"

"Sire, there is a fatality about it," murmured the minister, feeling that such a blow was sufficient to crush any mortal.

"Ah! what our enemies say about us is true, indeed," continued the King, "we have learnt nothing, and forgotten nothing! If I had been betrayed as *he* was, I should feel more consoled; but to be surrounded by those whom I have placed in important positions, and then to be lost miserably through incapacity and carelessness! Ah! monsieur, you are right, there is, indeed, a fatality about it!"

M. de Blacas wiped his moist brow, and Villefort smiled to himself, for he felt his importance increasing.

" To fall," Louis resumed, " and to learn one's fate by telegraph ! Oh ! I would a thousand times rather ascend the scaffold which my brother trod, than step down the staircase of the Tuileries, driven out by ridicule—ridicule, monsieur ; you hardly know the force of it in France—and yet you ought to know what it is. Come forward, M. de Villefort," continued the King, addressing the young man, " and tell this gentleman that it was possible to know beforehand all that he has not known."

" Sire, it was materially impossible to divine the projects which this man concealed from all the world."

" Materially impossible ! Yes, that is a fine word, monsieur ; unfortunately, fine words are like fine men, and I have measured them both. So it was materially impossible for a minister who has officers, agents, spies, and fifteen hundred thousand francs of private funds at his command, to know what was going on at a place sixty leagues from the coast of France ? Indeed ! Well then, see this gentleman here, who has no such resources at his disposal, who is simply a magistrate, and yet knows more than you do with all your staff of police, and who, if he had only had the command of the telegraph as you have, would have saved my crown."

The minister of police turned a look of bitter hatred on Villefort, who bowed his head in modest triumph.

Another person might have been carried away by such overwhelming praise ; but though he clearly perceived that the minister of police was irretrievably ruined, Villefort yet feared to make of him a mortal enemy. The minister had not succeeded in divining Napoleon's secret, but he might, in the tumult of his distress, gain some slight perception of his—Villefort's—and would only need to question Dantès on the matter. Instead, therefore, of overwhelming his rival, Villefort came to the rescue.

" Sire," said he, " what your Majesty considers an evidence of great penetration on my part, is in reality, a matter of accident : I have merely profited by the accident like a devoted subject, that is all. Credit me with no more than I deserve, Sire, and then you will never have to alter your estimate of me."

The minister, with an expressive look, thanked the young man, and Villefort perceived that, without losing a particle of the King's gratitude, he had made a friend on whom he might rely.

" Good," said the King ; " and now, gentlemen," continued he, turning towards M. de Blacas, and the minister of police. " I have no more need of you, and you can retire ; all that remains to do now, lies within the province of the minister of war."

" Happily, Sire," said M. de Blacas, " we can count upon the army. Your Majesty is aware that all reports declare the whole service as devoted to your government."

" Talk to me no more of reports ; I know, Duke, now, what they are worth. Ah ! by the by, though, speaking of reports, have you heard any news, Monsieur le Baron, of the affair in the Rue Saint Jacques ? "

" The affair in the Rue Saint Jacques ! " cried Villefort, unable to keep back the exclamation ; then checking himself immediately, he said, " Pardon, Sire, my devotion to your Majesty makes me constantly forget the rules of etiquette."

" Speak and act as you please, monsieur," returned Louis, " you have to-day fully earned the right to be heard."

" Sire," went on the minister, " I came to-day on purpose to give your majesty the news I have obtained of the matter, when the attention of your Majesty was distracted by this terrible catastrophe ; the information can now have no further interest."

" On the contrary, monsieur, on the contrary," observed Louis ; " the affair appears to me to have a very decided connection with the subject we are at present discussing ; and General Quesnel's death may perhaps put us on the track of some important secret conspiracy."

At the name of General Quesnel Villefort shuddered.

" The fact is, Sire," returned the minister, " everything leads to the supposition that the death is the result, not of suicide, but of assassination. General Quesnel had just left a Bonapartist club, when he disappeared. Some unknown individual had been inquiring for him that morning, and had arranged to meet him in the Rue Saint Jacques ; unfortunately, the General's valet, who was attending on his master when the stranger was ushered into the room, has forgotten the number. But we are on the track of the man who fixed the rendezvous. The servant gave a description of him ; a man of fifty, or fifty-two, of dark complexion, with black eyes, and bushy eyebrows, and wearing a moustache ; he was dressed in a blue frock coat, and wore a rosette of the Legion of Honour. Yesterday an individual was followed whose appearance exactly corresponded to this description, and he disappeared at the corner of the Rue de la Jussienne and the Rue de Coq-Héron."

Villefort felt his limbs sinking under him ; when, however, he heard that the stranger had eluded pursuit, he breathed more freely.

"You must hunt out this man, monsieur," said the King to the minister of police; "for if General Quesnel has been the victim of murder, whether by Bonapartists or others, his assassins shall be rigorously dealt with."

Villefort needed all his *sang froid* to avoid betraying the agony of terror with which this command of the King inspired him.

"It is a strange thing," continued the King, with an impulse of annoyance, "but the police think they have said all that is necessary when they have announced a murder has been committed, and done everything, when they have added : ' We are on the track of the criminals.' "

"Sire," said Blacas, "your Majesty will be satisfied on that point, I believe."

"Well, we shall see; I will detain you no longer, Baron; you, Monsieur de Villefort, must be fatigued with your long journey, go and rest.   You alighted, I imagine, at your father's residence ? "

A dazzling light seemed to flash before Villefort's eyes.

"No, Sire," said he; "I got down at the Hôtel de Madrid, in the Rue de Tournon."

"But you have seen him ? "

"Sire, I came immediately to M. de Blacas."

"But you will see him, I suppose ? "

"I do not think so, Sire."

"That is well," said Louis, showing by his smile that his questions had not been put without an object.   "I forgot that you were not on warm terms with M. Noirtier, and that it is another sacrifice to the royal cause, for which I must reward you."

"Sire, the goodness your Majesty testifies towards me is in itself a reward which so surpasses all my hopes, that I require nothing more."

"Nevertheless, Monsieur, you shall not be forgotten, depend upon it.   In the meantime," said Louis, taking off a cross of the Legion of Honour, which he usually wore with a cross of Saint Louis, and the orders of Notre Dame and Saint Lazare, "in the meantime, take this cross.   Blacas, you must see that the warrant is presented to M. de Villefort."

Villefort's eyes moistened with tears of joyful pride; he took the cross and kissed it.

"And now," he asked, "what commands does your Majesty honour me with ? "

"Take the repose you need, and recollect that though you have no power to assist me in Paris, you can be of the greatest use to me at Marseilles."

" Sire," replied Villefort bowing, " in an hour I shall have quitted Paris."

" Go, monsieur, and if I should forget you—for kings have short memories—do not hesitate to recall yourself to my remembrance. Now, Baron, order the minister for war to be sent for. You, Blacas, remain."

" Ah! monsieur," said the minister of police to Villefort, as the latter was leaving the Tuileries, " you have had a lucky entrée, and your fortune is made."

" But for how long ? " murmured Villefort to himself as he bowed to the minister, and looked round him for a conveyance. A cab was passing, and jumping in, he leant back, and in about ten minutes he reached his hotel, ordered breakfast, and required the horses to be ready by two o'clock. He was about to seat himself at the table, when there was a ringing of the bell, and on the valet opening the door, Villefort heard the sound of his own name.

" Who can possibly know that I am here, already ? "

The valet at this moment returned.

" A stranger, monsieur, who will not give his name, wishes to speak to monsieur."

" What sort of a man is he ? "

" About fifty years of age, perhaps ; very much about monsieur's own height ; dark, very dark ; black hair and eyebrows, and dark eyes."

" And how dressed ? " inquired Villefort, eagerly.

" In a large blue frock coat, buttoned from top to bottom ; decorated with the Legion of Honour."

" It is he ! " muttered Villefort, turning pale.

" Eh ! *pardieu* ! " cried a voice, as the individual. whose description has just been given, appeared in the doorway, " is it the custom at Marseilles for sons to leave their fathers in their ante-chambers ? "

" Oh! father ! " cried Villefort, " then I was not deceived ; I thought it must be you."

" Then if you guessed it was I," returned the new comer, resting his walking-stick in a corner, and placing his hat on a chair, ' permit me to tell you, my dear Gérard, that it was not very amiable of you to make me wait in this manner."

" You can leave us, Germain," said Villefort.

CHAPTER XII

FATHER AND SON

M. Noirtier carefully watched the servant out of the room; then, with a suspicion that he might listen in the antechamber, troubled himself to close the door of the antechamber, returned, and carefully shut and bolted the door of the bedroom, and then extended his hand to Villefort.

" Ah ! now, do you know, my dear Gérard, you do not look particularly delighted to see me ? "

" Indeed, father," said Villefort, " but I am delighted ; only I so little expected your visit that I was a little startled."

" Well, my dear fellow," returned M. Noirtier, seating himself, " I think I may say the same thing to you. How is this ? You announce your betrothal to take place at Marseilles on the 28th of February, and on the 3rd of March here you are in Paris."

" And if I am, father, do not complain ; for it is for your sake that I have come, and this journey may, perhaps, be the means of saving you. You have heard of a certain Bonapartist club in the Rue Saint Jacques ? "

" No. 53 ? Yes ; I am the vice-president."

" Father, your boldness makes me tremble."

" What would you have, my dear fellow ? When one has had to get out of Paris in a hay-cart, and been hunted round Bordeaux by Robespierre's bloodhounds, one has got accustomed to many things. But go on ! What about the club in the Rue Saint Jacques ? "

" It appears that General Quesnel was induced to go there, that he left his house at nine o'clock in the evening, and was found three days later in the Seine."

" And, pray, who told you this pretty story ? "

" The King himself, monsieur."

" Well, now, in exchange for your little tale, I will tell you some news," rejoined Noirtier. " Have you heard of the landing of his majesty the Emperor ? "

" Yes, I know the news ; indeed, I knew it before you. For the last three days I have been posting in hot haste from Marseilles to Paris, maddened by the thought that I could not send the intelligence like a flash, over the two hundred leagues."

" Three days ! Nonsense ! Three days ago the Emperor had not landed."

" No matter, I knew of the project by a letter which was addressed to you from the Island of Elba. I found it in a packet in possession of the messenger. If that letter had fallen into the hands of anyone else, you would probably have been shot by this time, father."

Noirtier began to laugh. "Shot? My dear fellow, what an idea! And this letter, where is it? I know you too well to have any fear that you have let it lie about."

"I burnt it, for fear that a single fragment should remain, for it would have been your condemnation."

"And the ruin of your future," replied Noirtier, coldly. "Yes, I understand; but I have nothing to fear since you protect me."

"I do more than that, I save you. I must refer again to the club in the Rue Saint Jacques. General Quesnel has been killed, and in every country of the world that is called murder."

"There is nothing to prove that the general has been the victim of a murder; people are picked up every day out of the Seine who have thrown themselves in, in despair, or have been drowned from not knowing how to swim."

"Father, you know very well that the general did not drown himself in a fit of despair, and people do not bathe in the Seine at this time of the year. Do not deceive yourself; this death is properly entitled a murder. The King himself says so."

"The King! I thought he was enough of a philosopher to know that there was no such thing as murder in politics. In politics we do not kill a man; we get rid of an obstacle, that is all. Would you like to know how this affair came about? It was generally believed that we could count on General Quesnel; he had been recommended at the Island of Elba; one of us went to ask him to attend a meeting in the Rue Saint Jacques, where he would find friends; he came; the whole plan was unfolded to him—the departure from the Island of Elba, the intended landing, and so on; then, when he had heard everything, he declared himself a Royalist. The matter was considered; they made him take an oath of secrecy, which he did, but with a bad grace. Well, the general was allowed to leave—free, perfectly free. He did not return home, however. My dear fellow, it is plain enough. He left us to go home, and missed the way—that is all. A murder, indeed! You surprise me, Villefort. Have I ever taken it upon myself to say to you, when you were carrying on your Royalist game, and causing the heads of my friends to fall beneath the knife: 'My son, you have committed a murder?' No! but I have said, 'Very well, monsieur, you have fought victoriously; revenge will come to-morrow!'"

" Ah ! but take care, father. When we take revenge, it will be terrible indeed ! "

" I do not understand you."

" You are counting on the Usurper's return ? He will not get through a distance of ten leagues before he will be pursued, trapped, and captured like a wild beast."

" My dear fellow, the Emperor at this moment is on the road to Grenoble ; he will be at Lyons on the 10th or 12th, and by the 20th or 25th he will be in Paris."

" He has but a handful of men, and the army will be sent against him."

" It will act as escort when he re-enters the capital. Really, my dear Gérard, you are a perfect child ! You believe you are well informed because you learn by telegraph three days after the landing that ' the Usurper has landed at Cannes with some followers ; he is being pursued.' But where he is, or what he is doing, you don't know in the least. Well, he will be pursued as far as Paris without a shot being fired. Grenoble will open its gates to him with enthusiasm, and all Lyons will go out to meet him. Believe me, we are as well informed as you are, and our police are as good as yours. Would you like a proof of it ? Well, then, you wished to conceal your journey from me, and yet I knew of your arrival half an hour after you had passed the barrier ; you gave your address to no one except the post-boy ; nevertheless, I knew your address, as is proved by the fact that I got here just as you were about to sit down to table. But ring and order covers for two, and we will dine together."

And so saying, Noirtier extended his hand to ring the bell and summon the servant. Villefort stayed his arm.

" Stop, father, one word ! Badly organized as the Royalist police may be, they have hold of the description of the man, who on the morning of the day that Quesnel disappeared, called to see him. Dark hair and complexion, whiskers, dark eyes, blue frock coat, buttoned to the chin, a rosette of an officer of the Legion of Honour in his button-hole, broad-brimmed hat, and malacca cane."

" Ah ! so they know all that. Then why have they not laid hands on the man ? "

" They lost sight of him yesterday, or the day before, at the corner of the Rue Coq-Héron ; but at any moment they may find him," returned Villefort.

" Yes," said Noirtier, glancing carelessly round, " yes. if the

man were not warned, but he is ; and," he added, smiling, " he
is about to change his appearance and costume."

With these words he rose, took off his coat and cravat, and
going to the table where were spread out the necessary preparations for his son's toilette, he took a razor, made a lather, and
with steady hand shaved off the whiskers which had given the
police such a valuable clue.

His whiskers destroyed, Noirtier rearranged his hair, and put
on a coloured cravat, which he found at the top of an open valise,
in place of his black one. He next arrayed himself in a coat
of chestnut colour belonging to Villefort, and proceeding to the
glass, tried on his son's hat, with a narrow turned-up brim, appearing quite satisfied with the result. He left his own walking-stick
in the corner, and switched in his vigorous hand a small bamboo
cane, which the elegant young deputy was in the habit of carrying
and twirling with a careless swagger, this being one of his distinguishing characteristics.

" Well," said Noirtier, turning to his stupefied son, " do you
think the police will recognize me now ? "

" I hope not, I am sure, father," stammered Villefort.

" And now I think of it, you are perhaps right after all, and
have possibly been the means of saving my life ; but never mind,
I will repay you before long. Shall you see the King again ? "

" Perhaps."

" If you do, tell him this : ' Sire, you have been deceived
regarding public feeling in France ; he, whom you designate
the Ogre of Corsica, and the Usurper, is already called Bonaparte at Lyons, and Emperor at Grenoble. You believe him
to be pursued, and surrounded on all sides—he is marching onwards, rapidly as the eagle which he bears. The soldiers are
increasing like the flakes of snow on a rolling ball. Sire, leave
at once ; abandon France to her true master who conquered her ;
leave, Sire, not that you run any danger ; your rival is sufficiently
strong to forgive, but because it would be humiliating for a grandson of Saint Louis to owe his life to the hero of Arcole, Marengo,
and Austerlitz.' Tell him that, Gérard ; or rather, go, and say
nothing at all ; post back to Marseilles ; go into your house by
the back entrance, and there remain quietly, humbly, and above
all inoffensively ; for this time, I swear to you, we shall act
vigorously, like people who know their enemies. Therefore, go,
my dear Gérard, and in return for this obedience to paternal
orders we will keep you in your post. That will be," he added
with a smile, " another reason for you to save me a second time,

if the political see-saw should, one day, raise you again, and let me down."

And with these words Noirtier quitted the room.

Villefort, pale and agitated, hastened to the window, and beheld him pass out, and calmly and impassively walk by two or three men of suspicious aspect, who were lying in wait at the corner of the street, placed there probably to arrest the individual with black whiskers, blue frock coat, and broad-brimmed hat. Villefort remained watching, with bated breath, until his father had disappeared at the Rue Bussy. Then he darted towards the articles of attire scattered about the room, placed the black cravat and frock coat at the bottom of his portmanteau, and twisting up the hat, thrust it into the back of the wardrobe. He next broke the stick into three pieces, which he flung into the fire, and calling his valet, whose questioning looks he over-awed with his stern expression, ordered his hotel bill to be sent for. His horses were waiting, he was told, so without further delay, he hastened downstairs, jumped into the chaise, and started off. At Lyons he learnt that Bonaparte had just entered Grenoble ; and after passing through varied scenes of excite-ment that continued throughout his entire journey, the young deputy at last reached Marseilles ; a prey to all the doubts and fears which beset the minds of men who are reaping in the harvest of long-coveted honours, the first fruits of a restless ambition.

CHAPTER XIII

THE HUNDRED DAYS

M. NOIRTIER was a true prophet, and affairs progressed quickly, as he had foretold. The monarchy trembled on its insecure basis, and at a mere sign from the Emperor, the shapeless structure, built up by a strange alliance between old prejudices and new ideas, crumbled away. Villefort, therefore, had only received from the King an expression of gratitude, useless, even if not dangerous for the moment, and the cross of the Legion of Honour, which he was careful not to exhibit. Napoleon would certainly have dismissed Villefort, but for the intervention of Noirtier, who was now an all-powerful personage at the court of the Hundred Days. Thus, as he had promised, the Girondist of '93, and the senator of 1806, returned the protection he had received.

During the reinstatement of the Empire all Villefort's efforts were directed towards concealing the secret which Dantès had been on the point of divulging. The King's Procureur alone was dismissed, he being suspected of lukewarm sentiments towards Bonapartism. Nevertheless the Imperial power was scarcely set up, when Marseilles, notwithstanding the attitude of the local magistrates, began to ferment with those fire-brands of civil war, which in the south are so difficult to extinguish ; indeed, the spirit of retaliation was hardly kept within the limit of caricaturing in the comic papers those Royalists who shut themselves up in their houses, and publicly affronting those who ventured to show themselves abroad.

By a natural change of circumstances, the worthy shipowner, whom we have remarked as belonging to the popular party, now found himself in a position to raise his voice to make a desired claim ; and we need hardly add that the claim M. Morrel brought forward referred to Dantès. Villefort had kept his post notwithstanding the removal of his superior, and his marriage was not broken off, though postponed till a more auspicious occasion. If the Emperor retained his power, some other alliance would be advisable for the young deputy. If, however, a second restoration should bring Louis XVIII back again to France, the influence of M. de Saint Méran, and consequently Villefort's, would be doubled ; in that case the union would be more desirable than ever.

It was at this period, when, for the time being, the deputy procureur was the first magistrate in Marseilles, that one morning his valet entered to announce to him M. Morrel. Anyone else in his position would probably have hastened to meet the shipowner, and by a certain anxiety, given palpable signs of weakness ; but Villefort had a shrewd intelligence, and though his experience had been limited, his instinct generally led him right. He therefore allowed Morrel to be left in the antechamber, and then, after a quarter of an hour, he ordered the shipowner to be ushered in. M. Morrel expected to find Villefort somewhat humbled ; he found him, however, calm, firm, and full of that cold politeness which is the most insuperable of all barriers between the educated and the common man. He had entered the room convinced that the magistrate would tremble at the sight of him, but now he himself felt chilled and disturbed before this stern inquisitor. He paused at the door. Villefort looked at him as though he scarcely recognized him ; then, after a few seconds of critical examination, during which the worthy shipowner stood twirling his hat in his hands, he remarked—

" M. Morrel, I believe ? To what circumstance do I owe the honour of your visit ? "

" Have you no suspicion, monsieur ? "

" Not the least in the world ; I am none the less, however, disposed to be agreeable to you, if it is within my power."

" It is a matter that depends entirely on you, monsieur," began the shipowner, regaining assurance as he spoke, and strengthened besides by the justice of his cause, and the honesty of his position. " Some days before the landing of his Majesty, the Emperor, I came to claim your indulgence for an unfortunate young man, a sailor, mate on board my ship ; he was accused, if you recollect, of having intercourse with the island of Elba. This intercourse, which was then considered a crime, is to-day a title for favour. You were then serving Louis XVIII, and did not spare the accused, monsieur ; it was your duty. To-day, however, you are serving Napoleon, and therefore ought to protect him ; this is also your duty. I am come here to ask you what has become of him."

Villefort composed himself with a violent effort.

" And the name of this man ? "

" Edmond Dantès ! "

Villefort would rather have stood the fire of an adversary in a duel at twenty-five paces than have heard this name. Nevertheless, he made no sign.

" They can certainly never accuse me," he murmured to himself, " of arresting this young man on a purely personal question." Then turning to Morrel, he repeated, " Dantès you said, did you ? "

" Yes, monsieur."

Villefort fetched a large register from a book-shelf near, and turning it over on the table, remarked in a perfectly natural manner—

" Are you quite sure you are not mistaken, M. Morrel ? "

" No, monsieur," replied the shipowner, " I am not mistaken ; I have known the poor fellow for ten years, and he has been in my service for four. I came, you must remember, six weeks ago to beg you to be merciful, as I come now to beg you to be just to the poor boy. You did not receive me then very graciously. Ah ! the Royalists were indeed hard upon the Bonapartists at that time."

" Stay a moment," returned Villefort, turning over a new register, " here it is !—a sailor, is it not ? who married a young Catalan. Yes, yes, I recollect now ; the affair was very serious indeed."

" How so ? "

You know that when he left me he was taken to one of the prisons in the Palais de Justice."

" Yes, and then ? "

" Then I sent my report to Paris, and enclosed the papers found on him. It was my duty, there was nothing for it, and eight days after his arrest the prisoner was taken off ; he has probably been sent to Fenestrelles, Pignerol, or the isles of Saint Margaret— sent abroad, as we call it in official terms ; and some fine morning you will see him back again to take the command of his ship."

"Whenever he returns his place will be ready for him," answered Morrel. " But why is he not back already ? The first duty of the Bonapartist administration should be to set at liberty those who were imprisoned under the government of the Royalists."

" Do not judge rashly, my dear Monsieur Morrel," replied Villefort, " we must proceed in a legal manner about everything."

" But," said Morrel, " is there no way of hurrying on the formalities now that we have triumphed ? I have friends and influence ; I can obtain a reversal of the sentence."

" There was no sentence."

" I can get him out of prison, then."

" In political matters," Villefort rejoined, " no prison-register is kept. Sometimes governments have reason to desire that some individual should disappear without leaving any trace, and a register would be a means of tracking him. The Emperor has always been more strict in the regulation of his prisons than even the ' Grand Monarque ' himself ; and the number of prisoners of whom there is no mention in the registers is incalculable."

Thus easily are kindly natures hoodwinked, and Morrel had not even a suspicion.

" Nevertheless, monsieur," said he, " what counsel can you give me to hurry on poor Dantès' release ? "

" Only this ; draw up a petition to the magistrate."

" Oh ! monsieur, you know what petitions end in ; the magistrate receives two hundred a day, and perhaps reads but four."

" Yes," returned Villefort, " but he will read a petition sent, endorsed, and directed by me. I will despatch one with the greatest pleasure. Dantès perhaps was then guilty, but to-day he is innocent ; and it is only my duty to assist in setting at liberty him whom I was compelled before to imprison."

In this manner Villefort anticipated the possible danger of any inquiry, which would inevitably have exposed him.

" But as to writing to the magistrate ? " resumed Morrel.

" Seat yourself here," said Villefort, giving up his place to the shipowner, " and I will dictate to you."

" I am ready, monsieur," said Morrel.

Villefort then dictated the petition, in which, with admirable cunning, he exaggerated Dantès' patriotism, and the services he had rendered to the Bonapartist cause ; in fact, Dantès was depicted as having been one of the most active agents in assisting Napoleon's return. It was evident that on receiving this document the magistrate could not but act justly and release the prisoner. When it was duly written, Villefort read it through aloud.

" There," said he, " now you can leave it to me. It will be sent off to-day, countersigned by me, and I will manage the rest."

This assurance raised Morrel's hopes, and he hastened to announce to old father Dantès that he would soon behold his son again. As for Villefort, instead of forwarding the petition to Paris, he carefully preserved it in his own keeping ; for though it would have been the means of releasing Dantès at that critical time, it might compromise him terribly in the event of a second Restoration, already foreshadowed by the aspect of Europe and the progress of events. He had gone too far to draw back, and Dantès must be broken on the wheel of his ambition. Dantès, therefore, remained a prisoner. Buried in the darkness of his dungeon, he heard neither the mighty disturbance caused by the fall of the throne of Louis XVIII, nor yet the more terrible collapse of the Empire. Twice during that short-lived Imperial phenomenon, entitled the Hundred Days, Morrel had returned to the charge, insisting always on the release of Dantès, and each time Villefort had pacified him with promises and expectations. At last the day of Waterloo arrived. Morrel came no more to seek Villefort ; he had done all for his young protégé that was humanly possible ; to make any fresh attempts, now that the second Restoration had come, was to compromise himself uselessly.

Louis XVIII re-ascended the throne. Villefort, for whom Marseilles had become associated with many painful and remorseful recollections, solicited and obtained the post of royal procureur, then vacant, at Toulouse. A fortnight after his installation his marriage took place with Mademoiselle de Saint Méran, whose father was now more influential than ever. Thus Dantès, during the Hundred Days, and also after Waterloo, still remained barred in his prison, forgotten, as it seemed, both by God and man.

Danglars, on hearing of Napoleon's return, comprehended its significance and its bearing on his affair with Dantès; he felt he had hit the mark in his accusation, and he called this curious coincidence a *decree of Providence.* But when Napoleon really reached Paris, Danglars began to be afraid; every moment he expected to see Dantès reappear, thirsting for vengeance. He therefore made known to M. Morrel his desire to leave the marine service, and obtained from him a recommendation to a Spanish merchant, in whose service he entered as clerk, towards the end of March, about ten or twelve days after the return of Napoleon to the Tuileries.

Fernando understood nothing but that Dantès was out of the way, which was all he cared for. He employed himself partly in misleading Mercédès as to the reason of his disappearance, and partly in meditating plans of emigration and abduction; now and then, also, when a gloomy fit was on him, he would sit on the summit of Cape Pharo, and look up and down the two roads to see if the handsome young fellow with the manly stride and haughty air was not returning, like a messenger of vengeance, to chastise him. Then all Fernando's schemes would be frustrated; he would shoot Dantès and kill himself afterwards to extenuate the murder. But in this he deceived himself; the man who has anything to hope for never takes his own life.

In the meantime, the Imperial Government issued a proclamation for a general conscription; and everyone capable of bearing arms was despatched out of France on active service. Among others, Fernando had to leave the country, and he quitted his home and Mercédès, tortured by the dark and terrible thought that in his absence his rival might return and wed her whom he loved. If Fernando ever really felt inclined to kill himself, it was when he was thus compelled to leave Mercédès. Moreover, his attention to the young girl, the compassion with which he appeared to regard her misfortune, and the readiness with which he gratified her smallest wish, had produced the usual effect on a generous nature. Mercédès had always felt a friendly attachment towards Fernando, and her friendship for him was now increased by an additional sentiment—gratitude.

"My brother," said she, as she fastened the young soldier's knapsack on his shoulders, "my brother, my only friend, you must not get killed and leave me all alone in the world; for what should I do without you?"

These words, spoken at the moment of departure, inspired Fernando with hope. If Dantès did not return, Mercédès might one day be his. Thus Mercédès was left alone on that barren spot, which had never before seemed so desolate. Often she was seen, her eyes bathed in tears, wandering alone on the outskirts of the little village, sometimes standing mute and motionless, gazing in the direction of Marseilles; or, again, seated on the shore, listening to the moaning of the sea—ceaseless and never-ending, like her own sorrow. It was not for want of courage that Mercédès did not resort to suicide as a solution of her woes, but religion came to her aid and saved her.

Caderousse, like Fernando, was called out for active service; but as he was eight years older than the young Catalan, and was, moreover, married, he was only sent to the frontier. Old Dantès, who had only been sustained by hope, lost heart altogether on the fall of the Emperor. Exactly five months from the day he was separated from his son, and almost at the same hour at which the arrest had taken place, the poor old man breathed his last in Mercédès' arms.

CHAPTER XIV

THE MAD AND THE FURIOUS PRISONER

ABOUT a year after the return of Louis XVIII, the inspector made a visit to all the prisons. Dantès heard the sounds and confusion of preparations, which, in the distance, would have been inappreciable to any other ear but that of a prisoner, accustomed in the silence of the night to listen for even the movements of a spider, or the dropping of water from the ceiling of the cell. He divined that something unusual was occurring above, among the *living*, as he mentally termed them; for he had inhabited a tomb so long, he almost felt himself numbered with the dead. The inspector questioned several of the prisoners, principally those whose mildness or stupidity recommended them to the favourable notice of the management; the inspector questioned them as to their food, and asked if they had any requests to make. They replied uniformly that the food was detestable, and that they requested to be set at liberty. The inspector then asked if they had anything else to say. They shook their heads. What else can prisoners solicit but their liberty? The inspector turned to the governor, and said with a smile : " I do not see the use of making these purposeless examinations. When you have seen one prisoner, you have seen a hundred, and when you have heard one, you have heard a thousand. It is always the same tale—badly fed, and innocent. Are there any others ? "

" Yes, we have the dangerous prisoners, and the lunatics, in the dungeons."

" Lead the way, then," said the inspector, with an air of profound weariness, " we must do it thoroughly, I suppose. To the dungeons."

" Wait one moment," said the governor, " we must have the escort of two men ; for the prisoners sometimes, from very disgust of life, and to obtain sentence of death, commit very violent acts, and you might be the victim."

Two soldiers were fetched, and they commenced to descend a flight of steps, so foul, and dark, and mouldy, that even in passing down it, the senses of sight, smell, and respiration were all most disagreeably affected.

" We have a very dangerous conspirator here, who is declared to be capable of anything."

" How long has he been here ? "

" Nearly a year."

" Was he put in this dungeon at first ? "

" No, monsieur, only after endeavouring to kill the warder who took his food to him. This man can tell you all about it ; can you not, Antoine ? "

" Certainly ; he tried to kill me," said the jailer ; " he is a perfect demon."

" Do you wish it complained about ? "

" It would be useless, and he is punished enough, monsieur ; I should say that before another year is out, he will be completely mad."

" And all the better for him," returned the inspector, " once completely mad, he will suffer less.

" You are right, monsieur," said the governor, " and your remark shows that you have profoundly studied the matter. For instance, in a dungeon about twenty feet from this spot, we have an old abbé, once the leader of a party in Italy, who has been here since 1811 ; his reason gave way towards the end of 1813, and since that time he is physically hardly recognizable ; he used to weep, now he laughs ; he grew thin, now he is fat. Perhaps you would rather see him than the other prisoner ? His madness is somewhat amusing, and will not sadden you."

" I will see both," returned the inspector. " I must fulfil my duty conscientiously. Let us visit the other first."

At the grinding of the massive bolts, and the grating of the rusty hinges, Dantès, who was squatting in a corner of the cell, drawing in the small ray of daylight which penetrated through a narrow grating, raised his head.

At the sight of the new comer, whom the governor addressed, hat in hand, ushered in by two turnkeys bearing torches, and followed by two soldiers, he instantly divined the meaning of the affair, and perceiving that, at last, an opportunity had presented itself for appealing to a superior authority, he bounded forward, with clasped hands.

The soldiers immediately advanced their bayonets, and the inspector also drew back a step.

Dantès instantly perceived that he had been represented as a dangerous individual. He therefore composed his features to an expression of perfect mildness and humility, and expressing himself with an eloquent fervour that astounded the attendants, he endeavoured to touch his visitor's heart.

The inspector listened to his story to the conclusion, then said, turning to the governor, in a low voice, " He will come round to loyalty ; he seems very well disposed. You see he is affected by fear ; he drew back before the bayonets ; now, a madman recoils before nothing. I have made some curious observations on that point at Charenton." Then turning towards the prisoner, he added, " Well, and what do you require ? "

" I require to know what crime I have committed ; I demand judges, and to have my case properly tried ; I demand to be shot if I am guilty, but also to be set at liberty if I am innocent."

" Do you have proper food ? " asked the inspector.

" Yes, I believe so, but I don't know, and it is of little importance. But it is of importance, not only to me, the unlucky prisoner, but also to the functionaries who dispense justice, and to the King who governs us, that an innocent man should not be the victim of an infamous accusation, and should not die under locks and bars, cursing his executioners."

" You spoke rather differently, my friend, the day you endeavoured to knock down your keeper."

" That is true, monsieur," said Dantès ; " and I humbly beg pardon of him, for he has always been good to me. But I could not help it—I was mad."

" And you are so no longer ? "

" No, monsieur, captivity has humbled me, and broken my spirit ; I have been here so long."

" So long ! When were you arrested, then ? " demanded the inspector.

" On the 28th of February, 1815, at two o'clock in the afternoon."

The inspector calculated.

"It is now the 30th of July, 1816; what do you say? you have only been a prisoner seventeen months."

"Only seventeen months!" cried Dantès. "Ah, monsieur, you do not know what seventeen months of prison means: it is seventeen years—seventeen centuries, particularly for a man situated as I was, about to marry the woman I loved, and with an honourable career open before me. To lose it all in a moment, to fall from the glory of the beautiful daylight into the darkest night, to see one's future destroyed, and not to know if one's beloved is still faithful, or if one's old father is living or dead! Monsieur, seventeen months in prison is more than even the most odious crimes deserve that it is possible to think of. Have pity on me, then, monsieur, I only ask to be tried, and they can never refuse me that."

"You are right; we will see about it," said the inspector. Then he added to the governor, "When we go up again you must show me the statement about him in the register."

"Monsieur," began Dantès again, "I am aware it does not rest with you to set me at liberty, but you can transmit my request to the authorities. A trial—that is all I ask—that I may know what crime I have committed, and to what punishment I am condemned, for uncertainty is the worst of tortures!"

"Light me upstairs again," said the inspector.

"Oh, monsieur!" cried Dantès, "I can tell by the sound of your voice that you have some compassion for me. Tell me that I may hope!"

"I cannot tell you that," replied the inspector; "I can only promise you to examine your record. Who arrested you?"

"M. de Villefort," answered Dantès. "See him and consult with him."

"M. de Villefort left Marseilles a year ago, and is now at Toulouse."

"Ah, now I understand it all," murmured Dantès; "my only protector was absent."

"Had M. de Villefort any motive of hatred against you?" asked the inspector.

"None, monsieur. Indeed, he was very kind to me."

"I can therefore rely on the information he has given about you?"

"Perfectly, monsieur."

"That is well; you must wait the result."

Dantès fell on his knees, and raising his clasped hands, he

breathed a prayer of blessing on the man who had thus penetrated to the depths of his prison like a saviour coming to deliver souls from hell. The door closed, but the hopes which the inspector had excited remained with Dantès and lightened his loneliness.

" Will you prefer to examine the register before going into the abbé's cell ? "

" No, we will finish the dungeons first."

" Well, this prisoner is very different from the other one, and his delusions are not so pitiful as the reasonable feelings of his neighbour. He believes himself the possessor of an immense treasure. The first year of his imprisonment he offered the government a million if he could be set at liberty, the second year two millions, the third three millions, and so on progressively. He is now in his fifth year, and he is sure to ask to speak to you privately and offer you five millions."

" And the name of this millionaire ? "

" Abbé Faria."

" No. 27 ? " said the inspector.

" Yes. Open the door, Antoine."

The inspector entered, looking curiously round the abode of the " mad abbé," as he was usually termed. In the middle of the cell, seated on the floor, in the centre of a circle traced with a piece of plaster from the wall, was a man in ragged and tattered garments. He was engaged in drawing some geometrical lines within the circle, and appeared as much absorbed in his problem as Archimedes, when he was assassinated by one of Marcellus' soldiers. He did not move until the blaze of torches cast a brilliant light on the damp ground where he was at work. Then he rose quickly, and taking a coverlet thrown across his miserable couch, he drew it round him, that he might appear more decently clothed to the eyes of strangers.

" What do you require ? " began the inspector, with his usual formula.

" I, monsieur ? " said the abbé, with an astonished air. " I require nothing."

" You do not understand," returned the inspector ; " I am an agent of the government, and it is my business to visit the prisoners and listen to their statements and requirements."

" Oh, that is another thing, monsieur ! " exclaimed the abbé, " and we shall understand each other, I hope. I am the Abbé Faria, and was born at Rome. I was for twenty years secretary to Cardinal Rospigliosi ; I was arrested, I scarcely know why, at the commencement of 1811 ; since that time I have continued

to demand my liberty from the Italian and French authorities."

"Why from the French authorities?" asked the governor.

"Because I was arrested at Piombino, and I suppose that, like
Milan and Florence, Piombino has become the chief town of a
French province."

"Good heavens!—my dear sir," said the inspector, "your
Italian news is not very recent."

"It dates from the day when I was arrested, monsieur," said
the Abbé Faria; "and as his Majesty, the Emperor, had created
the royalty of Rome for the son whom heaven had just sent him,
I presume that, continuing the course of his conquests, he has
by this time accomplished the dream of Machiavelli and Cæsar
Borgia, which was to make all Italy a single and united kingdom."

"Monsieur," said the inspector, "Providence has happily
interfered in the prosecution of that gigantic plan, of which you
appear to be so warm a partizan."

"It is the only means of making Italy a strong state—independent and prosperous," replied the abbé.

"That may be," rejoined the inspector, "but I did not come
here to go through a course of Ultramontane politics, but to ask
whether you have any requests to make regarding the manner
in which you are lodged and fed."

"The food is what it always is in prisons," returned the abbé,
"that is to say, extremely bad; as to the accommodation, as
you see, it is damp and unhealthy, but very well for a dungeon.
But there are certain revelations of the highest importance which
I have to make to the government. That is why I am glad to see
you," went on the abbé, "although you have disturbed me in
a calculation, which will very likely upset Newton's system
entirely. Will you grant me the favour of a private interview?"

"Monsieur, what you ask is impossible."

"But if it referred to an enormous sum of money—a sum of
five millions, for example, which the government might gain."

"*Ma foi*!" exclaimed the inspector, turning to the governor,
"you were right even to the figure."

"But see," said the abbé, observing that the inspector made
a movement to withdraw, "it is not necessary that we should
be alone. The governor may take part in our discussion."

"My dear monsieur," said the governor, "unfortunately we
know beforehand, and by heart, all that you are going to say.
It refers to your treasures, does it not?"

Faria regarded the jesting speaker with steadfast eyes, in

which any disinterested observer would have read at once an expression of truthfulness and unclouded reason.

"Certainly," said he. "Of what should I speak, if not of that?"

"My dear monsieur," said the inspector, "the government is rich and has no need, thank God, of your money. Keep it, then, for the time you come out of prison."

"But if, contrary to all justice, I am kept in this dungeon, if I die without having bequeathed my secret to anyone, this treasure will be lost! Is it not better that the government should profit by it? I will even offer six millions—yes, I will give up six millions, and will content myself with the rest, if only they will set me at liberty."

"Upon my word," said the inspector, "if one did not know that the man was mad, one would say he was speaking the truth, he talks with such sincere conviction."

"I am not mad, monsieur, and I am speaking the truth," said Faria. "This treasure of which I speak really exists, and I offer to sign an agreement with you, in virtue of which you shall conduct me to the spot indicated by me; the ground shall be dug under our eyes, and if I deceive you, if nothing is found there, and, if I am mad, you can bring me back again to this dungeon, and I will stay here for ever, and will die without asking anything further of you or anyone else."

The governor laughed. "And where is this treasure?"

"About a hundred leagues from here."

"That is not a bad idea; if the keepers were to consent to such a journey, there would be an excellent opportunity for the prisoners to bolt."

"That plan has been heard of before," said the inspector. "I have inquired whether you were properly fed."

"Monsieur," replied Faria, "swear you will set me free if I have spoken the truth, and I will show you where the treasure is buried."

"Are you properly fed?" reiterated the inspector.

"Monsieur, you would risk nothing, and as for myself, I will remain in prison until the expedition has been made."

"You do not reply to my question," returned the inspector, impatiently.

"Nor you to my request!" cried the abbé. "May you be cursed with all the other senseless creatures who would not believe me! You will not have my gold—well, I will keep it; you refuse me liberty—God will send it me! Go! I have no more

to say to you." And throwing off the coverlet, and taking up
again his piece of plaster, the abbé reseated himself at his circle,
and commenced anew his lines and figures.

"He must have possessed some wealth," observed the inspector as they ascended the stairs.

"Or dreamt that he did, and then woke up to find he had lost
his head," replied the governor.

"Certainly," said the inspector, with the *naïveté* that takes
corruption for granted, "if he had really been rich, he would
hardly be now in prison."

Thus the Abbé Faria remained a prisoner; and as a result of
this visit, his reputation as the happy madman was greater than
ever.

As to Dantès, the inspector kept his word, and had the prison
register brought for his inspection. The memorandum concerning the prisoner was couched in the following terms:

EDMOND DANTÈS. { Violent Bonapartist; took an active part in the return from Elba. To be kept in secret confinement, and under the strictest superintendence.

This note was in different writing from the remainder of the
register, which proved that it had been added since Dantès' imprisonment. The accusation was of too positive a character to
be set aside; the inspector, therefore, merely wrote underneath,
"Nothing to be done."

This visit had, so to speak, revived Dantès. Since he had been
in prison, he had forgotten to count the days; the inspector, however, had given him a new date, and he was careful not to forget
it. He wrote on the wall with a morsel of plaster, "July 30th,
1816," and each day he made a notch, that he might keep a
calculation. Days passed, then weeks, then months. Still
Dantès waited expectantly; he began by fixing the date of his
emancipation at the end of a fortnight. If the inspector prosecuted the matter with only half the interest which he had testified
on the occasion of his visit, he could certainly accomplish it in a
fortnight. When the fortnight had passed, however, Dantès told
himself that it was absurd to think that the inspector could set
about it until his return to Paris, which could not take place until
his tour of inspection was completed, which might probably last
a month or two; he therefore gave himself three months instead
of a fortnight. The three months also passed, and then another
idea occurred to him, and he prolonged the period to six months.
When this had also elapsed, he found, on closely calculating, that

D

he had been waiting altogether ten months and a half. During this period, nothing had been changed in the routine of his prison life ; he had received no consoling news, and the jailer, when questioned, was as mute as ever. Dantès began to doubt his senses, to believe that what he took for the remembrance of an event was nothing more than a mental hallucination, and that the consoling angel who had appeared in his prison, had only descended on the wings of a dream.

At the end of a year a new governor arrived ; and as it would have taken him too long to learn the names of all his prisoners, they were represented to him merely by their numbers. Thus the unfortunate youth ceased to be known by his own name of Edmond, or Dantès, and was called Number 34.

CHAPTER XV

NUMBER 34 AND NUMBER 27

DANTÈS slowly passed through every stage of suffering that could be endured by a prisoner, left forgotten in a dungeon. First his pride, resulting from his consciousness of innocence, supported him ; then he began to doubt his innocence, fell from his pedestal of pride, and prayed—not yet to God, Who is the last resource—but to men. Dantès prayed that they would take him from his dungeon, and place him in another, even though darker, and drearier. A change, even for the worse, was still a change, and would give him slight excitement for a few days. He also begged that he might walk in the open air, and have books or tools. None of his petitions was granted ; nevertheless, he still went on imploring. He was in the habit of talking to his new jailer, though the man was, if possible, even more silent than the last ; but to address a human being, even though a mute, was still a gratification. Dantès spoke that he might hear the sound of his own voice ; he tried to talk, too, when he was alone, but he felt afraid. Often in the days of his freedom he had been horrified at witnessing an assembly of prisoners, composed of bandits, assassins, and vagabonds, who, with coarse merriment, joined in wild orgies and noisy fellowship. Now he would have been glad to be himself thrust into one of these fearful dens, where he would, at any rate, behold other countenances than that of his impassive jailer ; he even envied the galley-slave, with his garb of infamy, shoulder-brand, and heavy chains : for the prisoners in the galleys had, at least, the society of their fellows ; they breathed the air, they could gaze into the skies ; they were indeed to be envied. He one day implored the jailer to ask for a companion for him ; it did not matter who—even that mad abbé whom he had heard mentioned. Under the rough exterior of the jailer there still lingered a touch of human feeling. Though he had given no sign, he had often, in the depths of his heart, pitied the unfortunate young fellow who felt his captivity so keenly. He made known the request of Number 34 to the governor ; but the latter imagined that Dantès wished to excite the prisoners to hatch some plot, or obtain an ally in some plan of escape, and he therefore refused.

Thus Dantès had exhausted the circle of human resources, and turned at last to heavenly aid. All the pious thoughts of unhappy and afflicted souls recurred to his mind and refreshed his wounded spirit ; he recalled the prayers his mother had taught him, and found in them a new meaning. Dantès prayed then ; not only fervently, but violently. He prayed aloud, no longer terrified at the sound of his own voice, and then he fell into a kind of ecstasy.

But notwithstanding his prayers, Dantès remained a prisoner. Then his spirit became clouded, and shadows gathered round his vision. He was simple-minded and without education. He had only his brief past, his dark present, and his doubtful future— a few years of light with which to meditate through an eternal night ! It was the only distraction that remained to him ; his energetic mind was cramped like an eagle in a cage. He clung to the thought of his past happiness, destroyed without apparent cause, and by a strange fatality. Dantès had but a transient faith, based on a sense of power ; he lost it, as others have lost it ; neither had he profited by it. Rage succeeded to asceticism. He hurled blasphemies at the jailer which made the man recoil with horror. He dashed himself against the walls of his prison, and vented his fury on such of his surroundings as excited his annoyance.

Then the letter of accusation which Villefort had shown him returned to his recollection. He told himself that it was through the hatred of men, not the vengeance of God, that he had been plunged into such an abyss of misery ; and he mentally consigned his enemies to every form of suffering that his ardent imagination could devise, feeling that the most terrible were yet too mild and too brief ; for, after suffering comes death, and with death insensibility. From frequently repeating to himself that death was not an evil to be shunned, he fell at last into a gloomy train of thought on suicide.

This idea has an intoxicating kind of consolation ; it shows the yawning gulf, but at the bottom of the gulf, oblivion. Edmond found some relief in the thought; all his sorrows and sufferings, and the procession of spectres which followed in their train, appeared to fly from the corner of his cell, where the Angel of Death silently rested his foot. Dantès regarded his past life with calmness, his future with terror, and chose that middle point, which appeared to be a haven of rest.

"How often," said he to himself, "in my long voyages, when I was free and independent, have I watched the sky get overcast, the waves wild and boisterous, and seen the storm beat the horizon with outspread wings! Sometimes the threatening rocks seemed to foreshadow approaching death, and I was terrified; I made every effort to escape it; for I was happy, and to retain life was to retain happiness. But now it is different. I have lost all that makes life dear, and death smiles on me as a nurse on the infant she is about to lull to sleep."

After this thought had started in his mind the young man became calmer and more resigned; he felt his existence almost supportable, as he realized that he could at any time put an end to it, and leave it off like a worn-out garment. There were two ways of cutting short his existence. The simpler plan was to tie his handkerchief to a bar of the window and hang himself; the other, to pretend to partake of his food, and slowly starve himself to death. Dantès recoiled from the first. It appeared to him a death full of ignominy; so he determined to adopt the second, and to put it into execution at once.

Nearly four years had passed in the manner we have just related. Now he had said to himself, "I wish to die!" and had determined the kind of death; he had thoroughly faced it, and for fear of altering his decision had vowed to himself to die. He decided that when his repast was served to him, morning and evening, he would throw it out of the window, and pretend to have eaten it. And this he carried out. Twice a day, through the little grating, by means of which he could look upward to the sky, he threw out his provisions; first freely, then thoughtfully, then with regret, and he needed the full remembrance of his vow to keep his resolution in carrying out this terrible design. The food which he had formerly regarded with disgust, now that hunger had seized him, appeared both appetizing and exquisite. He would stand sometimes for nearly an hour with the plate in his hand, his eyes fixed on the piece of tainted meat, fish, or black and mouldy bread. At times his dungeon appeared less dreary, and his prospects less desperate; he was still young, and had probably fifty years to

live. During that period what unforeseen events might not force
his prison doors and give him back his liberty ? Then he would
take a morsel of food, and hold it dangling before his lips ; but the
recollection of his vow would flash across him, and he had too
great a dread of self-contempt to forego his resolution. He persisted, therefore, with inexorable determination until at last the
day came when he had no longer the strength to raise himself
and throw his provisions out of the loophole. The jailer thought
he was dangerously ill. Edmond hoped he was dying. Thus the
day passed. Dantès felt a slight torpor steal over him, which
was not without an element of comfort. The nervous twitching
of his stomach was relieved ; his burning thirst assuaged ; when
he closed his eyes a number of bright lights danced before him ;
it was the twilight of that unknown land called Death. Suddenly, towards nine o'clock in the evening, he heard a muffled
sound on the other side of the wall against which his bed was
placed. So many unclean creatures made noises in this dark abode
that Dantès had been accustomed to sleep without noticing them ;
but on this occasion either his senses were sharpened by abstinence,
or the noise was louder than usual, or at this supreme moment
everything was magnified in importance, and he raised his head
that he might hear better. It was the scratching sound, either
of a powerful claw, or strong teeth, or the rubbing of some kind
of instrument on the stones.

Enfeebled as he was, the young man's mind was instantly
struck with that overpowering idea constantly arising in the
minds of prisoners—liberty ! The noise caught his ear so suddenly at the moment when all sounds seemed about to cease for
ever, that it appeared as if the Almighty had sent this warning to
stay him on the very verge of the tomb, towards which his feet
were slowly tottering. This might be one of his friends, one of
those loved ones who was now exerting himself and endeavouring
to reach him. The sounds continued nearly three hours ; then
Dantès heard the noise of something falling, after which they entirely ceased. A few hours later they began again, louder and
nearer.

Dantès was getting interested in the work, which was a distraction for him, when suddenly the jailer entered. Since a week
ago, when Dantès had resolved to die, and during the four days
he had been putting his project into execution, he had never
addressed a single word to his keeper, not even replying when he
was questioned as to what was the matter with him, and turning
his face to the wall if he were looked at attentively. But to-day

the jailer might hear this dull sound, become suspicious, put an end to it, and thus destroy the undefined hope which had begun to soothe Dantès. The man brought in his breakfast. Dantès lifted himself upon his bed, and, raising his voice, began to talk on all imaginable subjects—the bad quality of the food, the coldness of the cell, and so on, grumbling and scolding as an excuse for talking loudly, and wearying the patience of the jailer, who had that very day begged for a roll of fresh bread for the invalid prisoner. Fortunately, he fancied that Dantès was delirious, so he put down the food on the rickety table and retired. Freed from this danger, Edmond commenced listening again eagerly. The sound had become so distinct that the young man could now hear it without any effort.

"Doubtless," said he to himself, "it is some unfortunate prisoner like myself who is attempting to work his way out. Oh ! if I were near him, how I would help him !"

Then all at once a dark cloud overshadowed the dawn of hope, for his mind was so accustomed to misery that it could not easily realize any human joy. It occurred to him that the sound might be that of some workmen making repairs in the next cell. It would be easy to ascertain, but how could he risk a question ? Certainly, he might wait for the jailer, let him listen to the noise, and watch his expression ; but that would be to betray most precious hopes. Unfortunately, he was so feeble, and his mind so vacillating, that he could not grapple with a single thought.

At last he saw but one means of giving clearness to his reflections and firmness to his judgment ; he turned his eyes towards the hot broth, which the jailer had just placed on the table, rose, tottered towards it, raised the bowl to his lips, and swallowed the contents with an unspeakable sensation of relief.

Soon he felt clearness return to his brain, and could now think connectedly, and fortify his thought with judgment.

"I must," he said to himself, "make an experiment, but without compromising anybody. If it is but an ordinary workman, I have only to knock on the wall ; he will stop, perhaps, to try to find out who knocks, but as his work is not only lawful, but the carrying out of orders, he will soon resume it. A prisoner, on the contrary, will be alarmed : he will fear to be discovered, and will discontinue his work until the evening, when he will believe everyone in bed and asleep."

Edmond therefore got up again. He went to a corner of the prison, broke off a piece of loose stone, and struck the wall in the place where the sounds were most perceptible. He struck three blows. At the first, the noise ceased as though by magic. Edmond listened with all his might. An hour passed, two hours, but no further sound was heard. Full of hope, he ate a few mouthfuls of bread, and swallowed a little water ; and, thanks to the strong constitution with which nature had endowed him, he felt nearly as strong as ever.

The day passed, and the silence still continued. Night came, but the sound did not recommence.

" It is a prisoner," said Edmond to himself, with unspeakable joy.

The night passed without the slightest sound being heard. Edmond never once closed his eyes. Morning came, and the jailer entered with his food. Edmond had eaten his previous supply, and he now devoured the fresh plateful, while he never ceased to listen for the sounds, impatient at the prudence of the prisoner who seemed incapable of guessing that he had only been disturbed by a fellow prisoner, as anxious to be free as himself.

Three days passed, seventy-two mortal hours, counted minute by minute ! At last, one evening, when the jailer had just paid his last visit, and Dantès, for the hundredth time, bent his ear to the wall, it seemed to him that his head received a slight shock, when placed against the silent stones. He drew back to recover himself, took another turn up and down his room, and placed his ear against the wall. He had now no doubt about it ; something was being done on the other side.

The prisoner had been made aware of the danger of his manœuvre, and had adopted another ; to continue the work with more security, he had substituted the lever for the chisel.

Emboldened by this discovery, Edmond resolved to come to the aid of the indefatigable labourer. He began by removing his bed, behind which it seemed to him that the work of deliverance was being carried on ; and looked round for an instrument with which he might cut out some of the damp cement, and loosen a stone. He could find nothing, however. He had neither a knife, nor any other sharp implement ; there were only the iron bars of his grating, but he had assured himself so often that they were immovable, that it was not worth while trying to shake them. His furniture consisted of a bed, a chair, a table, a pail, and a small pitcher. There were iron staples in the bedstead, but they were fastened with screws into the wood, and could only be got out with a screwdriver. The table and chair were of no use. There had formerly been a handle to the pail, but this had been removed, Dantès had but one resource, which was to break his pitcher, and set to work with one of the broken pieces. He therefore dashed it to the ground, shivering it to atoms ; and proceeded to select two or three of the sharpest pieces, which he hid under his mattress, leaving the rest scattered on the ground.

Dantès had the whole night in which to work ; but in the dark he made but little progress, and he soon felt that his instrument was getting blunted against some harder substance. He, therefore, pushed back the bed, and waited for daylight. With hope, patience had also returned to him.

Day came at last, and the jailer paid his visit. Dantès told him that the evening before he had dropped the pitcher whilst drinking from it, and had broken it to atoms. The man went out, scolding, to fetch another, but without troubling to remove the fragments of the old one. He came back quickly, advised the prisoner to be more careful in future, and left again. Dantès listened with indescribable joy to the grating of the drawn bolt, whereas, formerly, the sound had made his heart sink with despair, and when silence reigned, he drew out his bed.

By the aid of the feeble morning light he saw that he had been working at the body of the stone, instead of the cement which surrounded it. Dampness had rendered this cement soft and powdery, and Dantès found that it could be detached in fragments ; they were but small pieces, it is true, but at the end of half an hour, he had loosened nearly a handful. The prisoner now reproached himself with not having thus employed the long hours which had passed so slowly, and which he had wasted in hope, and prayer, and despair.

During the years he had been a prisoner in that cell, what an amount of work he might have achieved ! This thought gave him new ardour. At the end of three days he succeeded, with incredible precautions, in removing all the cement, and leaving the stone bare. The wall was composed of rough loose stones, with here and there, to give it solidity, a large hewn stone. It was one of these hewn stones which he had laid bare, and which he now endeavoured to shake and loosen. He tried with his nails, but in vain. The pieces of pitcher broke off when used as levers in the crevices. After an hour spent in useless attempts, Dantès rose, the sweat of anguish on his brow. Then a thought flashed across his mind ; he stood upright and smiling, and his brow cleared.

The jailer was in the habit of bringing his soup in a tin saucepan. This saucepan had an iron handle, and it was this handle which Dantès desired, and for which he would willingly have given in exchange ten years of his life. The jailer always emptied the contents of the saucepan into a plate ; and the prisoner, after eating, washed the plate ready for the next day. This evening Dantès placed his plate half way between the door and the table, so that the jailer, as he entered, trod on it, breaking it into a thousand pieces.

He then looked round for something in which to pour the broth, but Dantès did not possess another plate.

" Why not leave the saucepan ? " said Dantès, " you can take it away when you bring my breakfast in the morning."

This was an agreeable suggestion to the jailer, who was thus saved the trouble of fetching another plate. He left the saucepan. Dantès trembled with joy. He quickly ate the broth and meat, and after waiting for an hour to be certain that the jailer did not think better of it, he moved his bed, took the saucepan, and inserting the end of the handle between the hewn stone and the loose fragments that surrounded it, tried to raise it by leverage. It moved slightly, and at the end of an hour the stone was drawn from the wall, where it left an opening of about a foot and a half in diameter.

Dantès carefully collected all the plaster, carried it into a corner of his prison, scratched a hole with a fragment of the pitcher, and covered the plaster with earth. Then he continued his work of boring with desperate ardour.

At dawn he replaced the stone in its hole, pushed back his bed, and lay down. His breakfast consisted of a piece of bread, which the jailer laid upon the table.

" Ah ! so you have not brought me another plate," said Dantès.

" No," replied the turnkey, " you broke your pitcher, and caused me to break your plate. You can keep the saucepan, and your food can be poured into it, and then perhaps you will not break anything else."

Dantès raised his eyes to heaven. This piece of iron inspired him with a more lively sense of gratitude than he had ever experienced in his past life for any benefit or happiness. He had remarked, however, that since he had begun to work the other prisoner had ceased altogether. No matter, that was no reason why he also should cease ; if his neighbour would not come to him, he must go to his neighbour. All day long he worked without intermission, and by evening, thanks to his useful weapon, he had extracted from the wall more than ten handfuls of loose stones, plaster, and cement.

When the hour for the jailer's visit arrived, he straightened the bent handle of the saucepan as well as he could, and put it in the accustomed place. The turnkey poured out the allowance of broth and fish; for three times a week the prisoners did not have meat. After the jailer had retired, Dantès listened earnestly, for he wished to assure himself if his neighbour had really ceased working. All was silent. Dantès sighed; his neighbour distrusted him. Nevertheless, he was not discouraged; but after two or three hours' hard labour, he met with an obstacle, and found on feeling it with his hands that it was a beam. This beam extended completely across the hole he had been making. Now he must bore a passage either above or below. The unfortunate young man had not anticipated this difficulty.

" Oh, my God ! " he cried, " I have prayed to Thee, and thought that Thou heardest me. Thou hast deprived me of liberty, Thou hast denied me the oblivion of death, and hast recalled me to life. Oh ! God, have pity on me, and leave me not to die in despair ! "

" Who speaks of God and of despair at such a time ? " said a voice, which seemed to proceed from below the ground, and which, deadened by the thickness of the wall, sounded to the young man almost sepulchral.

Edmond felt his hair stand on end, and shrank down on to his knees.

" Ah ! " he murmured, " I hear a human voice."

It was four or five years since he had heard any voice but that of his jailer, and to the poor prisoner the jailer hardly seemed a human being.

" In the name of heaven ! " he cried, " I beseech you, though your voice terrified me, tell me who you are."

" Who are you, then ? " demanded the voice.

" An unfortunate prisoner," replied Dantès, who made no difficulty about answering the question. " Edmond Dantès, a sailor."

" How long have you been here ? "

" Since the 28th February, 1815."

" Of what are you accused ? "

" Of having conspired for the return of the Emperor."

" What ! the return of the Emperor ! He is then no longer on the throne ? "

" He abdicated at Fontainebleau in 1814, and was banished to the Island of Elba. But how long have you been here, that you are ignorant of all this ? "

" Since 1811."

Dantès shuddered. This man, then, had been a prisoner four years longer than himself.

" Now, cease your work," the voice went on, speaking quickly, " and tell me at what height from the ground is the opening you have made."

" It is on a level with the ground, and is concealed behind my bed."

" What does your cell open into ? "

" The corridor."

" And the corridor ? "

" Leads to the courtyard."

" Alas ! " sighed the voice. " I have been deceived ; the want of a compass has led me astray, and a single crooked line on my plan has been equivalent to fifteen feet of reality ; and finally, I mistook the wall that you have been boring at for the outer wall of the prison."

" But then you would only get to the sea ? "

" That was what I wanted. I should have thrown myself into the waves, gained one of the islands near the Château d'If —either the Isle of Daume or Tiboulen, or perhaps reached the coast—and then I should have been safe ; but now all is lost. Cover up the hole carefully ; give up working, and wait till you hear from me."

" Tell me, at any rate, who you are ! "

" I am—I am No. 27."

" You mistrust me, then ? I am a good Christian," Dantès cried, divining that his companion thought of abandoning him, " and I swear I would kill myself rather than betray anything to your tormentors and mine ; but in the name of heaven, do not deprive me of your company, or of the sound of your voice, for I am almost desperate, and shall dash my head against the wall, and then you will have my death to reproach yourself with."

" How old are you ? Your voice sounds that of a young man."

" I do not know, for I have not counted the time since I have been here. All I know is, that I was arrested when I was nearly nineteen, on the 28th February, 1815."

" Not quite six-and-twenty, then," muttered the voice. " Come, one is rarely a deceiver at that age. You did well to speak to me and petition me, for I had formed another plan, and should have kept away from you. But your age reassures me, and I will join you."

" Ah ! you will not abandon me, you will not leave me alone, you will come to me or let me come to you ? We will escape

together, or, if we cannot, we can talk—you of the people you
love, and I of those I love.   You care for someone ? "

" I am alone in the world."

" Then you must love me. If you are young, I will be your
comrade ; if you are old, I will be your son. I have a father who
must be seventy, if he is still alive, and I love him and a young
girl named Mercédès. My father has not forgotten me, I feel
sure ; but she——. Heaven knows if she still thinks of me !
I will love you as I loved my father."

" That is well," answered the prisoner. " To-morrow then ! "

Dantès asked no more, but rose, and taking the same precautions as before, pushed the bed back against the wall. Then the
young man gave himself up to the thought of his happiness ; he
should now no longer be alone ; perhaps even he should be free ;
at the worst, if he remained a prisoner, he would have a comrade,
and captivity shared is captivity shorn of half its horrors.

The whole day Dantès walked up and down his cell, his
heart beating with delight. Once or twice the fear that he would
be separated from this man, whom he did not know, but whom
he already loved, occurred to him. In that case, he made up
his mind ; if the jailer removed his bed and discovered the opening,
he would at that very moment break his head with one of the
heavy stones. He would be condemned to death, that he knew ;
but had he not been about to die of despair at the moment this
wonderful noise called him back to life ?

The jailer came, as usual, in the evening. Dantès was on
his bed, for so, he thought, he should the better conceal the
unfinished opening. He, however, regarded the unwelcome
intruder with a curious glance, for the man inquired, " Well,
are you going to be crazy again ? "

Dantès made no reply, fearing that his voice would betray his
emotion. The jailer retired, shaking his head.

When night arrived, Dantès believed that his neighbour would
profit by the silence and the darkness to renew the conversation,
but he was mistaken ; the night passed without any sound striking on his ear to satisfy his feverish expectation. But the next
day, after the keeper's morning visit, as he was proceeding to
remove his bed from the wall, he heard three knocks at equal
intervals. He fell on his knees.

" Is it you ? " he cried ; " here I am."

" Has your jailer gone ? " asked the voice.

" Yes," replied Dantès ; " he will not return till evening ;
we have twelve hours of liberty."

" I can come, then ? "

" Yes, yes, at once ! Come this instant, I beseech you ! "

Then a portion of the opening on which Dantès was resting his hands, gave way ; he drew back, as a mass of earth and loose stones fell from a hole which appeared below the opening he himself had made ; then through the dark aperture he saw first a head, then the shoulders, and finally the whole form of a man emerging with considerable dexterity through the fallen rubbish.

CHAPTER XVI

A CLEVER ITALIAN

DANTÈS took in his arms this new friend, so long and impatiently awaited, and drew him to the window, where a little daylight penetrated the dark dungeon.

He was a man of small stature, his hair whitened more by suffering than age, with penetrating eyes, almost hidden beneath bushy grey eyebrows, and a beard descending to his breast. The thinness of his face, with its deep furrows and marked lines, seemed to indicate that he was a man more accustomed to exercise his moral than his physical faculties. His brow was moist from his exertions. As regards his clothes, it was impossible to distinguish their primitive form, for he was literally in rags. He appeared to be about five and sixty, though a certain vigour in his movements seemed to indicate that he was younger than his long captivity made him look. His chilled heart seemed to warm and melt in contact with this young ardent soul.

" Let us see, first," said he, " if there is any means of concealing from the jailers all traces of the opening."

Then he bent down to the hole, took the stone, which he easily raised, notwithstanding its weight, and fitted it into the opening.

" This stone has been very carelessly excavated," he remarked, shaking his head ; " you had no tools, I suppose ? "

" Had you any ? " inquired Dantès with astonishment.

" I made them myself. Except a file, I have all that is necessary—chisel, pincers, and lever. See, here is the chisel," said the new-comer, exhibiting a strong, pointed piece of iron, set in a wooden handle.

" How did you make that ? " said Dantés.

" With one of the iron pins of my bed. With this instrument I bored through the passage I have made, a distance of nearly fifty feet."

" And you say you have bored through a distance of fifty feet, to get here ? "

" Yes, that is about the distance that separates my room from yours ; only I believed, as I have told you, that I should reach the outer wall, bore through it, and throw myself into the sea. I bored along the corridor outside, instead of passing under it ; and now all my labour is lost, for this corridor opens on to a courtyard full of soldiers."

" That is true," said Dantès, " but the corridor only runs along one side of my cell, and there are four sides."

" Yes, of course ; in the first place, there is this one which rests against the rock ; it would take ten miners, properly furnished with tools, ten years to pierce through that rock.   Then this one evidently is built against the foundations of the governor's room ; we should fall through into the cellars and be caught. This other side, wait, let us see what it looks on to."

The wall in question contained the loop-hole, an opening of such contracted dimensions, that it only served to let in the smallest gleams of daylight ; while its rows of iron bars were strong enough to set at rest any fear of attempted escape.   The new comer proceeded to drag the table underneath the window.

" Now get up," said he to Dantès.

Edmond obeyed and stood upright on the table, resting his back against the wall, and extending his two hands.

Then the individual who called himself No. 27, climbed up on the table and, with the agility of a cat, or a lizard, crept up from Dantès' hands to his shoulders ; then, almost bent double, for the ceiling of the prison prevented him from standing upright, he passed his head between the bars to make a complete inspection.   In a moment he drew his head in quickly.

" Ah ! " he exclaimed, " I was afraid so— " and he slipped down from Dantès' shoulders on to the table, whence he jumped on to the ground.   " The fourth wall of your prison looks on to an outside walk, a kind of sentinel's beat, in fact, where the patrols are constantly passing up and down.   I saw a soldier's shako and the end of a gun, and drew back because I was afraid he might see me.   So you see it is impossible to escape from your cell."

" Therefore ? " continued the young man, interrogatively.

" Therefore, God's will be done ! " and an expression of profound resignation spread over the old man's features.

Dantès regarded this man, who renounced his long-cherished hopes so philosophically, with astonishment mingled with admiration.

" Now, will you not tell me who you are ? " he presently asked. His companion smiled sadly.

" I am the Abbé Faria," said he, " and have been a prisoner here since 1811 ; but for three years I was confined in the fortress of Fenestrelle. In 1811, I was transferred from Piedmont to France. I then learnt that fate had given to Napoleon a son, and that this infant had been styled King of Rome. I was far from suspecting what you have told me, namely, that four years later, the Colossus would be overturned. Who is it that now governs France ? Napoleon the Second ? "

" No. Louis XVIII."

" Louis ! the brother of Louis XVI ? The decrees of heaven are indeed strange and mysterious. What can have been the design of Providence in thus abasing the man who had been exalted, and exalting him who had been abased ? And so it was in England ; after Charles I, Cromwell ; after Cromwell, Charles II ; and after James II, the Prince of Orange. And then came fresh concessions to the people—a constitution—liberty ! You will see such days, young man," he added, turning on Dantès his brilliant and penetrating eyes, almost prophetic in their expression. " You are still young ; you will see all that."

" Yes, if I ever leave here."

" Ah ! true," returned the abbé. " We are prisoners ; there are moments when I forget it, and because my mental vision overleaps my prison walls, I fancy myself at liberty."

" But why were you imprisoned ? " asked Dantès.

" Because I dreamed in 1807 of the project which Napoleon endeavoured to realize in 1811 ; because, like Macchiavelli, I wished to unite in a single, compact, and strong empire, all those principalities which make of Italy a nest of little tyrannical and feeble kingdoms ; because I believed I had found my Cæsar Borgia in a crowned simpleton, who only pretended to understand me that he might the better betray me. It was the project of Alexander VI and Clement VII ; it will now never be realized, since they undertook it in vain, and since Napoleon could not accomplish it. Italy is cursed ! " and the old man bent his head.

Dantès could not understand how a man could risk his life for such interests.

" Are you not," said Dantès, beginning to share the jailer's opinion, in fact, the accepted opinion at the Château d'If, " the priest who is said to be ill ? "

" Mad, you mean, do you not ? "

"I did not like to say it," said Dantès, smiling.

"Yes," continued Faria, with a bitter laugh; "yes, I have passed for a madman a long time; it serves to divert the keepers of the prison, and to amuse the children, if there are children in this wretched abode."

"Then you give up the idea of escape?" said Dantès.

"I see that flight is impossible; and it is flying in the face of Providence to attempt the impossible."

"But why be discouraged? Can you not set about it in some other way?"

"You do not know all that I have accomplished when you talk so. Do you know that it took me four years to make the tools I possess? that for two years I have been scraping and digging in ground that was as hard as granite? that I have, by degrees, laid bare stones, which I at first thought it impossible to remove, and passed whole days in this gigantic labour, happy if, at night, I had succeeded in clearing away a square inch of the old cement, which had become as hard as the stone itself? Do you know that, to hide away all the earth and stones I had dug out, I had to cut through the arch of a staircase, and within it bury all the accumulation of rubbish, so that now it is quite full, and I no longer know where to put even a handful of dust? And then, at last, when I believed I had reached the goal of all my labour, the Almighty shuts me out from all hope of reaching it. Ah! I declare to you, I can no longer struggle for my liberty, for the will of God seems to be that it is lost for ever."

The abbé seated himself on Dantès' bed while Edmond himself remained standing. The young man had not previously dreamt of escape. To devote the labour of three years to burrowing a distance of fifty feet under the ground, only to reach a precipice rising perpendicularly from the sea, with the intention of jumping some fifty or sixty feet, to fall, perhaps, bruised and injured, head foremost on the rocks, and then if one escaped the fire of the sentinels, to have to swim a league to reach a place of safety, seemed like resigning oneself to death at once, and Dantès had never dreamt of such a desperate undertaking. The sight, however, of this old man who had clung to life with so much tenacity afforded him such a lively example of indomitable resolution, that he felt inspired with new courage and energy. If another had done so much, what might not he, Dantès, accomplish! Faria had bored through fifty feet; he would bore through a hundred! Faria had devoted three years to the task; he would give six! Faria had not dreaded the idea of crossing from the

Château d'If to the Isle of Daumo, Ratonneau, or Lemaire ; and should he, Edmond, a sailor, a fearless swimmer, hesitate on such a venture ? Dantès only needed to be encouraged by an example. All that another had done, he would do ! The young man reflected for a moment. At last he said, " I think I have discovered what you were seeking."

Faria started.

" What have you discovered ? "

" The corridor, beneath which you penetrated to come here, extends in the same direction as the walk outside, does it not ? "

" Yes."

" There cannot be more than fifteen feet between them ? "

" At the most."

" Well, about the middle of the corridor, we must excavate and make a road branching like a cross. This time, you will calculate better. We shall open out on to the outer walk ; we will kill the sentinel, and escape. For this plan to succeed, courage is needed, which you certainly have, and vigour, of which I have plenty. I do not speak of patience ; you have given proof of yours, and I will of mine."

" One moment," said the abbé ; " you do not understand, my dear companion, the nature of my courage, and to what use I can devote my strength. I thought I was only serving God in attempting to free myself, an innocent creature, and therefore not eternally condemned. Until now I have had to encounter only material objects, but you now propose to me to deal with men. I could pierce through a wall and a staircase, but I cannot pierce a human breast, I cannot destroy an existence."

" What ! " said Dantès, " if you were able to get free, you would be kept back by a scruple like that ? "

" But tell me," said Faria ; " why have you never knocked down your jailer with the leg of your table, dressed yourself in his clothes, and fled ? "

" The idea never occurred to me."

" No, because you had an instinctive horror of such a crime," returned the old man ; " for in simple and lawful matters our natural instincts warn us not to pass the boundary line of right. The tiger who sheds blood obeys his instinct. But man recoils from shedding blood ; it is not the social laws that restrain murder so much as natural laws."

Dantès was confounded, though the abbé's words were but an expression of sentiments that almost unconsciously arose in his own mind.

"I have," continued Faria, "during the long years that I have been in prison thought over many celebrated escapes. Escapes that are crowned with complete success are generally meditated with great care and slowly prepared. There are also those which occur through an accident: those are the best. We must wait an opportunity, and when it occurs, profit by it."

"You have been able to wait," said Dantès, sighing, "this long work has given you ceaseless occupation, and when you have not had your work to distract you, you had your hopes to console you."

"But I have had other occupations," said the abbé. "I wrote or studied."

"They gave you ink, pens, and paper?" cried Dantès.

"No. I made them myself. When you come into my room, I will show you a work, the result of the combined researches and thoughts of my whole life, on which I have meditated under the shadow of the Coliseum at Rome, at the foot of St. Mark's column at Venice, and on the banks of the Arno at Florence, and which I little thought I should conclude some day between the four walls of the Château d'If. It is a *Treatise on the Possibility of a United Monarchy in Italy*, and will make a large quarto volume."

"And you wrote it?"

"On two of my shirts. I invented a preparation which renders linen as smooth and firm as parchment."

"But for such a work you needed books. Had you any?"

"At Rome I had nearly five thousand volumes in my library. After reading and re-reading them, I perceived that in about a hundred and fifty well-chosen works one has, if not a complete *resumé* of human knowledge, at least all that is necessary for a man to know. I devoted three years of my life to reading and re-reading these hundred and fifty volumes, so that, at the time of my arrest, I almost knew them by heart. Now that I am in confinement, I can, with a slight effort of memory, recall their contents. Thus I could recite to you Thucydides, Xenophon, Plutarch, Titus Livius, Tacitus, Strada, Jornandès, Dante, Montaigne, Shakespeare, Spinoza, Macchiavelli, and Bossuet. I only mention the most important."

"Then you know several languages?"

"I speak five modern languages—German, French, Italian, English, and Spanish; by means of ancient Greek I understand modern Greek; I speak it badly, but I am studying it at the present time. I have made a vocabulary of the words I am acquainted with; I have arranged and combined them, so that they suffice to express my thoughts. I know nearly a thousand words, which is all I really need, although there are, I believe, a hundred thousand in the dictionaries. I can make myself understood, and that satisfies me."

More and more astounded, Dantès began to think there was something supernatural in the faculties of this strange man; so he inquired—

" But if they gave you no pens, how could you write this voluminous treatise ? "

" I made some myself from the cartilage of the heads of those large whiting which they give us on the days we go without meat. Thus, I always welcome Wednesdays, Fridays, and Saturdays with great pleasure, because I hope to increase my stock of pens ; and my historical works are, I admit, my greatest solace.

" But ink," said Dantès, " how did you procure ink ? "

" There was formerly a chimney in my cell, which was stopped up some time before my arrival, but for many years there had been fires in it ; the interior, therefore, is covered with soot. I dissolve this soot in a little wine which they give me every Sunday, and it furnishes excellent ink. For particular foot-notes, to which I desire to attract attention, I scratch my finger and write with my own blood."

" And when can I see all this ? " asked Dantès.

" Come with me," said the Abbé Faria. And he entered the subterranean passage, Dantès following him.

CHAPTER XVII

THE ABBÉ'S CELL

AFTER creeping along the subterranean passage, Dantès at last reached the other extremity, which opened into the abbé's room. The cell was laid with flags, and it was by removing one of these flags in the darkest corner that he had begun the laborious operation of which Dantès had seen the conclusion. As soon as he stood upright, the young man looked attentively round the room ?

" Well," said the abbé, " it is only a quarter past twelve, so we have several hours before us."

Dantès glanced round to see by what clock the abbé had been able to tell the hour so exactly.

" Do you see that ray of light that comes through my window," said the abbé, " and these lines on the wall ? By means of these lines, which accord with the double movement of the earth, and the ellipsis it makes round the sun, I can tell the hour more exactly than if I had a watch ; for a watch gets out of order, whilst the sun and the earth never alter."

Dantès did not understand this explanation ; but in every word his companion uttered he perceived some wonderful mysteries of science.

" Now," said he, " I am anxious to examine your treasures."

The abbé went to the chimney-piece, removed with his chisel the stone which had formerly served as the hearthstone, and which covered up a deep cavity. In this cavity were hidden all the objects he had described to Dantès.

" Which will you see first ? " said he.

" Show me your great work on the kingdom of Italy."

Faria drew forth three or four rolls of linen, folded one over another like sheets of papyrus, about four inches wide and eighteen in length. The strips were all numbered, and covered with writing in the abbé's mother tongue, which Dantès, being a Provençal, understood perfectly.

" See," said the abbé, " here it all is ; and about a week ago I wrote *finis* at the bottom of the sixty-eighth strip. Two of my shirts and all my handkerchiefs have been used ; if I ever get my freedom, and there is to be found in Italy a printer who dare print it, my reputation will be made."

" Yes," said Dantès, " it will certainly be. And now, please, show me your pens."

" Here they are," said Faria ; and he handed to the young man a small stick, six inches in length and about as thick as a pencil, to the end of which was fastened with some thread one of the pieces of cartilage, still wet with ink, of which he had spoken to Dantès ; it was pointed into a nib and split like an ordinary pen. Dantès wondered with what instrument it could have been shaped.

" Ah ! the penknife did that ! " said Faria ; " it is my *chef-d'œuvre*. I made it, as well as this knife, from an old iron candlestick."

The penknife was as sharp as a razor, and the large knife possessed the double advantage of serving either as a knife or a dagger. Dantès examined all these different objects with the same interest with which he had often, in the curiosity shops of Marseilles, examined tools and other things manufactured by savages in the Southern Seas, and brought by captains from their long voyages.

" But one thing still astonishes me," said Dantès, " that daylight has sufficed to you for all this work."

" I had the nights, too," said Faria. " God has given man intelligence to supplement the weakness of his senses. I obtained a light. I separate all the fat from the meat they bring me, and melt it into oil. See, this is my candlestick ;" and the abbé exhibited a small lamp like those sometimes used at illuminations.

" But how do you procure a light ? "

" With two flints and a piece of burnt linen."

Dantès laid down the different articles on the table, and bent his head, overwhelmed by the perseverance and energy of this strong mind.

" This is not all," continued Faria ; " one must not put all one's treasures in the same hiding-place. We will shut this one up."

They lifted the stone into its place again, and the abbé scattered a little dust to obliterate any sign of irregularity ; then he approached his bed, and moved it from the wall. Concealed by a stone was a large hole, and in this hole a rope-ladder, twenty-five to thirty feet in length. Dantès examined it ; it was perfectly strong and secure.

" And how did you procure the rope for this wonderful work ? "

" By unravelling some of my shirts and the sheets from my bed during my three years' imprisonment at Fenestrelle ; when I was brought to the Château d'If I managed to bring it all with me, and continued the work here."

" But did they not notice that your sheets had no hem ? "

" I stitched them with this needle ;" and the abbé, opening his tattered coat, showed Dantès a long, sharp fish-bone, with a thread running through it.

" Yes," he continued, " I thought at first of loosening these bars and escaping through the window, which is a little larger than yours, as you see, and which I should have made larger still ; but I found that it opened on to an inner court, and I gave up the project as too dangerous. However, I preserved the ladder."

Dantès, while affecting to examine the ladder, was busily thinking of a very different matter. Might not this man, so intelligent, ingenious, and profound, be able to throw some light on the mystery of his own misfortune, the origin of which appeared so obscure to himself ?

" Well, what are you thinking of ? " said the abbé, smiling, imagining that Dantès' silence was due to intense admiration.

" I was thinking, first of all, that it was only by means of enormous intelligence that you have been able to reach such a point of success. What would you have done if you were free ? "

" Nothing, perhaps ; my capacious brain would have evaporated in futilities. Captivity has concentrated in one direction all my wandering faculties. They have clashed in a narrow space, and, as you know, from the collision of the clouds results electricity, from electricity a flash, and from the flash, light."

"Indeed, I know nothing," said Dantès, dejected by his own ignorance ; " half the words you utter are to me empty of meaning ; you are indeed fortunate to be so learned."

The abbé smiled. " But," said he, " you were thinking of two things, and have only told me the first."

" Yes, I was also thinking that you have related the story of your life to me, but do not at present know anything of mine."

" Your life, young man, is too short to embrace events of much importance."

" It nevertheless contains a great misfortune," said Dantès— " a misfortune I have not merited, and I would fain know what human wretches have been the authors of it, that I may not blaspheme heaven, as I have, alas ! sometimes done."

" But you declare yourself innocent of what is imputed to you ? "

" Completely innocent, by the name of my father and of Mercédès, the only two people whom I love."

Dantès then related the whole story of his life, ending with an account of his arrival at Marseilles, his interview with his father, his love for Mercédès, their betrothal feast, his arrest, examination, temporary prison at the Palais de Justice, and, finally, his transportation to the Château d'If. At this point the narrative came to an end. He knew no more, not even how long he had been there.

" That is a profound truth," the abbé presently observed, "that unless a wicked thought arises in a depraved mind, human nature recoils from crime. Nevertheless, civilization has given rise to many desires, vices, and factitious appetites, which sometimes stifle our good instincts and lead us astray. Therefore this maxim holds good : If you would discover the guilty one, seek for him to whom the crime would probably have been useful. Now, who would have benefited by your disappearance ? "

" No one, thank God ! I was not of sufficient consequence."

" Do not answer so ; such a reply is wanting both in logic and philosophy. Everything is relative, my dear friend, beginning with the King, who stands in the way of his successor, and ending with the *employé*, who fills a post longed for by the supernumerary. You were about to be made captain of the *Pharaon*, and to marry a beautiful young girl ? "

" Yes."

" Had anyone an interest in your not becoming captain of the *Pharaon* ? Did anyone wish to prevent you from marrying Mercédès ? Answer the first question, to begin with ; order is the key to all problems.   Had anyone any interest in your not being made captain of the *Pharaon* ? "

" No, I was beloved on board. If the sailors had had the power to choose, they would have chosen me. Only one man had a grudge against me. I had had a quarrel with him, and proposed a duel, which is refused."

" Ah ! what was this man's name ? "

" Danglars, the supercargo."

" If you had been made captain, should you have kept him in his post ? "

" Not if the matter had rested with me, for I had noticed some irregularities in his accounts."

" Good. Now was anyone present at your interview with Captain Leclère, or could anyone have heard your conversation ? "

" Yes, the door was open ;—and, now I think of it, Danglars went by just at the moment when Captain Leclère handed me the packet for the Grand Marshal."

" Exactly," said the abbé, " now we are on the track. Did you take anyone with you when you landed at the Island of Elba ? "

" No one."

" And you then received the letter ? "

" Yes, from the Grand Marshal."

" And what did you do with it ? "

" I put it in my pocketbook."

" Which you had on your person, I suppose ? But how could a pocketbook, large enough to contain an official letter, be got into a sailor's jacket pocket ? "

" You are right ; I had left my pocketbook on board."

" It was not till you came on board again, then, that you put the letter in your pocketbook ? "

" No."

" And coming back from Porto Ferrajo to the ship, what did you do with it ? "

" I held it in my hand."

" When you got on board, then, everyone, Danglars, as well as the others, could see that you held a letter ? "

" Yes."

" Now, attend to me ; exert your memory ; can you recall the terms in which the accusation was couched ? "

Dantès reflected a moment, and then said, " This is it, word for word :—' Monsieur the Procureur du Roi is warned by a friend to the throne and religion, that one, Edmond Dantès, mate of the ship *Pharaon*, which arrived in port this morning from Smyrna, after having touched at Naples and PortoFerrajo, has been commissioned by Murat with a letter for the Usurper, and by the Usurper with a letter for the Bonapartist Committee at Paris. Proof of this crime will be obtained on arresting him, for the letter will be found either on his person, or in his father's house, or in his cabin on board the *Pharaon.*' "

The abbé shrugged his shoulders.

" It is as clear as daylight," said he ; " what was Danglars' usual handwriting ? "

" A good running hand."

" And the writing of this anonymous letter was feigned ? "

" It was too bold to be feigned."

" Wait," said Faria, and taking his pen, he dipped it in the ink, and wrote with his left hand, on a piece of the prepared linen, the letter of accusation.

Dantès recoiled, and regarded the abbé almost with terror.

" Oh ! " he cried, " how extraordinary ! That writing exactly resembles the anonymous writing."

" That is because it has been written by the left hand ; I have observed that though handwritings of the right hand constantly vary, all writing with the left hand is alike. Now let us go on to the second point. Had anyone any interest in preventing your marrying Mercédès ? "

" Yes, a young man who was in love with her, Fernando, a Catalan."

" Do you think he was capable of writing this letter ? "

" Oh ! no ; he might have stabbed me, though. Besides, he was ignorant of all the details contained in the accusation."

" And you confided, then, to no one ; not even to your betrothed ? "

" Not even to Mercédès."

" It was Danglars, then ! "

" Yes, now I am sure of it," cried Dantès.

" Stay," said Faria ; " did Danglars know Fernando ? "

" No—and yet—I seem to recollect—— The night before my marriage I saw them seated together in old Pamphile's arbour ; Danglars was friendly and joking, but Fernando was pale and troubled."

" And were they alone ? "

" No, there was a third person, a tailor, named Caderousse, well known to me ; but he was tipsy. Why, now I think of it," continued Dantès, raising his hand to his head, " on the table, where they were drinking, there were pens, ink, and paper ! Oh ! the villains ! the villains ! "

" Is there anything else you want cleared up ? " said the abbé, smiling.

" Yes ; for you seem able to penetrate everything. Why was it I was only examined once, why was I not tried, and why was I condemned without a sentence ? "

" That," said the abbé, " is rather a weightier matter ; the ways of justice are dark and mysterious. What we have just discovered about your two friends is mere child's play ; but on this matter, you must give me very exact information. Who was it that examined you ? the Procureur du Roi, the deputy, or the magistrate ? "

" It was the deputy."

" Was he young or old ? "

" Young ; about twenty-seven or twenty-eight."

" Good ! then hardly corrupted, though, perhaps, ambitious. How did he behave towards you ? "

" Pleasantly, rather than sternly."

" And you told him everything ? "

" Everything."

" Did his manner change during the course of the examination ? "

" Yes, when he was reading the letter which compromised me. He seemed overwhelmed at my misfortune."

" You are sure it was your misfortune that touched him ? "

" Yes, and he certainly gave me a proof of his sympathy by burning the only evidence against me."

" Do you mean the accusation ? "

" No, the letter itself. He did it before my eyes, and he said, ' Now you see the only proof against you, I have destroyed.' "

" Such conduct was too sublime to be natural. How was the letter addressed ? "

" To M. Noirtier, 13, Rue Coq-Héron, Paris."

" Do you imagine this deputy had any interest in destroying the letter."

" It is possible ; for he made me promise two or three times— for my own sake, he said—not to speak to anyone about this letter, and made me swear never to utter the name of the person it was addressed to."

" ' Noirtier,' " repeated the abbé ; " ' Noirtier ' ; I knew a Noirtier at the court of the late Queen of Etruria, a Noirtier who had been a Girondist during the Revolution. What was the name of this deputy of yours ? "

" De Villefort."

The abbé burst out laughing.

" You can see that gleam of daylight ? " he said. " Well ! it is all now as clear to me as that is bright and luminous. Poor fellow ! and so this magistrate was kind to you ? And the worthy man burned—destroyed the letter ? This honest purveyor to the executioner also made you swear never to pronounce the name of Noirtier ? "

" Yes."

" And Noirtier—poor, blind soul that you were ! have you no idea who this Noirtier was ? Noirtier was his own father ! "

If a thunderbolt had fallen at Dantès' feet, the shock would have been less overwhelming than the effect of these unexpected words. He started up, clasping his head in his hands, as though it would burst.

" His father ! his father ! " he cried.

" Yes ; his father, whose name is Noirtier."

Then a bright light flashed across the young prisoner's brain, and what had formerly been obscure was now illumined by the light of day.

Villefort's tergiversation during the examination, the burnt letter, the exacted vow, the almost supplicating voice of the deputy, who, instead of menacing, seemed even to implore— all recurred vividly to his remembrance ; he staggered like a drunken man, and then cried : " Oh ! I must be alone ; I must think over all this ! "

On reaching his own cell, he flung himself on the bed, where the turnkey found him in the evening, lying with fixed eyes and contracted features, motionless and mute as a statue.

During these hours of meditation, which passed like so many seconds, he had made a terrible resolution, and taken a solemn oath !

At last a voice roused Dantès from his reverie. It was the Abbé Faria, who, having received the jailer's visit in his turn, came to invite Dantès to sup with him.

On account of his reputation as a harmless, and even amusing lunatic, the old prisoner obtained many little privileges, such as having white bread and a small bottle of wine on Sundays. He therefore came to invite his young companion to partake of his dainties.

Dantès rose and followed him.

"I am sorry," the abbé observed, "that I have told you so much, because a sentiment has arisen in your heart which was not there before—vengeance!"

"Let us talk of something else."

The abbé looked at him, shook his head sadly, then began to talk of other matters.

The old prisoner's conversation contained much useful information, and inspired a sustained interest; but it was not egotistical, for the poor abbé never spoke of his own misfortunes. Dantès listened with admiration; some of his observations came within his own limited range of knowledge, while others touched on things unknown to him, and showed him new, unexplored ranges of country, and many undreamt of fields of thought. Dantès could, however, comprehend the pleasure with which a more cultured mind than his own would have followed this educated man in the moral, philosophical, and social disquisitions in which he delighted.

"You must teach me a little of what you know," said he, "if only not to get tired of me. What will you teach me first? I am anxious to begin—I long to learn."

"You must learn everything," said the abbé.

And that same evening the two prisoners agreed on a plan of education which was put into execution on the following day. Dantès had a prodigious memory, and great readiness of conception; his aptitude for mathematics rendered him extremely quick in calculation, whilst his naturally romantic temperament coloured with a pleasing light everything that would otherwise have appeared dry and uninteresting in arithmetical or geometrical problems. He already knew Italian, and a little Romaic, picked up during his voyages in the East. By means of these two languages he soon comprehended the construction of all others, and at the end of six months he began to speak Spanish, English, and German. At the end of a year he was another being. As for the Abbé Faria, Dantès remarked that, notwithstanding the fresh interest he himself afforded him, he grew day by day more gloomy and more desponding. One thought appeared incessantly and eternally to burden his spirit; he fell into profound reveries, sighed involuntarily, would start up suddenly, and crossing his arms, pace sadly up and down his prison. One day he stopped suddenly in one of his restless walks round his room, and cried:

"Oh! if there were only no sentinel!"

"There would be no sentinel if you only desired it," said Dantès, who had penetrated the thought in his companion's mind.

"Ah! but I have told you that I have a horror of murder," returned the abbé.

"But this murder, supposing it were committed, would be from a motive of self-preservation, of personal defence."

"That makes no difference."

"You think about it, nevertheless?"

"Constantly, constantly," murmured the abbé.

"And have you thought of any means?" asked Dantès, quickly.

"Yes, if one could only put a blind and deaf sentinel in the passage."

"He would be blind—he would be deaf," answered the young man, with an accent of resolution that terrified the abbé.

"No, no," he cried, "impossible!"

Dantès would have continued the subject, but the abbé shook his head, and refused to say any more.

Three months passed. At last one day the abbé said:

"Are you strong, Edmond?"

Dantès took the chisel, bent it into the shape of a horseshoe, and then straightened it again.

"You will promise not to kill the sentinel except at the last extremity?"

"Yes, on my honour."

"Then," said the abbé, "we will carry out our plan."

"And how long will it take to accomplish?"

"A year, at least, but we can begin immediately. See, this is my plan." And he showed Dantès a plan of the two cells, with the passage that united them.

In the centre of this passage he proposed to cut a small opening, which should extend underneath the corridor where the sentinel walked. They could then commence an extensive excavation, and finally loosen one of the flags which formed the floor of the corridor; at a certain moment this flagstone would give way under the soldier's weight, who would suddenly fall through the opening. Then, while the man was still stunned with his fall, and unable to defend himself, Dantès would throw himself on him, bind and gag him. They would then get out of one of the windows of the corridor, and by means of the rope-ladder let themselves down the outer wall and escape.

Dantès clapped his hands, and his eyes sparkled with delight; the plan seemed so simple, it was sure to succeed.

The same day, the two miners began their work. They had no interruption till the hour arrived at which they were both obliged to re-enter their cells to receive the jailer's visit. They had become, however, by dint of habit, able to distinguish the almost imperceptible sound of the man's footsteps directly he began to descend the stairs, and neither the one nor the other had ever been taken by surprise. The earth extracted from the opening, which would have choked the narrow passage, was thrown by little and little, and with incredible precautions, through one or the other of the windows of their cells. It was pulverized with great care, and the wind bore it away, leaving no trace behind.

More than a year passed, and the work was still prosecuted, the only instruments used by the indefatigable miners being a chisel, a knife, and a wooden lever. During their employment Faria continued to instruct Dantès, conversing with him now in one language, now in another, and giving him much information concerning the history of nations, and of great men who, from time to time, have left behind them the luminous tracks we call glory.

At the end of fifteen months the hole was finished, and the excavation beneath the corridor completed. They could hear the sentinel pacing up and down, but they were obliged to wait for a dark and cloudy night to make their escape more secure ; and in the meantime they had but one fear—namely, that the ground should give way prematurely beneath the soldier's feet. They, however, obviated this danger by fixing a small beam, which they had discovered in the foundations, as a support beneath the weak structure.

Dantès was one day engaged in completing this fixture, having left the old prisoner in his room busy sharpening a peg for se- curing their rope-ladder, when he suddenly heard a sharp cry of distress, and hurrying in, found the abbé standing in the middle of the cell, pale as death, with streaming brow and clenched hands.

Dantès gazed at his livid countenance, his white lips, and the dark shadows round his eyes, and, overwhelmed with terror, dropped his chisel.

" Oh ! what is it ? " he cried.

" I am lost, lost ! " said the abbé ; " but listen to me. A terrible malady has seized me ; an attack is coming on ; I feel it. I was first seized with it the year preceding my imprison- ment. For this disease there is but one remedy ; turn up the foot of my bed; it is hollow, and you will find in it a small bottle half full of a reddish fluid, which bring to me; or, stay—no, I might be surprised here. Help me back to my own cell while I have the strength to move. Who knows what might happen during the time of the attack? "

Dantès led his companion through the corridor with infinite care, and on reaching the abbé's room, laid him on the bed.

" Thanks," said the old man, shivering in every limb, " the evil that is coming upon me is a cataleptic fit; perhaps I shall make no movement and not utter a sound; but perhaps I shall foam at the mouth, become stiff, and cry out; try to prevent my cries from being heard; it is important, for they might change my cell, and then we should be parted for ever. When you see me motionless, cold, and dead, so to speak—and only at that moment, understand—force open my teeth with a knife, and make me swallow eight or ten drops of that fluid, and perhaps I shall recover."

" Perhaps," cried Dantès, piteously.

" Help, help! " cried the abbé, " I am dying; I——"

The attack was so sudden and so violent that the unfortunate prisoner could not finish his sentence; a dark shade passed over his face; his eyes dilated, his mouth became contorted, his face grew purple; he writhed, foamed, and cried out. Dantès endeavoured to stifle his cries under the coverlet. This lasted two hours. Then, as pale and cold as marble, he stiffened again in a second convulsion, and became livid.

Edmond waited till this apparent death seemed to have crept over the entire body—till it reached the heart. Then he took a knife, introduced the blade between the abbé's teeth, pressed open the clenched jaws, administered the ten drops, and waited.

An hour passed without the old man making the slightest sign, and Dantès began to fear he had waited too long.

At last a slight colour appeared in the invalid's face; his eyes which had throughout remained fixed and open, regained their usual expression, a sigh escaped him, and he moved.

" Saved! saved! " ejaculated Dantès.

The sick man could not yet speak, but he motioned with his hand with visible anxiety towards the door.

Dantès listened, and heard the jailer's steps. It was seven o'clock, but the time had passed unnoticed. The young man darted towards the opening, disappeared, filled it up with the flagstone, and re-entered his own cell.

A moment later and the jailer entered, and as usual found

the prisoner seated on his bed. His back was scarcely turned when Dantès, without touching his food, again entered the abbé's chamber. The poor man had regained consciousness, but was lying extended on his bed, helpless.

" I hardly expected to see you again," he observed, as Dantès approached ; " everything was ready for flight, and I thought you would escape."

" Without you ? " Dantès cried. " You deemed me capable of that ? "

" But I was deceived," returned the sick man. " Ah! I am very feeble, shaken, and broken."

" Courage ! " said Dantès ; " your strength will return."

" The last time," said the abbé, " the attack lasted half an hour, after which I was hungry, and could raise myself unaided. To-day, I can move neither my right leg nor my right arm, my head is confused, which shows some injury to the brain. The third time I shall be paralysed entirely, or shall die under the shock."

" No, no, cheer up ; you will not die. The third attack, if it comes, will find you free ; and you will be cured as you were now ; indeed, you will be better off, for you will be able to have all the necessary remedies."

" My friend," said the old man, " do not deceive yourself, the attack which has just seized me has condemned me to a perpetual prison ; one must walk in order to escape."

" Well, we will wait a week, a month, two months ; in that time your strength will return. Everything is ready, and we have the liberty of choosing the moment. When you feel sufficiently strong to swim, that very day we will put our project into execution."

" I shall never swim again," said Faria, " this arm is paralysed—not for a day only, but for ever. Raise it, and see how helpless it is."

The young man lifted his arm, which fell like a dead weight on the coverlet.

" Now you are convinced, Edmond ? " said Faria ; " believe me, I know what I am talking about ; I expected it, for it is hereditary in our family : my father died at the third attack, my grandfather also. The physician who gave me this fluid, the famous Cabanis, predicted a like fate for myself."

" The physician made a mistake," cried Dantès ; " besides, as to your paralysis, I will take you on my shoulders and swim along with you."

"My boy," said the abbé, "cease deluding yourself with such chimeras. I shall remain here until the hour of my deliverance, which now can be no other than the hour of death! As for you— fly! escape! You are young, strong, and nimble; do not be uneasy about me. I give you back your promise!"

"If that is it," said Dantès, "I also shall remain." And, rising, he extended his hand solemnly towards the old man, adding, "By the blood of Christ, I swear never to leave you till your death!"

Faria looked up at the young fellow, so noble, simple, and elevated in his devotion, and read on his features the sincerity of his affection, and the loyalty of his vow.

"Thank you," said the sick man, "I accept your promise." Then stretching out his hand, he added, "You will perhaps be recompensed for this devotion, but as I cannot, and you will not escape, you must stop up the opening under the corridor; the soldier might discover the hollowness of the place, direct the attention of the inspector to it, and then we should be discovered and separated. Give the whole night to it, if necessary, and do not return till after the jailer's visit in the morning; I shall have something important to say to you."

CHAPTER XVIII

THE TREASURE

WHEN Dantès entered his companion's cell next morning he found him seated in his chair looking calm and collected. He was holding up to the light in his left hand, the only one he could use, a strip of paper, which had been so tightly rolled up that it was not very easily untwisted. Without speaking, he handed the paper to Dantès.

"Look at it carefully," said the abbé, smiling. "That paper, my friend, is my treasure, of which one half from this day belongs to you."

A cold perspiration covered Dantès' brow. Until that day, he had avoided speaking to Faria about this treasure which had been the source of the painful rumour of the poor abbé's insanity. With instinctive delicacy Edmond had preferred not to touch on the unfortunate subject, and Faria had been silent.

The young man had taken his companion's silence as an evidence of his return to his right mind, and now that these few

words escaped him after his terrible attack, a painful doubt
arose that they perhaps indicated a return of the delusion.

" Your treasure ? " he stammered.

" Yes," said he ; " you have a noble heart, Edmond, and I
understand what is passing in your mind. But I am not mad.
This treasure exists, Dantès, and as I have not been vouchsafed
to possess it, *you* shall possess it. No one has been willing to
listen to me or believe me, because I was thought to be mad ;
but you, who ought to know that I am nothing of the kind, must
listen, and believe me afterwards if you will."

" My friend, the attack has exhausted you ; will you not
first take a little rest ? To-morrow, if you wish it, I will listen
to the whole story, but to-day I want you to take care of yourself. Besides," he continued, smiling, " is it a very urgent
matter, this treasure ? "

" Very urgent, Edmond," replied the old man. " Who
knows but to-morrow, or the day after, I may be seized with the
third attack ? and then perhaps all will be over. Yes, it is true.
I have often thought with a bitter pleasure that these riches,
which would have made the fortune of ten families, are lost for
ever to my cruel persecutors ; but now that I think of all the
happiness that might result to you from my secret, I tremble at
any delay which may prevent my assuring myself of so worthy
a successor to my buried riches." Dantès turned his head away
and sighed. " You persist in your incredulity, Edmond," continued Faria ; " my voice has not convinced you ? I see that
you need proofs. Well, read this paper, which I have never
shown to anyone."

" To-morrow, my friend," said Edmond, anxious to avoid
lending himself to the old man's craze.

" We will not talk about it till to-morrow ; but read this paper
now."

" I will not irritate him," thought Dantès ; and taking the
torn piece of paper, which had apparently been partly burnt
by some accident, he read :

" This treasure, which amounts to two . . .
Roman crowns in the corner . . .
of the second opening, which . . .
bequeath to him as sole . . .
April 25, 149 . ."

" Well ? " said Faria, when the young man had finished.

" But all the lines are broken," said Dantès ; " and as a good
deal has been burnt, it is unintelligible."

E

" To you, my friend, who read it for the first time, but not to me, who have grown pale pondering it many long nights, reconstructing every phrase, and completing every thought."

" And you think you have found the hidden meaning ? "

" I am sure of it ; but you shall judge for yourself. First listen to the history of this paper."

" Silence ! " cried Dantés ; " I hear footsteps. Someone is coming—I must go, adieu ! " and happy to escape the story and explanation, which would but have confirmed in him the certainty of his friend's mental alienation, Edmond slipped like a snake along the narrow passage, whilst Faria, roused by terror to greater exertion than he could otherwise have made, pushed back the flagstone with his foot.

It was the governor, who, having heard from the jailer of Faria's illness, came to make inquiries as to its gravity.

Faria avoided every movement that would have betrayed him, and succeeded in concealing the paralysis which had numbed one half of his body. His great fear was lest the governor, touched by compassion, should desire to place him in a healthier cell, and thus separate him from his young companion. This, however, was not the case, and the governor retired, convinced that his poor lunatic had only been affected by slight indisposition.

All this time Edmond remained seated on his bed, endeavouring to collect his scattered thoughts. Was Faria deceived about this treasure ? or was everyone deceived about Faria ? Dantès kept to his room the whole day, trying thus to postpone the moment when he should acquire conclusive evidence of the abbé's insanity. Towards evening, however, after the jailer's visit, Faria attempted to traverse the distance between the cells. Edmond trembled as he heard the painful, stumbling efforts the old man made as he dragged himself along ; one leg was helpless, and he could no longer use his right arm. Dantès was at last obliged to go to his assistance, for he could not unaided get through the narrow opening into Dantès' cell.

" Here I am ! " exclaimed the old man, " relentlessly bent on pursuing you. You thought to escape my munificence, but you will do nothing of the kind. Now, listen."

Edmond placed the old man on his bed, and seated himself on the stool beside him.

" You are aware," began the abbé, " that I was the secretary, confidant, and friend of Cardinal Spada, the last of the princes of that name. To this noble lord I owe all the happiness that I have enjoyed. He was not rich, although the wealth of his family was proverbial, but had the reputation of opulence. His palace was my Paradise. I instructed his nephews, who both died ; and when he was alone in the world I endeavoured to repay, by absolute devotion to his wishes, all he had done for me during a period of ten years. The cardinal's house had soon no secrets for me ; and I was in the habit of seeing monsignor spend much time examining ancient books, and eagerly searching among dusty family manuscripts. One day, when I reproached him with his useless labours, and spoke of the fits of depression which generally followed them, he regarded me with a melancholy smile, and opened a volume of the history of Rome. There, in the twentieth chapter of the *Life of Pope Alexander the Sixth* were the following lines, which I have never been able to forget :

" ' The great wars of Romagna had terminated. Cæsar Borgia, who had completed his conquest, had now need of money to buy Italy entirely. The Pope had also need of money to arrange matters with Louis XII, King of France, who was still formidable, in spite of his recent reverses. It was therefore necessary to embark on some good speculation, which was a difficult matter in poverty-stricken Italy. His Holiness had an idea. He would appoint two cardinals.'

" By choosing two members of the highest aristocracy of Rome and men of wealth withal, the Holy Father gained two advantages : he had the proceeds of the sale of the large establishments and important posts held by the new cardinals, and he could also count on a handsome sum as the price of the two hats. There was yet a third point, of which more presently. The Pope and Cæsar Borgia first of all found the two cardinals —Jean Rospigliosi, who alone held four of the highest dignities of the Holy See ; and Cæsar Spada, one of the noblest and richest of the Romans. Both felt the value of such a favour from the Pope, for they were ambitious ; both paid handsomely for their hats ; and eight other individuals also paid for the posts previously held by the new cardinals, a sum of eight hundred thousand crowns thereby accruing to the speculators.

" We will now pass to the last part of the speculation. The Pope having conferred on Rospigliosi and Spada the insignia of cardinalship, and overwhelmed them with caresses, felt tolerably sure that they had been obliged to realize their property in order to meet the fictitious debt and settle themselves at

Rome; and in conjunction with Cæsar Borgia he invited them to dinner.

" The repast was at the Vinery, a charming residence which the Pope possessed near Saint-Pierre-ès-Liens, and which the cardinals, well knew by reputation. Rospigliosi, whose head was rather turned by his new dignity, willingly lent himself to the occasion. Spada, however, was prudent, and greatly attached to his nephew, a young captain and a very promising youth. He feared the possible consequences of a Papal banquet and therefore sat down, took pen and paper, and made his will. He also sent word to his nephew to await him near the Vinery, but the messenger could not find him. Spada set out towards two o'clock for the Vinery of Saint-Pierre-ès-Liens. The Pope was awaiting him. The first object that met Spada's eyes was his own nephew, elegantly dressed, and laughing pleasantly, standing near Cæsar Borgia, who was overwhelming him with attentions. Spada turned pale, and Cæsar glancing at him with a look full of irony, showed him that everything had been anticipated. Spada knew his fears had been realized. They sat down to dinner, and an hour later, a doctor declared them both poisoned by eating mushrooms. Spada died on the threshold of the Vinery; his nephew expired at his own door, making signs which his wife could not comprehend. Then Cæsar and the Pope immediately hastened to possess themselves of the uninherited wealth, under pretext of looking over the papers of the dead men. But the only will they could find, consisted of a morsel of paper, on which Spada had written ' I bequeath to my much-loved nephew, my coffers and books, among which is my beautiful breviary with the gold corners, which I desire he will keep as a souvenir from his affectionate uncle.' And this was all : Cæsar and his father searched and pried into every corner, but they found nothing but a thousand crowns or so, and a little jewellery; for the nephew had had time to say to his wife when he returned : ' Seek among my uncle's papers, for there is a will.' They had searched, therefore, even more actively than the august heirs, but their efforts were fruitless. There were two palaces, and a vineyard behind the Palatine, but at that time landed property had little value, and the palaces and vineyard remained in the family, as beneath the rapacity of the Pope and his son.

" Months and years rolled by. Alexander VI died from poison, administered by mistake; Cæsar afterwards quitted Rome, and was eventually killed in a nocturnal skirmish. The

Spadas remained in doubtful circumstances, a mystery hung over the dark deed, and public rumour declared that Cæsar, a better contriver than his father, had carried off the fortune of the two cardinals, for Cardinal Rospigliosi, who had taken no precaution, was completely despoiled."

Here Faria suddenly stopped.

" Well," said he, " so far it does not seem to you very insane, does it ? "

" Oh ! no, no," cried Dantès ; " I feel as though I were reading a most interesting narrative. Continue, I pray you."

" I will now speak of the last of the family, the Count Spada, to whom I was secretary. I so frequently heard him complain of the disparity between his fortune and his rank, that I recommended him to obtain a life annuity, which he did, thus doubling his income. The famous breviary had been handed down from father to son, for the remarkable clause of the only will that had been found had constituted it a valuable relic, regarded with superstitious veneration by the family. It was a volume illuminated in most beautiful Gothic characters, and so heavy from the weight of gold, that an attendant generally bore it in front of the cardinal on days of grand celebrations. When I saw the papers of all kinds, title-deeds, contracts, and rolls of parchment, kept in the family archives, which had been left by the poisoned cardinal, I began thoroughly to examine the formidable pile ; but I found absolutely nothing. I, however, read, and, indeed, wrote a true account of the family of the Borgias, with the object of assuring myself as to whether any increase of fortune had accrued to them on the death of Cardinal Cæsar Spada, but I discovered only the acquisition of the fortune of Cardinal Rospiliosi, his unfortunate companion. I was then convinced that the wealth had benefited neither the Borgias nor the Spada family themselves, but had probably remained unclaimed like those treasures described in the Arabian Nights, which lay buried in the earth guarded by a genie.

" My patron at last died. He had excepted from his life annuity, his family papers, his library, composed of five thousand volumes, and his famous breviary. All these he left to me, with a thousand crowns in ready money, on condition that I had anniversary masses in his memory, and that I prepared a genealogical tree and a history of his family, which I have scrupulously done.

" Do not be impatient, my dear Edmond, we are approaching the end. In 1807, shortly before my arrest, and a fortnight after the death of Count Spada, on the 25th December (you will learn soon why the date of that memorable day has for ever remained in my recollection), I was re-reading for the thousandth time the papers which I had arranged, when, fatigued by my constant labour, and somewhat indisposed by a heavy dinner, my head dropped on my hands, and I fell asleep. It was three o'clock in the afternoon. I awoke just as the clock struck six, and raising my head, found I was in complete darkness. I rang for a light, but as no one came, I resolved to help myself. I took a small lamp in one hand, and felt about with the other for a piece of paper to light at the grate ; but fearing I might accidentally destroy some precious document, I hesitated, until I recollected having seen in the breviary on the table near me, an old yellow piece of paper which was slipped in like a book-marker, and which had remained there for centuries, untouched by reverent heirs. I felt about for this useless sheet, tore it out, and holding it to the flame, set fire to it. Then, as if by magic, I saw yellow letters start forth on the paper ; terror seized me ; I twisted it in my hands and extinguished the flame. I then quickly lighted the lamp at the fire, and opening the crumpled letter with indescribable emotion, I discovered that it was written in that secret ink, which is only discernible when exposed to a powerful heat. Rather more than a third of the paper had been consumed by the flame ; it was the document which you read this morning, Dantès ; now, read it through again, and then I will complete the broken sentences, and interpret the meaning."

And Faria handed the paper to Dantès, who eagerly scanned the following lines, written in a red ink, of a curious, rusty colour :

" This, the 25th day of April, 1498, having . . . .
Alexander VI, and fearing that, not   . . .
he wishes to obtain my fortune, and   . . .
and Bentivoglio, who died from poison,   . . .
my sole heir, that I have   . . .
through having visited it with me, namely, in   . . .
island of Monte Cristo, all that I   . . .
diamonds and trinkets ; that I alone   . . .
probably amounts to nearly two mil   . . .
will find on lifting the twentieth stone   . . .
creek, towards the east, in a straight line   . . .
Two openings   . . .
in these grottoes ; the treasure is in the farthest   . . .

and this treasure I bequeath to him, whol   .   .   .
sole heir.

" 25th April, 1498.

" Cæs .   .   ."

"Now," said the abbé, "read this." And he handed to Dantès
a second sheet with some more fragmentary lines.

Dantès read the following :

" .   .   . been invited to dinner by His Holiness,
.   .   . content with making me pay for the hat,
.   .   . reserves for me the fate of Cardinals Caprara
.   .   . I make known to my nephew, Guido Spada,
.   .   . buried in a place which he knows,
.   .   . the grottoes of the little
.   .   . possess, ingots, coins, jewellery,
.   .   . know of the existence of this treasure, which
.   .   . lions of Roman crowns, and which he
.   .   . turning out of the little
.   .   . Two openings have been made
.   .   . corner of the second,
.   .   . ly and entirely as my
" ar † Spada."

Faria looked at him with eager eyes.

"Now, join the two pieces together and form your own opinion."

Dantès obeyed ; and the two pieces, when placed together,
read as follows :

"This, the 25th day of April, 1498, having been invited to dinner
by His Holiness, Alexander VI, and fearing that, not content
with making me pay for the hat, he wishes to obtain my
fortune, and reserves for me the fate of Cardinals Caprara and
Bentivoglio, who died from poison, I make known to my
nephew, Guido Spada, my sole heir, that I have buried in a place
which he knows, through having visited it with me, namely, in
the grottoes of the little island of Monte Cristo, all that I possess,
ingots, coins, jewellery, diamonds, and trinkets ; that I alone
know of the existence of this treasure, which probably amounts
to nearly two millions of Roman crowns, and which he will find
on lifting the twentieth stone, turning out of the little creek,
towards the east, in a straight line. Two openings have been
made in these grottoes ; the treasure is in the farthest corner

of the second, and this treasure I bequeath to him, wholly and entirely as my sole heir.

" 25th April, 1498.

" CÆSAR † SPADA."

" Well," said Faria, " now do you understand ? "

" This is the declaration of Cardinal Spada, the will that was searched for so long ? "

" Yes, a thousand times yes ! "

" And who put it together in this fashion ? "

" I did. By calculating the probable length of the lines from the fragment I had saved from the fire, and by guessing at the hidden meaning of the broken sentences, as in a subterranean passage one guides oneself by the gleam of light that penetrates the darkness."

" What did you do when you thought you had cleared up the matter ? "

" I intended to start at once. Indeed, I did set out, but for some time the Imperial police had kept a watch on me, for Napoleon had not then a son, and they desired the division of the provinces. My precipitate departure aroused their suspicions, and just as I was about to embark at Piombino, I was arrested. And now," continued Faria, looking at Dantès with an almost paternal expression, " now, my dear friend, you know as much as I do ; if we ever escape together, the half of my treasure is yours ; if I die here, and you escape alone, it is all yours."

" But," said Dantès, hesitating, " is there not a more legitimate owner to whom this wealth should revert ? "

" No, you may be assured as to that ; the family is extinct, and, moreover, the last Count Spada made me his heir ; in bequeathing to me the celebrated breviary, he bequeathed to me all that it contained. No, no, be easy on that score ; if we can ever possess ourselves of this fortune, we may enjoy it without misgiving."

" And you say that this wealth amounts to—— "

" Two millions of Roman crowns, or about thirteen millions of our money."

" Impossible ! " cried Dantès, overwhelmed by the immense sum.

" I have only kept the secret from you so long," continued Faria, " first, to prove you ; and, secondly, to surprise you. If we had escaped before my attack of catalepsy, I should have taken you to Monte Cristo ; as it is," he added, with a smile,

" you will take me there. Well, Dantès, you offer me no thanks."

" This wealth belongs to you, my friend," said Dantès, " it belongs to you alone, and I have no right to it; I am not your relative."

" You are my son, Dantès! " cried the old man; " you are the child of my captivity; my profession condemns me to celibacy; God has sent you to console both the man who can never be a father, and the prisoner who will never be free! " And Faria extended the hand which he could still use to the young man, who threw himself weeping on his neck.

CHAPTER XIX

THE THIRD FIT

Now that the treasure which had so long been the object of the abbé's meditation was assured for the use and benefit of the being whom Faria really loved as a son, its importance was doubled in his estimation. Every day he talked over the amount of the treasure, telling Dantès all that a man with thirteen or fourteen millions of money might do for the benefit of his friends; and then Dantès' face would darken, for the vow of vengeance that he had uttered would return to his mind, and he thought to himself how much evil a man with thirteen or fourteen millions might do to his enemies. The abbé did not know the island of Monte Cristo, but Dantès had often passed it, situated about twenty-five miles from Pianosa, between Corsica and the island of Elba. This island was, always had been, and still remains, completely barren; it is a rock of a nearly conical shape, which seems to have been thrust by some volcanic convulsion to the surface of the ocean.

Dantès made a plan of the island for Faria, who gave him advice as to the best means of searching for the treasure. But Dantès was far from being as enthusiastic as the old man. It is true he was now convinced that Faria was not mad; but he could not realize that this precious store, supposing it really had existed, existed still, and though he did not regard the idea of the treasure as chimerical, he scarcely believed it could any longer be there.

And now, as though Fate intended to deprive the prisoners of their last hope, and to make them feel that they were condemned to a perpetual prison, a fresh misfortune overtook them. The corridor on the side of the sea, which for some time had been getting out of repair, was reconstructed ; new foundations were made, and the hole which Dantès had already half stopped, was filled up with enormous blocks of rock. Thus they were shut in by a barrier, more impassable than the former one.

" You see," said the young man, with a gentle and sorrowful air to Faria, " that the Almighty even desires to deprive me of the merit of what you term my devotion to you. I promised you to remain with you for ever, and now I cannot but keep my promise ; I shall have no other treasure than you, and we shall never, either of us, leave this place. So, my friend, my real treasure is not that which awaits me under the dark rocks of Monte Cristo, but is your presence itself ; my treasures are those gleams of intelligence which you have called forth in my brain, those languages which you have implanted in my memory. The different sciences you have rendered so easy for me by the profundity of your knowledge, and the clearness of the principles to which you have reduced them—these are my treasures. To have had you near me all this time, to have listened to your eloquent voice as you instilled into me new ideas, strengthened my soul, and made me capable of great and terrible things ; to have had my thoughts so well directed that the despair which overwhelmed me before I knew you, has now no longer hold over me : this is my fortune, and it is a real one. I owe it all to you, and all the sovereigns of the world, were they even Cæsar Borgias, can never succeed in taking it from me."

Thus the days passed for the two unfortunate prisoners, if not happily, at least bearably. Faria, who had kept so closely the secret of his treasure, now spoke of it constantly. As he anticipated, his paralysis continued, and he had almost lost all hope for himself ; but he dreamt continually of deliverance and escape for his young companion, and rejoiced for his sake. Fearing that some day the letter might be mislaid or lost, he compelled Dantès to learn it by heart ; and then he destroyed the second part, convinced that the first might safely fall into any one's hands without the secret being divulged. Sometimes Faria occupied whole hours in giving Dantès instructions which might be useful to him when he regained his liberty. The very day, the very hour that he was free, he must have but one thought—to reach the island of Monte Cristo, search for the wonderful grottoes and examine the appointed spot. In the meantime the hours passed, if not quickly, at least tolerably. Faria, though he had not regained the use of his hand and foot, still retained all his intellect, and had by slow degrees not only instilled into his companion's mind the strictest principles of morality, but set him an example in the patient and sublime art of making an object of interest out of the merest trifle. Thus the time passed almost as calmly as in the lives of those who have had no evil lot to bear; but beneath this superficial calm there frequently arose in the heart of the young man, and also in that of his companion, many repressed desires and longings, and at times half-stifled sighs escaped them when separated in their different cells.

One night Edmond awoke with a start, fancying he heard himself called. He opened his eyes and tried to pierce the surrounding gloom. He thought he heard his own name, or rather a plaintive voice endeavouring to articulate it. He raised himself on his bed, the sweat of anguish on his brow, and listened. Without doubt the sound came from his companion's cell.

" Good God ! " exclaimed Dantès, " can it be that ? " and he lifted away the stone and darted along the narrow passage. At the other end, he found the stone removed, and by the light of the flickering lamp beheld the old man pale and trembling, holding on to his bed. His features were convulsed by those horrible symptoms which Dantès had already witnessed.

" Well, my friend," said Faria, in a resigned manner, " you see how it is with me. I have no need to tell you what is the matter."

Edmond, losing his head, rushed to the door, crying, " Help ! help ! "

Faria had just strength to detain him by the arm. " Silence," said he, " or we are lost. We must now only think of you, my friend, how to render your captivity supportable and your flight possible. It will take you years to do over again alone all that I have done here. Moreover, my friend, the cell which I shall soon leave will not long remain empty ; some other unfortunate will be put in my place ; and to this other you will appear as a saving angel. He may, perhaps, be young, strong, patient, like you, and will aid your flight as much as I have retarded it. Providence will reward your efforts ; He will give you more than He takes away ; and it is time I died."

Edmond could only clasp his hands and cry, " Oh ! my friend, my friend, do not say that ! " Then, recovering from the unnerved condition in which the old man's words had plunged him, he exclaimed, " But I saved you before, and I will save you again ! " and lifting up the foot of the bed, he drew out the bottle, still one-third full of the red fluid. " See," said he, " there is still some of this mighty restorative. Quick, quick ! tell me what I must do this time. Are there any fresh instructions ? Speak, my friend, and I will save you ; I will, indeed ! "

" You may try ; but I am getting cold ; I feel the blood flowing to my brain ; the dreadful trembling which makes my teeth chatter, and seems to dislocate my bones, already seizes my body ; in five minutes the attack will come on, and in a quarter of an hour a corpse will be all that is left of me."

" Alas ! " cried Dantès, in accents broken with grief.

" You must do what you did on the first occasion," resumed the abbé, " only do not wait so long. The springs of life are now nearly exhausted, and Death," he added, showing his paralysed arm and leg, " will only have half his business to do. If, after pouring twelve instead of ten drops down my throat, you see that I do not recover, you may give me the rest. Now help me to my bed, for I cannot stand any longer."

Edmond took the old man in his arms and laid him on the bed.

" And now, my friend," said Faria, " my only remaining consolation, now that I am about to leave you for ever, I pray that you may have all the happiness, all the prosperity that you deserve. My son, I bless you ! "

The young man threw himself on his knees and buried his face on the abbé's bed.

" But, now, listen carefully to what I tell you at this supreme moment : the treasure of the Spadas exists ; God has withdrawn every veil from my eyes. If you succeed in escaping, hasten to Monte Cristo, and appropriate this wealth ; take it ; you have suffered enough."

A spasmodic quivering seized the old man. Dantès looked up and beheld his eyes become bloodshot and fixed.

" Adieu, adieu ! " murmured the poor abbé, convulsively pressing the young man's hand ; " adieu ! "

" Oh ! not yet, not yet," cried Dantès ; " do not abandon us ; oh ! my God ! succour him ! help, help ! "

" Hush," muttered the dying man, " that they may not separate us, if you succeed in saving me ! "

" You are right. I will be quiet and save you ! Besides, although you suffer much, it does not seem so severe as the other attack."

" Ah ! you are deceived. I suffer less, because I have less power of resistance. At your age, one has so much faith in life, but the old see death more clearly. Ah ! it is coming, coming ! my sight fails me ! my thoughts are confused ! Your hand, Dantès ! Adieu ! adieu ! "

Then mustering all his strength for a final effort, he raised himself, and ejaculated, " Monte Cristo ! do not forget Monte Cristo ! " and fell backwards.

The crisis was terrible. The contorted limbs, swollen eyelids, and foaming lips were painful to see, until at last a stiff, motionless body was all that remained on the bed of suffering, in place of the intelligent being who had laid down there but a few minutes before.

Dantès took the lamp, and set it on a projecting stone near the head of the bed. With fixed and watchful eyes, he awaited the moment for administering the remedy. When he believed the proper time had arrived, he took a knife, opened the shut teeth, counted the drops, and administered them. The phial still contained nearly double what he had just poured from it. He waited ten minutes, a quarter of an hour, half an hour, but there was no movement. He sat trembling, his hair on end with terror, his forehead bedewed with perspiration, counting the seconds by the beating of his heart. At last he thought it was time to make the final attempt ; he raised the phial to the blue lips of the unfortunate man, and poured the remainder of the fluid between his parted teeth. The remedy produced a galvanic effect ; a violent quivering seized the limbs of the old man, his eyes rolled in a terrible manner, a sigh escaped him which was almost a wail, and then his quaking body became stark and stiff. The eyes, however, remained open. Half-an-hour—an hour, slowly passed. During this period of mental anguish, Edmond remained, bending over his friend, his hand pressed on his heart ; he felt its pulsations become fainter and fainter, and the body growing gradually cold. At last the feeble beats stopped, and the face became livid, the eyes remaining open with a vacant stare.

It was now six o'clock in the morning, the day began to dawn, and the feeble lamp light grew dim, as the cold, wan morning light penetrated the dark cell. So long as the conflict between light and darkness lasted, Dantès still doubted and hoped, but as soon as daylight fairly filled the chamber, he comprehended that he was alone with a corpse. Then a profound terror seized him. He extinguished the lamp, hid it carefully, and fled, replacing as well as he could the stone over the secret passage. It was time, for the jailer soon arrived. He visited Dantès first, and on leaving him, proceeded to Faria's cell, carrying his breakfast and some fresh linen. Dantès perceived from the man's expression that he had no knowledge of what had occurred, and as soon as the door was closed, he was seized with an uncontrollable desire to know what was taking place. He therefore crept along the underground passage, and reached the other end in time to hear the exclamations of the turnkey, who called aloud for help. Soon the other warders entered, then the soldiers with their heavy, regular tread, and last of all the governor. Edmond could hear the creaking of the bed, on which they moved the corpse; he heard the voice of the governor ordering cold water to be thrown on the face of the dead man, but finding that this had no effect, a doctor was sent for. The governor left the cell, and Dantès heard a few compassionate words mingled with coarse joking and mockery.

" Well," said one, " the madman has gone to seek his treasures at last. A pleasant journey to him! "

" He won't have enough to pay for his shroud, with all his millions," said another.

" Oh ! " rejoined a third, " shrouds at the Château d'If are not very expensive."

Edmond listened, and lost not a word of the conversation. Soon the voices ceased, and he fancied the attendants had quitted the cell. He dared not enter, however, for they might have left a turnkey to watch the dead, so he remained mute and motionless, hardly daring to breathe. At the end of an hour, the silence was broken by the sound of advancing footsteps. It was the governor returning, followed by the doctor and several officers. There was silence; the doctor had approached the bed, and was examining the corpse; then he asked several questions, investigated the symptoms of disease, and declared that the prisoner was dead.

" I am sorry to hear what you say," said the governor, " he was a gentle, inoffensive creature, happy in his own delusions, and very easily kept under control."

" Yes, indeed," remarked the jailer, " it was hardly necessary to keep guard over him at all; he would have remained here fifty years, without making a single attempt at escape."

" In spite of your conviction," said the governor, " it is most necessary to be certain that the prisoner is dead, for the sake of my own responsibility."

There was a short silence, during which Dantès imagined that the doctor was again examining the corpse.

" He is quite dead; I answer for it."

" You are nevertheless aware, monsieur," persisted the governor, " that we are not contented in cases such as this with a simple examination. In spite of appearances, then, be good enough to settle the matter by fulfilling the formalities prescribed by law."

"Certainly. Heat the irons," said the doctor, "though it is really unnecessary."

This order to heat the irons made Dantès shudder. He heard hurried footsteps, the opening of the door, and much going backwards and forwards, and at the end of a few moments a turnkey entered, saying:

"Here is the brazier and an iron, monsieur."

There was a moment's silence, then a slight crackling sound, and the nauseous odour of burnt flesh penetrated to where Dantès was standing. As this terrible odour reached him the perspiration burst forth on his brow, and he believed he should faint.

"You see," said the doctor, "that he is really dead; this burning of the heels is decisive; the poor fellow is now cured of his madness, and freed from his captivity. I hope, monsieur," he added, "that you will show him every respect."

"Yes, yes. He shall be decently deposited in the newest sack that we possess; you may be easy on that score."

"Shall we put the corpse in its shroud before you leave, monsieur?" inquired a turnkey.

"Certainly; but make haste, I cannot remain in this place all day."

Then Dantès again heard steps hastening backwards and forwards, the crumpling of stiff canvas, and creaking of the bed; then the heavy step of a man who seemed raising a heavy burden and laying it down again.

"It will be this evening," said the governor.

"Will there be mass?" inquired one of the officers.

"Impossible," answered the governor; "the chaplain has just been asking me for a week's leave of absence to make a short voyage to Hyères, and I promised to manage without him during that time. The poor abbé should not have been in such a hurry, if he wanted a requiem."

"Bah!" exclaimed the doctor, with the impiety common to his profession, "he was a priest. The Almighty will not give the Evil One a wicked satisfaction by sending him a churchman."

A burst of laughter greeted this coarse pleasantry. Meanwhile the operation of enshrouding the corpse was proceeded with.

"It must take place this evening," said the governor, when it was completed.

"At what time?" asked the turnkey. "About ten or eleven o'clock."

"Must anyone watch the dead ? "

"It is not necessary : the cell can be locked as usual."

Dantès then heard the sounds of retiring footsteps, the voices of the jailers were lost in the distance, the door was drawn to, on its grating hinges, and a silence more mournful than solitude, the silence of death, reigned over all, and overwhelmed the stricken soul of the young man. He cautiously raised the flag-stone and peered inquiringly into the cell. It was empty; slowly emerging from the passage, he entered.

CHAPTER XX

THE CEMETERY OF THE CHÂTEAU D'IF

STRETCHED out at full length on the bed, and perceptible by the morning light which penetrated the narrow window, was the sack of coarse canvas, through the heavy folds of which a stiff form was definable. It was the Abbé Faria's shroud—that shroud which, as the turnkey said, cost so little. A material separation now existed between Dantès and his old friend. He seated himself on the edge of the couch and gave himself up to melancholy. Alone ! he was again alone—again driven into silence : Alone ! No longer to see, no longer to hear the voice of the only creature who had attached him still to life ! Were it not better, like Faria, to solve the enigma of existence at once, even at the risk of passing through the dark gate of suffering ? The thought of suicide, dispelled by the abbé's presence and companionship, returned, and rose up like a spectre beside the corpse of his old friend.

"If I were to die," said Dantès, inwardly, "I should go where he is going, and I should then find him again. But how to die ? And yet it would be simple enough ; I can remain here, throw myself on the first person who enters, and strangle him, and then I shall be guillotined ! "

But Dantès recoiled from the idea of this infamous death, and passed suddenly from his despairing thoughts to an ardent longing for life and liberty !

"To die ! Oh, no ! " he cried. " It is not well having lived so long, having suffered so much, to die now ! To die ! It was well enough when I made the resolution some years ago, but now it would be but succumbing to my miserable destiny. No, I will live—I will reconquer the happiness that has been taken from me ! Before I die I have my persecutors to punish !—

and—who knows ?—some friends to recompense. Yet I shall assuredly be left here to die, and to leave my dungeon like Faria ! "

As he said this, Edmond started, then remained motionless, with fixed eyes, like a man struck with a sudden and terrible idea. He rose, raised his hand to his head as though seized with giddiness, walked two or three times up and down the cell, and then paused at the foot of the bed.

" Oh ! " he murmured, " who sent me this thought ? Is it Thou, O God ?—' Since none but the dead ever leave this place, why not take the place of the dead ? ' "

Then, without giving himself time to reconsider the matter, he bent over the sack, cut it open with the knife which Faria had made, slowly drew out the corpse of his dead friend, carried it to his own cell, and laid it on the bed. He covered the head with a strip of linen, kissed the cold brow for the last time, and endeavoured vainly to close the rebellious eyes which continued wide open, terrible in their vacant stare. He then turned the head towards the wall, that the jailer, when he brought his evening repast, might merely think he had followed his usual custom and gone to bed. After entering the narrow passage, he drew the bed close up against the opening, and made his way back to the other cell. He next took from the hiding-place the needle and thread, slipped off his rags that they might feel his naked body beneath the canvas, and getting into the open sack, stretched himself out and closed up the opening from within. He would have waited until after the jailer's evening visit, but was afraid the governor might change his mind, and have the corpse removed earlier, and then his last hope would have been destroyed. Now his plan was secured, he determined on his future action. If, during the transit, the grave-diggers found that they were carrying a living body instead of a dead one, he would not give them time to investigate, but with a vigorous slash of the knife would open the sack from top to bottom, and, profiting by their terror, escape. If they attempted to stop him, he would use the knife. They would probably take him to the cemetery and lay him in a grave. In that case, he would allow himself to be covered with the soil, and in the darkness of the night, make his way out of the damp earth and escape. If, however, the weight of earth were too heavy for him, and he should die of suffocation, so much the better ; all would then be over !

The first danger that threatened Dantès was the chance of the jailer discovering the ruse when he brought his supper at seven o'clock. Fortunately, Dantès had frequently received the jailer in bed, and the man generally placed the bread and broth on the table and retired without speaking. But on this occasion he might address Dantès and, receiving no reply, approach the bed and discover all.

When seven o'clock struck, Dantès' anguish of mind became intense. With one hand he tried to still the beatings of his heart, whilst with the other he wiped away the perspiration which streamed from his temples. From time to time a shudder seized his whole body, and his heart seemed in the grip of a frozen vice. The hours slowly passed, and there had been no stir or commotion in the Château, so Dantès knew he had escaped the first danger. At last, about the hour the governor had appointed, steps could be heard descending the staircase. Edmond summoned all his courage and held his breath, happy if he could at the same time have quieted the pulsations of his heart. There were evidently two persons and they paused at the door. Dantès thought they were the grave-diggers, and this suspicion became a certainty when he heard the noise they made in depositing the stretcher. The door opened, and by means of a bright light Dantès could distinguish two forms approaching his bed. A third remained near the door, holding a lantern in his hand.

The two figures slowly approached and took hold of the sack at each end.

" He is rather heavy, considering he was such a thin old man ! " said one of them, raising Dantès by the head.

" They say that the bones increase half a pound in weight every year," said the other, taking him by the feet.

" Have you made the knot ? " asked the first.

" No, it would be stupid to burden ourselves with an unnecessary weight," said the second ; " I will do it afterwards."

" A knot ! what is that for ? " said Dantès to himself.

They carried the supposed dead body from the bed to the stretcher, and Edmond stiffened himself that he might the better deceive them. The *cortège* then proceeded upstairs, lighted by the man with the lantern, who walked on in front. Suddenly they came out into the fresh, keen, night air. Dantès felt the cold wind, and experienced a sudden sensation of mingled delight and anguish.

The bearers proceeded about twenty paces, then stopped, and deposited the stretcher on the ground. One of them walked away, and Dantès heard his receding footsteps on the flags. The prisoner's first impulse was to escape, but happily he checked it.

Dantès heard the sound of some heavy weight being deposited beside him, and at the same moment, a rope was fastened round his feet with a tightness that was painful.

" Well, is the knot secure ? " inquired the grave-digger.

" Thoroughly secure."

" Well, then ; march."

And the stretcher was lifted, and once more carried on its way. After walking a short distance, there was a halt to open a door, through which they passed and then proceeded onwards. The sound of the waves beating against the rocks on which the Château is built, now reached Dantès' ears.

" It is bad weather," said one of the bearers ; " not a very pleasant night for a dip in the sea."

" The good abbé runs some risk of getting wet," returned the other, and they both laughed heartily.

Dantès could not comprehend this pleasantry, but his hair stood on end with apprehension, nevertheless.

" Well, here we are ! " exclaimed the first.

" No, farther on, farther on," rejoined the other ; " you know that the last one was caught in its fall, and dashed on to the rocks, and the governor told us the next morning we were lazy fellows."

They proceeded a little farther, and then Dantès felt that they were taking him by the head and feet, and swinging him to and fro.

" One ! two ! three ! " cried the grave-diggers, and at the same moment Dantès felt himself hurled into empty space, falling through the air like a wounded bird, with a terrific force that froze his very heart-blood. Although he was impelled downwards by some heavy weight, which precipitated his rapid descent, it seemed to him that this fall lasted for a century. Then, with a fearful splash, he fell like an arrow, through the ice-cold water, uttering a startled cry which was quickly stifled by immersion.

Dantès had been thrown into the sea, and was being dragged to the bottom by a heavy cannon-ball attached to his feet.

The sea is the cemetery of the Château d'If.

CHAPTER XXI

THE ISLAND OF TIBOULEN

DANTÈS, though stunned and nearly suffocated, had the presence of mind to hold his breath ; and with his right hand, in which he held the open knife ready for any emergency, he cut open the sack, and extricated his head and arm. In spite of every effort, however, he failed to free himself from the heavy bullet which kept him down. At last he arched his body, and groping for the rope which confined his legs, cut it with a desperate effort just as he felt himself suffocating. Then with a vigorous push of the foot, he propelled himself upwards to the surface, whilst the bullet dragged off the coarse covering, which had so nearly become his shroud.

Dantès took but a moment to regain his breath, and dived a second time, that he might avoid being seen.

When he next appeared above the water, he was at least fifty paces from the spot where he fell. Before him stretched the roaring ocean, its billowy waves seething as at the approach of a tempest, whilst behind him, like a threatening phantom, rose the terrible giant of granite, its black point stretching out like an arm extended to grasp its prey. On the rock, too, he could see a lantern lighting two shadowy forms. He fancied the figures turned towards the sea with some anxiety. Doubtless they had heard the cry, which he uttered as he fell!

He therefore took another plunge, and swam some distance beneath the surface. When he reappeared on the water the lantern had vanished. He must now look about him; the islands that were nearest to the Château d'If were inhabited; the safest haven would be Tiboulen or Lemaire, about a league from the Château d'If.

Dantès resolved to make for one of these islands; but how to find them in the darkness was the question.

At this moment he saw the beacon of Planier shining like a star. Turning straight towards this beacon, he knew he had the island of Tiboulen on the left; therefore if he bore a little to the left, he might reach it. He found, with joy, that his forced inaction had deprived him of none of his strength or agility, and he was still master of the element in which he had played as a child. Fear, too helped to double Dantès' vigour. He listened as he reached the summit of a wave for every sound, and endeavoured to penetrate with his eyes the surrounding darkness. Every large wave seemed to be a boat pursuing him, and he redoubled his efforts and gradually the terrible Château melted away in the dim night mist. He saw it no longer, but he still felt its presence and continued to cut through the waves in the direction of the island.

" I must have been swimming an hour," he said to himself,

" but as the wind is against me, a quarter of my energy has been thrown away. However, unless I have been deceived in the direction, I cannot be far from Tiboulen. But if I should be wrong ? "

A shudder ran through him ; he tried to float to gain a little rest, but the sea became more and more boisterous, and he found that this method of relief was impossible.

" But I will go on to the end," he vowed, " until my arms are wearied, until cramp seizes me, and then I will sink to the bottom." And he went on swimming with the energy of despair.

Suddenly it seemed to him that the sky became still darker, and at the same moment he felt a violent blow on the knee. He stretched out his hand and felt some resisting body and, moving forward carefully, found he was touching land.

Dantès lifted his head, advanced a few steps, and throwing himself on the rough granite rocks, which appeared to him softer than a couch of down, he thanked God for his deliverance. Then, in spite of wind and rain, he fell into the delicious sleep of a man whose body is numbed with fatigue, but whose soul still watches, rejoicing in the consciousness of unhoped-for happiness.

At the end of an hour he was roused by the roar of a tremendous thunder-clap. From time to time a lightning flash darted forth like a fiery serpent, illuminating the waves and clouds, which rolled one after another in fearful chaos.

Dantès had reached the first of the two islands, which is in reality the island of Tiboulen. He knew it was barren, exposed, and afforded no shelter ; he therefore determined, as soon as the storm was over, to plunge again into the waves and swim to the island of Lemaire, which was equally bare, but larger, and therefore a more suitable resting-place. He took refuge beneath a projecting rock, just as the tempest burst forth in all its fury.

Edmond felt the island tremble beneath him, and every moment fancied it would drift away like a vessel broken from its moorings, and carry him into the fearful whirlpool.

Presently a flash which seemed to open the heavens up to the mighty throne of God illumined the darkness, and about a quarter of a league distant Dantès beheld a small fishing-boat gliding like a spectre over the waves. Suddenly it vanished, then reappeared above another wave, driven along with a fearful rapidity.

Dantès endeavoured to cry out and signal danger. Another flash quickly following showed him four men clinging to the mast and rigging, while a fifth held on to the broken helm. Above the mast, a sail rent in tatters flapped violently in the wind, until the last link that held it snapped asunder, and it was carried off into the darkness of the night.

Immediately afterwards a crash was heard, and some despairing cries arose; and Dantès saw, by the light of another flash, that the little vessel was dashed to pieces, and that amid the wreck-strewn waves imploring faces and outstretched hands were raised piteously to heaven. Then again all was dark as night; the tragic spectacle had vanished like a flash.

Dantès threw himself on the slippery rock and gazed and listened, but he heard and saw no more; human cries and struggles were ended; the tempest alone continued to roar in the wind.

Little by little, however, the wind abated; large grey clouds rolled towards the west, disclosing a clear azure and bright patches of starlight; then, in the east, a long reddish strip of colour slowly stretched itself across the horizon, and mingled with the dark blue undulations of the clouds, while the waves danced in a glimmer that tinged their foaming peaks with gold.

It was day. Dantès stood mute and motionless before the grand spectacle, as though beholding it for the first time; he had almost forgotten the wonders of Nature during his long imprisonment in the Château d'If. He turned towards the frowning fortress, casting at the same time a searching glance over sea and land. The towering edifice rose from the bosom of the waves with imposing majesty and stateliness, seeming at the same time to watch and to command. It was probably five o'clock in the morning, and the sea was growing calmer.

" In two or three hours," thought Edmond, " the jailer will be going to my cell; he will find the corpse of my poor friend, will recognize it, seek for me in vain, and will give the alarm. Then the hole and the passage will be discovered, the men will be questioned who threw me into the sea, who must have heard me cry out. Then boats full of soldiers will be despatched after the unhappy fugitive, who they will know cannot be far off. The firing of the cannon will warn the whole coast not to give shelter to any man found wandering, naked and hungry. All the spies and police of Marseilles will scour the land, while the governor of the Château pursues me by sea. Then, entrapped and surrounded both by sea and land, what will become of me ? I am at the mercy of the first peasant who wishes to gain twenty francs by surrendering me. I have no longer strength, thought, or resolution. O my God ! have I not suffered enough ? and wilt Thou not do for me what I cannot do for myself ? "

Just as Edmond uttered this piteous prayer, turning as he did so to the Château d'If, he saw above the point of the island of Pommègue, a small barque, which his experienced eye told him was a Genoese tartan. She came from Marseilles, and was making for the open sea, scattering the white foam as she glided through the water.

" I might reach that vessel in half an hour did I not fear to be questioned, recognized as a fugitive, and taken back to Marseilles. What can I do ?   What story can I invent ?   They are probably smugglers or pirates, who scour the coast under pretext of trading ; they would rather sell me than do a kind action if it were unprofitable.   The alarm is not yet given, though, and they will suspect nothing ; I can pass for one of the sailors of the boat that was wrecked last night.   Now for it ! "   And with these words Dantès turned his eyes towards the spot where the little boat had gone down.

He trembled.   Caught on the edge of a rock was the Phrygian cap worn by one of the shipwrecked sailors, and close by floated some broken pieces of the keel, and a few planks which were dashed backwards and forwards against the base of the rock.

Dantès threw himself into the sea, swam towards the cap, which he placed on his head, and then, seizing one of the planks, swam out to cross the track of the vessel.

" Now I am saved ! " he murmured ; and the conviction renewed his strength.   The vessel was tacking between the Château d'If and the tower of Planier.   The vessel and the swimmer approached each other insensibly, until the boat came within a league of Dantès.   He raised himself in the water, waving his cap as a sign of distress, but no one observed him, and the vessel tacked in another direction.   Then he congratulated himself on having taken the precaution of securing the wooden plank. Enfeebled as he was, he would have been unable to sustain himself unaided in the water until he reached the vessel, and would have failed to reach the coast again, if the tartan passed without seeing him.   At last she tacked and stood towards him.   He now advanced to meet her, but before he had made much progress, she tacked about again.   Then Dantès, with a supreme effort, raised himself in the water, waved his cap, and uttered one of those piteous cries peculiar to shipwrecked mariners, which sound like the wail of some spirit of the sea.   This time they saw and heard him.   The tartan instantly steered towards him, and at the same moment he saw that they were launching a boat.   Then Dantès loosed his hold of the plank, and swam vigorously to meet them. But he had overestimated his strength, and the piece of wood which was now floating away had been of unspeakable value to him. His arms grew stiff, his legs lost their flexibility, his strokes became jerky and feeble, and his breath was almost gone. He uttered a great cry; the two sailors redoubled their efforts, and one of them called to him in Italian : " Courage ! "

The word reached him just as a wave covered him with foam. He reappeared, cried out a third time, and then sank again, as though he had once more the fatal bullet on his leg. Another violent effort, and he rose to the surface ; he felt himself seized by the hair, then he saw and heard no more, but fainted away.

On opening his eyes, Dantès found himself on the deck of the tartan ; his first glance was to see what direction she was following ; the Château d'If was left far behind. Dantès was so exhausted that his exclamation of joy was mistaken for a cry of suffering. He lay stretched on the deck ; one sailor was rubbing his limbs with a woollen covering. Another held a gourd to his mouth, while an old sailor, who was both pilot and captain, looked on with that pity which people feel when regarding a misfortune which they have just escaped, and which may overtake them on the morrow. The few drops of rum in the gourd revived the young man's heart and his limbs began to regain elasticity under the friction applied by the sailor.

" Who are you ? " inquired the captain in bad French.

" I am a Maltese sailor," said Dantès in bad Italian ; " we were coming from Syracuse, laden with wine and grain. Last night's squall overtook us near Cape Morgion, and we were shipwrecked against those rocks which you see there."

" Where are you come from now ? "

" From those rocks. My three companions are drowned ; I believe I am the only one who escaped. I saw your vessel and tried to come to you on a piece of our shattered boat. Thank you ! you have saved my life ! I was lost when one of your sailors seized me by the hair."

" It was I," said one of the crew, with a frank, open countenance, and long dark whiskers, " and it was time; you were just sinking."

" Yes, my friend," said Dantès, extending his hand, " and I thank you a second time."

" *Ma foi !* " said the sailor, " but I rather hesitated ; with your beard and hair about a foot long, you looked more like a brigand than an honest man."

Dantès now recalled to mind that since he had been in the Château d'If, his hair and beard had never been cut.

" Yes," he rejoined, " I made a vow to our Lady of Pie de la Grotta, in a moment of danger, to be ten years without cutting my hair. To-day is the expiration of the period, and I have signalized the anniversary by escaping from drowning."

" And now, what can we do for you ? " asked the captain.

" Just what you please. I am a good sailor ; put me out at the first port, and I shall easily get employment on a merchant vessel."

" You know the Mediterranean ? "

" There are very few ports that I could not enter with my eyes shut. Where are you going ? "

" To Leghorn."

" Then instead of tacking so frequently, and losing precious time, why do you not go with the wind ? "

" Because we should make straight for the island of Rion."

" You would pass about twenty fathoms from it."

" Take the helm," said the captain, " and let us test your knowledge."

The young man placed himself at the helm, assured himself by a slight pressure that the vessel answered the rudder, and then called out, " To the braces ! " The four sailors who composed the crew hastened to their posts, whilst the captain looked on.

" Haul in," cried Dantès. Now make fast ! "

The vessel, instead of altering her course, gradually approached the isle which she passed, as Dantès had predicted, at about twenty fathoms' distance.

" Bravo ! " cried the captain.

" Bravo ! " repeated the sailors, and they all regarded with astonishment this man, who now gave evidence of such vigour and intelligence.

" You see," said Dantès, quitting his post, " that I could be of some use to you during the voyage, at any rate. If you do not care to keep me at Leghorn, why, you can leave me there, and with the first month's pay that I earn I will repay you for my food, and the clothes you lend me. One man is as good as another, if you will give me the same as the others, it is settled."

" That is not fair," said the sailor who had pulled Dantès out of the sea, " for you know more than we do."

" Now why do you mix yourself up in the matter ? what concern is it of yours, Jacopo ? " said the captain ; " everyone is free to engage himself for what sum he pleases. You would be doing something better if you lent this poor fellow a jacket and pair of trousers ; that is, if you have a change of clothes."

"No," said Jacopo, "but I have a shirt and trousers."

"That is all I need; thank you, friend," said Dantès.

Jacopo disappeared through the hatchway, and returned with the two garments, in which Dantès clothed himself with unspeakable pleasure.

"Now, do you need anything else ?" inquired the captain.

"A piece of bread, if you please, and another draught of that excellent rum which I have already tasted, for it is a long time since I swallowed anything."

They brought Dantès some brandy, and Jacopo gave him the gourd, but as he was raising it to his lips he paused.

"Stay," said the captain, "what is going on at the Château d'If ?"

A small white cloud, which had attracted Dantès' attention, crowned the battlements of the southern bastion of the Château d'If. A second afterwards, and the sound of a distant gun was faintly perceptible. The sailors looked at one another.

"What is the meaning of that ?" inquired the captain.

"Some prisoners must have escaped last night," said Dantès, "and they are firing the alarm cannon."

The captain cast a glance at the young man, who, as he said this, raised the gourd to his lips, and drank off its contents with so much calmness and satisfaction, that the glimmer of suspicion that had arisen in the captain's breast died away immediately.

Under pretext of being tired, Dantès now asked to be allowed to seat himself at the helm. The steerman glanced towards the captain, who signalled to him to relinquish his post to his new companion. Dantès could now gaze in the direction of Marseilles.

"What day of the month is it ?" he asked of Jacopo, who seated himself near him, as they lost sight of the Château d'If.

"The twenty-eighth of February," replied the latter.

"And what year is it ?" inquired Dantès, again.

"What year is it ? You want to know that ? Why, 1829," said Jacopo.

It was then fourteen years, to the day, since Dantès had been arrested. He was nineteen when he entered the Château d'If, and now he was thirty-three. A sorrowful smile played round his lips. He asked himself what had become of Mercédès during this long period, in which she must have believed him dead ; and his eyes flashed as he thought of the three men to whom he owed such a long and cruel captivity. He uttered against Danglars, Fernando, and Villefort that vow of implacable vengeance which he had already formed when in prison. And this vow was no longer an empty menace, for at that hour the quickest sailer of the Mediterranean would have failed to catch the little tartan as she sped over the waters with full sail towards Leghorn.

CHAPTER XXII

THE SMUGGLERS

It will readily be guessed that Dantès was on board a smuggling vessel. The captain of the *Jeune Amélie*, as she was called, had at first received him with a certain amount of distrust; he was well known by all the custom-house officers on the coast; and as there was a constant exchange between these worthies and himself, of more or less cunning stratagems, he imagined that Dantès might be an agent for the salt tax, who made use of an ingenious trick to obtain some insight into the secrets of the trade. But the skilful manner in which Dantès had passed through the ordeal of guiding the vessel had entirely reassured him.

Edmond had therefore the advantage of knowing who his captain was, and yet maintaining complete secrecy as to his own antecedents. On whatever side he was attacked by the old mariner or his comrades, he still refrained from divulging his secret, giving many details of Naples and Malta, which he knew as well as Marseilles, and maintaining his original story with a clearness and decision that did honour to his memory. Thus matters stood when they reached Leghorn.

Edmond had now to undergo another test; he would see whether he knew himself again after the fourteen years since he beheld his own countenance; he had a clear idea of what he was as a youth; he would now see what he had become as a man. As soon as they reached Leghorn he made his way to a barber's whom he knew in the Rue Saint Ferdinand, and desired to have his hair and beard cut.

The barber gazed with astonishment at the long locks and thick black beard, but began his task without remark.

When the operation was concluded, and Dantès felt his chin shaven, and his hair reduced to its natural length, he asked for a mirror, and examined himself critically. He had gone to the Château d'If with the round, frank, smiling face of a happy youth, whose first steps in life have been easy, and who naturally infers that the future will be like the past. But now it was changed. The oval countenance was elongated, the once smiling mouth was set in fixed, hard lines, indicating great resolution; the brows were arched, the eyes expressed a profound melancholy, now and then lighted up by a dark flash of anger or misanthropy; his complexion had assumed that pallor, which, in combination with dark hair, is a mark of beauty. The knowledge he had acquired had imparted an aspect of intelligence to his countenance, and he had gained a certain vigour of body, and in place of nervous, slender elegance had more muscular rotundity. As to his voice, it seemed as though prayers, wailings, and imprecations had completely changed it to its present intonations of peculiar sweetness, now and then broken by an accent of sudden roughness and harshness. From force of habit, too, his eyes had acquired the singular faculty of distinguishing objects in the dark, like those of the hyæna and wolf.

He smiled as he looked at himself; it was impossible that his best friend, if he had one, should recognize him; he did not even recognize himself.

The captain of the *Jeune Amélie*, who much wished to keep Edmond in his service, had offered to advance him something on the future profits, which Dantès had accepted; and his first care on leaving the barber was to purchase a sailor's suit, composed of white trousers, striped shirt, and cap. Thus attired, and carrying in his hand the shirt and trousers Jacopo had lent him, Edmond presented himself to the captain of the *Jeune Amélie*, who at first failed to recognize, in this smart-looking young sailor, the shaggy-haired, long-bearded man whom he had received naked and dying on board his vessel. Carried away by his handsome appearance, he at once renewed his proposals of an engagement; but Dantès, who had his own projects, would only accept them for three months.

The *Jeune Amélie* was, however, a very expeditious vessel, and under the command of a captain who made a point of never losing his time. She had scarcely been a week at Leghorn before she was well loaded with coloured muslins, English powder, and tobacco, on which the excise had omitted to place its seal. She was to leave Leghorn, which was a free port, and to land at Corsica, where certain speculators undertook to transport the cargo to France. At last they sailed. Edmond left Gorgone on his right, Pianosa on his left, and made for the country of Paoli and Napoleon.

The following day, as the captain came on deck at his usual early hour, he found Dantès leaning against the side of the boat, regarding with a curious expression a pile of granite rocks which the rising sun bathed in a flood of rose-coloured light. It was the island of Monte Cristo. The *Jeune Amélie* passed it about three-quarters of a league to starboard, and continued on her way to Corsica. As they passed the island, Dantès thought to himself that he had only to leap into the sea, and in half an hour he would be on the promised territory. But then, what should he do, without tools to dig out the treasure, or arms to defend himself? Besides, what would the sailors say—what would the captain think? No, he must wait. Happily, Dantès knew how to wait; he had waited fourteen years for liberty; he could well wait, now that he was free, six months or a year for wealth. Night came on, and Dantès beheld the island tinged with all the changing shadows of twilight; but, with his eyes well tutored to obscurity, he could still distinguish it, and was the last to leave the deck.

Next morning they found themselves off the coast of Algeria. Throughout the day they frequently altered their course, until, in the evening, two fires were lighted on the coast, a lantern in place of the flag was hoisted on the mast of the little vessel, and they slowly approached within gunshot of land. Four long-boats quietly approached the vessel, which lowered her own shallop; and the five boats managed their business so well, that by two in the morning the whole of the cargo had been transferred from the *Jeune Amélie* to the coast. But the voyage was not yet concluded. They now made for Sardinia, to take in a fresh cargo; and this second operation was effected as successfully as the first. The new cargo was for the Duchy of Lucca, and was almost entirely composed of Havanna cigars and wine from Xeres and Malaga. But they did not escape a quarrel with the excise about the salt tax. A custom-house officer was stretched on the deck, and two sailors were wounded, one of whom was Dantès, whose shoulder had been grazed by a bullet. He was almost gratified by this skirmish, and pleased that he had been wounded. It showed him with what indifference he regarded danger and suffering. He examined the wounded exciseman, and, either from the excitement of the skirmish or the chilling of all his human sentiments, the sight had produced but a slight impression on him. Dantès was on the track that he wished to follow; his heart seemed petrified in his bosom. Jacopo, seeing his comrade fall, believed he was killed, and rushed to his assistance, and tended him like a good comrade. Happily, Edmond was but slightly wounded, and by means of certain herbs sold to the smugglers by old Sardinian women, the wound quickly healed.

Two months and a half passed in these different cruises, in the course of which Edmond massed nearly one hundred piastres. He had passed and re-passed twenty times by the island of Monte Cristo, but he had never found an opportunity of landing. At last he resolved that, as soon as his engagement with the captain of the *Jeune Amélie* was ended, he would hire a small boat on his own account, and under some pretext make for the island of Monte Cristo and carry on his researches. But though he eagerly sought in his fruitful imagination for some other means of reaching the island, he could think of none. He was still in a state of indecision, when the captain, who had great confidence in him, and much wished to retain his services, took him by the arm one evening, and led him to a tavern of La Via del Oglio, where the better class of the Leghorn smugglers were wont to assemble. On this occasion, a matter of importance was debated, regarding a vessel laden with Turkey carpets and cashmeres, and stuffs from the Levant. Some neutral spot must be found, where the exchange could be made, and then the different articles would be smuggled to the French coast.

The captain of the *Jeune Amélie* proposed, as a suitable landing-place the island of Monte Cristo, which was completely deserted, and therefore contained neither soldiers nor excisemen.

At the mention of Monte Cristo, Dantès trembled with joy; he rose to conceal his emotion, and walked up and down the smoky tavern where all the idioms of the known world mingled in the lingua Franca. When he again approached the Captain, it was decided to land at Monte Cristo and set out on the expedition the following night.

CHAPTER XXIII

THE ISLAND OF MONTE CRISTO

THUS Dantès, by one of those turns of luck which sometimes befall those whom Fate has hardly treated, obtained the longed-for opportunity by simple and natural means, and was about to put foot on the island without exciting a shadow of suspicion. One night only intervened before the time for departure. That night was one of the most feverish Dantès had ever passed. When he closed his eyes, he saw the letter of Cardinal Spada written in characters of fire on the wall; if he dozed, the wildest dreams disturbed his brain; he was entering grottoes paved with emeralds, the walls lined with rubies, and stalactites of diamonds. The pearls fell in drops like the filtering of water. He was astonished, enraptured, and filled his pockets with the gems; but when daylight came, the jewels had turned to common pebbles. Then he tried to re-enter the wonderful caves of which he had only had a glimpse, but the path twisted and turned in all directions, and he could not find the opening. In vain he searched his wearied memory for the mysterious magic word which opened for the Arab woodman, the caves of Ali Baba. All was useless, the vanished treasure had again become the property of the genii of the ground, from whom he had had a momentary hope of stealing it. The next morning he was almost as feverish as he had been during the night, but reason came to the aid of imagination, and he at last fixed on a plan which had for some time been vaguely floating in his brain. Night came, and with it the preparations for departure, and amid the bustle Dantès was able to conceal his excitement. By degrees he had assumed as much authority over his companions as if he were undisputed master of the vessel; and as his orders were always precise and to the point, his comrades obeyed him not only promptly but pleasantly.

At seven o'clock all was ready; at ten minutes past seven they had doubled the lighthouse, just as the beacon was kindled. The sea was calm, with a fresh wind blowing from the southeast. Dantès declared that he would take the helm, and that everyone might go to bed.

When the Maltese, as Dantès was called, took this upon himself, it was sufficient and everyone went to bed. Dantès, brought back from solitude into the world, often felt an imperious desire to be alone.

On this occasion the solitude was peopled by his thoughts, the night was illumined by his fancies, and the silence was broken by his reiterated vows. When the captain awoke, the ship had every sail set, every stitch of canvas was full with the breeze, and they were running at the rate of two and a half leagues an hour.

At last the island of Monte Cristo appeared on the horizon. Dantès relinquished his post to the master, and went to stretch himself in his hammock, but notwithstanding his sleepless night he could not close his eyes.

In two hours he again went on deck; the vessel was about to double the island of Elba. They were just off Mareciana, and above the green, flat island of Pianosa; against the blue sky the bright peak of Monte Cristo was visible Dantès ordered the helmsman to port the helm, leaving Pianosa on the right ; he calculated that this manœuvre would shorten the distance two or three knots.

Towards five o'clock in the evening they gained a clear view of the island, owing to the limpid quality of the atmosphere, noticeable when the sun is going down. Edmond devoured with his eyes the huge mass of rocks which were coloured with all the changing shades of twilight ; from a bright red to dark blue.

Evening drew on and at ten o'clock they touched land. The *Jeune Amélie* was the first at the *rendezvous*. Dantès, in spite of his self-control, could not contain himself ; he was the first to leap on shore, and, if he had dared, would have kissed the very ground.

It was a dark night, but at eleven o'clock the moon rose, tinging the quivering waves with silver, and casting her rays in a flood of light on the rocky points.

The island was well known to the crew of the *Jeune Amélie* —it was one of their ordinary stations ; but Dantès, though he had seen it in his voyages to the Levant, had never landed there before. He questioned Jacopo.

" Where shall we pass the night ? "

" On board the tartan, to be sure."

" Should we not be better in the grottoes on the island ? "

" I do not know of any grottoes," replied Jacopo.

Dantès stood dumbfounded for a moment ; then he bethought him that the grottoes might have been stopped up by some accident, or even filled in for greater safety by Cardinal Spada. But it was useless to search during the night ; he therefore put off the investigation till the following morning. Moreover, a signal given about half a league off, to which the *Jeune Amélie* quickly replied, indicated that the time had come for doing business. The boat which now arrived, reassured by the answering signal, soon appeared white and silent as a phantom, and cast anchor about a cable's length from the shore. Then the work of transfer began.

On the following morning, taking his gun, shot, and powder, Dantès expressed his desire to kill one of the wild goats which could be seen leaping from rock to rock ; this excursion was only attributed to his fondness for sport and desire for solitude. Jacopo alone insisted on accompanying him, and Dantès dared not oppose him, fearing that he might by so doing excite suspicion. But he had not gone far before he succeeded in killing a goat, and he then despatched Jacopo with it to his companions with the injunction to cook it, and, when it was ready, to fire a gun as a signal ; some dried fruits and a bottle of Montepulciano wine were to complete the repast.

Dantès still went on, looking back from time to time. When he reached the summit of a rock he saw a thousand feet below him Jacopo and his comrades engaged in preparing the breakfast. Dantès gazed down at them with the gentle, melancholy smile of a superior being.

" In two hours' time," he said to himself, " these people will have set out again, enriched by fifty piastres, to endeavour at the risk of life even to gain fifty more, and will then squander their money with the pride of sultans and ostentation of nabobs. To-day my own expectations make me despise their wealth which appears the merest poverty ; to-morrow I may be undeceived, and compelled to regard this poverty as supreme good fortune. But that cannot be ; the clever, infallible Faria can never have been deceived in this one matter. Besides, it were better to die than to continue this miserable, commonplace life ! "

Thus Dantès, who but three months ago longed only for liberty, was now not satisfied with liberty, but longed for wealth. The fault, however, was not his, since God, though limiting the powers of man, has yet instilled into him infinite desires.

Meanwhile, by a road hidden between the walls of rock, following a path hollowed out by the torrent, which in all probability had never before been trodden by human foot, Dantès was approaching the spot where he believed the grottoes existed.

As he kept to the line of the coast, examining the smallest objects with minute attention, he thought he remarked on certain rocks notches made by a human hand. Time seemed to have respected these signs, which were traced with a certain regularity, and probably with the intention of pointing out a track. Occasionally the marks disappeared under tufts of myrtle or clinging lichens.

Then Dantès raised the branches, or removed the moss, to seek for the landmarks which were his guides in the labyrinth. These marks had inspired him with hope. Might they not have been made by the Cardinal himself, that in case of accident they might serve as a guide to his nephew ? This solitary place was certainly one likely to be chosen by anyone who desired to bury a treasure.

At last, about sixty yards from the harbour, it seemed to Edmond, still hidden from his comrades by the rising ground,

F

that the notches came to an end; but they did not terminate at any grotto. A large circular rock was the sole object to which the path conducted. Edmond felt that instead of reaching the end he was perhaps but at the beginning; he therefore retraced his steps.

During this time his companions had been busy preparing the meal, drawing water from the spring, fetching bread and fruit from the boat, and cooking the goat. As they were removing it from the spit, they beheld Dantès, light and nimble as a chamois, leaping from rock to rock. They fired the gun, and the sportsman hastened back at full speed.

But just as all eyes were fixed on his flying descent, in which he heightened the effect of his agility by a show of rashness to inspire them with alarm, his foot slipped. They saw him totter over the summit of a rock and disappear, uttering a cry.

With one accord they all darted forward, for they were fond of Dantès in spite of his superiority.

Jacopo was the first to reach him. He found him lying bleeding and almost unconscious; he had fallen a distance of twelve or fifteen feet. They poured a few drops of rum into his mouth, and Edmond opened his eyes, complained of great pain in his knee, a heaviness in his head, and aching in his back. His comrades wished to carry him to the shore; but as soon as he was touched, even by Jacopo, he declared he could not bear to be stirred.

There was now, therefore, no question of breakfast for Dantès, but he insisted that his comrades should return and partake of it; he only needed rest, and by the time they came back would probably feel relieved. The sailors needed not a second pressing; they were hungry, the savoury smell of the goat reached them, and there is little ceremony among jack tars. In an hour's time they returned.

All that Dantès had been able to do, was to drag himself a few yards that he might lean against a mossy stone. But the pain seemed to increase in violence. The old captain who had arranged to deposit his cargo on the coast of Piedmont and France, between Nice and Fréjus, insisted on Dantès' rising.

Dantès made superhuman efforts to obey, but at every attempt he fell, pale and groaning.

" He has injured his back," said the captain, aside. " No matter, he is a good fellow, and we must not abandon him; let us carry him to the ship."

But Dantès declared he would rather die where he was than endure the torture that moving occasioned him.

"Well," said the captain, "whatever happens, it shall never be said that we deserted a brave comrade like you. We will not start till this evening."

But Dantès would not hear of this.

"No," he said, "I have been clumsy, and must bear the pain of my accident. Leave me a small provision of biscuits, a gun, powder, and shot, to shoot some goats and to defend myself, and a pickaxe that I may construct some kind of habitation if you are very long in coming to fetch me."

"But you will die of hunger," said the captain.

"I would rather do that," said Dantès, "than suffer the agony which movement causes me. If in a day or two you hail a fishing-boat, coming into these waters, ask them to call and fetch me. I will give them twenty-five piastres to take me to Leghorn."

The captain shook his head.

"Now, Captain Baldi, I know of a way of settling the matter," said Jacopo; "I will stay with the invalid and take care of him."

"And lose your share of the profits to remain with me?"

"Yes," said Jacopo, "and without regret."

"Come, you are a good fellow, Jacopo," said Edmond, "and God will recompense you for your kindness; but I need no one, thank you; a day or two's rest will put me right, and I hope to find in these rocks some herbs that are excellent for bruises;" and a curious smile passed over Dantès' face; he pressed Jacopo's hand warmly, but was immovable in his determination to remain, and remain alone. The smugglers then supplied him with all he needed and slowly withdrew.

When they were out of sight, he murmured to himself, smiling: "How strange that among such men one should meet with such proofs of friendship and devotion!"

Then he crept carefully up to the edge of a rock which hid him from the view of the sea, whence he beheld the tartan weigh anchor, and, balancing herself gracefully, set out on her voyage. At the end of an hour, she had disappeared.

Then Dantès rose, more supple and agile than the goats which were bounding among the rough-hewn rocks, took his gun in one hand, his pickaxe in the other, and hastened towards the rock at which the notches had disappeared.

"Now," he cried, the story of the Arab woodman which Faria had related to him returning to his mind, "Now, Sesame, open!"

CHAPTER XXIV

DAZZLED

THE sun was slowly rising in the heavens. Thousands of grass hoppers kept up a monotonous murmur; the myrtle and olive leaves trembled with a gentle rustle; at every step that Edmond took, startled lizards darted forth, as green as emeralds, while the wild goats bounded afar off on the steep incline. In a word, the island was alive, inhabited, and astir, and yet Dantès felt himself alone with God. He experienced, too, an indescribable emotion of fear, a certain dislike of the broad daylight, which gives the impression, even in a desert, of observing eyes. This sentiment was so strong, that just at the moment he was about to begin his work, Edmond stopped, put down the pickaxe, and taking his gun, climbed once more up the highest rock on the island, and then cast a searching glance all round him. The brigantine which had sailed in the morning was disappearing in the Strait of Bonifacio; the tartan was about to round Corsica.

The sight reassured Edmond. He turned his gaze on the objects more immediately at hand. He was standing on the highest point of the island, a narrow, slender statue on an immense pedestal. Not a creature was near him; there was nothing but blue sea which beat against the base of the rocks, covering them with a fringe of silvery foam. At last he descended, quickly but carefully, for he feared to meet with an accident like that he had so cleverly simulated. He now endeavoured to trace the marks in the opposite direction, and found that they led to a sort of little creek sufficiently large and deep for a little boat to pass over it, and yet remain concealed from observation. Continuing the thread of inferences which in the hands of the Abbé Faria had been such a valuable guide in the labyrinth of probabilities, it occurred to Dantès that Cardinal Spada, desiring to escape notice, had landed there, hidden the boat, and proceeded along the track to the spot where he buried his treasure. It was this idea that brought Dantès back again to the circular rock. One thing only threatened to upset his theory. How could this rock, which probably weighed several tons, have been moved without considerable force to the spot where it stood?

Suddenly a thought flashed across Dantès' mind: "Instead of being lifted up, it must have been pushed down;" and he sprang above the rock in order to discover where it originally stood. He soon perceived that a slight incline had been made, and the rock must have been rolled over, down to its present resting-place. A large stone had evidently been used as a wedge, and small blocks and pebbles had been carefully spread about to hide the gaps round it, and these, in course of time, had become covered with grass and moss, so that the old rock now appeared firmly wedged into the ground. Dantès raised some of the soil, and saw, or thought he saw, the whole of this ingenious artifice. He raised his pickaxe, and began to attack this wall of rock. After working ten minutes, it gave way a little, and an opening was made through which he could thrust his arm. Dantès then proceeded to cut down the strongest olive tree he could find, stripped it of its branches, and introduced it as a lever into the opening. But the rock was heavy and wedged too firmly into the lower one for human force to shake it. It then occurred to Dantès that he must attack the wedge itself. But how could it be done ? He looked round him in an embarrassed manner, and his eyes fell on a mouflon's horn, full of powder, that his friend Jacopo had left him. He smiled ; the infernal invention should do the work for him. By means of his pickaxe, Dantès hollowed out a mine between the upper and lower rock, such as is often made by pioneers to save human labour ; then he filled it with powder, and tearing up his handkerchief, soaked it in saltpetre, and set fire to it with a match. He retired to a distance. The explosion was not long in coming ; the upper rock was lifted instantaneously and with great violence, while the lower one was shattered to pieces. Through the small opening which Dantès had first made a whole world of startled insects crept forth, and a huge snake raised his head, and then slowly glided out of sight. The upper rock, now without support, inclined downwards to the sea below. The dauntless investigator examined it, selected the weakest part, inserted his lever, and, like a second Sisyphus, strained every nerve to shake the huge mass. The rock, already loosened by the explosion, tottered on its base. Dantès redoubled his efforts. At last the rock yielded, rolled, and fell over with a splash into the ocean. A circular opening was now disclosed, and in the centre a square stone with an iron ring attached to it. Dantès uttered a cry of delight ; never had more magnificent results crowned a first attempt. His legs trembled beneath him, his heart beat violently, and such a thick shadow passed before his eyes that he was compelled to pause.

This hesitation passed like a flash. Edmond inserted his

lever through the ring, and endeavoured, with a might effort, to raise it. The stone slowly yielded, and when removed, disclosed the steep incline of a kind of ladder, which led down into a grotto, and was lost in obscurity. Another might have hastened on at once with exclamations of joy, but Dantès paused, pale and doubtful.

" Come," he said to himself, " I must be a man. Accustomed as I am to adversity, I must not be overwhelmed by a deception, or I shall have suffered in vain. The heart that breaks after being unduly elated by the warm breath of hope is afterwards chilled by cold reality—Faria dreamt it all; Cardinal Spada buried nothing in this grotto, perhaps, indeed, never came here, or if he did, that bold, adventurous thief, Cæsar Borgia came here afterwards, discovered the track, followed it as I have done, raised the stone, went down, and took all the treasure away."

He still remained motionless and thoughtful, his eyes fixed on the dark opening, and continued, " and yet he who compared Italy to an artichoke which he could eat, leaf by leaf, knew the value of time too well to have wasted his own in replacing this rock; I will go down."

Then with a doubting smile on his lips, and murmuring that last word of human philosophy, " Perhaps," Dantès descended. But instead of the darkness and thick heavy atmosphere he expected, he found a soft bluish light pervading all the interior ; for air and light penetrated not only through the opening he had made, but through many chinks in the rock, invisible from the outside.

After standing a few seconds in this grotto, of which the atmosphere was rather warm and fragrant, than damp and unpleasant, Dantès' eyes penetrated to the farthest extremity of the cave ; it was of granite, the bright facets of which sparkled like diamonds.

Edmond now recalled the terms of the will, which he knew by heart : " In the farthest corner of the second opening." He had only reached the first grotto ; he must now seek the entrance of the second. He looked about him ; the second grotto must of necessity extend towards the interior of the island. He examined the blocks of stone, and sounded one of the walls, in which he fancied the opening might be concealed for precaution's sake. The blow of the pickaxe resounded, drawing forth a dull sound, the denseness of which made the perspiration start to Dantès' brow ; then, after repeated attempts, it seemed to the indefatigable miner, that one portion of the granite wall responded with a deeper reverberation to the blow; he examined the part, and from its appearance, judged it possible there might be some opening there. However, that he might not begin a fruitless task, Dantès sounded the other walls, struck the ground with the butt end of his gun, and removed the soil in suspicious-looking places; but finding nothing, he returned to that portion of the wall which yielded the hopeful sound. He struck again with more force. And now, a curious thing occurred. Under the blows of the weapon, a kind of stucco, such as is placed on walls intended for fresco painting, gradually fell off in fragments, discovering an ordinary-looking soft white stone. The opening had, evidently, been filled in with stones, on which had been placed a layer of stucco, painted in imitation of the crystalline granite. Dantès struck with the pointed end of his pickaxe, which entered about an inch into this door in the wall. This was certainly the spot to be excavated. By some strange freak of human nature, however, the more the proofs of the authenticity of Faria's story accumulated to reassure Dantès, the more his failing heart gave itself up to doubt and discouragement; this new discovery which should have inspired him with fresh energy, took from him his last remaining strength. The pickaxe fell heavily, dropping almost from his hands; he laid it down, wiped his brow, and ascended to the light of day, on the pretext of seeing if he were watched, but in reality, because he needed air and felt as though he should faint.

Dantès swallowed a mouthful of rum, and re-entered the grotto, strengthened and revived. The pickaxe, which before had seemed so heavy, now felt light in his hand. After a few blows, he perceived that the stones were not cemented, but merely placed one on the top of another. He inserted the point of his pickaxe in one of the crevices, pressed on the handle, and beheld the stone roll over and fall at his feet. He had now only to pick out one stone after another, and the space was soon sufficiently large to allow of his passing through. The appearance of this cave was darker, gloomier, and more dismal than the other; the air, which penetrated only by the opening Dantès had just made, had the mephitic odour that he had expected to find in the first. He paused, therefore, till the death-like atmosphere became purified by the current of outer air, and then entered.

To the left of the opening was a dim, obscure corner. Dantès cast a searching look round him; the grotto was empty like the other. The treasure, if it existed, was buried in the dark corner. The hour of anguish had indeed arrived!

Two feet of earth to excavate ! That was all that lay between
Dantès and supreme joy or supreme despair ! He attacked the
ground boldly with his pickaxe. At the fifth or sixth blow the
pickaxe resounded against an iron substance. Never did death-
knell or alarm-bell produce such an effect on the listener ! He
sounded again near the same spot ; but the blow produced a
different sound. " It is a wooden chest set in iron," he said to
himself.

At this moment a sudden shadow intercepted the light. Dantès
dropped his pickaxe, seized his gun, and darted through the first
grotto to the opening. A wild goat had bounded past, and was
now browsing at a little distance. It was a good opportunity to
assure himself of his dinner ; but Dantès feared that the report of
his gun might attract someone. He reflected a moment, then
cut down a resinous bough, lit it at the fire the smugglers had
made to cook their meal, and returned, bearing it as a torch.
Again entering the grotto, he held the torch to the unfinished
hole, and discovered that he had not been mistaken. The blows
of the pickaxe had alternately struck on iron and on wood. He
planted his torch on the ground and set to work. Very soon
Dantès beheld distinctly an oak chest, set in chased iron. In the
centre of the lid, on a silver plate which the soil had failed to
tarnish, were emblazoned the arms of the Spada family—namely,
a sword on an oval escutcheon, like most Italian armorial bearings,
surmounted by a cardinal's hat. Dantès readily recognized them.
How often had Faria drawn them for him !

By degrees the chest was exposed to view, with its lock set
between two padlocks, and handles at each side ; they were all
chased, as was usual at that period, when art made even the
commonest metals valuable. Taking it by both handles, Dantès
attempted to raise it ; but it was impossible. He tried to open it,
but the lock and padlocks were secure. Dantès then introduced
the point of the pickaxe beneath the lid and burst it open. A
large split in the wood rendered the iron hinges useless, and they
were easily wrenched off, fragments of old oak still clinging to
them. A feverish giddiness seized Dantès ; he took his gun,
loaded it, and placed it near him ; then he closed his eyes, as
children do, that they may see more stars in the brilliant night of
their imagination than they can count in the starry skies ; then
he reopened them. He stood dazzled at what he beheld.

The chest was divided into three compartments. In the first
shone bright golden coins, with their tawny glitter ; in the second,
unpolished ingots, arranged in regular order, possessing no attrac-

tion but their value as gold. In the third, which was half full, Edmond turned over diamonds, pearls, and rubies that fell from his hand in a sparkling shower with the sound as of hail pattering on the window panes. After having touched and handled the jewels with trembling excitement, Edmond rose and made his way back to the opening of the caves with the tumultuous exaltation of a half-frenzied man. He climbed a rock whence he could overlook the sea, but saw nothing. He was alone—alone with these incalculable, fabulous, incredible riches, which were all his own! But was it a passing illusion, or did he grasp a living reality? He pressed his hands to his head, as though to retain his fleeting senses; then he darted off across the island without following any particular line or track, making the wild goats fly out of his path, and startling the sea-birds by his cries and gesticulations; then, turning round, he retraced his steps, and dashed again into the grottoes, to find himself once more face to face with the gold and diamonds. This time he fell on his knees, pressing his hands convulsively on his palpitating heart, and murmuring a prayer intelligible to God alone. Soon he felt himself calmer, and consequently happier; for from that hour he began to realize his good fortune. He next set himself to count his wealth. He had a thousand gold ingots of two or three pounds' weight each; then he piled up twenty-five thousand gold crowns, each worth about twenty-five francs, bearing the heads of Pope Alexander VI and his predecessors; and after this was done, he perceived that the compartment was only half empty. Finally, he measured out ten times his two hands full of pearls, gems, and diamonds, many of which had been mounted by the best jewellers of the time, and possessed an artistic as well as an intrinsic value.

Day was slowly declining, and Dantès, fearing to be surprised if he remained in the cave, went out, gun in hand. A piece of biscuit and some mouthfuls of wine were his supper. He replaced the stone, lay down on it, and slept for several hours, covering with his body the entrance to the grotto.

CHAPTER XXV

THE UNKNOWN

WITH the first rays of morning Dantès rose and ascended, as on the previous evening, the highest rock on the island to explore the surrounding scene; but no living creature was in sight.

Edmond then descended, removed the stone, and entered the grotto. He filled his pockets with the jewels, replaced carefully the splintered wood and lock, covered the chest with soil, and trod the earth down with his feet, scattering some sand to conceal any irregularity; he then came out of the grotto, replaced the stone, piled up some small fragments, which he filled in with earth, and then planted a few myrtles and heaths, sprinkling them with water that they might not appear a recent growth; then effacing the traces of his footmarks, he awaited with impatience the arrival of his companions. He longed to return to social life, to mix with men, and take in society the rank, influence, and power that in this world can be procured by wealth alone.

On the sixth day came the smugglers. Dantès dragged himself to the landing-place, and declared to his companions that though much better he was not yet free from pain.

He then listened to the recital of their adventures. All things considered, the expedition had not been unsuccessful; and everyone, particularly Jacopo, regretted that Dantès had not taken part in it, so that he might have obtained a share of the profits which amounted to fifty piastres to each man.

Edmond did not even smile at the enumeration of the advantages he had missed, and as the *Jeune Amélie* only touched at Monte Cristo to fetch him, he embarked the same evening, and accompanied the captain to Leghorn.

At Leghorn he went to a Jew, and sold, for five thousand francs apiece, four of his smallest diamonds. The Jew might have inquired how a sailor possessed such gems, but he held his peace, for he had gained a thousand francs on each.

The following day Dantès purchased a new boat, which he presented to Jacopo, along with a hundred piastres, that he might get it properly equipped, on condition that he went to Marseilles and obtained news of an old man named Louis Dantès, living in the Allées de Meilhan, and of a girl named Mercédès living in the Catalans' village. Jacopo thought he must be dreaming.

Edmond told him that he had become a sailor from caprice, because his family refused money for his maintenance, but that on reaching Leghorn he had come into his uncle's property, to which he was the sole heir. Dantès' education gave such an air of probability to this story that Jacopo never doubted it.

The next day Jacopo sailed for Marseilles; he was to meet Edmond at Monte Cristo. Dantès, too, set out the same day, but without saying whither he was going. He took leave of the crew of the *Jeune Amélie*, dispensing splendid gratuities, and bade the captain farewell, with the promise of some day or other sending news of himself.

Then he started for Genoa. At the moment of his arrival there a small yacht, built for an Englishman, was being tried in the bay. The English gentleman had desired a yacht constructed after the best fashion, and had agreed to pay forty thousand francs for it.

Dantès at once offered sixty thousand, on condition that the boat should be given up to him immediately.

Dantès then took the shipbuilder with him to a Jew's, and after a short interview with the latter in a back room, the shipbuilder was paid sixty thousand francs down. He then offered his services in finding a crew for the vessel, but Dantès thanked him, saying that he was in the habit of cruising alone, and that the only thing he needed was a secret press in his cabin at the head of his bed, with three divisions opening with a concealed spring. He gave the measurements for these compartments, which were duly fitted on the following day.

When all was ready, Dantès set out from the harbour of Genoa, attended by the gaze of a crowd of people, who eagerly watched the movements of the Spanish *seigneur* who was accustomed to sail over the seas alone.

Dantès managed the boat to perfection. She glided along like an intelligent being, and the young sailor was constrained to admit to himself that the Genoese merited their reputation of being the first shipbuilders in the world. The curious followed the vessel until she disappeared, and then many discussions ensued as to her destination. None thought of the island of Monte Cristo. Yet it was to Monte Cristo that Edmond was bound. He arrived there late on the second day, and, instead of landing at the usual harbour, cast anchor in the little creek.

Dantès at once proceeded to his hidden treasure ; everything was in the same state in which he had left it. The following day his immense fortune was transported on board the yacht, and enclosed in the three compartments of the secret press.

Dantès, however, remained a week longer. During this time he sailed round the island, studying it as a skilful rider studies a horse, until he knew all its merits and all its defects, resolving in his own mind to increase the former and remedy the latter.

On the eighth day he beheld a small boat, which he recognized as the one he had given to Jacopo. He signalled, Jacopo replied, and in two hours' time the latter had reached the yacht.

There was a sad answer to both Dantès' inquiries. Old Dantes was dead. Mercédès had disappeared.

Edmond heard the news with a calm face ; then he once more

went on shore, forbidding anyone to follow him. Two hours later he returned, and then two of Jacopo's sailors went on board the yacht to aid in manœuvring her, and Dantès ordered that she should be steered for Marseilles.

He had expected his father's death, but Mercédès—what had become of her ? Edmond could not give proper instructions to an agent, without divulging his secret ; besides, there was other information that he required, which no one but himself must obtain.

At last, one morning, the yacht, followed by the little boat, entered the harbour of Marseilles, and anchored at the very spot where on that evening of fatal memory he had embarked for the Château d'If.

It was not, however, without a shudder that Dantès beheld a gendarme in the boat accompanying the officers of health. But with the ease of manner which he had acquired, he presented the English passport he had purchased at Leghorn, and by means of this foreign document, always regarded in France with respectful attention, he was allowed to land without delay.

The first person whom Dantès beheld on setting foot on La Canebière was one of the sailors belonging to the *Pharaon.* This man had served under him, and the opportunity therefore for Dantès to discover if he were recognizable was not to be lost. He therefore walked straight up to the sailor and put several questions to him, to which the man replied without evincing the smallest suspicion that he had ever beheld his interlocutor before.

Dantès gave the sailor a piece of money, and thanked him for his information. The next moment the honest fellow came runing after him.

" Pardon, monsieur," said he, " but you have made a mistake ; you no doubt intended to give me a two-franc piece, and, see, you have given me a double Napoleon."

" Well, my friend, I suppose I did make a mistake," said Dantès ; " but your honesty merits some recompense, so take this also and drink my health with your comrades."

The sailor gazed at Edmond, and was so lost in astonishment that he almost forgot to thank him, and looked after him as he moved away, exclaiming, " He must be a nabob from India, surely ! "

Dantès walked on. At every step his heart was oppressed with some new emotion. All the memories of childhood rose before him at every turn in the street, at every corner of the square, and every sign-post on the cross-road. At last he approached the house where his father had dwelt. The nasturtiums and other plants had disappeared from the window, where the old man had trained them with such care. Dantès leant against the trunk of a tree and gazed at the upper storey of the poor little house.

Presently he advanced to the door, crossed the threshold, and inquired if there were a lodging vacant; and although the house was full, he insisted so much on visiting the upper storey that the doorkeeper at last requested, on behalf of a stranger, permission from the occupants, a young man and woman who had only been married about a week, to inspect their two rooms. When he beheld these young people Dantès uttered a sigh.

Nothing in the room, however, reminded Edmond of the past; there was not even the same paper on the walls, and all the old furniture had disappeared. The four walls alone remained. Dantès turned towards the bed; it was in the same spot, and his eyes moistened with tears; there the old man must have breathed his last, murmuring the name of his son.

The two young people regarded with astonishment this stern-looking man, who stood motionless, two large tears rolling down his cheeks. But as sorrow is sacred the couple asked no questions, but retired to the background that he might not be disturbed in his grief, and when he withdrew, they followed him, saying he might come again whenever he felt inclined.

Passing down to the lower storey, Edmond knocked at another door, and inquired if the tailor, Caderousse, still lived there. But the doorkeeper informed him that the individual in question had got into difficulties, and now kept a small inn on the road from Bellegarde to Beaucaire.

Dantès left, after inquiring the name of the proprietor of the little house, whom he called upon. Announcing himself as Lord Wilmore, the name on his passport, he offered to purchase the house for the sum of twenty-five thousand francs. This was at least ten thousand more than the place was worth; but if the price had been half a million, Dantès would have given it willingly.

The same day the young couple on the fifth storey were informed by the notary who had drawn up the contract that the new proprietor gave them the choice of any other rooms in the whole house, without an increase of rent, on condition that they gave up their present lodging. This curious occurrence was the subject of discussion among the good folk of the Allées de Meilhan for nearly a week, and thousands of conjectures were made thereon; not one of which touched the truth, however.

But what excited the curiosity of the little community in the highest degree, was the fact that on the same evening, the stranger was seen to enter a poor fisherman's hut, where he remained for more than an hour asking news of many people who had been dead, or had disappeared, for more than fifteen or sixteen years.

On the following day the people of whom he had obtained his information received a present of a smart new boat, with two fishing-nets. The brave fellows would have been glad to thank their benefactor, but after taking leave of them, and giving some orders to a sailor, he had left Marseilles on horseback, taking the road to Aix.

CHAPTER XXVI

THE INN OF PONT DU GARD

THOSE who have ever made a pedestrian tour in the south of France, may have remarked half way between Bellegarde and Beaucaire, a small inn, in front of which hangs an iron sign-board, bearing a grotesque representation of the Pont du Gard. The inn has what, in Languedoc, is termed a garden ; that is to say, the back entrance opens on to an enclosure, where some stunted olives and wild fig trees raise their straggling branches, silvered over with dust. Between these grow vegetables, such as garlic, pimentos, and eschalots, while in a lonely corner, a large fir stands like an outpost sentinel, its fan-like boughs withering beneath the scorching sun. All the trees, both large and small, are bent by the force of the north-west wind, one of the scourges of Provence. Here and there, in the surrounding plain, which strongly resembles a lake of dust, a few straggling ears of wheat are to be seen, serving as perches for the grasshoppers, which pursue, with their harsh, monotonous song, any passers-by loitering in this dreary wilderness.

The master of this small inn was a man of about forty-five years of age, tall, thin, and vigorous, of the true Southern type, with deep-set, bright eyes, hook nose, and teeth as white as some carnivorous animal's. His hair, in spite of his years, had scarcely begun to turn grey, and like his beard, was thick and curly. His complexion, naturally sunburnt, had assumed a still deeper tinge through the poor fellow's habit of standing, from morning till evening, on the threshold of his door, waiting to see if any customer were coming that way, during which perform-ance, his face was only protected from the rays of the sun

THE INN OF PONT DU GARD

by a red handkerchief tied round his head, after the fashion
of the Spanish muleteers. This man was no other than our
old acquaintance, Gaspard Caderousse. His wife, whose maiden
name was Madeleine Radelle, was a pale, thin, sickly woman,
born at Carconte, by which name—following a local custom,
she was generally known—and preserving traces of the traditional beauty of her compatriots ; she had, nevertheless, seen
her good looks slowly decay under the influence of one of those
low fevers so common among the marshes of Aiguemortes and
Camargue. She kept nearly entirely to her own room, situated
on the first floor, where, shivering and complaining, she remained
propped up either on the bed or in an armchair, while her husband
posted himself at the door on his usual sentry duty, which he
prolonged all the more willingly, as he thereby escaped the eternal
lamentations on their hard fate, to which his better half continually subjected him—complaints to which he was in the habit of
replying in these philosophical words : " Hush, Carconte, it is
God's will ! "

On this particular day, Caderousse had been standing, according
to habit, in front of his inn, now more a place of shelter for his own
head than a house of business, gazing sadly at the fowls picking
among the patch of grass outside, and then up and down the road
which ran straight from north to south, when the sharp voice of
his wife calling him, forced him to leave his post.

At the moment Caderousse entered, the long road, which he
had scanned so eagerly, was as bare and solitary as a desert at
midday. No traveller, free to choose any other hour of the day
for his journey, would care to venture along this frightful Sahara.
Nevertheless, if he had remained at his post a minute longer,
Caderousse would have seen approaching from the direction of
Bellegarde, a man on horseback, coming along at that easy pace,
which indicates the best of relations between horse and rider.
The rider was a priest, dressed in black, and wearing a three-
cornered hat.

As they reached the door of the inn, it would have been difficult
to decide whether the horse was pulled up, or stopped of his own
accord ; but at any rate, the rider dismounted, and taking the
bridle, fastened it to the handle of an old dilapidated shutter ;
then advancing towards the door, and wiping his moist brow
with a red cotton handkerchief, the priest knocked three times
with the metal end of his whip. A large black dog thereupon
darted forward, barking, and displaying two rows of sharp teeth, a
hostile demonstration which proved that he was unaccustomed to

visitors. Then a heavy step was heard creaking on the stairs, and the landlord presented himself, bowing low to his guest.

"Here I am, monsieur!" he exclaimed, full of amazement; "be quiet, Margotin, will you! He will not hurt you, monsieur; he barks but does not bite. Any wine, monsieur? It is terribly hot. Ah! pardon!" he added, observing who his visitor was, "I was not aware whom I had the honour of receiving. What will your reverence please to take?"

The priest regarded him for two or three seconds with a strange attention, and appeared anxious also to attract the innkeeper's scrutiny to himself; then, seeing that Gaspard's face betrayed no other expression than that of surprise, at receiving no answer, he said, "Are you not M. Caderousse?"

"I am, monsieur," replied the landlord, still more surprised by the question than he had been by the long silence, "Gaspard Caderousse, at your service!"

"Gaspard Caderousse! yes, name and surname are the same. You carried on the business of a tailor, formerly, I believe, in the Allées de Meilhan, did you not, at Number 4?"

"Yes; but it did not turn out well; it is so hot at that wretched place, Marseilles, that I think the people will end with wearing no clothes at all. But, speaking of heat, what refreshment may I offer your reverence?"

"A bottle of your best wine, and let us continue the conversation."

Anxious not to lose this opportunity of bringing out one of his last bottles of Cahors wine, Caderousse hastened to open a trap-door in the floor of the room which served both as dining-room and kitchen. He reappeared at the end of five minutes, and found the abbé seated in a chair, his elbow resting on the table, whilst Margotin was seated between his knees, stretching up her thin neck and eager-looking eyes.

"Are you alone here?" inquired the abbé, whilst the landlord placed before him a glass and the bottle of wine.

"Alas! yes; or, at least, nearly alone, your reverence; for I have a wife who can give me no help in anything; she is a great invalid, poor Carconte."

"Ah! you are married?" said the priest with some interest.

"You see that I am not rich," said Caderousse, sighing, "but how can it be otherwise? To be an honest man does not suffice for obtaining prosperity in this world."

The abbé fixed on him a piercing look.

"Yes, an honest man. I can at least boast that I am that,

monsieur," said the innkeeper, without evading the abbé's glance, " and in these times it is not everybody who can say that ! "

" So much the better for you, if what you assert is true," said the abbé, " for I have conviction that sooner or later, the honest man will be recompensed, and the wicked man punished."

" It is part of your business to say that, monsieur," returned Caderousse bitterly, " but one is free to keep one's own opinion about it."

" You are wrong there," said the abbé, " as I may perhaps prove to you presently ; but first of all I must assure myself that you are the person I am looking for. Did you, in 1814 or 1815, know a young sailor named Dantès ? "

" Dantès ? Did I know him ? poor Edmond ! I should think so ! he was one of my best friends ! " cried Caderousse, a dark flush rising to his face, while the abbe's dilated eyes seemed to read his very soul. " And what has become of the poor fellow ? Did you know him, monsieur ? Have you seen him ? Is he free and happy ? "

" He died in prison, more desperate, and more miserable than the prisoners on the galleys at Toulon."

A mortal paleness succeeded the crimson flush which had covered Caderousse's face. He turned aside, and the abbé beheld him wiping away a tear with a corner of his red handkerchief.

" Poor young fellow ! " he murmured. " Alas ! monsieur, God is only good to the wicked. Ah ! the world goes from bad to worse. The best thing would be for heaven to send a deluge of gunpowder, then a flash of fire, and there would be an end of it all ! "

" You appear to have been fond of this young fellow ? " observed the abbé.

" Yes, I was indeed," returned Caderousse, " although I have to reproach myself with having for a moment envied his good fortune. But I have—I swear to you on my honour—most truly mourned his unhappy fate. And you knew him."

" I was called in to render him the last consolations of religion," replied the abbé.

" And what did he die of ? "

" Of what is a man likely to die, at the age of thirty, in prison if not of prison itself ? "

Caderousse dried the moisture streaming down his forehead.

" And the strangest thing was, that Dantès, on his death-bed even, swore to me by the name of Christ that he was ignorant of the cause of his imprisonment."

" That is true," murmured Caderousse ; " he could not know it. He did not deceive you in that, monsieur. Poor fellow ! "

" For which reason he charged me to clear up the mystery he had never himself been able to penetrate, and to remove any stigma resting on his good name ; " and the abbé, with a still keener look, fixed his eyes on Caderousse's dark physiognomy.

" A rich Englishman," he continued, " his companion in misfortune, who was let out of prison at the second Restoration, was the possessor of a diamond of great value. When bidding farewell to Dantès, who had tended him like a brother during an illness, he offered him this diamond as a token of gratitude. Dantès, instead of using it as a means of buying over his jailers, who would probably have taken it and betrayed him afterwards, preserved it carefully, in case he might at some future time be let out of prison, when his fortune would be made by the sale of this single diamond."

" Really ? " said Caderousse, with gleaming eyes ; " it was a diamond of great value, then ? "

" Everything is relative," replied the abbé ; " of great value to Edmond, I should say. It was worth, perhaps, fifty thousand francs ; but you shall judge for yourself."

The abbé drew from his pocket a small box of black leather, opened it, and held up to the dazzled gaze of Caderousse the sparkling gem, mounted in a ring of beautiful workmanship.

" And that is worth fifty thousand francs ? "

" Without the mounting, which is in itself of considerable value ; " and the abbé closed the case and put it away in his pocket ; but the diamond still sparkled in Caderousse's memory.

" And how came you to have the diamond in your possession, monsieur ?   Did Edmond make you his heir ? "

" Not his heir, but his executor. ' I have three good friends besides my betrothed,' he said to me ; ' four in all, who will, I am sure, regret me bitterly. One of these good friends is named Caderousse.' The second was called Danglars ; the third, though a rival, was much attached to him."

A diabolical smile passed over Caderousse's face, and he made a movement to interrupt the abbé.

" Wait," said the priest ; " let me finish. The individual, he said, who, though a rival, was yet attached to him, was called Fernando, and the name of the *fiancée* was Mercédès."

" Well ? " said Caderousse.

" Give me a glass of water first."

The abbé filled the glass and swallowed a few mouthfuls.

" Let me see—where were we ? " said he. " Ah ! yes. Then Dantès said to me, ' You must go to Marseillès, sell this diamond, and make an equal division between these five friends, the only beings who have ever loved me in the world.' "

" What ! five shares ? But you have only named four persons," said Caderousse.

" Because the fifth is dead, according to what I hear. The fifth was Dantès' father."

" Alas ! yes," said Caderousse, moved by conflicting emotions ; " yes, poor man ! he is dead."

" I learnt the news at Marseilles," said the abbé, making an effort to appear indifferent ; " but it is so long since his death occurred, that I have not been able to obtain any details of the affair. Perhaps you can enlighten me as to the old man's end ? "

" Ah ! indeed," said Caderousse, " who is likely to know better than I ? I lived in the same house with the old man ; and, alas ! scarcely a year had elapsed after his son's disappearance when he died. Poor old man ! The doctors called his malady gastric fever, I believe ; those who knew him said he died of a broken heart ; but I, who saw him die, say that he died of hunger."

" Of hunger ! " cried the abbé, starting out of his chair—" of hunger ! The vilest animals do not die of hunger. Even the stray dogs in the streets get a morsel of bread thrown to them by some compassionate hand ; and for a man, a Christian, to die of hunger in the midst of other men who call themselves Christians ! impossible ! impossible ! "

" What I have said, I have said," returned Caderousse.

" And all the worse for you ! " cried a voice on the stairs ; " why need you meddle in the matter ? "

The two men turned to look round, and saw through the banisters of the staircase the sickly countenance of Carconte. She had dragged herself so far to listen to the conversation, and was seated on the top step, resting her elbows on her knees.

" What business is it of yours, woman ? " said Caderousse. " This gentleman requests certain information, and politeness compels me to give it him."

" Yes, but prudence should compel you to refuse him. How do you know, you foolish fellow, what reason he may have for making you talk ? "

" A very excellent one, madame, I can assure you," said the abbé ; " your husband has nothing to fear, provided he speaks frankly. No misfortune will come to you through me, I answer for it."

Carconte grumbled a few unintelligible words, dropped her head again on her hands, and leaving her husband free to continue the conversation, placed herself so that she should not lose a word. The abbé meanwhile had swallowed a few mouthfuls of water, and composed himself.

" And was this poor old man," he continued, " so abandoned by all the world that he died such a death ? "

" Oh ! no, monsieur," returned Caderousse ; " he was not abandoned by Mercédès or M. Morrel. But the poor old man took a great antipathy to Fernando, whom Dantès mentioned as one of his friends," continued Caderousse, with an ironical smile.

" Then he was not a friend ? "

" Gaspard, Gaspard ! " called out the woman from the staircase, " take care what you say ! "

" Is one likely to be a friend of the man whose wife one covets, monsieur ? Dantès, who had a heart of gold, called everybody his friend. Poor Edmond ! Well, it is a good thing that he knew nothing about it, or he would have found forgiveness a difficult matter on his death-bed. And whatever people say," continued Caderousse, " I am more afraid of the curse of the dying than of the hatred of the living."

" Imbecile ! " cried Carconte.

" Do you know, then," said the abbé, " what Fernando did to Dantès ? "

" Gaspard, you can do as you like, as you are master ! " exclaimed the woman, " but if you take my advice you will say nothing ! "

" This time I think you are right, wife," said Caderousse.

" Then you will give me no information ? " said the abbé.

" Where is the use ? " said Caderousse. " If the poor fellow were alive, and came among us once more to find out who were his friends and who were his enemies, it would be different ; but now that he is in his grave, he can hate no longer, and cannot avenge himself. So let it all be forgotten."

" Then you allow me to give to these persons, whom you declare to have been false, unworthy friends, a recompense intended only for the faithful ? "

" That is true ; you are right," said Caderousse. " But what would poor Edmond's legacy be to them ?—a mere drop in the ocean."

" And they could crush you in a moment," added his wife.

" Then these individuals have become rich and powerful ? "
Caderousse reflected a moment.

"You are free, of course, to hold your tongue, my friend," said the abbé, with an accent of the profoundest indifference, "and I respect your scruples. We will talk no more about it. I was only charged with a formality. I must now sell the diamond."

And he drew the case again from his pocket, took out the ring and held it up to the admiring gaze of Caderousse.

"Come and look here, wife," cried the innkeeper, in a hoarse voice.

"What, a diamond!" exclaimed Carconte, looking up; and then descending the stairs with a sufficiently firm step, she entered the room. "And what is it for?"

"Did you not hear, woman?" said Caderousse; "it is a diamond bequeathed by poor Edmond to his father, to his three friends, Fernando, Danglars, and I, and to his betrothed, Mercédès. The diamond is worth fifty thousand francs! The fifth of that sum will come to us, monsieur?"

"Yes," said the abbé, "in addition to part of Dantès' father's share, which I imagine I shall have to divide among the four."

"Why among us four?"

"Because you are Edmond's four friends."

"Those that betray are not friends, though!" muttered the woman, in a low voice.

"Yes," said Caderousse, "that is just what I said; it is almost sacrilege, almost profanation, to recompense such treachery and crime!"

"Well, you would have it so," replied the abbé, calmly, putting the diamond back in the pocket of his cassock. "Now give me the address of these friends of Edmond's, so that I may execute his last wishes."

The perspiration rolled in large drops down Caderousse's face, while the abbé turned to the door to give a glance at his horse. The husband and wife looked at each other.

"The diamond would be ours entirely," said he. "A priest would never deceive us."

"Well, do as you like," she answered. "As for me, I will not mix myself up in the affair."

Then, shaking and shivering, she made her way upstairs again. On the top step she paused a moment.

"Think well about it, Gaspard," she cried.

Carconte re-entered her room, a sigh escaping her; her steps were audible as she walked across the floor and threw herself into her chair.

"Well, what have you decided?"

"To tell you everything, monsieur."

"I daresay that is the best thing to do," returned the priest; "not that I wish to know anything that you would conceal from me, but still it is best for you to aid me in distributing the legacy as the testator would have desired."

"Wait one moment," rejoined Caderousse, "we might be interrupted at the most interesting point; besides, it is not necessary for anyone to know that you are here." And he walked to the door, closed it and barred it for the night.

Meantime the abbé had placed himself that he might listen at his ease; he had chosen a corner where, in the shade himself, he could observe his companion's countenance. Then with head bent forward, and hands clasped, or rather clenched, he prepared to listen attentively.

CHAPTER XXVII

THE RECITAL

"BEFORE beginning, monsieur," said Caderousse, "I must beg you to promise that if ever you make any use of the details I am about to give you, you will never divulge that they came from me, for those of whom I shall speak are rich and powerful, and with a fillip of the little finger could annihilate me!"

"Put your mind at rest, my friend," said the abbé; "I am a priest, and all confessions are safe in my keeping. Therefore, speak without reserve, and also without animosity; speak the truth, the whole truth. I belong to God, not to man; and when this business is ended shall return to my convent, which I only quitted to fulfil the last wishes of a dying man!"

This assurance put Caderousse at ease.

"Well," said he, "I will speak out plainly, for I ought to undeceive you regarding these friendships which poor Edmond believed to be so sincere."

"If you please, however, let us begin with his father," said the abbé. "Edmond often spoke to me of the old man, for whom he had a profound affection."

"It is a very sad story, monsieur," said Caderousse, shaking his head; "you probably know the beginning?"

"Yes," replied the abbé, "Edmond related everything to me up to the moment when he was arrested at a small inn near Marseilles."

"At La Réserve! Ah, mon Dieu!—yes. I can see the whole

scene over again. It was at his betrothal feast, and the repast which began so merrily had a sad ending; a commissary and four soldiers entered the room, and Dantès was arrested."

"That is just where my information ceases," said the priest.

"Well, then, as soon as Dantès was arrested, M. Morrel set out to obtain some tidings, and the news he brought was sad indeed. Old Dantès returned alone to his house, put away his wedding finery, weeping as he did so, and passed the rest of the day, and the night too, walking up and down his room, for I lived in the apartment beneath, and could hear his steps. The following morning Mercédès came to Marseilles to implore the protection of M. de Villefort; she gained nothing. At the same time she paid a visit to the old man. When she saw him so dejected and overwhelmed, she wanted him to come home with her, that she might take care of him, but the old man would not consent. 'No,' he said, 'I will not leave this house; for my poor boy loves me beyond anyone, and if he comes out of prison he will be sure to hasten to me first; and what would he say if I were not here to receive him?' I heard all this as I stood on the landing; I was very anxious that Mercédès should persuade the old man to accompany her, for his steps constantly resounding above my head gave me not a moment's rest."

"But did you not yourself go up to the old man and console him?" asked the priest.

"Ah, monsieur, one can only console those who wish to be consoled, and he would accept no consolation; besides, I do not know why, but I fancied he had a dislike to seeing me. One night, however, when I heard his sobs, I could no longer resist, and went up to him; but when I reached the door he was no longer weeping, but praying. I cannot tell you, monsieur, how eloquent were his words, and pitiful his supplications. I could not help saying to myself at that moment, 'It is a happy thing the good God never sent me any children, for if I were a father, and overtaken with such a sorrow as this poor old man's, and sought in vain for the consolation he asks from God, I should fling myself into the sea rather than endure such misery!'"

"Poor father!" murmured the priest.

"As time went on he lived more and more to himself. M. Morrel and Mercédès often came to see him, but his door was always closed; and although he was within he never replied. One day, however, when, contrary to habit, he admitted Mercédès, and the poor girl, though despairing herself, endeavoured to cheer him, he said, ' Believe me, my girl, he is dead ; and instead of awaiting him, it is he who awaits us. I am, happily, the oldest, and shall therefore be the first to see him again.'

" One soon ceases to seek out those who make one sorrowful, however good one is ; and old Dantès was at length left entirely alone. I now never saw anyone going up to him except some unknown persons, who generally came down with a half-concealed bundle. I have since found out what these bundles were : he was selling, little by little, all that he had, for his maintenance. At last the poor man had to part with his clothes ; he owed three quarters' rent, and was threatened with ejectment. He begged for a week's respite, which was granted him. I heard every detail of the matter, because the landlord came into my room after leaving his. For the first three days I heard him pacing up and down, as before, but on the fourth all was silent. I ventured to go upstairs ; the door was closed, but through the keyhole I perceived him looking so pale and exhausted, that thinking he was seriously ill, I informed M. Morrel and hastened to tell Mercédès. Both hurried to the spot. M. Morrel brought a doctor, who declared it was gastric fever, and ordered a low diet. I was present, monsieur, and I shall never forget the old man's smile at this order. Thenceforward he opened the door ; he had now an excuse for not eating : the doctor had put him on a low diet."

The abbé uttered a half-stifled groan.

" At last Mercédès came. She found him so changed that she wished to take him away at once. M. Morrel also advised the same thing, and would have carried him off by force, but the old man cried and protested so much that they were afraid. Mercédès, therefore, remained by his bedside, and M. Morrel retired, with a sign that he had left a purse on the mantelpiece ; but, supported by the doctor's order, the old man persisted in taking nothing. At last, after nine days of despair and abstinence, he breathed his last, cursing those who had caused his misery, and saying to Mercédès, ' If you ever behold Edmond again, tell him that I died blessing him ! ' "

The abbé rose and paced once or twice up and down the room, pressing his trembling hand on his parched lips. " And you believe that he died——"

" Of hunger, monsieur, of hunger," said Caderousse, " on my word as a Christian."

The abbé convulsively seized a glass of water and swallowed it at a draught. " It was a terrible affair," he said.

" All the more so, monsieur, that it was not God's doing, but men's."

" Pass on, then, to these men," said the abbé; " but remember," he ádded, with an almost menacing air, " you promised to tell me everything. Who were these men who caused the son to die of despair and the father of hunger ? "

" Two men who were jealous of him, monsieur ; one through love, the other through ambition—Fernando and Danglars."

" And how did they manifest their ill-feeling ? "

" They denounced Edmond as a Bonapartist agent."

" But which of the two denounced him ? Which was the guilty one ? "

" They were both guilty, monsieur ; Danglars wrote the denunciation at La Réserve, the evening before the marriage, with his left hand to disguise the writing, and Fernando despatched it."

" But," cried the abbé, impulsively, " you were there yourself ! You must have been present to be so familiar with all these details."

" True," said Caderousse, in a stifled voice ; " I was there."

" And why, then, did you not oppose this infamy ? " said the abbé. " You were their accomplice ! "

" Monsieur," returned Caderousse, " they had made me drink so much wine that I had become half-stupefied. I saw everything through a cloud, a sit were. I said everything that a man in such a condition could say, but they both declared it was only a joke."

" But the next day," persisted the abbé, " you must have seen that it *had* been carried out ; yet you said nothing, though you were present when he was arrested."

" That is true, monsieur ; but I wished to tell everything, only Danglars kept me back. ' If he is guilty,' he said to me, ' if he did land at Elba, and undertake to deliver a letter for the Bonapartist Committee in Paris, and this letter is found on him, those who have upheld him will be regarded as his accomplices.' I had a terror of politics at that time, and I held my tongue ; it was cowardly, I acknowledge, but it was not a crime."

" I understand ; you allowed it to be done ; that was all."

" Yes, monsieur ; and it has been a matter of remorse to me night and day. I often pray God's forgiveness for this action, the only one for which I have seriously to reproach myself, and which has, I firmly believe, been the cause of my adversity. I am expiating a moment of selfishness, and thus I often say to Carconte, when she complains, ' It is God's will.' "

"Well," said the abbé, "you have spoken frankly; to acknowledge one's fault thus is to merit pardon."

"Unfortunately, though," said Caderousse, "Edmond is dead, and never pardoned me."

"But he did not know——"

"He knows now, though," returned Caderousse; "they say the dead know all."

The abbé paced the room thoughtfully, then sat down again.

"You have already," said he, "mentioned two or three times a certain M. Morrel. Who was he?"

"The owner of the *Pharaon*; Dantès' master."

"And what part did he play?"

"The part of an honest, courageous, kind-hearted man, monsieur. He interceded for Edmond, time after time. When the Emperor returned, he wrote, entreated, threatened—so much so, that at the second Restoration he was much persecuted for being a Bonapartist. Ten times or more, as I have said, he came to see old Dantès, and to offer to take him away; and he also left money enough to pay all the poor man's debts and meet the expenses of the funeral; so that the old man died as he had lived, without owing anything to any man. I still keep the purse which he left—a large purse of red thread."

"And this M. Morrel, is he still living?" inquired the abbé. "Such a man should indeed be blessed of God. Is he rich—prosperous?"

Caderousse smiled bitterly. "About as prosperous as I am," said he. "He is almost in complete poverty, monsieur; and not only that, but almost on the point of dishonour! After twenty-five years of hard work, and after having held a most honourable position in Marseilles, M. Morrel is ruined. He lost five ships in two years, has been a bankrupt three times, and his only hope is now in this same *Pharaon* that poor Dantès commanded, which is expected from India, laden with cochineal and indigo. If this ship is lost, like the others, he will be ruined."

"Poor fellow!" said the abbé. "Has he a wife and children?"

"Yes, he has a wife, who has borne herself like a saint; he has a daughter who was going to marry a man whom she loved, but the young man's friends object to the match, now that her father is ruined; he has also a son who is a lieutenant in the army. Thus the poor man's troubles are much aggravated. If he had only himself to think of, he would knock his brains out, and there would be an end of it."

"Sad, sad," murmured the priest.

"That is how God rewards virtue, monsieur," continued Caderousse; "for example, I, who never did a bad action besides the one I have confessed to you, am in poverty, and after seeing my poor wife die of fever, without being able to do anything for her, shall probably die of hunger like old Dantès, whilst Fernando and Danglars are rolling in money."

"Indeed!"

"Yes, everything has turned out well with them, whilst with honest people, everything turns out badly."

"What has become of Danglars?—the guiltiest, if not the instigator?"

"He left Marseilles, and on the recommendation of M. Morrel, who was ignorant of his crime, obtained the post of clerk with a Spanish banker. During the war, he was employed in the commissariat of the French army, and made his fortune. Then he speculated in the funds, trebled and quadrupled his capital, and his first wife, the daughter of the banker, having died, he married a widow lady, Madame de Nargonne, daughter of M. Servieux, the king's chamberlain, and an influential personage. Danglars, after becoming a millionaire, was made a baron, and at the present time, my Baron Danglars is living in a large house in the Rue de Mont Blanc, has ten horses in his stables, half-a-dozen lacqueys in his antechamber, and I know not how many millions in his coffers."

"Ah!" said the abbé with a curious accent; "then he is happy?"

"Happy! I don't know. Who can say? Happiness or sorrow is a secret, shut in by four walls; the walls have ears, but they have no tongue. If a large fortune brings happiness, why, Danglars is happy."

"And Fernando?"

"Fernando also has made his way. Fernando, some days before the Emperor's return, was drawn by the conscription. He was left in quiet in the Catalans' quarter, under the Bourbons, but when Napoleon returned, a general conscription was proclaimed, and Fernando was obliged to leave home. He was enrolled in a regiment on active service, and on reaching the frontier, took part in the battle of Ligny. On the night which followed the battle, he was engaged as sentry outside the camp of the general, who was carrying on secret negotiations with the enemy. That very night the general was about to go over to the English. He proposed to Fernando to accompany him; the latter agreed, abandoned his post, and followed his leader into the ranks of the enemy. That affair which would have brought Fernando to a court-martial if Napoleon had remained on the throne, served to raise him in the favour of the Bourbons. He returned to France with a sub-lieutenant's epaulette, and as he was still under the protection of his general, obtained the appointment of captain in 1823, during the Spanish war, just at the time when Danglars was beginning his pecuniary speculations. Fernando was a Spaniard; he was therefore sent to Madrid to study the spirit of his compatriots. He there met Danglars, had interviews with him, promised his general the support of the Royalists in the capital and in the provinces, and having imposed certain stipulations, entered on his own responsibility into engagements, guided his regiment through ways he knew into ravines guarded by Royalists, and finally, in this short campaign, rendered such signal services, that after the surrender of Trocadéro, he was made colonel, and received the cross of the Legion of Honour, with the title of Count."

" Destiny! destiny! " murmured the abbé.

" Yes, but listen; that is not all. The war with Spain ended, Fernando's career was checked by the long peace which promised to be lasting in Europe. Greece alone had risen against Turkey, and had just begun her struggle for independence. Fernando solicited, and obtained permission to enter into the service of Greece, still retaining his position in the French army. Soon afterwards, it was made known that the Count de Morcerf —that was his title—had entered into the service of Ali Pasha, with the rank of lieutenant-general. Ali Pasha was killed, but before he died, he recompensed Fernando for his services, bequeathing him a considerable sum of money, with which Fernando returned to France, where his rank of lieutenant-general was confirmed to him."

" So that now—— ? " interposed the abbé.

" So that now," Caderousse continued, " he possesses a splendid house in Paris, in the Rue de Helder."

The abbé opened his lips, hesitated, then with an effort, inquired, " And Mercédès? Has *she* made a fortune? "

" Mercédès at this moment," returned Caderousse, " is one of the grandest ladies in Paris. At first she was beside herself at the catastrophe which carried off Edmond. I have spoken of the entreaties she addressed to M. de Villefort, and of her devotion to Dantès' father. In the midst of her despair a fresh trouble came to overwhelm her: this was Fernando's departure

—Fernando, of whose crime she was ignorant, and whom she regarded as a brother. He set out, and Mercédès was left alone. Three months passed away, which she spent in continued lamentation. No news of Edmond; no news of Fernando; only the old man for a companion, slowly dying of despair. One evening, after having been seated the whole day, as was her habit, at the corner of the two roads from Marseilles and the Catalan village, she returned home more disheartened than she had ever been before. Suddenly she thought she heard a familiar step, and, as the door opened, beheld Fernando in his lieutenant's uniform. Though it was not all she wanted, it was a portion of her past life returned to her. She had never disliked Fernando, only she had not loved him; that was all. Another had possession of her heart, another who had disappeared—was dead, perhaps! As this last thought occurred to her, Mercédès burst into tears; for this idea, which she had repelled when suggested to her by anyone else, now returned to her with full force. Moreover, the old man had never ceased to say to her, ' Our Edmond is dead; if he were not he would return to us.' If the old man had lived, perhaps Mercédès would never have become the wife of another. Fernando felt this. When he heard of the old man's death he returned. He was now a lieutenant. On his first visit he had not breathed a word to Mercédès of his love; he now told her that he loved her. She begged for six months longer in which to mourn her Edmond."

" In point of fact," said the abbé, with a bitter smile, " it was eighteen months altogether. What more could the most adoring lover desire ? "

" Six months later," continued Caderousse, " the marriage took place at the church of Accoules."

" Ah, at the same church where she would have married Edmond," muttered the priest; " a change of bridegroom, that was all."

" Mercédès was married there," continued Caderousse. " But though to a casual observer she appeared calm enough, she nearly fainted as she passed La Réserve, where, eighteen months before, her betrothal had been celebrated with him whom she still loved. Fernando, though happy, was not at ease, for I could see that he was in constant dread of Edmond's return. He was anxious to get his wife away from the place, and to quit it himself. A week, therefore, after the wedding they departed."

" And did you ever see Mercédès again ? " inquired the priest.

' Yes, I saw her during the war at Perpignan, where Fernando had left her; she was then engaged in the education of her son."

" Her son ! "

" Yes," Caderousse rejoined, " the little Albert."

" But to instruct this son she must have received some education herself. I fancy from what Edmond intimated to me, that she was the daughter of a simple fisherman, beautiful, but uncultured."

" Oh ! " exclaimed Caderousse, " did he know his own bride no better than that ? Mercédès might have been a queen, monsieur, if crowns were only intended for the most beautiful and most intelligent heads ! As her fortune increased, so she increased in dignity and refinement. She learnt drawing, music, and many accomplishments. I believe, between ourselves, that she studied as a means of distraction from painful thoughts, and that she filled her brain that she might the better conquer her heart. But now, doubtless, wealth and honours have consoled her. She is rich, she is a countess—and yet——I am sure that she is not happy."

" Why do you think so ? "

" Well, when I first became unfortunate myself, I thought that my old friends would perhaps help me. I went to Danglars' house, but he would not even receive me. I went to Fernando, who sent me a hundred francs by his valet. But Madame de Morcerf saw me as I was leaving the house; a purse containing twenty-five louis fell at my feet. I looked up quickly, and beheld Mercédès drawing down the blind."

" And what has become of M. de Villefort ? " inquired the abbé.

" I only know that some time after the arrest he married Mademoiselle de Saint Méran, and then quitted Marseilles. Doubtless fortune has smiled on him as on the others; he is probably rich, like Danglars, and highly esteemed, like Fernando. I alone, as you see, am poor, miserable, and forsaken of God."

" You are deceived, my friend," said the abbé. " God appears sometimes to forsake when His justice is only delayed ; but a moment always comes when He remembers, and here is a proof." And with these words the abbé drew the diamond from his pocket, and presenting it to Caderousse, said, " Here, my friend, take this diamond ; it is yours."

" What ! mine ? " cried Caderousse. " Oh, monsieur, you are joking ! "

" No, this diamond was to have been divided between his

friends. Edmond, it seems, has but one friend, therefore the division cannot be made. Take the diamond, and sell it. It is worth fifty thousand francs, and this sum I hope will suffice to relieve your poverty."

" Oh, monsieur," said Caderousse, " do not make a joke of the happiness or despair of a poor fellow."

" I know what happiness and misery mean too well," returned the abbé, " to amuse myself at the expense of others. Take it, and in exchange give me that purse that M. Morrel left on old Dantès' mantelpiece, and which you said you still have in your keeping."

Caderousse walked up to an old oak cupboard, and took from it a long purse of red silk edged with tarnished gilt rings. The abbé took it, and then handed the diamond to Caderousse.

" Oh ! you are indeed a man of God, monsieur," cried Caderousse, " for no one knew that Edmond had given you this diamond, and you might have kept it."

The abbé rose and took up his hat and gloves.

" Then," said he, " everything that you have told me is true, and I can believe it implicitly ? "

" Listen, monsieur," said Caderousse. " Here in this corner is a crucifix, and on that trunk is my wife's Bible ; open it, and I will swear to you by its precious pages, with my hand extended towards the crucifix, on the salvation of my soul, and my faith as a Christian, that I have told you everything as it occurred, and as it will be known in the Day of Judgment ! "

" Good ! " said the abbé, convinced by his accent that Caderousse spoke the truth. " Good ! May the money be a blessing to you ! Farewell ; I shall now leave the haunts of men who work each other such evil."

And the abbé proceeded to unfasten the door. He mounted his horse, followed by the confused and exuberant protestations of the innkeeper, and started off, returning the same way that he had come. When Caderousse re-entered the house he found Carconte pale and trembling.

" Is all this true that I hear ? " she asked. " That he has given us the diamond entirely ? "

" Nothing can be more true—here it is ! "

" But supposing it is a mock one ? "

Caderousse turned pale. " Why should this man give me a mock diamond ? "

" To get your secret out of you, imbecile ! "

Caderousse paused a moment, stunned by the terrible idea.

"Oh !" he cried, at last, seizing his hat. "I will find out at once. There is a fair at Beaucaire, and some jewellers will be there from Paris ; I will show it to them. You, wife, take care of the house ; in two hours I shall be back."

Caderousse darted out of the house, in the opposite direction to that which the stranger had taken.

"Fifty thousand francs," murmured Carconte, "it is a good lump of money, but still it is not a fortune."

CHAPTER XXVIII

THE PRISON REGISTERS

On the day following that on which the scene at the wayside inn occurred, a man of about thirty years of age, dressed in a blue frock-coat, nankeen trousers and a white waistcoat, and having both the appearance and manner of an Englishman, presented himself before the mayor of Marseilles.

"Monsieur," said he, "I am the chief clerk of the firm of Thomson and French, at Rome. We have been connected in business with the firm of Morrel and Son, of Marseilles, for the last ten years. As we have about a hundred thousand francs at stake in these relations, we are uneasy at hearing that this establishment is on the brink of ruin. I have come, therefore, expressly from Rome to ask you to give me some particulars as to this firm."

"Monsieur," replied the mayor, "I am aware that, for four or five years, ill-luck has appeared to pursue M. Morrel. But it is not my business, though I myself am his creditor to the extent of ten thousand francs, to give any information as to his pecuniary position. Ask me, as mayor, my opinion of M. Morrel, and I can tell you that he is a man of most rigid honesty, who, up to the present time, has fulfilled his engagements in a strictly honourable manner. But that is all I can tell you, monsieur ; if you wish to know more, you must address yourself to M. de Boville, inspector of prisons, 15, Rue de Noailles. He has, I believe, two hundred thousand francs in Morrel's business, and as this sum is more considerable than my own, if there is anything to fear, you will find him better informed on the matter than I am."

The Englishman, appearing fully to appreciate this scrupulous delicacy, bowed, and withdrew, proceeding without delay to the address just mentioned.

M. de Boville was in his study. The Englishman, as he was ushered in, gave a slight start of surprise, which seemed to indicate that it was not the first time he beheld the individual before him. As to M. de Boville, he was in such a condition of mental distraction, that it was evident his whole faculties were absorbed in the thought that just then possessed him, leaving neither his memory nor imagination free to wander back to the past. The Englishman, with the phlegm characteristic of his nationality, stated his question in much the same terms as those he had used to the mayor of Marseilles.

" Oh ! monsieur," cried M. de Boville, " your fears are, unfortunately, only too well founded, and you see before you a ruined man ! I had placed two hundred thousand francs in the firm of Morrel ; this sum was to have been my daughter's dowry, who is to be married in a fortnight, and one hundred thousand was payable on the fifteenth of this month, the remainder on the fifteenth of next month. I notified to M. Morrel that I desired these payments made punctually ; and now, he has only just been here, monsieur, to tell me that if his vessel, the *Pharaon*, does not come into port by the 15th, he will not be able to meet the debt."

" You regard this debt with considerable apprehension ? "

" I regard it as lost."

" Well, then, I will purchase it from you."

" You ? But at a large discount ? "

" No ; for two hundred thousand francs ; our establishment," the Englishman added, laughing, " does not do business in that way."

And the Englishman drew from his pocket a bundle of bank notes, amounting, probably, to double the sum that M. de Boville feared to lose.

" Monsieur, I ought to warn you that, in all probability, you will not get six per cent. of the money."

" That is not my affair," said the Englishman ; " that concerns only Thomson and French, in whose name I am acting. But, monsieur, here I am, ready to count out this money for the transfer. I only ask a brokerage."

" Certainly, monsieur, that is only right ! " cried M. de Boville. " The commission is generally one and a half. Perhaps you wish two, three—five per cent ? What do you demand ? "

" Monsieur," returned the Englishman, " I am like my firm, and do not carry on business in that manner ; no, my request is of quite another nature. You are, I believe, an inspector of

G

prisons, and have possession of the registers of entries, etc. ? Now, I must tell you, monsieur, that I was educated at Rome by a poor fellow, the Abbé Faria, who suddenly disappeared. I have since learnt that he was imprisoned in the Château d'If, and I wish to obtain some information as to his death."

" I recollect him perfectly," cried M. de Boville; " he was mad. He pretended he knew of the existence of an immense treasure, and offered unheard of sums to the government if they would set him at liberty."

" Poor fellow ! And he is really dead ? "

" Yes, monsieur ; about six months back, last February, I believe. I recollect it because the poor fellow's death was connected with a singular circumstance. The fact is, the abbé's cell was separated by a distance of forty-five to fifty feet from that of a Bonapartist agent, one of those who contributed most to the Usurper's return in 1815. I had occasion to see this man myself, in 1816 or 1817, and we had then to go down to his cell with a guard of soldiers. He made a profound impression on me, and I will never forget his face."

The Englishman smiled perceptibly.

" And you were saying, monsieur," he rejoined, " that the two cells——"

" Were separated by a distance of fifty feet ; but it appears that this dangerous fellow, Edmond Dantès, managed to provide himself with tools, for a passage was discovered by means of which the prisoners communicated with each other."

" This passage, I suppose, had been made with the object of escaping ? "

" Exactly ; but unfortunately for the prisoners, the Abbé Faria was seized with a fit of catalepsy and died."

" Ah ! and so put an end to the project of escape ? "

" For the dead man, yes," replied M. de Boville ; " but not for the living one. On the contrary, Dantès found in it but a means of hastening his flight ; he no doubt thought that the prisoners who died in the Château d'If were buried in an ordinary cemetery ; he therefore conveyed the corpse to his own cell, placed himself in the sack in which the body had been concealed, and awaited the moment of removal."

" That was a hazardous proceeding, and indicated some courage," said the Englishman.

" Ah ! as I told you, monsieur, he was a very dangerous character ; happily, however, he himself has relieved the government of any further apprehensions on his behalf. The Château d'If has no burying-ground; the dead are thrown into the sea with a thirty-six pound ball tied to their feet."

"Well?" ejaculated the Englishman.

"Well, they tied a ball to Dantès' feet, and threw him into the sea."

"You don't say so," exclaimed the Englishman.

"Yes, monsieur," continued the inspector, "and you may imagine what must have been the surprise of the prisoner, when he felt himself hurled over the rocks. I should like to have beheld his face at that moment. I can picture it to myself!" and he laughed heartily.

"So can I," exclaimed the Englishman, and he, too, burst out laughing, but, like the English, with shut teeth. "So," he remarked, being the first to recover from the fit of hilarity, "so the fugitive was drowned, I suppose. And the governor of the Château was relieved at one and the same time of a dangerous prisoner and of a madman?"

"He was."

"But I suppose there was some statement drawn up of the affair?"

"Yes, a certificate of death. You see, Dantès' relations, if he had any, might be interested to know if he were living or dead."

"So that they might inherit anything from him, I presume? Then he is positively dead?"

"Oh! Mon Dieu! yes. And the certificate can be handed to them whenever they want it."

"Good!" said the Englishman. "Now let us return to the subject of the registers."

"Ah! yes, pardon; this little story has caused a digression. And now you wish to learn everything relating to the poor abbé, who certainly was gentleness itself? Come with me into my private room and I will show you the register;" and M. de Boville rose and led the way into the next apartment.

The inspector requested the Englishman to be seated; and placing the register and documents relating to the Château d'If in front of him, left him to look them over at his leisure.

The visitor speedily found the certificate relating to the Abbé Faria; but the story which M. de Boville had related, appeared to have greatly interested him, for he turned over the papers, until he came to the bundle of documents concerning Edmond Dantès.

There everything lay before him; the accusation, the examination, and Morrel's petition, countersigned by De Villefort.

He quietly folded up the paper containing the accusation, and put it in his pocket, read the account of the examination, observing that the name of Noirtier had been omitted, and glanced at the petition dated April, 1815, in which Morrel, following the deputy's advice, exaggerated with the best intentions the services Dantès had rendered to the Imperial cause, services which the signature of De Villefort also endorsed.

Everything now was plain to him. This petition to Napoleon, kept back by De Villefort, had become, at the second Restoration, a most powerful weapon in the hands of the deputy procureur.

As he slowly turned over the pages, he was no longer astonished to find this marginal note opposite his name—

EDMOND DANTÈS. { Violent Bonapartist; took an active part in the return from Elba. To be kept in secret confinement, and under the strictest superintendence.

Below these lines was another note in a different handwriting— "Nothing to be done."

On comparing the writing in the margin with that of the certificate, the investigator felt convinced that they were both by De Villefort. As to the added note, it must have been registered by some inspector who took a passing interest in Dantès, and, on reading the certificate given above, had found it impossible to move in the matter.

The inspector, busily engaged in reading *Le Drapeau Blanc*, did not observe the English gentleman abstract the accusation written by Danglars in the arbour of La Réserve, bearing the postmark of Marseilles, February 27th. But probably, if he had, he would have attached too little importance to the document, and too great importance to his two hundred thousand francs, to offer any opposition.

" Thank you," said the English gentleman, rising at last, and closing the register, noisily. " I have quite finished, and now I have to fulfil my promise ; write out the statement of the debt, and a receipt for the cash, and I will hand it over to you ; " and he relinquished his seat at the desk to M. de Boville, who drew up the required document, while the stranger counted over his bank notes on the table.

CHAPTER XXIX

THE FIRM OF MORREL

ANYONE who had known M. Morrel's office in the days of its prosperity, now entering it after a long absence, would hardly have recognized it as the same establishment. Instead of that atmosphere of bustle and excitement which permeates a flourishing house of business there was now only a scene of depressing desolation. Of the numerous employés two only remained. One of these was a young man of about four and twenty, named Emanuel Raymond, the affianced lover of M. Morrel's daughter. The other was an old one-eyed cashier, bearing the name of Coclès, a *sobriquet* invented by the young people who formerly thronged this business hive.

Coclès had remained in M. Morrel's service; but a singular change had come over his position. He had, at the same time, risen to the post of cashier and descended to that of servant. In the midst of the general calamities that had overtaken Morrel's establishment, Coclès was the only one who remained immovable. But do not let my readers imagine that this arose from any want of affection on his part : it proceeded, on the contrary, from an unshaken conviction.

He had been for twenty years in the house of M. Morrel, and had always seen the payments coming in with regularity. The last month's balance had been made with rigorous exactness.

Coclès had discovered an error made by M. Morrel of seventy centimes to his own prejudice, and had brought them to his master, who, with a melancholy smile, had taken them from him, and tossed them into a nearly empty drawer, saying, " Thanks, Coclès ; you are a jewel of a cashier."

But since the end of last month, when they had made such a successful struggle, M. Morrel had passed through many painful hours. In order to meet his next payments, he had collected all his resources and, fearing that the rumour of his distress might spread in Marseilles when he was seen to have recourse to such extremities, had made an expedition to the fair at Beaucaire, to sell some jewels belonging to his wife and daughter, and a part of his plate. By means of this sacrifice, he was still enabled to meet his liabilities, but the cash-box remained empty.

Matters were in this condition, when the clerk from the firm of Thomson and French presented himself at M. Morrel's establishment. Emanuel received him. The young man was anxious, if possible, to spare his patron the annoyance of an interview. He therefore questioned the new-comer ; but the stranger declared that he had nothing to say to M. Emanuel, that it was to M. Morrel in person he wished to speak. Emanuel sighed, and called Coclès. On the staircase they met a beautiful young girl, of about seventeen, who regarded the stranger with uneasiness.

Coclès did not appear to notice her expression, which, however, did not escape the visitor's observation.

"M. Morrel is in his study, is he not, Mademoiselle Julie?" inquired the cashier.

"Yes; at least I think so," said the young girl, with hesitation; "you had better see first, Coclès, and if my father is there, announce this gentleman."

"It will be of no use to announce me, mademoiselle," replied the English stranger; "this gentleman need only say that I am the head clerk from Thomson and French, of Rome."

The young lady turned pale, passed on downstairs, and entered the office where Emanuel had remained. In the meantime Coclès opened a door in the corner of the landing on the second floor, and leaving the stranger in an ante-room, opened a second door, which he closed behind him. He soon reappeared, and beckoned the stranger to enter.

M. Morrel was seated at a table, looking through some ledgers, and calculating his liabilities with pale, disconsolate looks. Fourteen years had wrought a great change in the appearance of the worthy merchant, who was now in his fiftieth year. His hair had turned white, his brow was wrinkled with lines of care, and his expression, formerly so energetic and decided, was now vague and irresolute, as though it were a trouble to him to determine on anything. The English gentleman regarded him with an expression of curiosity mingled with interest.

"Monsieur," said Morrel, the gaze of the stranger appearing to increase his uneasiness, "you desired to speak to me?"

"Yes, monsieur; you are aware, I believe by whom I am sent?"

"By Messrs. Thomson and French; at least so my cashier tells me."

"He tells you the truth, monsieur. Thomson and French have, in the course of this month and next, to pay off about 400,000 francs in France and, knowing how prompt your payments are, they have obtained every bill that came in their way bearing your signature, and have directed me, as those bills become due, to draw the money from you at once."

"What is the amount?" inquired the shipowner in a voice which he strove to render firm.

"First of all," said the stranger, drawing a bundle of papers from his pocket, "there is an assignment of 200,000 francs made to our house by M. de Boville, inspector of prisons. You, of course, acknowledge this debt?"

" Certainly, monsieur ; he deposited it with me, at four and a half per cent., nearly five years ago."

" And which you have to meet——"

" Half on the fifteenth of this month, and half on the fifteenth of next month."

" Exactly. Then, here are bills amounting to 32,500 francs ; they are all signed by you, and handed over to us by the holders."

" I recognize them," said Morrel, " and is this all ? "

" No, monsieur ; I have, besides these, securities of 287,500 francs in all."

It is impossible to describe the sufferings of the unfortunate Morrel during this enumeration of his liabilities.

" 287,500 francs," he repeated mechanically.

" Yes, monsieur," replied the Englishman ; " and I cannot conceal from you, M. Morrel, that public rumour in Marseilles declares that you are not in a condition to meet your liabilities."

At this almost brutal speech Morrel turned pale.

" Monsieur," said he, " up to the present time not a single bill signed by Morrel and Son has ever been presented to us without being honoured."

" Yes, I am aware of that," replied the Englishman ; " but can you meet these liabilities with the same promptness ? "

Morrel trembled, but nevertheless regarded the speaker with more assurance than he had previously shown.

" Yes, monsieur, I can meet them if, as I venture to hope, my vessel arrives safely in port. But if, through any accident, the *Pharaon*, my last resource, should be lost I shall be forced to suspend payment."

" Have you no friends who can help you in this strait ? "

Morrel smiled sadly.

" In matters like these, as you know, monsieur, one has no friends, only correspondents."

" Just as I was coming to you I believe a vessel did come into port," observed the stranger.

" I know it, monsieur. I heard of the arrival of a ship."

" And is it not yours ? "

" No, it is a Bordeaux vessel, *La Gironde*."

" Perhaps the crew may bring news of the *Pharaon*, though."

" To tell you the truth, monsieur, I am almost as much afraid of hearing news of my three-master as of remaining in suspense. As long as suspense lasts there is hope."

" What is that ? " said the Englishman, listening ; " what is the meaning of that noise ? "

There were, in fact, sounds of a great disturbance on the staircase, steps hurrying to and fro, and then a cry of lamentation.

The two men remained facing each other, Morrel trembling in every limb, the stranger regarding him with an expression of profound pity. A key was placed in the lock, and the outer door opened. Almost immediately the second door opened, and the young girl appeared, looking very pale, and her cheeks wet with tears.

" Oh, father ! " cried the young girl, clasping her hands, " pardon your child for being the messenger of bad news ! "

Morrel turned terribly pale and Julie threw herself in his arms.

" Then the *Pharaon* has foundered ? " said Morrel, in a stifled voice.

The girl said nothing, but nodding sadly in the affirmative, laid her head on her father's breast.

" And the crew ? " asked Morrel.

" Are saved," she replied, " saved by the Bordeaux vessel that has just come into the harbour."

Morrel raised his clasped hands to heaven with an expression of resignation and gratitude that was sublime.

" I thank Thee, my God," he murmured, " at least Thou strikest me only ! "

Phlegmatic as was the Englishman, a tear moistened his eyelids.

" Come in all of you," said Morrel, at last, " for I presume you are waiting outside."

Scarcely had he spoken when Madame Morrel entered weeping bitterly. Emanuel followed her and, at the back of the ante-room, the bronzed, rugged faces of seven or eight sailors were visible.

" How did it happen ? " inquired Morrel.

" Come forward, Penelon," said the young man, " and give the particulars of the event."

Penelon turned over a quid of tobacco in his mouth, put one foot forward, and balancing himself to and fro, began his story.

" Well, then, Monsieur Morrel, I must tell you that we were somewhere between Cape Blanc and Cape Boyador, sailing with a pretty stiff breeze from south-south-west, after nearly a week's calm, when Captain Gaumard came up to me as I was standing at the helm, and said, ' Penelon, what do you think of those clouds over there on the horizon ? ' ' What do I think, captain ? ' said I. ' I think they are rising much more quickly than they have any right to do.' ' That is my opinion also,' said the captain. ' Halloa there ! slacken sail and lower the flying jib ! ' It was quite time ; the order was only just executed when the gale was on us and the vessel began to heel. ' Good,' said the captain ; ' but we have still too much canvas. All hands to lower the mainsail ! ' Five minutes later, and the mainsail was lowered, and we had now only the topsails and topgallant sails. ' Well, Penelon,' said the captain to me, ' why are you shaking your head ? ' ' I'll tell you what it is, captain,' said I, ' it will be a tremendous tempest, or I do not know my own name ; ' and as I spoke the wind came on us like the dust at Montredon. Happily the captain knew what he was about. ' All hands to take in two reefs in the topsails,' he cried, ' let go the bow lines, brace to, and lower the topgallant sails ! ' "

" That was not enough in those waters," observed the Englishman. " I should have taken in four reefs and lowered the mizen."

Everyone started at the unexpected interruption, uttered in a firm, decided voice.

" We did better than that, monsieur," said the old seaman, respectfully, " for we struck topsails and set the helm to run before the wind. Ten minutes later we scudded along under bare poles."

" The boat was rather old to risk that," observed the Englishman.

" Ah ! that was just what lost us ! We sprang a leak. ' Penelon,' said the captain to me, ' I believe we shall sink, old man ; give me the helm, and do you go down to the hold.' I gave up my place at the helm and went below ; there were already three feet of water. I ran up again, crying, ' To the pumps ! to the pumps ! ' But, alas ! it was already too late ! We set to work, but the faster we pumped out, the faster it came in."

" Well ? " said the Englishman.

"The water rose continually—not more than two inches an hour, perhaps, but still it rose. At last the captain said, ' Come ! we have done enough, and M. Morrel cannot reproach us for anything. Let down the long-boat, my boys, at once ! '

" You see, M. Morrel," continued Penelon, " though we all loved the *Pharaon*, yet, however much a sailor loves his ship, he loves himself better. Therefore, in a twinkling, the long-boat was launched, and we all eight got into it. The captain left the last; but, no ! I should say rather that he would not leave ; but I seized him round the waist and threw him over to my comrades, and then jumped down after him. We were just in time. As I leaped from the vessel, there was a fearful crash, like a broadside from a man-of-war. Brrou ! it was all over ! As for us sailors, we had been three days without eating or drinking when we sighted *La Gironde.* We signalled; she saw us, made immediately towards us, let down her boat, and took us all on board. That is how it all came about, M. Morrel, on my word of honour as a sailor!"

"Well, my friends," said M. Morrel, "you are brave fellows, and I knew from the beginning that I had only destiny to blame for my misfortune. Now tell me how much pay is owing to you?"

"Well, there is three months' pay owing to us," said Penelon.

"Coclès, pay two hundred francs to each of these brave fellows. At any other time, my friends, I should have added 'and give them each a gratuity of two hundred francs'—but the times are bad, and the little money I have left does not belong to me. Excuse me, therefore, and do not love me the less."

Penelon pulled a compassionate grimace, turned towards his companions and, having interchanged a few words, came forward again.

"The fact is, monsieur, my comrades all say that, for the time being, they will have enough with fifty francs each, and that they will wait for the rest."

"Thank you, thank you, my friends," cried M. Morrel, touched to the heart; "you are indeed good-hearted fellows; but take the money, and if a good opening occurs you are free to leave my service."

The latter part of this speech produced a mighty effect on the worthy mariners. They looked at each other in a scared manner. Penelon, almost breathless with surprise, narrowly escaped swallowing his quid.

"What, Monsieur Morrel!" cried he, in a stifled voice. "What! you dismiss us—you are dissatisfied with us?"

"No, my brave fellows," said the shipowner, "no, I am not dissatisfied with you, quite the contrary, and I am not dismissing you. But what can I do? I have no more ships and I need no more sailors."

"What! you have no more ships?" replied Penelon. "Well, then, you will have some others built, and we can wait, thank God!"

"But I have no money for building any more ships, Penelon," said the shipowner, with a melancholy smile. "I cannot, therefore, accept your offer, though it is so kindly meant."

"Well, if you have no money, why do you pay us? We shall only be like the poor *Pharaon*, going along under bare poles."

"Enough, enough, my friends," said Morrel, struggling with his emotion. "Now go, I beg of you at once. Things will perhaps right themselves in time. You, Emanuel, go with these good fellows and see that my wishes are carried out."

And the shipowner signed to Coclès, who led the way.

" Now," said Morrel to his wife and daughter, " leave me for a moment ; I have to speak with this gentleman." And he glanced towards the agent of Thomson and French.

The two women raised their eyes to look at the stranger, whom they had completely forgotten, and then withdrew from the room.

" Now, monsieur," said Morrel, dropping back into his chair, " you have seen all, and heard all, and nothing remains for me to tell you."

" I have seen, monsieur," replied the Englishman, " that a fresh misfortune, as unmerited as the others, has overtaken you, and it has confirmed in me the desire to do you a kindness."

" Oh, monsieur ! " cried Morrel.

" Let me see," continued the stranger, " I am one of your principal creditors ; is it not so ? "

" You are, at any rate, the one who possesses bills expiring at the earliest date."

" You wish for a delay in paying me ? "

" A delay would save my honour and consequently my life."

" How long do you require ? "

Morrel hesitated.

" Two months," said he

" Good," said the stranger. " I give you three. Renew all these bills till the 5th of September ; and on the 5th of September, at eleven o'clock in the morning—that is the time now—I will present myself to you."

" I shall expect you, monsieur," said Morrel, " and you shall be paid, or I shall die ! "

These last words he uttered under his breath and the stranger could not hear them.

The bills were then renewed, the old ones destroyed, and the poor shipowner found himself with at least three months before him to collect his scattered resources.

On the staircase the stranger encountered Mademoiselle Julie. The young girl appeared to be descending, but in reality she had been awaiting him.

" Oh, monsieur ! " said she, clasping her hands.

" Mademoiselle," said he, " you will receive some day a letter signed Sindbad the Sailor. Do exactly, point for point, what this letter tells you, however strange it may appear."

" Yes, monsieur," said Julie.

" Good ! And now farewell, mademoiselle. Remain always the good girl you are, and I doubt not God will reward you by giving you Emanuel for a husband."

The stranger passed on downstairs, waving his hand in adieu. In the court he met Penelon, who held a hundred francs in each hand, seeming undecided as to carrying them away.

" Come, along with me, my friend," said the English gentleman, " I wish to speak to you."

CHAPTER XXX

THE FIFTH OF SEPTEMBER

THE respite granted by the agent of the firm of Thomson and French at the moment when Morrel least expected it, appeared to the shipowner one of those spells of good fortune which indicate to a man that ill luck has at last given up pursuing him. When he thought over the matter, he could not in the least understand the generous conduct displayed towards him by Messrs. Thomson and French. He could only explain it to himself on the grounds that this apparently friendly firm had been determined in their course of action by the selfish reflection : " Better try to sustain a man who owes us nearly 300,000 francs, and have the 300,000 francs at the end of three months, than hasten his ruin and have the paltry remnant of his capital."

Unfortunately, either from uncharitableness or blindness to their own interests, all M. Morrel's correspondents were not influenced by a similar conviction. The opinion of the business community of Marseilles was that he could not stand against the successive reverses that had overtaken him. Great then was the astonishment when at the end of the month he was seen to be meeting his debts with customary promptness.

Nevertheless, confidence was far from being generally restored, and it was almost a unanimous opinion that at the end of the following month his balance-sheet would show a large deficit.

The month passed, and the most incredible efforts were made on the part of Morrel to unite all his scattered resources. Formerly, any bill of his, of whatever date, had been accepted with confidence, or even alacrity. He now tried to negotiate bills at ninety days, but found every bank closed. Happily, however, he could count on some ready money shortly to be paid in to him, and he thus found himself prepared in a measure to meet his engagements when the end of July approached.

On the other hand, the clerk from the firm of Thomson and French had never been seen again in Marseilles ; and as to the sailors of the *Pharaon*, it appeared as though they had taken some other engagement, for they had all disappeared.

August passed in ceaseless attempts on the part of Morrel to renew his former credit. It was known at Marseilles that on the 20th of August he had taken a place in the mail-coach ; and the rumour was current that at the end of the month payments would be finally suspended, and that Morrel had left beforehand in order not to be present on such a trying occasion, leaving everything doubtless to his cashier, Coclès, and his head clerk, Emanuel. But, in spite of all these prophecies, when the 31st of August came round, the establishment opened for business as usual. Coclès appeared behind the grating, calm and immovable, examined the bills presented to him with the same attention, and paid them from first to last with the same punctuality. The public could not understand it at all, and with the tenacity peculiar to prophets of bad news, postponed the expected bankruptcy to the end of September.

On the first of the month Morrel returned from Paris. He was awaited by his family with great anxiety, for it was hoped this journey might have some happy result.

It had occurred to Morrel that he might possibly receive some assistance from Danglars, now a millionaire, and formerly under obligations to him for the recommendation to the Spanish banker through whom Danglars had amassed such a large fortune.

The worthy shipowner had for some time thought of applying to Danglars, but, held back by an instinct of repulsion he could not account for, had delayed as long as possible having recourse to this last means of relief. He had been right in his apprehensions, for he now returned overwhelmed by the humiliation of a refusal. Yet he breathed not a word of complaint or recrimination, but shut himself in his private room, ordering Coclès to be sent to him.

" Now," said the two women to Emanuel, " we are indeed lost."

Then, in a short consultation, it was agreed that Julie should write to her brother, who was in garrison at Nîmes, begging him to come at once. The poor women felt instinctively that they had need of every friendly presence to support them under the threatening blow. Moreover, Maximilian Morrel, though scarcely twenty-two, had great influence with his father. He was a steady, upright young man, and when there had been a question as to the choice of his career, his father had allowed him freely to consult his own taste.

Maximilian had declared that he would enter the military profession ; he had, therefore, studied hard, and gone through the course at the École Polytechnique, leaving it as sub-lieutenant of the 53rd of the line. For a year he had held this grade, with the early prospect of being promoted to lieutenant.

In the regiment, Maximilian Morrel was known as a rigid observer of every duty pertaining to an honourable man, and had earned the appellation of " the Stoic."

Such was the young man whom his mother and sister now called to their assistance, to sustain them in the grave position in which they were placed. They were not deceived as to the gravity of the situation ; almost immediately after M. Morrel had entered his room with Coclès, the latter had been seen by Mademoiselle Julie coming out again, pale and trembling, and looking extremely disturbed. A moment later, the young girl saw him return, carrying two or three large ledgers, a portfolio, and a bag of money.

Morrel consulted the registers, opened the portfolio, and counted the money. His entire resources amounted to 14,000 francs, with which to meet a debt of 287,500 francs.

At dinner Morrel appeared tolerably calm ; but this calmness terrified the two ladies more than the most profound distress would have done. Night came. The two women remained watching, hoping that, as he left his room, Morrel might look in upon them ; but they heard him pass the door, as softly as possible, doubtless to avoid being called. They listened ; he entered his room and closed the door.

Madame Morrel sent her daughter to bed, then half an hour afterwards, she rose, took off her slippers, and gliding along the corridor, looked through the keyhole to see what her husband was doing. In the corridor she noticed a figure hastily retiring It was Julie, who now approached her mother.

" He is writing," she said.

The same thought occurred to them both—that he was making his will.

The following morning, M. Morrel still appeared perfectly calm ; he remained as usual in his study, only taking his breakfast with the family, but after dinner, in the evening, he called his daughter to sit beside him, embraced her, and made her rest her head upon his breast.

The same evening, Julie remarked to her mother, that though

her father appeared outwardly so calm, she had noticed that his heart was beating violently. Two more days passed in much the same fashion. On the evening of the 4th of September, M. Morrel demanded from his daughter the key of his room. Julie started at the request, which seemed to her ominous. Why should her father ask for this key, which she had always kept, and which had only been taken from her, as a child, to punish her ?

She glanced at him.

" Ah ! I have left it in my room," she said, and went out ; but instead of going to her own apartment, she hastened downstairs to consult Emanuel.

" Do not give up that key to your father," said he, " and tomorrow morning, if possible, do not leave him."

The girl tried to question her lover, but he could, or rather would say no more.

Until three o'clock in the morning Madame Morrel heard her husband pacing up and down the room in an agitated manner. At last he threw himself on his bed. The two sorrowful women spent the night together. Since the previous evening they had been expecting Maximilian.

At eight o'clock in the morning, M. Morrel came down. He was calm, but the agitation of the night was plainly written on his pale, worn countenance. Morrel seemed kinder to his wife, and more loving to his daughter than he had ever been.

Julie recalled Emanuel's advice, and when her father went out, endeavoured to accompany him ; but he put her aside gently.

" Remain with your mother," he said.

It was the first time Morrel had ever spoken to his daughter so decidedly, but his manner was so full of paternal affection that Julie dared not resist him.

A moment later, the door suddenly opened, she felt herself clasped in two arms, and a kiss imprinted on her forehead. She looked up and uttered an exclamation of joy.

" Maximilian ! my brother ! " she cried.

Hearing her exclamation, Madame Morrel hastened into the room and threw herself into her son's arms.

" Julie," said Madame Morrel, with a sign to the young man, " inform your father that Maximilian has arrived."

The young girl darted out of the room, but on the staircase she met a man with a letter in his hand.

" You are Mademoiselle Julie, I believe ? " said the man, with a pronounced Italian accent.

" Yes, monsieur," said Julie.

" Read this letter," said the man. " It concerns your fatner's safety."

The young girl tore the letter out of his hands, quickly opened it, and read as follows :—

" Go at once to No. 15 in the Allées de Meilhan, enter the house, and ask the doorkeeper for the key of the room on the fifth floor. In this room you will find, on a corner of the mantel-piece, a purse of red silk. Take it to your father. It is important that he should have it before eleven o'clock. You have promised to obey me blindly. Remember your promise.

" SINDBAD THE SAILOR."

The young girl uttered a cry of joy, and looked up to seek and question the messenger, but he had disappeared. She glanced again at the letter, and perceived a postscript :—

" It is important that you fulfil this mission in person and alone. If you come accompanied by anyone, or send another person to represent you, the doorkeeper will reply that he knows nothing about it."

This postscript was a sudden check to the young girl's delight. Was there nothing to fear ? or was it some trap laid for her ? Her innocence made her ignorant of the dangers that surround a young girl of her age. Julie hesitated and resolved to ask advice ; but, strangely enough, it was not to her mother or her brother that she applied for counsel, but to Emanuel.

" You must go, certainly, mademoiselle," said Emanuel, " and I will accompany you."

" But do you not see that I have to go alone ? " said she.

" You can go in alone," the young man replied, " and I will await you at the corner of the Rue du Musée, and if you are so long that I become uneasy, I shall come to you at once."

" Then, Emanuel," continued the young girl, " your advice is that I attend to the invitation ? "

Emanuel paused a moment, but the wish to urge the young girl to a prompt decision overcame him.

" Listen," said he ; " to-day is the 5th of September, is it not ? "

" Yes."

" If before eleven o'clock to-day your father has not found someone to assist him, he will be obliged to declare himself bankrupt."

" Oh ! come, then ! come at once ! " cried Julie.

In the meantime Madame Morrel had unfolded the story of their sad circumstances to her son. Astounded, he hastened up to his father's study and knocked at the door. As he stood there, he turned round and beheld his father coming upstairs. Instead of proceeding at once to his study, M. Morrel entered his bedroom, and then came out again, closing the door behind him. On perceiving his son, he uttered an exclamation of surprise, for he was ignorant of the young man's arrival. Maximilian descended the stairs, and threw himself on his father's neck ; but he recoiled quickly, and placed his right hand on M. Morrel's breast.

" Father," said he, turning pale as death, " why have you a pair of pistols under your coat ? "

" Maximilian," replied the shipowner, looking fixedly at his son, " you are a man, and a man of honour; I will tell you."

Morrel opened his study door, and closed it after his son had entered, then, crossing the room, walked to his desk, laid his pistols on a corner of the table, and pointed with his finger to the open ledger. In this ledger the exact position of affairs was plainly set forth. In half an hour Morrel had to pay 287,500 francs. He possessed altogether 15,257 francs.

" Read that," said Morrel.

The young man perused the balance-sheet and stood overwhelmed.

" And you have done everything to meet this misfortune ? "

" Yes," replied Morrel.

" In half an hour, then," said Maximilian, in a gloomy tone, " our name is dishonoured ! "

" Blood washes out dishonour," said Morrel.

" You are right, father ; I understand ; " then stretching out his hand to the pistols, he added, " there will be one for you, and one for me ; thank you."

But Morrel stopped his hand.

" Your mother and your sister ; who will take care of them ? "

The young man reflected for a moment, then an expression of resignation came into his eyes, and he proceeded, slowly and sadly, to remove his epaulettes, the insignia of his rank.

" So be it," said he, extending his hand to his father ; " die in peace, father ! I will live ! "

Morrel made a half movement to throw himself on his knees. Maximilian clasped him in his arms, and these two noble hearts beat against each other.

" You know that it has not been my fault," said Morrel.

"I know, father, that you are, as you have always been, the most honest of men."

"That is well; it is all over. Now return to your mother and sister."

"Father!" said the young man, bending his knee, "bless me!"

Morrel took his son's head between his hands, bent down and pressed it with his lips.

"Yes, yes," said he; "I bless you in my name, and in the name of three generations of upright men. Listen to what they say with my voice: 'The edifice that misfortune has destroyed, Providence may, perhaps, rebuild.' Seeing me die such a death, the most inexorable will have pity on me; to you, perhaps, may be given the respite that has been refused me. Set to work, labour hard, young man, struggle boldly and courageously. Live all of you, your mother and sister alike, on the strictest principles of economy, so that, day by day, the money that I leave, may gradually increase and fructify in your hands. Think what a grand, what a solemn day will that be, when you are able to stand up and say in this very office: 'My father died because he could not do what I am doing to-day; but he died peacefully, because he knew that I should do it.'"

The young man groaned, but he seemed resigned. For the second time in the interview, the conviction of his mind overpowered the tenderest feelings of his heart.

"Now," said Morrel, "leave me, and endeavour to keep your mother and sister away."

"And have you no particular injunctions to give me, father?" inquired the young man, in broken accents.

"Yes, my son, a sacred injunction."

"Speak, father."

"The firm of Thomson and French is the only one that, either from humanity or selfishness—but it is not for me to read the hearts of men,—has had compassion on me. Their agent, who will shortly be here, to present a bill for 287,500 francs, granted—no, I should rather say, offered—me a delay of three months. Let this debt be paid first, my son, and respect that man."

"I will, father," said Maximilian.

"Once more, farewell: go, I need to be alone; you will find my will in the writing-desk in my room."

The young man still lingered; the power of movement seemed to fail him.

"Listen, Maximilian," said his father, "supposing I were a

soldier, like you, that I had received the command to carry a redoubt, and that you knew I should be killed in the attempt, would you not say to me at once : ' Go, father; for you are dishonoured by delay, and death is better than shame ? ' "

" Yes, yes," cried the young man ; then pressing Morrel convulsively in his arms, he exclaimed, " Go, father ! " and rushed out of the room.

Morrel remained standing, his eyes fixed on the door which had closed on his son, and then he rang the bell.

In a moment or so, Coclès appeared. He looked a different being. The three days of painful conviction had crushed him. The thought that the firm of Morrel would suspend payment had bowed him down more than twenty years would have done.

" My good Coclès," said Morrel, in an accent it is impossible to describe, " I wish you to remain in the antechamber. When the agent from Messrs. Thomson and French, whom you saw three months back, arrives, you must announce him."

Coclès made no reply ; he merely bowed his head, went out, and seated himself in the antechamber.

Morrel fell back in his chair, his eyes wandered to the clock. He had seven minutes longer. The minute hand appeared to move with incredible speed.

What now passed through the mind of this man, who, though in the prime of days, yet overcome by a false, if specious course of reasoning, was about to separate himself from the love of his family and all he held dear in life, it is impossible to say. Yet his countenance, though covered with the sweat of agony, was resigned, and his tear-dimmed eyes were raised to heaven.

The minute hand moved on ; the pistols were ready loaded. He stretched out his hand and took one, murmuring the name of his daughter. Then he put down the dreadful weapon, took a pen and wrote a few words. He felt as though he had not taken a sufficient farewell of his beloved daughter. Then he glanced again at the clock. He no longer counted by minutes, but by seconds. He took up the pistol, his lips parted, his eyes fixed on the minute hand ; then he started as he clicked the trigger.

At this moment, a deathlike dampness covered his brow, a mortal anguish seized him. He heard the door on to the staircase open, then that of his own room. The hand of the clock was on eleven. Morrel did not turn round. He expected to hear Coclès' voice announcing the agent from Thomson and French. He raised the pistol to his mouth. Suddenly he heard a cry; it was his daughter's voice. He looked round, and beheld Julie; and the pistol dropped from his hands.

"Father! father!" cried the young girl, breathless, and half-dying with joy, "you are saved! saved!" and she threw herself into his arms, holding up to his astonished gaze a purse of red silk.

Morrel took the purse with a start, for he had a vague recollection that it had once belonged to himself. He opened it. On one side was the bill of 287,500 francs. *It was receipted!* On the other side was a diamond, as large as a hazel-nut, with these words inscribed on a piece of parchment: "Julie's dowry."

Just then the clock struck eleven. Each stroke seemed to vibrate on his very heart.

"But tell me, my child," said he; "where did you find this purse?"

"In a house in the Allées de Meilhan, on the corner of the chimney-piece, in a poor little room on the fifth floor."

"Monsieur Morrel!" cried a voice on the staircase, "Monsieur Morrel!"

"It is his voice," said Julie; and almost immediately, Emanuel entered, his face radiant with joyous emotion.

"The *Pharaon!*" he cried, "the *Pharaon!*"

"What do you say?—the *Pharaon?*—you are mad, Emanuel. You know she is lost!"

"It is the *Pharaon*, monsieur; they are signalling now; the *Pharaon* is coming into port!"

Morrel fell back in his chair, for his strength failed him. His intelligence faltered before this succession of extraordinary, incredible, events.

His son now entered.

"Father," he cried, "why did you say the *Pharaon* was lost? She has just been signalled, and is coming into port."

"My friends, if that were so," said Morrel, "it would be nothing short of a divine miracle! Impossible! impossible!"

"Why, monsieur," said Coclès, also approaching, "what is this about the *Pharaon?*"

"Come, my children," said Morrel, rising, "come, we will go and see; and may God have mercy on us if it is false news!"

They proceeded downstairs. On the way they encountered Madame Morrel, who had not dared to come up to her husband. In a few moments they had reached the Canebière. There was a great crowd on the pier, but as Morrel and his friends approached it opened to let them pass through. "The *Pharaon!* the *Pharaon!*" was heard on every side; and there, strange to relate, in front of the town of Saint Jean, was a vessel, bearing on her stern these words, inscribed in white letters: "The *Pharaon*, Morrel and Son, Marseilles," perfectly resembling the other *Pharaon* in appearance, and laden in like manner with cochineal and indigo. She cast anchor and furled her sails; and on deck Captain Gaumard could be seen giving orders, and Penelon waving to M. Morrel. There could no longer be any doubt about it; there was the testimony of his own senses, and ten thousand persons assembled as witnesses to the wonderful fact.

As Morrel and his son embraced each other on the pier, amid the applause of the multitude, a man, with his face half covered by a thick, black beard, was standing partly concealed behind a sentry-box, contemplating the scene with an expression of tender emotion.

"Be happy, noble heart," he murmured, "be blessed for all the good thou hast done and shalt do hereafter!" He descended one of the flights of steps on the landing-stage, calling out, "Jacopo! Jacopo! Jacopo!" A boat immediately came up to him, took him on board, and conducted him to a handsomely-rigged yacht. He sprang on deck with the agility of a sailor, and once more looked back towards Morrel, who, weeping with joy, was shaking hands cordially with all the crowd round him, and appearing, with a vague, upward look, to be seeking his unknown benefactor in the heavens.

"Now," muttered the stranger to himself, "farewell to kindness, humanity, and gratitude—farewell to all the gentler sentiments of the heart! I have been Heaven's substitute to recompense the good! may I also be the substitute of an avenging Providence to punish the wicked!"

CHAPTER XXXI

ITALY. SINDBAD THE SAILOR

TOWARDS the beginning of the year 1838, two young men were visiting Florence. They belonged to the highest society of Paris —one, Viscount Albert de Morcerf; the other, Baron Franz d'Epinay. They agreed that they would be present at the Carnival at Rome. Now, as it is no small matter to spend the Carnival in Rome, particularly if one has no desire to sleep in the Piazza del Popolo or in the Campo Vaccino, they wrote to M. Pastrini, proprietor of the Hôtel de Londres, to request him to reserve for them some comfortable rooms. Then, wishing to make the best use of the intervening time, Albert set off for Naples, leaving Franz at Florence. Having partaken of the hospitality of some of the wealthy aristocrats of Florence, Franz decided that he would visit the island of Elba, Bonaparte's celebrated resting-place.

One evening, therefore, a boat was loosed from its moorings in the harbour of Leghorn, and the traveller gave this order to the sailors : " To the island of Elba." The boat glided out of port like a sea-bird from its nest, and the following morning Franz landed at Porto Ferrajo. He traversed the island, following every trace that the mighty giant of history had left behind him, and then re-embarked for Marciana. Two hours afterwards he landed at Pianosa, where he had been assured there was plenty of red partridges. But the sport was bad. Franz scarcely succeeded in killing a few small birds, and, like most sportsmen who have fatigued themselves for nothing, he came on board again in a rather bad temper.

" Well, if your Excellency cares about it," said the captain, " you might have capital sport."

" Where, pray ? "

" Do you see that island ? " said the captain, pointing southwards to a conical pile rising out of the deep blue of the sea.

" Yes. What island is that ? "

" That is the island of Monte Cristo," replied the captain.

" But I have not got permission to shoot on that island."

" Your Excellency does not need that, for the island is uninhabited."

" And to whom does this island belong ? "

" To Tuscany."

" What game shall I find there ? "

" Thousands of wild goats."

" But where could I sleep ? "

" In one of the grottoes, or on deck, wrapped up in your cloak."

As Franz had still plenty of time before rejoining his companion, and had no longer any anxiety regarding his quarters in Rome, he accepted the proposal.

After he had signified his acquiescence, the sailors began putting their heads together and conversing in undertones.

" Well," he inquired, " is there any difficulty in the way ? "

" No," returned the captain ; " only we ought to warn your Excellency that the island is in a state of outlawry."

" What do you mean ? "

" We mean that Monte Cristo, though uninhabited, is some-times used as a landing-place by smugglers and pirates, who come from Corsica, Sardinia, or Africa, and if it should become known that you had been staying on the island, we should be compelled on our return to Leghorn, to remain in quarantine for six days."

" That is rather long, my good fellows."

" But who would be likely to tell that your Excellency had been to Monte Cristo ? "

" Well, I shall not, of course," said Franz.

" Nor will we ! " exclaimed the sailors.

" Well, then, be it for Monte Cristo."

The captain gave his orders, and the little boat now made sail in the direction of the island. After all the manœuvres were completed, Franz renewed the conversation.

" My dear Gaetano," said he to the captain, " you have just been telling me that the island of Monte Cristo serves as a refuge for pirates ; I thought that since the taking of Algiers and the end of the regency, pirates no longer existed."

" Then your Excellency was mistaken. There are pirates, like the bandits, who waylay travellers every day at the very gates of Rome. Did not your Excellency hear that about six months ago the French Ambassador was robbed but five hundred yards from Velletri ? "

" Indeed ! "

" Well, if your Excellency lived at Leghorn, you would hear from time to time of some little boat laden with merchandise, or a smart English yacht, daily expected at Bastia, Porto Ferrajo, or Civita Vecchia. The boat does not arrive. People imagine that it has perhaps been dashed to pieces on a rock. And as a matter of fact, it *has* met with a rock, for a flat, narrow boat, manned by six or eight sailors, has surprised and plundered it on a dark stormy night, just as bandits stop and rifle a post-chaise at the corner of a wood."

" But," said Franz, as he lay back wrapped in his cloak, " why do not those individuals who are treated in this manner demand vengeance from the French, Sardinian, or Tuscan governments ? "

" Because they first of all take from the boat or yacht every-thing that is worth taking ; then they tie the hands and feet of all the crew, fastening to each 'man's neck a ball of twenty-four pounds' weight, make a large hole in the keel of the vessel, close the hatch-way, and return to their own boat. Now," said the captain, smiling, " you understand how it is the boat never comes into port, and the crew never make any complaint."

If Gaetano had described this affair before proposing the expedition, it is probable that Franz would have thought twice before undertaking it; but now they had set out it seemed cowardice to draw back. He was moreover one of those men who do not run into danger, but if any occasion of danger occurs, prepare with perfect *sang froid* for the conflict.

" Bah ! " he exclaimed, " I have travelled through Sicily and Calabria, and sailed for two months in the Archipelago, and I have never seen the shadow of a bandit or a pirate."

" I did not tell your Excellency all this to deter you from the expedition," said Gaetano; " I was asked a question and replied, that is all."

" Yes, my good Gaetano, and your conversation is most interesting; and as I wish to enjoy it as long as possible we will go to Monte Cristo."

They were now rapidly approaching the end of the voyage; a fresh breeze was blowing, and the boat made from six to seven miles an hour. As they came nearer, the island seemed to rise slowly out of the sea, and through the limpid atmosphere of the waning sunlight one could distinguish the heap of rocks, piled one above another, like cannon-balls in an arsenal, in the crevices of which bloomed heather and green trees.

They were within fifteen miles of Monte Cristo when the sun began to go down behind the Corsican mountains, whose dark peaks were carved in clear outline against the sky. Half an hour later it was black night.

Happily the sailors were in familiar waters, and knew every small rock of the Tuscan archipelago, or in the midst of such profound darknessFranz would not have been free from uneasiness.

An hour nearly had passed since the sun went down, when Franz thought he perceived, a quarter of a mile to the left, a dark mass. Suddenly a bright light shone on the shore; the strip of land looked like a cloud, but the light was certainly not a meteor.

" What is that light ? " he inquired.

" Hush ! " said the captain, " it is a fire ! "

" But you said the island was uninhabited."

" But I also said that it was a halting-place for smugglers."

" And for pirates ? "

" And for pirates," repeated Gaetano; " that is why I gave the order to pass the island; for, as you see, the fire is behind us."

" But this fire," said Franz, " seems to me rather a reason for security than alarm ; people who feared to be discovered would not light a fire."

" Oh, that has nothing to do with it," replied Gaetano ; " if you were able to perceive the position of the island through the darkness, you would see that this fire cannot be seen either from the coast or Pianosa, but only from the open sea."

" Then you are afraid this fire is a sign that there are bad characters about ? "

" That is what we must find out," replied Gaetano.

With these words Gaetano turned to consult with his companions. After five minutes' discussion a manœuvre was silently executed ; they tacked about, went back in the direction they had come, and in a few seconds the fire was out of sight, hidden behind rising ground. Then the pilot again changed the course of the little boat, which gradually approached the island till it was within a distance of fifty paces.

Gaetano lowered the sail, and the boat became stationary. This was all done in perfect silence ; since the boat had changed its course not a word had been uttered on board. Gaetano, who had proposed the expedition, took all the responsibility on himself.

As to Franz, he examined his firearms with the greatest coolness ; he had two double-barrelled guns and a rifle ; he loaded them, looked at the locks, and waited the course of events. Meanwhile the captain threw off his jacket and shirt, and secured his trousers round his waist ; then putting his finger to his lips as a sign of perfect silence, he jumped into the sea, and swam towards the shore with so much precaution that not the slightest ripple was audible. In half an hour, with a couple of strokes, Gaetano had again reached the boat.

" They are Spanish smugglers," returned the captain, " and have two Corsican bandits with them."

" And what are these Corsican bandits doing with Spanish smugglers ? "

" Well, your Excellency," returned Gaetano in a tone of profound Christian charity, " men must help each other ! "

" Indeed ! " said Franz, " then you are something of a smuggler yourself, my dear Gaetano ? "

" Ah ! what would you have, your Excellency ? " returned the captain with a curious smile, " we do a little of everything ; one must live, you know."

" Then you are probably acquainted with the people who are at present occupying the island of Monte Cristo ? "

"Yes, in a sort of way. We sailors are like the freemasons, and recognize each other by certain signs."

"And you think we have nothing to fear in landing, then ? "

"Nothing; smugglers are not robbers."

"But these two Corsican bandits," continued Franz, calculating in advance all the chances of danger.

"Eh! Mon Dieu!" said Gaetano, "it is not their fault if they are bandits, it is the fault of the authorities."

"How so ? "

"They are pursued for having taken a skin, and nothing else ; as though it were not a Corsican's nature to avenge himself ! "

"What do you mean by having taken a skin ? Having killed a man, eh ? " said Franz, continuing his investigations.

"I mean having killed an enemy," returned the captain, "which is very different."

"How many are there ? "

"Four, your Excellency, and the two bandits make six."

"Well, that is just our figure; in case these people show any evil disposition, we are in equal force, and consequently can check them. Thus, for the last time, make for Monte Cristo."

"Then silence ! " cried Gaetano, and everyone held his peace.

For a man regarding everything from Franz's point of view, the situation, without being dangerous, was not wanting in a certain amount of gravity. He found himself on the darkest night, isolated in the sea, with sailors who did not know him, and had no motive for being devoted to him; who, moreover, knew that he had in his belt some thousands of francs. Further, he was about to land, with no other escort than these men, on an island bearing a religious name, it is true, but owing to the pirates and bandits who infested it, unlikely to offer him any particular hospitality.

Thus placed, between a double, though possibly imaginary danger, he kept his gaze steadily fixed on the men, and did not relax hold of his pistol.

The sailors had now hoisted their sails anew, and returned on their track. Franz, becoming somewhat accustomed to the obscurity, could distinguish the giant of granite round which the barque coasted, then passing the angle of the rock, he perceived the fire which shone more brilliantly than ever, and round this fire, five or six persons were seated. The reflection of the light extended some distance over the sea. Gaetano skirted round the light, then turned and boldly entered the luminous circle; at the same time striking up a fishers' song, of which his companions sustained the chorus.

At the first sound of the singing, the men seated round the fire rose, and approached the landing-place, gazing eagerly at the boat, of which they evidently sought to judge the size, and divine the intentions.

They soon appeared satisfied with their examination, and, with the exception of one man, who remained near the water's edge, returned to their fire, before which a goat was roasting.

When the boat came within twenty paces or so, the man on the shore made mechanically with his rifle the gesture of a sentinel who awaits a patrol, and cried, " Qui vive ! " in Sardinian patois.

Franz coolly prepared his firearms. Gaetano then exchanged with the man a few words, incomprehensible to the traveller, but evidently concerning him.

" Does your Excellency," demanded the captain, " wish to give your name or to remain incognito ? "

" My name would be strange to them; say merely that I am a Frenchman travelling for pleasure."

When Gaetano had transmitted this reply, the sentinel gave an order to one of the men seated before the fire, who at once got up and disappeared among the rocks. He presently returned from an opposite direction, and signed to the sentinel, who turned to the crew, merely uttering these words, " S'accommodi," a phrase meaning " Make yourselves at home."

The sailors did not need to be told twice; in four strokes of the oar the boat was brought to land. Gaetano leaped on the beach and his companions followed one after another; and last of all came Franz.

The boat was made fast, and they then proceeded a short distance to find a convenient bivouac; but the direction they took was evidently not suited to the smugglers' convenience, for one called out to Gaetano :

" Not that way, if you please."

Gaetano muttered an excuse, and without persisting further, turned in the opposite direction, while two of the sailors approached to light their torches at the fire, that they might have a beacon in the darkness. They had not advanced thirty yards before they paused on a little esplanade surrounded by rocks, in which had been hollowed some seats like small sentry-boxes.

Franz lowered his torch, and recognized by a heap of cinders that he was not the first to discover this spot, which was evidently one of the habitual resorts of nomadic visitors to the island of

Monte Cristo. All his suspicions had disappeared since he set foot on the island, and his prejudices gave way before the eager demands of appetite. He intimated as much in a few words to Gaetano, who replied that it would be an easy matter to prepare a supper, for they had bread, wine, and six partridges in the boat, and only needed to make a good fire.

"Nevertheless," he added, "if your Excellency finds the smell of this goat so tempting, I can offer our neighbours two of our birds for a slice of their quadruped."

"Do so, Gaetano, pray do so," said Franz; "you were certainly born with a genius for negotiation."

Franz, still scenting the odour of the goat, awaited impatiently the return of the captain, who, when he reappeared, came up with a very preoccupied air.

"Well," said Franz, "what news? Do they refuse the offer?"

"On the contrary," said Gaetano. "The chief, hearing that you are a young Frenchman, invites you to supper, but attaches a curious stipulation to receiving you in his abode."

"And what is the condition?"

"That you allow yourself to be blindfolded, and do not remove the bandage till he himself tells you."

Franz endeavoured to penetrate Gaetano's expression, to discover the hidden meaning of this proposition.

"I know well enough," continued Gaetano, as though replying to Franz's look; "I know that it requires reflection."

"What would you do in my place?" inquired the young man.

"I—I have nothing to lose; I should go."

"There is something curious to be seen in this chief's abode?"

"They say he lives in an underground cave, compared with which the Pitti Palace dwindles into insignificance."

"Oh, it must be fancy," said Franz, reseating himself.

"No, it is not fancy," returned the captain; "it is quite true, Cama, the pilot of Saint Ferdinand, went in one day, and he came out perfectly amazed, saying that he had never heard of such treasures but in fairy tales."

"Then you advise me to accept?"

"Oh! as to that, your Excellency must do as you please. I can give no counsel in the matter."

Franz reflected a few moments, reasoned that this wealthy man could have no designs on him, seeing that he had only a few thousand francs on his person, and as he saw his way to an excellent supper, accepted. Gaetano took his reply. Nevertheless, Franz turned to a sailor and inquired of him how all these men could have landed, since neither speronares, tartans, nor any other boats were to be seen.

" I have no doubt about that," replied the sailor, " for I know their vessel. It is a fancy vessel, a ' yacht ' the English call it —but built to stand any weather."

" And where was it built ? "

" I do not know, but I imagine at Genoa."

" But how is it," continued Franz, " that a smuggler chief dare give an order for a yacht destined for his line of business in the port of Genoa ? "

" I have not said that the proprietor of this yacht was a smuggler," returned the sailor.

" But if this man is not a smuggler chief, what is he ? "

' A rich lord, who travels for pleasure."

" What is his name ? "

" When he is asked," replied the sailor, " he answers that he is called Sindbad the Sailor."

" His Excellency awaits you, monsieur," said a voice behind him, which he recognized as that of the sentinel. The new-comer was accompanied by two men belonging to the yacht's crew.

Franz merely replied by drawing out his handkerchief and handing it to the speaker. Without speaking, the men bandaged his eyes with an amount of precaution that indicated their fear that he might commit some indiscretion ; after which they made him swear that he would not attempt in any way to remove the bandage. He swore solemnly. Then the two men took him by each arm, and he walked away between them, the sentinel going in advance.

After a few steps, Franz perceived, by the appetizing odour of the goats, that they were passing the bivouac, then advancing fifty yards or so, he fancied they were bearing off in the direction that had been forbidden to Gaetano. In a short time he comprehended, from the change of atmosphere, that he was entering a cavern. He then felt that his feet were treading a soft, thick carpet, and suddenly his guides released him. There was a moment's silence, and then a voice said, in good French, but with a foreign accent, " You are very welcome, monsieur, and you may now remove your handkerchief."

As one may suppose, Franz did not wait for the invitation to be renewed ; he loosened the handkerchief, and found himself face to face with a man of about forty years of age, wearing the Tunisian costume—namely, a red cap with a long tassel of blue silk, a jacket of black cloth embroidered with gold, puffed pantaloons of deep crimson, gaiters of the same colour embroidered with gold like the jacket, and yellow slippers. Although of almost livid pallor, the man had a handsome face; his eyes were bright and piercing; his nose was straight, and almost on a line with his forehead, denoting the Greek type in all its purity; his teeth showed themselves with pearly whiteness beneath his black moustache. There was something curious about his pallor; it was like that of a man who has been a long while enclosed in a tomb, and is unable to regain his natural colouring. Without being tall, he was well-made, and like most men of the South, had small hands and feet. But what astonished Franz, who had treated Gaetano's recital as a fanciful narrative, was the sumptuous magnificence of the surroundings. The whole apartment was spread with Turkish stuffs of crimson embroidered with flowers of gold. In a recess was a kind of divan, surmounted by a trophy of Arabic weapons, with gilt scabbards, and hilts resplendent with precious stones; from the ceiling hung a lamp of Venetian glass, of exquisite form and colour, while on the ground was a magnificent Turkey carpet. Curtains hung from the door through which Franz had entered, and also before another door opening into a second room, which appeared to be brilliantly illuminated. The stranger allowed Franz to remain for a moment in his bewilderment, and meanwhile returned scrutiny for scrutiny.

" A thousand pardons, monsieur," said he at last, " for the precautions that have been taken in bringing you to me; but as this island is generally deserted, if the secret of my dwelling became known, I should probably, on my return, find it in rather bad condition, which would be very annoying to me."

" *Ma foi!* my dear host," replied Franz, " there is no need for apology. I am aware that people who enter enchanted palaces always have their eyes bandaged, like Raoul, for instance, in the ' Huguenots '; and I have no reason to complain, for what I see here is a worthy sequel to the marvels of the Arabian Nights."

At the same instant, the curtain was raised, and Ali, a Nubian negro, as black as ebony, and clad in a simple white tunic, signed to his master to walk into the banqueting-room.

" Now, I do not know if you are of my opinion," said the stranger to Franz, " but I think that nothing is more tiresome than to remain two or three hours *tête-à-tête*, without knowing each other's name. Recollect, however, that I respect the laws of hospitality too much to inquire your name or title; I only

ask you to tell me by what appellation I may address you. As
for myself, I may as well tell you at once that I am accustomed
to be called Sindbad the Sailor."

" And I," returned Franz, " beg to inform you, that as only
the wonderful lamp is wanting to put me in the situation of Aladdin, I see no reason why, for the time being, you should not call
me Aladdin."

" Well, then, Signor Aladdin, supper is ready ; be kind enough
to enter the *salle-à-manger*."

The young Frenchman passed from one enchantment to another. The table was splendidly laid, and having noticed this,
Franz turned to look round him. The *salle-à-manger* was not less
magnificent than the boudoir he had just left ; it was of marble
with antique *bas reliefs* of priceless value, and at each end of the
room, which was oblong in shape, were two magnificent statues
bearing baskets on their heads. These baskets contained pyra-
mids of splendid fruit ; there were pine apples from Sicily, pome-
granates from Malaga, oranges from the Balearic Isles, peaches
from France, and dates from Tunis. As to the supper, it was
composed of a roast pheasant, garnished with Corsican blackbirds,
a boar's ham, *à la gelée*, a quarter of a kid, *à la tartare*, a magnificent turbot, and a gigantic lobster.

Franz rubbed his eyes to make sure that he was not dreaming.
Ali alone served at table, and acquitted himself so well that the
Frenchman complimented his host thereon.

" Yes," replied the latter, while doing the honours of the table
with much ease and grace, " yes, poor fellow, he is greatly devoted
to me, and does his best. He bears in mind that I saved his
life."

" Shall you consider it indiscreet, Signor Sindbad," said Franz,
" if I inquire the circumstances in which you rendered that kind
action ? "

" Oh, no ! it was a simple affair," returned the host ; " it
appeared that the fellow had been found prowling nearer the
seraglio of the Bey of Tunis than is permitted to one of his colour.
He was therefore condemned by the Bey to have his tongue cut
off the first day, his hand the second, and his head the third. I
had always desired to have a mute in my service ; I therefore
waited till he had had his tongue cut out, and then proposed to
the Bey to give him to me in exchange for a magnificent double-
barrelled gun, which, the evening before, had apparently excited
his Highness's desire. He hesitated a moment, so anxious was he
to make an end of the poor devil. Then I offered in addition an

English hunting-knife, with which I had shivered his Highness's dagger to pieces, and the Bey at last consented to let him off, but on condition that he never again set foot in Tunis."

Franz was pensive for a few moments pondering the half unfeeling jocularity with which his host had related the incident. At last he observed, changing the conversation, " Then like the worthy sailor, from whom you take your name, you pass your time in travelling ? "

" Yes, in accordance with a vow I made at a time when I little thought I should ever be able to accomplish it," said the stranger, smiling. " I made others too, which I hope will also be fulfilled in their turn."

As Sindbad pronounced these words with perfect coolness, his eyes shot forth a glance of strange ferocity.

" You have suffered much, monsieur," said Franz.

Sindbad started and looked at him fixedly.

" How can you tell that ? " he asked, quickly.

" By your voice," replied Franz, " your expression, your pallor, and also the life you lead."

" Indeed ? Why, I lead the happiest life possible—the veritable life of a pasha. I am a lord of creation. If I am pleased with a place, I stay there; if wearied, I depart; I am free as a bird, and have wings like one ; those who surround me obey me at a sign. Ah, if you had ever tasted my life you would wish for no other, and you would never return to the world, unless you had some great project to carry out."

" An act of vengeance, for example," said Franz.

" And why vengeance ? "

" Because," said Franz, " you appear to me to have the air of a man who has been persecuted by society, and has a terrible reckoning to settle with it."

" Indeed," said Sindbad, laughing his strange laugh, which exposed his row of white teeth, " then you are wrong. In fact, I am a kind of philanthropist, and perhaps some day I shall go to Paris as a rival to M. Appert."

" I hope I shall be there at the time," returned Franz, " so that I may endeavour to return the hospitality you have so generously shown me at Monte Cristo."

" I should avail myself of your invitation with great pleasure," returned his host, " but unfortunately, if I go there, it must be *incognito*."

Meanwhile the supper was partaken of, though it appeared to have been served solely for the benefit of Franz ; for his host scarcely touched any of the dainty dishes to which his guest did such ample justice.

At last Ali laid the dessert, or rather took the two baskets from the statues, and placed them on the table. Between the baskets he put a small silver cup, closed with a lid. The care with which Ali brought this cup excited Franz's curiosity. He lifted the lid, and beheld a greenish-coloured paste, somewhat resembling preserved angelica, but he had no idea what it was. He replaced the lid, as ignorant of the contents as he was before. Then glancing towards his host, he observed he was smiling at his disappointment.

" I see you cannot guess," said the stranger, " what kind of eatable that little vase contains, and you are puzzled, are you not ? "

" I am."

" Well, then, that greenish sweetmeat is neither more nor less than the ambrosia that Hebe served at Jupiter's table."

" But," said Franz, " this ambrosia, passing through men's hands, has doubtless lost its celestial name for a human one ; in vulgar phrase, what do you style this ingredient, for which I must confess, I do not feel any great desire ? "

" Ah ! " cried Sindbad, " if you are a practical man, and gold is your god, taste this, and mines of Peru, of Guzerat, and Golconda are opened to you. Are you a man of imagination, a poet, taste it, and all material barriers disappear ? Are you ambitious ? Do you covet worldly greatness ? Taste it still, and in an hour you will be sovereign, not of a small kingdom hidden away in a corner of Europe like France, Spain, or England, but of the world, the universe, creation. Now, is not this tempting, and is it not a simple matter, since there is only this to be done ?—See."

With these words, he opened the cup, and taking a spoonful of the magic preserve, raised it to his lips, and swallowed it slowly, his eyes half closed, and his head thrown backwards.

" It must be hasheesh ! " cried Franz.

" Exactly, Signor Aladdin, it is hasheesh."

" Do you know," said Franz, " I should much like to judge for myself as to the truth of your praises ? "

" Judge for yourself, my dear guest, certainly ; but do not decide by a first trial ; like everything else, one must accustom oneself to a new impression of any kind. Nature struggles against this divine substance—nature, which is not made for joy, and clings to pain."

By way of reply, Franz took a spoonful of the marvellous paste.

H

" The devil ! " he exclaimed, after swallowing the divine confectionery. " I don't know yet whether the result will be as agreeable as you say, but the thing itself does not seem to me so succulent as you declare."

" Because your palate has not yet risen to the sublimity of the substance it is tasting. Tell me, did you, the first time, like oysters, tea, truffles, all the things that you adored afterwards ? Do you understand the Romans, who used to season pheasants with asafœtida, and the Chinese, who eat swallows' nests ? Certainly not. Well, it is the same with hasheesh ; only take it every day for a week, and no food in the world will seem to you to be comparable in flavour to this, which, perhaps, now seems to you sickly and nauseating. However, let us pass into the next room, that is to say, into your room, and Ali will serve you with coffee, and give us pipes."

Both rose ; and while he who had given himself the name of Sindbad, issued certain orders to his servant, Franz entered the neighbouring room.

It was more simply, but not less richly furnished. It was circular in shape, with a great divan extending all round. But divan, walls, ceiling, and floor, were all spread with magnificent furs, soft and yielding, like the richest carpets.

Both stretched themselves on the divan ; chibouques, or Turkish pipes, with jasmine tubes and amber mouth-pieces lay ready to hand, and all prepared, so that one needed not to smoke twice out of the same chibouque. Each took a pipe, and Ali lit them, and went out to get the coffee.

" How will you take your coffee ? " asked the unknown, " in the French or in the Turkish manner ? "

" I shall take it in the Turkish fashion," answered Franz.

" And you are right," cried his host ; " that proves that you have an inclination for Oriental life. Ah, the Orientals, you see, are the only men who know how to live ! As for myself, when I have settled my affairs in Paris, I shall retire to the East ; and if you want to find me then, you will have to seek me out at Cairo, Baghdad, or Ispahan."

" On my word," said Franz, " that will be the easiest thing in the world, for I seem to be mounting on eagles' wings, and with those wings I'd fly round the world in four and twenty hours."

" Ah, ah ! It's the hasheesh operating ; very well, open your wings and fly away into sublime regions."

Then he said some Arabic words to Ali, who made a gesture of obedience, and retired, without going far off.

As to Franz, a strange transformation was going forward within him. His body seemed to acquire an ethereal lightness, his mind was illumined in an unheard-of manner, his senses seemed to be doubled in their faculties ; the horizon grew wider and wider, but not that gloomy horizon, on which floated a vague terror, and which he had seen before his sleep, but a blue horizon, transparent, vast, with all the azure of the sea, with all the radiance of the sun, with all the perfumes of the breeze ; then, amid the songs of his sailors, songs so limpid and so clear that no man would have made a divine harmony of them, if he could have noted them down, he saw the island of Monte Cristo, no longer like a threatening rock amid the waves, but like an oasis hidden in the desert ; then, as the barque approached nearer, the songs became more numerous, for an enchanting and mysterious harmony rose from the island to God, as if some fairy like Lorelei, or some enchanter like Amphion, had wanted to attract a soul thither, or to build a town.

At last the barque touched the shore, but without effort, without shock, as lips touch lips, and he entered the grotto, without any cessation of this charming music. He descended some steps, and he saw once more all that he had beheld before his sleep, from Sindbad, the fantastic host, to Ali, the dumb servant ; then everything seemed to be effaced and confounded before his eyes, and he found himself once more in a hall of statues. They were rich in form, fulness, and poetry, with magnetic eyes, licentious smiles, and flowing hair. They were statues of Phryne, Cleopatra, Messalina—those three great courtesans ; then among these immodest figures there glided, like a pure ray, one of those chaste faces, one of those calm shadows, one of those sweet visions, seeming to veil the virginal forehead amid all these marble impurities.

Then it seemed to him that these three statues had become enamoured of one man, and that he was that man ; that they approached the bed where he was dreaming in a second sleep, their feet hidden in their long white robes, with throats bare, and their locks floating like waves, with attitudes to which the gods yielded, but which the saints resisted.

Then all these mouths of stone quivered with life, the bosoms became warm ; and Franz, for the first time under the dominion of the hasheesh, experienced an ecstasy that was almost torture, when he felt his fevered mouth swept by the lips of these statues, cold and lissome as the rings of a serpent. But the more his arms endeavoured to thrust from him this unknown love, the more did his senses experience the charm of the mysterious dream ; so that after a struggle for which a man would have given his soul, he abandoned himself without reserve, and fell back exhausted under the enchantment of this marvellous dream.

CHAPTER XXXII

THE AWAKENING

WHEN Franz came to himself, the outward objects around seemed a continuation of his vision. He fancied himself in a sepulchre, into which scarcely penetrated a ray of the sun. He stretched forth his hand, and it lighted on stone. He sat upright ; he had been lying, in his burnous, on a very soft and fragrant bed of dry heather.

The whole vision had vanished ; and, as if the statues had been but shadows that had issued from their tombs during his dream, they had fled at his awakening.

He took a few steps in the direction in which the daylight appeared ; to all the agitation of the dream succeeded the calm of reality. He found himself in a grotto, and through the door, which stood ajar, could see the blue sky and an azure sea. The firmament and the water sparkled in the rays of the morning sun ; on the beach, the sailors sat chatting and laughing, ten yards from the shore the barque was riding gracefully at anchor.

Then for a time he enjoyed the fresh breeze that blew upon his brow ; he listened to the faint murmur of the wave and gave himself up to the impression of the moment, without reflecting on the divine charm that exists in the objects of nature, especially on awakening from a fantastic dream ; then little by little this outward life reminded him of the unreality of his sleep, and recollections began to return.

He remembered his arrival at the island, his introduction to the smuggler chief, the subterranean palace full of splendour, the excellent supper, and the spoonful of hasheesh.

Only in the face of this reality of the broad day, it seemed to him as if at least a year had elapsed since all these things happened, so lively was the dream he had dreamt in his recollection, and so deep an impression had it made on his mind. From time to time also, his imagination caused one of those shadows which had lighted up his night with their looks and their kisses, to appear, sitting among the sailors, or traversing a rock, or hovering over the vessel. Beyond this, his head was perfectly clear and his body completely rested ; he was conscious of a general feeling of physical comfort, a greater faculty than ever of absorbing the air and the sunlight.

Accordingly, he went up to the sailors with an air of gaiety. Directly they perceived him they rose, and the captain came towards him.

" The Seigneur Sindbad," he said, " has commissioned us to make his best compliments to your Excellency, and to inform you of the regret he feels at being unable to pay his adieux in person ; but he trusts you will excuse him when you learn that very urgent business calls him to Malaga."

" Ah, indeed, my dear Gaetano," said Franz ; " then all this is truly a reality ; a man actually exists who received me in this island, who extended to me a royal hospitality, and who went away while I slept ? "

" He has such a real existence, that yonder is his yacht under full sail ; and if you choose to use your glass, you will in all probability recognize your host standing among his crew."

Franz took up his glass. Gaetano was not mistaken. Near the stern of the vessel the mysterious stranger was standing, his face turned towards him, and, like himself, holding a telescope in his hand. He was attired exactly as he had appeared to his guest the evening before, and was waving his handkerchief in token of farewell.

Franz returned his salute by drawing forth his own handkerchief and waving it as the stranger was doing.

A second afterwards, a light cloud of smoke became visible on the poop of the vessel, detached itself gracefully from the quarter, and floated slowly towards the sky ; then a faint report penetrated to Franz's ear.

" There—do you hear him ? " said Gaetano ; " he is bidding you good-bye. And, now, what are your Excellency's orders ? "

" In the first place, that you light me a torch."

" Ah ! yes, I understand," answered the captain, " to seek out the entrance to the enchanted chamber. With much pleasure, your Excellency. But I also have had the idea you entertain, and tried to carry out my fancy three or four times ; but I have given it up at last. Giovanni, light a torch, and bring it to his Excellency."

Giovanni obeyed. Franz took the torch and went into the underground cavern, followed by Gaetano.

He recognized his couch of bushes, which was still all tumbled ; but in vain did he pass his torch across all the exterior surface of the grotto—he saw nothing, except that he realized by the traces of smoke, that others before him had attempted the same investigation.

Nevertheless, he did not leave unexamined one foot of the granitic wall. He encountered not a single fissure into which he did not thrust the blade of his hunting-knife ; he did not notice a single projection on which he did not press, in the hope that it would yield ; but all was useless ; and he lost two hours in this search without result.

At the expiration of that time he gave it up.

Gaetano reminded him that he had come to hunt the goats, a circumstance he had completely forgotten. He took his gun, and began traversing the island, and within a quarter of an hour he had killed a she-goat and two kids. But these goats, though wild, and as nimble as the chamois, bore too great a resemblance to domestic goats, and Franz did not look upon them as game.

Moreover far more urgent thoughts occupied his mind. He felt irresistibly drawn towards the grotto, and in spite of the uselessness of his first search, began a second, after giving directions to Gaetano to roast one of the kids. That second visit lasted a tolerably long time ; for when he came back the kid was roasted, and the breakfast ready.

Franz sat down in the place where, the evening before, he had received the invitation to supper from that mysterious host ; and he could still see the yacht making for Corsica.

" But," said Franz, " you told me that the Seigneur Sindbad was setting sail for Malaga, while it seems to me that he is bending his course towards Porto Vecchio."

" Do you not remember," answered the captain, " that I told you there were among his crew, at this time, two Corsican bandits ? Well, he is going to land them on the coast. Ah ! he fears neither God nor devil, and would turn fifty leagues out of his way to do a poor man a service."

" But services of this kind might easily bring him into collision with the authorities," said Franz.

" Ah, indeed ! " replied Gaetano, laughing, " what does he care for the authorities ? He laughs at them ; let them only try to pursue him ! First of all, his yacht is not a ship ; it's a bird, and would give a frigate three knots in twelve ; and then, he has only to throw himself upon the coast, and he will find friends everywhere."

There was nothing more to keep Franz at Monte Cristo. He had lost all hope of finding out the secret of the grotto

Accordingly, he took his breakfast, ordering his men to have their ship in readiness.

Half an hour afterwards he was on board. He cast a last glance at the yacht; it was just about to disappear in the bay of Porto Vecchio. Then he gave the signal for departure.

At the moment their ship began to move, the yacht disappeared. With it vanished the last reality of the preceding night; and the supper, Sindbad, hasheesh, and statues, began to be confounded in the same dream.

The boat continued under sail the whole day and the whole night, and the next morning when the sun rose, the island of Monte Cristo had disappeared in its turn.

When Franz once again set foot on shore, he forgot, for the moment, at least, the events which had just passed, whilst he finished his affairs of pleasure at Florence; then he determined to rejoin his companion, who was awaiting him at Rome.

He set out, and on the Saturday evening reached the Place de la Douane. Apartments had been retained beforehand, and he had but to go to the hotel of Maître Pastrini; but this was not so easy a matter, for the streets were thronged with people, and Rome was already a prey to that feverish murmur which precedes all great events; and at Rome there are four great events in every year : the Carnival, the Holy Week, the Fête-Dieu, and the St. Peter. At last he made his way through this mob, which was continually increasing and growing more agitated, and reached the hotel. On his first inquiry he was told that there was no room for him at the Hôtel de Londres. Then he sent his card to Maître Pastrini, and demanded Albert de Morcerf. This plan succeeded, and Maître Pastrini himself ran to him, excusing himself for having made his Excellency wait, and was ready to lead him to Albert, when Morcerf himself appeared. The apartments consisted of two small rooms and a closet. The two rooms looked on to the street, a fact which Maître Pastrini commented upon as an appreciable advantage. The remainder of the storey was hired by a very rich gentleman, who was supposed to be a Sicilian or Maltese.

"Very good, Maître Pastrini," said Franz; "but we must have some supper instantly, and a carriage for to-morrow, and the following days."

"As to supper," replied the landlord, "you shall be served immediately; but as for the carriage, we will do all in our power to procure you one, but I am afraid, even if we offer Drake and Aaron's double money, that we shall not procure a carriage."

" Then they must put horses to mine ; it is a little the worse for the journey, but that's no matter."

" There are no horses. They have been all hired this fortnight, and there are none left, but those absolutely necessary for posting."

" What are we to say to this ? " asked Franz.

" I say, that when a thing passes my comprehension I am accustomed not to dwell on it, but to pass to another. Is supper ready, Maître Pastrini ? "

" Yes, your Excellency."

" Well, then, let us sup."

" But the carriage and horses ? " said Franz.

" Be easy, my dear boy, they will come in due season ; it is only a question of how much shall be charged for them." Morcerf then, with that delighted philosophy which believes that nothing is impossible to a well-lined pocket-book, supped, went to bed, slept soundly, and dreamed he was racing all over Rome at Carnival time in a coach with six horses.

CHAPTER XXXIII

ROMAN BANDITS

NEXT morning Franz woke first, and instantly rang the bell. The sound had not yet died away when Maître Pastrini himself entered.

" Well, Excellency," said the landlord, triumphantly, " I feared yesterday, when I would not promise you anything, that you were too late ; there is not a single carriage to be had,— that is for the last three days."

" Yes, the very days it is most necessary."

" What is the matter ? " said Albert, entering ; " no carriage to be had ? "

" Just so," returned Franz, " you have guessed it."

" Well ! your Eternal City is a devilish nice city."

" That is to say, Excellency," replied Pastrini, " that there are no carriages to be had from Sunday to Tuesday evening, but from now till Sunday you can have fifty if you please."

" Ah ! that is something," said Albert ; " to-day is Thursday, and who knows what may arrive between this and Sunday ? "

" Ten or twelve thousand travellers will arrive," replied Franz, " which will make it still more difficult. At least we can have a window ? "

" Where ? "

" Looking on the Corso."

" Ah, a window ! " exclaimed Maître Pastrini,—" utterly impossible ; there was only one left on the fifth floor of the Doria Palace, and that has been let to a Russian prince for twenty sequins a day."

The two young men looked at each other with an air of stupefaction.

" Well," said Franz to Albert ; " the best thing we can do is to pass the Carnival at Venice ; there we are sure of obtaining gondolas if we cannot have carriages. "

" Ah ! the devil ! no," cried Albert ; " I came to Rome to see the Carnival, and I will, though I see it on stilts."

" Do your Excellencies still wish for a carriage from now to Sunday morning ? "

" Parbleu ! " said Albert, " do you think we are going to run about on foot like lawyers' clerks ? "

" I hasten to comply with your Excellencies' wishes ; when do you wish the carriage to be here ? "

" In an hour."

An hour later the vehicle was at the door ; it was a hack conveyance, which was elevated to the rank of a private carriage in honour of the occasion ; but, in spite of its humble exterior, the young men would have thought themselves happy to secure it for the last three days of the Carnival.

Franz and Albert took their places, and the cicerone sprang into the seat behind. " Where do your Excellencies wish to go ? " asked he.

" To St. Peter's first, and then to the Colosseum," returned Albert. But Albert did not know that it takes a day to see Saint Peter's and a month to study it. The day was passed at St. Peter's alone. Suddenly the daylight began to fade ; Franz took out his watch—it was half-past four. They returned to the hotel ; at the door Franz ordered the coachman to be ready at eight. He wished to show Albert the Colosseum by moonlight, as he had shown him Saint Peter's by daylight. He was to leave the city by the Porta del Popolo, skirt the outer wall, and re-enter by the Porta San Giovanni ; thus they would behold the Colosseum without being in some measure prepared by the sight of the Capitol, the Forum, the arch of Septimius Severus, the Temple of Antoninus and Faustina, and the Via Sacra. They sat down to dinner. Maître Pastrini had promised them a banquet : he gave them a tolerable repast. At the end of the dinner he entered in person. Franz concluded he came to hear his dinner praised, and began accordingly, but at the first words he interrupted him. "Excellency," said he, "I am delighted to have your approbation, but it was not for that I came. You have ordered your carriage at eight o'clock precisely? You intend visiting the Colosseum, and have told your coachman to leave the city by the Porta del Popolo, to drive round the walls, and re-enter by the Porta San Giovanni?"

"Those are my words exactly."

"Well, this route is impossible."

"Impossible!"

"Very dangerous, to say the least. On account of the famous bandit, Luigi Vampa."

"But what has this bandit to do with the order I have given the driver to leave the city by the Porta del Popolo, and return by the Porta San Giovanni?"

"This!" replied Maître Pastrini, "that you will go out by one, but I very much doubt your returning by the other."

"Why?" asked Franz.

"Because, after nightfall, you are not safe fifty yards from the gates."

"My dear fellow," said Albert, turning to Franz, "here is an admirable adventure; we will fill our carriage with pistols, blunderbusses, and double-barrelled guns. Luigi Vampa comes to take us, and we take him—we bring him back to Rome, and present him to his holiness the Pope, who asks how he can repay so great a service; then we merely ask for a carriage and a pair of horses, and we see the Carnival in the carriage, and doubtless the Roman people will crown us at the Capitol, and proclaim us, like Curtius and Horatius Cocles, the preservers of the country." Whilst Albert proposed this scheme, Maître Pastrini's face assumed an expression impossible to describe.

"Your Excellency knows," said the host, "that it is not customary to defend yourself when attacked by bandits. It would be useless. What could you do against a dozen bandits who spring out of some pit, ruin, or aqueduct, and level their pieces at you?"

"Eh, *parbleu!*—they should kill me."

"My dear Albert," returned Franz, "your answer is sublime, but as for us, it would be ridiculous to risk our lives." Albert poured himself out a glass of *lacryma Christi*, which he sipped at intervals.

"Well, Maître Pastrini," said Franz, "now you see how peace-

ful my intentions are, tell me who is this Luigi Vampa. Is he
a shepherd or a nobleman ?—young or old ?—tall or short ?
Describe him so that if we meet him by chance we may recognize him."

"You could not apply to anyone better able to inform
you on all these points, for I knew him when he was a child ;
and one day that I fell into his hands, going from Ferentino to
Alatri, he, fortunately, recollected me, and set me free, not only
without ransom, but gave me a very handsome watch, and told
me his history."

"Let us see the watch," said Albert.

Maître Pastrini drew from his fob a magnificent Bréguet, bearing the name of its maker and a count's coronet.

"*Peste !*" returned Albert, "I compliment you on it ; I have
its fellow "—he took his watch from his waistcoat pocket—"and
it cost me 3,000 francs."

"Let us hear the history," said Franz, motioning Maître
Pastrini to seat himself. "You tell me that you knew Luigi
Vampa when he was a child—he is still a young man, then ?"

"A young man! he is only two-and-twenty ;—he will gain
himself a reputation."

"Is he tall or short ?"

"Of the middle height—about the same stature as his Excellency," returned the host, pointing to Albert. "He was a
shepherd-boy attached to the farm of the Comte de San Felice,
situated between Palestrina and the lake of Gabri ; he was born
at Pampinara, and entered the count's service when he was
five years old. When quite a child, Vampa was of a most extraordinary disposition. One day, when he was seven years old,
he came to the curé of Palestrina, and prayed him to teach him
to read ; it was somewhat difficult, for he could not quit his
flock ; but the good curé went every day to say mass at a little
hamlet called Borgo ; he told Luigi that he might meet him on
his return, and that then he would give him a lesson, warning him
that it would be short, and that he must profit as much as possible
by it. Every day Luigi led his flock to graze on the road that
leads from Palestrina to Borgo ; every day, at nine o'clock in the
morning, the priest and the boy sat down on a bank by the wayside, and the little shepherd took his lesson out of the priest's
breviary. At the end of three months he had learned to read.
At the end of another three months he had learned to write.
The curé, astonished at his quickness and intelligence, related
this to the Comte de San Felice, who sent for the little shepherd,

made him read and write before him, ordered his attendant to let him eat with the domestics, and to give him two piastres a month. With this Luigi purchased books and pencils. He applied to everything his imitative powers, and, like Giotto, when young, he drew on his slate sheep, houses, and trees. Then, with his knife, he began to carve all sorts of objects in wood; it was thus that Pinelli, the famous sculptor, had begun.

" A girl, a little younger than Vampa, tended sheep on a farm near Palestrina : she was an orphan, born at Valmontone, and was named Teresa. The two children met, and thus grew up. Vampa was twelve and Teresa eleven. And yet their natural disposition revealed itself. Besides his taste for the fine arts, which Luigi had carried as far as he could in his solitude, he was sad by fits, ardent by starts, angry by caprice, and always sarcastic. His disposition kept him aloof from all friendships, Teresa alone ruled this impetuous character, which yielded beneath the hand of a woman, and which beneath the hand of a man might have been broken, but would never have bent. Teresa, on the contrary, was lively and gay, but coquettish to excess. The two piastres that Luigi received every month from the Comte de San Felice's steward, and the price of all the little carvings in wood he sold at Rome, were expended in earrings, necklaces, and gold hair-pins. So that, thanks to her friend's generosity, Teresa was the most beautiful and the best attired peasant near Rome.

" One day the young shepherd told the count's steward he had seen a wolf come out of the Sabine mountains, and prowl around his flock. The steward gave him a gun ; this was what Vampa longed for. From this moment he devoted all his leisure time to perfecting himself in the use of this precious weapon ; he purchased powder and ball, and everything served him for a mark. Thus he soon became so expert that Teresa overcame the terror she at first felt at the report, and amused herself by watching him direct the ball wherever he pleased, with as much accuracy as if placed by the hand.

" One evening a wolf emerged from a pine-wood near which they were usually stationed ; but the wolf had scarcely advanced ten yards ere he was dead. Proud of this exploit, Vampa took the dead animal on his shoulders, and carried him to the farm. All these circumstances had gained Luigi considerable reputation. The man of superior abilities always finds admirers, go where he will. He was spoken of as the most adroit, the strongest and most courageous *contadino* for ten leagues round ;

and although Teresa was universally allowed to be the most
beautiful girl of the Sabines, no one had ever spoken to her
of love, because it was known that she was beloved by Vampa.
And yet the two young people had never declared their affection.   Only their wish to see each other had become a necessity,
and they would have preferred death to a day's separation.

" About this time, a band of brigands that had established
itself in the Lepini mountains began to be much spoken of.
The brigands have never been really extirpated from the neighbourhood of Rome.   Sometimes a chief is wanted, but when a
chief presents himself he rarely wants a band.

" The celebrated Cucumetto, pursued in the Abruzzo, driven
out of the kingdom of Naples, where he had carried on a regular
war, had crossed the Garigliano, like Manfred, and had come
between Sonnino and Juperno, to take refuge on the banks of
the Amasine.   He it was who strove to reorganize a band, and
who followed the footsteps of Decesaris and Gasperone, whom
he hoped to surpass.   Many young men of Palestrina, Frascati,
and Pampinara disappeared.   Their disappearance at first
caused much inquietude ; but it was soon known they had joined
the band of Cucumetto.   After some time Cucumetto became
the object of universal attention ; the most extraordinary traits
of ferocious daring and brutality were related of him, and everyone trembled at his name.

" These narratives were frequently the themes of conversation between Luigi and Teresa.   The young girl trembled very
much, but Vampa reassured her with a smile, tapping the butt
of his good fowling-piece, which threw its ball so well ; and if
that did not restore her courage, he pointed to a crow perched
on some dead branch, took an aim, touched the trigger, and the
bird fell dead at the foot of the tree.   Time passed on, and the
two young people settled to be married, when Vampa should be
twenty and Teresa nineteen years of age.   One day, when they
were talking over their plans for the future, they heard two or
three reports of firearms, and suddenly a man came out of the
wood near which the two young persons used to graze their
flocks, and hurried towards them.   When he came within hearing he exclaimed, ' I am pursued ; can you conceal me ? '   They
knew full well that this fugitive must be a bandit ; but there is
an innate sympathy between the Roman brigand and the Roman
peasant, and the latter is always ready to aid the former.   Vampa,
without saying a word, hastened to the stone that closed up the
entrance to their grotto, drew it away, made a sign to the fugi-

tive to take refuge there, closed the stone upon him, and then resumed his seat by Teresa.   Instantly afterwards four carbineers on horseback, appeared on the edge of the wood; three of them seemed to be looking for the fugitive, whilst the fourth dragged a brigand prisoner by the neck.   The three carbineers saw the young peasants, and galloping up, interrogated them.   They had seen no one.   ' That is very annoying,' said the brigadier; ' for the man we are looking for is the chief.'

"' Cucumetto ? ' cried Luigi and Teresa at the same moment.

"' Yes,' replied the brigadier; ' and as his head is valued at a thousand Roman crowns there would have been five hundred for you, if you had helped us to catch him.'   The two young persons exchanged looks.   The brigadier had a moment's hope. Five hundred Roman crowns are three thousand francs, and three thousand francs is a fortune for two poor orphans who are going to be married.

"' It is very annoying,' said Vampa; ' but we have not seen him.'

"The carbineers scoured the country in different directions, but in vain; then, after a time, they disappeared.   Vampa then removed the stone, and Cucumetto came out.   He had seen, through the crevices in the granite, the two young peasants talking with the carbineers, and guessed the subject of their parley.   He had read in the countenances of Luigi and Teresa their steadfast resolution not to surrender him, and he drew from his pocket a purse full of gold, which he offered to them.   But Vampa raised his head proudly; as for Teresa, her eyes sparkled when she thought of all the fine gowns and gay jewellery she could buy with this purse of gold.

"Cucumetto was a cunning fiend, and had assumed the form of a brigand instead of a serpent, and this look of Teresa revealed to him that she was a worthy daughter of Eve, and he returned to the forest, pausing several times on his way, under the pretext of saluting his protectors.   Several days elapsed, and they neither saw nor heard of Cucumetto.   The time of the Carnival was at hand.   The Comte de San Felice announced a grand masked ball, to which all that were distinguished in Rome were invited.   Teresa had a great desire to see this ball, Luigi asked permission of his protector, the steward, that she and he might be present amongst the servants of the house.   This was granted.   The ball was given by the count for the particular pleasure of his daughter Carmela, whom he adored.   Carmela was precisely of the age and figure of Teresa, and Teresa was as handsome as Carmela. On the evening of the ball Teresa was attired in her best, her most brilliant hair ornaments, and gayest glass beads,—she was in the costume of the women of Frascati. Luigi wore the very picturesque garb of the Roman peasant at holiday time. They both mixed, as they had leave to do, with the servants and peasants.

" Carmela was attired like a woman of Sonnino. Her cap was embroidered with pearls, the pins in her hair were of gold and diamonds, her girdle was of Turkey silk, with large embroidered flowers, her bodice and skirt were of cashmere, her apron of Indian muslin, and the buttons of her corset were of jewels. Two of her companions were dressed, the one as a woman of Nettuno, and the other as a woman of La Riccia. Four young men of the richest and noblest families of Rome accompanied them with that Italian freedom which has not its parallel in any other country of the world. They were attired as peasants of Albano, Velletri, Civita Castellana, and Sora. We need hardly add that these peasant costumes, like those of the females, were brilliant with gold and jewels.

" Carmela wished to make a uniform quadrille, but there was one lady wanting. Carmela looked all around her, but not one of the guests had a costume similar to her own, or those of her companions. The Comte de San Felice pointed out to her, in the group of peasants, Teresa, who was hanging on Luigi's arm.

" ' Will you allow me, father ? ' said Carmela.

" ' Certainly,' replied the Comte ; ' are we not in Carnival time ? '

" Carmela turned towards the young man who was talking with her, and saying a few words to him, pointed with her finger to Teresa. The young man followed with his eyes the lovely hand which made this indication, bowed in obedience and then went to Teresa, and invited her to dance in a quadrille directed by the Count's daughter. Teresa felt something like a flame pass over her face, she looked at Luigi, who could not refuse his assent. Luigi slowly relinquished Teresa's arm, which he had held beneath his own, and Teresa, accompanied by her elegant cavalier, took her appointed place with much agitation in the aristocratic quadrille. Certainly, in the eyes of an artist, the exact and strict costume of Teresa had a very different character from that of Carmela and her companions ; and Teresa was frivolous and coquettish, and thus the embroidery and muslins, the cashmere waist-girdles, all dazzled her and the reflection of sapphires and diamonds almost turned her giddy brain.

" Luigi felt a sensation hitherto unknown arising in his mind. It was like an acute pain which gnawed at his heart, and then passed thrillingly throughout his frame. He followed each movement of Teresa and her cavalier; when their hands touched, he felt as though he should swoon. When they spoke it seemed as if the whole world were turning round, and all the voices of hell were whispering ideas of murder and assassination. Then fearing that his paroxysm might get the better of him, he clutched with one hand the branch of a tree against which he was leaning, and with the other convulsively grasped the dagger with a carved handle, which was in his belt, and which, unwittingly, he drew from the scabbard from time to time. Luigi was jealous. He felt that, influenced by her ambition and coquettish disposition, Teresa might escape him.

" The young peasant girl, at first timid and scared, soon recovered herself. I have said that Teresa was handsome, but this was not all; she was replete with all those wild graces which are so much more potent than affected and studied elegances. She had almost all the honours of the quadrille, and if she were envious of the Comte de San Felice's daughter, I will not undertake to say that Carmela was not jealous of her. And with overpowering compliments, her handsome cavalier led her back to the place whence he had taken her, and where Luigi awaited her. Twice or thrice during the dance the young girl had glanced at Luigi, and each time she saw he was pale and his features agitated; once even the blade of his knife, half drawn from its sheath, had dazzled her eyes with its sinister glare. Thus, it was almost trembling that she resumed her lover's arm. The quadrille had been perfect, and it was evident there was a great demand for a second edition, Carmela alone objecting to it; but the Comte de San Felice begged his daughter so earnestly that she acceded to it. One of the cavaliers hastened to invite Teresa, without whom it was impossible the quadrille could be formed, but the young girl had disappeared. The truth was, that Luigi had not felt the strength to support another such trial, and, half by persuasion, and half by force, he had removed Teresa to another part of the garden. Teresa had yielded in spite of herself, but when she looked at the agitated countenance of the young man she understood by his silence and trembling voice that something strange was passing within him. She herself was not exempt from internal emotion, and without having done anything wrong, she fully comprehended that Luigi was right in reproaching her. However, to Teresa's great astonishment, Luigi remained mute, and not a word escaped his lips the rest of the evening. When the chill of the night had driven the guests from the gardens, and the gates of the villa were closed on them for the fête indoors, he took Teresa away, and as he left her at her home he said,—

" ' Teresa, what were you thinking of as you danced opposite the daughter of the Comte de San Felice ? '

" ' I thought,' replied the young girl, with all the frankness of her nature, ' that I would give half my life for a costume such as she wore.'

" ' And what said your cavalier to you ? '

" ' He said it only depended on myself to have it, and I had only one word to say.'

" ' He was right,' said Luigi. ' Do you desire it as ardently as you say ? '

" ' Yes.'

" ' Well then, you shall have it.'

" The young girl, much astonished, raised her head to look at him, but his face was so gloomy and terrible that her words froze to her lips. As Luigi spoke thus he left her. Teresa followed him with her eyes into the darkness as long as she could, and when he had disappeared she entered her apartment with a sigh.

" That night a great accident happened, no doubt from the imprudence of some servant who had neglected to extinguish the lights. The Villa de San Felice took fire in the rooms adjoining the very apartment of the lovely Carmela. Awakened by the light of the flames, she had sprung out of bed, wrapped herself in a dressing-gown, and attempted to escape by the door, but the corridor by which she hoped to fly was already a prey to the fire. She had then returned to her room, calling for help as loudly as she could, when suddenly her window, which was twenty feet from the ground, was opened, a young peasant jumped into the chamber, seized her in his arms, and with superhuman skill and strength conveyed her to the turf of the grass-plot, where she fainted. When she recovered, her father was by her side. All the servants surrounded her, offering her assistance. An entire wing of the villa was burnt down ; but what did that matter, as Carmela was safe and uninjured ? Her preserver was everywhere sought for, but could not be found ; he was inquired for everywhere, but no one had seen him. Carmela was greatly troubled that she had not recognized him.

" The next day, at the usual hour, the two young peasants

were on the borders of the forest. Luigi arrived first. He came towards Teresa in high spirits, and seemed to have forgotten the events of the previous evening. He took her arm beneath his own, and led her to the door of the grotto. Then he paused.

" ' Teresa,' he said, ' yesterday evening you told me you would give all the world to have a costume similar to that of the Count's daughter.'

" ' Yes,' replied Teresa, with astonishment ; ' but I was mad to utter such a wish.'

" ' And I replied, " Very well, you shall have it." '

" ' Yes,' replied the young girl, whose astonishment increased at every word uttered by Luigi, ' but of course your reply was only to please me.'

" ' I have promised no more than I have given you, Teresa,' said Luigi, proudly. ' Go into the grotto and dress yourself.'

" At these words he drew away the stone, and showed Teresa the grotto, lighted up by two wax lights, which burnt on each side of a splendid mirror ; on a rustic table, made by Luigi, were spread out the pearl necklace and the diamond pins, and on a chair at the side was laid the rest of the costume.

" Teresa uttered a cry of joy, and, without inquiring whence this attire came, or even thanking Luigi, darted into the grotto transformed into a dressing-room. Luigi pushed the stone behind her. for he saw on the crest of a small adjacent hill which prevented him from seeing Palestrina from where he was, a traveller on horseback, who stopped a moment as if uncertain of his road, and thus presented, in the blue sky, that perfect outline peculiar to the distances of southern climes. When he saw Luigi, he put his horse into a gallop and advanced towards him. The traveller, who was going from Palestrina to Tivoli, had mistaken his way : the young man directed him ; but as at a quarter of a mile distance the road again divided into three ways, and on reaching these the traveller might again stray from his route, he begged Luigi to be his guide. In ten minutes they reached the cross-roads alluded to by the young shepherd. On arriving there, with an air as majestic as that of an emperor, he stretched his hand towards that one of the roads which the traveller was to follow.

" ' That is your road, Excellency, and now you cannot again mistake.'

" ' And here is your recompense,' said the traveller, offering the young herdsman some pieces of small money.

" ' Thank you,' said Luigi, drawing back his hand ; ' I render a service, I do not sell it.'

" ' Well,' replied the traveller, who seemed used to this difference between the servility of a man of the cities and the pride of the mountaineer, ' if you refuse pay, you will, perhaps, accept of a present. Take these two Venice sequins and give them to your bride, to make herself a pair of earrings.'

" ' And then do you take this poniard,' said the young herdsman ; ' you will not find one better carved between Albano and Civita Castellana.'

" ' I accept it,' answered the traveller, ' but then the obligation will be on my side, for this poniard is worth more than two sequins.'

" ' For a dealer, perhaps ; but for me, who engraved it myself, it is hardly worth a piastre.'

" ' What is your name ? ' inquired the traveller.

" ' Luigi Vampa,' replied the shepherd, with the same air as he would have replied, Alexander, King of Macedon.

" ' And yours ? '

" ' I,' said the traveller, ' am called Sindbad the Sailor.' "

Franz d'Épinay started with surprise. The name of Sindbad the Sailor, as may well be supposed, awakened in him a world of recollections.

" Proceed ! " said he to the host.

" Vampa put the two sequins haughtily into his pocket, and slowly returned by the way he had gone. As he came within two or three hundred paces of the grotto, he thought he heard a cry. A moment afterwards and he heard his own name pronounced distinctly. The cry proceeded from the grotto. He bounded like a chamois, cocking his carbine as he went, and in a moment reached the summit of a hill opposite to that on which he had perceived the traveller. Thence cries of help came more distinctly on his ear. He cast his eyes round him, and saw a man carrying off Teresa. This man was already three-quarters of the way on the road from the grotto to the forest. Vampa measured the distance, the man was at least two hundred paces in advance of him, and there was not a chance of overtaking him. The young shepherd stopped, as if his feet had been rooted to the ground ; then he put the butt of his carbine to his shoulder, took aim at the ravisher, followed him for a second in his track, and then fired. The ravisher stopped suddenly, his knees bent under him, and he fell with Teresa in his arms. The young girl rose instantly, but the man lay on the earth in the agonies of death. Vampa then rushed towards Teresa ; for at ten paces from the dying man her legs had failed her, and she had dropped on her knees, so that the young man feared the ball that had brought down his enemy, had also wounded his betrothed. Fortunately, she was unscathed; fright alone had overcome Teresa. When Luigi had assured himself that she was safe, he turned towards the wounded man. He had just expired. His eyes remained open and menacing. Vampa approached the carcase and recognized Cucumetto. From the day on which the bandit had been saved by the two young peasants, he had been enamoured of Teresa, and had sworn she should be his. From that time he had watched them, and profiting by the moment when her lover had left her alone, had carried her off, and believed he at length had her in his power, when the ball, directed by the unerring skill of the young herdsman, had pierced his heart. Vampa gazed on him without betraying the slightest emotion. Then suddenly he turned towards his mistress :—' Ah ! ah ! ' said he—' good, good ! you are attired, it is now my turn to dress myself.'

" Teresa was clothed from head to foot in the garb of the Comte de San Felice's daughter. Vampa took Cucumetto's body in his arms and conveyed it to the grotto, whilst in her turn Teresa remained outside. At the end of a quarter of an hour Vampa quitted the grotto ; his costume was no less elegant than that of Teresa. He wore a vest of garnet-coloured velvet, with buttons of cut gold ; a silk waistcoat covered with embroidery ; a Roman scarf tied round his neck ; a cartouche-box worked with gold, and red and green silk ; sky-blue velvet breeches, fastened above the knee with diamond buckles ; garters of deer-skin, worked with a thousand arabesques, and a hat whereon hung ribands of all colours ; two watches hung from his girdle, and a splendid poniard was in his belt. Teresa uttered a cry of admiration. Vampa had assumed the costume of Cucumetto. The young man saw the effect produced on his betrothed, and a smile of pride passed over his lips.

" ' Now,' he said to Teresa, ' are you ready to share my fortune, whatever it may be ? '

" ' Oh, yes ! ' exclaimed the young girl, enthusiastically.

" ' And follow me wherever I go ? '

" ' To the world's end.'

" ' Then take my arm, and let us on ; we have no time to lose.' "

" The young girl did so without questioning her lover as to where he was conducting her. They went towards the forest, and soon entered it. At the end of an hour and a half they had reached the thickest of the forest. A torrent, whose bed was dry, led into a deep gorge, which seemed, but for the difficulties of its descent, that path to Avernus of which Virgil speaks. Teresa, alarmed at the wild and deserted look of the place, pressed closely against her guide, uttering not a syllable ; but as she saw him advance with composed countenance, she endeavoured to repress her emotion. Suddenly, about ten paces from them, a man advanced from behind a tree and aimed at Vampa.

" ' Not another step,' he said, ' or you are a dead man.'

" ' What ! ' said Vampa, raising his hand with a gesture of disdain, whilst Teresa, no longer able to restrain her alarm, clung closely to him ; ' do wolves rend each other ? '

" ' Who are you ? ' inquired the sentinel.

" ' I am Luigi Vampa, shepherd of the farm of San Felice, and I would speak with your companions who are in the recess at Rocca Bianca.'

" ' Follow me, then,' said the sentinel : ' or, as you know your way, go first.'

" Vampa smiled disdainfully at this precaution of the bandit, went before Teresa, and at the end of ten minutes the bandit made them a sign to stop. Then the bandit thrice imitated the cry of a crow. A croak answered this signal.

" ' Good ! ' said the sentry : ' you may advance.'

" Luigi and Teresa again set forward ; as they advanced, Teresa clung tremblingly to her lover, as she saw through the trees arms appear, and the barrels of carbines shine. When Teresa and Luigi reached Rocca Bianca, they found themselves in the presence of twenty bandits.

" ' Here is a young man who wishes to speak to you,' said the sentinel.

" ' What has he to say ? ' inquired the young man who was in command in the chief's absence.

" ' I wish to say that I am tired of a shepherd's life,' was Vampa's reply.

" ' Ah, I understand,' said the lieutenant ; ' and you seek admittance into our ranks ? '

" ' Welcome ! ' cried several bandits of Ferrusino, Pampinara, and Anagni, who had recognized Luigi Vampa.

" ' Yes, but I come to ask something more than to be your companion.'

" ' And what may that be ? ' inquired the bandits, with astonishment.

' ' I come to ask to be your captain,'

" The bandits shouted with laughter.

" ' And what have you done to aspire to this honour ? ' demanded the lieutenant.

" ' I have killed your chief, Cucumetto, whose dress I now wear ; and I set fire to the Villa San Felice to procure a wedding-dress for my betrothed.' An hour afterwards Luigi Vampa was chosen captain, *vice* Cucumetto deceased."

" Well, my dear Albert," said Franz, turning towards his friend, " what think you of citizen Luigi Vampa ? "

" I say he is a myth," replied Albert, " and never had an existence."

" But you, landlord, say that Vampa exercises his profession at this moment in the environs of Rome ! "

" And with a boldness of which no bandit before him ever gave an example."

" Then the police have vainly tried to lay hands on him ? "

" Why, you see, he has a good understanding with the shepherds in the plains, the fishermen of the Tiber, and the smugglers of the coast. They seek for him in the mountains, and he is on the waters ; they follow him on the waters, and he is on the open sea ; they pursue him, and he has suddenly taken refuge in the isle of Giglio, of Guanouti, or Monte Cristo ; and when they hunt for him there he reappears suddenly at Albano, Tivoli, or La Riccia."

" And how does he behave towards travellers ? "

" It depends on the distance he may be from the city, whether he gives eight hours, twelve hours, or a day wherein to pay the ransom ; and when that time has elapsed he allows another hour's grace. At the sixtieth minute of this hour, if the money is not forthcoming, he blows out the prisoner's brains, or plants his dagger in his heart."

The clock struck nine as the door opened, and a coachman appeared. " Excellencies," said he, " the coach is ready."

" Well, then," said Franz, " let us to the Colosseum."

" By the Porta del Popolo or by the streets, your Excellencies ? "

" By the streets, *morbleu !* by the streets," cried Franz.

" Ah, my dear fellow," said Albert, lighting his third cigar ; " really, I thought you had more courage."

CHAPTER XXXIV

THE COLOSSEUM

FRANZ had so managed his route, that during the ride to the Colosseum, they passed not a single ancient ruin, so that no gradual preparation was made on the mind for the colossal proportions of the building they came to admire. This itinerary possessed another great advantage, that of leaving Franz at full liberty to indulge his deep reverie upon the subject of the story recounted by Maître Pastrini, in which his mysterious host of the isle of Monte Cristo was so strangely mixed up. Seated with folded arms in a corner of the carriage, he continued to ponder the singular history he had so lately listened to, and to ask himself an interminable number of questions touching its various circumstances, without, however, arriving at a satisfactory reply to any of them. One fact more than the rest brought his friend "Sindbad the Sailor" back to his recollection, and that was the mysterious intimacy that seemed to exist between the brigands and sailors; and Pastrini's account of Vampa's having found refuge on board the vessels of smugglers and fishermen, reminded Franz of the two Corsican bandits he had found supping so amicably with the crew of the little yacht which had even deviated from its course and touched at Porto Vecchia for the sole purpose of landing them. The very name assumed by his host of Monte Cristo, and repeated by the landlord of the Hôtel de Londres, proved that his island friend was playing his philanthropic part equally on the shores of Piombino, Civita Vecchia, Ostia, and Gaëta, as on those of Corsica, Tuscany, and Spain; and Franz thought he had heard his entertainer speak both of Tunis and Palermo, proving thereby how largely his circle of acquaintances extended.

But however the mind of the young man might be absorbed in these reflections, they were at once dispersed at the sight of the frowning ruins of the stupendous Colosseum, through the various openings of which the pale moonlight played and flickered like the unearthly gleam from the eyes of the wandering dead. The carriage door was opened, and the young men eagerly alighting, found themselves opposite a cicerone, who appeared to have sprung up from the ground, so unexpected was his appearance.

The usual guide from the hotel having followed them, they had paid two conductors; nor is it possible, at Rome, to avoid this abundant supply of guides; besides the ordinary cicerone who seizes upon you directly you set foot in your hotel, and never quits you while you remain in the city, there is also a special cicerone belonging to each monument—nay, almost to each part of a monument.

As for Albert and Franz, they essayed not to escape from their ciceronian tyrants. And, indeed, it would have been so much the more difficult to break their bondage, as the guides alone are permitted to visit these monuments with torches in their hands ; thus the young men made no attempt at resistance, but confidingly surrendered themselves into the care of their conductors. No adequate notion of these ruins can be formed, save by such as have visited them, and more especially by moonlight, at which time the vast proportions of the building appear twice as large, when viewed by the mysterious beams of a southern moonlit sky, whose radiance is sufficiently clear and vivid to gild the horizon with a glow equal to the soft twilight of an Eastern clime. Scarcely, therefore, had the reflective Franz walked a hundred steps beneath the interior porticoes of the ruin, than he abandoned Albert to the guides, and to escape a mechanical survey of the wonders by which he was surrounded, ascended a half-dilapidated staircase. Here, leaving the others to follow their monotonous round he seated himself at the foot of the column, immediately opposite a large chasm, which permitted him to enjoy an undisturbed view of the dimensions of this majestic ruin.

Franz had remained for nearly a quarter of an hour hidden by the shadow of the vast column at whose base he had found a resting-place, and from whence his eyes followed Albert and his guides, who, holding torches in their hands, resembled, as they glided along, restless shades following the flickering glare of so many ignes fatui, when all at once his ear caught a sound resembling that of a stone rolling down the staircase opposite the one by which he had himself ascended. There was nothing remarkable in the circumstance of a morsel of granite giving way and falling heavily below ; but it seemed to him that the substance that fell gave way beneath the pressure of a foot ; and also that someone, who endeavoured to prevent his footsteps from being heard, was approaching the spot where he sat. Conjecture soon became certainty, for the figure of a man was visible, gradually emerging from the staircase opposite, upon which the moon was pouring a full tide of silvery brightness.

The stranger thus presenting himself was probably a person who, like Franz, preferred the enjoyment of solitude and his own thoughts to the frivolous gabble of the guides ; and his appearance had nothing extraordinary in it ; but the hesitation with which he

proceeded onwards, stopping and listening with anxious attention
at every step, convinced Franz he expected the arrival of some
person.   By a sort of instinctive impulse, Franz withdrew as much
as possible behind his pillar.   About ten feet from the spot where
himself and the stranger were placed the roof had given way,
leaving a large round aperture.   Around this opening grew a
quantity of creeping plants, whose delicate green branches stood
out in bold relief against the clear azure of the firmament, while
large masses of thick strong fibrous shoots forced their way
through the chasm, and hung floating to and fro like so many
waving strings.   The person whose mysterious arrival had attracted the attention of Franz stood in a kind of half-light, that
rendered it impossible to distinguish his features, although his
dress was easily made out.   He wore a large brown mantle, one
fold of which, thrown over his left shoulder, served to mask the
lower part of his countenance, the upper part of which was hidden
by his broad-brimmed hat ; the lower part of his dress was more
distinctly visible by the bright rays of the moon, which fell on
feet cased in elegantly-made boots of polished leather, over which
descended fashionably-cut trousers of black cloth.

Franz could only come to one conclusion—that the person he
was thus watching belonged to no humble station of life.   Some
few minutes had elapsed, and the stranger began to show signs
of impatience, when a slight noise was heard outside the aperture
in the roof, and almost immediately a dark shadow seemed to
obstruct the flood of light that had entered it, and the figure of a
man was clearly seen gazing with eager scrutiny on the immense
space beneath him ; then, as his eye caught sight of the man in
the mantle, he grasped a floating mass of thickly-matted boughs,
and glided down by their help to within three or four feet of the
ground, and then leaped lightly on his feet.   The new-comer wore
the costume of Trastevere.   " I beg your Excellency's pardon
for keeping you waiting," said the man, in the Roman dialect ;
"but I don't think I'm many minutes after my time ; ten o'clock
has just struck."

" Say not a word about being late," replied the stranger, in pur-
est Tuscan, " 'tis I who am too soon ; but even if you had caused
me to wait a little, I should have felt sure the delay was not occasioned by any fault of yours."

" Your Excellency is perfectly right in so thinking," said the
man ; " I came here direct from the Castle of St. Angelo, and I had
an immense deal of trouble before I could get to speak to Beppo."

" And who is Beppo ? "

" Oh ! Beppo is employed in the prison, and I give him so much a year to let me know what is going on within his Holiness's Castle. You see no one knows what may happen ; perhaps some of these days I may be entrapped, like poor Peppino, and may be very glad to have some little mouse gnaw the meshes of my net, and so help me out of prison."

" Briefly, what did you glean ? "

" That two executions of considerable interest will take place the day after to-morrow at two o'clock, as is customary at Rome at the commencement of all great festivals ; one of the culprits will be *mazzolato*,—he is an atrocious villain, who murdered the priest who brought him up ; the other sufferer is sentenced to be *decapitato*, and he is poor Peppino."

" The fact is, you have inspired not only the Pontifical government, but also the neighbouring States, with such extreme fear, that they are glad of an opportunity of making an example."

" But Peppino did not even belong to my band ; he was merely a poor shepherd, whose only crime consisted in furnishing us with provisions."

" Which makes him your accomplice to all intents and purposes ; but mark the distinction with which he is treated ; instead of being knocked on the head, as you would be if once they caught hold of you, he is simply sentenced to be guillotined, by which means, too, the amusements of the day are diversified, and there is a spectacle to please everyone."

" Without reckoning the wholly unexpected one I am preparing to surprise them with.   One thing I have resolved on, and that is, to stop at nothing to restore a poor devil to liberty, who has got into this scrape solely from having served me."

" And what do you mean to do ? "

" To surround the scaffold with twenty of my best men, who, at a signal from me, will rush forward directly Peppino is brought for execution, and drive back the guard and carry off the prisoner."

" That seems to me as hazardous as uncertain, and convinces me my scheme is far better than yours."

" And what is your Excellency's project ? "

" Just this ! I will so advantageously bestow 2,000 piastres that the person receiving them shall obtain a respite till next year for Peppino ; and during that year another skilfully-placed 1,000 piastres shall afford him the means of escaping from his prison."

" And do you feel sure of succeeding ? "

" *Pardieu !* " exclaimed the man in the cloak, suddenly expressing himself in French, " I would do more single-handed by the means of gold than you and all your troop could effect with stilettos, pistols, carbines, and blunderbusses included. Leave me, then, to act, and have no fear for the result."

" At least there can be no harm in myself and party being in readiness, in case your Excellency should fail. Remember, the execution is fixed for the day after to-morrow, and that you have but one day to work in."

" And what then ? Is not a day divided into twenty-four hours, each hour into sixty minutes, and every minute into sixty seconds ? Now in 86,400 seconds very many things can be done."

" And how shall I know whether your Excellency has succeeded or not ?

" Oh ! that is very easily arranged ; I have engaged the three lower windows at the Café Rospoli ; should I have obtained pardon for Peppino, the two outside windows will be hung with yellow damasks, and the centre with white, having a large cross in red marked on it."

" And whom will you employ to carry the reprieve to the officer directing the execution ? "

" Send one of your men disguised as a penitent friar, and I will give it to him : his dress will procure him the means of approaching the scaffold itself, and he will deliver the order to the officer, who in his turn will hand it to the executioner. In the meantime acquaint Peppino with what we have determined on, if only to prevent his dying of fear or losing his senses, because in either case a very useless expense will have been incurred."

" Your Excellency," said the man, " only fulfil your promise of rescuing Peppino, and henceforward you shall receive the most absolute obedience from myself and those under me that one human being can render to another."

" Have a care how far you pledge yourself, my good friend, for I may remind you of your promises at some perhaps not very distant period."

" Your Excellency will find me what I have found you in this my heavy trouble ; and if from the other end of the world you but write me word to do such or such a thing, conclude it done, on the word and faith of——"

" Hush ! I hear a noise. 'Twere better we should not be seen together ; those guides are nothing but spies, and might recognize you ; and, however I may be honoured by your friendship, if once the extent of our intimacy were known, I am afraid my reputation and credit would suffer thereby."

" Well, then, if you obtain the reprieve ? "

" The middle window at the Café Rospoli will be hung with white damask, bearing on it a red cross."

" And if you fail ? "

" Then, all three windows will have yellow draperies."

" And then ? "

" Use your daggers in any way you please ; and I promise to be a spectator of your prowess."

" All is then understood between us. Adieu, your Excellency ! "

Saying these words, the Trastevere one disappeared down the staircase, while his companion, muffling his features more closely than before in the folds of his mantle, passed almost close to Franz, and descended to the arena by an outward flight of steps. The next minute Franz heard himself called by Albert, who made the lofty building re-echo with the sound of his friend's name. Franz, however, did not obey the summons till he felt certain that the two individuals, whose conversation he had thus surprised, were at a sufficient distance to prevent his encountering them in his descent.

In ten minutes from the parting of the strangers Franz was on the road to the Hôtel de Londres, listening with indifference to the learned dissertation delivered by Albert, touching the iron-pointed nets used to prevent the ferocious beasts from spring-ing on the spectators. Franz longed to be at home, and able, undisturbedly, to ponder all that had occurred. One of the two men, whose mysterious rendezvous in the Colosseum he had witnessed, was an entire stranger to him, but not so the other ; and though Franz had been unable to distinguish his features, the tones of his voice had made too powerful an impression on him the first time he heard them for him ever again to forget them. It was more especially when speaking in a manner half jesting, half bitter, that Franz's ear recalled most vividly the deep, sonor-ous, yet well-pitched voice, which had spoken to him in the grotto of Monte Cristo, and which he heard for the second time amid the ruined grandeur of the Colosseum !

Next day Albert employed part of his time in arranging for the evening's diversion ; he had sent to engage a box at the Teatro Argentino, and Franz having a number of letters to write, relin-quished the carriage to his friend. At five o'clock Albert returned, delighted with his day's work ; he had been occupied in leaving his letters of introduction, and had received in return more in-vitations to balls and soirées than he could fulfil ; besides this he had seen (as he called it) all the remarkable sights at Rome.

The opera of " Parisina " was announced for representation at the Teatro Argentino. and the principal actors were Coselli, Moriani, and La Spech. The young men, therefore, had reason to consider themselves fortunate in having the opportunity of hearing one of the best works of the composer of " Lucia di Lammermoor," supported by three of the most renowned vocalists of Italy. Albert had never been able to endure the Italian theatres, with their absence of balconies, or open boxes. Still, in despite of this, he displayed his most dazzling and most effective costume each time he visited the theatres ; but, alas ! his *recherché* toilette was wholly thrown away ; and one of the most admired representatives of Parisian fashion had the mortifying reflection that he had nearly overrun Italy without making a single conquest.

However, he hoped to indemnify himself for all slights during the Carnival, knowing that among the different states and kingdoms in which this festivity is celebrated, Rome is the spot where even the wisest and gravest relax the usual severity of their lives, and deign to mingle in the follies of this season of liberty and mirth. The Carnival was to begin on the morrow ; therefore Albert had not an instant to lose in setting forth the programme of his hopes, expectations, and claims to notice. With this design he had engaged a box in the most conspicuous part of the theatre, in the first circle, and exerted himself to set off his personal attractions by the aid of the most elaborate toilette. He hoped that thus advantageously placed he could not fail to attract the notice of some fair Roman ; and an introduction might ensue that would procure him the offer of a seat in a carriage, or a place in a princely balcony, from which he might behold the gaieties of the Carnival. These united considerations made Albert more anxious to please than he had hitherto been. Totally disregarding the business of the stage, he leaned from his box and began scrutinizing the beauty of each pretty woman, aided by a powerful *lorgnette ;* but, alas ! it was but too apparent that the lovely creatures into whose good graces he was desirous of stealing were all so much engrossed with themselves, their lovers, or their thoughts, that they had not so much as remarked him or the pointing of his glass.

Towards the close of the first act of " Parisina " the door of a box which had been hitherto vacant was opened ; and a lady entered, to whom Franz had been introduced in Paris, where, indeed, he had imagined she still was. The quick eye of Albert caught the involuntary start with which his friend beheld the new arrival, and turning to him he said hastily—

"Do you know the woman who has just entered the box?"

"Yes; what do you think of her?"

"Oh, she is perfectly lovely, what a complexion! And such magnificent hair! Is she French?"

"No; she is a Venetian. Countess G——."

"Ah! I know her by name," exclaimed Albert; "she is said to possess as much wit and cleverness as beauty! I was to have been presented to her at Madame de Villefort's ball."

"Shall I assist in repairing your negligence?" asked Franz.

"My dear fellow, are you really on such good terms with her as to venture to take me to her box?"

"Well, I have only had the honour of being in her society and conversing with her three or four times in my life; but you know that even such an acquaintance as that might warrant my doing what you ask."

At this instant the Countess perceived Franz, and graciously waved her hand to him, to which he replied by a respectful inclination of the head.

"Upon my word," said Albert, "you seem to be on excellent terms with the beautiful Countess!"

"You are mistaken in thinking so," returned Franz, calmly; "believe me, nothing is more fallacious than to form an estimate of the intimacy existing between persons from the familiar terms on which they seem to stand towards each other."

"Is that so, my good fellow? But are you not going to keep your promise of introducing me to her?"

"Certainly, directly the curtain falls!"

"What a confounded time this first act takes! I believe, on my soul, that they never mean to finish it!"

"Oh, yes! they will! only listen to that charming finale! How exquisitely Coselli sings his part! and did you ever see anything more perfect than La Spech's acting?"

"Why, you know, my dear fellow, when one has been accustomed to Malibran and Sonntag, these kind of singers don't make the same impression on you."

"At least you must admire Moriani's style and execution."

"I never fancied men of his dark, ponderous appearance singing with a voice like a woman's."

"My good friend," said Franz, turning to him, while Albert continued to point his glass at every box in the theatre, "you seem determined not to approve; you are really too difficult to please." The curtain at length fell on the performances, to the infinite satisfaction of the Viscount de Morcerf, who seized his hat, rapidly passed his fingers through his hair, arranged his cravat and wristbands, and signified to Franz that he was waiting for him to lead the way. Franz, who had mutely interrogated the Countess, and received from her a gracious smile in token that he would be welcome, sought not to retard the gratification of Albert's eager impatience, but began at once the tour of the house, to the Countess's box; at the knock the door was immediately opened and the young man who was seated beside the Countess in the front of the *loge*, in obedience to the Italian custom, instantly rose and surrendered his place to the strangers, who, in turn, would be expected to retire upon the arrival of other visitors.

Franz presented Albert as one of the most distinguished young men of the day, both as regarded his position in society and extraordinary talents; nor did he say more than the truth, for in Paris and the circle in which the viscount moved he was looked upon and cited as a model of perfection. The Countess bowed gracefully to Albert, and extended her hand with cordial kindness to Franz; then, inviting Albert to take the vacant seat beside her, she recommended Franz to take the next best, if he wished to view the ballet, and pointed to the one behind her own chair. Albert was soon deeply engrossed in discoursing upon Paris and Paris matters, speaking to the Countess of the various persons they both knew there. Franz perceived how completely he was in his element; and, unwilling to interfere with his pleasure, took up Albert's enormous *lorgnette*, and began in his turn to survey the audience. Sitting alone, in the front of a box immediately opposite, but in the third row, was a woman of exquisite beauty, dressed in a Greek costume, which, from the ease and grace with which she wore it, was her national attire. Behind her, in deep shadow, was the outline of a male figure; but the features of this latter personage it was not possible to distinguish. Franz could not forbear breaking in upon the conversation between the Countess and Albert, to inquire of the former if she knew who was the fair Albanian opposite, since beauty such as hers was worthy of being remarked by either sex.

"All I can tell you about her," replied the Countess, "is, that she has been at Rome since the beginning of the season; for I saw her where she now sits the very first night of the theatre's opening, and since then she has never missed a performance. Sometimes she is accompanied by the person who is with her, and at others attended by a black servant."

"And what do you think of her personal appearance?"

" Oh, I consider her perfectly lovely,—she is just my idea of what Medora must have been."

Franz and the Countess exchanged a smile, and then the latter resumed her conversation with Albert, while Franz returned to his survey of the house and company. The curtain rose on the ballet *Poliska*, one of those excellent specimens of the Italian school—masterly productions of grace, method, and elegance, in which the whole *corps de ballet*, from the principal dancers to the humblest supernumerary, are all engaged on the stage at the same time ; and a hundred and fifty persons may be seen exhibiting the same attitude, or elevating the same arm or leg with a simultaneous movement that would lead you to suppose but one mind, one act of volition, influenced the moving mass. However much the ballet might have claimed his attention, Franz was too deeply occupied with the beautiful Greek to take any note of it, while she seemed to experience an almost childlike delight in watching it ; her eager, animated looks contrasting strongly with the utter indifference of her companion, who, during the whole time the piece lasted, never even moved, in spite of the furious crashing din produced by the trumpets, cymbals, and Chinese bells. The companion of the fair Greek took no heed of the deafening sounds that prevailed, but was, as far as appearances might be trusted, enjoying soft repose and bright celestial dreams. The ballet at length came to a close, and the curtain fell amidst the plaudits of an enthusiastic and delighted audience.

The overture to the second act began ; and as the curtain drew up, the attention of Franz was attracted by the actors ; his eyes quitted their gaze at the box containing the Greek girl and her strange companion to watch the business of the stage.

Most of my readers are aware that the second act of " Parisina " opens with the celebrated duet in which Parisina, while sleeping, betrays to Azzo the secret of her love for Ugo. The injured husband goes through all the workings of jealousy, until conviction seizes on his mind, and then, in a frenzy of rage and indignation, he awakens his guilty wife to tell her he knows her guilt, and to threaten her with his vengeance. This duet is one of the finest conceptions that has ever emanated from the fruitful pen of Donizetti. Franz now listened to it for the third time : yet its notes, so tenderly expressive and fearfully grand, as the wretched husband and wife give vent to their different griefs and passions, thrilled through the soul of Franz with an effect equal to his first emotions upon hearing it. Excited beyond his usual calm, Franz rose with the audience, and was about to join the enthusiastic applause that followed ; but his purpose was arrested, his hands fell by his sides, and the half-uttered " bravos " expired on his lips. The occupant of the box in which the Greek girl sat appeared to share the universal animation that prevailed, for he left his seat to stand up in the front, so that, his countenance being fully revealed, Franz had no difficulty in recognizing him as the mysterious inhabitant of Monte Cristo, and the very same person he had encountered the preceding evening in the ruins of the Colosseum, and whose voice and figure had seemed so familiar to him. All doubt of his identity was now at an end ; his singular host evidently resided at Rome. The surprise and agitation occasioned by this confirmation of Franz's former suspicion had no doubt imparted a corresponding expression to his features, for the Countess, after gazing with a puzzled look on his speaking countenance, burst into a fit of laughter, and begged to know what had happened.

" Madame la Comtesse," returned Franz, unheeding her raillery, " I asked you a short time since if you knew any particulars respecting the Albanian lady opposite ; I must now beseech you to inform me who and what is her husband."

" Nay," answered the Countess, " I know no more of him than yourself. All I can say is, that the gentleman, whose history I am unable to furnish, seems to me as though he had just been dug up ; he looks more like a corpse permitted by some friendly gravedigger to quit his tomb for a while, and revisit this earth of ours, than anything human. How ghastly pale he is ! "

" Oh, he is always as colourless as you now see him," said Franz.

" Then you know him ? " almost screamed the Countess. " Oh ! pray do, for Heaven's sake, tell us all about him ; is he a vampire or a resuscitated corpse, or what ? "

" I fancy I have seen him before ; and I even think he recognizes me."

" I can well understand," said the Countess, shrugging her beautiful shoulders, as though an involuntary shudder passed through her veins, " that those who have once seen that man will never be likely to forget him."

" Well," inquired Franz, after the Countess had a second time directed her *lorgnette* at the *loge* of their mysterious *vis-à-vis* " what do you think of him ? "

" Why, that he is no other than Lord Ruthven himself in living form." This fresh allusion to Byron drew a smile to Franz's countenance ; although he could but allow that if anything were likely to induce belief in the existence of vampires it would

I

be the presence of such a man as the mysterious personage before him.

"I must find out who and what he is," said Franz, rising from his seat.

"No, no!" cried the Countess, "you must not leave me. I depend upon you to escort me home. Oh, indeed, I cannot permit you to go."

"Is it possible," whispered Franz, "that you entertain any fear?"

"I'll tell you," answered the Countess. "Byron had the most perfect belief in the existence of vampires, and even assured me he had seen some. The description he gave me perfectly corresponds with the features and character of the man before us. Oh! it is the exact personification of what I have been led to expect. The coal-black hair, large glittering eyes, in which a wild, unearthly fire seems burning,—the same ghastly paleness. Then observe, too, that the very woman he has with him is unlike all others of her sex. She is a foreigner—a stranger. Nobody knows who she is, or where she comes from. No doubt she belongs to the same horrible race, and is, like himself, a dealer in magical arts. I entreat of you not to go near him—at least, to-night; and if to-morrow your curiosity still continue as great, pursue your researches if you will; but to-night you neither can nor shall. For that purpose I mean to keep you all to myself."

Franz protested he could not defer his pursuit till the following day. "Listen to me," said the Countess, "and do not be so headstrong. I am going home. I have a party at my house to-night, and cannot remain till the conclusion of the opera. Now, I cannot believe you so devoid of gallantry as to refuse a lady your escort when she even condescends to ask for it."

Franz could not do less than take up his hat, open the door of the *loge*, and offer the Countess his arm. The Countess's manner showed that her uneasiness was not feigned; Franz could feel her arm tremble as he assisted her into the carriage. Upon arriving at her hotel, Franz perceived that she had deceived him when she spoke of expecting company; on the contrary, her own return before the appointed hour seemed greatly to astonish the domestics. "Excuse my little subterfuge," said the Countess, "but that horrid man had made me feel uncomfortable, and I longed to be alone, that I might compose my mind. However, promise me one thing."

"I will do anything you desire, except relinquish my determination to find out who this man is. I have more reasons than you can imagine for desiring to know who he is, whence he came, and whither he is going. But what is the promise you wished me to make ? "

" Give me your word to return immediately to your hotel, and make no attempt to follow this man to-night. There are certain affinities between persons. For heaven's sake, do not serve as a conductor between that man and me. Pursue your chase after him to-morrow as eagerly as you please ; but never bring him near me if you would not see me die of terror. And now, good-night ; try to sleep away all recollections of this evening. For my own part, I am sure I shall not be able to close my eyes." So saying, the Countess quitted Franz, leaving him unable to decide whether she were merely amusing herself at his expense, or whether her fears were genuine.

Upon his return to the hotel Franz found Albert in his dressing-gown and slippers, listlessly extended on a sofa, smoking a cigar. " My dear fellow ! " cried he, springing up, " is it really you ? Why, I did not expect to see you before to-morrow."

" My dear Albert ! " replied Franz, " I am glad of this opportunity to tell you, once and for ever, that you entertain a most erroneous notion concerning Italian women. I should have thought the repeated failures you have met with in your love affairs might have taught you better by this time."

" Upon my soul ! these women would puzzle the very devil. Why,—they give you their hand—press yours in return—keep up a whispering conversation—permit you to accompany them home ! If a Parisian were to indulge in a quarter of these marks of attention her reputation would be gone for ever."

" The very reason why Italian women put so little restraint on their words and actions is because they live so much in public, and have nothing to conceal. Besides, you must have perceived that the Countess was really alarmed."

" At what ? At the sight of that respectable gentleman sitting opposite to us in the same *loge* as the lovely Greek girl ? Now, for my part, I met them in the lobby after the conclusion of the piece ; and, hang me, if I can guess where you took your notions of the other world from ! This hobgoblin of yours is a deuced fine-looking fellow—admirably dressed. Indeed, I feel quite sure his clothes are made by a first-rate Paris tailor—probably Blin or Humann. He was rather too pale ; but, you know, paleness is looked upon as a strong proof of descent and breeding." Franz smiled ; for he remembered that Albert prided himself on the absence of colour in his own complexion.

"Well, that tends to confirm my own ideas," said Franz, "that the Countess's suspicions were destitute alike of sense and reason. Did he speak in your hearing? and did you catch any of his words?"

"I did; but they were uttered in the Romaic dialect. I knew that from the mixture of Greek words. When I was at college I was rather strong in Greek."

"He spoke the Romaic language, did he?" murmured Franz. "'Tis he, past all doubt."

"What do you say?"

"Nothing, nothing. But tell, what were you thinking about when I came in?"

"Why, you know, it is impossible to procure a carriage."

"Certainly; we have done all we could to get one."

"Now, then, in this difficulty, a bright idea has flashed across my brain. What do you say to a cart? I daresay such a thing might be had."

"Very possibly."

"And a pair of oxen?"

"As easily found as the cart."

"Then, you see, my good fellow, with a cart and a couple of oxen our business can be managed. The cart must be tastefully ornamented; and if you and I dress ourselves as Neapolitan reapers we may get up a striking tableau. It would add greatly to the effect if the Countess would join us in the costume of a peasant from Pozzuoli or Sorrento."

"Well," said Franz, "this time, Albert, I give you credit for having hit upon a most capital idea."

"Quite a national one, too," replied Albert, with gratified pride. "A mere masque borrowed from our own festivities. Ha! ha! Messieurs les Romains; you thought to make us, unhappy strangers, trot at the heels of your processions, like so many lazzaroni, because no carriages or horses are to be had in your beggarly city. But you don't know us; when we can't have one thing we invent another."

"Have you communicated your idea to any person?"

"Only to our host. He assured me that nothing would be easier than to furnish all I desired. One thing I was sorry for; when I bade him have the horns of the oxen gilded, he told me there would not be time, as it would require three days to effect that; so you see we must do without this little superfluity."

At this instant the door opened, and the head of Maître Pastrini appeared. "*Permesso?*" inquired he.

" Now, then," asked Albert, eagerly ; " have you found the cart and oxen ? "

" Better than that ! " replied the Maître Pastrini, with the air of a man well satisfied with himself. " Your Excellencies are aware that the count of Monte Cristo is living on the same floor as yourselves. Hearing of the dilemma in which you are placed, the Count has sent to offer you seats in his carriage and two places at his windows in the Palace Rospoli." The friends looked at each other with unutterable surprise.

" But do you think," asked Franz, " that we ought to accept such an offer from a stranger ? What sort of person is this count of Monte Cristo ? "

" A very great nobleman, but whether Maltese or Sicilian I cannot exactly say ; but this I know, that he is noble as a Borghese and rich as a gold mine."

" It seems to me," said Franz, speaking in an undertone to Albert, " that if this person merited the panegyrics of our landlord, he would have conveyed his invitation through another channel, and not permitted it to be brought to us in this unceremonious way. He would have written—or—— "

At this instant someone knocked at the door.

" Come in ! " said Franz. A servant, wearing a livery of considerable style and richness, appeared at the threshold, and, placing two cards in the landlord's hands, said, " Please to deliver these, from M. le comte de Monte Cristo, to M. le vicomte Albert de Morcerf and M. Franz d'Epinay. M. le comte de Monte Cristo begs these gentlemen's permission to wait upon them as their neighbour, and he will be honoured by an intimation at what time they will please to receive him."

" Tell the count," replied Franz, " that we will do ourselves the pleasure of calling on him." The servant bowed and retired.

" That is what I call an elegant mode of attack," said Albert. " You were quite correct in what you stated, Maître Pastrini. The count of Monte Cristo is a man of first-rate breeding and knowledge of the world."

" Then you accept his offer ? " said the host.

" Of course we do," replied Albert. " Still I must own I am sorry to be obliged to give up the cart and the group of reapers —it would have produced such an effect ! Were it not for the windows at the Palace Rospoli, by way of recompense for the loss of our beautiful scheme, I don't know but that I should have held on to my original plan. What say you, Franz ? "

" Oh, I agree with you ; the windows in the Palace Rospoli

alone decided me." The truth was, that the mention of two places in the Palace Rospoli had recalled to Franz's mind the conversation he had overheard in the ruins of the Colosseum. If this muffled-up person proved (as Franz felt sure he would) the same as the man he had seen in the Teatro Argentino, then he should be able to establish his identity and prosecute his researches respecting him with facility and freedom. Franz passed the night in confused dreams respecting the two meetings he had already had with his mysterious tormentor, and in waking speculations as to what the morrow would produce. Eight o'clock found him up and dressed, while Albert, who had not the same motives for early rising, was still asleep. The first act of Franz was to summon his landlord.

" Pray, Maître Pastrini," asked Franz, " is not some execution appointed to take place to-day ? "

" Yes, your Excellency ; but if you wish to procure a window to view it from, you are much too late."

" Oh, no ! " answered Franz, " I had no such intention ; and even if I had felt a wish to witness the spectacle I might have done so from Monte Pincio. Very possibly I may not go, but in case I feel disposed, tell me the number of persons condemned to suffer, their names, and the kind of death they are to die."

" Luckily, your Excellency, only a few minutes ago they brought me the *tavolettas*."

" What are they ? "

" Wooden tablets hung up at the corners of streets the evening before an execution, on which is pasted a paper containing the names of the condemned persons, their crimes, and mode of punishment. The reason for publicly announcing this is, that all good Catholics may offer up prayers for the culprits, and beseech of Heaven to grant them repentance."

" And these tablets are brought to you that you may add your prayers to those of the faithful, are they ? " asked Franz, somewhat incredulously.

" Oh dear, no, your Excellency ; I have not time for anybody's affairs but my own and those of my honourable guests ; but I make an agreement with the man who pastes up the papers, and he brings them to me, as he does the playbills, for the information of my guests."

" Oblige me by a sight of the *tavoletta*."

" Nothing can be easier than to comply with your Excellency's wish," said the landlord, opening the door of the chamber ; " I have caused one to be placed on the landing, close by your apartment." Taking the tablet from the wall, he handed it to Franz, who read as follows :—

" ' The public is informed that on Wednesday, February 23rd, being the first day of the Carnival, executions will take place in the Piazza del Popolo, by order of the Tribunal de la Rota, of two individuals, named Andrea Rondola, and Peppino, otherwise called Rocca Priori ; the former found guilty of the murder of a venerable and exemplary priest, named Don César Torlini, canon of the church of San Giovanni in Laterano ; and the latter convicted of being an accomplice of the atrocious and sanguinary bandit Luigi Vampa and his troop. The first-named malefactor will be *mazzolato*, the second culprit, *decapitato*. The prayers of all good Christians are entreated for these unfortunate men, that it may please God to awaken them to a sense of their guilt, and to grant them a hearty and sincere repentance for their crimes.' "

This was precisely what Franz had heard in the ruins of the Colosseum. No part of the programme differed—the condemned persons—their crimes and mode of punishment—all agreed with his previous information. In all probability, therefore, the person from Trastevere was no other than the bandit Luigi Vampa, and the man shrouded in the mantle Sindbad the Sailor, who, no doubt, was still pursuing his philanthropic expedition in Rome as he had already done at Porto Vecchia and Tunis.

Time was getting on, however, and Franz deemed it advisable to awaken Albert ; but at that moment his friend entered the saloon in perfect costume for the day. The anticipated delights of the Carnival had so run in his head as to make him leave his pillow long before his usual hour.

" Now, my excellent Maître Pastrini," said Franz, " since we are ready, do you think we may visit the count of Monte Cristo ? "

" Most assuredly," replied he. " The count is always an early riser."

The landlord preceded the friends across the landing, which was all that separated them from the apartments of the count, rang at a bell, and upon the door being opened by a servant, said, " *I Signori Francesi.*"

The domestic bowed respectfully, and invited them to enter. They passed through two rooms, furnished with a style and luxury they had not calculated on finding under the roof of Maître Pastrini, and were shown into an elegantly fitted-up saloon. The richest Turkey carpets covered the floor, and the softest and most inviting couches invited repose. Splendid paintings hung on the walls, intermingled with magnificent trophies of war, while heavy curtains of costly tapestry were suspended before the different doors of the room. "If your Excellencies will please to be seated," said the man, "I will let M. le Comte know you are here."

And with these words he disappeared behind one of the tapestried *portières*. As the door opened, the sound of a *guzla* reached the ears of the young men, but was almost immediately lost, for the rapid closing of the door merely allowed one rich swell of harmony to enter the saloon. Franz and Albert looked at each other, and then at the gorgeous appointments.

"Well," said Franz, "what think you of all this?"

"Why, upon my soul, it strikes me our neighbour must either be some stock-jobber who has speculated in the fall of the Spanish funds or some prince travelling *incog.*"

"Hush! hush!" replied Franz, "we shall ascertain who and what he is—he comes!" As Franz spoke, he heard the sound of a door turning on its hinges, and almost immediately the tapestry was drawn aside, and the owner of all these riches stood before the two young men. Albert instantly rose to meet him, but Franz remained on his chair, in a manner spellbound, for in the person who had just entered he recognized not only the mysterious visitant to the Colosseum, and the occupant of the *loge* at the Teatro Argentino, but also his host of Monte Cristo.

CHAPTER XXXV

LA MAZZOLATA

"GENTLEMEN," said the count of Monte Cristo as he entered, "I pray you excuse me for suffering my visit to be anticipated; but I feared to disturb you by presenting myself earlier at your apartments."

"Franz and I have to thank you a thousand times, M. le Comte," returned Albert; "you extricated us from a great dilemma, and we were on the point of inventing some very fantastic vehicle when your friendly invitation reached us."

"Indeed!" returned the count, motioning the two young men to sit down. "It was the fault of that blockhead Pastrini that I did not sooner assist you in your distress. As soon as I learned I could in any way help you, I seized the opportunity of offering my services." The two young men bowed. Franz had, as yet, found nothing to say; and as nothing in the count's manner manifested the wish that he should recognize him, he did not know whether to make any allusion to the past, or wait until he had more proof. Besides, although sure it was he who had been in the box the previous evening, he could not be equally positive that he was the man he had seen at the Colosseum. He resolved, therefore, to make no direct overture to the count, but to lead the conversation to a subject which might clear up his doubts.

"M. le Comte," said he, "you have offered us places in your carriage, and at your windows of the Rospoli Palace. Can you tell us where we can obtain a sight of the Piazza del Popolo?"

"Ah!" said the count, negligently, looking attentively at Morcerf, "is there not an execution at the Piazza del Popolo?"

"Yes," returned Franz, finding that the count was coming to the point he wished.

"Stay, I think I told my steward yesterday to attend to this; perhaps I can render you this slight service also." He extended his hand, and rang the bell thrice. "Did you ever occupy yourself," said he to Franz, "with the employment of time and the means of simplifying the summoning your servants? I have: when I ring once, it is for my valet; twice, for my maître d'hôtel; thrice, for my steward: thus I do not waste a minute or a word. Here he is!" A man of about five-and-forty to fifty entered, exactly resembling the smuggler who had introduced Franz into the cavern; but he did not appear to recognize him. "M. Bertuccio," said the count, "have you procured me windows looking on the Piazza del Popolo, as I ordered yesterday?"

"Yes, Excellency," returned the steward; "but it was very late."

"Did I not tell you I wished for one?" replied the count, frowning.

"And your Excellency has one, which was let to Prince Loba-nieff; but I was obliged to pay a hundred——"

"That will do—that will do, Monsieur Bertuccio; spare these gentlemen all such domestic arrangements. You have the window that is sufficient. Give orders to the coachman; and be in readiness on the stairs to conduct us to it." The steward bowed, and was about to quit the room. "Ah!" continued the count, "be good enough to ask Pastrini if he has received the *tavoletta*, and if he can send us an account of the execution."

"There is no need to do that," said Franz, taking out his notebook; "for I saw the account, and copied it down."

"Very well, you can retire, Maître Bertuccio; let us know

when breakfast is ready; lay covers for three." He took Franz's memorandum. "'To-day,' he read, in the same tone with which he would have read a newspaper, 'the 23rd of February, will be executed Andrea Rondola, guilty of murder on the person of the respectable and venerated Don César Torlini, canon of San Giovanni in Laterano, and Peppino, called Rocca Priori, convicted of complicity with the bandit Luigi Vampa, and the men of his troop.' Hum! 'The first will be *mazzolato*, the second *decapitato*.' Yes," continued the count, "it was at first arranged in this way; but I think since yesterday some change has taken place in the order of the ceremony."

"Really!" said Franz.

"Yes, I passed the evening at the Cardinal Rospigliosi's, and mention was made of a pardon for one of the men."

"For Andrea Rondola?"

"No," replied the count, carelessly; "for the other (he glanced at the notes as if to recall the name) for Peppino, called Rocca Priori. You are thus deprived of seeing a man guillotined; but the *mazzolato* still remains, which is a very curious punishment. The *mandaïa* never fails, never trembles, never strikes thirty times ineffectually. Ah!" added the count, in a contemptuous tone, "do not tell me of European punishments; they are in the infancy, or rather the old age, of cruelty."

"Really, M. le Comte," replied Franz, "one would think you had studied the different tortures of all the nations of the world."

"There are few I have not seen," said the count, coldly.

"And you took pleasure in beholding these dreadful spectacles?"

"My first sentiment was horror, the second indifference, the third curiosity."

"Curiosity! that is a terrible word."

"Why so? In life, our greatest preoccupation is death; is it not, then, curious to study the different ways by which the soul and body can part; and how, according to their different characters, temperaments, and even the customs of their countries, individuals bear the transition from life to death; from existence to annihilation? The more men you see die, the easier it becomes to die; and, in my opinion, death may be a torture, but is not an expiation."

"I do not understand you," replied Franz.

"Listen," said the count, and deep hatred mounted to his face, as the blood would to the face of any other. "If a man had by unheard-of and excruciating tortures destroyed your father, your mother, your mistress, would you think the reparation that society gives you by means of the knife of the guillotine adequate, seeing that he who has caused years of moral sufferings can only undergo a few moments of physical pain ? "

" Yes, I know," said Franz, " that human justice is insufficient to console us ; she can give blood in return for blood, that is all ; but you can only demand from her what it is in her power to grant."

" I will put another case," continued the count, " where society, attacked by the death of a person, avenges death by death. But are there not a thousand tortures which a man may suffer without society taking the least cognizance of them, or offering him even the insufficient means of vengeance, of which we have just spoken ? Are there not crimes for which the empalement of the Turks, the augers of the Persians, the stake and the brand of the Iroquois Indians, are inadequate tortures, and which are unpunished by society ? Answer me, do not these crimes exist ? "

" Yes," answered Franz ; " and it is to punish them that duelling is tolerated."

" Ah, duelling ! " cried the count ; " a pleasant manner, upon my soul, of arriving at your end when that end is vengeance ! A man has carried off your mistress, or seduced your wife, or dishonoured your daughter ; he has rendered the whole life of one who had the right to expect from heaven that portion of happiness God has promised to everyone of His creatures, an existence of misery and infamy ; and you think you are avenged because you send a ball through his head, or pass a sword through his breast. Nay, it is often he who comes off victorious from the strife, absolved of all crime in the eyes of the world ! No, no," continued the count ; " had I to avenge myself, it is not thus I would take revenge."

" Then you would not fight a duel ? " asked Albert in his turn, astonished at this strange theory.

" Oh, yes," replied the count ; " I would fight a duel for a trifle, for an insult, for a blow ; and the more so that, thanks to my skill and indifference to danger, I should be almost certain to kill my man. I would fight for such a cause ; but in return for a slow, profound, eternal torture, I would give back the same, were it possible : an eye for an eye, a tooth for a tooth, as the Orientalists say,—our masters in everything."

" But," said Franz to the count, " with this theory, which renders you at once judge and executioner of your own cause, it would be difficult to adopt a course that would for ever prevent your falling under the power of the law. Hatred is blind; rage carries you away; and he who pours out vengeance runs the risk of tasting a bitter draft."

"Yes, if he be poor and inexperienced: not if he be rich and skilful; besides, the worst that could happen to him would be the punishment of which we have already spoken. What matters this punishment, as long as he is avenged? On my word, I almost regret that in all probability this miserable Peppino will not be *decapitato*, as you might have had an opportunity then of seeing how short a time the punishment lasts, and whether it is worth even mentioning. But, really, this is a singular conversation for the Carnival, gentlemen; how did it arise? Ah! I recollect, you asked for a place at my window; you shall have it; but let us sit down to table, for here comes the servant to inform us breakfast is ready."

During the meal, which was excellent and admirably served, Albert ate like a man who for the last four or five months had been condemned to partake of Italian cookery—that is, the worst in the world. As for the count, he just touched the dishes; he seemed as if he fulfilled the duties of an entertainer by sitting down with his guests, and awaited their departure to be served with some strange or more delicate food. This brought back to Franz, in spite of himself, the recollection of the terror with which the count had inspired the Countess G——, and her firm conviction that the man in the opposite box was a vampire. At the end of the breakfast Franz took out his watch.

"Well," said the count, "what are you doing?"

"You must excuse us, M. le Comte," returned Franz, "but we have still much to do. We have no disguises, and it is necessary to procure them."

"Do not concern yourself about that; we have, I think, a private room in the Piazza del Popolo; I will have whatever costumes you choose brought to us, and you can dress there."

"I thank you for your courtesy, but I shall content myself with accepting a place in your carriage and at your window at the Rospoli Palace, and I leave you at liberty to dispose of my place at the Piazza del Popolo."

"But I warn you, you will lose a very curious sight," returned the count.

"You will relate it to me," replied Franz, "and the recital from your lips will make as great an impression on me as if I had witnessed it. I have more than once intended witnessing an execution, but I have never been able to make up my mind : and you, Albert ? "

" I," replied the viscount—" I saw Castaing executed, but I think I was rather intoxicated that day, for I had quitted college the same morning, and we had passed the previous night at a tavern."

" Besides, it is no reason because you have not seen an execution at Paris that you should not see one anywhere else ; when you travel it is to see everything. Think what a figure you will make when you are asked, ' How do they execute at Rome ? ' and you reply, ' I do not know ! ' If you went to Spain, would you not see the bull-fights ? Well, suppose it is a bull-fight you are going to see ? Recollect the ancient Romans of the Circus, and the sports where they killed three hundred lions and a hundred men. Think of the eighty thousand applauding spectators, the sage matrons who took their daughters, and the charming Vestals who made with the thumb of their white hands the fatal sign that said, ' Come, despatch this man, already nearly dead.' "

" Shall you go, then, Albert ? " asked Franz.

" Ma foi ! yes : like you, I hesitated, but the count's eloquence decides me ! "

" Let us go, then," said Franz, " since you wish it ; but on our way to the Piazza del Popolo I wish to pass through the Corso. Is this possible, M. le Comte ? "

" On foot, yes ! in a carriage, no ! "

" I will go on foot, then ! There is something I wish to see ! "

" Well, we will pass by the Corso. We will send the carriage to wait for us on the Piazza del Popolo, by the Via del Babuino, for I shall be glad to pass, myself, through the Corso, to see if some orders I have given have been executed."

" Excellency," said a servant, opening the door, " a man in the dress of a penitent wishes to speak to you."

" Ah ! yes ! " returned the count, " I know who he is, gentlemen ; will you return to the salon ? you will find on the centre table some excellent Havanna cigars. I will be with you directly." The young men rose and returned into the salon, whilst the count, again apologizing, left by another door.

" Well," asked Franz, " what think you of the count of Monte Cristo ? "

" What do I think ? " said Albert, surprised at such a question ; ' I think that he is a delightful fellow, who does the honours of his table admirably; who has travelled much, read much, is like Brutus, of the Stoic school, and, moreover," added he, sending a volume of smoke up towards the ceiling, " who has excellent cigars."

" But," said Franz, " did you remark how attentively he looked at you ? "

" At me ? "

" Yes."

" Ah ! " replied Albert sighing, " that is not very surprising ; I have been more than a year absent from Paris, and my clothes are of a most antiquated cut; the count takes me for a provincial. The first opportunity you have, undeceive him, I beg, and tell him I am nothing of the kind." Franz smiled ; an instant later the count entered.

" I am now at your service, gentlemen," said he. " The carriage is going one way to the Piazza del Popolo, and we will go another ; and if you please, by the Corso. Take some cigars, M. de Morcerf."

" With all my heart," returned Albert. " Italian cigars are horrible. When you come to Paris I will return all this."

" I will not refuse ; I intend going there soon, and since you allow me, I will pay you a visit. Come ! we have no time to lose, it is half-past twelve ! " All three descended ; the coachman received his master's orders, and drove down the Via del Babuino. Whilst the three gentlemen walked towards the Piazza di Spagna and the Via Fratina, which led directly between the Fiano and Rospoli Palaces, all Franz's attention was directed towards the windows of that last palace, for he had not forgotten the signal.

" Which are your windows ? " he asked of the count, with as much indifference as he could assume. " The three last," he returned, casually. Franz glanced rapidly towards the three windows. The side windows were hung with yellow damask, and the centre one with white damask and a red cross. The man in the mantle had kept his promise to the visitor from Trastevere, and there could now be no doubt that he was the count.

Franz, Albert, and the count continued to descend the Corso : as they approached the Piazza del Popolo the crowd became more dense, and above the heads of the multitude two objects were visible ; the obelisk surmounted by a cross, which marks the centre of the Piazza, and before the obelisk, at the point where the three streets, del Babuino, the Corso, and di Ripetta, meet, the two uprights of the scaffold, between which glittered the curved knife of the *mandaia*. At the corner of the street they met the count's steward, who was awaiting his master. The window was on the second floor of the great palace, situated between the Via del Babuino and the Monte Pincio. The apartments consisted of a small dressing-room, opening into a bedroom, and when the door of communication was shut the inmates were alone. On two chairs were laid as many elegant costumes of *paillasse*, in blue and white satin. " As you left the choice of the costumes to me," said the count to the two friends, " I have had these brought, as they will be the most worn this year; and they are most suitable on account of the *confetti* (sweetmeats), as they do not show the flour."

Franz heard the words of the count but imperfectly, and he perhaps did not fully appreciate this new attention to their wishes; for he was wholly absorbed by the spectacle that the Piazza del Popolo presented, and by the terrible instrument that was in the centre. It was the first time Franz had ever seen a guillotine—we say guillotine because the Roman *mandaia* is formed on almost the same model as the French instrument; the knife is shaped like a crescent that cuts with the convex side and falls from a lesser height, and that is all the difference. Two men, seated on the movable plank, on which the culprit is laid, were eating their breakfasts, whilst waiting for the criminal. Their repast consisted, apparently, of bread and sausages. One of them lifted the plank, took thence a flask of wine, drank some, and then passed it to his companion. These two men were the executioner's assistants.

The prisoners, transported the previous evening from the Carcere Nuovo to the little church of Santa Maria del Popolo, had passed the night, each accompanied by two priests, in a chapel closed by a grating, before which were two sentinels, relieved at intervals. A double line of carbineers, placed on each side of the door of the church, reached to the scaffold, and formed a circle round it, leaving a path about ten feet wide, and around the guillotine a space of nearly a hundred feet. All the rest of the Piazza was paved with heads. Many women held their infants on their shoulders, and thus the children had the best view. The Monte Pincio seemed a vast amphitheatre filled with spectators; the balconies of the two churches at the corners of the Via del Babuino and the Via di Ripetta were crammed; every niche in the wall held its living statue. What the count said was true—the most curious spectacle in life is that of death. And yet, instead of the silence and the solemnity demanded

by the occasion, a noise of laughter and jest arose from the crowd ;
it was evident that this execution was, in the eyes of the people,
only the beginning of the Carnival.

Suddenly the tumult ceased, as if by magic ; the doors of the
church opened. A brotherhood of penitents, clothed from head
to foot in robes of grey sackcloth, with holes for the eyes alone,
and holding in their hand a lighted taper, appeared first ; the
chief marched at the head. Behind the penitents came a man
of vast stature, and proportions. He was naked, with the exception of cloth drawers, at the left side of which hung a large
knife in a sheath, and he bore on his right shoulder a heavy mace.
This was the executioner. Behind him came, in the order in
which they were to die, first Peppino, and then Andrea, each
accompanied by two priests. Neither had his eyes bandaged.
Each kissed, from time to time, the crucifix a confessor held
out to him. At this sight Franz felt his legs tremble under him,
and Albert cast away his cigar, although he had not half smoked
it. The count alone seemed unmoved—nay, more, a slight
colour seemed striving to rise in his pale cheeks. His nostrils
dilated like those of a wild beast that scents its prey, and his lips,
half open, disclosed his white teeth, small and sharp, like those
of a jackal. And yet his features wore an expression of smiling
tenderness, such as Franz had never before witnessed in them ;
his black eyes especially were full of kindness and pity. The
two culprits advanced. Peppino was a handsome young man
of four or five and twenty, bronzed by the sun, and carried his head
erect. Andrea was short and fat. His visage, marked with brutal
cruelty, did not indicate age ; he might be thirty. In prison
he had suffered his beard to grow—his head fell on his shoulder
—his legs bent beneath him, and he seemed to obey a mechanical
movement, of which he was unconscious.

" I thought," said Franz to the count, " that you told me there
would be but one execution ! yet here are two culprits."

" Yes ; but only one is about to die !—the other has long
years to live."

" If the pardon is to come there is no time to lose."

" And see, here it is," said the count. At the moment when
Peppino arrived at the foot of the *mandaïa*, a penitent, who
seemed to arrive late, forced his way through the soldiers, and
advancing to the chief of the brotherhood, gave him a folded paper.

The chief took the paper, unfolded it, and, raising his hand,
" Heaven be praised ! and his Holiness also ! " said he, in a loud
voice. " Here is a pardon for one of the prisoners."

" A pardon ! " cried the people with one voice. " A pardon ! " At this cry Andrea raised his head—" Pardon for whom ? " cried he.

" A pardon for Peppino, called Rocca Priori," said the principal friar. And he passed the paper to the officer commanding the carbineers, who read and returned it to him.

" For Peppino ! " cried Andrea, " why for him and not for me ? We ought to die together. I was promised he should die with me. You have no right to put me to death alone. I will not die alone—I will not ! " And he broke from the priests, struggling and raving like a wild beast. The executioner made a sign, and his assistant leaped from the scaffold and seized him.

" Look !—look ! " cried the count, taking the young men's hands ; " look for, on my soul, it is curious. Here is a man who has resigned himself to his fate ; who was going to the scaffold to die—like a coward, it is true, but he was about to die without resistance. Do you know what gave him strength ?—do you know what consoled him ? It was that another partook of his punishment, that another partook of his anguish—that another was to die before him ! Lead two sheep to the butcher's, two oxen to the slaughter-house, and make one of them understand that his companion will not die ; the sheep will bleat for pleasure, the ox will bellow with joy. But man—man, whom God created in His own image—man, upon whom God has laid His first, His sole commandment, to love his neighbour—man, to whom God has given a voice to express his thoughts— what is his first cry when he hears his fellow-man is saved ? A blasphemy ! Honour to man—this masterpiece of nature— this king of the creation ! " And the count burst into a laugh ; but a terrible laugh, that showed he must have suffered horribly to be able thus to laugh. However, Andrea's struggle still continued, and it was dreadful to witness.

The people took part against Andrea, and twenty thousand voices cried, " Put him to death !—put him to death ! "

Franz sprang back, but the count seized his arm, and held him before the window. " What are you doing ? " said he. " Do you pity him ? If you heard the cry of ' Mad dog ! ' you would unhesitatingly shoot the poor beast, who, after all, was only guilty of having been bitten by another dog. And yet you pity a man who, without being bitten by one of his race, has yet murdered his benefactor ; and who now, unable to kill anyone, because his hands are bound, wishes to see his companion in captivity perish. No, no ; look ! look ! "

This recommendation was needless; Franz was fascinated by the horrible spectacle. The two assistants had borne Andrea to the scaffold, and there, in spite of his struggles, his bites, and his cries, had forced him to his knees. During this time the executioner had raised his mace, and signed to them to get out of the way; the criminal strove to rise, but ere he had time, the mace fell on his left temple. A dull and heavy sound was heard, and the man dropped like an ox on his face, and then turned over on his back. The executioner dropped his mace, drew his knife, and with one stroke opened his throat; and, mounting on his stomach stamped violently on it with his feet. At every stroke a jet of blood sprang from the wound.

This time Franz could sustain himself no longer, but sank, half fainting, into a seat. Albert, with his eyes closed, was standing grasping the window curtains. The count was erect and triumphant, like the Avenging Angel!

CHAPTER XXXVI

THE CARNIVAL AT ROME

When Franz recovered his senses he saw Albert drinking a glass of water, of which his paleness showed he stood in great need, and the count assuming a costume of *paillasse*. He glanced mechanically towards the Piazza; all had disappeared,—scaffold, executioners, victims. Nought remained but the people, full of noise and excitement. The bell of Monte Citorio, which only sounds on the pope's decease and the opening of the Carnival, was ringing a joyous peal.

" Well," asked Franz of the count, " what has happened ? "

" Nothing," replied the count; " only, as you see, the Carnival has commenced."

" But Peppino, what has become of him ? "

" Peppino is a lad of sense, who, unlike most men who are furious if they pass unnoticed, was delighted to see that the general attention was directed towards his companion. He profited by this distraction to slip away amongst the crowd, without even thanking the worthy priests who accompanied him. But dress yourself; see M. de Morcerf sets you the example." Albert was in reality drawing on the satin pantaloon over his black trousers and varnished boots.

" Well, Albert," said Franz, " do you feel much inclined to join the revels ? Come, answer frankly ! "

" *Ma foi !* no," returned Albert. " But I am really glad to have seen such a sight ; and I understand what M. le Comte said, that when you have once habituated yourself to such spectacles, the first is the only one that causes you any emotion."

Franz assumed his costume, and fastened on his mask that scarcely equalled the pallor of his own face. Their toilette finished, they descended ; the carriage awaited them at the door, filled with sweetmeats and bouquets. They fell into the line of carriages. It is difficult to form an idea of the perfect change that had taken place. Instead of the spectacle of death, the Piazza del Popolo presented a spectacle of mirth and revelry. A crowd of masks flowed in from all sides, emerging from doors, descending from windows. From every street and every turn appeared carriages filled with pierrots, harlequins, dominoes, marquises, Trasteveres, knights, and peasants—screaming, fighting, gesticulating, whirling eggs filled with flour, confetti, nosegays,—attacking, with sarcasms and missiles, friends and foes, companions and strangers, indiscriminately, without any one taking offence, or doing anything else than laugh. Little by little, the general vertigo seized Franz and Albert, and they felt obliged to take part in the noise and confusion. From a neighbouring carriage, came a handful of confetti which, whilst covering Morcerf and his two companions with dust, pricked his neck and that portion of his face uncovered by his mask like a hundred pins, and plunged him into the general combat, in which all the masks around were engaged. He rose in his turn, and seizing handfuls of confetti and sweetmeats, with which the carriage was filled, cast them with all the force and address he was master of.

The strife had begun, and the recollection of what they had seen was gradually effaced from the young men's minds. Imagine the Corso bordered from end to end with palaces, their balconies hung with carpets and their windows with flags ; at these balconies three hundred thousand spectators—Romans, Italians, strangers from all parts of the world—the united aristo-cracy of birth, wealth, and genius ; lovely women who, yielding to the influence of the scene, bent over their balconies, or leaned from their windows, and showered down confetti, which were returned by bouquets. In the streets the lively crowd was garbed in the most fantastic costumes. Gigantic cabbages walked gravely about, buffalos' heads bellowed from men's shoulders, dogs walked on their hind legs. In the midst of all this a mask is lifted, and a lovely face is exhibited which we would fain follow, but from which we are separated by troops of fiends. Such a scene gives a faint idea of the Carnival at Rome. At the second turn, the count stopped the carriage, and requested permission to quit them, leaving the vehicle at their disposal. Franz looked up; they were opposite the Rospoli Palace. At the centre window, the one hung with white damask with a red cross, was a blue domino, beneath which Franz's imagination easily pictured the beautiful Greek.

"Gentlemen," said the count, springing out, "when you are tired of being actors, and wish to become spectators of this scene, you know you have places at my windows. In the meantime, dispose of my coachman, my carriage, and my servants."

Franz thanked the count for his attention. As for Albert, he was busy throwing bouquets at a carriage full of Roman peasants that was passing. Unfortunately, the line of carriages moved on again, and whilst he descended the Piazza del Popolo, the other ascended towards the Palazzo di Venezia.

"Ah! my dear fellow!" said he to Franz, "you did not see that calèche filled with Roman peasants. I am convinced they are all charming women."

"How unfortunate you were masked, Albert!" said Franz; "here was an opportunity of making up for past disappointments."

"Oh! I hope the Carnival will not pass without some amends in one shape or the other."

But, in spite of Albert's hope, the day passed unmarked by any incident except meeting two or three times the calèche with the Roman peasants. At one of these encounters, accidentally, or purposely, Albert's mask fell off. He instantly rose and cast the remainder of the bouquets into the carriage. Doubtless one of the charming females Albert had divined beneath their coquettish disguise was touched by his gallantry, for, in her turn, as the carriage of the two friends passed her, she threw a bunch of violets into it. Albert placed it in his button-hole, and the carriage went triumphantly on.

"Well," said Franz; "here is the beginning of an adventure."

"Laugh if you please—I really think so. So I will not abandon this bouquet."

The jest, however, soon appeared to become earnest, for when Albert and Franz again encountered the carriage with the *contadini*, the one who had thrown the violets to Albert clapped her hands when she beheld them in his button-hole.

"Bravo! bravo!" said Franz; "things go wonderfully. Shall I leave you? Perhaps you would prefer being alone?"

" No," replied he ; " If the fair peasant wishes to carry matters farther, we shall find her, or rather, she will find us to-morrow : then she will give me some sign and I shall know what to do."

Albert was right ; the fair unknown had resolved, doubtless, to carry the intrigue no farther ; for although the young men made several more turns, they did not again see the calèche. They returned to the Rospoli Palace ; but the count and the blue domino had disappeared ; the two windows, hung with yellow damask, were still occupied by the persons whom the count had invited. At this moment the bell that had proclaimed the beginning of the mascherata sounded the retreat. The file on the Corso broke the line, and in a second all the carriages had disappeared. Franz and Albert were opposite the Via delle Maratte : the coachman, without saying a word, drove up it, passed along the Piazza di Spagna and the Rospoli Palace, and stopped at the door of the hotel. Maître Pastrini came to the door to receive his guests. Franz's first care was to inquire after the count, and to express his regret that he had not returned in sufficient time to take him ; but Pastrini reassured him by saying that the count of Monte Cristo had ordered a second carriage for himself, and that it had gone at four o'clock to fetch him from the Rospoli Palace. The count had, moreover, charged him to offer the two friends the key of his box at the Argentino. Franz questioned Albert as to his intentions ; but Albert had great projects to put into execution before going to the theatre, and inquired if Maître Pastrini could procure him a tailor to make by to-morrow two costumes of Roman peasants.

The host shook his head. " I ask your Excellencies' pardon, but next week you will not find a single tailor who would consent to sew six buttons on a waistcoat if you paid him a crown apiece for each button ! But leave all to me ; and to-morrow, when you wake, you shall find a collection of costumes with which you will be satisfied."

" My dear Albert," said Franz, " leave all to our host ; let us dine quietly, and afterwards go and see ' l' Italienne à Alger ! ' "

" Agreed," returned Albert ; " but recollect, Maître Pastrini, that my friend and myself attach the greatest importance to having to-morrow the costumes we have asked for."

The host again assured them they might rely on him, and that their wishes should be attended to ; upon which Franz and Albert mounted to their apartments, and proceeded to disencumber themselves of their costume. Albert, as he took off his dress, carefully preserved the bunch of violets ; it was his sign of recognition for the morrow. The two friends sat down to table ; but they could not refrain from remarking the difference between the table of the count of Monte Christo and that of Maître Pastrini. During dessert, the servant inquired at what time they wished for the carriage. " His Excellency the count of Monte Cristo had," he said, " given positive orders that the carriage was to remain at their lordships' orders all the day, and they could therefore dispose of it without fear of indiscretion."

They resolved to profit by the count's courtesy, and ordered the horses to be harnessed, whilst they substituted an evening costume for that which they had on, and which was somewhat the worse for the numerous combats they had sustained. This precaution taken, they went to the theatre, and installed themselves in the count's box. During the first act the Countess G—— entered hers. Her first look was at the *loge* where she had seen the count the previous evening, so that she perceived Franz and Albert in the box of the very person concerning whom she had expressed so strange an opinion to Franz. Her opera-glass was so fixedly directed towards them, that Franz saw it would be cruel not to satisfy her curiosity, and the two friends quitted their box to pay their respects to the Countess. Scarcely had they entered the *loge*, when she motioned to Franz to assume the seat of honour. Albert, in his turn, sat behind.

" Well," said she, hardly giving Franz time to sit down, " it seems you have nothing better to do than to make the acquaintance of this new Lord Ruthven, and you are the best friends in the world."

" Without being so advanced as that, Madame la Comtesse," returned Franz, " I cannot deny we have abused his good nature. This morning we breakfasted with him ; we rode in his carriage all day, and now we have taken possession of his box."

" What is his name ? for, of course, you know."

" The count of Monte Cristo : it is the name of the isle he has purchased."

" What sort of a man is he ? "

" We should be very hard to please madam," said Albert, " did we not think him delightful ; a friend of ten years' standing could not have done more for us, or with a more perfect courtesy."

" Come," observed the Countess, smiling ; " I see my vampire is only some millionaire, who has taken the appearance of Lara in order to avoid being confounded with M. de Rothschild ; and have you seen the beautiful Greek ? "

" No ; we heard, I think, the sound of her *guzla*, but she remained invisible."

" When you say invisible," interrupted Albert, " it is only to keep up the mystery ; for whom do you take the blue domino at the window of the Rospoli Palace ? "

" The count had three windows of the Rospoli Palace ? "

" Yes. Did you pass through the Corso, and did you remark two windows hung with yellow damask, and one with white damask with a red cross ? These were the count's windows."

" Why, he must be a nabob ! "

" In reality," observed Albert, " he seemed to me somewhat eccentric ; were he at Paris, and a frequenter of the theatres, I should say he was a poor devil, literally mad. This morning he made two or three exits worthy of Didier or Anthony."

At this moment a fresh visitor entered and, according to custom, Franz gave up his seat to him. This circumstance had, moreover, the effect of changing the conversation ; an hour afterwards the two friends returned to their hôtel.

Maître Pastrini had already set about procuring their disguises for the morrow ; and next morning, at nine o'clock, he entered Franz's room, followed by a tailor, who had eight or ten costumes of Roman peasants on his arm ; they selected two exactly alike, and charged the tailor to sew on each of their hats about twenty yards of riband, and to procure two of those long silken sashes of different colours with which the lower orders decorate themselves on fête days. Albert was impatient to see how he looked in his new dress : it was a jacket and breeches of blue velvet, silk stockings with clocks, shoes with buckles, and a silk waistcoat. This picturesque attire set him off to great advantage ; and when he had bound the scarf around his waist, and when his hat, placed coquettishly on one side, let fall on his shoulder a stream of ribands, Franz was forced to confess that costume has much to do with the physical superiority we accord to certain nations. He complimented Albert, who looked at himself in the glass with an unequivocal smile of satisfaction. They were thus engaged when the count of Monte Cristo entered.

" Gentlemen," said he, " although a companion is agreeable, perfect freedom is sometimes still more agreeable. I come to say that to-day, and for the remainder of the Carnival, I leave the carriage at your disposal. I have three or four more, so that you do not deprive me in any way of it."

Albert was charmed with the count's manners, and the leave to do what he liked with the carriage pleased him above all, for the fair peasants had appeared in a most elegant carriage the preceding evening, and Albert was not sorry to be upon an equal footing with them. At half-past one they descended, Albert with the faded bunch of violets in his button-hole. At the first sound of the bell they hastened into the Corso by the Via Vittoria. At the second turn, a bunch of fresh violets, thrown from a carriage filled with *paillassines*, indicated to Albert that, like himself and his friend, the peasants had changed their costume also ; and whether it was the result of chance, or whether a similar feeling had possessed them both, whilst he had changed his costume they had assumed his.

Albert placed the fresh bouquet in his button-hole, but he kept the faded one in his hand ; and when he again met the calèche he raised it to his lips, an action which seemed greatly to amuse not only the fair lady who had thrown it, but her joyous companions also. The day was as gay as the preceding one, perhaps even more animated and noisy. It is almost needless to say that the flirtation between Albert and the fair peasant continued all day. At ten minutes past five Albert returned overjoyed. The *paillassine* had resumed her peasant's costume, and as she passed had raised her mask. She was charming. Franz congratulated Albert, who received his congratulations with the air of a man conscious they are merited. He had recognized, by certain unmistakable signs, that his fair *incognita* belonged to the aristocracy. He had made up his mind to write to her, and begged the favour of being allowed to occupy the carriage alone next day. Franz said that he would be content to witness the Carnival from the windows of the Rospoli Palace.

The next morning he saw Albert pass and repass. He held an enormous bouquet, which was doubtless meant to be the medium of his amorous epistle. This belief was changed into certainty when Franz saw the bouquet (remarkable by a circle of white camelias) in the hands of a charming *paillassine* dressed in rose-coloured satin. The evening was no longer joy, but delirium. Albert did not doubt but that the fair unknown would reply in the same manner. Franz anticipated his wishes by telling him the noise fatigued him, and that he should pass the next day in writing and looking over his journal. Albert was not deceived, for the next evening Franz saw him enter, shaking triumphantly a folded paper he held by one corner.

" Read ! " This word was pronounced in a manner impossible to describe. Franz took the letter, and read :—

" ' Tuesday evening, at seven o'clock, descend from your carriage opposite the Via de Pontefici, and follow the Roman peasant who snatches your *moccoletto* from you. When you arrive at the first step of the church of San Giacomo, be sure to fasten a knot of rose-coloured ribands to the shoulder of your costume of *paillasse*, in order that you may be recognized. Until then you will not see me—CONSTANCY AND DISCRETION.'"

"Well," asked he, when Franz had finished, "what do you think of that?"

"You are born to good fortune," said Franz, as he returned the letter.

"Laugh as much as you will," replied Albert, "I am in love."

"You alarm me," cried Franz. "I see that I shall not only go alone to the Duke of Bracciano's ball, but also return to Florence alone."

"If my unknown be as amiable as she is beautiful," said Albert, "I shall fix myself at Rome for six weeks, at least. I adore Rome, and I have always had a great taste for archæology."

"Come, two or three more such adventures, and I do not despair of seeing you a member of the Academy." Doubtless Albert was about to discuss his right to an Academic chair when they were informed that dinner was ready. Albert's love had not taken away his appetite, and after dinner the count of Monte Cristo was announced. They had not seen him for two days. Maître Pastrini informed them that business had called him to Civita Vecchia. This man was an enigma to Franz. The count must feel sure he recognized him and yet he had not let fall a single word that indicated he had seen him anywhere. On his side, however great Franz's desire was to allude to their former interview, the fear of its being disagreeable to the man who had loaded him and his friend with kindness prevented him from mentioning it. The count had learned the two friends had sent to secure a box at the Argentino Theatre, and were told they were all let. In consequence, he brought them the key of his own— at least, such was the apparent motive of his visit. Franz and Albert made some difficulty, but the count replied that, as he was going to the Palli Theatre, the box at the Argentino Theatre would be lost if they did not profit by it.

Franz had become by degrees accustomed to the count's paleness, which had so forcibly struck him the first time he saw him. He could not refrain from admiring the severe beauty of his features, the only defect, or rather the principal quality of which was the pallor. Veritable hero of Byron! His forehead was marked by the line that indicates the constant presence of a bitter thought; he had those fiery eyes that seem to penetrate to the heart; and the haughty and disdainful upper lip that gives to the words it utters a character that impresses them on those to whom they are addressed. The count was no longer young. He was at least forty; and yet it was easy to understand he was formed to rule the young men with whom he associated at present. In reality, to complete his resemblance to the fantastic heroes of the English poet, the count seemed to have the power of fascination. Albert was constantly expatiating on their good fortune in meeting such a man. Franz was less enthusiastic; but the count exercised over him also the ascendancy a strong mind always wields. He thought several times of the project the count had of visiting Paris; and he had no doubt but that with his eccentric character, his remarkable face, and his colossal fortune, he would produce a great effect. Yet he did not wish to be at Paris when the count was there.

At length arrived the Tuesday, the last and most tumultuous day of the Carnival. On the Tuesday, the theatres open at ten o'clock in the morning, as Lent begins after eight at night. On this day all who, through want of money, time, or enthusiasm, have not been to see the Carnival before, mingle in the gaiety, and contribute to the noise and excitement. From two o'clock till five Franz and Albert followed in the fête, exchanging confetti with the other carriages and the pedestrians, who crowded amongst the horses' feet and the carriage wheels without a single accident, a single dispute, or a single fight. Albert was triumphant in his costume of *paillasse*. A knot of rose-coloured ribands fell from his shoulder almost to the ground. In order that there might be no mistake, Franz wore his peasant's costume.

As the day advanced, the tumult became greater. There was not on the pavement, in the carriages, at the windows, a single tongue that was silent, a single arm that did not move. It was a human storm, composed of a thunder of cries, and a hail of sweetmeats, flowers, eggs, oranges, and nosegays. At three o'clock the sound of fireworks, let off on the Piazza del Popolo and the Palazzo di Venezia (heard with difficulty amid the din and confusion), announced that the races were about to begin. The races, like the *moccoli*, are one of the features peculiar to the last days of the Carnival. At the sound of the fireworks, the carriages instantly broke the ranks, and retired by the adjacent streets, all these evolutions being executed with inconceivable address and rapidity, without the police interfering in the matter. The pedestrians ranged themselves against the walls ; then the trampling of horses and the clashing of steel were heard. A detachment of carbineers, fifteen abreast, galloped up the Corso in order to clear it for the *barberi*. When the detachment arrived at the Palazzo di Venezia, a second volley of fireworks was discharged to announce that the street was clear. Almost instantly seven or eight horses, excited by the shouts of three hundred thousand spectators, passed by like lightning. Then the Castle of Saint Angelo fired three cannons to indicate that number three had won. Immediately the carriages moved on, towards the Corso, like torrents pent up for a while, which again flow into the parent-river.

A new source of noise and movement was added to the crowd. The sellers of *moccoletti* entered on the scene. The *moccoli*, or *moccoletti*, are candles which vary in size, from the Pascal taper to the rushlight, and which excite two simple problems : 1st, How to preserve the *moccoletto* alight ; 2nd, How to extinguish the *moccoletti* of others. The *moccoletto* is kindled by approaching it to a light. But who can describe the thousand means of extinguishing the *moccoletto* ?—the gigantic bellows, the monstrous extinguishers, the superhuman fans. Everyone hastened to purchase *moccoletti*—Franz and Albert among the rest.

The night was rapidly approaching ; and already at the cry of " *Moccoletto !* " repeated by the shrill voices of a thousand vendors, two or three stars began to burn among the crowd. In ten minutes fifty thousand lights glittered ; it seemed the fête of Jack-o'-lanterns. The *facchino* follows the prince, the Trastevere the citizen, everyone blowing, extinguishing, relighting. This flaming race continued for two hours ; the Corso was light as day ; the features of the spectators on the third and fourth storeys were visible. Every five minutes Albert took out his watch ; at length it pointed to seven. The two friends were in the Via de Pontefici. Albert sprang out, bearing his *moccoletto* in his hand. Two or three masks strove to knock his *moccoletto* out of his hand ; but Albert, a first-rate pugilist, sent them rolling in the street, and continued his course towards the church of San Giacomo. The steps were crowded with masks, who strove to snatch each other's flambeau. Franz followed Albert with his eyes, and saw him mount the first step. Instantly a mask, wearing the familiar costume of a female peasant, snatched his *moccoletto* from him without his offering any resistance Franz was too far off to hear what they said, but he saw Albert disappear arm-in-arm with the peasant girl He watched them pass through the crowd, but lost sight of them in the Via

Macello. Suddenly the bell that gives the signal for the Carnival sounded, and at the same instant all the *moccoletti* were extinguished as if by enchantment. Franz found himself in utter darkness. No sound was audible save that of the carriages that conveyed the masks home; nothing was visible save a few lights that burnt behind the windows. The Carnival was finished.

CHAPTER XXXVII

THE CATACOMBS OF SAINT SEBASTIAN

IN his whole life, perhaps, Franz had never before experienced so rapid a transition from gaiety to sadness, as in this moment. It seemed as though Roim had suddenly changed into a vast tomb. By a chance, which added yet more to the intensity of the darkness, the moon, which was on the wane, did not rise until eleven o'clock, and the streets the young man traversed were plunged in deepest obscurity. The distance was short; and at the end of ten minutes his carriage stopped before the Hôtel de Londres. Dinner was waiting; but as Albert had told him that he should not return so soon, Franz sat down without him. Maître Pastrini, who had been accustomed to see them dine together, inquired into the cause of his absence, but Franz merely replied that Albert had received on the previous evening an invitation which he had accepted. The sudden extinction of the *moccoletti*, the silence which had succeeded, and the turmoil, had left on Franz's mind a depression which was not free from uneasiness.

Franz ordered the carriage for eleven o'clock, desiring Maître Pastrini to inform him the moment Albert returned to the hôtel. At eleven o'clock Albert had not come back. Franz dressed himself and went out, telling his host that he was going to pass the night at the Duke of Bracciano's. The Duke's house is one of the most delightful in Rome; his lady does its honours with the most consummate grace, and their fêtes have a European celebrity. The first question on Franz's arrival was to ask him where his companion was. Franz replied that he had lost sight of him in the Via Macello.

" And do you know whither he went ? "

" No, not precisely," Franz replied, " however, I think it was something very like an assignation."

" Diavolo ! " said the duke ; " this is a bad day, or night rather, to be out late in the streets of Rome, is it not, countess ? " These

words were addressed to the Countess G——, who had just
arrived on the arm of M. Torlonia, the duke's brother.

" Ah ! " asked the countess, " who is out in the streets of Rome
at this hour, unless it be to go to a ball ? "

" Our friend, Albert de Morcerf, countess, whom I left in pursuit of his unknown about seven o'clock this evening," said Franz,
" and whom I have not since seen."

" You should not have allowed him to go," said the duke to
Franz ; " you know Rome better than he does."

" You might as well have tried to stop number three of the
barberi who gained the prize in the race to-day," replied Franz ;
" and then, moreover, what could happen to him ? "

" Who can tell ? The night is gloomy, and the Tiber is very
near the Via Macello."

" I informed them at the hôtel that I had the honour of passing
the night here, duke," said Franz, " and desired them to tell me
of his return."

" Ah ! " replied the duke, " here, I think, is one of my servants
who is seeking you."

The duke was not mistaken ; the servant came up to Franz.
" Your Excellency," he said, " the master of the Hôtel de Londres has sent to let you know that a man is waiting for you
with a letter from the Viscount de Morcerf."

" A letter from the viscount ! " exclaimed Franz. " Who is the
man ? Why did he not bring it to me here ? "

" The messenger did not say. He went away directly he
saw me enter the ball-room to find you."

" Oh ! " said the Countess to Franz, " go with all speed—poor
young man ! Perhaps some accident has happened to him."

Franz took his hat and departed in haste. He had sent away
his carriage with orders for it to fetch him at two o'clock : fortunately the Palazzo Bracciano is hardly ten minutes' walk from
the Hôtel de Londres. As he came near the hôtel Franz saw a
man in the centre of the street : he had no doubt that it was the
messenger from Albert. The man was wrapped up in a large
cloak. He went up to him, but to his extreme astonishment the
individual addressed him first.

" Your Excellency's name——"

" Is the Baron Franz d'Epinay."

" Then it is to your Excellency that this letter is addressed."

" Is there any answer ? "

" Your Excellency will know when you have read the letter."

" Shall I find you here ? "

"Certainly." Franz entered the hotel. On the staircase he met Maître Pastrini.

"You have seen the man who desired to speak with you from your friend?" he asked of Franz.

"Yes, I have seen him," he replied, "and he has handed this letter to me. Light my apartment, if you please."

The innkeeper gave orders to a servant to go before Franz with a candle. The young man had found Maître Pastrini looking very much alarmed, and this had only made him the more anxious to read Albert's letter. It was written and signed by Albert. Franz read it twice before he grasped what it contained :—

"MY DEAR FELLOW,—The moment you receive this have the kindness to take from my pocket-book, which you will find in the square drawer of the secrétaire, the letter of credit ; add your own to it, if it be not sufficient. Run to Torlonia, draw from him instantly four thousand piastres, and give them to the bearer. I must have this money without delay. I do not say more, relying on you as you may rely on me.—Your friend,
"ALBERT DE MORCERF.

"P.S.—I now believe in Italian banditti."

Below these lines was written, in a strange hand, the following in Italian :—

"Se alle sei della mattina le quattro mila piastre non sono nelle mie mani, alle sette il Conte Alberto avrà cessato di vivere. "LUIGI VAMPA."

"*If by six in the morning the four thousand piastres are not in my hands, by seven o'clock the Viscount Albert will have ceased to live.*"

Albert, then, had fallen into the hands of the famous chief of banditti in whose existence he had for so long refused to believe. There was no time to lose. Franz hastened to the secrétaire, and found the pocket-book and in it the letter of credit ; there had been six thousand piastres, but of these Albert had already expended three thousand. As to Franz, he had no letter of credit, as he lived at Florence, and had only come to Rome to pass seven or eight days ; he had brought but a hundred louis, and of these he had not more than fifty left. Thus seven or eight hundred piastres were wanting to make up the sum that Albert required. True, he might in such a case rely on the kindness of M. Torlonia. He was, therefore, about to return to the Palazzo Bracciano, when suddenly a luminous idea crossed his mind. He remembered the

count of Monte Cristo. Franz was about to ring for Maître
Pastrini when that worthy presented himself. " My dear sir,"
he said, hastily, " do you know if the count is within ? "

" Yes, your Excellency ; he has this moment returned."

" Then ring at his door, if you please, and request him to be so
kind as to give me an audience."

Maître Pastrini did as he was desired, and, returning five
minutes afterwards, he said, " The count awaits your Excellency."

Franz went along the corridor, and a servant introduced him
to the count. He was in a small cabinet which Franz had not
yet seen, and which was surrounded with divans. The count
came towards him. " Well, what good wind blows you hither at
this hour ? " said he ; " have you come to sup with me ? it would
be very kind of you."

" No ; I have come to speak to you of a very serious matter."

" A serious matter ! " said the count, looking at Franz with
the earnestness usual to him ; " and what may it be ? "

Franz gave him Albert's letter. " Read that," he said. The
count read it.

" What do you think of it ? " inquired Franz.

" Have you the money he demands ? "

" Yes, all but eight hundred piastres."

The count went to his secrétaire, opened it, and, pulling out a
drawer filled with gold, said to Franz, " I hope you will not offend
me by applying to anyone but myself. Have what you will," and
he made a sign to Franz to take what he pleased.

" Is it absolutely necessary to send the money to Luigi Vampa ? "
asked the young man, looking fixedly in his turn at the count.

" Judge for yourself," replied he, " The postscript is explicit."

" I think that if you would take the trouble of reflecting, you
could find a way of simplifying the negotiation," said Franz.
" If we were to go together to Luigi Vampa, I am sure he would
not refuse you Albert's freedom."

" What influence can I have over a bandit ? "

" Have you not just rendered him one of those services that are
never forgotten ? Have you not saved Peppino's life ? "

" Ah ! " said the count ; " who told you that ? "

" No matter, I know it."

The count knit his brows, and remained silent an instant.
" And if I went to seek Vampa, would you accompany me ? "

" If my society would not be disagreeable."

" Be it so ; it is a lovely night, and a walk without Rome will
do us both good."

" Shall I take any arms ? or money ? "

" It is useless. Where is the man who brought the letter ? "

" In the street, awaiting the answer."

" I must learn where we are going. I will summon him hither."

The count went to the window of the apartment that looked on to the street, and whistled in a peculiar manner. The man in the mantle quitted the wall, and advanced into the centre of the street. " *Salite !* " said the count, in the same tone in which he would have given an order to his servant. The messenger obeyed with alacrity, and mounting the steps of the passage at a bound, entered the hotel.

" Ah ! it is you, Peppino," said the count. But Peppino, instead of answering, threw himself on his knees, seized the count's hand, and covered it with kisses.

" Ah ! " said the count, " you have not forgotten that I saved your life ; that is strange, for it is a week ago."

" No, Excellency, and never shall I forget it," returned Peppino, with an accent of profound gratitude.

" Never ! that is a long time : but it is something that you believe so. Rise and answer."

Peppino glanced anxiously at Franz.

" Oh, you may speak before his Excellency," said he. " He is one of my friends."

" Good," returned Peppino ; " I am ready to answer any questions your Excellency may address to me."

" How did the Viscount Albert fall into Luigi's hands ? "

" Excellency, the Frenchman's carriage passed several times the one in which was Teresa."

" The chief's mistress ? "

" Yes ; the Frenchman threw her a bouquet, Teresa returned it ; all this with the consent of the chief, who was in the carriage. It was he who drove, disguised as the coachman."

" Well ? " said the count.

" Well, then, the Frenchman took off his mask. Teresa, with the chief's consent, did the same. The Frenchman asked for a rendezvous ; Teresa gave him one ; only instead of Teresa it was Beppo who was on the steps of the church of San Giacomo."

" What ! " exclaimed Franz, " the peasant girl who snatched his moccoletto from him——"

" Was a lad of fifteen," replied Peppino ; " but it was no disgrace to your friend to have been deceived. Beppo has taken in plenty of others."

And Beppo led him outside the walls ? " said the count.

" Exactly so ; a carriage was waiting at the end of Via Macello. Beppo got in, inviting the Frenchman to follow him, and he did not wait to be asked twice. He gallantly offered the righthand seat to Beppo, and sat by him. Beppo told him he was going to take him to a villa a league from Rome ; the Frenchman assured him he would follow him to the end of the world. The coachman went up the Via di Ripetta and the Porta San Paolo ; and when they were two hundred yards outside, as the Frenchman became somewhat too forward, Beppo put a brace of pistols to his head, the coachman pulled up and did the same. At the same time four of the band, who were concealed on the banks of the Almo, surrounded the carriage. The Frenchman made some resistance, and nearly strangled Beppo ; but he could not resist five armed men, and was forced to yield ; they made him get out, walk along the banks of the river, and then brought him to Teresa and Luigi, who were waiting for him in the catacombs of St. Sebastian."

" Well," said the count, turning towards Franz, " it seems to me that this is a very likely story. What do you say to it ? "

" Why, that I should think it very amusing," replied Franz, " if it had happened to anyone but poor Albert."

" And, in truth, if you had not found me here," said the count, it might have cost your friend dearly ; but now, be assured, his alarm will be the only serious consequence."

" And shall we go and find him ? " inquired Franz.

" Oh ! decidedly, sir ; he is in a very picturesque place. Do you know the catacombs of St. Sebastian ? "

" I was never in them, but I have often resolved to visit them."

" Well, here is an opportunity made to your hand. Have you a carriage ? "

" No."

" That is of no consequence ; I always have one ready, day and night."

" Always ready ? "

" Yes ; I am a very capricious being, and I should tell you that sometimes when I rise, or after my dinner, or in the middle of the night, I resolve on starting for some particular point, and away I go." The count rang, and a footman appeared. " Order out the carriage," he said, " and remove the pistols which are in the holsters. Ali will drive." In a very short time the carriage stopped at the door. The count took out his watch. " Half-past twelve," he said ; " we might start at five and be in time, but the delay may cause your friend an uneasy night ; therefore,

K

we had better go with all speed to extricate him from the hands of the infidels. Come along."

Franz and the count went downstairs, accompanied by Peppino. Franz and the count got into the carriage. Peppino placed himself beside Ali on the box, and they set off at a rapid pace. Ali had received his instructions, and went down the Corso, crossed the Campo Vaccino, went up the Via San Gregorio, and reached the gates of St. Sebastian. There the porter raised some difficulties ; but the count of Monte Cristo produced an authority from the governor of Rome to quit or enter the city at any hour of the day or night ; the portcullis was therefore raised, the porter had a louis for his trouble, and they went on their way. The road which the carriage now traversed was the ancient Appian Way. From time to time, by the light of the moon which began to rise, Franz imagined that he saw something like a sentinel appear at various points and suddenly retreat into the darkness on a signal from Peppino. A short time before they reached the circus of Caracalla the carriage stopped. Peppino opened the door, and the count and Franz alighted.

" In ten minutes," said the count to his companion, " we shall arrive there."

He then took Peppino aside, gave him some order in a low voice, and Peppino went away, taking with him a torch, brought with them in the carriage. Five minutes elapsed, during which Franz saw the shepherd advance along a narrow path, in the midst of the irregular ground which forms the convulsed soil of the plain of Rome, and disappear in the midst of the high red herbage.

Franz and the count in their turn advanced along the same path, which, at the end of a hundred paces, led them by declivity to the bottom of a small valley. They then perceived two men conversing in the shade.

One of these two men was Peppino, and the other a bandit on the lookout.

" Your Excellency," said Peppino, addressing the count, " if you will follow me the opening of the catacombs is close at hand."

They came to an opening behind a clump of bushes, and in the midst of a pile of rocks by which a man could scarcely pass. Peppino glided first into this crevice ; but after advancing a few paces the passage widened. Then he paused, lighted his torch, and turned round to see if they came after him. The count first reached a kind of square space, and Franz followed him closely. They went on a hundred and fifty paces thus, and then were

stopped by " Who goes there ? "   At the same time they saw
the reflection of a torch on the barrel of a carbine.

" A friend ! " responded Peppino.

Behind the sentinel was a staircase with twenty steps. Franz
and the count descended these, and found themselves in a kind of
cross-roads, forming a burial-ground.   Five roads diverged like
the rays of a star, and the walls, dug into niches, placed one
above the other in the shape of coffins, showed that they were at
last in the catacombs.   In one of the cavities some rays of light
were visible.   The count laid his hand on Franz's shoulder.

" Would you like to see a camp of bandits in repose ? "

" Exceedingly," replied Franz.

" Come with me, then.   Peppino, extinguish the torch."

Peppino obeyed, and fifty paces in front of them there played
along the wall some reddish beams of light, more visible since Peppino had put out his torch.   They walked silently, the count guiding Franz as if he had the faculty of seeing in the dark.   Franz,
however, distinguished his way more plainly as he advanced
towards the rays of light which served them for guides.   Three
arcades, of which the middle served as the door, offered themselves.
These arcades opened on one side to the corridor, in which were
the count and Franz, and on the other to a large square chamber,
entirely surrounded by niches similar to those of which we have
spoken.   In the midst of this chamber were four stones, which
had formerly served as an altar, as was evident from the cross
which still surmounted them.   A lamp, placed at the base of a
pillar, lighted up the singular scene which presented itself to the
two visitors concealed in the shadow.   A man was seated with his
elbow leaning on the column, and was reading with his back
turned to the arcades, through the openings of which the new-
comers contemplated him.   This was the chief of the band, Luigi
Vampa.   Around him, lying in their mantles, or with their backs
against a kind of stone bench, which went all round the Columbarium, were to be seen twenty brigands or more, each having
his carbine within reach.   At the bottom, silent, scarcely visible,
and like a shadow, was a sentinel, who was walking up and down
before a kind of opening.   When the count thought Franz had
gazed sufficiently on this picturesque tableau, he raised his finger
to his lips, to warn him to be silent, and ascending the three steps
which led to the corridor of the Columbarium, entered the chamber
by the centre arcade, and advanced towards Vampa, who was so
intent on his book that he did not hear the noise of footsteps.

' Who goes there ? " cried the sentinel, less occupied, and who saw by the lamp's light a shadow which approached his chief. At this sound, Vampa rose quickly, drawing at the same moment a pistol from his girdle. In a moment all the bandits were on their feet, and twenty carbines were levelled at the count.

" Well, my dear Vampa, you receive a friend with a great deal of ceremony ! "

" Ground arms ! " exclaimed the chief, with an imperative sign of the hand, whilst with the other he took off his hat respectfully. " Your pardon, M. le Comte, but I was so far from expecting the honour of a visit, that I did not recognize you."

' Your memory is equally short in everything, Vampa," said the count ; " not only do you forget people's faces, but also the conditions you make with them. Was it not agreed that my person, and that of my friends should be respected by you ? "

" And how have I broken that treaty, your Excellency ? "

" You have this evening carried off and conveyed hither the Viscount Albert de Morcerf. Well," continued the count, in a tone that made Franz shudder, " this young gentleman is one of *my friends*, lodges in the same hotel as myself, has been up and down the Corso for eight hours in my private carriage, and yet you have carried him off, and," added the count, taking the letter from his pocket, " have set a ransom on him as if he were an indifferent person."

" Why did you not tell me all this, you ? " inquired the brigand chief, turning towards his men, who retreated before his look. " Why have you made me fail in my word towards the count, who has our lives in his hands ? By heavens ! if I thought one of you knew that the young gentleman was the friend of his Excellency, I would blow his brains out ! "

" Well," said the count, turning towards Franz, " I told you there was some mistake in this."

" Are you not alone ? " asked Vampa, with uneasiness.

" I am with the person to whom this letter was addressed, and to whom I desired to prove that Luigi Vampa was a man of his word. Come, your Excellency, here is Luigi Vampa, who will himself express to you his deep regret at the mistake."

Franz approached, the chief advancing several steps to meet him. " Welcome amongst us, your Excellency," he said to him ; " you heard what the count just said, and also my reply ; let me add that I would not have had this happen for the four thousand piastres at which I had fixed your friend's ransom."

" But," said Franz, " where is the viscount ? I do not see him."

" The prisoner is there," replied Vampa, pointing to the hollow place in front of which the bandit was on guard, " and I will go myself and tell him he is free."   The chief went towards the place, and Franz and the count followed him.   " What is the prisoner doing ? " inquired Vampa of the sentinel.

" *Ma foi !* captain," replied the sentry, " I do not know ; for the last hour I have not heard him stir."

" Come in, your Excellency," said Vampa.

By the gleam of a lamp, similar to that which lighted the Columbarium, Albert could be seen wrapped up in a cloak which one of the bandits had lent him, lying in a corner in profound slumber.

" Come ! " said the count, smiling his peculiar smile, " not so bad for a man who is to be shot at seven o'clock to-morrow morning ! "   Vampa looked at Albert with a kind of admiration ; he was not insensible to such courage.

" You are right, M. le Comte," he said ;   " this must be one of your friends."   Then going to Albert, he touched him on the shoulder, saying,—" Will your Excellency please to awaken ? " Albert stretched out his arms, rubbed his eyelids, and opened his eyes.   " Ah ! " said he, " is it you, captain ?   You should have allowed me to sleep.   I had such a delightful dream ;   I was dancing the galop at Torlonia's with the Countess G——."   Then he drew from his pocket his watch, which he had preserved, that he might see how time sped.

" Half-past one only," said he.   " Why the devil do you rouse me at this hour ? "

" To tell you that you are free, your Excellency."

" My dear fellow," replied Albert, at perfect ease, " remember for the future Napoleon's maxim, ' Never awaken me but for bad news.'   So they have paid my ransom ? "

" No, your Excellency !   A person to whom I can refuse nothing has come to demand you."

" Really ! then that person is a most amiable person."   Albert looked round, and perceived Franz.   " What ! " said he, " is it you, my dear Franz, whose devotion and friendship are thus displayed ? "

" No, not I," replied Franz, " but our neighbour, the count of Monte Cristo."

" Ah ! M. le Comte," said Albert, gaily, " you are really most kind, and I hope you will consider me as your eternally obliged, in the first place for the carriage, and in the next for this ! " and he put out his hand to the count, who shuddered as he gave his own, but who nevertheless did give it.   The bandit gazed on this scene with amazement, and Franz was enchanted at the way in which Albert had sustained the national honour in the presence of the bandit. "My dear Albert," he said, "if you will make haste, we shall yet have time to finish the night at Torlonia's. You may conclude your interrupted galop, so that you will owe no ill-will to Signor Luigi, who has, indeed, throughout this whole affair, acted like a gentleman."

"You are right, and we may reach the Palazzo at two o'clock. Signor Luigi," continued Albert," "is there any formality to fulfil before I leave?"

"None, sir," replied the bandit : "you are as free as air."

"Well, then, a happy and merry life to you! Come, gentlemen, come!"

Albert, followed by Franz and the count, crossed the square chamber, where the bandits stood, hat in hand. "Peppino," said the chief, "give me the torch. I will show you the way back myself," said the captain to the count ; "that is the least honour I can testify to your Excellency."

Taking the lighted torch from the hand of the herdsman, he preceded his guests, not as a servant, but as a king who precedes ambassadors. On reaching the door, he bowed. "And now, M. le Comte," added he," allow me to repeat my apologies, and to hope you will not entertain any resentment at what has occurred."

"No, my dear Vampa," replied the count ; "besides, you compensate for your mistakes in so gentlemanly a way, that one almost feels obliged to you for having committed them."

"Gentlemen," added the chief, turning towards the young men, "perhaps the offer may not appear very tempting to you ; but if you should ever feel inclined to pay me a second visit, wherever I may be, you shall be welcome." Franz and Albert bowed. The count went out first, then Albert, ; Franz paused for a moment. "Has your Excellency anything to ask me?" said Vampa.

"Yes, I have," replied Franz. "I am curious to know what work you were perusing with so much attention as we entered?"

"Cæsar's *Commentaries*," said the bandit ; "it is my favourite work."

"Now, M. le Comte," Albert exclaimed, "let us on with all the speed we may. I am enormously anxious to finish my night at the Duke of Bracciano's."

It was just two o'clock when the two friends entered the dancing room. "Madame," said the Viscount Morcerf, advancing to the Countess, "yesterday you were so condescending as to promise me a galop; I am rather late in claiming this gracious promise, but here is my friend, whose character for veracity you well know, and he will assure you the delay arose from no fault of mine." And as at this moment the music gave the warning for the waltz, Albert put his arm round the waist of the Countess, and disappeared with her in the whirl of dancers.

In the meanwhile Franz was considering the singular shudder that had pervaded the count of Monte Cristo's frame when he had been forced to give his hand to Albert.

CHAPTER XXXVIII

THE RENDEZVOUS

NEXT morning, Albert asked his friend to go with him to see the Count. Franz, attracted by some strange magnetism, in which terror was mingled, and reluctant to expose his friend alone to the Count's influence, accompanied him, and presently the Count joined them in the salon. " M. le Comte," said Albert, " permit me to repeat the poor thanks I offered last night, and to assure you that the remembrance of all I owe you will never be effaced from my memory. I am indebted to you even for my life."

" My very good friend and excellent neighbour," replied the count, with a smile, " you exaggerate my small exertions. You owe me nothing but some trifle of 20,000 francs, which have been saved out of your travelling expenses, so that there is not much of a score between us ;—but you must permit me to congratulate you on the unconcern with which you resigned yourself to your fate, and the indifference you manifested as to the turn events might take."

" I deserve no credit for what I could not help, namely, a determination to let those bandits see that the French can smile even in the face of Death. All that, however, has nothing to do with my obligations to you, and I now come to ask whether I can in any way serve you ? My father, the Comte de Morcerf, although of Spanish origin, possesses influence at the courts of France and Madrid, and I place the best services of myself, and all to whom my life is dear, at your disposal."

" M. de Morcerf," replied the count, " your offer, far from surprising me, is precisely what I expected of you, and I accept it in the same spirit of hearty sincerity in which it is made ;—nay, I will go still farther, and say that I had made up my mind to ask a great favour at your hands. I am wholly a stranger to Paris— it is a city I have never yet seen."

" Is it possible," exclaimed Albert, " that you have not yet visited the finest capital in the world ? I can scarcely credit it."

" Nevertheless, it is true ; still my ignorance of the first city in Europe is a reproach to me in every way, and calls for immediate correction ; and I should have beheld the wonders and beauties of your celebrated capital ere now, had I known any person who would introduce me into the fashionable world."

" So distinguished a person as yourself," cried Albert, " could scarcely have required an introduction."

" You are most kind ; but I can find no merit I possess, save that, as a millionaire, I might have become a partner in the speculations of M. Rothschild ; but as my motive in travelling to your capital was not for the pleasure of dabbling in the funds, I have stayed away till some favourable chance should arise of carrying out my wishes. Your offer, however, removes all difficulties, and I have only to ask you, my dear M. de Morcerf " (these words were accompanied by a most peculiar smile), " whether you undertake, upon my arrival in Paris, to open to me the doors of that fashionable world of which I know no more than a Huron or native of Cochin China ? "

" Oh, that I do, and with infinite pleasure ! " answered Albert ; " and so much the more readily, as a letter received this morning from my father summons me to Paris, in consequence of a treaty of marriage (my dear Franz, do not smile, I beg of you) with a family of high standing, connected with the very *élite* of Parisian society."

" Connected by marriage, you mean," said Franz, laughingly.

" Well, never mind how it is," answered Albert, " it comes to the same thing in the end. But as regards your wish to visit our city, my dear count, I can only say that you may command me and mine to any extent you please."

" Then it is settled," said the count ; " and I give you my solemn assurance that I only waited an opportunity like the present to realize schemes I have long meditated."

" Tell me now, count," exclaimed Albert, delighted at the idea of having to chaperone so distinguished a person as Monte Cristo ; " tell me truly whether you are in earnest, or if this project of visiting Paris is merely one of those chimerical plans of which we make so many in the course of our lives."

" I pledge you my honour," returned the count, " that both inclination and necessity compel me to visit Paris. When shall you be there ? "

" In a fortnight or three weeks."

" Nay," said the count, " I will give you three months ere I join you ; you see I make an ample allowance for all delays and difficulties."

" And in three months," said Albert, " you will be at my house ? "

" Shall we make an appointment for a particular day and hour ? " inquired the cóunt ; " only let me warn you that I am punctilious in keeping my engagements."

" The very thing ! " exclaimed Albert.

" So be it, then," replied the count, and extending his hand towards an almanack, suspended near the chimney-piece, he said, " To-day is the 21st of February : " and drawing out his watch, added, " it is exactly half-past ten o'clock. Now, promise to expect me on the 21st of May at the same hour in the forenoon."

" Capital ! " exclaimed Albert ; " and you shall find everything and everybody ready to receive you. Your breakfast shall be smoking hot awaiting your arrival."

" Where do you live ? "

" No. 27, Rue du Helder. I reside in my father's hôtel, but occupy a pavilion at the farther side of the courtyard, separated from the main building."

" Quite sufficient," replied the count, as, taking out his tablets, he wrote down, " No. 27, Rue du Helder, 21st May, half-past ten in the morning. Now, then," said the count, returning his tablets tc his pocket, " make yourself perfectly easy ; the hand of your timepiece will not be more accurate in marking the time than myself. When do you set off ? "

" To-morrow afternoon, at five o'clock."

" In that case I must say adieu to you ; as I am compelled to go to Naples, and shall not return hither before Saturday evening or Sunday morning. And you, M. le Baron," pursued the count, addressing Franz, " do you also depart to-morrow ? "

" Yes, I go to Venice ; I shall remain in Italy for another year or two."

" We shall not meet in Paris ? "

" I fear not."

" Well, since we must part," said the count, holding out a hand to each of the young men, " allow me to wish you both a safe and pleasant journey." It was the first time the hand of Franz had come in contact with that of the Count, and unconsciously he shuddered at his touch, for it felt cold and icy as that of a corpse.

The young men then rose, and, courteously bowing to their acquaintance, quitted the room.

" What is the matter ? " asked Albert of Franz, when they had returned to their own apartment ; " you seem more than commonly thoughtful."

" I will confess that I am puzzled to unravel the character of this count ; and the appointment to meet him in Paris fills me with a thousand apprehensions."

" My dear fellow," exclaimed Albert, " what is there to excite uneasiness ? You must have lost your senses to imagine danger can spring from it ! "

" Whether in my senses or not," answered Franz, " such is my fear of the evil effects that may arise from your meeting with this incomprehensible count, that I would give much you had not crossed his path."

" Listen to me, Franz," said Albert ; " our present conversation gives me an opportunity of remarking that I have been struck with the difference between your manner towards the count and that with which you treat your friends in general ; to him you are frigid and polite, while to myself, for instance, you are as cordial as a friend should be. Have you any reasons for so acting ? Did you ever meet him before ? "

" Will you promise not to repeat a single word of what I am about to tell you ? And will you pledge your honour that nothing shall induce you to divulge it ? "

" I pledge my honour."

" Well, listen to me."

Franz then related to his friend the history of his excursion to the isle of Monte Cristo, and of his finding a party of smugglers there, with whom were two Corsican bandits. He dwelt on the almost magical hospitality he had received from the count, and the magnificence of his entertainment in the grotto. He recounted all particulars of the supper ; the hacheesh, the statues, the dream, and reality, and how, at his awakening, there remained no proof or trace of all these events, save the small yacht hastening with spread sails towards Porto Vecchio. Then he detailed the conversation he had overheard at the Colosseum, in which the count had promised Vampa to obtain the release of the bandit Peppino. At last he came to the adventure of the preceding night, when he had applied to the count to furnish the money in which he was deficient, and the Count's successful intervention to secure Albert's release.

" Well," said Albert, when Franz had concluded, " what do you find to object to in all you have related ? The count is fond of travelling, and, being rich, possesses a vessel of his own. Now, by way of having a resting-place during his excursions at which he might be sure of a decent cookery and a comfortable bed, Monte Cristo has furnished the abode where you found him ; but, to prevent the Tuscan Government from taking a fancy to his enchanted palace, and depriving him of the advantages to be derived from so large an outlay of capital, he has purchased the island, and assumed the title of its count. Just ask yourself, my good fellow, whether there are not many persons of our acquaintance who assume the names of lands and properties they never in their lives were master of."

" But," said Franz, " how do you account for the Corsican bandits being among the crew of his vessel ? I suppose you will allow that such men as Vampa and his band are villains, who have no other motive than plunder when they seize your person. How do you explain the influence the count possessed over these ruffians ? "

" My good friend, as in all probability I owe my present safety to that influence, it would ill become me to search too closely into its source ; therefore, instead of condemning him for his intimacy with outlaws, you must give me leave to excuse any little irregularity there may be in such a connexion ; not altogether for preserving my life, for my own idea is that it never was in much danger ; but certainly for saving me 4,000 piastres, which, being translated, means neither more nor less than 24,000 livres of our money,—a sum at which, most assuredly, I should never have been estimated in France ; proving, most indisputably," added Albert, with a laugh, " that no prophet is honoured in his own country."

" Talking of countries," replied Franz, " can you tell me what country produced this mysterious person, what is his native tongue, his means of existence, whence he derives his immense fortune, and what were those events of his early life—a life as marvellous as unknown,—that have tinctured his succeeding years with so gloomy a misanthropy ? These are questions, which in your place, I should like to have answered."

" My dear Franz," replied Albert, " when, upon receipt of my letter, you found the necessity of asking the count's assistance, you promptly went to him, saying, " My friend Albert de Morcerf is in danger ; help me to deliver him.' Did he ask you, ' Who is M. Albert de Morcerf ? what are his means of existence ? of what country is he a native ? ' Tell me, did he put all these questions to you ? "

"I confess he asked me none."

"No; he merely came and freed me from the hands of Signor Vampa, where, I assure you, in spite of all my outward appearance of ease and unconcern, I did not very particularly care to remain. Now, then, Franz, when, in return for services so promptly and unhesitatingly rendered, he but asks me to do for him what is done daily for any Russian prince or Italian noble who may pass through Paris, would you have me refuse? My good fellow, you must have lost your senses to think I could act in such a cold-blooded manner."

"Well," said Franz, with a sigh, "do as you please, my dear viscount, for your arguments are beyond my powers of refutation. Still, you must admit that this count is a most singular being."

"He is a philanthropist," answered the other; "and no doubt his motive in visiting Paris is to compete for the Monthyon prize, given to the person who shall be proved to have most materially advanced the cause of virtue and humanity. If my vote and interest can obtain it for him, I will give him the one and promise the other. And now, my dear Franz, let us talk of something else. Come, shall we take our luncheon, and pay a last visit to St. Peter's?"

Franz assented; and the following afternoon, at half-past five o'clock, the young men parted, Albert de Morcerf to return to Paris, and Franz d'Épinay to pass a fortnight at Venice. But ere he entered his travelling carriage, Albert, lest his guest might forget the engagement, placed in the care of the waiter of the hotel a card to be delivered to the count of Monte Cristo, on which, beneath the name of Albert de Morcerf, he had written in pencil,—

"27, Rue du Helder, on the 21st May, half-past ten a.m."

CHAPTER XXXIX

THE GUESTS

IN the house in the Rue du Helder everything was being prepared on the morning of the 21st of May. Albert de Morcerf occupied a pavilion situated at the corner of a large court, and directly opposite another building, in which were the servants' apartments. Two windows only of the pavilion faced the street; three other windows looked into the court, and two at the back into the garden. Between the court and the garden stood the large and fashionable dwelling of the Count and Countess de Morcerf. A high wall surrounded the whole of the hôtel, surmounted at intervals by vases filled with flowers, and broken in the centre by a large gate of gilt iron, which served as the carriage entrance. A small door, close to the lodge of the concierge, gave ingress and egress to the servants and masters when they were on foot.

By means of the two windows, looking into the street, Albert could see all that passed ; and should anything appear to merit a more minute examination, Albert de Morcerf could follow up his researches by means of a small gate, similar to that close to the concierge's door. It was a little entrance that seemed never to have been opened since the house was built, so entirely was it covered with dust and dirt ; but the well-oiled hinges and lock announced a frequent and mysterious employment. This door laughed at the concierge, from whose vigilance and jurisdiction it escaped, opening at a cabalistic word or a concerted tap without from the sweetest voices or whitest fingers in the world. At the end of a long corridor, with which the door communicated, and which formed the antechamber, were, on the right, Albert's breakfast-room, looking into the court, and, on the left, the salon, looking into the garden. Shrubs and creeping plants covered the windows, and hid from the garden and court these two apartments, the only rooms into which, as they were on the ground floor, the prying eyes of the curious could penetrate. On the first floor were similar rooms, with the addition of a third, formed out of the antechamber ; these three rooms were a salon, a boudoir, and a bedroom. The salon downstairs was only an Algerian divan, for the use of smokers. The boudoir upstairs communicated with the bedchamber by an invisible door on the staircase ;—it was evident every precaution had been taken. Above this floor was a large *atelier*, which had been increased in size by pulling down the partitions. In it were collected and piled up signs of all Albert's successive fads,—hunting-horns, bass-viols, flutes,—a whole orchestra, for he had not a taste but a fancy for music ; easels, palettes, brushes, pencils,—for music had been succeeded by painting ; foils, boxing-gloves, broadswords, and singlesticks,—for Albert de Morcerf cultivated, with far more perseverence than music and drawing, the three arts that complete a dandy's education, *i.e.*, fencing, boxing, and singlestick ; and it was in this apartment that he received Grisier, Cook, and Charles Lecour. The rest of the furniture of this privileged apartment consisted of ancient cabinets and old armchairs, on which were thrown splendid stuffs, dyed beneath Persia's sun, or woven by the fingers of the women of Calcutta or Chandernagore. In the centre of the room was a piano in rosewood, and on the walls were swords, daggers, Malay krises, maces, battle-axes, suits of armour, gilded, damasked, and inlaid; dried plants, minerals, and stuffed birds, opening their flame-coloured wings as if for flight, and their beaks that never close. This was the favourite sitting-room of Albert.

However, on the morning of the appointment, the young man had established himself in the small salon downstairs. There, on a table, surrounded at some distance by a large and luxurious divan, every species of tobacco known was exposed in those pots of crackled earthenware of which the Dutch are so fond; beside them, in boxes of fragrant wood, were ranged, according to their size and quality, pueros, regalias, havannas, and manillas; and, in an open cabinet, a collection of pipes from all countries awaited the fancy or the sympathy of the smokers. At a quarter to ten, a valet entered; his name was Germain, and he enjoyed the entire confidence of his young master, and now he held in one hand a number of papers, and in the other a packet of letters, which he gave to Albert. Albert glanced carelessly at the different missives, selected two written in a small and delicate hand, and enclosed in scented envelopes, opened them, and perused their contents with some attention.

" How did these letters come ? " said he.

" One by the post ; Madame Danglars' footman left the other."

" Let Madame Danglars know that I accept the place she offers me in her box. Wait ; then, during the day, tell Rosa that when I leave the Opera I will sup with her, as she wishes. Take her six bottles of different wines,—Cyprus, sherry, and Malaga, and a barrel of Ostend oysters ; get them at Borel's, and be sure you say they are for me."

" At what o'clock, sir, do you breakfast ? "

"At half-past ten. Debray will, perhaps, be obliged to go to the Home Office,—and besides (Albert looked at his tablets), it is the hour I told the count ; and though I do not much rely upon his promise, I wish to be punctual. Is Madame la Comtesse up yet ? "

" If M. le Vicomte wishes, I will inquire."

" Yes, ask her for one of her liqueur cellarets, mine is complete ; and tell her I shall have the honour of seeing her about three o'clock, and that I request permission to introduce someone to her." Presently a carriage stopped and the servant announced M. Lucien Debray. A tall young man, with light hair, clear grey eyes, and thin compressed lips, dressed in a blue coat with buttons of gold, beautifully carved, a white neckcloth, and a tortoiseshell eye-glass, suspended by a silken thread, entered, with a half-official air, without smiling or speaking. "Good morning, Lucien! good morning!" said Albert; "your punctuality alarms me. What do I say? punctuality! You, whom I expected last, you arrive at five minutes to ten, when the time fixed was half-past! Have ministers resigned?"

"No, my dear fellow," returned the young man, seating himself on the divan; "reassure yourself; we are tottering always, but we never fall; and I begin to believe that we shall pass into a state of immobility, and then the affairs of the Peninsula will completely consolidate us."

"Ah, true! you drive Don Carlos out of Spain."

"My dear fellow, do not confound our plans. We take him to the other side of the French frontier, and offer him hospitality at Bourges. He has not much to complain of; Bourges is the capital of Charles VII. Don't you know that all Paris knew it yesterday, and the day before it had already transpired on the Bourse, and M. Danglars made £40,000?"

"And you gained another order; for I see you have a blue riband at your button-hole."

"Yes, they sent me the order of Charles III.," returned Debray, carelessly. "It is very well as a finish to the toilette. It looks very neat on a black coat buttoned up. It is for that reason you see me so early."

"Because you have the order of Charles III. and wish to announce the good news to me?"

"No, because I passed the night writing letters,—five-and-twenty despatches. I returned home at daybreak and strove to sleep; but my head ached and I got up to have a ride for an hour. At the Bois de Boulogne, *ennui* and hunger attacked me at once. I then recollected you gave a breakfast this morning and here I am. I am hungry, feed me; I am bored, amuse me."

"It is my duty as your host," returned Albert, ringing the bell. "Germain, a glass of sherry and a biscuit. In the meantime, my dear Lucien, here are cigars—contraband, of course—try them, and persuade the minister to sell us such instead of poisoning us with cabbage-leaves."

"*Peste!* I will do nothing of the kind; the moment they come from Government you would find them execrable. Besides, that does not concern the Home but the Financial Department. Address yourself to M. Humann, section of the Indirect Contributions, Corridor A, No. 26."

"On my word," said Albert, "you astonish me by the extent of your acquaintance."

"Really, my dear count," replied Lucien, lighting a manilla at a rose-coloured taper that burnt in a beautifully enamelled stand, "how happy you are to have nothing to do!"

"And what would you do, my dear diplomatist," replied Morcerf, with a slight degree of irony in his voice, "if you did nothing? What! private secretary to a minister, plunged at once into European cabals and Parisian intrigues; having kings and, better still, queens, to protect, parties to unite, elections to direct; making more use of your cabinet with your pen and your telegraph than Napoleon did of his battle-fields with his sword and his victories; possessing five and twenty thousand francs a year, besides your place; a horse, for which Château-Renaud offered you four hundred louis, and which you would not part with; a tailor who never disappoints you; with the opera, the jockey club, and other varieties, can you not amuse yourself? Well, I will amuse you by introducing you to a new acquaintance." But I hear Beauchamp in the next room; you can dispute together about the papers, and that will pass away the time."

"My dear friend," said Lucien, with an air of sovereign contempt, "do I ever read the papers?"

"M. Beauchamp," announced the servant.

"Enter," said Albert, advancing to meet the young man. "Here is Debray, who detests you without reading you, so he says."

"He is quite right," returned Beauchamp, "for I criticise him without knowing what he does. Good-day, commander!"

"Ah! you know that already," said the private secretary, smiling and shaking hands with him. "And what do they say of it in the world?"

"They say that it is quite fair, and that you sow so much red, that you must reap a little blue."

"Come, come; that is not bad!" said Lucien. "Why do you not join our party, my dear Beauchamp? With your talents you would make your fortune in three or four years."

"I only await one thing before following your advice; that is, a minister who will hold office for six months. My dear Albert, one word; for I must get poor Lucien a respite. Do we breakfast or dine? I must go to the Chamber, for our life is not an idle one."

"You only breakfast; I await two persons; and the instant they arrive, we shall sit down to table."

THE BREAKFAST

CHAPTER XL

THE BREAKFAST

" What sort of persons do you expect ? " said Beauchamp.

" A gentleman and a diplomatist."

" Then we shall have to wait two hours for the gentleman, and three for the diplomatist. I shall come back to dessert ; save me some strawberries, coffee, and cigars. I shall take a cutlet on my way to the Chamber."

" Nothing of the sort ; for were the gentleman a Montmorency, and the diplomatist a Metternich, we will breakfast at eleven ; in the mean time, follow Debray's example, and take a glass of sherry and a biscuit."

" Be it so ; I will stay. I must do something to distract my thoughts. You do not know with what I am threatened. I shall hear this morning M. Danglars make a speech at the Chamber of Deputies ; and at his wife's this evening I shall hear the tragedy of a peer of France."

" Do you run down M. Danglars' speeches," said Debray ; " he votes for you, for he belongs to the Opposition."

" *Pardieu !* that is exactly the worst of all : I am waiting until you send him to speak at the Luxembourg, to laugh at my ease."

" My dear friend," said Albert to Beauchamp, " it is plain the affairs of Spain are settled, for you are most desperately out of humour this morning. Recollect that Parisian gossip has spoken of a marriage between myself and Mlle. Eugénie Danglars ; I cannot, in conscience, therefore, let you run down the speeches of a man who will one day say to me, ' M. le Vicomte, you know I give my daughter eighty thousand pounds.' "

" Ah, this marriage will never take place," said Beauchamp. " The king has made him a baron, and can make him a peer, but he cannot make him a gentleman : and the Count de Morcerf is too aristocratic to consent to a *mésalliance* for the paltry sum of eighty thousand pounds. The Viscount de Morcerf can only wed a marchioness."

" But eighty thousand pounds is a nice little sum," replied Morcerf.

" Never mind what he says, Morcerf," said Debray, " do you marry her. You marry the ticket of a money-bag, it is true, but what does that matter ? It is better to have a blazon less and a figure more on it. You have seven martlets on your arms, give three to your wife and you will still have four ; that is one more than M. de Guise had, who so nearly became king of France, and whose cousin was emperor of Germany."

"On my word, I think you are right, Lucien," said Albert, absently.

"M. de Château-Renaud! M. Maximilian Morrel!" said the servant, announcing two fresh guests.

"Morrel!" muttered Albert,—"Morrel! who is he?" But before he had finished, M. de Château-Renaud, a handsome young man of thirty, took Albert's hand. "My dear Albert," said he, "let me introduce to you M. Maximilian Morrel, captain of Spahis, my friend; and what is more, my preserver. Salute my hero, viscount." And he stepped on one side, exhibiting a fine and noble young man with large and open brow, piercing eyes, and black moustache. A rich uniform, half French, half Oriental, set off his broad chest, which was decorated with the order of the Legion of Honour, and his graceful and stalwart figure. The young officer bowed with easy politeness. "Monsieur," said Albert, with affectionate courtesy, "M. le Comte de Château-Renaud knew how much pleasure this introduction would give me; you are his friend, be ours also."

"Well said!" interrupted Château-Renaud; "and pray that, if you should ever be in a similar predicament, he may do as much for you as he did for me."

"What has he done?" asked Albert.

"Oh! nothing worth speaking of."

"Not worth speaking of?" cried Château-Renaud; "life is not worth speaking of!"

"M. le Capitaine Morrel saved your life?"

"Exactly so."

"On what occasion?" asked Beauchamp.

"You all know that I had a fancy for going to Africa. In consequence, I embarked for Oran, and went thence to Constantine, where I arrived in time to witness the raising of the siege. I retreated with the rest during eight-and-forty hours. I supported the rain during the day and the cold during the night tolerably well, but the third morning my horse died of cold. Poor brute! accustomed to be covered up and to have a stove in the stable, an Arabian finds himself unable to bear ten degrees of cold in Algeria. I was retreating on foot. Six Arabs came up at full gallop to cut off my head. I shot two with my double-barrelled gun, and two more with my pistols, but I was then disarmed, and two were still left, one seized me by the hair (that is why I now wear it so short, for no one knows what may happen).

the other encircled my neck with the yataghan, when this gentle-man, whom you see here, charged them, shot the one who held me by the hair, with a pistol, and cleft the skull of the other with his sabre. He had assigned himself the task of saving the life of a man that day, and chance caused that man to be myself ; when I am rich I will order a statue of Chance from Klugmann or Maro-chetti."

" Yes," said Morrel, smiling, " it was the 5th of September, the anniversary of the day on which my father was miraculously preserved ; therefore I endeavour to celebrate it by some——"

" Heroic action," interrupted Château-Renaud. " I was chosen. But this is not all : after rescuing one from the sword, he rescued me next from the cold, not by sharing his cloak with me, like St. Martin, but by giving me it all ; and finally from hunger, by sharing with me—guess what ? "

" A Strasbourg pie ? " asked Beauchamp.

" No, his horse : of which each of us ate a slice with a hearty appetite ; it was very hard."

" The horse ? " said Morcerf, laughing.

" No, the sacrifice," returned Château-Renaud : " ask Debray if he would sacrifice his English steed for a stranger ? "

" Not for a stranger," said Debray, " but for a friend, perhaps."

" I divined that you would become mine, M. le Comte," replied Morrel ; " besides, as I had the honour to tell you, heroism or not, sacrifice or not, that day I owed an offering in recompense for the favours good fortune had on other days granted to us."

" The history to which M. Morrel alludes," continued Château-Renaud, " is an admirable one, which he will tell you some day when you are better acquainted with him ; to-day let us fill our stomachs, and not our memories. What time do you breakfast, Albert ? "

" At half-past ten ; but you will give me five minutes' grace," replied Morcerf, " for I also expect a preserver. *Parbleu !* do you think I cannot be saved as well as anyone else, and that there are only Arabs who cut off heads ? Our breakfast is a philan-thropic one ; and we shall have at table—at least, I hope so—two benefactors of humanity."

" And where does he come from ? " asked Debray.

" Really," said Albert, " I do not know ; when I invited him three months ago, he was then at Rome, but since that time, who knows where he may have gone ? "

"And you think him capable of being exact?" demanded Debray.

" I think him capable of everything."

" Well, with the five minutes' grace, we have only ten left."

" I will profit by them to tell you something about my guest.
When I was at Rome the last Carnival, I was carried off by
brigands, who conducted me to a most gloomy spot, called the
Catacombs of Saint Sebastian. I was informed I was a prisoner
until I paid the sum of 4,000 Roman crowns. Unfortunately,
I was at the end of my journey and of my credit. I wrote to
Franz that if he did not come with the money before six in the
morning, at a few minutes past I should have joined the blessed
saints and glorious martyrs, in whose company I had the honour
of being ; and Luigi Vampa—such was the name of the chief of
these bandits—would have scrupulously kept his word. Franz
came along with the guest I am going to present to you, a man
about my own size, without even a knitting-needle. He said
two words to the chief, and I was free."

" And they apologized to him for having carried you off ? "
said Beauchamp.

" Just so : his name is the count of Monte Cristo."

" There is not a count of Monte Cristo," said Debray.

" I think I can assist you," said Maximilian. " Monte Cristo
is a little island I have often heard spoken of by the old sailors my
father employed."

" Precisely ! " cried Albert. " Well, he of whom I speak is the
lord and master of this islet; he has purchased the title of count
somewhere in Tuscany."

" He is rich, then ? "

" Have you read the *Arabian Nights* ? "

" What a question ! "

" Well, do you know whether the persons you see there are
rich or poor, whether their sacks of wheat are rubies or diamonds ?
They seem like poor fishermen, and suddenly they open some
mysterious cavern filled with the wealth of the Indies. My count
of Monte Cristo is one of those fishermen. He has even a name
taken from the book, since he calls himself Sindbad the Sailor, and
has a cave filled with gold."

" I, also," said Morrel, thoughtfully, " have heard something
like this from an old sailor named Penelon."

" Ah ! " cried Albert, " it is very lucky that M. Morrel comes
to aid me ; you are vexed—are you not ?—that he thus gives a
clue to the labyrinth ? "

" My dear Albert," said Debray, " what you tell us is extraordinary ; but does not prevent the count of Monte Cristo from
existing."

" *Pardieu !* everyone exists."

" He eats, then ? "

" Yes, but so little, it can hardly be called eating."

" He must be a vampire."

" Laugh, if you will : the Countess G——, who had known Lord Ruthven, declared the count *was* a vampire."

" Wild eyes, the iris of which contracts or dilates at pleasure," said Debray ; " facial angle strongly developed, magnificent forehead, livid complexion, black beard, sharp and white teeth, politeness unexceptionable."

" Just so, Lucien," returned Morcerf ; " you have described him feature for feature. Yes, keen and cutting politeness. This man has often made me shudder ; and one day when we were viewing an execution, I thought I should faint, more from hearing the cold and calm manner in which he spoke of every description of torture than from the sight of the executioner and the culprit. When I look at you Parisians, idlers on the Boulevard de Gand or the Bois de Boulogne, and think of this man, it seems to me we are not of the same race."

" At the same time," added Château-Renaud, " your count of Monte Cristo is a very fine fellow, always excepting his little arrangements with the Italian banditti."

" There are no Italian banditti ! " said Debray.

" No vampire ! " cried Beauchamp.

" No count of Monte Cristo ! " added Debray. " There is half-past ten striking, Albert ! Confess you have dreamed this, and let us sit down to breakfast."

But the sound of the clock had not died away when Germain announced, " His Excellency the Count of Monte Cristo."

The involuntary start everyone gave proved how much Morcerf's narrative had impressed them, and Albert himself could not avoid a sudden emotion. He had not heard a carriage stop in the street, or steps in the antechamber ; the door had itself opened noiselessly. The count appeared, dressed with the greatest simplicity, but the most fastidious dandy could have found nothing to cavil at in his toilette, every article of dress, hat, coat, gloves, and boots, being from the best makers. He seemed scarcely five-and-thirty ; but what struck everybody was his extreme resemblance to the portrait Debray had drawn. The count advanced smiling into the centre of the room and approached Albert, who hastened towards him holding out his hand.

" Punctuality," said Monte Cristo, " is the politeness of kings—according to one of your sovereigns, I think ; but it is not the same with travellers. However, I hope you will excuse the two or three seconds I am behindhand ; five hundred leagues are not to be accomplished without some trouble, and especially in France, where, it seems, one must not beat the postillions."

" M. le Comte," replied Albert, " I was announcing your visit to some of my friends, whom I now present to you. They are M. le Comte de Château-Renaud, whose nobility goes back to the twelve peers, and whose ancestors had a place at the Round Table ; M. Lucien Debray, private secretary to the Ministre de l'Intérieur ; M. Beauchamp, editor of a paper which is the terror of the Government, and M. Maximilian Morrel, captain of Spahis."

At this name the count, who had hitherto saluted everyone with courtesy, but at the same time with coldness and formality, stepped forward, and a tinge of red coloured his pale cheeks.

" You wear the uniform of the new French conquerors, monsieur," said he. " It is a handsome uniform."

No one could have said what caused the count's voice to vibrate so deeply, and what made his eye flash.

" You have never seen our Africans, M. le Comte ? " said Albert.

" Never," replied the count, who was by this time perfectly master of himself again.

" Well, beneath this uniform beats one of the bravest and noblest hearts in the whole army. We have just heard, of a fresh action of monsieur, and so heroic a one, that, although I have seen him to-day for the first time, I request you to allow me to introduce him as my friend."

At these words it was still possible to remark in Monte Cristo that fixed gaze, that passing colour, and that slight trembling of the eyelid, which showed his emotion.

" Ah ! you have a noble heart ! " said the count ; " so much the better."

This exclamation, which corresponded to the count's own thought rather than to what Albert was saying, surprised everybody, and especially Morrel, who looked at Monte Cristo with surprise.

" Why should he doubt it ? " said Beauchamp to Château-Renaud.

" In reality," replied the latter, who had penetrated all that was penetrable in Monte Cristo, " Albert has not deceived us, for the count is a most singular being. What say you, Morrel ? "

" Ma foi ! he has an open look that pleases me, in spite of the strange remark he made about me."

"Gentlemen," said Albert, " Germain informs me that breakfast is ready." They passed silently into the breakfast-room ; everyone took his place. " Gentlemen," said the count, seating himself, " permit me to make a confession which must form my excuse for any *inconvenance* I may commit. I am a stranger, and this is the first time I have ever been in Paris. The French way of living is unknown to me, and up to the present I have followed the Eastern customs, which are entirely in contrast to the Parisian. I beg you, therefore, to excuse if you find anything in me too Turkish, too Italian, or too Arabian. Now, then, let us breakfast."

"My dear count," said he, " I fear one thing, and that is, that the fare of the Rue du Helder is not so much to your taste as that of the Piazza di Spagna. I ought to have consulted you on the point, and have had some dishes prepared expressly."

" Did you know me better," returned the count, smiling, " you would not think of such a thing for one who has successively lived on macaroni at Naples, polenta at Milan, olla podrida at Valencia, pilau at Constantinople, curry in India, and swallows' nests in China. I eat everywhere, and of everything, only I eat but little ; and to-day, when you reproach me with my want of appetite, is my day of appetite, for I have not eaten since yesterday morning. I was forced to go out of my road to obtain some information near Nîmes, so that I was somewhat late, and, therefore, I did not choose to stop."

" And you ate in your carriage ? " asked Morcerf.

" No ; I slept, as I generally do when I am weary without having the courage to amuse myself, or when I am hungry without feeling inclined to eat."

" But you can sleep when you please, monsieur ? " said Morrel.

" Yes."

" You have a receipt for it ? "

" An infallible one. I make no secret of it ; it is a mixture of opium, which I fetched from Canton in order to have it pure, and the best hasheesh which grows in the East, that is, between the Tigris and Euphrates. These two ingredients are mixed in equal proportions, and formed into pills. Ten minutes after one is taken, the effect is produced. Ask M. le Baron Franz d'Épinay ; I think he tasted them one day."

" Yes," replied Morcerf ; " he said something about it to me."

" But," said Beauchamp, who, in his capacity of journalist, was very incredulous, " you always carry this drug about you ? "

" Always."

" Would it be an indiscretion to ask to see those precious pills ? " continued Beauchamp, hoping to take him at a disadvantage.

" No, monsieur," returned the count ; and he drew from his pocket a marvellous *bonbonnière*, formed out of a single emerald, and closed by a golden lid, which unscrewed and displayed a small ball of greenish colour, and about the size of a pea. This ball had an acrid and penetrating odour. There were four or five more in the emerald, which would contain about a dozen. The *bonbonnière* passed round the table ; but it was more to examine the beautiful emerald than to see the pills that it passed from hand to hand. " And is it your cook who prepares these pills ? " asked Beauchamp.

" Oh, no, monsieur," replied Monte Cristo ; " I do not thus betray my enjoyments to the vulgar ; I am a tolerable chemist, and prepare my pills myself."

" This is a magnificent emerald, and the largest I have ever seen," said Château-Renaud.

" I had three," returned Monte Cristo ; " I gave one to the Grand Seigneur, who mounted it in his sabre ; another to our holy father the Pope, who had it set in his tiara, opposite one given by the Emperor Napoleon to his precedessor, Pius VII. I kept the third for myself, and I had it hollowed out, which reduced its value, but rendered it more commodious for the purpose I intended it for." Every one looked at Monte Cristo with astonishment ; he spoke with so much simplicity that it was evident he spoke the truth, or was mad.

" And what did the sovereigns give you in exchange for these magnificent presents ? " asked Debray.

" The Grand Seigneur the liberty of a woman," replied the Count ; " the Pope the life of a man ; so that once in my time I have been as powerful as if Heaven had made me come into the world on the steps of a throne."

" And it was Peppino you saved, was it not ? " cried Morcerf.

" Perhaps," returned the count, smiling.

" Monsieur le Comte, you have no idea what pleasure it gives me to hear you speak thus," said Morcerf. " I had announced you beforehand to my friends as an enchanter of the *Arabian Nights*, a wizard of the Middle Ages ; but these excellent Parisians are people so subtle in paradox, that they mistake for caprice of the imagination the most incontestable truths, when these truths do not form a part of their daily existence. Tell them yourself that I was taken by bandits, and that without your generous intercession I should now have been sleeping in the Catacombs of St. Sebastian, instead of receiving them in my humble abode in the Rue du Helder."

"It seems to me," returned the count, smiling, "that you played a sufficiently important part to know as well as myself what happened."

"Well, you promise me if I tell all I know, to relate in your turn all that I do not know."

"That is but fair," replied Monte Cristo.

"Well," said Morcerf, "for three days I believed myself the object of the attention of a mask, whom I took for a descendant of Tullia or Poppæa, whilst I was simply the object of the attentions of a *contadine*, and I say *contadine* to avoid saying peasant. What I know is, that like a fool, I mistook for this peasant a young bandit of fifteen or sixteen, with a beardless chin and slim waist, and who, as I was about to imprint a chaste salute on his lips, placed a pistol to my head, and, aided by seven or eight others, dragged me to the Catacombs of St. Sebastian, where I found a highly educated chief of brigands perusing Cæsar's *Commentaries*. He deigned to leave off reading to inform me, that unless the next morning, before six o'clock, four thousand piastres were paid in to his account at his bankers, at a quarter-past six I should have ceased to exist. The letter is still to be seen, for it is in Franz d'Epinay's possession, signed by me, and with a postscript by Luigi Vampa. This is all I know, but I know not, M. le Comte, how you contrived to inspire with such respect the bandits of Rome, who have so little respect for anything; I assure you, Franz and I were lost in admiration."

"Nothing more simple," returned the count. "I had known the famous Vampa for more than ten years. When he was a child and only a shepherd, I gave him, for having shown me the way to a place, some pieces of gold; he, in order to repay me, gave me a poniard, the hilt of which he had carved with his own hand. In after years, whether he had forgotten this interchange of presents, which ought to have cemented our friendship, or whether he did not recollect me, he sought to take me, but, on the contrary, it was I who captured him, and a dozen of his band. I might have handed him over to Roman justice, which is somewhat expeditious, and which would have been still more so with him; but I suffered him and his band to depart upon the simple condition that they should respect myself and my friends. Perhaps what I am about to say may seem strange to you, who are Socialists, and vaunt humanity and your duty to your neighbour: but I never seek to protect people who do not protect me, and who I will even say, in general, occupy themselves about me only to injure me; and thus giving them a low place in my esteem, and preserving a neutrality towards them, it is society and my neighbour who are indebted to me."

"Bravo!" said Château-Renaud; "you are the first man I ever met sufficiently courageous to preach egotism. Bravo! M. le Comte, bravo!"

"It is frank, at least," said Morrel. "But I am sure that M. le Comte does not regret having once deviated from the principles he has so boldly avowed."

"How have I deviated from these principles, monsieur?"

"Why, it seems to me," replied Morrel, "that in delivering M. de Morcerf, whom you did not know, you did good to your neighbour and to society."

"Monsieur le Comte," cried Morcerf, "you are at fault: you, one of the most formidable logicians I know, and you must see it clearly proved that, instead of being an egotist, you are a philanthropist. Ah! you call yourself Oriental, Levantine, Maltese, Indian, Chinese; your family name is Monte Cristo; Sindbad the Sailor is your appellation, and yet the first day you set foot in Paris, you instinctively possess the greatest virtue, or rather the chief defect, of us eccentric Parisians—that is, you assume the vices you have not, and conceal the virtues you possess."

"My dear vicomte," returned Monte Cristo, "I do not see in all I have done anything that merits the eulogies I have received. You are no stranger to me, for I knew you, since I had given up two rooms to you, had invited you to breakfast with me, had lent you one of my carriages, had witnessed the Carnival with you, and had also seen from a window of the Piazza del Popolo the execution that affected you so much that you nearly fainted. I will appeal to any of these gentlemen, could I leave my guest in the hands of a bandit, as you term him? Besides, you know, I had the idea that you could introduce me into some of the Paris salons when I came to France. You might, some time ago, have looked upon this resolution as a vague project, but to-day you see it was a reality, and you must submit to it under penalty of breaking your word."

"I will keep it," returned Morcerf; "but I fear that you will be much disappointed, accustomed as you are to picturesque events and to fantastic horizons. Amongst us you will not meet with any of those episodes with which your adventurous existence has so familiarized you; France is so prosaic, and Paris so

civilized a city, that you will not find in the eighty-five departments
a single hill on which there is not a telegraph, or a grotto in which
the commissary of police has not put up a gas-lamp. There is
but one service I can render you, and for that I place myself
entirely at your orders; that is to present, or make my friends
present, you everywhere. If knowledge of Parisian habits, of
the means of rendering yourself comfortable, or of the bazaars,
can assist, you may dispose of me to find you a fitting dwelling
here. I dare offer to share my apartments with you, as I shared
yours at Rome—I, who do not possess egotism, but am yet egotistical *par excellence;* for, except myself, these rooms would not
contain a shadow, unless it were the shadow of a female."

"Ah," said the count, "that is a most conjugal reservation;
I recollect that at Rome you said something of a projected
marriage. May I congratulate you?"

"The affair is still *in posse.* My father is most anxious about
it; and I hope, ere long, to introduce you, if not to my wife, at
least to my intended—Mademoiselle Eugénie Danglars."

"Eugénie Danglars!" said Monte Cristo; "tell me, is not her
father M. le Baron Danglars?"

"Yes," returned Morcerf; "a baron of a new creation. Do
you know him?"

"I do not know him," returned Monte Cristo; "but I shall
probably soon make his acquaintance, for I have a credit opened
with him by the house of Richard and Blount, of London, Arstein
and Eskeles, of Vienna, and Thomson and French, of Rome."

As he pronounced the two last names, the count glanced
at Maximilian Morrel. If the stranger expected to produce an
effect on Morrel, he was not mistaken—Maximilian started as if
he had been electrified.

"Thomson and French!" said he; "do you know this house,
monsieur?"

"They are my bankers in the capital of the Christian world,"
returned the count, quietly. "Can my influence with them be
of any service to you?"

"Oh, M. le Comte, you could assist me perhaps in researches
which have been, up to the present, fruitless. This house, in past
years, did ours a great service, and has, I know not for what
reason, always denied having rendered us this help."

"I shall be at your orders," said Monte Cristo, inclining himself.

"But," continued Morcerf, "*à propos* of Danglars,—we have
strangely wandered from the subject. We were speaking of a
suitable habitation for the count of Monte Cristo. Come, gentle-

men, let us all propose some place : where shall we lodge this new guest in our great capital ? "

"Faubourg Saint Germain," said Château-Renaud. "The count will find there a charming hotel, with a court and garden."

"Bah ! Château-Renaud," returned Debray, "you only know your dull and gloomy Faubourg Saint Germain ; do not pay any attention to him, M. le Comte—live in the Chaussée d'Antin, that's the real centre of Paris."

"Boulevard de l'Opéra," said Beauchamp ; "on the first floor —a house with a balcony. M. le Comte will have his cushions of silver cloth brought there and, as he smokes his chibouque, see all Paris pass before him."

"You have no idea, then, Morrel ? " asked Château-Renaud ; "you do not propose anything ? "

"Oh, yes," returned the young man, smiling ; "on the contrary, I have one ; but I expected the count would be tempted by one of the brilliant proposals made him, yet as he has not replied to any of them, I will venture to offer him a suite of apartments in a charming hotel, in the Pompadour style, that my sister has inhabited for a year, in the Rue Meslay."

"You have a sister ? " asked the count.

"Yes, monsieur, a most excellent sister."

"Married ? "

"Nearly nine years."

"Happy ? " asked the count again.

"As happy as it is permitted to a human creature to be," replied Maximilian. "She married the man she loved, who remained faithful to us in our fallen fortunes—Emanuel Herbaut."

Monte Cristo smiled imperceptibly.

"I live there during my leave of absence," continued Maximilian ; "and I shall be, together with my brother-in-law Emanuel, at the service of M. le Comte, whenever he thinks fit to honour us."

"Thanks, monsieur," said Monte Cristo, "I shall content myself with being presented to your sister and her husband, if you will do me the honour to introduce me ; but I cannot accept the offer of any of these gentlemen, since my habitation is already prepared. As I determined to have a house to myself, I sent on my valet, and he ought by this time to have bought the house and furnished it."

"You have a valet who knows Paris ? " said Beauchamp.

"It is the first time he has ever been in Paris. He is black, and cannot speak," returned Monte Cristo.

" It is Ali ! " cried Albert, in the midst of the general surprise.

" Yes, Ali himself, my Nubian mute, whom you saw at Rome."

" I recollect him perfectly. But how could you charge a Nubian to purchase a house, and a mute to furnish it ? He will do everything wrong."

" Undeceive yourself, monsieur," replied Monte Cristo ; " I am sure he will choose everything I wish. He knows my tastes, my caprices, my wants ; he has been here a week, with the instinct of a hound, hunting by himself ; he will organize everything for me. He knew I should arrive to-day at ten o'clock ; he awaited me at the Barrière de Fontainebleau. He gave me this paper ; it contains the number of my new abode ; read it yourself," and Monte Cristo passed a paper to Albert.

" What ! do you not know your house ? " asked Debray.

" No," said Monte Cristo ; " I told you I did not wish to be late ; I dressed myself in the carriage, and descended at the vicomte's door."

" We must content ourselves, then," said Beauchamp, " with rendering M. le Comte all the little services in our power. I, in my quality of journalist, open all the theatres to him."

" Thanks, monsieur," returned Monte Cristo ; " my steward has orders to take a box at each theatre. You know him, M. de Morcerf."

" It is M. Bertuccio, who understands hiring windows so well ? "

" Yes, you saw him the day I had the honour of receiving you ; he has been a soldier, a smuggler—in fact, everything. I am not sure that he has not been mixed up with the police for some trifle—a stab with a knife, or something of the sort. He answers my purpose, knows no impossibility, and so I keep him."

" Then," continued Château-Renaud, " since you have an establishment, a steward, and a hôtel in the Champs Élysées, you only want a mistress."

Albert thought of the fair Greek he had seen in the count's box at the Argentino.

" I have something better than that," said Monte Cristo ; " I have a slave. You procure your mistresses from the Opera, the Vaudeville, or the Variétés. I purchased mine at Constantinople : it cost me more, but I have nothing to fear."

" But you forget," replied Debray, laughing, " that we are Franks by name and franks by nature, as King Charles said ; and that the moment she puts her foot in France your slave becomes free."

" Everyone who surrounds me is free to quit me, and when they leave me will no longer have any need of me or anyone else ; it is for that reason, perhaps, that they do not quit me." They had long since passed to dessert and cigars.

Albert rose as his friends proposed to depart.

" My dear Albert," said Debray, " it is half-past two. Your guest is charming ; but you leave the best company to go into the worst sometimes. I must return to the minister's. I will tell him of the count, and we shall soon know who he is."

" Bravo ! " said Beauchamp to Albert ; " I will not go to the Chamber ; I have something better to offer my readers than a speech of M. Danglars."

" Beauchamp," returned Morcerf, " you must not deprive me of the merit of introducing him everywhere. Is he not peculiar ? "

" He is more than that," replied Château-Renaud ; " he is one of the most extraordinary men I ever saw in my life. Are you coming, Morrel ? "

" Directly I have given my card to M. le Comte, who has promised to pay us a visit at Rue Meslay, No. 14."

" Be sure I will not fail to do so," said the count, bowing. And Maximilian Morrel retired with the Baron de Château-Renaud, leaving Monte Cristo alone with Morcerf.

CHAPTER XLI

THE PRESENTATION

WHEN Albert found himself alone with Monte Cristo, " M. le Comte," said he, " allow me to show you a specimen of a bachelor's apartment. You, who are accustomed to the palaces of Italy, can amuse yourself by calculating in how many square feet a young man who is not the worst lodged in Paris can live. As we pass from one room to another I will open the windows to let you breathe." Monte Cristo had already seen the breakfast-room and the salon on the ground-floor. Albert led him first to his *atelier*, which was, as we have said, his favourite apartment. Monte Cristo was a connoisseur of all that Albert had collected—old cabinets, Japan porcelain, Oriental stuffs, Venice glass, arms from all parts of the world,—everything was familiar to him ; and at the first glance he recognized their date, their country, and their origin. Morcerf had expected he should be the guide ; on the contrary it was he who, under the count's guidance, followed a course of archæology, mineralogy, and natural history. They descended to the first floor ; Albert led his guest into the salon where he expected to have something new to show to the traveller, but, to his great surprise, the latter named instantly the author of every picture in such a manner that it was easy to see that each of their styles had been appreciated and studied by him. From the salon they passed into the bed-chamber : it was a model of taste and simple elegance. A single portrait shone in its carved and gilded frame. This portrait attracted the count of Monte Cristo's attention, for he made three rapid steps in the chamber, and stopped suddenly before it. It was the portrait of a young woman of five or six and twenty, with a dark complexion, and light and lustrous eyes veiled beneath their long lashes. She wore the picturesque costume of the Catalan fisherwomen, a red and black bodice, and golden pins in her hair. The light was so faint in the room that Albert did not perceive the paleness that spread over the count's visage, or the nervous heaving of his chest and shoulders. Silence prevailed, during which Monte Cristo gazed intently on the picture.

" You have there a most charming mistress, viscount," said the count in a perfectly calm tone : " and this costume—a ball costume, doubtless,—becomes her admirably."

" Ah, monsieur ! " returned Albert, " I would never forgive you this mistake if you had seen another picture besides this. You do not know my mother ; she had her portrait painted thus six or eight years ago. This costume is a fancy one, and the resemblance is so great that I think I still see my mother as she was in 1830. The countess had this portrait painted during the count's absence. She intended giving him an agreeable surprise ; but, strange to say, the portrait seemed to displease my father, and the value of the picture, one of the best works of Leopold Robert, could not overcome his dislike to it. So my mother, who paints exceedingly well, and was unwilling to part with so valuable a picture, gave it to me to hang here, where it would be less likely to displease M. de Morcerf, whose portrait, by Gros, I will also show you. Excuse my talking of family matters : but as I shall have the honour of introducing you to the count, I tell you this to prevent you from making any allusions to this picture. My mother rarely comes here without looking at it, and still more rarely does she look at it without weeping. This disagreement is the only one that has ever taken place between the count and the countess, who are still as much united, although married more than twenty years, as on the first day of their wedding."

Monte Cristo glanced rapidly at Albert, as if to seek a hidden meaning in his words ; but it was evident the young man uttered them in the simplicity of his heart. "Now," said Albert, "that you have seen all my treasures, allow me to offer them to you unworthy as they are. Consider yourself as in your own house : and to put yourself still more at your ease, pray accompany me to the apartments of M. de Morcerf, to whom I wrote from Rome an account of the services you rendered me. I may say that both the count and countess anxiously desire to thank you in person. You are somewhat *blasé*, I know, and family scenes have not much effect on Sindbad the Sailor, who has seen so many others. However, accept what I propose to you as an initiation into Parisian life—a life of politeness, visiting, and introductions."

Monte Cristo bowed without making any answer ; he accepted the offer without enthusiasm and without regret, as one of those conventions of society which every gentleman looks upon as a duty. Albert summoned his servant, and ordered him to acquaint M. and Madame de Morcerf with the arrival of the count of Monte Cristo. Albert followed him with the count. When they arrived at the antechamber, above the door was visible a shield, which, by its rich ornaments and its harmony with the rest of the furniture indicated the importance the owner attached to this blazon. Monte Cristo examined it attentively.

"Azure, seven merlets, or, placed bender," said he. "These are, doubtless, your family arms ? Except the knowledge of blazons, that enables me to decipher them, I am very ignorant of heraldry. Excuse my putting such a question to you."

"You have guessed rightly. These are our arms ; that is, those of my father ; but they are, as you see, joined to another shield, which has gules, a silver tower, which are my mother's. On her side I am Spanish, but the family of Morcerf is French, and I have heard, one of the oldest of the south of France."

"Yes," replied Monte Cristo, "these blazons prove that almost all the armed pilgrims that went to the Holy Land took for their arms either a cross, in honour of their mission, or birds of passage, in sign of the long voyage they were about to undertake. One of your ancestors had joined the Crusades ; and supposing it to be only that of St. Louis, that takes you back to the thirteenth century, which is tolerably ancient."

Morcerf thanked him with a smile, and pushed open the door above which were his arms, and which opened into the salon. In the most conspicuous part of the salon was another portrait. It was that of a man, from five to eight-and-thirty, in the uniform of a general officer, wearing the double epaulet *en torsade*, that indicates superior rank ; the riband of the Legion of Honour round his neck, which showed he was a commander; and on the breast, on the right, the star of a grand officer of the order of the Saviour, and on the left that of the grand cross of Charles III, which proved that he had served in the wars of Greece and Spain, or had fulfilled some diplomatic mission in the two countries.

Monte Cristo was engaged in examining this portrait with no less care than he had bestowed upon the other when another door opened, and he found himself opposite to the Count de Morcerf himself. He was a man of forty to forty-five years, but he seemed at least fifty, and his black moustache and eyebrows contrasted strangely with his almost white hair, which was cut short in the military fashion. He was dressed in plain clothes, and wore at his button-hole the ribands of the different orders of which he was a member. He entered with a tolerably dignified step, and with a species of haste. Monte Cristo saw him advance without making a single step on his part. It seemed as if his feet were rooted to the ground, and his eyes on the Count de Morcerf. "Father," said the young man, "I have the honour of presenting to you M. le comte de Monte Cristo, the generous friend whom I had the good fortune to meet in the critical juncture of which I have told you."

"You are most welcome, monsieur," said the Count de Morcerf, saluting Monte Cristo with a smile; "and monsieur has rendered our house, in preserving its only heir, a service which ensures him our eternal gratitude."

Monte Cristo, whilst he took the seat Morcerf offered him, placed himself in such a manner as to remain concealed in the shadow of the large velvet curtains, and read on the careworn and livid features of the count a whole history of secret griefs. "Madame la Vicomtesse," said Morcerf, "will be in the salon in ten minutes."

"It is a great honour for me," returned Monte Cristo, "to meet, on the first day of my arrival in Paris, a man whose merit equals his reputation, and to whom fortune has for once been equitable; but has she not still on the plains of Mitidja, or in the mountains of Atlas, a marshal's staff to offer you?"

"Oh," replied Morcerf, reddening slightly, "I have left the service, monsieur. Made a peer at the Restoration, I served through the first campaign under Marshal Bourmont. I could, therefore, expect a higher rank, and who knows what might have happened had the elder branch remained on the throne? But the revolution of July was, it seems, sufficiently glorious to allow itself to be

L

ungrateful. I tendered my resignation; for when you have gained your epaulets on the battlefield, you do not know how to manœuvre on the slippery ground of the salons. I have hung up my sword, and cast myself into politics. I have devoted myself to industry; I study the useful arts. During the twenty years I served, I often wished to do so, but I had not the time."

"These are the ideas that render your nation superior to any other," returned Monte Cristo. "A gentleman of high birth, possessor of an ample fortune, you have consented to gain your promotion as an obscure soldier, step by step; this is uncommon; then, become general, peer of France, commander of the Legion of Honour, you consent to begin again a second apprenticeship, without any other hope or desire than that of one day becoming useful to your fellow-creatures; this, indeed, is praiseworthy,—nay, more, it is sublime. Alas! we do not act thus in Italy; we grow according to our race and our species, and we pursue the same lines, and often the same uselessness, all our lives."

"But, monsieur," said the Count de Morcerf, "for a man of your merit, Italy is not a country, and France opens her arms to receive you; respond to her call. France will not, perhaps, be always ungrateful! She treats her children ill, but she always welcomes strangers."

"Ah, father!" said Albert, with a smile, "it is evident you do not know M. le comte de Monte Cristo; he despises all honours and contents himself with those that are written on his passport."

"That is the most just remark," replied the stranger, "I have ever heard concerning myself!"

"You have been free to choose your career," observed the Count de Morcerf, with a sigh; "and have chosen the path strewed with flowers."

"Precisely, monsieur," replied Monte Cristo.

"If I did not fear to fatigue you," said the general, charmed with the count's manners, "I would have taken you to the Chamber."

"I shall be most grateful, monsieur, if you will, at some future time, renew your offer; but I have been flattered with the hope of being introduced to the countess and I will therefore wait."

"Ah! here is my mother," cried the viscount. Monte Cristo turned round hastily, and saw Madame de Morcerf, pale and motionless, at the entrance of the salon, at the door opposite to that by which her husband had entered; when Monte Cristo turned round, she let fall her arm, which for some unknown reason had been resting on the gilded doorpost. She had been there some moments, and had overheard the last words of the visitor. The latter rose and bowed to the countess, who inclined herself without speaking.

"Are you ill, mother?" cried the viscount, springing towards her.

"No," she said, "but I feel some emotion on seeing, for the first time, the man without whose intervention we should have been in tears and desolation. Monsieur," continued the comtesse, advancing with the majesty of a queen; "I owe to you the life of my son, and for this I bless you."

The count bowed again, but lower than before; he was even paler than Mercédès. "Madame," said he, "M. le Comte and yourself recompense too generously a simple action. To save a man, to spare a father's feelings, or a mother's sensibility, is not to do a good action, but a simple deed of humanity."

"It is very fortunate for my son, monsieur, that he found such a friend." And Mercédès raised her fine eyes to heaven with so fervent an expression of gratitude, that the count fancied he saw tears in them.

M. de Morcerf approached her. "Madame," said he, "I have already made my excuses to M. le Comte for quitting him, and I pray you to do also. The sitting began at two; it is now three, and I am to speak."

"Go, then, and monsieur and I will strive our best to forget your absence!" replied the countess. "M. le Comte," continued she, turning to Monte Cristo, "will you do us the honour of passing the rest of the day with us?"

"Believe me, madame, I feel most grateful for your kindness, but I got out of my travelling carriage at your door this morning, and I am ignorant how I am installed in Paris; this is but a trifling inquietude, I know, but one that may be appreciated."

"We shall have this pleasure another time!" said the countess; "you promise that?" Monte Cristo inclined himself without answering. "I will not detain you, monsieur: I would not have our gratitude become indiscreet or importunate."

"My dear count," said Albert, "I will endeavour to return your politeness at Rome, and place my coupé at your disposal until your own be ready."

"A thousand thanks for your kindness, viscount, but I suppose that M. Bertuccio has employed the four hours and a half I have given him, and that I shall find a carriage at the door."

Albert was used to the count's manner of proceeding; but wishing to see how far the count's orders had been executed, he accompanied him to the door of the hôtel. Monte Cristo was not deceived. As soon as he appeared in the Count de Morcerf's antechamber, a footman sprang into the vestibule, and when he arrived at the door the traveller found his carriage awaiting him. It was a coupé of Koller's building, with horses and harness, for which Drake had refused on the previous day seven hundred guineas.

"Monsieur," said the count to Albert, " I do not ask you to accompany me to my house, as I can only show you a habitation fitted up in a hurry, and I have, as you know, a reputation to keep up as regards not being taken by surprise. Give me, therefore, one more day before I invite you; I shall then be certain not to fail in my hospitality."

"If you ask me for a day, count, I know what to anticipate; it will not be a house I shall see, but a palace."

"*Ma foi!* spread that idea," replied the count of Monte Cristo, putting his foot on the velvet-lined step of the splendid carriage, "and that will be worth something to me among the ladies."

As he spoke, he sprang into the vehicle, the door was closed but not so rapidly that Monte Cristo detected the almost imperceptible movement which stirred the curtains of the apartment in which he had left Madame de Morcerf. When Albert returned to his mother, he found her in the boudoir reclining in a large armchair. Albert could not see her face, which was lost in a thin veil which descended around her features like a cloud of vapour; but it seemed as though her voice had altered. He could distinguish amidst the perfumes of the roses and heliotropes the sharp odour of volatile salts, and he remarked, in one of the chased cups on the mantelpiece, the countess's smelling-bottle, taken from its shagreen case, and exclaimed in a tone of uneasiness, as he entered—

"My dear mother, have you been unwell during my absence?"

"No, no, Albert! but you know these roses, tuberoses, and orange-flowers throw off at first, before one is used to them, such violent perfumes."

"Then, my dear mother," said Albert, putting his hand to the bell, "they must be taken into the antechamber. You are really unwell, and just now were so pale when you came into the room—"

A servant entered, summoned by Albert's ring of the bell.

"Take these flowers into the anteroom or dressing-room," said the viscount; "they make the countess unwell."

"What is this name of Monte Cristo?" inquired the countess, when the servant had taken away the last vase of flowers; "is it a family name, or the name of the estate, or a simple title?"

" I believe, mother, it is merely a simple title. The count purchased an island in the Tuscan Archipelago, and founded a commandery. Except this, he has no pretension to nobility, although the general opinion at Rome is that he is a man of very high distinction."

" His manners are admirable ! " said the countess.

" They are perfect, mother, so perfect, that they surpass by far all I have known in the leading aristocracy of the proudest *noblesse* of Europe."

" You have seen, my dear Albert—I ask the question as a mother—you have seen M. de Monte Cristo in his house ; you have much knowledge of the world, more tact than is usual at your age ; do you think the count is really what he appears to be ? I do not refer to his origin, but what he is."

" Ah ! what he is ; that is quite another thing. I have seen so many remarkable things of him, that if you would have me say what I think, I shall reply that I look upon him as one of Byron's heroes, whom Misery has marked with a fatal brand—some Manfred, Lara, Werner, or some wreck of ancient family who, disinherited of his patrimony, has achieved one by the force of his adventurous genius."

" And what do you suppose is the count's age ? " inquired Mercédès, evidently attaching great importance to this question.

" Thirty-five or thirty-six, mother."

" So young ! it is impossible," said Mercédès, replying to what Albert said as well as to her own private reflection.

" It is the truth, however. Three or four times he has said to me, without the slightest premeditation, at such a period I was five years old, at another ten years old, at another twelve, and I, induced by curiosity, which kept me alive to these details, have compared the dates, and never found him inaccurate. Besides mother, remark how vivid his eye, how raven black his hair, and his brow, though so pale is free from wrinkles—he is not only vigorous but young."

" And has this man displayed a friendship for you, Albert ? " she asked with a nervous shudder.

" I am inclined to think so."

" And—do—you—like—him ? "

" Why, he pleases me, in spite of Franz d'Epinay, who tries to convince me that he is a being from the other world."

" Albert," she said, in a voice which was altered by emotion ; " I have always put you on your guard against new acquaintances.

Now you are a man, and able to give me advice, yet I repeat to you, Albert, be prudent."

" Why, my dear mother, in order to turn your advice to account, I must know beforehand what I have to distrust. The count never plays, he only drinks water tinged with a little sherry, and is so rich that he cannot, without intending to laugh at me, try to borrow money. What, then, have I to fear from him ? "

" You are right," said the countess, ".and my fears are weakness, especially when directed against a man who has saved your life. How did your father receive him, Albert ? "

" Nothing could be in better taste than my father's demeanour, madame," said Albert; ". nay, more, he seemed greatly flattered at two or three compliments which the count paid him with as much ease as if he had known him these thirty years. Thus they parted the best possible friends ; and M. de Morcerf even wished to take him to the Chamber to hear the speakers." The countess made no reply. She fell into so deep a reverie that her eyes gradually closed. The young man, standing up before her, gazed upon her with that filial affection which is more tender and more endearing with children whose mothers are still young and handsome. Then, after seeing her eyes closed, and hearing her breathe gently, he believed she had dropped asleep, and left the apartment on tiptoe. " This devil of a fellow," he muttered, shaking his head ; " I said at the time he would create a sensation here, and I measure his effect by an infallible thermometer. My mother has noticed him, and he must, therefore, perforce, be remarkable."

CHAPTER XLII

MONSIEUR BERTUCCIO

DURING this time the count had arrived at his house ; it had taken him six minutes to cover the distance ; but these six minutes were sufficient to induce twenty young men who knew the price of the equipage they had been unable to purchase themselves, to put their horses to a gallop in order to see the rich foreigner who could afford to give 20,000 francs apiece for his horses. The house Ali had chosen was situated on the right hand as you ascended the Champs Elysées. A thick clump of trees and shrubs rose in the centre, and masked a portion of the front ; around this shrubbery two alleys, like two arms, extended right and left, and formed a carriage-drive from the iron gates to a double portico, on every step of which stood a porcelain vase, filled with flowers.

This house had, besides the main entrance, another in the Rue Ponthieu. Even before the coachman had hailed the concierge, the massive gates rolled on their hinges ; at Paris, as everywhere else, the Count was served with the rapidity of lightning. The carriage stopped at the left side of the portico and two men presented themselves ; the one was Ali, and the other the steward, who bowed respectfully and offered his arm to assist the count in descending.

" Thanks, Monsieur Bertuccio," said the count, springing lightly up the three steps of the portico ; " and the notary ? "

" He is in the small salon, Excellency," returned Bertuccio.

" And the cards I ordered to be engraved ? "

" I have been myself to the best engraver of the Palais Royal, who did the plate in my presence. The first card struck off was taken, according to your orders, to M. le Baron Danglars, Rue de la Chaussée d'Antin, No. 7 ; the others are on the mantelpiece of your Excellency's bed-room."

" Good ; what o'clock is it ? "

" Four o'clock."

Monte Cristo handed his hat, cane, and gloves to the French footman who had called his carriage at the Count de Morcerf's, and then passed into the small salon, preceded by Bertuccio.

The notary was a simple-looking lawyer's clerk, elevated to the dignity of a provincial scrivener.

" You are the notary empowered to sell the country-house that I wish to purchase, monsieur ? " asked Monte Cristo.

" Yes, M. le Comte," returned the notary.

" Is the deed of sale ready ? "

" Yes, M. le Comte."

" Very well ; and where is this house that I purchase ? "

The steward made a gesture that signified, " I do not know."

The notary looked at the count with astonishment. " What ! " said he, " does not M. le Comte know where the house he purchased is situated ? "

" No," returned the count. " How should I know it ? I have arrived from Cadiz this morning. I have never before been at Paris, and it is the first time I have ever even set foot in France."

" Ah ! that is different ; the house you purchase is situate at Auteuil." At these words Bertuccio turned pale.

" And where is Auteuil ? " asked the count.

" Near here, monsieur," replied the notary, " a charming situation, in the heart of the Bois de Boulogne."

" So near as that ? " said the count ; " but that is not in the country. What made you choose a house at the gates of Paris, Monsieur Bertuccio ? ”

" I ! " cried the steward, with a strange expression. " M. le Comte did not charge me to purchase this house. If M. le Comte will recollect—if he will think——"

" Ah, true," observed Monte Cristo ; " I recollect now. I read the advertisement in one of the papers, and was tempted by the false title, ' a country house.' ”

" It is not yet too late," cried Bertuccio, eagerly ; " and if your Excellency will entrust me with the commission, I will find you a better at Enghien, at Fontenay-aux-Roses, or at Bellevue.”

" Oh, no," returned Monte Cristo, " since I have this I will keep it.”

" And you are quite right," said the notary, who feared to lose his fee. " It is a magnificent place, well supplied with spring water and fine trees ; a comfortable habitation, without reckoning the furniture, which is valuable, now that old things are so much sought after. I suppose M. le Comte has the tastes of the day ? ”

" *Peste !* let us not lose such an opportunity," returned Monte Cristo. " The deed, if you please." He signed it, after having run his eye over that part of the deed in which were specified the situation of the house and the names of the proprietors.

" Bertuccio," said he, " give fifty-five thousand francs to monsieur.”

The steward left the room with a faltering step, and returned with a bundle of bank-notes, which the notary counted like a man who never gives a receipt until after legal examination.

" And now," demanded the count, " are all the forms complied with ? ”

" All, M. le Comte.”

" Have you the keys ? ”

" They are in the hand of the concierge, who takes care of the house ; but here is the order I have given to instal Monsieur le Comte in his new possession.”

" Very well," and Monte Cristo with his hand dismissing him.

" But," observed the honest notary, " you are mistaken, M. le Comte ; it is only fifty thousand francs, everything included.”

" And your fee ? ”

" Is included in this sum.”

" But have you not come from Auteuil here ? ”

" Yes, certainly.”

" Well, then, it is but fair that you should be paid for your loss of time and trouble," said the count.

Scarcely was the count alone when he drew from his pocket a book closed with a lock, and opened it with a key which he wore round his neck and which never left him. After having sought for a few minutes, he stopped at a leaf which had several notes, and compared them with the deed of sale which lay on the table:—

" 'Auteuil, Rue de la Fontaine, No. 28 ; ' it is indeed the same," said he.; " and now, am I to rely upon an avowal extorted by religious or physical terror ? However, in an hour I will know all. Bertuccio ! "

The steward appeared at the door.

" Monsieur Bertuccio," said the count, " did you ever tell me that you had travelled in France ? "

" In some parts of France—yes, Excellency."

" You know the environs of Paris, then ? "

" No, Excellency, no," returned the steward.

" It is unfortunate," returned he, " that you have never visited the environs, for I wish to see my new property this evening, and had you gone with me, you could have given me some useful information."

" To Auteuil ! " cried Bertuccio.

" Well, what is there surprising in that ? When I live at Auteuil, you must come there, as you belong to my service. Why, what has happened to you ? Am I to ring a second time for the carriage ? "

Bertuccio made but one bound to the antechamber, and cried in a hoarse voice, " His Excellency's horses ! "

Monte Cristo wrote two or three notes and, as he sealed the last, the steward appeared.

" Your Excellency's carriage is at the door," said he.

" Well, take your hat and gloves," returned Monte Cristo.

The steward followed his master and sat himself respectfully on the front seat.

CHAPTER XLIII

THE HOUSE AT AUTEUIL

MONTE CRISTO had remarked that, as they descended the staircase, Bertuccio signed himself in the Corsican manner, that is, had formed the sign of the cross in the air with his thumb, and as he seated himself in the carriage muttered a short prayer. In twenty minutes they were at Auteuil ; the steward's emotion had continued to augment as they entered the village. " Tell them to stop at Rue de la Fontaine, No. 28," said the count, fixing his eyes on the steward, to whom he gave this order. Bertuccio obeyed and, leaning out of the window, cried to the coachman—" Rue de la Fontaine, No. 28." The carriage stopped, the footman sprang off the box and opened the door. Bertuccio knocked, the door opened, and the concierge appeared.

" What is it ? " asked he.

" It is your new master, my good fellow," said the footman. And he held out to the concierge the notary's order.

" What was the name of your old master ? " said Monte Cristo.

" M. le Marquis de Saint Méran : he had an only daughter, who married M. de Villefort, who had been the *procureur du roi* at Nîmes, and afterwards at Versailles." Monte Cristo glanced at Bertuccio, who became whiter than the wall against which he leaned to prevent himself from falling.

" And is not this daughter dead ? " demanded Monte Cristo ; " I fancy I have heard so."

" Yes, monsieur, one-and-twenty years ago ; and since then we have not seen the poor marquis three times."

" Thanks, thanks," said Monte Cristo, judging from the steward's utter prostration that he could not stretch the cord farther without danger of breaking it.

" Take one of the carriage lamps, Bertuccio, and show me the apartments."

The steward obeyed in silence ; but it was easy to see, from the manner in which the hand that held the light trembled, how much it cost him to obey. They went over a tolerably large ground-floor, a first floor consisting of a salon, a bath-room, and two bedrooms ; by one of these bedrooms they arrived at a winding staircase that opened on to the garden.

" Ah ! here is a private staircase," said the count ; " that is convenient. Light me, M. Bertuccio, and go first ; we will see where it leads to."

" Monsieur," replied Bertuccio, " it leads to the garden."

" Well, let us be sure of that."

Bertuccio sighed, and went on first ; the stairs led, in reality, to the garden. At the outer door the steward paused.

" Go on, Monsieur Bertuccio," said the count. But he to whom he spoke was stupefied, bewildered, stunned ; his haggard eyes glanced round, as if in search of the traces of some terrible event, and with his clenched hands he seemed striving to shut out some horrible recollections.

" Well ! " insisted the count.

" No, no," cried Bertuccio, setting down the lantern at the angle of the interior wall. " No, monsieur, it is impossible; I can go no farther."

" What does this mean ? " demanded the irresistible voice of Monte Cristo.

" Why, you must see, M. le Comte," cried the steward, " that this is not natural ; that, having to purchase a house, you purchase it exactly at Auteuil ; and that, purchasing it at Auteuil, this house should be No. 28 Rue de la Fontaine. Oh ! why did I not tell you all ? I am sure you would not have forced me to come. I hoped your house would have been some other one than this ; as if there were not another house at Auteuil than that of the assassination ! "

" Ah ! ah !" cried Monte Cristo, stopping suddenly, " what words did you utter ? Come, take the lantern, and let us visit the garden ; you are not afraid of ghosts with me, I hope ? " Bertuccio raised the lantern and obeyed. The steward wished to turn to the left. " No, no, monsieur," said Monte Cristo. " What is the use of following the alleys ? Here is a beautiful lawn, let us go straight forward."

Bertuccio wiped the perspiration from his brow, but obeyed ; however, he continued to take the left hand. Monte Cristo on the contrary, took the right hand, arrived near a clump of trees, he stopped. The steward could not restrain himself. " Move, monsieur,—move away, I entreat you ; you are exactly on the spot ! "

" What spot ? "

" Where he fell."

" I think you are going mad, Bertuccio," said the count, coldly. " If that is the case, I warn you I shall have to put you in an asylum ! "

" Alas ! " Excellency," returned Bertuccio, " the evil has arrived ! "

" M. Bertuccio," said the count, " I am very glad to tell you that whilst you gesticulate, you wring your hands and roll your eyes like a man possessed by a devil who will not leave him ; and I have always remarked that the devil most obstinate to be expelled is a secret one. I knew you were a Corsican, I knew you were gloomy, and always brooding over some old history of the vendetta ; I overlooked that in Italy, because in Italy those things are thought nothing of. But in France they are considered in very bad taste ; there are gendarmes who occupy themselves with such affairs, judges who condemn, and scaffolds which avenge. The Abbé Busoni, then, told me an untruth, when, after his journey in France, in 1829, he sent you to me, with a letter of recommendation, in which he enumerated all your valuable qualities. Well, I will write to the abbé; I will hold him responsible for his *protégé's* misconduct, and I will soon know all about this assassination. Only I warn you, that when I reside in a country, I conform to its code, and I have no wish to put myself within the compass of the French laws for your sake."

"I have always served you faithfully," cried Bertuccio, in despair. "I have always been an honest man, and, as far as lay in my power, I have done good."

"I do not deny it," returned the count; "but why are you thus agitated?"

"M. le Comte," replied Bertuccio, hesitatingly, "did not the Abbé Busoni, who heard my confession in the prison at Nîmes, tell you I had a heavy reproach to make against myself?"

"Yes; but as he said you would make an excellent steward, I concluded you had stolen, that was all."

"Oh, Monsieur le Comte!" returned Bertuccio, contemptuously.

"Or, as you are a Corsican, that you had been unable to resist the desire of making a *peau*, as you call it."

"Yes, my good master," cried Bertuccio, casting himself at the count's feet, "it was simply a vengeance—nothing else."

"I understand that; but I do not understand what it is that galvanizes you in this manner."

"But, monsieur, it was in this house that my vengeance was accomplished."

"What, my house?"

"Oh, M. le Comte, it was not yours then."

"Whose, then? M. le Marquis de Saint Méran, I think, the concierge said. What had you to revenge on the Marquis de Saint Méran?"

"Oh, it was not on him, monsieur; it was on another."

"This is strange," returned Monte Cristo, seeming to yield to his reflections, "that you should find yourself without any preparation in the house where the event happened that causes you so much remorse."

"Monsieur," said the steward, "it is fatality, I am sure. First, you purchase a house at Auteuil; this house is the one where I have committed an assassination; you descend to the garden by the same staircase by which he descended; you stop at the spot where he received the blow ; and two paces farther is the grave in which he had just buried his child. This is not chance ; for chance, in this case, resembles Providence too much."

" Well, let us suppose it is Providence. Come, collect yourself, and tell me all."

" I have never related it but once, and that was to the Abbé Busoni. Such things," continued Bertuccio, shaking his head, " are only related under the seal of confession."

" Then," said the count, " I refer you to your confessor ; turn Chartreux or Trappist, and relate your secrets ; but as for me, I do not like anyone who is alarmed by such phantasms, and I do not choose that my servants should be afraid to walk in the garden of an evening. *Peste !* I thought you somewhat Corsican, a great deal smuggler, and an excellent steward : but I see you have other strings to your bow. You are no longer in my service, Monsieur Bertuccio."

" Oh, M. le Comte ! " cried the steward, struck with terror at this threat, " if that is the only reason I cannot remain in your service, I will tell all ; for if I quit you, it will only be to go to the scaffold."

" That is different," replied Monte Cristo ; " but if you intend to tell an untruth, reflect, it were better not to speak at all."

" No, monsieur, I will tell you all, for the Abbé Busoni himself only knew a part of my secret ; but, I pray you, go away from that plane-tree ; standing where you do, and wrapped in the cloak that conceals your figure, you remind me of M. de Villefort."

" What ! " cried Monte Cristo, " it was M. de Villefort ? "

" Your Excellency knows him ? "

" The former *procureur du roi* at Nîmes ? "

" Yes."

" Who married the Count de Saint Méran's daughter ? "

" Yes."

" Who enjoyed the reputation of being the most severe, the most upright, the most rigid magistrate on the bench ? "

" Well, monsieur," said Bertuccio, " this man with this spotless reputation was a villain."

" Ah ! really," said Monte Cristo. " Have you proof of this ? "

" I had it."

" And you have lost it. How stupid ! "

" Yes, but by careful search it might be recovered."

" Really," returned the count ; " relate it to me, for it begins to interest me." And the count humming an air from " Lucia di Lammermoor," sat down on a bench.

CHAPTER XLIV

THE VENDETTA

" At what point shall I begin, M. le Comte ? " asked Bertuccio.

" From where you please," returned Monte Cristo, " since I know nothing of it."

" The story begins in 1815."

" Ah ! " said Monte Cristo, " 1815 is not yesterday."

" No, monsieur ; and yet I recollect all things as clearly as if they had happened but then. I had a brother, he had become lieutenant in a regiment composed entirely of Corsicans. We became orphans, I at five, he at eighteen. He brought me up as if I had been his son ; and, in 1814, he married. When the emperor returned from Elba, my brother joined the army, was wounded at Waterloo, and retired with the army behind the Loire. One day we received a letter. I should tell you that we lived in the little village of Rogliano, at the extremity of Cape Corse. This letter was from my brother. He told us that the army had disbanded, and that he should return by Châteauroux, Clermont-Ferrand, le Puy, and Nîmes ; and, if I had any money, he prayed me to leave it for him at Nîmes, with an innkeeper with whom I had dealings. I possessed a thousand francs. I left five hundred with Assiunta, my sister-in-law, and with the other five hundred I set off for Nîmes. It was easy to do so ; as I had my boat and a cargo to take in at sea, everything favoured my project. But, after we had taken in our cargo, the wind became contrary, so that we were four or five days without being able to enter the Rhone. At last, however, we succeeded, and worked up to Arles. I left the boat between Bellegarde and Beaucaire, and took the road to Nîmes."

" We are getting to the story now ? "

" Yes, your Excellency. Just at this time, the famous massacres of the south of France took place. Three brigands, called Tretsaillon, Truphemy, and Graffan, publicly assassinated everybody whom they suspected of Bonapartism. You heard of these massacres, M. le Comte ? "

" Vaguely : I was far from France at that period. Go on."

" As I entered Nîmes, I literally waded in blood. At the sight of this slaughter and devastation, I became terrified for my brother, a soldier of the empire, returning from the army of the Loire, with his uniform and his epaulets. I hastened to the innkeeper. My presages had been but too true ; my brother had arrived the previous evening at Nîmes, and, at the very door of the house where he was about to demand hospitality, he had been assassinated. I did all in my power to discover the murderers, but no one durst tell me their names, so much were they dreaded. I then thought of that French justice of which I had heard so much, and which feared nothing, and I went to the *procureur du roi.*"

" And this *procureur du roi* was named Villefort ? " asked Monte Cristo, carelessly.

" Yes, your Excellency ; he came from Marseilles, where he had been deputy procureur. His zeal had procured him advancement, and he was said to be one of the first who had informed the government of the departure from the island of Elba."

" Then," said Monte Cristo, " you went to him ? "

" Monsieur," I said, ' my brother was assassinated yesterday in the streets of Nîmes, I know not by whom, but it is your duty to find out. You are the head of justice here ; and it is for justice to avenge those she has been unable to protect.'

" ' Who was your brother ? ' asked he.

" ' A lieutenant in the Corsican battalion.'

" ' A soldier of the Usurper, then ? '

" ' A soldier of the French army.'

" ' Well,' replied he, ' he has smitten with the sword, and has perished by the sword.'

" ' You are mistaken, monsieur,' I replied ; ' he has perished by the poniard.'

" ' What do you want me to do ? ' asked the magistrate.

" ' I have already told you ; avenge him.'

" ' On whom ? '

" ' On his murderers.'

" ' Why, your brother has been involved in a quarrel, and killed in a duel. The people here do not like soldiers of such disorderly conduct.'

" ' Monsieur,' I replied, ' it is not for myself that I entreat your interference,—I should grieve for him or avenge him ; but my poor brother had a wife. Pray, try to obtain a small pension for her.'

" ' Every revolution has its catastrophes,' returned M. de Villefort. ' Your brother has been the victim of this ; it is a misfortune, and government owes nothing to his family."

" ' What ! ' cried I, ' do you, a magistrate, speak thus to me ? '

" ' All these Corsicans are mad, on my honour,' replied M. de Villefort ; ' they fancy that their countryman is still Emperor. Depart instantly, or I will compel you to do so.'

" I looked at him an instant to see if, by renewed entreaties, there was anything to hope. But this man was of stone. I approached him and said in a low voice,—' Well ! since you know the Corsicans so well, you know that they always keep their word. You think that it was a good deed to kill my brother, who was a Bonapartist, because you are a Royalist ! Well ! I, who am a Bonapartist, also, declare one thing to you, which is, that I will kill you : from this moment I declare the vendetta against you : so protect yourself, as well as you can, for the next time we meet your last hour has come.' And before he had recovered from his surprise, I opened the door and left the room."

" Ah ! " said Monte Cristo. " With your innocent appearance you do these things, M. Bertuccio ; and to a *procureur du roi !* moreover, did he know what was meant by this terrible word ' vendetta ' ? "

" He knew so well that from that moment he shut himself in his house and never went out unattended, seeking me high and low. Fortunately, I was so well concealed that he could not find me. Then he became alarmed, and dared not reside any longer at Nîmes ; so he solicited a change of residence, and as he was in reality very influential, he was nominated to Versailles ; but, as you know, a Corsican who has sworn to avenge himself cares not for distance. The most important thing was, not to kill him only, for I had an opportunity of doing so a hundred times, but to kill him without being discovered—at least, without being arrested. During three months I watched M. de Villefort. At length, I discovered that he went mysteriously to Auteuil, I followed him thither, and I saw him enter the house where we now are ; only, instead of entering by the great door that looks into the street, he came on horseback, or in his carriage, left the one or the other at the little inn, and entered by the gate you see there ! " Monte Cristo made a sign with his head that he could discern amid the darkness the door to which Bertuccio alluded.

" As I had nothing more to do at Versailles, I went to Auteuil and gained all the information I could. The house belonged, as the concierge informed your excellency, to M. de Saint Méran, Villefort's father-in-law ; it was reported to be let to a young widow, known only by the name of the baroness.

" One evening, as I was looking over the wall, I saw a young and handsome woman, who was walking alone in the garden, which was not overlooked by any windows, and I guessed that she was awaiting M. de Villefort. When she was sufficiently near to distinguish her features, I saw she was from eighteen to nineteen, tall, and very fair. As she had a loose muslin dress on, and as nothing concealed her figure, I saw she would ere long become a mother. A few moments later a man entered; the young female hastened to meet him; they threw themselves into each other's arms, embraced tenderly, and returned together to the house. This man was M. de Villefort."

" And," asked the count, " did you ever know the name of this woman ? "

" No, Excellency," returned Bertuccio.

" Go on."

" That evening," continued Bertuccio, " I could have killed the *procureur du roi ;* but as I did not know the locality well, I was afraid that if I did not kill him outright, his cries might raise an alarm and I should be caught. Three days afterwards, about seven in the evening, I saw a servant leave the house at full gallop, and take the road to Sèvres. In three hours the man returned : and ten minutes later, another man on foot, muffled in a mantle, opened the little door of the garden, which he closed after him. Although I had not seen Villefort's face, I recognized him by the beating of my heart. I crossed the street, and stopped at a post placed at the angle of the wall, by means of which I had once before looked into the garden. This time I did not content myself with looking, but I took my knife out of my pocket, felt that the point was sharp, and sprang over the wall. My first care was to run to the door ; he had left the key in it, taking the simple precaution of turning it twice in the lock. Nothing preventing my escape by this means, I examined the place. The garden formed a long square, a terrace of smooth turf extended in the middle, and at the corners were clumps of trees with dense foliage, that mingled with the shrubs and flowers. In order to go from the door to the house, or from the house to the door, M. de Villefort was compelled to pass by one of these clumps.

" It was the end of September : the wind blew violently. The faint glimpses of the pale moon were unable to pierce the obscurity of the thick shrubberies, in which a man could conceal himself without any fear of discovery. I hid myself in the one nearest to the path Villefort must take ; and scarcely was I there when, amidst the gusts of wind, I fancied I heard groans. Two hours passed thus, during which I imagined I heard these moans repeated   Midnight struck. As the last stroke died away, I saw a faint light shine through the windows of the private staircase by which we have just descended. The door opened, and the man in the mantle reappeared. I drew my knife from my pocket again, opened it, and prepared to strike. The man in the mantle advanced towards me, but as he drew near I saw he had a weapon in his hand. When he was only a few paces from me, I saw that what I had taken for a weapon was only a spade. I was still unable to define for what reason M. de Villefort had this spade in his hands, when he stopped close to the clump, glanced round, and began to dig a hole in the earth. I then perceived that he hid something beneath his mantle, which he laid on the grass to dig more freely. An idea crossed my mind, which was confirmed when I saw the *procureur du roi* lift from under his mantle a box, two feet long and six or eight inches deep. I let him place the box in the hole he had made; then, while he stamped with his feet to remove all traces of his occupation, I rushed on him and plunged my knife into his breast, exclaiming, 'I am Giovanni Bertuccio; thy death for my brother's; thy treasure for his widow; thou seest that my vengeance is more complete than I had hoped.' He fell without a cry. In a second I had disinterred the box; then I filled up the hole, threw the spade over the wall, and rushed through the door, which I double-locked, carrying off the key."

"Ah!" said Monte Cristo. "I recollect," replied the count; "did you not say something of an infant?"

"Yes, Excellency; I hastened to the river, sat down on the bank, and with my knife forced open the lock of the box. In a fine linen cloth was wrapped a new-born child. Its purple visage, and its violet-coloured hands, showed it had perished by suffocation; but as it was not yet cold I hesitated to throw it into the water that ran at my feet; in reality, at the end of an instant, I fancied I felt a slight pulsation of the heart; and as I had been assistant at the hospital at Bastia, I did what a doctor would have done—I inflated the lungs and at the expiration of a quarter of an hour, I saw the breathing begin, and a feeble cry was heard. In my turn I uttered a cry, but a cry of joy. 'God has not cursed me, then,' I cried, 'since He permits me to save the life of a human creature, in exchange for the life I have taken away.'"

"And what did you do with the child?" asked Monte Cristo. "It was an embarrassing load for a man seeking to escape."

"I had not for a moment the idea of keeping it, but I knew that at Paris there was a hospital where they receive these poor creatures. After taking the precaution to cut the linen in two pieces, so that one of the two letters which marked it was wrapped round the child whilst the other remained in my possession, I rang the bell and fled with all speed. A fortnight later I was at Rogliano, and I said to Assiunta, ' Console thyself, sister, Israel is dead, but he is avenged.' She demanded what I meant, and when I had recounted all to her,—' Giovanni,' said Assiunta, ' you should have brought this child with you ; we would have replaced the parents it has lost, have called it Benedetto, and then in consequence of this good action God would have blessed us.' In reply I gave her the half of the linen I had kept in order to reclaim him if we became rich."

" What letters were marked on the linen ? " said Monte Cristo.

" H and N, surmounted by a baron's coronet."

" What became of this little boy ? and what was the crime of which you were accused when you asked for a confessor, and the Abbé Busoni came to visit you in the prison at Nîmes."

" The story will be very long, Excellency."

" What matter ? you know I take but little sleep, and I do not suppose you are very much inclined for it either."

Bertuccio bowed and resumed his story.

" Partly to drown the recollections of the past that haunted me, partly to supply the wants of the poor widow, I returned to my trade of smuggler. We profited by the kind of respite Government gave us to make friends everywhere. Since my brother's assassination in the streets of Nîmes, I had never entered the town ; the result was, the innkeeper with whom we were connected seeing we would no longer come to him, was forced to come to us, and had established a branch to his inn, on the road from Bellegarde to Beaucaire, at the sign of the Pont du Gard. We had thus, both on the side of Aiguesmortes, Martigues, or at Bouc, a dozen places where we left our goods, and where, in case of necessity, we concealed ourselves from the gendarmes and custom-house officers. Smuggling is a profitable trade when a certain degree of vigour and intelligence is employed ; as for my-self, brought up in the mountains, I had a double motive for fearing the gendarmes and custom-house officers, as my appearance before the judges would cause an inquiry, and an inquiry always looks back into the past. And in my past life they might find something far more grave than the selling of smuggled cigars, or barrels of brandy without a permit. So, preferring death to capture, I accomplished the most astonishing deeds ; when you have once devoted your life, you are no longer the equal of other men, or, rather, other men are no longer your equals ; and whosoever has taken this resolution feels his strength and resources doubled."

" Philosophy, Monsieur Bertuccio," interrupted the count; " you have done a little of everything in your life."

" O Excellency ! "

" No, no, but philosophy at half-past ten at night is somewhat late ; yet I have no other observation to make, for what you say is correct, which is more than can be said for all philosophy."

" My journeys became more and more extensive and more productive. Assiunta took care of all, and our little fortune increased. One day when I was setting forth on an expedition, ' Go,' said she ; ' at your return I will give you a surprise.' We ran our cargo without opposition, and returned home full of joy. When I entered the house, the first thing I beheld in the centre of Assiunta's chamber was a cradle that might be called sumptuous compared with the rest of the furniture, and in it a baby of seven or eight months old. I uttered a cry of joy ; the only moments of sadness I had known since the assassination of the *procureur du roi* were caused by the recollection that I had abandoned this child. For the assassination itself I had never felt any remorse. Poor Assiunta had guessed all. She had profited by my absence, and furnished with one half of the linen, and having written down the day and hour at which I had deposited the child at the hospital, had set off for Paris and reclaimed it. No objection was raised, and the infant was given up to her. Ah, I confess, M. le Comte, when I saw the poor creature sleeping in its cradle, my eyes filled with tears. ' Ah, Assiunta,' cried I, ' you are a good woman, and Heaven will bless you.' "

" This," said Monte Cristo," is less correct than your philosophy ; it is only faith."

" Alas ! your Excellency is right," replied Bertuccio, " and God made this infant the instrument of our punishment. Never did a perverse nature declare itself more prematurely ; and yet it was not owing to any fault in his bringing up. He was a most lovely child, with large blue eyes, of that deep colour that harmonizes so well with the general fairness of the complexion ; only his hair, which was too light, gave his face a most singular expression, which redoubled the vivacity of his look and the malice of his smile. Unfortunately, there is a proverb that says, that ' red is either altogether good or altogether bad.' The proverb was but too correct as regarded Benedetto, and even in his infancy he manifested the worst disposition. It is true, that the indulgence of his mother encouraged him. This child, for whom my poor sister would go to the town, five or six leagues off, to purchase the earliest fruits and the most tempting sweetmeats, preferred to the grapes of Palma, or the preserves of Genoa, the chestnuts stolen from a neighbour's orchard, or the dried apples in his loft, when he could eat as well of the nuts and apples that grew in my garden. One day, when Benedetto was about five or six, our neighbour, Wasilio complained that he had lost a louis out of his purse; we thought he must have made a mistake in counting his money, but he persisted in the accuracy of his statement. One day, Benedetto did not return until late in the evening, dragging a monkey after him, which he said he had found chained to the foot of a tree. For more than a month past, the mischievous child, who knew not what to wish for, had taken it into his head to have a monkey. A boatman who had passed by Rogliano, and who had several of these animals, whose tricks had greatly diverted him, had, doubtless, suggested this idea to him. 'Monkeys are not found in our woods chained to trees,' said I; 'confess how you obtained this animal.' Benedetto maintained the truth of what he had said, and accompanied it with details that did more honour to his imagination than to his veracity. I became angry; he began to laugh; I threatened to strike him and he made two steps backwards. 'You cannot beat me,' said he; 'you have no right, for you are not my father.'

"We never knew who had revealed this fatal secret, which we had so carefully concealed from him; however, this answer, in which the child's whole character revealed itself, terrified me, and my arm fell without touching him. The boy triumphed; no sooner was my back turned than Benedetto became master, and everything went ill. When he was only eleven, he chose his companions from among the young men of eighteen or twenty, the worst characters in Bastia, or, indeed, in Corsica. I became alarmed, as prosecution might be attended with serious consequences, I was compelled, at this period, to leave Corsica on an important expedition; I resolved that Benedetto should accompany me. I spoke to Benedetto alone, and proposed to him to accompany me, endeavouring to tempt him by all the promises most likely to dazzle the imagination of a child of twelve years old. He heard me patiently, and, when I had finished, burst out laughing.

"'Are you mad, uncle?' (he called me by this name when he was in a good humour); 'do you think I am going to change the life I lead for your mode of existence? Why, I have as much money as I want: mother Assiunta always supplies me when I ask for it. You see that I should be a fool to accept your offer.' The arguments and this audacity stupefied me. Benedetto rejoined his associates, and I saw him from a distance point me out to them as a fool."

"Sweet child!" murmured Monte Cristo.

"Oh! had he been my own son," replied Bertuccio, "or even my nephew, I would have brought him back to the right road; but the idea that I was striking the boy whose father I had killed, made it impossible to punish him. I gave my sister, who constantly defended the unfortunate boy, good advice; and as she confessed that she had several times missed money to a considerable amount, I showed her a safe place in which to conceal our little treasure for the future. My mind was already made up; Benedetto could read, write, and cypher perfectly; for when the fit seized him he learned more in a day than others in a week; my intention was to enter him as a clerk in some ship, and without letting him know anything of my plan, to convey him some morning on board: by this means his future treatment would depend upon his own conduct. I set off for France after having fixed upon the plan. All our cargo was to be landed in the Gulf of Lyons, and this was the more difficult, since peace had been restored. The vigilance of the custom-house officers was redoubled, and this strictness was increased at this time, in consequence of the fair of Beaucaire.

"Our expedition began favourably. We anchored our barque, which had a double hold, where our goods were concealed, amidst a number of other vessels that bordered the banks of the Rhone from Beaucaire to Arles. On our arrival there we began to discharge our cargo in the night, and to convey it into the town, by the help of the innkeepers with whom we were connected. Whether success rendered us imprudent, or whether we were betrayed, I know not; but one evening, about five o'clock, our little cabin-boy hastened, breathless, to inform us that he had seen a detachment of custom-house officers advancing in our direction. In an instant we were on the alert, but it was too late, our vessel was surrounded, and amongst the custom-house officers I observed several gendarmes. I sprang into the hold, opened a port, dropped into the river, dived, and only rose at intervals to breathe, until I reached a cutting that led from the Rhone to the canal that runs from Beaucaire to Aiguesmortes. I reached the canal in safety. I had designedly taken this direction. I have already told your Excellency of an innkeeper of Nîmes who had set up a little inn on the road from Bellegarde to Beaucaire. He had, seven or eight years before this period, sold his establishment to a tailor at Marseilles. Of course we made the same arrangements with the new landlord that we had with the old; and it was of this man that I intended to ask shelter."

" What was his name ? " inquired the count.

" Gaspard Caderousse; he had married a woman from the village of Carconte, whom we did not know by any other name than that of her village.

" And you say," interrupted Monte Cristo, " that this took place towards the year——"

" 1829, M. le Comte."

" In what month ? "

" June."

" The beginning or the end ? "

" The evening of the third."

" Ah," said Monte Cristo, " the evening of the 3rd of June, 1829. Go on."

" It was from Caderousse that I intended demanding shelter ; and as we never entered by the door that opened on to the road, I resolved not to break through the rule, and, climbing over the garden hedge, I crept amongst the olive and wild fig trees ; and, fearing that Caderousse might have some one there, I entered a kind of shed in which I had often passed the night, and which was only separated from the inn by a partition, in which holes had been made in order to enable us to watch an opportunity of announcing our presence. I stepped into the shed, and it was fortunate I did so, for at that moment Caderousse entered with a stranger.

" I waited patiently, not to overhear what they said, but because I could do nothing else ; besides, the same thing had occurred often before. The man who was with Caderousse was evidently a stranger to the South of France ; he was one of those merchants who come to sell jewellery, at the fair of Beaucaire. Caderousse entered hastily. Then, seeing that the room was, as usual, empty, and only guarded by the dog, he called to his wife ; ' Hilloa, Carconte ! ' said he, ' the worthy priest has not deceived us, the diamond is real.' An exclamation of joy was heard, and the staircase creaked beneath a feeble step. ' What do you say ? ' asked his wife, pale as death.

" ' I say that the diamond is real, and that this gentleman, one of the first jewellers of Paris, will give us 50,000 francs for it. Only, in order to satisfy himself it really belongs to us, he wishes you to relate to him, as I have done already, the miraculous manner in which the diamond came into our possession. In the meantime, please to sit down, monsieur, and I will fetch you some refreshment.' The jeweller examined attentively the interior of the inn and visible poverty of the persons who were about to sell him a diamond that seemed to have come from the casket of a prince. 'Relate your story, madame,' said he.

"'Oh!' returned she, 'it was a gift of Heaven! My husband was a great friend, in 1814 or 1815, of a sailor named Edmond Dantès. This poor fellow, whom Caderousse had forgotten, had not forgotten him, and at his death bequeathed this diamond to him.'

"'But how did he obtain it?' asked the jeweller; 'was it in his possession before he was imprisoned?'

"'No, monsieur; but it appears that in prison he made the acquaintance of a rich Englishman; and as in prison he fell sick, and Dantès took the same care of him as if he had been his brother, the Englishman, when he was set free, gave this stone to Dantès, who, less fortunate, died, and in his turn left it to us, and charged the excellent abbé who was here this morning to deliver it.'

"'The same story!' muttered the jeweller; 'and, improbable as it seems at first, the history may be true. There's only the price we are not agreed about.'

"'How not agreed about?' said Caderousse; 'I thought we agreed for the price I asked.'

"'That is,' replied the jeweller, 'I offered 40,000 francs.'

"'Forty thousand!' cried La Carconte; 'we will not part with it for that sum. The abbé told us it was worth 50,000 without the setting.'

"'What was the abbé's name?' asked the indefatigable questioner.

"'The Abbé Busoni,' said La Carconte.

"'He was a foreigner?'

"'An Italian from the neighbourhood of Mantua, I believe.'

"'Let me see this diamond again,' replied the jeweller; 'the first time you are often mistaken as to the value of a stone.' Caderousse took from his pocket a small case of black shagreen, opened, and gave it to the jeweller. At the sight of the diamond, which was as large as a hazel nut, La Carconte's eyes sparkled with cupidity."

"And what did you think of this fine story, eavesdropper?" said Monte Cristo; "did you credit it?"

"Yes, your Excellency."

"That did more honour to your heart than to your experience,

M. Bertuccio. Had you known this Edmond Dantès of whom they spoke ? "

" No, your Excellency, I had never heard of him before, and never but once afterwards, and that was from the Abbé Busoni himself, when I saw him in the prison at Nîmes."

" Go on."

" The jeweller took the ring, and, drawing from his pocket a pair of steel pliers and a small set of copper scales, taking the stone out of its setting, he weighed it carefully.

" ' I will give you 45,000 francs,' said he, ' but not a sou more ; besides, as that is the exact value of the stone, I brought just that sum with me.'

" ' No matter,' observed Caderousse, replacing the box in his pocket, ' someone else will purchase it.'

" ' Yes,' continued the jeweller ; ' but someone else will not be so easy as I am, or content himself with the same story. It is not natural that a man like you should possess such a diamond. He will inform against you. You will have to find the Abbé Busoni ; and abbés who give diamonds worth two thousand louis are rare. Justice will seize it, and put you in prison ; if at the end of three or four months you are set at liberty, the ring will be lost, or a false stone, worth three francs, will be given you instead of a diamond worth 50,000 or perhaps 55,000 francs ; but which you must allow one runs considerable risk in purchasing.'

" Caderousse and his wife looked eagerly at each other. ' No,' said Caderousse, ' we are not rich enough to lose 5,000 francs.'

" ' As you please, my dear sir,' said the jeweller ; ' I had, however, as you see, brought you the money in bright coin.' And he drew from his pocket a handful of gold.

" There was evidently a severe struggle in the mind of Caderousse. He turned towards his wife, ' What do you think of this ? ' he asked, in a low voice.

" ' Let him have it—let him have it,' she said.

" ' Well, then, so I will ! ' said Caderousse ; ' so you may have the diamond for 45,000 francs. But my wife wants a gold chain, and I want a pair of silver buckles.'

" The jeweller drew from his pocket a long flat box, which contained several samples of the articles demanded. ' Here,' he said, ' I am very plain in my dealings—take your choice.' The woman selected a gold chain worth about five louis, and the husband a pair of buckles worth perhaps fifteen francs. ' I hope you will not complain now ? ' said the jeweller.

"And the five-and-forty thousand francs,' inquired Caderousse in a hoarse voice, 'where are they? Come—let us see them!"

"'Here they are,' replied the jeweller; and he counted out upon the table 15,000 francs in gold and 30,000 francs in banknotes.

"'Wait whilst I light the lamp,' said La Carconte; 'it is growing dark, and there may be some mistake.' Caderousse counted and again counted the gold and the notes; then handed them to his wife, who counted and counted them again in her turn. 'Well,' inquired the jeweller, 'is the cash all right?'

"'Yes,' said Caderousse. 'Give me the pocket-book, La Carconte, and find a bag somewhere.'

"La Carconte went to a cupboard, and returned with an old leather pocket-book, from which she took some greasy letters, and put in their place the bank-notes, and a bag, in which were, at the moment two or three crowns of six livres each, and which, in all probability, formed the entire fortune of the miserable couple. 'There,' said Caderousse; 'and now, although you have wronged us of perhaps 10,000 francs, will you have your supper with us? I invite you with goodwill.'

"'Thank you,' replied the jeweller; 'it must be getting late, and I must return to Beaucaire,—my wife will be getting uneasy.' He drew out his watch and exclaimed, ' Morbleu! nearly nine o'clock!—why, I shall not get back to Beaucaire before midnight! Good night, my dears. If the Abbé Busoni should by any accident return, think of me.'

"'In another week you will have left Beaucaire,' remarked Caderousse, 'for the fair finishes in a few days.'

"'True; but that is of no consequence. Write to me at Paris, to M. Joannes, in the Palais Royal, Stone Gallery, No. 45: I will make the journey on purpose to see him, if it is worth while.'

"At this moment there was a tremendous clap of thunder, accompanied by a flash of lightning so vivid that it quite eclipsed the light of the lamp.

"'Oh dear!' exclaimed Caderousse. 'You cannot think of going out in such weather as this.'

"'Oh, I am not afraid of thunder!' said the jeweller.

"'Well, then, a good journey to you,' said Caderousse.

"'Thank ye,' replied the jeweller. At the moment when he opened the door, such a gust of wind came in that the lamp was nearly extinguished. 'Oh!' said he, 'this is very nice weather, and two leagues to go in such a storm!'

" ' Remain,' said Caderousse. ' You can sleep here.'

" ' No; I must sleep at Beaucaire. So once more, good night.'

" Caderousse followed him slowly to the threshold.

" ' Close the door,' said La Carconte; ' I do not like open doors when it thunders.'

" ' Particularly when there is money in the house, eh ? ' answered Caderousse, double-locking the door.

" He came into the room, went to the cupboard, took out the bag and pocket-book, and both began, for the third time, to count their gold and bank-notes. ' Why,' she inquired, in a hoarse voice, ' did you invite him to sleep here to-night ? '

" ' Why ? ' said Caderousse, with a shudder; ' why, that he might not have the trouble of returning to Beaucaire.'

" ' Ah ! ' responded the woman, with an expression impossible to render; ' I thought it was for something else.'

" ' Woman, woman, why do you have such ideas ? ' cried Caderousse; ' or, if you have them, why don't you keep them to yourself ? '

" ' Well,' said La Carconte, after a moment's pause, ' you are not a man ! '

" ' What do you mean ? ' added Caderousse.

" ' If you had been a man you would not have let him go from here.'

" ' Woman ! '

" ' Or else he should not have reached Beaucaire.'

" ' Woman ! '

" ' The road takes a turn, he is obliged to follow it, whilst alongside of the canal there is a shorter road.'

" ' Woman !—you offend the *bon Dieu !* There !—listen ! ' And at this moment there was heard a tremendous peal of thunder, whilst the livid lightning illumined the room. ' Mercy ! ' said Caderousse, crossing himself.

" At the same moment, and in the midst of the silence so full of terror which usually follows claps of thunder, they heard a knocking at the door. Caderousse and his wife started and looked aghast at each other.

" ' Who's there ? ' cried Caderousse, rising, and drawing up in a heap the gold and notes scattered over the table, and covering them with his two hands.

" ' It is I,' shouted a voice.

" ' And who are you ? '

" ' Eh, *pardieu !* Joannes, the jeweller.'

" ' Well, and you said I offended the *bon Dieu*,' said Carconte, with a horrid smile. ' Why, it is the *bon Dieu* Who sends him back again.'

" Caderousse fell back, pale and breathless, in his chair. La Carconte, on the contrary, rose, and going with a firm step towards the door, opened it, saying as she did so,—' Come in, dear M. Joannes.'

" ' *Ma foi!* ' said the jeweller, drenched with rain, ' it seems as if I was not to return to Beaucaire to-night. The shortest follies are best, my dear Caderousse. You offered me hospitality and I have returned to sleep beneath your friendly roof.'

" Caderousse stammered out some words whilst he wiped away the damp that started to his brow. La Carconte double-locked the door behind the jeweller."

CHAPTER XLV

THE RAIN OF BLOOD

" As the jeweller returned to the apartment, he cast around him a glance—but there was nothing to excite suspicion.

" ' Heyday! ' said the jeweller, ' you seem, my good friends, to have had some fears respecting the accuracy of your money, by counting it over so carefully directly I was gone.'

" ' No, no,' answered Caderousse, ' that was not my reason, I can assure you ; but the circumstances by which we have become possessed of this wealth are so unexpected, as to make us scarcely credit our good fortune, and it is only by placing the actual proof of our riches before our eyes that we can persuade ourselves the whole affair is not a dream.'

" The jeweller smiled. ' Have you any other guests in your house ? ' inquired he.

" ' Nobody but ourselves,' replied Caderousse ; ' the fact is we do not lodge travellers—indeed, our inn is so near to the town that nobody would think of stopping here.'

" ' Then I am afraid I shall very much inconvenience you ! '

" ' Oh, dear me, no ! indeed, good sir, you will not,' said La Carconte in her most gracious manner. ' I vow and protest your passing the night under shelter of our poor roof will not make the slightest difference in the world to us.'

" ' But where will you manage to stow me ? '

" ' In the chamber overhead.'

" ' Surely that is where you yourselves sleep ? '

" ' Never mind that, we have a bed in the adjoining room.' Caderousse stared at his wife.

" The jeweller, meanwhile, was humming a song as he stood warming himself by the bright, cheering blaze of a large fagot kindled by Carconte, to dry his wet garments. And this done, she next occupied herself in arranging his supper. Caderousse had once more parted with his treasures—the bank notes were replaced in the pocket-book, the gold put back into the bag, and the whole carefully locked in the *armoire*, which formed his stronghold ; he then began pacing the room with a pensive and gloomy air, glancing from time to time at the jeweller.

" ' Now then, my dear sir,' said La Carconte, as she placed a bottle of wine on the table, ' supper is ready whenever you are inclined to partake of it.'

" ' But you are going to sit down with me, are you not ? ' asked Joannes.

" ' I shall not take any supper to-night,' said Caderousse.

" ' Then it seems I am to eat alone,' remarked the jeweller.

" ' Oh, we shall have the pleasure of waiting upon you,' answered La Carconte, with an attention she was not accustomed to manifest even to guests who paid for what they took.

" From one minute to another, Caderousse darted on his wife keen, searching glances, but rapid as the lightning-flash. The storm still continued.

" ' There ! there ! ' said La Carconte ; ' do you hear that ? Upon my word, you were wise to return.'

" ' Well,' said the jeweller, as he placed himself at table, ' all I can say is, so much the worse for those who are abroad and cannot obtain shelter.'

" ' Ah ! ' chimed in La Carconte, ' they will have a wretched night of it, be they who they may.'

" The jeweller began eating his supper, while Caderousse continued in gloomy silence to pace the room, sedulously avoiding the sight of his guest ; but as soon as the stranger had completed his repast, the agitated innkeeper went eagerly to the door and opened it. ' The storm seems over,' said he. But as if to contradict his statement, at that instant a violent clap of thunder seemed to shake the house to its very foundation, while a sudden gust of wind, mingled with rain, extinguished the lamp he held in his hand. Trembling and awe-struck, Caderousse hastily shut the door and returned to his guest, while La Carconte lighted a candle by the smouldering ashes that glimmered on the hearth. ' You must be tired,' said she to the jeweller ; ' I have spread a pair of my finest and whitest sheets on your bed, so you have nothing to do but to sleep as soundly as I wish you may—you can easily find your room, it is exactly over this.'

"Joannes remained a short time listening whether the storm seemed to abate in its fury, but a brief space of time sufficed to assure him that, far from diminishing, the violence of the rain and thunder increased; resigning himself, therefore to what seemed inevitable, he bade his host good-night, and mounted to his sleeping apartment. As he passed over my head, the flooring seemed to creak beneath his tread, proving how slight must be the division between us. The quick eager glance of La Carconte followed him as he ascended the staircase, while Caderousse, on the contrary, turned his back, and most anxiously avoided even glancing at him.

"All these particulars did not strike me as painfully at the time as they have since done; worn out as I was with fatigue, and fully purposing to proceed onwards directly the tempest ceased, I determined to take advantage of the comparative silence and tranquillity that prevailed to obtain the refreshment of a few hours' sleep. Overhead I could accurately distinguish every movement of the jeweller, who, after making the best arrangements in his power for passing a comfortable night, threw himself on his bed, and I could hear it creak and groan beneath his weight. Insensibly my eyelids grew heavy, deep sleep stole over me, and having no suspicion of anything wrong, I sought not to shake it off. For the last time I looked in upon the room where Caderousse and his wife were sitting; the former—his head buried between his hands—was seated upon one of those low wooden stools which in country places are frequently used instead of chairs. La Carconte continued to gaze on him for some time in contemptuous silence and then, shrugging her shoulders, took her seat immediately opposite to him. But as he made no sign of changing his position, she extended her hard, bony hand, and touched him on the forehead.

"Caderousse shuddered. The woman's lips seemed to move, as though she were talking; but whether she merely spoke in an undertone, or whether my senses were dulled by sleep, I did not catch a word she uttered. How long I had been asleep I know not, when I was suddenly aroused by the report of a pistol, followed by a fearful cry. Weak and tottering footsteps resounded across the chamber above me, and the next instant a dull, heavy weight seemed to fall powerless on the staircase I had not yet fully recovered my recollection, when again I heard groans, mingled with half-stifled cries, as if from persons engaged in a deadly struggle. Hastily raising myself on one arm, I looked around, but all was dark; and it seemed to me as if the rain must have penetrated through the flooring of the room above, for some kind of moisture appeared to fall, drop by drop, upon my forehead, and when I passed my hand across my brow, I felt it wet and clammy.

" To the fearful noises that had awakened me had succeeded the most perfect silence, unbroken save by the footsteps of a man walking about in the chamber above. By the creaking of the staircase I judged the individual, whoever he was, was proceeding to the lower apartment. In another minute I heard some person moving there, and, looking through, saw a man stooping towards the fire to light a candle he held in his hand. As he turned round, I recognized the features of Caderousse—pale, ghastly, and convulsed—while the front and sleeves of his dress were covered with blood. Having obtained the light, he hurried upstairs again. Ere long he came below, holding in his hand the small shagreen case. He placed it in his red handkerchief, which he carefully rolled round his head. After this he took from his cupboard the bank notes and gold he had put there, thrust the one into the pocket of his trousers, and the other into that of his waistcoat, hastily tied up a small bundle of linen, and rushing towards the door, disappeared in the darkness of the night.

" Then all became clear and manifest to me; I fancied that I still heard faint moans, and imagining that the unfortunate jeweller might not be quite dead, I determined to go to his relief. Hastily snatching up the lighted candle, I hurried to the staircase; towards the middle of it I stumbled over a human body lying across the stairs. As I stooped to raise it, I discovered in the agonized features those of La Carconte. The pistol I had heard had doubtless been discharged at the unfortunate woman whose throat it had frightfully lacerated, leaving a gaping wound from which, as well as the mouth, the blood was welling in streams. Finding the miserable creature past all human aid, I strode past her, and ascended to the sleeping chamber, which presented an appearance of the wildest disorder. The murdered man lay on the ground, his head leaning against the wall, weltering in a gory stream, poured forth from three large wounds in his breast; there was a fourth gash, but the blood was prevented from escaping in consequence of the weapon (a large table knife) still sticking in it.

" I approached the jeweller, who was not quite dead, and at the sound of my footsteps he opened his eyes, fixed them on me

with an anxious and inquiring gaze, moved his lips as though trying to speak, then, overcome by the effort, fell back and expired.
I rushed towards the staircase, clasping my burning temples
with both hands, and uttering cries of horror. Upon reaching
the room below, I found five or six custom-house officers, accompanied by soldiers, who immediately seized me, ere, indeed, I had
sufficiently collected my ideas to offer any resistance ; in truth,
my senses had forsaken me, and when I strove to speak, a few
inarticulate sounds alone escaped my lips.

"As I noticed the significant manner in which the whole party
pointed to my blood-stained garments, I involuntarily surveyed
myself, and then I discovered that the thick warm drops that had
so bedewed me as I lay beneath that staircase must have been
the blood of La Carconte. Paralysed with horror, I could barely
indicate by a movement of my hand the spot where I had concealed myself. 'What does he mean ? ' asked a gendarme.
One of the custom-house officers went to the place I directed.
' He means,' replied the man upon his return, ' that he effected his
entrance by means of this hole,' showing the place where I had
broken my way through the planks into the house.

"Then, and not before, the true nature of my situation flashed
on me, and I saw that I was considered the author of all that
had occurred ; with this frightful conviction of my danger,
I recovered force and energy enough to free myself from the hands
of those who held me, while I managed to stammer forth—
' I did not do it ! Indeed, indeed I did not ! ' A couple of
gendarmes held the muzzles of their carbines against my breast,
—' stir but a step,' said they, ' and you are a dead man ! '

"Alas ! resistance was far from my thoughts. I was overpowered by surprise and terror ; and without a word I suffered
myself to be handcuffed and tied to a horse's tail, in which disgraceful plight I arrived at Nîmes.

"It seems I had been tracked by a custom-house officer, who
had lost sight of me near the inn ; feeling sure that I intended
to pass the night there, he had returned to summon his comrades, who just arrived in time to hear the report of the pistol,
and to take me in the midst of such circumstantial proofs of my
guilt as rendered all hope of proving my innocence utterly at an
end. One only chance was left me, that of beseeching the magistrate before whom I was taken to cause every inquiry to be made
for an individual named the Abbé Busoni, who had stopped at
the inn of the Pont du Gard on the morning previous to the
murder. If Caderousse had invented the story relative to the dia-

mond, and there existed no such person as the Abbé Busoni, then, indeed, I was lost past redemption. Two months passed away in hopeless expectation on my part, while I must do the magistrate the justice to say that he used every means to obtain information of the person who I declared could exculpate me if he would. Caderousse still evaded pursuit, and I had resigned myself to what seemed my inevitable fate. My trial was to come on at the approaching sessions; when, on the 8th of September, the Abbé Busoni, whom I never ventured to believe I should see, presented himself at the prison doors, saying he understood one of the prisoners wished to speak to him; he added, that having learned the particulars of my imprisonment, he hastened to comply with my desire. You may easily imagine with what eagerness I welcomed him, and how minutely I related the whole of what I had seen and heard. I felt some degree of nervousness as I entered upon the history of the diamond; but, to my inexpressible astonishment, he confirmed it in every particular, and, to my equal suprise, he seemed to place entire belief in all I stated. And then it was that I besought him to receive my confession, under the seal of which I recounted the affair of Auteuil, in all its details, as well as every other transaction of my life. My voluntary confession of the assassination at Auteuil proved to him that I had not committed that with which I stood accused. When he quitted me, he bade me be of good courage, and rely upon his doing all in his power to convince my judges of my innocence.

"I had speedy proofs that the excellent abbé was engaged in my behalf, for the rigours of my imprisonment were alleviated by many trifling though acceptable indulgences; and I was told that my trial was to be postponed to the assizes following those then being held. In the interim it pleased Providence to cause the apprehension of Caderousse, who was discovered in some distant country, and brought back to France, where he made a full confession, refusing to make the fact of his wife's having suggested and arranged the murder any excuse for his own guilt. The wretched man was sentenced to the galleys for life, and I was immediately set at liberty."

"And then it was, I presume," said Monte Cristo, "that you came to me as the bearer of a letter from the Abbé Busoni?"

"It was, your Excellency; the benevolent abbé took an interest in all that concerned me."

"'Your mode of life as a smuggler,' said he to me one day, 'will be the ruin of you if you persist in it.'

M

" ' But how,' inquired I, ' am I to maintain myself and my poor sister ? '

" ' A person, whose confessor I am,' replied he, ' applied to me a short time since to procure him a confidential servant. Would you like such a post ? If so, I will give you a letter of introduction to the friend I allude to. Here, take this,' continued he, after rapidly writing the few lines I brought to your Excellency, and upon receipt of which you deigned to receive me into your service, and I venture most respectfully, and humbly, to ask whether your Excellency has ever had cause to repent having done so ? ' "

" On the contrary, Bertuccio, I have ever found you faithful, honest, and deserving. One fault I find with you, and that is your not having placed sufficient confidence in me. How comes it, that having both a sister and an adopted son, you have never spoken to me of either ? "

" Alas ! I have still to recount the most distressing period of my life. When I arrived at Rogliano I found a house of mourning and of desolation, the consequences of a scene so horrible that the neighbours remember and speak of it to this day. Acting by my advice, my poor sister had refused to comply with the unreasonable demands of Benedetto, who was continually tormenting her for money, as long as he believed there was a sou left in her possession. One morning, after he had demanded money, threatening her with the severest consequences if she did not supply him with what he desired, he disappeared throughout the whole of the day. As the eleventh hour struck, he entered with two of the most dissolute and reckless of his ordinary companions. As poor Assiunta rose to clasp her truant in her arms, forgetting all but the happiness of seeing him again, she was seized by the three ruffians, while the unnatural Benedetto exclaimed—' Come, if the old girl refuses to tell us where she keeps her money, let us just give her a taste of the torture ; that will make her find her tongue, I'll engage.'

" It unfortunately happened that our neighbour, Wasilio, was at Bastia, leaving no person in his house but his wife ; no other human creature could hear or see anything that took place within our dwelling. Two of the brutal companions of Benedetto held poor Assiunta, who, unable to conceive that any harm was intended to her, smiled innocently and kindly in the faces of those who were soon to become her executioners, while the third ruffian proceeded to barricade the doors and windows, then returning to his infamous accomplices, the three united in stifling the cries uttered by the poor victim at the sight of these alarming preparations. This effected, they dragged the unoffending object of their barbarity towards the fire, on which they forcibly held her feet, expecting by this diabolical expedient to wring from her where her supposed treasure was secreted ; in the struggles made by my poor sister, her clothes caught fire, and her fiendish and cowardly tormentors were compelled to let go their hold in order to preserve themselves from sharing the same fate. Covered with flames, Assiunta rushed wildly to the door, but it was fastened ; tortured by the agony she endured, the unfortunate sufferer flew to the windows, but they were also strongly barricaded ; then her cries and shrieks of anguish filled the place, to these succeeded convulsive sobs, and deep groans, which, subsiding in faint moans, at length died away, and all was still as the grave. Next morning, as soon as the wife of Wasilio could muster up courage to venture abroad, she caused the door of our dwelling to be opened by the public authorities, when Assiunta, although dreadfully burnt, was found still breathing ; every drawer and closet in the house had been forced open, and everything worth carrying off stolen. Benedetto never again appeared at Rogliano, neither have I since that day either seen or heard anything concerning him.

" It was subsequently to these dreadful events that I waited on your Excellency, to whom it would have been folly to have mentioned Benedetto, since all trace of him seemed entirely lost, or of my sister, since she was dead.

" And now," resumed Bertuccio, " your Excellency may, perhaps, be able to comprehend that this place, which I revisit for the first time—this garden, the positive scene of my crime—must have given rise to reflections of no very agreeable nature."

" It may be so," said Monte Cristo, rising from the bench on which he had been sitting ; " but," added he, in a lower tone, " whether the *procureur du roi* be dead or not, the Abbé Busoni did right to send you to me, and you have also acted extremely properly in relating to me the whole of your history. As for that Benedetto, who so grossly belied his name, have you never made any effort to trace out whither he has gone, or what has become of him ? "

" No ; far from wishing to learn whither he had betaken himself, I should have shunned the possibility of meeting him, as I would a wild beast or a savage monster.

" Flatter not yourself that such is the case," replied the count ; " an All-wise Providence permits not sinners to escape thus easily from the punishment they have merited on earth, but reserves them to aid His own designs, using them as instruments whereby to work His vengeance on the guilty."

"I am content to have him live," continued Bertuccio, "so long as he spares me the misery of ever again beholding him. And now, M. le Comte," added the steward, bending humbly forward, "you know every secret of my life—you are my judge on earth, as the Almighty is in heaven; have you no words of consolation to bestow on a repentant sinner?"

"My good friend, I know of none more calculated to calm your mind than the expressions employed by the Abbé Busoni when speaking of you to me; Villefort, the man you killed, merited the punishment he received at your hands, as a just reward for the wrongs he had done you, and it may be for other crimes likewise. Benedetto, if still living, will become the instrument of Divine retribution in some way or other, and then be duly punished in his turn. As far as you yourself are concerned, I see but one point in which you are really guilty. Ask yourself, wherefore, after rescuing the infant from its living grave, you did not restore it to his mother? There was the crime, Bertuccio! That was where you became really culpable."

"True, my lord! there, as you say, I acted wickedly, and, moreover, cowardly. My first duty directly I had succeeded in recalling the babe to life should have been to restore it to its mother; but in order to do so, I must have made close and careful inquiry, which would, in all probability, have led to my own apprehension; and I clung to life, partly on my sister's account, and partly from that feeling of pride inborn in our hearts of desiring to come off untouched and victorious in the execution of our vengeance. Perhaps, too, the natural and instinctive love of life made me wish to avoid endangering my own. And then again, I was not formed as brave and courageous as my poor brother." Bertuccio hid his face in his hands as he uttered these words, while Monte Cristo fixed on him a long and indescribable gaze. After a brief silence, rendered still more solemn by the time and place, the count said, in a tone of melancholy wholly unlike his usual manner—"In order to bring this conversation to a befitting termination (as I promise you never again to revert to it), I will repeat to you some words which I have heard from the lips of the Abbé Busoni himself, and which I recommend you to treasure up for your consolation—'Every earthly ill yields to two all-potent remedies, time and silence.' And now leave me. I would enjoy the cool solitude of this place.

Here, I am agreeably surprised by the sight of a garden laid out in such a way as to afford the fullest scope for the imagination, and furnished with thickly-grown trees, beneath which leafy screen a visionary like myself may conjure up phantoms at will, and revel in the dreamy reveries of his own mind. Retire, Bertuccio, and tranquillize your mind; should your confessor be less indulgent to you in your dying moments than you found the Abbé Busoni, send for me, if I am still on earth, and I will soothe your ear with words that shall effectually calm your parting soul ere it goes forth to that ' bourne from whence no traveller returns.' "

Bertuccio bowed respectfully and turned away, sighing heavily as he quitted his patron.

When he had disappeared, Monte Cristo arose, and taking three or four steps onwards, he murmured—" Here, beneath this plane-tree, the infant's grave must have been dug. There is the little door opening into the garden. At this corner is the private staircase communicating with the sleeping-apartment. There will be no necessity for me to make a note of these particulars." After making the tour of the garden a second time, the count regained the house, and re-entered his carriage; while Bertuccio, who perceived the thoughtful expression of his master's features, took his seat beside the driver without uttering a word. The carriage proceeded rapidly towards Paris.

That same evening, upon reaching his abode in the Champs Élysées, the count of Monte Cristo went over the whole building with the air of one long acquainted with each nook and corner. Ali was his principal attendant during the somewhat late hour of his survey. Having given various orders to Bertuccio about the improvements and alterations he desired to make in the house, the count, drawing out his watch, said to the Nubian— " It is half-past eleven o'clock; it will not be long ere Haidée arrives; have the French attendants been summoned to await her coming ? "

Ali extended his hands towards the apartments destined for the fair Greek, which were at a distance from the habitable part of the dwelling, and so effectually concealed by means of a tapaltried entrance, that it would have puzzled the most curious to divine that beyond that spot lay hid a suite of rooms, fitted up with a magnificence worthy of the lovely being who was to tenant them. Ali, having pointed to the apartments, counted three on the fingers of his right hand, and then, placing it beneath his head, shut his eyes, and feigned to sleep.

" I understand," said Monte Cristo, well acquainted with Ali's pantomime ; " you mean to tell me that three female attendants await their new mistress in her sleeping-chamber."

" The young lady must needs be fatigued with her journey," continued Monte Cristo, " and will, no doubt, wish to retire to rest immediately upon her arrival. Desire the French attendants not to weary her with questions, but merely pay their respectful duty and retire. You will also see that the Greek servants hold no communication with these of this country."

At that moment voices were heard hailing the concierge. The count hastily descended, and presented himself at the already opened carriage-door to assist a young woman to alight. She raised the hand extended towards her to her lips, and kissed it with a mixture of love and respect. Some few words passed between them in that sonorous language in which Homer makes his gods converse. The woman spoke with an expression of deep tenderness, while the count replied with gentle gravity.

Preceded by Ali, who carried a rose-coloured flambeau in his hand, the lovely Greek, who had been Monte Cristo's companion in Italy, was conducted to her apartments, while the count retired to the pavilion reserved for himself. In another hour every light in the house was extinguished, and it might have been thought that all its inmates slept.

CHAPTER XLVI

UNLIMITED CREDIT

ABOUT two o'clock on the following day, a calèche, drawn by a pair of magnificent English horses, stopped at the door of the Count of Monte Cristo's house, and a person dressed in a blue coat, with buttons of a similar colour, a white wastcoat, over which was displayed a massive gold chain, brown trousers, and a quantity of black hair, a person, in a word, who, although evidently past fifty, desired to be taken for not more than forty, bent forwards from the carriage-door, on the panels of which were emblazoned the armorial bearings of a baron, and directed his groom to inquire at the porter's lodge whether the count of Monte Cristo resided there, and if he were within. The glance of this person was keen, but evincing rather cunning than intelligence ; his lips were straight, and so thin that, as they closed, they were compressed within the mouth ; his cheekbones were broad and projecting, while the flatness of his forehead, and the enlargement of the back of his skull, combined to form a physiognomy anything but prepossessing.

The groom, in obedience to his orders, tapped at the window of the porter's lodge, saying, " Pray, does not the count of Monte Cristo live here ? "

" His Excellency does reside here," replied the concierge, " but does not receive visitors to-day."

" Then take my master's card to the count, and say that, although in haste to attend the Chamber, he has come out of his way to have the honour of calling upon him."

" I never speak to his Excellency," replied the concierge ; " the valet will carry your message."

The groom returned to the carriage.

" Bless me ! " murmured M. le Baron Danglars ; " this must surely be a prince instead of a count by their styling him ' Excellency,' and only venturing to address him by the medium of his valet. However, it does not signify ; he has a letter of credit on me, so I must see him when he requires his money."

Then, throwing himself back in his carriage, Danglars called out to his coachman, in a voice that might be heard across the road, " To the Chambre des Députés."

Apprised in time of the visit paid him, Monte Cristo had, from behind the blinds of his pavilion, as minutely observed the baron by means of an excellent *lorgnette* as Danglars himself had scrutinized the house, garden, and servants.

" That fellow has a decidedly bad countenance," said the count, in a tone of disgust, as he shut up his glass into its ivory case. " How comes it that all do not retreat in aversion from that flat, receding, serpent-like forehead, round, vulture-shaped head, and sharp-hooked nose, like the beak of a buzzard ? Ali ! " cried he, " summon Bertuccio."

Almost immediately Bertuccio entered the apartment.

" Did your Excellency desire to see me ? "

" I did," replied the count. " You no doubt observed the horses standing a few minutes since at the door ? "

" Certainly, your Excellency : I noticed them for their remarkable beauty."

" Then how comes it," said Monte Cristo, with a frown, " that, when I desired you to purchase for me the finest pair of horses to be found in Paris, you permitted so splendid a couple to be in the possession of anyone but myself ? "

At the look of displeasure added to the angry tone in which the count spoke, Ali turned pale and hung down his head.

" It is not your fault, my good Ali," said the count in the Arabic language, " it is not your fault. You do not profess to understand the choice of English horses."

" Permit me to assure your Excellency," said Bertuccio, " that the horses you speak of were not to be sold when I purchased yours. M. le Comte is not, perhaps, aware that M. Danglars gave 16,000 francs for his horses ? "

" Very well ! then offer him double that sum ; a banker never loses an opportunity of doubling his capital."

" Is your Excellency really in earnest ? "

" I have to pay a visit this evening," replied he. " I desire that these horses, with completely new harness, may be at the door with my carriage."

Bertuccio bowed. " At what o'clock does your Excellency wish the carriage and horses ready ? "

" At five o'clock," replied the count.

Then turning towards Ali, he said, " Let all the horses in my stables be led before the windows of your young lady, that she may select those she prefers for her carriage. Request her also to oblige me by saying whether it is her pleasure to dine with me. Now leave me, and bid my valet come."

Scarcely had Ali disappeared when the valet entered the chamber.

" M. Baptistin," said the count, " you have been in my service one year, the time I generally give myself to judge of the merits or demerits of those about me. You suit me very well," Baptistin bowed low. " It only remains for me to know whether I also suit you ? "

" Oh, M. le Comte ! " exclaimed Baptistin, eagerly.

" Listen, if you please, till I have finished speaking," replied Monte Cristo. " You receive 1,500 francs per annum for your services. You live in a manner far superior to many clerks and placemen who work ten times harder than you do for their money, and are quite as faithful in the discharge of their duties as you may be. You make a profit also upon each article you purchase for my toilette, amounting in course of the year to a sum equalling your wages."

" Nay, indeed, your Excellency ! "

" Do not interrupt me, M. Baptistin. You know as well as myself, that were I to dismiss you it would be long ere you found so lucrative a post as that you have now the good fortune to fill. I neither ill-use nor ill-treat my servants by word or action. An error I readily forgive, but wilful negligence or forgetfulness of my orders I never look over. I am rich enough to become acquainted with whatever I desire to know, and I can promise you I am not wanting in curiosity. If, then, I should learn that you have taken upon yourself to speak of me to anyone favourably or unfavourably, to comment on my actions, or watch my conduct, that very instant you would quit my service. You may now retire. You have been duly admonished, and if the warning is given in vain you will have nobody to blame but yourself." Baptistin bowed, and was proceeding towards the door when the count bade him stay. " I forgot to mention to you," said he, ' I lay yearly aside a certain sum for each servant in my establishment; those whom I am compelled to dismiss lose (as a matter of course) all participation in this money, while their portion goes to the fund accumulating for those who remain with me, and among whom it will be divided at my death. You have been in my service a year and your fortune has begun ; do not prevent its growth by your own folly."

" I assure your Excellency," said Baptistin, " at least it shall be my study to merit your approbation in all things, and I will take M. Ali as my model."

" Pray do no such thing," replied the count, in the most frigid tone ; " Ali has many faults mixed with most excellent qualities ; he cannot serve you as a pattern for your conduct, not being as you are a paid servant, but a mere slave—a dog ! who, should he fail in his duty towards me, I should not discharge from my service, but kill ! "

Baptistin opened his eyes with unfeigned astonishment.

" You seem incredulous," said Monte Cristo, who repeated to Ali in Arabic what he had been saying to Baptistin in French. The Nubian smiled assentingly to his master's words, then, kneeling on one knee, respectfully kissed the hand of the count. This corroboration of the lesson he had just received put the finishing stroke to the wonder and stupefaction of M. Baptistin. The count then motioned the valet to retire, and to Ali to follow him into his study, where they conversed long and earnestly together. As the hand of the clock pointed to five o'clock, the count struck thrice upon his gong. The steward entered.

" My horses ! " said Monte Cristo.

" They are at the door harnessed to the carriage as your Excellency desired. Does M. le Comte wish me to accompany him ? "

" No, Ali and Baptistin will be sufficient." The count descended to the door of his mansion, and beheld his carriage drawn by the very pair of horses he had so much admired in the morning as the property of Danglars.

" Whither does M. le Comte desire to be driven ? "

" To the residence of M. le Baron Danglars, Rue de la Chaussée d'Antin." As Bertuccio was moving away, the count called him back. " I have another commission for you, M. Bertuccio," said he ; " I am desirous of having an estate by the sea in Normandy, for instance between Havre and Boulogne. It is absolutely necessary that the place you may select should have a small harbour or bay, in which my vessel can remain at anchor. She must be kept in constant readiness to sail immediately I think proper to give the signal. Make the requisite inquiries for a place of this description, and when you have heard of an eligible spot, visit it, and if it possess the advantages desired, purchase it at once in your own name. The corvette must now, I think, be on her way to Fécamp, must she not ? "

" Certainly, your Excellency ; I saw her put to sea the evening we quitted Marseilles."

" And the yacht ? "

" Was ordered to remain at Martigues."

" 'Tis well ! I wish you to write from time to time to the captains in charge of the two vessels so as to keep them on the alert."

" And the steamboat ? "

" The directions I gave you for the other two vessels may suffice for the steamboat also."

" I understand, my lord."

" When you have purchased the estate, I mean to establish constant relays of horses at ten leagues' distance one from the other along the northern and southern road."

" Your Excellency may fully depend upon my zeal and fidelity in all things." The count gave an approving smile, descended the terrace steps, and sprang into his carriage, which was whirled along with incredible swiftness, and stopped only before the hôtel of the banker. Danglars was at that moment presiding over a railway committee. But the meeting was nearly concluded when the name of his visitor was announced. As the count's title sounded on his ear he rose, and addressing his colleagues, many of whom were members of either Chamber, he said—

" Gentlemen, I must pray you to excuse my quitting you thus ; but a most ridiculous circumstance has occurred, which is this— Thomson and French, the bankers at Rome, have sent me a certain individual calling himself the count of Monte Cristo, who is desirous of opening an account with me to any amount he pleases. I confess this is the drollest thing I have ever met with in the course of my foreign transactions, and you may suppose it has roused my curiosity. I took the trouble this morning to call on the pretended count, for his title is a mere fiction—of that I am persuaded. But would you believe, upon arriving at the residence of the *soi-disant* count of Monte Cristo, I was very coolly informed, ' He did not receive visitors that day ! Upon my word, such airs are ridiculous, and befitting only some great millionaire or a capricious beauty. I made inquiries, and found that the house where the said count resides in the Champs Elysées is his own property. But," pursued Danglars, with one of his sinister smiles, " an order for unlimited credit calls for something like caution on the part of the banker on whom that order is given. I suspect a hoax, but the good folk who thought fit to play it off on me little knew whom they had to deal with. Well ! we shall see. ' They laugh best who laugh last ! ' "

Having delivered himself of this pompous address, he bowed to the assembled party, and withdrew to his drawing-room, whose sumptuous fittings-up of white and gold had caused an admiring sensation in the Chaussée d'Antin. The count turned round as he heard Danglars enter the room. With a slight inclination of the head Danglars signed to the count to be seated, pointing significantly to a gilded armchair, covered with white satin embroidered with gold. The count obeyed.

" I have the honour, I presume, of addressing M. de Monte Cristo ? "

The count bowed. " And I of speaking to Baron Danglars, Chevalier de la Légion d'Honneur, and Member of the Chamber of Deputies ? "

With an air of extreme gravity Monte Cristo slowly enumerated the various titles engraved on the card left by the baron.

Danglars felt all the irony contained in the address of his visitor. For a minute or two he compressed his lips as though seeking to conquer his rage ere he trusted himself to speak, then turning to his visitor he said—

" You will, I trust, excuse my not having called you by your title when I first addressed you, but you are aware we are living under a popular form of government, and that I am myself a representative of the liberties of the people."

" So much so," replied Monte Cristo, " that while preserving the habit of styling yourself baron you have deemed it advisable to lay aside that of calling others by their titles."

" Upon my word," said Danglars, with affected carelessness,

" I attach no sort of value to such empty distinctions ; but the fact is, I was made baron, and also Chevalier de la Légion d'Honneur, in consequence of some services I had rendered Government, but——"

" You have abdicated your titles after the example set you by Messrs. de Montmorency and Lafayette ? Well, you cannot possibly choose more noble models ! "

" Why," replied Danglars, " I do not mean to say I have altogether laid aside my titles ; with the servants for instance—I think it right to preserve my rank with all its outward forms."

" I see : to your domestics you are ' my lord ' ' M. le Baron ; ' the journalists of the day style you ' monsieur,' whilst your constituents term you ' citizen.' " Again Danglars bit his lips with baffled spite ; he saw well enough that he was no match for Monte Cristo in an argument of this sort, and hastened to turn to subjects more familiar to him, in which he calculated on having all the advantages on his side.

" Permit me to inform you, M. le Comte," said he, bowing, " that I have received a letter of advice from Thomson and French, of Rome."

" I am glad to hear it, M. le Baron, for I must claim the privilege of so addressing you as well as your servants. But as regards the letter of advice, I am charmed to find it has reached you ; that will spare me the troublesome and disagreeable task of coming to you for money myself. You have received a regular letter of advice, therefore my cheques will be duly honoured, and we shall neither of us have to go out of our way in the transaction."

" There is one slight difficulty, " said Danglars," and that consists in my not precisely comprehending the letter itself ! "

" Indeed ? "

" And for that reason I did myself the honour of calling upon you, in order to beg you would explain some part of it to me."

" With much pleasure ! Pray, now I am here, let me know what is was that baffled your powers of comprehension ? "

" Why," said Danglars, " this letter gives M. le comte de Monte Cristo unlimited credit on our house."

" And what is there that requires explaining in that simple fact, may I ask, M. le Baron ? "

" Merely the term *unlimited*—nothing else."

" Is not that word known in France ? Perhaps, indeed, it does not belong to the language ; for the persons from whom you received your letter of advice are a species of Anglo-Germans, and very probably do not write very choice or accurate French."

"Oh, as for the composition of the letter, there is not the smallest error in it ; but as regards the competency of the document, I certainly have doubts."

"Is it possible ? " asked the count, assuming an air and tone of the utmost simplicity and candour. "Is it possible that Thomson and French are not looked upon as solvent bankers ? Pray tell me what you think, M. le Baron, for I feel uneasy, I can assure you, having considerable property in their hands."

"Thomson and French are bankers of the highest repute," replied Danglars with an almost mocking smile ; " and it was not of their solvency I spoke, but of the word *unlimited*, which, in financial affairs, is so extremely vague a term—that—that——"

"In fact," said Monte Cristo, " that its sense is also without limitations."

"Precisely what I was about to say," cried Danglars. " Now what is vague is doubtful ; and, says the wise man, ' where there is doubt there is danger ! ' "

"Meaning to say," rejoined Monte Cristo, " that however Thomson and French may be inclined to commit acts of imprudence and folly, M. le Baron Danglars is not disposed to follow their example."

"How so, M. le Comte ? "

"Simply thus : the banking house of Thomson and Co. set no bounds to their engagements, while that of M. Danglars has its limits ; truly he is wise as the sage whose prudent apophthegm he quoted just now."

"Monsieur ! " replied the banker, drawing himself up with a haughty air, " the amount of my capital, or the extent and solvency of my engagements have never yet been questioned."

"It seems, then, reserved for me," said Monte Cristo, coldly, " to be the first to do so."

"By what right, sir ? "

"By right of the objections you have raised, which certainly imply considerable distrust on your part either of yourself or me —the former most probably." Again did Danglars, by a forcible effort, restrain himself from betraying the vindictive passions which possessed his mind at this second defeat by an adversary who calmly fought him with his own weapons.

"Well, sir," resumed Danglars, after a brief silence, " I will endeavour to make myself understood, by requesting you to inform me for what sum you propose to draw upon me ? "

"Why, truly," replied Monte Cristo, determined not to lose an inch of the ground he had gained, " my reason for desiring an 'unlimited' credit was precisely because I did not know what money I might expend."

The banker now thought it his turn to show off, and make a display of wealth and consequence. Flinging himself back therefore in his armchair, he said, with an arrogant and purse-proud air :—" Let me beg of you not to hesitate in naming your wishes ; you will then be convinced that the resources of the house of Danglars, however limited, are still equal to meeting the largest demands ; and were you even to require a million francs——"

" I beg your pardon ! " interposed Monte Cristo.

" I observed," replied Danglars, with a patronizing and pompous air, " that should you be hard pressed, the concern of which I am the head would not scruple to accommodate you to the amount of a million."

" A million ! " retorted the count ; " and what use can you suppose so pitiful a sum would be to me ? Excuse my smiling when you speak of a sum I am in the habit of carrying in my pocket-book or dressing-case." And with these words Monte Cristo took from his pocket a small case containing his visiting-cards, and drew forth two orders on the Treasury for 500,000 francs each, payable at sight to the bearer. A man like Danglars was only assailable by blows dealt with the force and vigour of the present *coup ;* its effect on the banker was perfectly stunning ; and, as though scarcely venturing to credit his senses, he continued gazing from the paper to the count with a mystified air.

" Come, come," said Monte Cristo, " confess honestly that you have not perfect confidence in the responsibility of the house of Thomson and French. See, here are two similar letters to that you have yourself received ; the one from the house of Arstein and Eskeles, of Vienna, to Baron de Rothschild ; the other drawn from Baring, of London, to M. Laffitte. Now, sir, you have but to say the word, and I will spare you all uneasiness and alarm on the subject, by presenting my letter of credit at one or other of the establishments I have named." The blow had struck home, and Danglars was entirely vanquished ; with a trembling hand he took the two letters from Vienna and London from the count, who held them carelessly between his finger and thumb, as though to him they were mere everyday matters to which he attached very little importance. Having carefully perused the documents in question, the banker proceeded to ascertain the genuineness of the signatures, and this he did with a scrutiny so severe as might have appeared insulting to the count, had it not suited his present purpose to mislead the banker in every respect.

"Well, sir," said Danglars, rising after he had convinced himself of the authenticity of the documents he held, "you have there signatures worth untold wealth; although your conversation and vouchers put an end to all mistrust in the affair, you must pardon me, M. le Comte, for confessing the most extreme astonishment."

"Nay, nay," answered Monte Cristo, with the easiest and most gentlemanly air imaginable, "'tis not for such trifling sums as these to startle or astonish the banking-house of M. le Baron Danglars. Then, as all is settled as to forms between us, I will thank you to send a supply of money to me to-morrow."

"By all means, M. le Comte; what sum do you want?"

"Why," replied Monte Cristo, "since we have come to so clear an understanding, we may as well fix a sum as the probable expenditure of the first year:—suppose we say six millions to——"

"Six millions!" gasped out Danglars, "certainly, whatever you please."

"Then if I should require more," continued Monte Cristo, in a careless, indifferent manner, "why, of course, I should draw upon you; but my present intention is not to remain in France more than a year, and during that period I scarcely think I shall exceed the sum I mentioned. However, we shall see."

"The money you desire shall be at your house by ten o'clock to-morrow morning, M. le Comte," replied Danglars. "How would you like it—in gold, silver, or notes?"

"Half in gold, and the other half in bank notes, if you please," said the count, rising from his seat.

"I must confess to you, M. le Comte," said Danglars, "that I have hitherto imagined myself acquainted with the degree of fortune possessed by all the rich persons of Europe, but wealth such as yours has been wholly unknown to me. May I presume to ask whether you have long possessed it?"

"It has been in the family a very long while," returned Monte Cristo, "a sort of treasure expressly forbidden to be touched for a certain period of years, and only employed by me within the last few years. Your ignorance on the subject, therefore, is easily accounted for. However, you will be better informed as to me and my possessions ere long." And the count, while pronouncing these latter words, accompanied them with one of those ghastly smiles that used to strike terror into Franz d'Epinay.

"With your tastes, and means of gratifying them," continued

Danglars, " you will exhibit a splendour that must put us poor miserable millionaires quite in the background. If I mistake not, you are an admirer of paintings. If you will permit me, I shall be happy to show you my picture-gallery, composed entirely of works by the ancient masters—warranted as such. Not a modern picture among them. I cannot endure the modern school of painting."

" You are perfectly right in objecting to them, for this one great fault—that they have not yet had time to become old."

" But perhaps you will prefer putting off your inspection of my poor pictures, until another opportunity, when we shall be better known to each other. For the present I will confine myself (if perfectly agreeable to you) to introducing you to Madame la Baronne Danglars,—excuse my impatience, M. le Comte, but a person of your wealth and influence cannot receive too much attention." Monte Cristo bowed, in sign that he accepted the proffered honour, and the financier immediately rang a small bell, which was answered by a servant in a showy livery. " Is Madame la Baronne at home ? " inquired Danglars.

" Yes, M. le Baron," answered the man.

" And alone ? "

" No, M. le Baron, madame has visitors."

" Have you any objection to meet any persons who may be with madame, or do you desire to preserve a strict incognito ? "

" No, indeed," replied Monte Cristo, with a smile. " I do not arrogate to myself the right of so doing."

" And who is with madame ?—M. Debray ? " inquired Danglars.

" Yes, M. le Baron," Danglars nodded his head ; then, turning to Monte Cristo, said, " M. Lucien Debray is an old friend of ours, and private secretary to the Ministre de l'Intérieur. As for my wife, she belongs to one of the most ancient families in France. Her maiden name was De Servières, and her first husband was M. le Colonel Marquis de Nargonne."

" I have not the honour of knowing Madame Danglars ; but I have already met M. Lucien Debray."

" Ah ! indeed ! " said Danglars ; " and where was that ? "

" At the house of M. de Morcerf."

" Madame la Baronne is waiting to receive you, gentlemen," said the servant, who had gone to inquire the pleasure of his mistress.

" With your permission," said Danglars, bowing, " I will show you the way."

" By all means," replied Monte Cristo ; " I follow you."

CHAPTER XLVII

THE DAPPLED GREYS

THE baron traversed a long suite of apartments, in which the prevailing characteristics were heavy magnificence and the gaudiness of ostentatious wealth, until he reached the boudoir of Madame Danglars—a small octagonal-shaped room, hung with pink satin, covered with white Indian muslin ; the chairs were of ancient workmanship and materials : over the doors were painted sketches of shepherds and shepherdesses, after the style and manner of Boucher ; and at each side pretty medallions in crayons harmonizing well with the fittings-up of this charming apartment, the only one throughout the vast hôtel in which any distinctive taste prevailed. The decoration of Madame Danglars' boudoir had been left entirely to herself and Lucien Debray. M. Danglars, however, entertained the most sovereign contempt for the simple elegance of his wife's favourite sitting-room.

As Danglars now entered he found Madame la Baronne seated at the piano, a most elaborate piece of cabinet and inlaid work, while Lucien Debray, standing before a small work-table, was turning over the pages of an album. Lucien had found time to relate many particulars respecting the Count to Madame Danglars. Monte Cristo had made a lively impression on the minds of the party at the breakfast given by Albert de Morcerf ; and although Debray was not in the habit of yielding to such feelings, he had never been able to shake off the influence of the impressive look and manner of the Count.

" Baroness," said Danglars, " give me leave to present to you the count of Monte Cristo, who has been most warmly recommended to me by my correspondents at Rome. I need but mention one fact to make all the ladies in Paris court his notice, and that is, that the noble individual before you has come to take up his abode in our capital for one year, during which brief period he proposes to spend six millions of money—think of that ! "

In spite of the vulgarity of this address, Madame Danglars could not forbear gazing with interest on a man who had selected Paris for the scene of his princely extravagance. " And when did you arrive here ? " inquired she.

" Yesterday morning, madame."

" You have selected a most unfavourable moment for your first visit to our city. Paris is a horrible place in summer ! The only amusement left us are the indifferent races held in the Champ de Mars and Satory. Are you fond of horses, Monsieur le Comte ? "

" I have passed a considerable part of my life in the East, madame, where they value two things—the fine breeding of their horses and the beauty of their women."

" Nay, M. le Comte," said the baroness, " it would have been somewhat more gallant to have placed the ladies before the animals."

" Ah ! madame, I require a preceptor to guide me in all my sayings and doings here."

At this instant the favourite attendant of Madame Danglars entered the boudoir ; approaching her mistress, she spoke some words in an undertone.

Turning impatiently towards her husband, Madame Danglars demanded,—" Is this true ? "

" Is what true, madam ? " inquired Danglars, visibly agitated.

" That when my coachman was about to prepare my carriage he discovered that the horses had been removed from the stables without his knowledge. I desire to know the meaning of this."

" Be kind enough, madame, to listen to me," said Danglars.

" Fear not my listening,—ay, and attentively too. These two gentlemen shall decide between us ; but, first, I will state the case to them. Gentlemen," continued the baroness, " among the horses in the stables of M. le Baron Danglars are two that belong exclusively to me—a pair of the handsomest and most spirited creatures to be found in Paris. Well ! I had promised Madame de Villefort the loan of my carriage to drive to-morrow to the Bois de Boulogne ; but when my coachman goes to fetch the greys from the stables they are gone. No doubt M. Danglars has sacrificed them to the selfish consideration of gaining some thousands of paltry francs."

" Madame," replied Danglars, " the horses were not sufficiently quiet for you ; they were scarcely four years old, and they made me extremely uneasy on your account."

The baroness shrugged her shoulders with an air of ineffable contempt, while her husband, affecting not to observe it, turned towards Monte Cristo, and said,—" Upon my word, M. le Comte, I am sorry I was not sooner aware of your establishing yourself in Paris, because I should have liked to offer you these horses. I have almost given them away, as it is ; but I was anxious to get quit of them upon any terms. They were only fit for a young man ; not suited for a person at my time of life."

" I am much obliged by your kind intentions towards me," said

Monte Cristo; " but this morning I purchased a very excellent pair of carriage-horses. There they are. Come, M. Debray, you are a connoisseur I believe, let me have your opinion."

As Debray walked towards the window, Danglars approached his wife. " I could not tell you before others," said he, in a low tone, " the reason of my parting with the horses; the fact is, I have gained 16,000 francs by the sale of them. Come, don't look so angry, and you shall have 4,000 francs of the money to do what you like with, and Eugénie shall have 2,000. Wasn't I right to part with the horses ? "

" What do I see ? " suddenly exclaimed Debray. " I cannot be mistaken; there are your horses ! The very animals we were speaking of harnessed to the count's carriage ! "

" My dear, beautiful dappled greys ? " demanded the baroness, springing to the window. " 'Tis indeed they," said she.

" How very singular ! " cried Monte Cristo, with well-feigned astonishment.

Madame Danglars whispered a few words in the ear of Debray, who approached Monte Cristo, saying, " The baroness wishes to know what you paid her husband for the horses."

" I scarcely know," replied the count; " it was a little surprise prepared for me by my steward; he knew how desirous I was of acquiring precisely such a pair of horses,—and—so he bought them. I think, if I remember rightly, he hinted that he had given about 30,000 francs."

Debray conveyed the count's reply to the baroness.

Danglars looked so crestfallen that Monte Cristo assumed a pitying air towards him.

" See," said the count, " how very ungrateful women are ! Your kind attention in providing for the safety of the baroness by disposing of the horses does not seem to have made the least impression on her."

Danglars made no reply; he was occupied in anticipation of the coming scene between himself and the baroness. Debray, feeling no desire to witness the explosion of Madame Danglars' rage, suddenly recollected an appointment that compelled him to take his leave; while Monte Cristo, unwilling by prolonging his stay to destroy the advantages he hoped to obtain, made a farewell bow and departed, leaving Danglars to endure the angry reproaches of his wife.

" Excellent ! " murmured Monte Cristo to himself, as he retraced the way to his carriage. " All has gone according to my wishes. Now, then, to gain the heart of both husband and wife—

delightful ! Still," added he, " amid all this, I have not yet been presented to Mademoiselle Eugénie Danglars, whose acquaintance I should have been glad to make."

The count's meditations were interrupted by his arrival at his own abode. Two hours afterwards Madame Danglars received a most flattering epistle from the count, in which he entreated her to accept her " dappled greys," protesting that he could not endure the idea of making his *début* in the Parisian world of fashion with the knowledge that his splendid equipage had been obtained at the price of a lovely woman's regrets. The horses were sent back wearing the same harness they had done in the morning ; the only difference consisted in the rosettes on the animals' heads being adorned with a large diamond in the centre of each.

To Danglars, Monte Cristo also wrote, requesting him to excuse the whimsical gift of a capricious millionaire, and to beg of Madame la Baronne to pardon the Eastern fashion adopted in the return of the horses.

During the evening Monte Cristo quitted Paris for Auteuil. Next day, about three o'clock, a single blow on the gong summoned Ali to the presence of the count.

" Ali," observed his master, " you have frequently explained to me how skilful you are in throwing the lasso ? "

Ali drew himself up proudly and made a sign in the affirmative.

" But could you arrest the progress of two horses rushing forward with ungovernable fury ? "

The Nubian smiled.

" It is well," said Monte Cristo ; " then listen to me. Ere long a carriage will dash past here, drawn by the pair of dappled grey horses you saw me with yesterday ; now at the risk of your own life you must manage to stop those horses before my door."

Ali descended to the street, and marked a straight line on the pavement at the entrance of the house, and then pointed out the line to the count, who was watching him. The count patted him gently on the back—his usual mode of praising Ali—who walked calmly towards a projecting stone forming the angle of the street and house, and seating himself thereon, began to smoke his chibouque, while Monte Cristo re-entered his dwelling, assured of the success of his plan. He stationed himself in a room commanding a view of the street, pacing the chamber with restless steps, stopping merely to listen from time to time for the sound of approaching wheels, then to cast an anxious glance on Ali. Suddenly a distant sound of rapidly-advancing wheels was heard, and almost immediately a carriage appeared, drawn by a pair of wild ungovernable horses, who rushed forward as though urged by the fiend himself, while the terrified coachman strove in vain to restrain their furious speed.

In the vehicle was a woman, apparently young, and a child of about seven or eight years of age. The carriage creaked and rattled as it flew over the rough stones ; and had it encountered the slightest impediment to its progress it must inevitably have upset.

Ali knew the right moment had come ; he threw the lasso so skilfully as to catch the forelegs of the near horse in its triple fold, suffered himself to be dragged for a few yards, by which time the tightening of the lasso had so hampered the furious animal as to bring it to the ground ; the horse falling on the pole, snapped it, and prevented the other animal from pursuing its headlong career. Gladly availing himself of this opportunity, the coachman leaped from his box ; but Ali had seized the nostrils of the second horse, and held them in his iron grasp, till the maddened beast, snorting with pain, sunk beside his companion. The count rushed from the house, and opened the door of the carriage, from which he led a lady who was convulsively grasping the cushions with one hand, while with the other she pressed to her bosom her young companion, who had lost all consciousness of what was passing.

Monte Cristo carried them both to the salon, and deposited them on a sofa. "Compose yourself, madame," said he ; "all danger is over. I understand the nature of your alarms, but I assure you there is no occasion for uneasiness ; your little charge has not received the least injury,—his insensibility is merely the effect of terror, and will soon cease."

"Are you quite sure you do not say so to tranquillise my fears ? See how deadly pale he is ! My child ! my darling Edward ! speak to your mother ; open your dear eyes and look on me once again ! Oh, sir, in pity send for help ! my whole fortune shall not be thought too much for the recovery of my blessed boy."

With a calm smile and gentle wave of the hand, Monte Cristo drew forth from a casket that stood near a phial composed of Bohemian glass, containing a liquid of the colour of blood, of which he let fall a single drop on the child's lips. Scarcely had it reached them, ere the boy opened his eyes, and eagerly gazed around him At this unhoped-for sight the wild delight of the mother equalled her former despair. "Where am I ?" exclaimed she, when her first raptures at her son's recovery were past.

"Madame," answered the count, "you are under the roof of

one who deems himself fortunate in having been able to save you from a continuance of sufferings."

"My wretched curiosity has brought all this about," pursued the lady. "All Paris rang with the praises of Madame Danglars' beautiful horses, and I had the folly to desire to know whether they merited the high character given of them."

"Is it possible that these horses belong to Madame la Baronne?"

"They do, indeed. May I inquire if you are acquainted with Madame Danglars?"

"I have that honour; and I have been the unwilling and unintentional cause of all the peril you have incurred. I yesterday purchased these horses of the Baron; but as the baroness regretted parting with them, I sent them back to her, with a request that she would gratify me by accepting them."

"You must be the count of Monte Cristo, of whom Hermine has told me so much?"

"You have guessed rightly, madam."

"I am Madame Héloïse de Villefort." The count bowed with the air of a person who hears a name for the first time. "How grateful will M. de Villefort be for all your goodness! But for the prompt assistance of your servant this dear child and myself must have perished. I trust you will not object to my offering a recompense to your noble-hearted servant, proportionate to the service he has rendered me and mine."

"I beseech you, madame," replied Monte Cristo, "not to spoil Ali, either by too great praise or rewards. He is my slave, and in saving your life he was but discharging his duty to me."

Madame de Villefort made no further reply; she was absorbed in contemplating the singular man, who had made so powerful an impression on her. Monte Cristo scrutinized the features and appearance of the boy on whom she lavished the most tender endearments. The child was small for his age, and unnaturally pale. His mouth was large, and the lips which had not yet regained their colour were particularly thin; in fact, the deep and crafty look, forming the principal character of the child's face, belonged rather to a boy of twelve or fourteen years of age, than to one so young. His first movement was to free himself by a violent push from the arms of his mother, and to pull the corks out of all the bottles in the casket out of which the count had taken the elixir of life.

"Touch nothing, my little friend," cried the count, eagerly; "some of those liquids are not only dangerous to taste, but even to smell."

Madame de Villefort became very pale, and drew her son anxiously towards her ; but when satisfied of his safety, she also cast an expressive glance at the casket, which was not lost upon the count. At this moment Ali entered. At sight of him Madame de Villefort uttered a cry of pleasure and holding the child still closer towards her, she said : " Edward, dearest ! do you see that good man ? Thank him, my child, in your every best manner ; for had he not come to our aid neither you nor I would have been alive to speak our thanks."

The child stuck out his lips and turned away his head disdainfully, saying—" I don't like him—he's too ugly for me ! "

The count witnessed all this with internal satisfaction, and a smile stole over his features as he thought that such a child bade fair to realize one part of his hopes ; while Madame de Villefort reprimanded her son with a gentleness very far from conveying the least hint of fault.

" This lady," said the count, speaking to Ali in the Arabic language, " is desirous that her son should thank you for saving both their lives ; but the boy refuses, saying ' You are too ugly ! ' "

Ali turned his intelligent countenance towards the boy, on whom he gazed without any apparent emotion ; but the sort of spasmodic working of the nostrils showed to the practised eye of Monte Cristo how deeply the Arab was wounded by the unfeeling remark.

" Will you permit me to inquire," said Madame de Villefort, as she rose to take her leave, " whether you usually reside here ? "

" No, I do not," replied Monte Cristo ; " it is a small place I have purchased quite lately. My place of abode is No. 30, Avenue des Champs Élysées. I am delighted to see you have recovered from your fright, and are desirous of returning home. Anticipating your wishes, I have desired the same horses you came with to be put to one of my carriages, and Ali will have the honour of driving you home, while your coachman remains here to attend to the repairs of your calèche. As soon as he is finished, I will have a couple of my own horses harnessed to convey it direct to Madame Danglars."

" I dare not return with those dreadful horses," said Madame de Villefort.

" You will see," replied Monte Cristo, " that they will be as different as possible in the hands of Ali. With him they will be meek as lambs."

After the animals had been got upon their legs (with considerable difficulty), Ali rubbed their foreheads and nostrils with a sponge soaked in aromatic vinegar, and quietly harnessed the pacified animals to the count's chariot. He then mounted the box, took the reins, and lo! was actually compelled to apply his whip in no very gentle manner ere he could induce them to start; and even then all that could be obtained from the celebrated dappled greys, was such a slow, pottering pace, that Madame de Villefort was more than a couple of hours returning to her residence in the Faubourg St. Honoré.

Scarcely had the first congratulations upon her miraculous escape been gone through when she retired to her room to write the following letter to Madame Danglars :—

"DEAR HERMINE,—I have just had a wonderful escape from the most imminent danger, and I owe my safety to the very count of Monte Cristo we were talking about yesterday, but whom I little expected to see to-day. But I must endeavour to render the account of my adventures intelligible. You must know, then, my dear friend, that when I had proceeded with your horses as far as Ranelagh, they darted forward like mad things, and galloped away at so fearful a rate that there seemed no other prospect for myself and my poor Edward but that of being dashed to pieces, when a strange-looking man, an Arab or a Nubian, at a signal from the count, whose domestic he is, suddenly stopped the infuriated animals, even at the risk of being trampled to death himself. The count then hastened to us, and carried myself and son into his house, where he recalled my poor Edward (who was quite insensible) to life. When we were sufficiently recovered he sent us home in his own carriage. Yours will be returned to you to-morrow. I am fearful you will not be able to use your horses for some days; they seem thoroughly stupefied, as if sulky at having allowed this black man to conquer them after all. Do not let them endanger your life, dear Hermine, as they did mine; for Providence may not send a Monte Cristo, or his Nubian servant to preserve you from destruction, as it did me. Adieu! I cannot return you many thanks for the drive of yesterday; but, after all, I ought not to blame you for the misconduct of your horses, more especially as it procured me the pleasure of an introduction to the count of Monte Cristo. Nay, so bent am I on following up my acquaintance with this remarkable personage, that if all other means fail, I really believe I shall have to borrow your horses again, and make another excursion to the Bois de Boulogne. Valentine sends many affectionate remembrances to your dear

Eugénie—and with best love to her and yourself, I remain, ever
yours truly,

"HÉLOÏSE DE VILLEFORT."

"P.S.—Do, pray, contrive some means for my meeting the
count of Monte Cristo at your house. I must and will see him
again. I have just made M. de Villefort promise to call on him,
and I flatter myself my husband's visit will be returned by the
count."

Nothing was talked of throughout the evening, but the adventure at Auteuil. Albert related it to his mother, Château-Renaud
recounted it at the Jockey Club, and Debray detailed it at length
in the salons of the minister ; even Beauchamp accorded twenty
lines in his journal to the narrative of the count's courage and
gallantry, thereby placing him as the greatest hero of the day before
the eyes of all the fair members of the aristocracy of France.
Vast was the crowd of visitors and inquiring friends who left their
names at the hôtel of Madame de Villefort, with the design of
hearing from her lips all the interesting circumstances of this most
romantic adventure, and, as Héloïse had stated, M. de Villefort
forthwith drove to the hôtel of the count in the Avenue des
Champs Elysées.

CHAPTER XLVIII

IDEOLOGY

IF the count of Monte Cristo had lived for a very long time in
Parisian society he would have fully appreciated the value of the
step which M. de Villefort had taken. Standing well at court,
M. de Villefort held a high position in the magistracy. His drawing-room was still one of those well-regulated Paris salons where
the worship of traditional customs and the observance of rigid
etiquette were carefully maintained. Ordinarily, M. de Villefort
made and returned very few visits. His wife visited for him, and
this was regarded as *comme il faut* in Society, which attributed
to his multifarious occupations what was really only studied
pride, in fact, the application of the axiom, "*Pretend to think
well of yourself and the world will think well of you,*" an axiom
a hundred times more useful than that of the Greek, '*Know thyself,*' a knowledge for which, in our days, we have substituted
the less difficult and more advantageous science of *knowing others.*

Of his friends M. de Villefort was a powerful protector; of his enemies he was a silent, but bitter foe; of those who were neither the one nor the other he was the personification of Law. M. de Villefort had the reputation of being the least curious and least wearisome man in France. He gave a ball every year, at which he appeared for a quarter of an hour only,—that is to say, five-and-forty minutes less than the king was visible at his balls. He was never seen at the theatres, at concerts, or in any place of public resort. Such was the man whose carriage had now stopped before the count of Monte Cristo's door. The valet announced M. de Villefort at the moment when the count, leaning over a large table, was tracing on a map the route from St. Petersburg to Peking.

The *procureur du roi* entered with the grave and measured step he would have employed in entering a court of justice. He was the same man, or rather the completion of the same man, whom we have heretofore seen as deputy at Marseilles. From slender he had become meagre; from pale yellow, his deep-set eyes were now hollow, and gold spectacles, as they shielded his eyes, seemed to form a portion of his face. All his costume was black, excepting his white cravat, and his funereal appearance was only broken in upon by the slight line of red riband which passed almost imperceptibly through his button-hole, and which appeared like a streak of blood traced with a pencil.

"Sir," said Villefort, in the tone assumed by magistrates in their oratorical periods—" sir, the signal service which you yesterday rendered to my wife and son has made it a duty in me to offer you my thanks. Allow me, therefore, to discharge this duty, and express to you all my gratitude."

"Monsieur," replied the count, with a chilling air, "I am very happy to have been the means of preserving a son to his mother, for they say that the sentiment of maternity is the most holy of all; and the good fortune which happened to me, monsieur, might have enabled you to dispense with a duty which, in its discharge, confers an undoubtedly great honour; for I am aware that M. de Villefort is not lavish of the favour he bestows on me, which, however estimable, is unequal to the satisfaction which I internally experience."

Villefort was astonished at this reply, which he by no means expected. He glanced around, in order to seize on something on which the conversation might turn, and thus let him fall easily. He saw the map which Monte Cristo had been examining when he entered, and said—" You seem geographically engaged, sir."

" Yes, sir," replied the count ; " I have sought to make of the human race, as a whole, what you practise every day on individuals—a physiological study. But sit down, sir, I beg of you."

Monte Cristo pointed to a chair, which the *procureur du roi* was obliged to take the trouble to draw forwards himself, whilst the count merely fell back into his own, on which he had been kneeling when M. Villefort entered. Thus the count was half turned towards his visitor, having his back towards the window, and his elbow on the geographical chart which afforded the conversation for the moment.

" Ah, you philosophise," replied Villefort, after a moment's silence, " well, sir, really if, like you, I had nothing else to do, I should seek a more amusing occupation."

" Why, sir," was Monte Cristo's reply, " man is but an ugly caterpillar for him who studies him through a solar microscope ; but you said, I think, that I had nothing else to do. Now, let me ask, sir, have you ?—do you believe you have anything to do ? or to speak in plain terms, do you think that what you do deserves being called anything ? "

Villefort's astonishment redoubled at this second thrust, and the *procureur du roi* exerted himself to reply.

" Sir," he responded, " you are a stranger, and I believe you say yourself that a portion of your life has been spent in Oriental countries ; thus, then, you are not aware how human justice, so expeditious in barbarous countries, takes with us a prudent and well-studied course."

" Oh, yes, I am aware of it, sir ; it is the *pede claudo* of the ancients. I know all that, for it is with the criminal procedure of all nations that I have compared natural justice, and I must say, sir, that it is the law of primitive nations, that is, the law of retaliation, that I have most frequently found to be according to the law of God."

" In the meanwhile," rejoined the magistrate, " our codes are in full force with all their contradictory enactments derived from Gallic customs, Roman laws, and Frank usages ; the knowledge of all which, you will agree, is not to be had without lengthened labour."

" I agree with you entirely, sir ; but all that even you know with respect to the French code I know, not only in reference to that code, but as regards the codes of all nations ; and thus I was right when I said to you, that relatively to what I have done you have very little to do ; but that relatively to all I have learned you have yet a great deal to learn."

" But with what motive have you learned all this ? " inquired Villefort, astonished.

Monte Cristo smiled. " Really, sir," he observed, " I see that in spite of your reputation as a superior man, you contemplate everything in the material and vulgar view of society, beginning with man, and ending with man."

" Pray, sir, explain yourself," said Villefort, more and more astonished. " I really do—not—understand you—perfectly."

" I say, sir, that you do not recognize any but those placemen whose brevets have been signed by the minister or the king, the men whom God has put above these titulars, ministers, and kings, escape your narrow ken. It is thus that human weakness fails from its debilitated and imperfect organs. Tobias took the angel who restored him to light for an ordinary young man."

" Then," said Villefort, more and more amazed, " you consider yourself as one of those extraordinary beings whom you have mentioned ? "

" And why not ? " said Monte Cristo, coldly.

" Your pardon, sir," replied Villefort, quite astounded, " but you will excuse me, if, when I presented myself to you, I was unaware that I should meet with a person whose knowledge and understanding so far surpass the usual knowledge and understanding of men. It is not usual for such privileged and wealthy beings to waste their time in speculations on the state of society, in philosophical reveries, intended at best to console those whom fate has disinherited from the goods of this world."

" Really, sir," retorted the count, " have you attained your eminent situation without having admitted or even met with exceptions ? and do you never use your eyes, which must have acquired so much *finesse* and certainty to divine, at a glance, the kind of man who has come before you ? Should not a magistrate be not merely the best administrator of the law, but a steel probe to search hearts, a touchstone to try the gold which in each soul is mingled with more or less of alloy ? "

" Sir," said Villefort, " you overcome me. I never heard a person speak as you do."

" Because you remain eternally encircled in a round of general conditions, and have never dared to raise your wing into those upper spheres which God has peopled with invisible or marked beings."

" You allow that spheres exist, and that these marked and invisible beings mingle amongst us ? "

" Why snould they not ? Can you see the air you breathe ? Yet without it you could not for a moment exist."

" Then we do not see those beings to whom you allude ? "

" Yes, we do ; you see them whenever God pleases to allow them to assume a material form. You touch them, come in contact with them, speak to them and they reply to you."

" Ah ! " said Villefort, smiling, " I confess I should like to be warned when one of these beings is in contact with me."

" You have been served as you desire, monsieur, for you have been warned just now, and I now again warn you."

" Then you yourself are one of these marked beings ? "

" Yes, monsieur, I believe so ; for until now no man has found himself in a position similar to mine. What men call the chances of fate—namely, ruin, change, circumstances—I have anticipated them all ; and if any of them should overtake me, yet they will not overwhelm me. Unless I die, I shall always be what I am, and therefore it is that I utter the things you have never heard, even from the mouths of kings—for kings have need, and other persons have fear of you. For who is there who does not say to himself, in society, as incongruously organized as ours, ' Perhaps some day I shall have to do with the *procureur du roi ?* ' "

" But can you not say that, sir ? For the moment you become an inhabitant of France you are naturally subjected to the French law."

" I know it, sir," replied Monte Cristo; " but when I visit a country I begin to study, by all the means which are available, the men from whom I may have anything to hope or to fear until I know them as well as, perhaps better than, they know themselves. It follows from this that the *procureur du roi*, be he who he may, with whom I should have to deal would assuredly be more embarrassed than I should."

" That is to say," replied Villefort, with hesitation, " that human nature being weak, every man, according to your creed, has committed faults."

" Faults or crimes," responded Monte Cristo, with a negligent air.

" And that you alone are perfect ? "

" No, not perfect," was the count's reply ; " only impenetrable, that's all. But let us leave off this strain, sir, if the tone of it is displeasing : I am no more disturbed by your justice than are you by my second sight."

" No ! no ! by no means," said Villefort, who was afraid of seeming to abandon his ground. " No ; by your conversation you have elevated me above the ordinary level; we no longer talk, we rise to dissertation. I will say to you, rude as it may seem, ' My brother, you sacrifice greatly to pride; you may be above others, but above you there is God."

" Above us all, sir," was Monte Cristo's response, in a tone and with an emphasis so deep that Villefort involuntarily shuddered. " I have my pride for men. But I lay aside that pride before God, Who has taken me from nothing to make me what I am."

" Then, M. le Comte, I admire you," said Villefort, who for the first time in this strange conversation used the aristocratical form to the unknown personage whom, until now, he had only called monsieur. " Yes, and I say to you, if you are really strong, really superior, really pious, or impenetrable, which you were right in saying amounts to the same thing—yet be proud, sir; that is the characteristic of predominance—still you have unquestionably some ambition."

" I have, sir.'

" And what may it be ? "

" I, too, as happens to every man once in his life, have been taken by Satan into the highest mountain in the earth, and shown all the kingdoms of the world; and, as he said before, so said he to me, ' Child of earth, what wouldst thou have to make thee adore me ? ' I reflected long, and then I replied, ' Listen,— I have always heard tell of Providence, and yet I have never seen Him, nor anything that resembles Him, or which can make me believe that He exists. I wish to be Providence myself, for I feel that the most beautiful, noblest, most sublime thing in the world is to recompense and punish.' Satan bowed his head and groaned. ' You mistake,' he said, ' Providence does exist, only you have never seen Him, because the child of God is as invisible as the parent. All I can do for you is, to make you one of the agents of that Providence.' The bargain was concluded. I may sacrifice my soul, but what matters it ? " added Monte Cristo. " If the thing were to do again, I would again do it."

Villefort looked at Monte Cristo with extreme amazement. " Monsieur le Comte," he inquired, " have you any relations ? "

" No, sir, I am alone in the world."

" So much the worse."

" Why ? " asked Monte Cristo.

" Because then you might witness a spectacle calculated to break down your pride. You fear nothing but death ? "

" I do not say I fear it; but that alone could check me."

" And madness ? "

" I have been nearly mad ; and you know the axiom—*non bis in eodem*. It is an axiom of criminal law, and, consequently, you understand its full application."

" Sir," continued Villefort, " there is something to fear besides death, old age, and madness. For instance, there is apoplexy— that lightning-stroke which strikes but does not destroy you, and yet after which all is ended. Come, if so you will, M. le Comte and continue this conversation at my house, any day you may be willing to see an adversary capable of understanding and anxious to refute you, and I will show you my father, M. Noirtier de Ville- fort, one of the most fiery Jacobins of the French Revolution ; a man who, perhaps, has not, like yourself, seen all the kingdoms of the earth, but who has helped to overturn one of the most powerful. Well, sir, the rupture of a blood-vessel on a lobe of the brain has destroyed all this—not in a day, not in an hour—but in a second. M. Noirtier, for whom France was a vast chessboard, from which pawns, rooks, knights, and queens were to disappear, so that the king was checkmated,—M. Noirtier, so redoubted, was the next morning poor M. Noirtier, the helpless old man, at the tender mercies of the weakest creature in the household, that is, his grandchild, Valentine."

" Alas, sir ! " said Monte Cristo, " this spectacle is neither strange to my eye nor my thought. A hundred writers since Socrates, Seneca, St. Augustine, and Galen, have made, in verse and prose, the comparison you have made, and yet I can under- stand that a father's sufferings may effect great changes in the mind of a son. I will call on you, sir, since you bid me contem- plate, for the advantage of my pride, this terrible spectacle which must spread so much sorrow throughout your house."

" It would have done so unquestionably, had not God given me so large a compensation. In presence of the old man, who is dragging his way to the tomb, are two children just entering into life—Valentine, the daughter by my first wife, Mademoiselle Renée de Saint Méran, and Edward, the boy whose life you have this day saved."

" And what is your deduction from this compensation, sir ? " inquired Monte Cristo.

" My deduction is," replied Villefort, " that my father, led away by his passions, has committed some fault unknown to human justice, but marked by the justice of God ; that God, desirous in His mercy to punish but one person, has visited this justice on him alone."

Monte Cristo, with a smile on his lips, had yet a groan at his heart, which would have made Villefort fly had he but heard it.

"Adieu, sir," said the magistrate, who had risen from his seat; "I am not a man to bore my friends, as you will learn. Besides, you have made an eternal friend of Madame de Villefort." The count bowed, and contented himself with seeing Villefort to the door of his room. When he had gone, Monte Cristo drew a hard breath from his oppressed bosom, and said—"Enough of this poison, let me now seek the antidote." Then sounding his bell, he said to Ali, who entered, "I am going to madame's chamber—have the carriage ready at one o'clock."

CHAPTER XLIX

HAIDÉE

IT will be recollected that the new, or rather old, acquaintances of the count of Monte Cristo, residing in the Rue Meslay, were no other than Maximilian, Julie, and Emanuel. The very anticipations of delight to be enjoyed in his forthcoming visits illumined his whole countenance as, immediately after the departure of Villefort, his thoughts flew back to the cheering prospect before him, of tasting, at least, a brief respite from the fierce and stormy passions of his mind.

It was the hour of noon, and Monte Cristo had set apart one hour to be passed in the apartments of Haidée. The young Greek occupied apartments wholly unconnected with those of the count. The rooms had been fitted up in strict accordance with the Eastern style. Haidée's establishment consisted of three French attendants, and a fourth, who was, like herself, a native of Greece. The first three women remained constantly in a small waiting-room, ready to obey the first sound of a small golden bell, or to receive the orders of the Romaic slave, who just knew sufficient French to be enabled to transmit her mistress's orders to the three other waiting-women, who had received most peremptory instructions from Monte Cristo to treat Haidée with the respect and deference they would show to a queen.

The fair Greek herself generally passed her time in the apartment forming the extremity of the suite of rooms assigned to her. It was a species of boudoir, circular, and lighted only from above through pale pink glass. Haidée was reclining upon soft downy cushions, covered with blue satin spotted with silver, her head, supported by one of her exquisitely moulded arms, rested on the divan immediately behind her, while the other was employed in adjusting to her lips the coral tube of a rich nargile. Her dress, which was that of the women of Epirus, consisted of a pair of white satin trousers, embroidered with pink roses, displaying feet so exquisitely formed and so delicately fair that they might well have been taken for Parian marble, had not the eye been undeceived by their constantly shifting in and out of the fairy-like slippers in which they were encased; her blue and white-striped vest, with long open sleeves, was trimmed with silver loops and buttons of pearls. She also wore a species of bodice, which, closing only from the centre to the waist, exhibited the whole of the ivory throat and upper part of the bosom; three magnificent diamond clasps fastened it where requisite. Around her waist she wore one of those many-coloured scarfs whose brilliant hues and rich silken fringe have rendered them so precious in the eyes of Parisian belles. She wore a small cap of gold, embroidered with pearls, and her luxuriant raven-black hair was lit up by a natural rose of dark crimson. The extreme beauty of her countenance was peculiarly and purely Grecian: there were the large, dark, melting eyes, the finely-formed nose, the coral lips, and pearly teeth that belonged to her race and country. And to complete the whole, Haidée was in the very springtide and fulness of youthful charms.

Upon Monte Cristo entering the apartments of the fair girl he summoned her Greek attendant, and bade her inquire whether it would be agreeable to her mistress to receive his visit. Haidée's only reply was to direct her servant by a sign to withdraw the tapestried curtain that hung before the door of her boudoir. As Monte Cristo approached she leaned upon the elbow of the arm that held the nargile, and extending to him her other hand, said with a smile of captivating sweetness, in the sonorous language of Athens and Sparta, " Why demand permission ere you enter ? Are you no longer my master, or have I ceased to be your slave ? "

" Listen to me, Haidée," replied the count. " I was about to remind you of a circumstance you are perfectly acquainted with ; namely, that we are now in France, and that you are consequently free ! "

" Free ! " repeated the fair girl. " Of what use would freedom be to me ? "

" It would enable you to quit me."

" Quit you ! Wherefore should I do so ? "

" That is not for me to say ; but we are now about to mix in society—to visit and be visited."

" I desire to see no one but yourself."

N

" Nay, but hear me, Haidée.　You cannot remain in seclusion in the midst of this gay capital ; and should you see one whom you could prefer, think not I would be so selfish or unjust as to——"

" No, no ! " answered Haidée, with energetic warmth, " that can never be.　No man could appear charming in my eyes but yourself.　None save yourself and my father have ever possessed my affection ; nor will it be bestowed upon any other."

" My poor child ! " replied Monte Cristo, " that is merely because your father and myself are the only men with whom you have ever conversed."

" And what care I for all others in the world ?　My father called me ' his joy '—you style me your ' love,'—and both of you bestowed on me the endearing appellation of ' your child ' ! "

" Do you remember your father, Haidée ? "

The young Greek smiled.　" He is here, and here," said she, touching her eyes and her heart.

" And where am I ? " inquired Monte Cristo, laughingly.

" You ? " cried she, with tones of thrilling tenderness, " you are everywhere ! "

Monte Cristo took the delicate hand of the young girl in his, and was about to raise it to his lips, when the simple child of nature hastily withdrew it, and presented her cheek instead.

" You now understand, Haidée," said the count, " that from this moment you are absolutely free.　Within this mansion you are mistress of your actions, and may go abroad or remain in your apartments as may seem most agreeable to you.　A carriage waits your orders, and Ali and Myrta will accompany you whithersoever you desire to go.　There is but one favour I would entreat of you.　Make no allusion to the past ; nor be induced to pronounce the names of your illustrious father or ill-fated mother ! "

" I have already told my lord it is not my intention to hold converse with anyone save himself."

" It is possible, Haidée, that so perfect a seclusion may not be practicable in Paris.　Endeavour, then, to accustom yourself to our manner of living in these northern climes as you did to those of Rome, Florence, Milan, and Madrid ; it may be useful to you one of these days, whether you remain here or return to the East."

The fair girl raised her tearful eyes towards Monte Cristo, as she said with touching earnestness, " My lord would mean whether we return to the East or continue here, would he not ? "

" My child," returned Monte Cristo, " you know full well that whenever we part it will be by no fault or wish of mine."

" My lord," replied Haidée, " never will I quit you, for sure

I am I could not exist if banished your presence; alas! what would life be worth then?"

"My poor girl, you forget that ten years will effect a change in both of us; to you they will bring the perfection of womanly graces, while they will wrinkle my brows and whiten my hair."

"My father had numbered sixty years, and the snows of age were on his head, but I admired and loved him far better than all the gay, handsome youths I saw about his court."

"Then tell me, Haidée, do you believe you will be able to accustom yourself to our present mode of life!"

"Shall I see you?"

"Every day."

"Then what does my lord apprehend for me?"

"I fear your growing weary."

"Nay, my lord, that cannot be. Oh, believe me, when three great passions, such as sorrow, love, and gratitude, fill the heart, *ennui* can find no place."

"You are a worthy daughter of Epirus, Haidée, and of this be well assured, that if you love me as a father, I, in my turn, feel for you all the affection of the fondest parent."

"Let not my lord be deceived; the love I bear you resembles in no degree my feelings towards my father; I survived *his* death; but were any evil to befall you, the moment in which I learned the fatal tidings would be the last of my life."

The count, with a look of indescribable tenderness, extended his hand to the animated speaker, who carried it affectionately to her lips.

Monte Cristo, thus calmed into a befitting state of mind to pay his visit to the Morrels, departed. Stepping lightly into his carriage, the count drove off at his usual rapid pace.

CHAPTER L

THE MORREL FAMILY

In a very few minutes the count reached the Rue Meslay. In the concierge that opened the gate the count recognized Coclès; but as he had but one eye, and this eye had considerably weakened in the course of nine years, Coclès did not so readily recognize the count. The carriages that drove up to the door were compelled to turn, to avoid a fountain that played in a basin of rockwork, and had gained for the house the appellation of "*le Petit Versailles.*" The house, raised above the kitchens and cellars, had, besides the ground-floor, two storeys and attics. The whole of the property, consisting of an immense workshop, two pavilions at the bottom of the garden, and the garden itself, had been purchased by Emanuel, who had reserved the house and half the garden, and building a wall between the garden and the workshops, had let them upon lease with the pavilions at the bottom of the garden. The breakfast-room was of oak; the salon of mahogany and blue velvet; the bedroom of citron wood and green damask; there was a study for Emanuel, who never studied, and a music-room for Julie, who never played. The whole of the second storey was set apart for Maximilian. He was superintending the dressing of his horse, and smoking his cigar at the entrance of the garden, when the count's carriage stopped at the door.

Coclès opened the gate, and Baptistin, springing from the box, inquired whether Monsieur and Madame Herbault, and Monsieur Maximilian Morrel, would see M. le comte de Monte Cristo.

" M. le comte de Monte Cristo ? " cried Morrel, throwing away his cigar and hastening to the carriage ; " I should think we would see him. Ah ! a thousand thanks, M. le Comte, for not having forgotten your promise." And the young officer shook the count's hand so warmly that the latter could not be mistaken as to the sincerity of his joy, and he saw that he had been expected with impatience and was received with pleasure.

" Come, come ! " said Maximilian, " I will serve as your guide ; such a man as you are ought not to be introduced by a servant."

At the sound of their steps, a young woman of twenty to five-and-twenty dressed in a silk robe-de-chambre, and busily engaged plucking the dead leaves off a splendid rose-tree, raised her head. This female was Julie, who had become, as the clerk of the house of Thomson and French had predicted, Madame Emanuel Herbault. She uttered a cry of surprise at the sight of a stranger, and Maximilian began to laugh.

" Don't disturb yourself, Julie," said he. " M. le Comte has only been two or three days in Paris, but he already knows what a woman of fashion of the Marais is, and if he does not, you will show him."

" Ah, monsieur ! " returned Julie, " it is treason in my brother to bring you thus, but he never has any regard for his poor sister. Penelon ! Penelon ! "

An old man approached, cap in hand, and striving to conceal a quid of tobacco he had just thrust into his cheek. A few locks of grey mingled with his hair, which was still thick and matted, whilst his bronzed features and determined glance announced the old sailor who had braved the heat of the equator and the storms of the tropics. " I think you hailed me, Mademoiselle Julie ? " said he.

" Penelon," replied Julie, " inform M. Emanuel of this gentleman's visit, and Maximilian will conduct him to the salon." Then, turning to Monte Cristo,—" I hope you will permit me to leave you for a few minutes," continued she ; and without awaiting any reply, disappeared behind a clump of trees, and entered the house by a lateral alley.

" I am sorry to see," observed Monte Cristo to Morrel, " that I cause no small disturbance in your house."

" Look there," said Maximilian, laughing ; " there is her husband changing his jacket for a coat. I assure you, you are well known in the Rue Meslay."

" Your family appears to me a very happy one ! " said the count, as if speaking to himself.

" Oh, yes, I assure you, M. le Comte, they want nothing that can render them happy : they are young and cheerful, they are tenderly attached to each other, and with twenty-five thousand francs a year they fancy themselves as rich as Rothschild."

" Five-and-twenty thousand francs is not a large sum, however," replied Monte Cristo, " but they will not be content with that : your brother-in-law is a barrister ? a doctor ? "

" He was a merchant, M. le Comte, and had succeeded to the business of my poor father. M. Morrel, at his death, left 500,000 francs which were divided between my sister and myself, for we were his only children. Her husband laboured and toiled until he had amassed 250,000 francs ; six years sufficed to achieve this object. At last, one day, Emanuel came to his wife, who had just finished making up the accounts. ' Julie,' said he to her, ' Coclès has just given me the last rouleau of a hundred francs ; that completes the 250,000 francs we had fixed as the limits of our gains. We can dispose of the business, if we please, in an hour, for I have received a letter from M. Delaunay, in which he offers to purchase the goodwill of the house, to unite with his own, for 300,000 francs. Advise me what I had better do.' ' Emanuel,' returned my sister, ' the house of Morrel can only be carried on by a Morrel. Is it not worth 300,000 francs to save our father's name from the chances of evil fortune and failure ? ' ' I thought so,' replied Emanuel ; ' but I wished to have your advice." ' This is my counsel : our accounts are made up and our bills paid ; all we have to do is to stop the issue of any more and

close our office.' This was done instantly. It was three o'clock ;
at a quarter past a merchant presented himself to insure two
ships; it was a clear profit of 15,000 francs. 'Monsieur,' said
Emanuel, 'have the goodness to address yourself to M. Delaunay.
We have given up business.' And this is the reason, monsieur,"
continued Maximilian, " of my sister and brother-in-law having
only 25,000 francs a year."

Maximilian had scarcely finished his story, when Emanuel
entered, clad in a hat and coat. He saluted the count with the
air of a man who is aware of the rank of his guest; then, after
having led Monte Cristo round the little garden, he returned to
the house. Julie, suitably dressed, and her hair arranged (she
had accomplished this feat in less than ten minutes), received
the count on his entrance. Everything in this charming retreat,
from the warble of the birds to the smile of the mistress, breathed
tranquillity and repose.

The count had felt, from the moment he entered the house, the
influence of this happiness. "Madame," said he at length,
" I pray you to excuse my emotion, which must astonish you
who are daily accustomed to the happiness I meet here; but
satisfaction is so new a sight to me that I could never be weary
of looking at yourself and your husband."

" We are very happy, monsieur," replied Julie; " but we
have also known unhappiness, and few have ever undergone more
bitter sufferings than ourselves."

" And God has poured balm into your wounds, as He does to all
those who are in affliction ? " said Monte Cristo, inquiringly.

" Yes, M. le Comte," returned Julie, " we may indeed say He
has, for He has done for us what He grants only to His chosen :
He sent us one of His angels."

Monte Cristo rose and, without making any answer (for the
tremulousness of his voice would have betrayed his emotion),
walked up and down the apartment with a slow step.

" Our magnificence makes you smile, M. le Comte," said Maximilian, who had followed him with his eyes.

" No, no," returned Monte Cristo, pale as death, pressing one
hand on his heart to still its throbbings, while with the other
he pointed to a crystal cover, beneath which a silken purse lay on a
black velvet cushion. " I was wondering what could be the
use of this purse, which contains a paper at one end and at the
other a large diamond."

" Oh, the articles contained in this purse are the relics of the
angel I spoke of just now."

" I do not understand ; and yet may I not ask for an explanation, madame ? " replied Monte Cristo, bowing.

" Monsieur," returned Maximilian, raising the glass cover, and respectfully kissing the silken purse, " this has touched the hand of a man who saved my father from suicide, us from ruin, and our name from shame and disgrace. This letter " (as he spoke, Maximilian drew a letter from the purse and gave it to the count " this letter was written by him the day my father had taken a desperate resolution, and this diamond was given by the generous unknown to my sister, as her dowry."

Monte Cristo opened the letter and read it with an indescribable feeling of delight. " Unknown, you say, is the man who rendered you this service—unknown to you ? "

" Yes ; we have never had the happiness of pressing his hand," continued Maximilian.

" Oh," cried Julie, " I have not lost all hope of some day kissing that hand, as I now kiss the purse he has touched. Four years ago, Penelon when he was at Trieste, saw on the quay an Englishman, who was on the point of embarking on board a yacht, and he recognized him as the person who called on my father on the 5th of June, 1829, and who wrote me this letter on the 5th of September. He felt convinced of his identity, but he did not venture to address him."

" An Englishman ! " said Monte Cristo, who grew uneasy at the attention with which Julie looked at him. " An Englishman, you say ? "

" Yes," replied Maximilian, " an Englishman, the confidential clerk of the house of Thomson and French, at Rome. It was this that made me start when you said the other day, at M. de Morcerf's, that Messrs. Thomson and French were your bankers. For God's sake, tell me, did you know this Englishman ? "

" What was his name ? " asked Monte Cristo.

" He gave no other name," answered Julie, looking earnestly at the count, " than that at end of his letter—' Sindbad the Sailor.' "

" Which is evidently not his real name, but a fictitious one."

Then noticing that Julie was struck with the sound of his voice—

" Tell me," continued he, " was he not about my height, perhaps a little taller, his chin imprisoned, to use the word, in a high cravat ; his coat closely buttoned up, and constantly taking out his pencil ? "

" Oh, do you know him ? " cried Julie, whose eyes sparkled with joy.

"No," returned Monte Cristo, "I only guessed. I knew a Lord Wilmore, who was constantly doing actions of this kind."

"And do you know this gentleman, monsieur?" inquired Emanuel.

"Alas!" replied Monte Cristo, striving to repress his emotion, "if Lord Wilmore was your unknown benefactor I fear you will never again see him. I parted from him two years ago, at Palermo, and he was then on the point of setting out for the most remote regions; so that I fear he will never return."

"O monsieur," said Julie, much affected, "Lord Wilmore had a family or friends, he must have known someone, can we not——"

"It is useless to inquire," returned the count; "he was not the man you seek for, he was my friend; he had no secrets from me, and he would have confided this also to me."

"And yet you instantly named him."

"Ah, in such a case one supposes——"

"Sister, sister," said Maximilian, coming to the count's aid, "monsieur is quite right. Recollect what our excellent father so often told us, ' It was no Englishman that thus saved us.' "

Monte Cristo started. "What did your father tell you, M. Morrel?" said he, eagerly.

"My father thought that this action had been miraculously performed—he believed that a benefactor had arisen from the grave to save us. Oh, it was a touching superstition, monsieur, and although I did not myself believe it, I would not for the world have destroyed my father's faith in it. On his death-bed this thought, which had, until then, been but a doubt became a conviction, and his last words were, ' Maximilian, it was Edmond Dantès.' "

At these words the count's paleness, which had for some time been increasing, became alarming. He could not speak; he looked at his watch like a man who has forgotten the time; spoke a few hurried words to Madame Herbault; then, pressing the hands of Emanuel and Maximilian, he said, " Madame, I trust you will allow me to visit you from time to time; I value your friendship, and feel grateful to you for your welcome, for this is the first time for many years that I have thus yielded to my feelings; " and he hastily quitted the apartment.

"This count de Monte Cristo is a singular man," said Emanuel.

"Yes," answered Maximilian; " but I feel sure he has an excellent heart and likes us."

"His voice went to my heart," observed Julie; " and two or three times I fancied I had heard it before."

CHAPTER LI

PYRAMUS AND THISBE

ABOUT the centre of the Faubourg Saint-Honoré, and at the back of one of the most distinguished-looking mansions in this rich neighbourhood, extended a large garden, whose spreading chestnut trees raised their heads above the walls, scattering, each spring, a shower of delicate pink and white blossoms into the large stone vases placed at equal distances upon the two square pilasters, supporting an iron gate, curiously wrought, after the style and manner of the reign of Louis XIV. This noble entrance, however, had fallen into utter disuse, from the period when the proprietors—and many years had elapsed since then—had confined themselves to the possession of the hôtel with its thickly-planted court-yard, opening into the Faubourg Saint-Honoré, and the garden shut in by this gate, which formerly communicated with a fine kitchen-garden of about an acre in extent. But the demon of speculation having projected a street, at the extremity of this kitchen-garden, it occurred to the then possessor of the hôtel that a handsome sum might be obtained for the ground now devoted to fruits and vegetables, for the purpose of adding it to the street intended to form a great branch of communication with the Faubourg Saint Honoré itself, one of the most important thoroughfares in the city of Paris.

In matters of speculation, however, though " man proposes," yet " money disposes." From some such difficulty the newly-named street died almost in birth, and the purchaser of the kitchen-garden, still clinging to the belief that at some future day he should obtain a sum for it that would repay him, contented himself with letting the ground temporarily to market-gardeners, at a yearly rent of 500 francs.

Horticulture seemed, however, to have been abandoned in the deserted kitchen-garden. A small, low door gave egress from the wall-enclosed area into the projected street. Towards the hotel the chestnut trees rose high above the wall. At one corner, where the foliage became so thick as almost to shut out day, a large stone bench and sundry rustic seats indicated that this sheltered spot was either in general favour or particular use by some inhabitant of the hôtel, which was faintly discernible through the dense mass of verdure that partially concealed it, though situated but a hundred paces off.

Whoever had selected this retired portion of the grounds as

the boundary of their walks or scene of their meditative musings, was abundantly justified in their choice by the absence of all glare, by the incessant and melodious warbling of birds, and by the seclusion from the noise of the street or the bustle of the hôtel. On the evening of one of the warmest days spring had yet bestowed on the inhabitants of Paris might be seen a young girl, standing close to the iron gate, endeavouring to discern something on the other side by means of the openings in the planks which boarded up the entrance.

At that instant the little side-door leading from the waste ground to the street was noiselessly opened by a tall, powerful young man, who was dressed in a common grey blouse and velvet cap, but whose carefully-arranged hair, beard, and moustaches, all of the richest, glossiest black, ill accorded with his plebeian attire. After casting a rapid glance around him, in order to assure himself he was unobserved, he carefully closed and secured the door and proceeded with a hurried step towards the iron gate.

At the sight of him she expected, though probably not in such a costume, the girl started in terror, and was about to make a hasty retreat. But the eye of love had already seen, even through the narrow chinks of the wooden palisades, the movement of the white robe and the fluttering of the blue sash fastened around the slender waist of his fair neighbour. Pressing his lips close to the planks that prevented further progress, he exclaimed,—

" Fear nothing, Valentine—it is I ! "

The timid girl found courage to return to the gate.

" And wherefore come you so late to-day ? Pray excuse yourself as well as you can and, after that, tell me why I see you in so singular a dress that at first I did not recognize you ? "

" Dearest Valentine ! " said the young man, " the difference between our stations makes me fear to offend you by speaking of my love, but yet I cannot find myself in your presence without longing to pour forth my soul, and to tell you how fondly I adore you. You ask me the cause of my being late, as also why I come thus disguised. I will candidly explain the reason of both, and I trust to your goodness to pardon me. But first let me tell you I have chosen a trade—have become a gardener."

" What nonsense, Maximilian ! "

" Do not call the wisest action of my life by such a name. By becoming a gardener I screen our meetings from danger."

" Cease trifling, Maximilian, and tell me what you mean."

" Simply that, having learned that the piece of ground on which I stand was to let, I applied for it, was accepted by the proprietor, and am now master of this fine crop of lucerne ! Think of that, Valentine ! There is nothing now to prevent my building myself a little hut on my plantation, and residing not twenty yards from you. I may also enjoy the precious privilege of assuring you of my unalterable affection, whenever you visit your bower ; unless it offend your pride to listen to professions of love from the lips of a poor working-man in blouse and cap."

A faint cry of mingled pleasure and surprise escaped from the lips of Valentine, who almost instantly said, in a saddened tone, as though some envious cloud darkened her joy—" Alas ! no, Maximilian, this must not be. We should presume too much on our strength of will and, like others, be led astray by blind confidence in each other's prudence."

" How can you for an instant entertain so unworthy a thought, dear Valentine ? When you spoke to me of your experiencing a vague sense of coming danger, I placed myself at your service, asking no other reward than the pleasure of being useful to you ; and have I ever since, by word or look, given you cause to regret your preference for my humble but devoted self ? "

" It is, indeed, most true," said Valentine, as she passed her slender fingers through a small opening in the planks, thus permitting her lover to press his lips to her hand ; " and you are a faithful friend. You promised to bestow on me the affection of a brother—on me who have no friend but yourself upon earth, who am neglected by my father, worried by my stepmother, and left to the sole companionship of a paralysed and speechless old man, whose eye alone converses with me, while, doubtless, there still lingers in his heart the warmest tenderness for his poor grandchild. Indeed, Maximilian, I am very miserable, and you are right to love me for myself alone."

" Dear Valentine ! " replied the young man, deeply affected, " I will not say you are all I love in the world, for I dearly prize my sister and brother-in-law. M. d'Épinay, to whom your father has engaged you, is not expected home for a year, I am told ; in that time many favourable and unforeseen chances may befriend us. Meanwhile, think a little what you have been to me—the beautiful but cold resemblance of a marble Venus. Oh, Valentine ! were I in your place, and did I feel conscious, as you do, of being worshipped, adored, with such a love as mine, a hundred times at least should I have passed my hand between these bars, and said to poor Maximilian, ' Take this hand, dearest Maximilian, 'and believe that, living or dead, I am yours,—yours only, and for ever ! ' " The poor girl made no reply, but her lover could hear her sobs and tears. A rapid change took place in the young man's feelings. " Dearest, dearest Valentine ! " exclaimed he, " forgive me if I have offended you, and forget the words I spoke if they have unwittingly caused you pain."

" No, Maximilian, I am not offended," answered she ; " but do you not see what a poor, helpless being I am ? In the eyes of the world I am surrounded by kindness and affection ; but the reverse is the case. My father neglects me from utter indifference, while my stepmother detests me with a hatred, the more terrible that it is veiled beneath a continual smile."

" Hate you, sweet Valentine ! " exclaimed the young man ; " how is it possible for any one to do that ? "

" Nay, I know not ; but though I don't want to talk about money, I will just say this much, that my stepmother envies me the fortune I enjoy in right of my mother, which will be more than doubled at the death of M. and Madame St. Méran, whose sole heiress I am. Alas ! how gladly would I exchange the half of this wealth for the happiness of sharing my father's love ! God knows, I would prefer sacrificing the whole, so that it would obtain me a happy home."

" But why view everything through a gloomy medium—why picture the future as fraught with evil ? "

" Because I judge it from the past."

" Still, consider that although I may not be what is termed a brilliant match for you, I am not altogether beneath your alliance. The aristocracy of the lance has allied itself with the nobility of the cannon before now, and certainly my prospects of preferment are most encouraging. My fortune, though small, is free and unfettered, and the memory of my father is respected in our country, Valentine, as that of the most upright and most honourable merchant of the city ; I say our country, because you were born not far from Marseilles."

" Name not Marseilles, I beseech you, Maximilian ; that one word brings back my mother to my recollection,—my angel mother, who died too soon for me and all who knew her. Ah, were she still living, we need fear nothing, Maximilian, for I would confide our love to her, and she would aid us."

" I fear, Valentine," replied her lover, " that were she living I should never have had the happiness of knowing you ; you would then have been too happy to stoop from your grandeur to bestow a thought on a humble person like myself."

" It is you who are unkind, ay, and unjust too, now, Maximilian," cried Valentine ; " but there is one thing I wish to know."

" And what is that ? "

" Tell me truly, Maximilian, whether in former days, when our fathers dwelt in Marseilles, there ever existed any misunderstanding between them ? "

" Not that I am aware of," replied the young man, " unless any ill-feeling might have arisen from their being of opposite parties ; your father being, as you know, a zealous partisan of the Bourbons, while mine was wholly devoted to the Emperor. There could not be any other difference between them ; tell me, dearest, why you ask ? "

" I must begin by referring to the time when you were made an officer of the Legion of Honour. We were all sitting in the apartments of my grandfather, M. Noirtier ; M. Danglars was there also. While the rest of the company were discussing the approaching marriage of Mademoiselle Danglars, I was occupied in reading the paper aloud to my grandfather ; but when I came to the paragraph concerning you, I felt so happy, and yet so nervous, that I really think I should have passed it over, but for the fear that my so doing might create suspicions as to the cause of my silence."

" Dear Valentine ! "

" Well, would you believe it ? directly my father caught the sound of your name, he turned round hastily, and, like a poor silly thing, I was so persuaded that everyone must be as much affected as myself, by the utterance of your name, that I was not surprised to see my father start, and almost tremble ; but I even thought that M. Danglars underwent a similar emotion. ' Morrel ! Morrel ! ' cried my father, ' stop a bit ' ; then knitting his brows, he added, ' Surely this cannot be one of the Morrel family who lived at Marseilles, and gave us so much trouble from their being such violent Bonapartists—I mean about the year 1815 ! ' ' I fancy,' replied Mr. Danglars, ' that the individual alluded to in the journal mademoiselle is reading is the son of the large shipowner.' ' Ah,' continued my father, still frowning, ' their idolized emperor treated these madmen as they deserved ; he called them " *food for cannon*," which was precisely all they were good for.'

" The sentiments expressed were somewhat unfeeling, I must confess," said Maximilian ; " but do not let that tinge your fair cheek with the blush of shame, my gentle Valentine ; for I can assure you that, although in a different way, my father was not a jot or tittle behind yours in the heat of his political expressions : 'Why,' says he, ' does not the Emperor form a regiment of lawyers, judges, and legal practitioners, sending them in the hottest fire the enemy could maintain, and using them to save better men ? ' But what said M. Danglars to this burst on the part of the *procureur du roi ?* "

" Oh, he laughed, and almost immediately rose and took his leave ; then, for the first time, I observed the agitation of my grandfather, and I must tell you, Maximilian, that I am the only person capable of discerning emotion in the paralysed frame of the poor afflicted old man. I suspected that the conversation had made a strong impression on his mind ; for, naturally enough, it must have pained him to hear the Emperor he so devotedly loved and served spoken of in that manner."

" The name of M. Noirtier," interposed Maximilian, " is celebrated throughout Europe ; he was a statesman of high standing and took a leading part in every Bonapartist conspiracy during the restoration of the Bourbons."

" Oh, I have often heard whispers of things that seem to me most strange—the father a Bonapartist, the son a Royalist ; what can have been the reason of so singular a difference in parties and politics ? But to resume my story ; I turned towards my grandfather, as though to question him as to the cause of his emotion. ' What is the matter, dear grandfather ? ' said I, ' are you pleased ? ' He gave me a sign in the affirmative. ' With what my father said just now ? ' He returned a sign in the negative. ' Perhaps you liked what M. Danglars remarked ? ' Another sign in the negative. ' Oh, then, you were glad to hear that M. Morrel had been made an officer of the Legion of Honour ; was that it, dear grandpapa ? ' He signified assent in a way that convinced me he was more than glad—that he was delighted. Perhaps, though, it was a mere whim on his part, for he is almost falling into second childhood ! But, for all that, I love him dearly, and pray that he may long be spared to me."

" How singular," murmured Maximilian, " that your father should hate the very mention of my name, while your grandfather, on the contrary——"

" Hush," cried Valentine suddenly, " conceal yourself ! Some one comes ! " Maximilian leaped at one bound into his crop of lucerne, which he began pulling up in the most pitiless manner, under the pretext of weeding it.

" Mademoiselle ! mademoiselle ! Madame is searching for you everywhere ; there are visitors in the drawing-room."

" Who is it ? " inquired Valentine, much agitated, " are they ladies ? "

" Oh, no, mademoiselle ! I believe it is the count of Monte Cristo, and he wishes particularly to see you."

" I will come directly," said Valentine aloud. The name caused an electric shock to the man on the other side of the iron gate, on whose ear the " I will come ! " of Valentine sounded the usual parting knell of all their interviews.

" Now," said Maximilian, " I would give much to know how the count of Monte Cristo is acquainted with M. de Villefort."

CHAPTER LII

TOXICOLOGY

THE count of Monte Cristo had arrived at Madame de Villefort's for the purpose of returning the visit of the *procureur du roi*, and at this name the whole house was in confusion. Madame de Villefort, who was alone in her drawing-room when the count was announced, desired that her son might be brought thither instantly to renew his thanks to the count ; and Edward made all haste to come to him, not from obedience to his mother, not from any feeling of gratitude to the count, but from sheer curiosity, and that he might find an opportunity for saying one of those small pertnesses which made his mother say,—" Oh, that sad child ! but pray excuse him, he is really *so* clever."

The count inquired after M. de Villefort.

" My husband dines with the chancellor," replied madame, " he has just gone, and he'll be exceedingly sorry not to have had the pleasure of seeing you before he went. What is your sister Valentine doing ? " she inquired of Edward ; " tell someone to bid her come here, that I may have the honour of introducing her to the count."

" You have a daughter, then, madame ? " asked the count ; " very young, I presume ? "

" The daughter of M. de Villefort," replied the young wife, " by his first marriage, a fine, well-grown girl."

" But melancholy," interrupted Master Edward, snatching the feathers out of the tail of a splendid parroquet in order to make a plume for his hat. Madame de Villefort merely cried, " Silence, Edward ! " She then added, " This young madcap is, however, very nearly right, for Mademoiselle de Villefort is, in spite of all we can do to rouse her, of a melancholy disposition and taciturn habit, which frequently injure the effect of her beauty. But what detains her ? Go, Edward, and see."

" Because they are looking for her where she is not to be found."

" And where are they looking for her ? "

" With grandpapa Noirtier."

" And where is she, then ?   If you know, why don't you tell ? "

" She is under the great chestnut tree," replied the spoiled brat.

When the young lady entered the apartment, she appeared much dejected ; and anyone who considered her attentively might have observed traces of recent tears.

Valentine was a tall and graceful girl of nineteen years of age, with bright chestnut hair, deep blue eyes, and that languishing air so full of distinction which characterized her mother.   She entered the apartment, and seeing near her stepmother the stranger of whom she had already heard so much, saluted him without any girlish awkwardness, or even lowering her eyes, and with an elegance that redoubled the count's attention.   He rose to return the salutation.

" Mademoiselle de Villefort, my stepdaughter," said Madame de Villefort to Monte Cristo, leaning back on her sofa and motioning towards Valentine with her hand.

" And M. de Monte Cristo, king of China, emperor of Cochin China," said the young imp, looking slyly towards his sister.

" But, madame," replied the count, continuing the conversation, and looking by turns at Madame de Villefort and Valentine, " have I not already had the honour of meeting yourself and mademoiselle ? "

" I do not think it likely, sir ; Mademoiselle de Villefort is not fond of society, and we seldom go out."

" Then it was not in society that I met with mademoiselle or yourself, madame, or this charming little boy."   The count placed his hand on his brow as if to collect his thoughts.   " No —it was somewhere—away from here—it was—I do not know— my recollection is connected with a lovely sky and some religious fête.   Pray come to my aid, madame.   Do not these circumstances bring to your mind some reminiscences ? "

" No, indeed," replied Madame de Villefort ; " and yet it appears to me, sir, that if I had met you anywhere, the recollection of you must have been imprinted on my memory."

" Perhaps M. le Comte saw us in Italy," said Valentine, timidly.

" Ah, yes—true, mademoiselle," exclaimed Monte Cristo, as if this simple indication were sufficient to determine his recollections. " It was at Perugia, on the day of the Fête-Dieu in the garden of the Hôtel des Postes, when chance brought us together ; you, Madame de Villefort, and your son I now remember, having had the honour of meeting you."

" I perfectly well remember Perugia, sir, and the Hôtel des Postes, and the fête to which you allude," said Madame de Villefort, " but in vain do I tax my memory, of whose treachery I am ashamed, for I really do not recall to mind that I ever had the pleasure of seeing you before."

" I will assist your memory, madame," continued the count ; " the day had been burning hot ; you were waiting for horses which were delayed in consequence of the festival. Mademoiselle was walking in the shade of the garden, and your son was chasing a peacock."

" And I caught it, mamma, don't you remember ? " interposed Edward, " and pulled three such beautiful feathers out of his tail."

" You, madame, remained under an arbour covered with vine ; do you not remember sitting on a stone bench and conversing for a considerable time with somebody ? "

" Yes, yes," answered madame, turning very red, " I do remember conversing with a person wrapped in a long woollen mantle ; he was a medical man, I think."

" Precisely, madame ; that man was myself ; for a fortnight I had been at that hotel, during which period I had cured my valet of a fever and my landlord of the jaundice, so that I acquired a reputation as a skilful physician. You, too, fell into the general error and consulted me about mademoiselle's health."

" But, sir, you were a medical man," said Madame de Villefort, " since you had cured the sick."

" Molière or Beaumarchais would reply to you, madame, that it was precisely because I was not, that I had cured my patients ; for myself, I am content to confess that I have studied chemistry and the natural sciences somewhat deeply, but still only as an amateur, you understand."

At this moment the clock struck six.

" It is six o'clock," said Madame de Villefort, evidently agitated. " Valentine, will you see whether your grandpapa will have his dinner ? "

Valentine rose and, saluting the count, left the apartment without a single word.

" Oh, madame ! " said the count, when Valentine had left the room, " was it on my account that you sent Mademoiselle de Villefort away ? "

" By no means ; she has gone to see that her grandfather has his evening meal. You are aware of the deplorable condition of my husband's father ? "

" M. de Villefort spoke of it to me—paralysis, I think ? "

" Alas, yes ! there is an entire want of movement in the frame of the poor old gentleman. `But excuse me, sir, for talking of our domestic misfortunes ; I interrupted you when you were telling me you were a skilful chemist."

" No, madame, I did not say so much as that," replied the count, with a smile ; " quite the contrary. I have studied chemistry, because, having determined to live in Eastern climates, I have been desirous of following the example of King Mithradates."

" *Mithradates, rex Ponticus*," said the young scamp, as he tore some beautiful portraits out of a splendid album, " the individual who breakfasted every morning with a cup of poison *à la crème*."

" Edward, you naughty boy ! " exclaimed Madame de Villefort, snatching the mutilated book from the urchin's grasp ; " you are positively past bearing ; leave us and join Valentine in dear grandpapa Noirtier's room."

" The album ! " said Edward, sulkily.

" What do you mean ?—the album ! "

" I won't go unless you give me the album," said the boy, seating himself doggedly in an armchair.

" Take it, then, and disturb us no longer," said Madame de Villefort, giving the album to Edward, who went to the door, led by his mother.

The count followed her with his eyes. " Let us see if she shuts the door after him," he muttered.

Madame de Villefort closed the door carefully after the child, the count appearing not to notice her.

" Allow me to observe, madame," said the count, with that kind tone, he could assume so well, " you are very severe with that dear child."

" Oh, sometimes severity is necessary," replied Madame de Villefort with all a mother's firmness.

" You interrupted him in a quotation from his *Cornelius Nepos*, which proves that his tutor has not neglected him, for your son is advanced for his years."

" The fact is, M. le Comte," answered the mother, agreeably flattered, " he has great aptitude, and learns all that is set before him. He has but one fault, he is somewhat wilful ; but on referring to what he said, do you really believe that Mithradates used these precautions, and that these precautions were efficacious ? "

" I think so, madame, because I—I who now address you, have

made use of them, that I might not be poisoned at Naples, Palermo and Smyrna—that is to say, on three several occasions, when, but for these precautions, I must have lost my life."

" Yes, I remember now your mentioning to me at Perugia something of this sort."

" Indeed ! did I ? " said the count, with an air of surprise, " I did not remember it."

" You said that poisons acted more certainly on Southerners than on the more sluggish Northern races."

" That is so," remarked the count, " I have seen Russians devour with impunity vegetables that would have killed a Neapolitan roan Arab."

" And do you think the result would be still more sure with us than in the East ? In the midst of our fogs and rains a man would habituate himself more easily than in a warm latitude to this progressive absorption of poison ? "

" Unquestionably. Suppose you knew beforehand the poison that would be made use of against you ; suppose the poison was brucine, and you were to take a milligramme the first day, two milligrammes the second day, and so on. Well ! at the end of ten days you would have taken a centigramme ; at the end of twenty days, increasing another milligramme, you would have taken three hundred centigrammes, that is to say, a dose which would be very dangerous for any other person who had not taken the same precautions as yourself. Well, then, at the end of a month, a person drinking water from the same *carafe* as yourself would be killed, without your perceiving, otherwise than from slight inconvenience, that there was any poisonous substance mingled with this water."

" Do you know any other counter-poison ? "

" I do not."

" I have often read, and read again, the history of Mithradates, and had always considered it as a fable."

" No, madame, contrary to most history, it is a truth ; but what you inquire of me is not the result of a chance remark ; for two years since you asked me the same questions, and said, too, that this history of Mithradates had long occupied your mind."

" True, sir. The two favourite studies of my youth were botany and mineralogy ; I have regretted I was not a man, that I might have been a Flamel, a Fontana, or a Cabanis."

" Orientals have gone farther than Mithradates went," said the count, " for they have raised the use of poisons into a fine art

Science becomes in their hands, not only a defensive weapon, but an offensive one also; the one serves against their physical sufferings, the other against their enemies. With opium, belladonna, brucæa, snake-wood, the cherry-laurel, they put to sleep those who would arouse them."

"Really! said Madame de Villefort, whose eyes sparkled at this conversation.

"Yes, indeed! madame," continued Monte Cristo, "the secret dramas of the East begin with the plant which can create love, and end with the plant that can cause death."

"But, sir," remarked the lady, "these Eastern societies, in the midst of which you have passed a portion of your existence, are visionary as the tales that come from their strange land."

"By no means, madame; the fanciful exists no longer in the East. Amongst us a simpleton possessed by the demon of hate or cupidity, who has an enemy to destroy, or some near relation to dispose of, goes straight to the grocer's or druggist's, gives a false name, which leads more easily to his detection than his real one, and purchases, under the pretext that the rats prevent him from sleeping, five or six pennyworth of arsenic. If he is really a cunning fellow, he goes to five or six different druggists or grocers, and thereby becomes only five or six times more easily traced. Then, when he has acquired his specific, he administers duly to his enemy, or near kinsman, a dose of arsenic which would make a mammoth or mastodon burst, and which, without rhyme or reason, makes his victim utter groans, which alarm the entire neighbourhood. Then arrive a crowd of policemen and constables. They fetch a doctor, who opens the dead body, and collects from the entrails and stomach a quantity of arsenic in a spoon. Next day a hundred newspapers relate the fact, with the names of the victim and the murderer. The same evening, the grocer or grocers, druggist or druggists, come and say, ' It was I who sold the arsenic to the gentleman accused;' and rather than not recognize the guilty purchaser, they will recognize twenty. This is the way in which you Northerns understand chemistry, madame."

"What would you have, sir?" said the lady, laughing; "we do what we can. All the world has not the secret of the Medicis or the Borgias."

"Now," replied the count, shrugging his shoulders, "shall I tell you the cause of all these stupidities? It is because at your theatres people see persons swallow the contents of a phial, or suck the button of a ring, and fall dead instantly. Five minutes afterwards the curtain falls and the spectators depart. They are ignorant of the consequences of the murder; they see neither the commissary of police with his badge of office, nor the corporal with his four men; and that leads weak brains to believe that poison can be used with impunity. But go out of France—go to Aleppo or Cairo, or only to Naples or Rome, and you will see people passing by you in the streets—people erect, smiling, and fresh-coloured, of whom Asmodeus, if you were holding on by the skirt of his mantle, would say, ' That man was poisoned three weeks ago, he will be a dead man in a month.' "

" Then," remarked Madame de Villefort, " they have again discovered the secret of the famous *aqua tofana* that they said was lost at Perugia ? "

" Ah ! does mankind ever lose anything ? Poison acts particularly on one organ or the other—one on the stomach, another on the brain, another on the intestines. Well, the poison brings on a cough, the cough inflammation of the lungs; and then there is a human being killed according to all the rules of art and skill, of whom justice learns nothing, as was said by a chemist of my acquaintance, the worthy Abbé Adelmonte of Taormina, in Sicily, who had studied these phenomena profoundly."

" It is quite frightful, but deeply interesting," said Madame de Villefort. " I thought, I must confess, that these tales were inventions of the Middle Ages."

" Yes, no doubt, but improved upon by ours. Yet man will never be perfect until he learns to create and destroy; he does know how to destroy, and that is half way on the road."

" So," added Madame de Villefort, constantly recurring to her subject, " the poisons of the Borgias, the Medicis——"

" Were objects of art, madame, nothing more," replied the count. " Do you suppose that the real *savant* addresses himself stupidly to the mere individual ? Science loves eccentricities, leaps and bounds, trials of strength, if I may be allowed so to term them. Thus the excellent Abbé Adelmonte, of whom I spoke just now, made some marvellous experiments."

" Really ! "

" Yes; I will mention one to you. He had a remarkably fine garden full of vegetables, flowers, and fruit. Out of the vegetables he would choose the most simple, say, a cabbage. For three days he watered this cabbage with a distillation of arsenic ; on the third, the cabbage began to droop and turn yellow. At that moment he cut it. Next, the Abbé Adelmonte took a rabbit, and made it eat a leaf of the cabbage. The rabbit died. What magistrate would find, or even venture to insinuate

anything against this ? So then, the rabbit dies, and justice
takes no notice. This rabbit dead, the Abbé Adelmonte has its
entrails taken out by his cook and thrown on the dunghill ; on
this dunghill was a hen, which, pecking these intestines, was,
in turn, taken ill, and dies next day. At the moment when it
was struggling in the convulsions of death, a vulture was flying
by ; this bird darts on the dead bird and carries it away to a rock,
where it dines off its prey. Three days afterwards, this poor
vulture falls heavily into a fish-pond. The pike, eels, and carp,
feast on the vulture. Well, next day one of these eels, or pike, or
carp, is served at your table, poisoned as they are to the third
generation. Well, then, your guest will be poisoned and die, at
the end of eight or ten days, of pains in the intestines, sickness, or
abscess of the pylorus. The doctors open the body and say, with
an air of profound learning, ' The subject has died of a tumour
on the liver, or typhoid fever ! ' "

Madame de Villefort was deep in thought, yet listened attentively.

" But," she exclaimed suddenly, " arsenic is indelible, indestructible ; in what way soever it is absorbed, it will be found
again in the body of the creature from the moment when it has
been taken in sufficient quantity to cause death."

" Precisely so," cried Monte Cristo, —" precisely so ; and this is
what I said to Adelmonte. He reflected, smiled, and replied
to me by a Sicilian proverb, which I believe is also a French
proverb, ' My son, the world was not made in a day—but in
seven. Return on Sunday.' On the Sunday following I did
return to him. Instead of having watered his cabbage with
arsenic, he had watered it this time with a solution of salts,
having their basis in strychnine, *strychnos colubrina*, as the learned
term it. Now, the cabbage had not the slightest appearance of
disease in the world, and the rabbit had not the smallest distrust ;
yet five minutes afterwards, the rabbit was dead. The fowl
pecked at the rabbit, and next day was a dead hen. This time
we were the vultures, so we opened the bird, and this time all
particular symptoms had disappeared ; there were only general
symptoms. The fowl had not been poisoned—it had died of
apoplexy. Apoplexy is a rare disease amongst fowls, I believe,
but very common amongst men." Madame de Villefort appeared
more and more reflective.

" It is very fortunate," she observed, " that such substances
can only be prepared by chemists ; else all the world would be
poisoning each other."

" By chemists and persons who have a taste for chemistry," said Monte Cristo carelessly.

" And then," said Madame de Villefort, endeavouring by an effort to get away from her thoughts, " however skilfully it is prepared, crime is always crime : and if it avoid human scrutiny, it does not escape the eye of God. The Orientals are stronger than we are in cases of conscience, and, very prudently, have no hell— that is the point."

" Really, madame, this is a scruple which naturally must occur to a pure mind like yours, but which would easily yield before sound reasoning. Man's whole life passes in doing these things, and his intellect is exhausted by reflecting on them. You will find very few persons who will brutally thrust a knife in the heart of a fellow-creature or administer to him, in order to remove him from the surface of the globe, that quantity of arsenic of which we just now talked. Such a thing is really out of rule—eccentric or stupid. But if, instead of committing an ignoble assassination, you merely remove from your path the individual who is in your way, and that without shock or violence, if there be no blood, no groans, no convulsions, and, above all, not that horrid and com- promising moment of accomplishing the act, then one escapes the clutch of the human law, which says to you, ' Do not disturb society ! ' This is the mode in which they manage these things in Eastern climes."

" Yet conscience remains ! " remarked Madame de Villefort, in an agitated voice, and with a stifled sigh.

" Yes," answered Monte Cristo,—" happily, yes ! conscience does remain ; and if it did not, how wretched we should be ! After every action requiring exertion, it is conscience that saves us, for it supplies us with a thousand good excuses of which we alone are judges ; and these reasons, how excellent soever in producing sleep, would avail us but very little before a tribunal, when we were tried for our lives. Thus was Lady Macbeth served by her conscience, when she sought to give her son, and not her husband (whatever Shakespeare may say) a throne ! Ah ! maternal love is a great virtue, a powerful motive, so powerful that it excuses a multitude of things, even if, after Duncan's death, Lady Macbeth had been at all pricked by her conscience."

Madame de Villefort listened with avidity to these appalling maxims and horrible paradoxes, delivered by the count with that ironical simplicity which was peculiar to him.

" Do you know," she said, " M. le Comte, that you are a very terrible reasoner, and that you look at the world through a distempered medium ? For, truth to say, you are a great chemist, and the elixir you administered to my son, which recalled him to life almost instantaneously——"

" Oh, do not place any reliance on that, madame ; *one* drop of that elixir sufficed to recall life to a dying child, but three drops would have impelled the blood into his lungs in such a way as to have produced most violent palpitations ; six would have suspended respiration, and caused syncope more serious than that in which he was ; ten would have destroyed him. You recollect how suddenly I snatched him from those phials which he so imprudently touched ? "

" Is it, then, so terrible a poison ? "

" Oh, no ! "

" What, then, is it ? "

" A skilful preparation of my friend's the worthy Abbé Adelmonte, who taught me the use of it."

" Oh ! " observed Madame de Villefort ; " it must be an admirable antispasmodic."

" Perfect, madame, as you saw," replied the count ; " and I frequently make use of it ; but with all possible prudence."

" Most assuredly," responded Madame de Villefort ; " as for me, so nervous, and so subject to fainting fits, I should require a Doctor Adelmonte to invent some means of breathing freely, and tranquillizing my mind, because of my fear of dying of suffocation. Meanwhile I must be satisfied with the usual remedies. Here are some lozenges which I have had made up ; they are compounded doubly strong."

Monte Cristo opened the tortoise-shell box, which the lady handed to him, and imbibed the odour of the lozenges with the air of an amateur who understood their composition.

" They are exquisite," he said ; " but as they must be submitted to the process of deglutition, a function which is frequently impossible in a fainting person, I prefer my own specific."

" And so should I, after the effects I have witnessed ; but of course it is a secret, and I am not so indiscreet as to ask it of you."

' But," said Monte Cristo, rising as he spoke, " I am gallant enough to offer it you."

" Oh, sir ! "

" Only remember one thing, a small dose is a remedy, a large one is poison. But I say no more, madame ; it is really as if I were advising you."

The clock struck half-past six, and a lady was announced, a friend of Madame de Villefort, who came to dine with her.

" If I had had the honour of seeing you for the third or fourth time, M. le Comte, instead of only for the second," said Madame de Villefort, " I should insist on detaining you to dinner, and not allowing myself to be daunted by a refusal."

" A thousand thanks, madame," replied Monte Cristo, " but I have an engagement which I cannot break ; I have promised to escort to the Académie a Greek princess of my acquaintance who has never seen your Grand Opera, and who relies on me to conduct her thither."

" Adieu, then, sir ! and do not forget to prescribe for me."

" Ah, in truth, madame, to do that, I must forget our conversation, which is indeed impossible."

Monte Cristo bowed, and left the house. Madame de Villefort remained immersed in thought. " He is a very strange man," she said ; " and in my opinion is himself the Adelmonte he talks about." As to Monte Cristo, the result had surpassed his utmost expectations. " Good ! " said he, as he went away ; " this is a fruitful soil, and I feel certain that the seed sown will not be cast on barren ground." Next morning, faithful to his promise, he sent the prescription requested.

CHAPTER LIII

" ROBERT LE DIABLE "

THE count's pretext of an opera engagement was the more feasible as there chanced to be on that very night a more than ordinary attraction at the Académie Royale. Morcerf, like most other young men of rank and fortune, had his orchestral stall ; he had, moreover, his right of entry into the omnibus-box. Château-Renaud rented a stall beside his own, while Beauchamp, in his editorial capacity, had unlimited range all over the theatre. It happened that on that particular night the minister's box was placed at the disposal of Lucien Debray, who offered it to the count de Morcerf, who, upon his mother's rejection of it, sent it to Danglars, with an intimation that he should probably do himself the honour of joining the baroness and her daughter during the evening, in the event of their accepting the box. The ladies received the offer with too much pleasure to dream of a refusal. To no class of persons is the presentation of a gratuitous opera-box more acceptable than to the wealthy millionaire, who still hugs economy while boasting of carrying a king's ransom in his waistcoat-pocket.

Danglars had, however, protested against showing himself in a ministerial box, declaring that his political principles, besides his being a member of the Opposition party, would not permit him so to commit himself; the baroness had, therefore, despatched a note to Lucien Debray, bidding him call for them, it being impossible for her to go alone with her daughter to the opera. Though an unfavourable construction would have been put upon the circumstance of two women going together to a public place, the addition of a third person, in the shape of her mother's lover, enabled Mademoiselle Danglars to defy malice and ill-nature.

The curtain rose, as usual, to an almost empty house, it being one of the absurdities of Parisian fashion never to appear at the Opera until after the beginning of the performance. The noise of opening and shutting doors, with the mingled buzz of conversation, effectually prevents even those few who would listen to the orchestra from being able to do so.

" Surely! " said Albert, as the door of a box on the first circle opened, and a lady entered, resplendent with beauty and jewels, " that must be the Countess G——."

" And who may she be, pray? " inquired Château-Renaud, carelessly.

" What a question! Now, do you know, baron, I have a great mind to pick a quarrel with you for asking it; as if all the world did not know who the Countess G—— was."

" Ah, to be sure! " replied Château-Renaud, " I remember now —your lovely Venetian, is it not? "

" Herself."

At this moment the countess perceived Albert, and returned his salutation with a graceful smile.

" You are acquainted with her, it seems? " said Château-Renaud.

" Franz introduced me to her at Rome," replied Albert.

" Well, then, will you do as much for me in Paris as he did for you in the ' Queen of Cities? ' "

" With much pleasure."

" Silence! " exclaimed the audience, a remonstrance of which the two young men took no notice.

" The Countess was at the races in the Champ de Mars to-day," said Château-Renaud.

" There were three races, were there not? "

" Yes; there was the prize given by the Jockey Club—a gold cup, you know—and a very singular circumstance occurred about that race."

" What was it ? "

" Silence ! " again vociferated the music-loving part of the audience.

" Why, that it was gained by a horse and rider utterly unknown on the course."

" Is that possible ? "

" True as day ; the fact was, nobody had observed a beautiful roan entered by the name of Vampa, or that of a jockey styled Job, who outstripped Ariel and Barbaro, against whom he ran, by at least three lengths."

" You say that the horse was entered under the name of Vampa ? "

" Exactly ; that was the title."

" Then," answered Albert, " I am better informed than you are, and know who the owner of that horse was ! "

" Silence there ! " cried the whole collective force of the pit. And this time the tone in which the command was given betokened such hostility that the young men deemed it prudent to obey the mandate.

At this moment the door of the minister's box opened, and Madame Danglars, accompanied by her daughter, entered, escorted by Lucien Debray.

" Ha, ha ! " said Château-Renaud, " here come some friends of yours, viscount ! What are you looking at ? don't you see they are trying to catch your eye ? "

Albert turned round just in time to receive a gracious wave of the fan from Madame la Baronne : as for Mademoiselle Eugénie, she scarcely vouchsafed to waste the glances of her large black eyes even upon the business of the stage.

" I tell you what, my dear fellow," said Château-Renaud, " I cannot imagine what objection you have to Mademoiselle Danglars. I call her a deuced fine girl."

" Handsome, certainly," replied Albert, " but not to my taste, which inclines to a softer, gentler, and more feminine style than that possessed by the young lady."

Indeed, it required but one glance at Mademoiselle Danglars to comprehend the justness of Morcerf's remark—" she was certainly handsome." But her beauty was of too marked and decided a character to please a fastidious taste ; her hair was raven black, but amid its natural waves might be seen a species of rebellion to the hand that sought to band and braid it ; her eyes, of the same colour as her hair, were richly fringed and surmounted by well-arched brows, whose great defect, however, consisted in an almost habitual frown; while her whole physiognomy wore an expression of firmness and decision little in accordance with the gentler attributes of her sex. But that which completed her almost masculine look was a large dark mole at the corner of her mouth; and the effect tended to increase the expression of unbending resolution and self-dependence that formed the characteristics of her face. As regarded her attainments, the only fault to be found with them was that they were too erudite and masculine for so young a person; she was a perfect linguist; a firstrate artist; wrote poetry and composed music. In the study of the latter she was assisted by a schoolfellow, who, having been educated with the view of turning her talents to account, was now busily engaged in improving her vocal powers, in order to take a leading position at the Academy of Music. But this decided Mademoiselle Danglars never to be seen in public with one destined for a theatrical life; and acting upon this principle the banker's daughter, though perfectly willing to allow Mademoiselle Louise d' Armilly to practise with her through the day, took care not to compromise herself by being seen in her company. Still, Louise was treated with far more kindness and consideration than is usually bestowed on that most unfortunate class of deserving women styled governesses.

The curtain fell almost immediately after the entrance of Madame Danglars into her box and the audience were at liberty to promenade the salon or lobbies, or to pay and receive visits in the boxes.

Morcerf and Château-Renaud were amongst the first to avail themselves of this opportunity. For an instant the idea struck Madame Danglars that this eagerness on the part of the young viscount arose from his impatience to join her party, and she whispered her expectations to her daughter.

Mademoiselle Eugénie, however, merely directed the attention of her mother to an opposite *loge*, in the first circle, in which sat the Countess G——, and where Morcerf had just made his appearance.

" So we meet again, my travelling friend, do we ? " cried the Countess. " It was really very good of you to recognize me so quickly, and still more so to bestow your first visit on me."

"Allow me to introduce my friend Baron de Château-Renaud, from whom I have learned that you were a spectator of the races in the Champ de Mars."

Château-Renaud bowed to the countess.

" Were you at the races, then, M. le Baron ? "

" I was."

" Well, then," pursued Madame G——, " you can tell me to whom the winner of the Jockey Club Stakes belonged."

" I am sorry I cannot," replied the baron ; " I ask the same question of my friend Albert."

" Are you very anxious to know, Madame la Comtesse ? " asked Albert.

" Excessively : you must know I felt so interested in the splendid roan horse and his elegant little rider so tastefully dressed in a pink satin jacket and cap, that I could not help praying for their success with as much earnestness as though the half of my fortune were at stake ; and when I saw them outstrip all the others, and come to the winning-post in such gallant style, I clapped my hands with joy. Imagine my surprise when, upon returning home, the first object I met on the staircase was the identical jockey in the pink jacket ! But that was not all, for when I entered my apartments I beheld the very gold cup awarded as a prize to the unknown horse and rider. Inside the cup was a small piece of paper, on which were written these words— ' From Lord Ruthven to Countess G——.' "

" Precisely : I was sure of it," said Morcerf.

" Sure of what ? "

" That the owner of the horse was Lord Ruthven himself."

" Mercy upon me ! " exclaimed the Countess ; " is he here too ? "

" He is my most intimate friend, and M. de Château-Renaud also has the honour of his acquaintance."

" But what convinces you he was the winner of the Jockey Club prize ? "

" Was not the winning horse entered by the name of Vampa ? "

" What of that ? "

" I argue from the fact of the horse and bandit bearing the same singular name that the count was the owner of the unknown horse."

" But what could have been his motive for sending the cup to me ? "

" Because I had spoken much of you to him, as you may believe ; and because he delighted to see a countrywoman take so lively an interest in his success."

" I trust you never repeated all our foolish remarks about him ? "

" I should not like to affirm upon oath that I have not. Besides, his presenting you the cup under the name of Lord Ruthven proves his knowledge of the comparison instituted between himself and that individual."

" And so he is in Paris ? What effect does he produce ? "

" Why," said Albert, " during the first week of his arrival he was the great lion of the day ; nothing else was thought of or talked about but the wonderful count of Monte Cristo and his extraordinary actions."

" My good fellow," said Château-Renaud, " interest in the count has not abated one jot. His first act upon coming amongst us was to present a pair of horses, worth 32,000 francs, to Madame Danglars ; his second, the almost miraculous preservation of Madame de Villefort's life ; now it seems that he has carried off the prize awarded by the Jockey Club ! Not only is the count the object of universal remark and curiosity, but he will continue to be so while he pleases to exhibit an eccentricity of conduct which, after all, may be his ordinary mode of amusing himself as well as the world."

At this moment the bell rang to announce the raising of the curtain for the second act. Albert prepared to return to his place.

" Shall I see you again ? " asked the countess.

" If you will permit me to make a second visit between the next pause in the opera, I will do myself the honour to inquire whether I can be useful to you in Paris."

" Pray take notice," said the countess, " that my residence is 22, Rue de Rivoli, and that I am at home to my friends every Saturday evening. So now you gentlemen cannot plead ignorance both of when and where you may see me."

The young men bowed and quitted the box. Upon reaching their stalls they found the whole of the audience in the *parterre* standing up and directing their gaze towards the box formerly possessed by the ambassador of Russia. " By heavens ! " said Albert, " it is Monte Cristo himself with his fair Greek ! "

The strangers were, indeed, no other than the count and Haidée. The second act passed away during one continued buzz of voices—one deep whisper—intimating that some great and universally-interesting event had occurred ; all eyes—all thoughts were occupied with the young and beautiful woman, whose gorgeous apparel and splendid jewels threw an air of insignificance upon all the fair visitants of the theatre. An unmistakable sign from Madame Danglars intimated her desire to see Albert in her box directly the curtain fell on the second act, and neither the politeness nor good taste of Morcerf would permit his neglecting an invitation so unequivocally given. He therefore proceeded to the baroness's *loge*. Having bowed to the two ladies, he extended his hand to Debray. By the baroness he was most graciously welcomed, while Eugénie received him with her accustomed coldness.

"My dear fellow!" said Debray, "you have just come in the very nick of time to help a fellow-creature regularly beaten and at a standstill. There is madame overwhelming me with questions respecting the count; she insists upon it that I can tell her his birth, education, and parentage, where he came from, and whither he is going. By way of getting out of the difficulty, I said, 'Ask Morcerf; he has the whole history of his beloved Monte Cristo at his fingers' ends;' and now I leave the solution of her questions in your hands."

"Have you remarked the extreme beauty of that young girl by whom he is accompanied, M. Lucien?" inquired Eugénie.

"I never met a woman so ready to do justice to the charms of another as yourself; let us see how far she merits your praises," continued Lucien, raising his lorgnette to his eye. "A most lovely creature, upon my soul!" cried he, after a long and searching scrutiny.

"Who is this young person, M. Morcerf?" inquired Eugénie; "does anybody know?"

"Allow me to state," said Albert, replying to this direct appeal, "that I can give you very tolerable information on that subject; the young person is a Greek."

"So I should presume by her dress; if, therefore, you know no more than that one self-evident fact, the whole of the spectators in the theatre are as well informed as yourself."

"I am extremely sorry you find me so ignorant a cicerone," replied Morcerf, "but I am reluctantly obliged to confess I have nothing further to communicate—yes, stay, I do know one thing more, namely, that she is a musician, for one day when breakfasting with the count I heard the sound of a guzla—it is impossible it could have been touched by any other finger than her own."

"I must persuade M. Danglars to invite him to dinner, that he may be obliged to ask us in return."

"What!" said Debray laughing; "would you go to his house?"

"Why not? my husband could accompany me."

"But this mysterious count is a bachelor."

"You have ample proof to the contrary, if you look opposite," said the baroness.

" No, no ! " exclaimed Debray ; " that is not his wife, he told us himself she was his slave ; do you not recollect, Morcerf, his telling us so at your breakfast ? "

" Well, then," said the baroness, " if slave she be, she has all the air and manner of a princess."

" What do you think of the count ? " inquired Debray ; " he is not much amiss, according to my ideas of good looks."

" The count ? " repeated Eugénie, as though it had not occurred to her to observe him sooner : " the count ? oh !—he is so dreadfully pale."

" I quite agree with you," said Morcerf ; " and in that very paleness consists the secret we want to find out. The Countess G—— insists he is a vampire."

" Then the Countess G—— has returned to Paris, has she ? " inquired the baroness.

" Is that she, mamma ? " asked Eugénie ; " almost opposite to us, with that profusion of beautiful light hair ? "

" Yes, yes, there she is ! " cried Madame Danglars ; " shall I tell you what you ought to do, Morcerf ? "

" Command me, madame."

" Well, you should bring your count of Monte Cristo to us."

" What for ? " asked Eugénie.

" What for ? why, to converse with him, of course. Have you really no desire to be introduced to this singular being ? "

" None whatever," replied Eugénie.

" He will very probably come of his own accord," said Morcerf. " There ! madame, he recognizes you, and bows."

The baroness returned the salute most graciously.

" Well," said Morcerf, " adieu ; I will see whether there is any means of speaking to him."

As Albert was passing the count's box, the door opened and Monte Cristo came forth. After giving some directions to Ali, who stood in the lobby, the count observed Albert, and taking his arm, walked onwards with him. Carefully closing the box door, Ali placed himself before it, while a crowd of wondering spectators assembled round the unconscious Nubian.

" Upon my word," said Monte Cristo, " Paris is a strange city, and the Parisians a very singular people ; now I will pledge myself that a Frenchman might show himself in public, either in Tunis, Constantinople, Baghdad, or Cairo, without drawing a circle of gazers around him."

" That shows that the Eastern nations have too much good sense to waste their time and attention on objects undeserving of either. However, as far as Ali is concerned, the interest he excites is merely due to the fact of his being your attendant; you are at this moment the most celebrated person in Paris."

"Really! and what has procured me so flattering a distinction?"

"What? why, yourself, to be sure! You give away horses worth a thousand guineas; you save the lives of ladies of high rank; you send thoroughbred racers to contest the prize of the Jockey Club, the horses being ridden by urchins not larger than marmots; then, when you have carried off the golden trophy of victory, instead of setting any value on it, you give it to the first handsome woman you think of. Why, if you sought concealment, did you call your horse Vampa?"

"That was an oversight, certainly," replied the count; "but tell me, does the count de Morcerf never visit the Opera?"

"He will be here to-night."

"In what part of the house?"

"In the baroness's *loge*, I believe."

"Is the charming young woman with her her daughter?"

"Yes."

"Indeed! then I congratulate you."

"We will discuss that subject at some future time," said he. "But what think you of the music?"

"What music?"

"That which you have just heard."

"Oh, it is admirable as the production of a human composer, sung by a party of bipeds without feathers, as Diogenes styled mankind. But when I wish to listen to sounds so exquisitely attuned to melody as mortal ear never yet listened to I go to sleep."

"I know—the famous hasheesh!"

"Precisely. Now you know my secret, my dear viscount, come and sup with me whenever you wish to be regaled with music really worth listening to."

"I have already enjoyed that treat when breakfasting with you," said Morcerf.

"Ah, then I suppose you heard Haidée's guzla; the poor exile frequently beguiles a weary hour in playing the airs of her native land."

The bell rang for the rising of the curtain.

"You will excuse my leaving you," said the count. "Pray, say everything that is kind to Countess G—— on the part of her friend the Vampire."

"And what message shall I convey to the baroness?"

o

" That, with her permission, I propose paying my respects in the course of the evening."

The third act had now begun, and during its progress the count de Morcerf made his appearance in the box of Madame Danglars. His presence was wholly unnoticed, save by the occupants of the box. The quick eye of Monte Cristo, however, marked his coming ; and a slight, though meaning smile, passed over his lips as he did so. Haidée, whose soul seemed centred in the business of the stage, like all unsophisticated natures, delighted in whatever addressed itself to the eye or ear.

The third act passed off as usual. Mesdemoiselles Noblet, Julie, and Lesroux executed the customary quantity of pirouettes ; Robert duly challenged the Prince of Granada ; and the royal parent of the Princess Isabella, taking his daughter by the hand, swept round the stage with majestic strides, after which the curtain again fell, and the spectators poured forth from the theatre into the lobbies and salon. The count also, quitting his, proceeded at once to the box of Madame Danglars.

" Welcome, M. le Comte," exclaimed she as he entered. " I have been most anxious to see you, that I might repeat verbally those thanks writing can so ill express."

" Surely so trifling a circumstance cannot deserve a place in your remembrance. Believe me, madame, I had entirely forgotten it ! "

" But it is not so easy to forget, M. le Comte, that the very day following the one in which you kindly prevented my disappointment respecting the horses, you saved the life of my dear friend Madame de Villefort, whom I had placed in danger by lending her the very animals your generosity restored to me."

" This time, at least, I cannot accept of your flattering acknowledgments ; in the latter affair you owe me nothing. Ali, my Nubian slave, was the fortunate person who enjoyed the privilege of rendering to your friend the assistance you allude to."

" Was it Ali," asked the Count de Morcerf, " who rescued my son from the hands of bandits ? "

" No, M. le Comte," replied Monte Cristo, " in this instance I may fairly and freely accept your thanks ; but I feel almost mortified to find you still revert to the trifling aid I was able to render your son. May I beg of you, Madame la Baronne, to honour me with an introduction to your charming daughter ? "

" Oh ! you are no stranger—at least not by name," replied Madame Danglars. " Eugénie," continued the baroness, turning towards her daughter, " M. le comte de Monte Cristo." The count bowed, while Mademoiselle Danglars returned a slight inclination of the head. " You have a charming young person with you to-night, M. le Comte," said Eugénie. " Your daughter, I presume ? "

" No, indeed," said Monte Cristo, astonished at the coolness and freedom of the question. " The girl you allude to is a poor unfortunate Greek left under my care."

" And what is her name ? "

" Haidée," replied Monte Cristo.

" A Greek ? " murmured the count de Morcerf.

" Yes, indeed, count," said Madame Danglars ; " and tell me, did you ever see at the court of Ali Tebelin a more exquisite beauty or richer costume than is displayed in the fair Greek ? "

" Did I hear rightly, M. le Comte," said Monte Cristo, " that you served at Janina ? "

" I was inspector-general of the Pasha's troops," replied Morcerf ; " and I seek not to conceal that I owe my fortune, such as it is, to the liberality of the illustrious Albanian chief."

" But look ! pray look," exclaimed Madame Danglars.

" Where ? " stammered out Morcerf.

" There, there ! " said Monte Cristo, as, throwing his arms around the count, he leaned with him over the front of the box, just as Haidée perceived his pale marble features close to the countenance of Morcerf, whom he was holding in his arms. She bent forward as though to assure herself of the reality of what she beheld, then, uttering a faint cry, threw herself back in her seat. " Bless me ! " exclaimed Eugénie, " what has happened to your ward, M. le Comte ? She is taken suddenly ill."

" Very probably ! " answered the count. " But do not be alarmed on her account ! Haidée's nervous system is delicately organized, and she is peculiarily susceptible. However," continued Monte Cristo, drawing a small phial from his pocket, " I have an infallable remedy for such attacks." So saying, he quitted the box. Upon his return to Haidée he found her extremely pale and agitated. Directly she saw him she seized his hand, while the icy coldness of her own made Monte Cristo start. ' With whom was my lord conversing a few minutes since ? " asked she in a trembling voice.

" With the count de Morcerf," answered Monte Cristo. ' He tells me he served your illustrious father, and that he owes his fortune to him."

" Base, cowardly traitor that he is ! " exclaimed Haidée. " He sold my beloved parent to the Turks, and the fortune he boasts of was the price of his treachery! Let us go hence, I beseech you. I feel as though it would kill me to remain longer near that dreadful man." So saying, Haidée rose and quitted the box when the curtain was rising upon the fourth act.

CHAPTER LIV

THE RISE AND FALL OF THE STOCKS

SOME days after this meeting, Albert de Morcerf visited the count of Monte Cristo at his house in the Champs Elysées. He was accompanied by Lucien Debray, who, joining in his friend's conversation, adding some passing compliments, the source of which the count's talent for finesse easily enabled him to guess. He was convinced that Lucien's visit was to be attributed to a double feeling of curiosity, the larger half of which sentiment emanated from the Rue de la Chaussée d'Antin.

" You are in constant communication, then, with the Baron Danglars ? " inquired the count of Albert de Morcerf.

" Yes, count; you know what I told you! "

" All remains the same, then, in that quarter ? "

" It is more than ever a settled thing," said Lucien, as he began to make the tour of the apartment, examining the arms and the pictures.

" Ah ! " said Monte Cristo, " I did not expect the affair would have been so promptly concluded."

" Oh, things take their course without our assistance ; whilst we are forgetting them they are falling into their appointed order ; and when again our attention is directed to them we are surprised at the progress they have made towards the proposed end. My father and M. Danglars served together in Spain, my father in the army and M. Danglars in the commissariat department. It was there they laid the foundation of their fortunes."

" Yes," said Monte Cristo, " I think M. Danglars mentioned that, and," he continued, " Mademoiselle Eugénie is pretty."

" Very pretty, or rather, very beautiful," replied Albert, " but of that style of beauty which I do not appreciate ; I am an ungrateful fellow."

" Really," said Monte Cristo, lowering his voice, " you do not appear to me to be very enthusiastic on the subject of this marriage."

" Mademoiselle Danglars is too rich for me," replied Morcerf.

" Bah ! " exclaimed Monte Cristo, " that's, surely, no reason. Are you not rich yourself ? "

" My father's income is about 50,000 francs per annum ; and he will give me, perhaps, ten or twelve thousand when I marry."

" That might not be considered a large sum, in Paris especially," said the count ; " but everything does not depend on wealth, and it is a fine thing to have a good name, and to occupy a high station in society."

Albert shook his head, and looked thoughtful. " My mother entertains some prejudice against the Danglars."

" Ah ! " said the count, in a somewhat forced tone, " that may be easily explained ; Madame la Comtesse does not relish the idea of being allied by your marriage with one of ignoble birth."

" I do not know if that is her reason," said Albert ; " but one thing I do know, this marriage would render her quite miserable. There was to have been a meeting six weeks ago in order to settle the affair ; but I had such a sudden attack of indisposition that they postponed the rendezvous for two months. There is no hurry, you know, but the two months will expire next week. It must be done. You cannot imagine how my mind is harassed. How happy you are in being exempted from all this ! "

" Well, and why should you not be free, too ? "

" Oh ! it will be too great a disappointment to my father."

" Marry her, then," said the count, with a significant shrug of the shoulders.

" Yes," replied Morcerf, " but that will plunge my mother into positive grief."

" Then do not marry her," said the count.

" Well, I shall see : you will give me your advice, will you not ? I think, rather than give pain to my excellent mother, I would run the risk of offending the count."

Monte Cristo turned away ; he seemed moved by this last remark. " Ah ! " said he to Debray, who held a pencil and an account book, " what are you doing there ? "

" I am engaged with arithmetic."

" Arithmetic ! "

" Yes ; I am calculating what the house of Danglars must have gained by the last rise in Haïti stock ; the prudent banker must have made 300,000 livres."

" That is not his best stroke of policy," said Morcerf ; " did he not gain a million from the Spaniards last year ? "

" But you were speaking of Haïti ! " said Monte Cristo.

" Ah, Haïti !—Haïti is the écarté of French stock-jobbing.

That is the game *par excellence*. M. Danglars sold yesterday at 405, and pockets 300,000 francs. Had he but waited till to-day, the stocks would have fallen to 205, and instead of gaining 300,000 francs, he would have lost 20,000 or 25,000."

" And what has caused the sudden fall from 405 to 205 ? " asked Monte Cristo."

" Because," said Albert, laughing, " one piece of news follows another, and there is often great dissimilarity between them."

" Ah," said the count, " I see that M. Danglars is accustomed to play at gaining or losing 300,000 francs in a day ; he must be enormously rich."

" It is not he who plays," exclaimed Lucien, " it is Madame Danglars."

" Ah, if I were in your place," said Albert, " I would reform her."

" How would you set about it."

" Ah, that would be easy enough. You never open your mouth but the stockbrokers immediately stenograph your words. Cause her to lose 200,000 or 300,000 francs in a short space of time, and that would teach her prudence."

" I do not understand," stammered Lucien.

" It is very clear, notwithstanding," replied the young man ; " tell her, for instance, that Henri IV. was seen yesterday at the house of Gabrielle. That will cause the funds to rise ; she will lay her plans accordingly, and she will certainly lose when Beauchamp announces next day, in his gazette, ' The report, stating the king to have been seen yesterday at Gabrielle's house, is totally without foundation. We can positively assert that his majesty did not quit the Pont Neuf.' " Lucien half smiled. Monte Cristo, although apparently indifferent, had not lost one word of this conversation, and his penetrating eye had even read a hidden secret in the embarrassed manner of the secretary. This embarrassment had completely escaped Albert, but it caused Lucien to shorten his visit ; he was evidently ill at ease. The count, in taking leave of him, said something in a low voice, to which he answered, " Willingly, M. le Comte ; I accept your proposal." The count returned to young De Morcerf.

" Do you not think on reflection," said he to him, " that you have done wrong in thus speaking of your mother-in-law in the presence of M. Debray ? "

" M. le Comte," said Morcerf, " I beg of you not to apply that title so prematurely."

"Is your mother really so very much averse from this marriage?"

"So much so that the baronne very rarely comes to the house, and my mother has not, I think, visited Madame Danglars twice in her whole life."

"Then," said the count, "I am emboldened to speak openly to you. I have thought of inviting M. and Madame Danglars and M. and Madame de Villefort to my country-house at Auteuil. If I were to invite you and the count and countess de Morcerf to this dinner it would give it the air of a matrimonial rendezvous. In that case your mother would hold me in aversion, and I do not at all wish that; on the contrary, I desire to occupy a prominent place in her esteem."

"Indeed, count," said Morcerf, "I gratefully accept the exclusion which you propose to me. You say you desire my mother's good opinion; I assure you it is already yours to a very unusual extent. We talked of you an hour after you left us the other day. If my mother could know of this attention on your part—and I will venture to tell her—I am sure that she will be most grateful to you; it is true that my father will be equally angry."

The count laughed.

"Well," said he to Morcerf, "but I think your father will not be the only angry one; M. and Madame Danglars will think me a very ill-mannered person. They know that I am intimate with you, and they will not find you at my house! They will certainly ask me why I did not invite you. Be sure to provide yourself with some previous engagement, and communicate the fact to me in writing."

"I will do better than that," said Albert; "my mother wishes to go to the sea-side—what day is fixed for your dinner?"

"Saturday."

"This is Tuesday—well, to-morrow evening we shall leave, and the day after we shall be at Tréport. I will immediately call on M. Danglars, and tell him that my mother and I will leave Paris to-morrow. I have not met you, consequently I know nothing of your dinner."

"How foolish you are! M. Debray has just seen you at my house."

"Ah, true!"

"On the contrary, I invited you without ceremony, and you instantly answered you could not accept, as you were going to Tréport."

" Well, that is settled ; but you will come and call on my mother before to-morrow."

" Before to-morrow ? That will be a difficult matter to arrange."

" You are to-day free as air—come and dine with me ; we shall be a small party—only yourself, my mother, and I. You have scarcely seen my mother ; you shall have an opportunity of observing her more closely. As to my father, you will not see him. We will talk over our travels ; and you, who have seen the whole world, will relate your adventures. Come, accept my invitation and my mother will thank you."

" A thousand thanks," said the count, " your invitation is most gracious, and I regret exceedingly that I cannot accept it."

" Ah, take care, you were teaching me just now how one might creditably make an excuse. I require the proof of a pre-engagement."

" I am going to give you a proof," replied the count, and he rang the bell.

" Humph ! " said Morcerf, " this is the second time you have refused to dine with my mother; it is evident you wish to avoid her." Monte Cristo started. " Oh, you do not mean that," said he ; " besides, here comes the confirmation of my assertion." Baptistin entered, and remained standing at the door.

" Baptistin, what did I tell you this morning when I called you into my laboratory ? "

" To close the door against visitors as soon as the clock struck five," replied the valet.

" What then ? "

" Then to admit no one except M. le Major Bartolomeo Cavalcanti and his son."

" You hear ? Major Bartolomeo Cavalcanti is a man who ranks amongst the most ancient nobility of Italy. His son, a charming young man, is making his *entrée* into the Parisian world, aided by his father's millions. The Major will bring his son this evening. If he prove worthy of it, I will do what I can to advance his interests ; you will assist me in the work ? "

" Most undoubtedly ! This Major Cavalcanti is an old friend ? "

" By no means. I have met him several times at Florence, Bologna, and Lucca, and he has now communicated to me the fact of his arrival in this place. Major Cavalcanti is come to take a second view of Paris, which he only saw in passing through in the time of the Empire ; he will confide his son to my care ; I will promise to watch over him ; I shall let him follow wherever his folly may lead him, and then I shall have done my part."

" Certainly ; I see you are a precious Mentor," said Albert.
" Good-bye, we shall return on Sunday. By the way, I have
received news of Franz. He misses you extremely."

" His opinion of me is altered for the better, then ? "

" No, he still persists in looking upon you as the most incomprehensible of beings."

" He is a charming young man," said Monte Cristo. " He is,
I think, the son of General d'Épinay, who was so shamefully
assassinated in 1815 ? "

" By the Bonapartists."

" Yes !—really I like him extremely ; is there not also a
matrimonial engagement contemplated for him ? "

" Yes, he is to marry Mademoiselle de Villefort."

" Indeed ! "

" And you know I am to marry Mademoiselle Danglars,"
said Albert, laughing.

" You smile ? "

" I think there is as much inclination to carry out this engagement as there is to carry out my own." Albert rose.

" Are you going ? "

" Really, that is a good idea of yours !—For two hours have I
been boring you to death, and then you ask if I am going. Indeed,
count, you are the most polished man in the world ! And your
servants, too, how very well behaved they are. If you part with
M. Baptistin, give me the refusal of him."

" Agreed, viscount."

" My compliments to your illustrious visitor, and if by any
chance he should wish to establish his son, and find him a wife
very rich, very noble on her mother's side at least, and a baroness
in right of her father, I will help you in the search. I should like
you a hundred times better, if, by your intervention, I could
manage to remain a bachelor, even were it only for ten
years."

" Nothing is impossible," gravely replied Monte Cristo. He
returned into the house, and struck the gong three times.

" M. Bertuccio, you understand that I intend to entertain company on Saturday at Auteuil. It is a beautiful house, or at all
events may be made so."

" There must be a good deal done, M. le Comte, for the tapestried
hangings are very old."

" Let them be taken away and changed, then, with the exception of the sleeping-chamber, which is hung with red damask ;
you will leave that exactly as it is." Bertuccio bowed. " You

will not touch the garden either; as to the yard, you may do what you please with it."

"I will carry out your wishes, M. le Comte. I should be glad, however, to receive your Excellency's commands concerning the dinner."

"Really, my dear M. Bertuccio," said the count, "you no longer seem to understand me."

"But surely your Excellency will be so good as to inform me whom you are expecting to receive?"

"I do not yet know myself, neither is it necessary that you should do so. 'Lucullus dines with Lucullus,' that is quite sufficient."

Bertuccio bowed and left the room.

CHAPTER LV

MAJOR CAVALCANTI

BOTH the count and Baptistin had told the truth when they announced to Morcerf the proposed visit of the major, which had served Monte Cristo as a pretext for declining Albert's invitation. At seven o'clock a *fiacre* deposited its fare at the Count's house. The person who alighted was about fifty-two years of age. He wore a green surtout, blue cloth trousers, not too brightly polished boots, buckskin gloves, and a hat rather resembling the kind usually worn by gendarmes. He had scarcely time to announce himself when the count was apprised of his arrival. He was ushered into a simple drawing-room, and the count met him with a smiling air. "Ah, my dear sir, you are most welcome; I was expecting you."

"Was your Excellency aware of my visit?"

"Yes; I had been told I should see you to-day at seven o'clock."

"Ah, so much the better; I feared this little precaution might have been forgotten."

"What precaution?"

"That of informing you beforehand of my coming."

"Oh, no, it has not."

"It really was I whom your Excellency expected at seven o'clock this evening?"

"Yes," said Monte Cristo. His visitor appeared slightly uneasy. "Let me see," said the count; "are you not M. le

Marquis Bartolomeo Cavalcanti, ex-major in the Austrian service ? "

" Was I a major ? " timidly asked the old soldier.

" Yes," said Monte Cristo ; " you were a major ; that is the title the French give to the post which you filled in Italy."

" Very good," said the major ; " I do not demand more, you understand——"

" You were sent here to-day by some other person ? "

" Yes."

" By the Abbé Busoni ? "

" Exactly so," said the major.

" And you have a letter ? "

" Yes ; there it is."

" Give it me, then," and Monte Cristo took the letter, which he opened and read.

The major looked at the count with his large staring eyes.

" Yes, yes, I see. ' Major Cavalcanti, possessing an income of half a million.' " Monte Cristo raised his eyes from the paper and bowed. " Half a million," said he, " magnificent ! "

" Half a million, is it ? " said the major.

" Yes, in so many words."

" Be it half a million ; but I had no idea that it was so much."
Monte Cristo resumed the perusal of the letter :—

" ' And who only needs one thing more to make him happy.' "

" Yes, indeed ! but one ! " said the major, with a sigh.

" ' Which is, to recover a lost and adored son, stolen in his infancy."

" At the age of five years, sir ! " said the major, with a deep sigh.

" Unhappy father ! " said Monte Cristo.   The count continued :
—" ' I have given him renewed life and hope, in the assurance that you have the power of restoring the son whom he has vainly sought for, for fifteen years.' "

The major looked at the count with an indescribable expression of anxiety.

" I have the power of so doing," said Monte Cristo.

The major recovered his self-possession. " Ah ! ah ! " said he, " the letter was true, then, to the end ? But your Excellency has not read all."

" Ah ! true ! " said Monte Cristo, " there is a postscript. ' In order to save Major Cavalcanti the trouble of drawing on his banker, I send him a draft for 2,000 francs to defray his travelling expenses, and credit on you for the further sum of 48,000, which you still owe me.' "

The major awaited the conclusion of the postscript, apparently with great anxiety.

" Very good," said the count.

" He said ' very good,' " muttered the major ; " then—sir—" replied he.

" Then what ? " asked Monte Cristo.

" Then the postscript is as favourably received by you as the rest of the letter ? "

" Certainly. You attach great importance, then, to this postscript, my dear M. Cavalcanti ? "

" I must explain to you," said the major, " that if this resource had failed me, I should have found myself very unpleasantly situated in Paris."

" Is it possible, that a man of your standing should be embarrassed anywhere ? " said Monte Cristo.

" Why, really, I know no one," and the major paused.

" Proceed, my dear M. Cavalcanti ! "

" So that you will remit to me these 48,000 francs ? "

" Certainly, at your first request."

The major's eyes dilated with pleasing astonishment.

Monte Cristo rang ; Baptistin appeared. The count advanced to meet him. " Well ? " said he, in a low voice. " The young man is here," said the valet in the same tone.

" That's right ; bring some Alicante and biscuits."

Baptistin left the room. " Really," said the major, " I am ashamed of the trouble I am giving you."

" Pray don't mention such a thing," said the count. Baptistin re-entered with glasses, wine, and biscuits. The count filled one glass, but in the other he only poured a few drops of the ruby-coloured liquid. The major made a wise choice ; he took the full glass and a biscuit.

" So, sir, you inhabited Lucca, did you ? you were rich, noble, held in great esteem, had all that could render a man happy ? "

" All," said the major, hastily swallowing his biscuit, " positively all."

" And one thing was wanting to complete your happiness ? "

" Ah ! " said the major, taking a second biscuit, " that consummation of my happiness was indeed wanting." The worthy major raised his eyes to Heaven and sighed.

" Let me hear, then," said the count, " who this deeply-regretted son was ? For I always understood you were a bachelor ? "

" That was the general opinion, sir," said the major, " and I——"

"Yes," replied the count, "and you confirmed the report. A youthful indiscretion, I suppose, which you were anxious to conceal from the world at large?"

"Yes," said the major, "I did wish this fault to be hidden."

"But for the sake of the mother?" said the count.

"Yes, for the mother's sake—his poor mother!" cried the major, taking a third biscuit.

"Take some more wine, my dear Cavalcanti," said the count, pouring out a second glass of Alicante; "your emotion has overcome you."

"His poor mother!" murmured the major, trying if the will was powerful enough to act on the lachrymal gland.

"Oliva Corsinari, was it not?"

'Oliva Corsinari!"

"A marchioness?"

"A marchioness!"

"And you married her at last, notwithstanding the opposition of her family?"

"Yes, I did so."

"And you have doubtless brought all your papers with you?" said Monte Cristo.

"M. le Comte, I regret to say that not knowing it was necessary to come provided with these papers, I neglected to bring them with me."

"They were indispensable."

"O peccato!"

"You must know that in France they are very particular on these points; it is not sufficient, as in Italy, to go to the priest and say, 'We love each other, and want you to marry us.' Marriage is a civil affair in France, and you must have papers which establish your identity."

"That is unfortunate! I have not the papers."

"Fortunately, I have them," said Monte Cristo.

"Ah, indeed!" said the major, "that is lucky, for it never occurred to me to bring them."

"I do not at all wonder at it, one cannot think of everything; but happily, the Abbé Busoni thought for you."

The major clasped his hands in token of admiration. "You married Oliva Corsinari, in the church of San Paolo del Monte Cattini; here is the priest's certificate."

"Yes, indeed, there it is truly," said the Italian, looking on with astonishment. "And here is Andrea Cavalcanti's baptismal register, given by the curé of Saravezza."

"Take these documents, then, they do not concern me; you will give them to your son, who will, of course, take great care of them."

"I should think so, indeed! If he were to lose them——"

"Well, and if he were to lose them?" said Monte Cristo.

"In that case," replied the major, "it would be necessary to write to the curé for duplicates, and it would be some time before they could be obtained."

"I am very glad you understand the value of these papers."

"I regard them as invaluable."

"Now," said Monte Cristo, "as regards la Marquise Corsinari, has she not paid the last debt of nature?"

"Alas!" returned the Italian.

"I knew that," said Monte Cristo; "she has been dead these ten years."

"And I am still mourning her loss," exclaimed the major.

"What would you have?" said Monte Cristo; "we are all mortal. Now, you understand, my dear M. Cavalcanti, that it is useless to tell people in France that you have been separated from your son for fifteen years. You sent him for his education to a college in one of the provinces, and now you wish him to complete his education in the Parisian world. That is why you left Via Reggio, where you have lived since the death of your wife. That will be sufficient."

"Very well, then."

"If they should hear of the separation——"

"Ah, yes; what could I say?"

"That an unfaithful tutor, bought over by the enemies of your family had stolen away this child, in order that your name might become extinct."

"That will do well, since he is an only son."

"Now that all is arranged, do not let these newly-awakened remembrances be forgotten. You have already guessed that I was preparing a surprise for you."

"An agreeable one?" asked the Italian.

"Someone has told you the secret; or, perhaps, you guessed that he was here."

"That who was here?"

"Your child—your son—your Andrea."

"Ah, very well! very well!" said the major.

"My dear sir," said Monte Cristo, "I understand your emotion; you must have time to recover yourself. I will, in the meantime, prepare the young man for this much-desired interview, for I presume he is not less impatient for it than yourself."

" By the way," said the major, " you know I have only the 2,000 francs which the Abbé Busoni sent me; this sum I have expended upon travelling expenses, and——"

" And you want money—that is a matter of course, my dear M. Cavalcanti. Well, here are 8,000 francs on account."

The major's eyes sparkled.

" I now owe you 40,000 francs," said Monte Cristo."

" Does your Excellency wish for a receipt ? " said the major, slipping the money into an inner pocket.

" When you receive the remaining 40,000 francs you shall give me a receipt in full. Between honest men such excessive precaution is quite unnecessary."

" Yes, so it is between perfectly upright people."

" One word more," said Monte Cristo. " You will permit me to make one remark ? "

" Certainly, pray do so."

" Then I should advise you to leave off that style of dress."

" But what shall I wear ? "

" What you find in your trunks."

" In my trunks. I have but one portmanteau."

" I daresay you have nothing else with you. What is the use of boring one's self with so many things ? Besides, an old soldier always likes to march with as little baggage as possible. But you are a man of foresight and prudence, and sent your luggage on before you. It has arrived at the Hôtel des Princes, Rue de Richelieu, where you will take up your quarters."

" Then, in these trunks——"

" I presume you gave orders to your valet to put in all you are likely to need—your plain clothes and your uniform. On grand occasions you must wear your uniform ; it will look very well. Do not forget your crosses. They laugh at them in France, and yet always wear them." Saying which, Monte Cristo bowed, and disappeared behind the tapestry.

CHAPTER LVI

ANDREA CAVALCANTI

THE count of Monte Cristo entered the adjoining room, and found there a young man, of graceful demeanour and elegant appear-

ance. Baptistin had no difficulty in recognizing the person who
presented himself at the door for admittance. When the count
entered the room the young man was carelessly stretched on a
sofa, tapping his boot with a gold-headed cane. On perceiving
the count he rose quickly.

" You are charged with a letter of introduction, are you not ? "
said the count.

" I did not mention that, because the signature seemed so
strange."

" The letter is signed ' Sindbad the Sailor,' is it not ? "

" Exactly so. Now, as I have never known any Sindbad
except the one celebrated in the *Thousand and One Nights*——"

" Well ! it is one of his descendants, and a great friend of mine ;
he is a rich Englishman, eccentric almost to insanity ; and his
real name is Lord Wilmore."

" Ah ! indeed ! then that explains everything," said Andrea,
" that is extraordinary."

" Perhaps you will give me some account of yourself and your
family ? "

" Certainly, I will do so," said the young man. " I am (as you
have said) the count Andrea Cavalcanti, son of Major Bartolomeo
Cavalcanti, a descendant of the Cavalcanti, whose names are inscribed in the golden book of Florence. Our family, although
still rich, has experienced many misfortunes, and for fifteen years
I have not seen the author of my existence. Since I have arrived
at years of discretion and become my own master I have been
constantly seeking him, but in vain. At length I received this
letter from your friend, which states that my father is in Paris,
and authorizes me to address myself to you for information
respecting him."

" Really, what you have related is exceedingly interesting,"
said Monte Cristo, " your father is indeed here, and is seeking
you."

" My father ! is my father here ? "

" Most undoubtedly," replied Monte Cristo, " your father,
Major Bartolomeo Cavalcanti."

" Ah ! that is the name—Major Bartolomeo Cavalcanti.
And my dear father is really here ? "

" Yes, sir, I have only just left him. The history which he
related to me of his lost son touched me to the quick. One day
he received a letter stating that the parties who had deprived him
of his son, now offered to restore him, on condition of receiving
a large sum of money, by way of ransom. Your father did not

hesitate an instant and the sum was sent. You were in the south of France, I think ? "

" Yes," replied Andrea, with an embarrassed air, " I was in the south of France."

" Then your father ought to have met you on the road."

" But," said Andrea, " if my father had met me, I doubt whether he would have recognized me ; I must be somewhat altered since he last saw me."

" Oh ! the voice of nature," said Monte Cristo.

" True," interrupted the young man, " I had forgotten that point of view."

" Now," replied Monte Cristo, " there is only one source of uneasiness left in your father's mind, which is this—he is anxious to see whether you have been fortunate enough to escape the bad moral influence to which you have been exposed, and which is infinitely more to be dreaded than any physical suffering ; whether you consider yourself capable of resuming and retaining the high position to which your rank entitles you."

" Sir," exclaimed the young man, quite astounded, " I hope no false report——"

" As for myself, I first heard you spoken of by my friend Wilmore, the philanthropist. He told me that he was anxious to restore you to the position you had lost, and that he would seek your father until he found him. My friend Wilmore is an original, but he is sincere, and as rich as a gold mine ; consequently, he may indulge his eccentricities without any fear of their ruining him, and I have promised to adhere to his instructions. I would wish to know whether your misfortunes have not, in some measure. contributed to render you a stranger to the world in which your fortune and your name entitle you to make a conspicuous figure ? "

" Sir," returned the young man, " make your mind easy on this score. I have received a very good education, and have been treated by these kidnappers very much as the slaves were treated in Asia Minor, in order that they might fetch a higher price in the Roman market."

" Well," said Monte Cristo, in an indifferent tone, " you will do as you please, but if I were you, I would not divulge a word of your adventures. Your history is a romance, and the world strangely mistrusts those which are bound in living parchment, even though they be gilded like yourself. Your touching history would be deemed unlikely and unnatural. You might be regarded as an upstart rather than a restored son."

" I agree with you, M. le Comte."

" Nevertheless, you must not exaggerate the risk," said Monte Cristo, " or by endeavouring to avoid one fault you will fall into another. You must form honourable friendships, and by that means counteract the prejudice which may attach to the obscurity of your former life."

Andrea changed countenance.

" Ah ! " said the count, watching Andrea, " I do not demand any confession from you ; it is precisely to avoid that necessity that your father was sent for from Lucca. You will find your father a very presentable person, I assure you."

" Then," said the young man, with anxiety, " I shall be sure to be placed in an agreeable position."

" One of the most pleasant possible ; he will allow you an income of 50,000 francs per annum during your stay in Paris."

" In that case I shall always choose to remain here."

" You cannot control circumstances, my dear sir, ' Man proposes, but God disposes.' "

" Does my father mean to remain long in Paris ? " asked Andrea.

" Only a few days," replied Monte Cristo. " His service will not allow him to absent himself more than two or three weeks together."

" Ah ! my dear father ! " exclaimed Andrea, evidently charmed at the prospect of his speedy departure.

" Therefore," said Monte Cristo, feigning to mistake his meaning—" therefore, I will not, for another instant, retard the pleasure of your meeting. If you are prepared to embrace your worthy father, go into the drawing-room, where you will find him awaiting you."

Monte Cristo watched him till he disappeared, and then touched a spring made to look like a picture, which revealed all that passed in the drawing-room now occupied by Cavalcanti and Andrea.

" Ah ! my dear father ! " said Andrea in a loud voice, in order that the count might hear him in the next room, " Is it really you ? "

" How do you do, my dear son ? " said the major, gravely.

" Will you not embrace me, sir ? " said Andrea.

" If you wish it, my son," said the major ; and the two men embraced each other after the fashion of actors on the stage ; that is to say, each rested his head on the other's shoulder.

" Then we are never more to be separated ? "

" Why, as to that—I think, my dear son, you must be by this time so accustomed to France as to look upon it almost as a second country."

" The fact is," said the young man, " that I should be exceedingly grieved to leave it."

" As for me, you must know I cannot live out of Lucca ; therefore, I shall return to Italy as soon as I can."

" But before you leave France, my dear father, I hope you will give me the documents necessary to prove my descent."

" I am here on that very account."

" Where are these papers ? "

" Here they are."

Andrea took the certificate of his father's marriage and his own baptismal register. When he had perused the documents, an indefinable expression of pleasure lighted up his countenance, and looking at the major with a most peculiar smile, he said, in very excellent Tuscan, " Then there is no longer any such thing in Italy as being condemned to the galleys ? "

" Will you be good enough to explain your meaning ? " said the major, endeavouring to assume an air of the greatest majesty.

" My dear M. Cavalcanti," said Andrea, taking the major by the arm in a confidential manner, " how much are you paid for being my father ? They give me 50,000 francs a year to be your son ; consequently, you can understand that it is not at all likely I shall ever deny my parent."

" Well, then," replied the major, " they paid me 50,000 francs down."

" You think I may rely on the count's promises ? "

" To the letter ; but, remember, we must play our respective parts. I, as a tender father——"

" And I as a dutiful son, since they choose that I shall be descended from you."

" Whom do you mean by they ? "

" *Ma foi !* I can hardly tell, but I was alluding to those who wrote the letter ; you received one, did you not ? "

" Yes."

" From whom ? "

" Abbé Busoni."

" Have you any knowledge of him ? "

" No, I have never seen him."

" What did he say in the letter ? "

The major gave a letter into the young man's hand.

Andrea read in a low voice :—

" You are poor ; a miserable old age awaits you. Would you like to become rich, or at least independent ? Set out immediately for Paris, and demand of the count of Monte Cristo, Avenue des Champs Élysées, No. 30, the son whom you had by the Marquise Corsinari, and who was taken away from you at five years of age. This son is named Andrea Cavalcanti. Remember to go to the count on the 26th of May, at seven o'clock in the evening.

(Signed) " ABBÉ BUSONI."

" I received a letter almost to the same effect."

" From whom ? '

" From an Englishman called Lord Wilmore, who takes the name of Sindbad the Sailor."

" And what did the letter contain ? "

" Read it."

" You are poor, and your future prospects are dark and gloomy. Do you wish for a name ? should you like to be rich, and your own master ? Go to the count of Monte Cristo, Avenue des Champs Elysées, on the 26th of May, at seven o'clock in the evening, and demand of him your father. You are the son of the Marquis Cavalcanti and the Marquise Oliva Corsinari. The marquis will give you some papers which will certify this fact, and authorize you to appear under that name in the Parisian world. As to your rank, an annual income of 50,000 francs will enable you to support it admirably. I enclose a letter of introduction to the count of Monte Cristo, whom I have directed to supply all your wants.

" SINDBAD THE SAILOR."

" Humph ! " said the major ; " very good ! You have seen the count ? "

" I have just left him."

" Do you understand the case ? "

" Not in the least."

Monte Cristo chose this moment for re-entering the drawing-room. On hearing the sound of his footsteps, the two men threw themselves in each other's arms ; and in the midst of this embrace the count appeared.

" Happy father ! happy son ! " said the count.

" There is only one thing which grieves me," observed the major, " and that is the necessity to leave Paris so soon."

" Ah ! my dear M. Cavalcanti, I trust you will not leave before I have had the honour of presenting you to some of my friends."

" I am at your service, sir," replied the major.

" Now, sir," said Monte Cristo, addressing Andrea, " make your confession."

" To whom ? "

" Tell M. Cavalcanti something of the state of your finances."

" *Ma foi!* M. le Comte, you have touched upon a tender chord."

" Well ! what would you have me do ? " said the major.

" You should furnish him with funds, of course," replied Monte Cristo.

" I ? "

" Yes, you ! " said the count, at the same time advancing towards Andrea, and slipping a packet of bank-notes into the young man's hand.

" What is this ? "

" It is from your father."

" I fully appreciate his delicacy," said Andrea, cramming the notes hastily into his pocket.

" And now, gentlemen, I wish you good day," said Monte Cristo.

" When shall we have the honour of seeing you again, M. le Comte ? " asked Cavalcanti.

" Ah ! " said Andrea, " when may we hope for that pleasure ? "

" On Saturday, if you will—yes. Let me see— Saturday—I am to dine at my country-house, at Auteuil, on that day, Rue la Fontaine, No. 28. Several persons are invited and, amongst others, M. Danglars, your banker. I will introduce you to him ; for he should know you, as he is to pay your money."

" At what hour shall we come ? " asked the young man.

" About half-past six."

" We will be with you at that time," said the major.

The two Cavalcanti bowed to the count, and left the house. Monte Cristo went to the window, and saw them crossing the street arm-in-arm.

" There go two miscreants ! "

CHAPTER LVII

THE TRYSTING-PLACE

OUR readers must now allow us to transport them again to the enclosure surrounding M. de Villefort's house, where we shall find some persons of our acquaintance. This time Maximilian was the first to arrive. He was awaiting with anxiety the sound of a light step on the gravel walk. At length he perceived that two were approaching him. The delay had been occasioned by a visit from Madame Danglars and Eugénie. Valentine proposed to Mademoiselle Danglars that they should take a walk in the garden, being anxious to show that the delay was not occasioned by any neglect on her part. The young man, with the intuitive perception of a lover, understood the circumstances in which she was placed and was comforted. Maximilian employed himself in mentally contrasting the two girls, and Valentine did not suffer by the contrast. In about half an hour the ladies retired, and Maximilian understood that Mademoiselle Danglars' visit had at last come to a conclusion. In a few minutes Valentine re-entered the garden alone, and—to avert suspicion—in leisurely fashion proceeded towards Maximilian.

"Good evening, Valentine."

"Good evening, Maximilian ; you saw the cause of my delay."

"Yes ; I recognized Mademoiselle Danglars. I was not aware you were so intimate with her."

"We were having a confidential chat," returned Valentine ; "she was telling me of her repugnance to the marriage with M. de Morcerf ; and I was confessing how wretched it made me to think of marrying M. d'Epinay."

"Ah ! how good you are to say so, Valentine ! You possess that indefinable charm, which is to a woman what perfume is to the flower and flavour to the fruit ; for the beauty of either is not the only quality we seek."

"Love makes you look upon everything in that light."

"No, Valentine, such is not the case. I was observing you both in the garden, and I cannot understand how any man can love Mademoiselle Danglars."

"The fact is, Maximilian, my presence rendered you unjust in your comparison."

"Does Mademoiselle Danglars object to this marriage with M. de Morcerf on account of loving another ? "

"She told me she loved no one," said Valentine ; "she dislikes the idea of being married, and would prefer leading an unfettered life. She almost wished her father might lose his fortune, that she might become an artist, like her friend, Mademoiselle Louise d'Armilly."

"Ah, well, enough of mademoiselle ; you are the subject on which I wish to speak."

"But we must be quick, for we have scarcely ten minutes more to pass together. Madame de Villefort requests my presence, as she has a communication to make on which a part of my fortune depends. You would love me as much if I were poor, would you not, Maximilian ? "

"Oh! I will always love you. But do you not fear that this communication may relate to your marriage? I met M. de Morcerf the other day. He has received a letter from Franz announcing his immediate return."

"Can it really be true, and is that why Madame de Villefort has sent for me? I hardly think so."

"Why not?"

"Because—I scarcely know why—but it has appeared as if Madame de Villefort secretly objected to the marriage, although she did not choose openly to oppose it."

"If she objects to your marrying M. d'Epinay she would be all the more likely to listen to any other proposal."

"No, Maximilian, it is not suitors Madame de Villefort objects to; it is marriage itself."

"Marriage! if she dislikes that so much, why did she ever marry herself?"

"You do not understand me, Maximilian. About a year ago I talked of retiring to a convent; Madame de Villefort, in spite of all the remarks which she considered it her duty to make, secretly approved of the proposition; my father consented to it, at her instigation, and it was only on account of my poor grandfather that I abandoned the project. I will never forget the reproachful look he cast on me, and the tears of utter despair he shed. Ah, Maximilian, I experienced such remorse for my intention, that, throwing myself at his feet, I exclaimed,— 'Forgive me, pray, forgive me, my dear grandfather; they may do what they will with me, I will never leave you.'"

"Dear Valentine, you are a perfect angel! I am sure I do not know what I have done to merit your love. But what interest can Madame de Villefort have in your remaining unmarried?"

"Did I not tell you just now that I was rich, Maximilian— too rich? Now, if I had taken the veil, my fortune would have gone to my father, and, in reversion, to his son."

"Ah! how strange that such a young and beautiful woman as your stepmother should be so avaricious."

"It is for her son."

"But could you not compromise matters?"

"How could I, especially with a woman who always professes to be so disinterested?"

"Valentine, I have regarded our love in the light of something sacred; will you permit me to make a confidant of a friend, and reveal to him the love I bear you?"

Valentine started. " A friend, Maximilian ? and who is this friend ? I tremble to give my permission."

" My dear girl ! you know him already. It was he who saved the life of your stepmother and her son."

" The count of Monte Cristo ? "

" The same."

" Ah ! " cried Valentine, " he is too much the friend of Madame de Villefort ever to be mine."

" The friend of Madame de Villefort ! That cannot be, Valentine ; you are mistaken."

" I am not ; I assure you his power over our household is almost unlimited. M. de Monte Cristo appears to exert a mysterious and almost uncontrollable influence over all the members of our family."

" If such be the case, my dear Valentine, you must yourself have felt, or at all events will soon feel, the effects of his presence. He meets Albert de Morcerf in Italy—it is to rescue him from the hands of the banditti ; he introduces himself to Madame Danglars—it is that he may give her a royal present ; your stepmother and her son pass before his door—it is that his Nubian may save them from destruction. His smile is so sweet when he addresses me that I forget it can ever be bitter to others. Ah ! Valentine, tell me if he ever looked on you with one of those sweet smiles ? If so, depend on it you will be happy."

" Me ! " said the young girl, " he never even glances at me." You say he loves you, Maximilian ; how do you know that ? All would pay deference to an officer like you, with a fierce moustache and a long sabre ; but they think they may crush a poor girl with impunity."

" Valentine ! you are mistaken."

" If it were otherwise—if he treated me diplomatically,—that is to say, like a man who wishes, by some means or other, to obtain a footing in the house, so that he may ultimately gain the power of dictating to its occupants,—he would, if it had been but once, have honoured me with the smile which you extol so loudly."

" Well, Valentine," said Morrel, with a sigh, " we will not discuss the matter further. I will not make a confidant of him."

" Alas ! " said Valentine, " I see that I have given you pain. I can only say how sincerely I ask pardon for having grieved you. But, indeed, I am not prejudiced beyond the power of conviction. Tell me what this count of Monte Cristo has done for you."

" I own that your question embarrasses me, Valentine, for I

cannot say that the count has rendered me any ostensible service. You will perhaps smile at me when I tell you that, ever since I have known this man, I have involuntarily entertained the idea that all the good fortune which has befallen me originated from him. I will endeavour to illustrate my meaning. He invited me to dine with him on Saturday, which was a very natural thing for him to do. Well, what have I learned since? That your mother and M. de Villefort are both coming to this dinner. I shall meet them there, and who knows what future advantages may follow? This may appear to you to be no unusual combination of circumstances; nevertheless, I perceive in it something more than is apparent on the surface."

"My good friend," said Valentine, "I should take you for a visionary and tremble for your reason, if I were always to hear you talk in a strain similar to this. Is it possible that you can see anything more than the merest chance in this meeting? No, no! it is as I have said, Maximilian; there is no one in the world of whom I can ask for help but yourself and my poor grandfather."

"You are right, logically speaking," said Maximilian; "but the gentle voice which usually has such power over me fails to convince me to-day."

"I feel the same as regards yourself," said Valentine; "and I own that, if you have no stronger proof to give me——"

"I have another," replied Maximilian, "which is conclusive to my mind. My ten years of service have also confirmed my ideas on the subject of sudden inspirations; for I have several times owed my life to one of those mysterious impulses which directed me to move at once in order to escape the ball which killed the comrade fighting by my side, whilst it left me unharmed."

"Dear Maximilian, why not attribute your escape to my constant prayers for your safety? But let me hear this second example."

"Well, look through this opening, and you will see the beautiful new horse which I rode here."

"Ah! what a beautiful creature!" cried Valentine.

"It is a very valuable animal," said Maximilian. "You know that my means are limited. Well, I went to a horse-dealer's, where I saw this horse, which I have named Medea. I asked the price of it; they told me it was 4,500 francs. I was therefore obliged to give it up, as you may imagine. The same evening some friends visited me, M. de Château-Renaud, M. de

Bray, and five or six other choice spirits, whom you do not know, even by name. They proposed *la bouillotte.* Just as they were sitting down to table M. de Monte Cristo arrived. He took his seat amongst them ; they played and I won. I am almost ashamed to say that my gains amounted to 5,000 francs. We separated at midnight. I could not defer my pleasure, so I took a cabriolet and drove to the horse-dealer's. Medea was standing at the rack, eating her hay. I immediately put on the saddle and bridle ; then, putting the 4,500 francs into the hands of the astonished dealer, I proceeded to fulfil my intention of passing the night in riding in the Champs Élysées. As I rode by the count's house I fancied I saw the shadow of his figure moving behind the curtain. Now, Valentine, I believe that he knew of my wish to possess this horse, and that he lost expressly to give me the means of procuring it."

"My dear Maximilian, you are really too fanciful. But they are calling me. Do you hear ? "

"Ah, Valentine ! " said Maximilian, " give me but one finger through this opening in the grating, that I may have the happiness of kissing it."

Valentine mounted the bank, and passed her whole hand through the opening. Maximilian seized the hand extended towards him, and imprinted on it an impassioned kiss. The little hand was then immediately withdrawn, and the young man saw Valentine hurrying towards the house, as though terrified at her own sensations.

CHAPTER LVIII

M. NOIRTIER DE VILLEFORT

WE will now relate what was passing in the house of the *procureur du roi* after the departure of Madame Danglars and her daughter. M. de Villefort entered his father's room, followed by Madame de Villefort. Both of the visitors took their places on either side of the paralytic.

M. Noirtier was sitting in an armchair, in which he was wheeled into the room in the morning, and in the same way removed at night. M. Noirtier, although almost immovable and helpless, looked at the new-comers with a quick and intelligent expression, perceiving at once that they were come on business of an unexpected and official character. Sight and hearing were the only senses remaining, and they appeared left, like two solitary sparks, to animate the miserable body which seemed fit for nothing but the grave. Noirtier's hair was long and white, and flowed over his shoulders; whilst in his eyes, shaded by thick black lashes, were concentrated, as happens with an organ which is used to the exclusion of the others, the activity, address, force, and intelligence, which were formerly diffused over his whole body; certainly the movement of the arm, the sound of the voice, and the agility of the body, were wanting; but the speaking eye sufficed for all. He commanded with it; it was the medium through which his thanks were conveyed. Three persons only could understand this language of the poor paralytic; these were Villefort, Valentine, and his old attendant, Barrois. Valentine, by means of her love, her patience, and her devotion, had learned to read in Noirtier's look all the varied feelings, which were passing in his mind. She was able to interpret his thoughts, and to convey her own in return, and it was seldom that she failed to anticipate the wishes of the living, thinking mind or the wants of the almost inanimate body. As to Barrois, he had been with his master for five-and-twenty years, and it was seldom that Noirtier found it necessary to ask for anything, so prompt was he in administering to all the wants of the invalid. Villefort perfectly understood the old man's vocabulary; he therefore allowed Valentine to go into the garden, sent away Barrois, and after having taken a place on the right hand of his father, whilst Madame de Villefort seated herself on the left, he addressed him thus :—

"I trust you will not be displeased, sir, that Valentine has not come with us, or that I dismissed Barrois; Madame Villefort and I have a communication to make to you."

Noirtier's face remained perfectly passive during this long preamble; but the eye of Villefort was endeavouring to penetrate into the inmost recesses of the old man's heart.

"Sir," resumed Villefort, "we are thinking of marrying Valentine. The marriage will take place in less than three months." Noirtier's eye still retained its lack-lustre expression.

Madame de Villefort now took her part in the conversation, and added, "We thought this news would possess an interest for you, sir, who have always entertained a great affection for Valentine; it therefore only now remains for us to tell you the name of the young man for whom she is destined. The person to whom we allude is, M. Franz de Quesnel, Baron d'Épinay."

When Madame de Villefort pronounced the name of Franz the pupil of M. Noirtier's eye began to dilate, his eyelids trembled, and he darted a lightning glance at Madame de Villefort and his son. The *procureur du roi* who knew the political hatred which had formerly existed between M. Noirtier and the elder d'Epinay, well understood the agitation and anger which the announcement had produced, but, feigning not to perceive either, he immediately resumed the conversation commenced by his wife. " Sir," said he, " you are aware that Valentine is in her nineteenth year, which renders it important that she should lose no time in forming a suitable connection. Nevertheless, you have not been forgotten in our plans, and we have fully ascertained beforehand that Valentine's future husband will consent that you should live with them ; so that you would be able to pursue exactly the same course of life which you have hitherto done, and two children instead of one will watch over and comfort you."

Noirtier's look was furious. Villefort opened a window, saying, " It is very warm, and the heat affects M. Noirtier." He then returned to his place, but did not sit down.

" This marriage," added Madame de Villefort, " is quite agreeable to the wishes of M. d'Epinay and his family ; besides he had no relations nearer than an uncle and aunt, his mother having died at his birth, and his father having been assassinated in 1815, that is to say, when he was but two years old."

" That assassination was a mysterious affair," said Villefort, " and the perpetrators escaped detection."

Noirtier made such an effort that his lips expanded into a smile.

" Now," continued Villefort, " those to whom the guilt really belongs would rejoice in the opportunity of bestowing such a peace-offering as Valentine on the son of him whose life they so ruthlessly destroyed."

Noirtier had succeeded in mastering his emotion. " Yes, I understand," was the reply contained in his look ; and this glance expressed a feeling of strong indignation, mixed with profound contempt.

Villefort motioned to his wife to take leave.

" Now, sir," said Madame de Villefort, " I must bid you farewell. Would you like me to send Edward to you for a short time ? "

It was understood among them that when the old man approved of a thing he closed his eyes, when otherwise he winked several times. Now he instantly winked his eyes. Provoked at his disapproval, Madame de Villefort bit her lip and said, " Then shall I send Valentine to you ? " The old man closed his eyes eagerly

M. and Madame de Villefort bowed and left the room, giving

orders that Valentine should be summoned to her grandfather's presence.

Valentine, with a colour still heightened by emotion, entered the room. One look was sufficient to tell her that her grandfather was suffering, and that there was something he wished to communicate to her.

" Dear grandpapa," cried she, " what has happened ? They have vexed you, and you are angry ? "

The paralytic closed his eyes in token of assent.

" Has anyone been speaking to you against me ? "

" Yes," said the old man's look, with eagerness.

" Let me think a moment. I do assure you, grandpapa—— Ah !—M. and Madame de Villefort have just left this room, have they not ? "

" Yes."

" What can they have said ? " and she tried to think what it could be.

" Ah ! I know," said she, lowering her voice, and going close to the old man, " they have been speaking of my marriage,—have they not ? "

" Yes."

" I understand ; you are displeased at the silence I have preserved on the subject. Pray forgive me."

But there was no look calculated to reassure her ; all it seemed to say was, " It is not only your reserve which afflicts me."

" What is it, then ? " asked the young girl. " You are vexed with the engagement ? "

" Yes."

" Well, listen," said Valentine, throwing herself on her knees, and putting her arm round her grandfather's neck, " I am vexed, too, for I do not love M. Franz d'Epinay." An expression of intense joy illumined the old man's eyes. " Then the idea of this marriage grieves you, too ? Ah ! if you could but help me—if we could both together defeat their plan ! Alas ! you, who would have been such a powerful protector to me in the days of your health and strength, can now only sympathize in my joys and sorrows."

At these words there appeared in Noirtier's eyes an expression of such deep meaning that the young girl thought she could read these words there, " You are mistaken ; I can still do much for you."

" Do you think you can help me, dear grandpapa ? " said Valentine.

" Yes." Noirtier raised his eyes ; it was the sign agreed on between him and Valentine when he wanted anything.

She recited all the letters of the alphabet from A down to N. When she arrived at that letter the paralytic made her understand that was the initial letter of the thing he wanted.

" Ah ! " said Valentine. " Well, let me see what you can want which begins with N ? Na—Ne—Ni—No—— "

" Yes, yes," said the old man's eyes.

Valentine fetched a dictionary, which she placed on a desk before Noirtier ; she opened it, and seeing the old man's eye fixed on its pages, she ran her finger quickly up and down the columns. At the word " Notary " Noirtier made a sign to her to stop.

" You wish a notary to be sent for ? " said Valentine.

" Yes."

" Shall my father be informed of your wish ? "

" Yes."

" Is that all you want ? "

" Yes."

Valentine rang the bell, and ordered the servant to tell Monsieur or Madame de Villefort that they were requested to come to M. Noirtier's room.

M. de Villefort entered, followed by Barrois. " What do you want me for, sir ? " demanded the former of the paralytic.

" Sir," said Valentine, " my grandfather wishes for a notary."

At this strange and unexpected demand M. de Villefort and his father exchanged looks.

" Do you wish for a notary ? " asked Villefort.

" Yes."

" What to do ? "

Noirtier made no answer.

" To do us an ill turn ? do you think it worth while ? " said Villefort.

" Still," said Barrois, with the freedom of an old servant, " if M. Noirtier asks for a notary, I suppose he really wishes it ; therefore I shall go at once, and fetch one."

" Yes, I do want a notary," motioned the old man, shutting his eyes with a look of defiance.

" You shall have a notary, as you wish for one, sir," said Villefort ; " but the case cannot fail to be ridiculous."

" Never mind that," said Barrois, " I will fetch a notary, nevertheless ; " and the old servant departed on his mission.

CHAPTER LIX

THE WILL

As soon as Barrois had left the room Noirtier looked at Valentine with that peculiar expression which conveyed so much deep meaning. The young girl understood the look, and so did Villefort, for his countenance became clouded, and he knitted his eyebrows angrily. He took a seat and awaited the arrival of the notary. In three-quarters of an hour Barrois returned with a notary.

" Sir," said Villefort, " you were sent for by M. Noirtier, whom you see here. All his limbs are completely paralysed; he has lost his voice also, and we ourselves find much trouble in endeavouring to catch some fragments of his meaning." Noirtier cast an appealing look on Valentine.

" Sir," said she, " I understand my grandfather always."

" That is true," said Barrois; " as I told the gentleman while we walked along."

" Permit me," said the notary, turning first to Villefort and then to Valentine, " permit me to state that the case in question is just one of those in which a public officer like myself cannot act without incurring a grave responsibility. I cannot be sure of the approbation or disapprobation of a client who cannot speak: and as the object of his desire cannot be clearly proved to me, my services here would be useless, and cannot be legally exercised." The notary then prepared to retire. Noirtier looked at Valentine with an expression so full of grief that she arrested the departure of the notary.

" Sir," said she, " the means whereby I speak with my grandfather may be easily learnt; and I can teach you. What will set your conscience at ease on the subject ? "

" In order to render an act valid I must be certain of the approbation or disapprobation of my client."

" Well, sir, by the help of two signs, with which I will acquaint you presently, you may ascertain with perfect certainty that my grandfather is in full possession of his mental faculties. M. Noirtier being deprived of voice and motion, is accustomed to convey his meaning by closing his eyes when he wishes to signify ' yes,' and to wink when he means ' no.' These signs will enable you to converse with M. Noirtier; try."

Noirtier gave Valentine such a look of tenderness and gratitude that it was comprehended even by the notary himself. " You have heard and understood what your granddaughter has been saying, sir, have you ? " asked the notary. Noirtier closed his eyes. " And you approve of what she said ; that is to say, you declare that the signs which she mentioned are really those by means of which you are accustomed to convey your thoughts ? "

" Yes."

" It was you who sent for me ? "

" Yes."

" To make your will ? "

" Yes."

" Let us try what we can do, then," said the notary. " You accept this young lady as your interpreter, M. Noirtier ? "

" Yes."

" Well, sir, what do you require of me, and what document is it that you wish drawn up ? " Valentine named all the letters of the alphabet till she came to W. At this letter the eloquent eye of Noirtier gave her notice that she was to stop.

" It is the letter W which M. Noirtier wants," said the notary.

" Wait," said Valentine ; and turning to her grandfather, she repeated, " Wa—We—Wi— " the old man stopped her at the last syllable. Valentine then took the dictionary, and when she came to the word " Will," M. Noirtier's eye bade her stop.

" Will ! " cried the notary ; " it is evident that M. Noirtier is desirous of making his will ! "

" Yes, yes, yes ! " motioned the invalid.

" Really, sir, you must allow that this is most extraordinary," said the astonished notary, turning to M. de Villefort.

" Yes," said the procureur, " and I think the will promises to be yet more extraordinary ; for I cannot see how it is to be drawn up without the intervention of Valentine, and she may, perhaps, be too much interested in its contents to allow of her being a suitable interpreter of the ill-defined wishes of her grandfather."

" No, no, no ! " replied the eye of the paralytic.

" What ! " said Villefort, " do you mean to say that Valentine is not interested in your will ! "

" No."

What is he going to do ? " thought Villefort. He left the room to give orders for another notary to be sent, but Barrois had already gone to fetch one. The *procureur du roi* then told his wife to come up. In the course of a quarter of an hour every one had assembled in the chamber of the invalid ; the second notary had also arrived. They read to Noirtier the formal copy of a will, in order to give him an idea of the terms in which such documents are generally couched ; then, in order to test the capacity of the testator, the first notary said, turning towards him, " When a person makes a will it is generally in favour or in prejudice of some person ! "

" Yes."

" Have you an exact idea of the amount of your fortune ? "

" Yes."

" I will name to you several sums, which will increase by graduation : you will stop me when I reach the one representing the amount of your own possessions."

" Yes."

There was a kind of solemnity in this interrogation. The witnesses had formed a circle round the invalid ; the second notary was sitting at a table ready to write, and his colleague was standing before the testator in the act of interrogating him.

" Your fortune exceeds 300,000 francs, does it not ? " asked he. Noirtier made a sign that it did.

" Do you possess 400,000 francs ? " inquired the notary. Noirtier's eye remained immovable.

" 500,000 ? " The same expression continued. " 600,000,—700,000,—800,000,—900,000 ? " Noirtier stopped him at the last-named sum.

" You are in possession of 900,000 francs ? " asked the notary.

" Yes."

" In stock ? "

" Yes."

" The stock is in your own hands ? "

The look which M. Noirtier cast on Barrois showed that there was something wanted which he knew where to find ; the old servant left the room, and presently returned with a small casket.

" Do you permit us to open this casket ? " Noirtier gave his assent. They opened it, and found 900,000 francs in bank script. The first notary handed over each note as he examined it to his colleague.

The total amount was found to be as M. Noirtier had stated.

" It is all as he has said ; it is clear that the mind still retains its full force and vigour." Then turning towards the paralytic, he said. " To whom do you desire to leave this fortune ? "

" Oh ! " said Madame de Villefort, " there is not much doubt on that subject. M. Noirtier tenderly loves his granddaughter, Mademoiselle de Villefort ; it is she who has nursed and tended him for six years, and has, by her devoted attention, won the affection, I had almost said the gratitude, of her grandfather ;

P

and it is but just that she should reap the fruit of her devotion."

The eye of Noirtier clearly showed by its expression that he was not deceived by the false assent given by Madame de Villefort's words and manner to the motives which she supposed him to entertain.

"It is, then, to Mademoiselle Valentine de Villefort that you leave these 900,000 francs ?" demanded the notary. The old man significantly winked his eye in token of dissent.

"You are not making any mistake, are you ? " said the notary ; "you really mean to declare that such is not your intention ? "

"No, no."

The old man's declaration that Valentine was not the destined inheritor of his fortune had excited the hopes of Madame de Villefort ; she gradually approached the invalid, and said : "Then, doubtless, dear M. Noirtier, you intend leaving your fortune to your grandson, Edward ? "

The winking of the eyes which answered this speech was most decided and expressed a feeling almost amounting to hatred.

"No ! " said the notary ; "then perhaps it is to your son, M. de Villefort ? "

"No."

Villefort and his wife blushed and changed colour.

"What have we all done, then, dear grandpapa ? " said Valentine ; " you no longer seem to love any of us ? "

Noirtier fixed his intelligent eyes on Valentine's hand.

"My hand ? " said she.

"Yes."

"Ah ! " cried Valentine, suddenly, " I understand ! it is my marriage you mean, is it not, dear grandpapa ? "

"Yes, yes," he signalled, casting on Valentine a look of gratitude for having guessed his meaning.

"You are angry with us all on account of this marriage, are you not ? "

"Yes."

"You do not wish me to marry M. Franz d'Epinay ? "

"I do not wish it," said the eye of her grandfather.

"And you disinherit your granddaughter," continued the notary, " because she has contracted an engagement contrary to your wishes ? "

"Yes."

"So that, but for this marriage, she would have been heiress ? "

"Yes."

" But," said Villefort, " I consider that I am the best judge of the propriety of the marriage in question. I am the only person possessing the right to dispose of my daughter's hand. It is my wish she should marry M. Franz d'Épinay—and she shall marry him ! "

Valentine sank weeping into a chair.

" Sir," said the notary, " how do you intend disposing of your fortune in case Mademoiselle de Villefort still determines on marrying M. Franz ? "

The old man gave no answer.

' You will, of course, dispose of it in some way or other ? "

" Yes."

' But," said the notary, " you are aware that the law does not allow a son to be entirely deprived of his patrimony ! "

" Yes."

" You only intend, then, to dispose of that part of your fortune which the law allows you to deduct from the inheritance of your son ? "

Noirtier made no answer.

" Do you still wish to dispose of all ? "

" Yes."

" What do you decide on, sir ? " asked the notary of Villefort.

" Nothing, sir ; it is a resolution which my father has taken, and I know he never alters his mind. I am quite resigned. These 900,000 francs will go out of the family in order to enrich some hospital ; but it is ridiculous thus to yield to the caprices of an old man ; and I shall, therefore, act according to my conscience."

Having said this, Villefort quitted the room. The same day the will was made, and given in charge to M. Des Champs, the family notary.

CHAPTER LX

THE TELEGRAPH

M. DE VILLEFORT found the count of Monte Cristo in the drawing-room, into which the latter had been shown, whilst the *procureur* was engaged with his father. The count remarked M. de Villefort's preoccupied look.

" *Ma foi !* " said Monte Cristo. " Have I arrived at the moment that you were drawing up a capital indictment ? "

" No, M. le Comte," replied M. de Villefort. " I am the only victim in this case."

" To what do you allude ? " said Monte Cristo, with well-affected interest. " Have you met with some misfortune ? "

" Oh ! M. le Comte," said Villefort, with a bitter smile, " it is only a loss of money which I have sustained. It is not so much the loss of the money which vexes me, though 900,000 francs is not a trifle, as the fact that this ill luck may blast the prospects of my child. It is all occasioned by an old man in second childhood."

" And who is the cause of all this annoyance ? "

" My father. I left him a few minutes ago dictating his will to two notaries."

" But to do this he must have spoken."

" He has done more than that ; he has made himself understood."

" How was such a thing possible ? "

" By the help of his eyes, which are still full of life, and, as you have heard, possess the power of inflicting serious injury."

" My dear," said Madame de Villefort, who had just entered the room, " perhaps you exaggerate the evil."

" What is this that M. de Villefort has been telling me ? " demanded Monte Cristo ; " and what incomprehensible misfortune——"

" Incomprehensible is not the word ! " interrupted the *procureur du roi*, shrugging his shoulders. " It is an old man's caprice."

" And is there no means of making him revoke his decision ? "

" Yes," said Madame de Villefort ; " it is in the power of my husband to cause the will, which is now in prejudice of Valentine, to be altered in her favour."

" My dear," said Villefort, in answer to his wife, " my wishes must be respected in my family. The folly of an old man and the caprice of a child shall not overturn a project which I have entertained for so many years. The Baron d'Épinay was my friend, as you know, and an alliance with his son is in every sense desirable."

" Do you think," said Madame de Villefort, " that Valentine is in league with him ? I should not be surprised if what we have just seen and heard is only the execution of a plan concerted between them."

" Madame," said Villefort, " a fortune of 900,000 francs is not so easily renounced."

" But she could make up her mind to renounce the world, sir ; only a year ago she proposed entering a convent."

" Never mind," replied Villefort, " I say that this marriage
shall be arranged. I can truly say that I have always entertained
a high respect for my father, but in the present circumstances,
I am justified in doubting the wisdom of an old man who, because
he hated the father, vents his anger on the son. My mind
is fully made up : my daughter shall marry the Baron Franz
d'Épinay.'

" What ! " said the count, " do you say that M. Noirtier
disinherits Mademoiselle de Villefort because she is going to
marry M. le Baron Franz d'Épinay ? "

" Yes, sir, that is the reason," said Villefort, shrugging his
shoulders.

" I believe I know M. Franz d'Épinay," said the count ; " is
he not the son of General de Quesnel, who was created Baron
d'Épinay by Charles X. ? "

" The same," said Villefort.

" But," said Monte Cristo, " do you know of any cause for
this hatred ? Perhaps it is some political difference."

" My father and the Baron d'Épinay lived in those stormy
times of which I only saw the last days," said De Villefort.

" Was not your father a Bonapartist ? " asked Monte Cristo ;
" I think I remember that you told me something of that kind."

" My father was a Jacobin more than anything else," said
Villefort, carried by his feelings beyond the bounds of prudence.
" When my father conspired, it was not for the Emperor, it was
against the Bourbons ; for M. Noirtier possessed this peculiarity,
that he never projected any Utopian schemes but strove for
possibilities, and never shrank from means which he deemed
necessary to their accomplishment."

" Well," said Monte Cristo, " it is just as I thought ; it was
politics which brought Noirtier and General Quesnel into personal
conflict. Although the General served under Napoleon, did he
not retain Royalist sentiments ? And was he not assassinated
one evening on leaving a Bonapartist meeting to which he had
been invited under the impression that he favoured the cause of
the Emperor ? "

" The facts were precisely as you have stated," said Madame
de Villefort ; " and it was to prevent the renewal of old feuds
that M. de Villefort formed the idea of uniting in the bonds of
matrimony the children of these inveterate enemies."

" It was a sublime and charitable thought," said Monte Cristo,
" It would be noble to see Mademoiselle Noirtier de Villefort
assuming the title of Madame Franz d'Épinay."

" Although," said De Villefort, " it will be a serious thing for Valentine to lose the fortune of her grandfather, I do not think the marriage will be prevented on that account, nor do I believe that M. d'Épinay will be alarmed at this pecuniary loss ; besides, he knows that Valentine is rich in right of her mother, and that she will, in all probability, inherit the fortune of M. and Madame de Saint Méran her mother's parents, who both love her tenderly."

" And who are fully as well worth loving and tending as M. de Noirtier," said Madame de Villefort; " besides, they are to come to Paris in about a month, and Valentine, after the affront she has received, need not consider it necessary to continue to bury herself alive with M. Noirtier."

" But it seems to me," said Monte Cristo, " that if M. Noirtier disinherits Mademoiselle de Villefort on account of her marrying a man whose father he detested, he cannot have the same cause of complaint against this dear Edward."

" True," said Madame de Villefort ; " is it not unjust—shamefully unjust ? Poor Edward is as much M. Noirtier's grandchild as Valentine."

The count listened and said no more.

" However," said Madame de Villefort, returning to the one idea which incessantly occupied her mind, " perhaps it would be better to represent this unlucky affair to M. d'Épinay, to give him the opportunity of renouncing his claim to Valentine."

" Ah, that would be a great pity," said Villefort. " A marriage once concerted and then broken off throws a sort of discredit on a young lady ; no, all will go well ; M. d'Épinay, if he is an honourable man, will consider himself more than ever pledged to Mademoiselle de Villefort."

" I agree with M. de Villefort," said Monte Cristo; " and if I were sufficiently intimate with him to allow of tendering advice, I would persuade him, since I have been told M. d'Épinay is coming back, to settle this affair at once beyond all possibility of revocation."

The *procureur du roi* was delighted with the proposition, but his wife changed colour.

" Well, that is all I wanted, and I will be guided by a counsellor such as you are," said he, extending his hand to Monte Cristo.

The count rose to depart.

" Are you going to leave us, M. le Comte ? " said Madame de Villefort.

" I am sorry I must do so, madame ; I only came to remind you of your promise for Saturday."

"Ah," said Villefort, "is it at your house in the Champs Élysées that you receive your visitors?"

"No," said Monte Cristo, "at my house in Auteuil."

"At Auteuil?" said Villefort; "and in what part of Auteuil do you reside?"

"Rue de la Fontaine, No. 28."

"Then," cried Villefort, "you bought M. de Saint Méran's house?"

"Did it belong to M. de Saint Méran?" demanded Monte Cristo.

"Yes," replied Madame de Villefort; "and, would you believe it? my husband would never live in it."

"A singular prejudice, M. de Villefort!"

"I do not like Auteuil, sir," said the *procureur du roi*, making an effort to remain calm.

"But I hope you will not carry your antipathy so far as to deprive me of the pleasure of your company, sir!" said Monte Cristo.

"No, M. le Comte—I hope—I assure you I will do all I can," stammered Villefort.

"Oh," said Monte Cristo, "I allow of no excuse. On Saturday, at six o'clock, I shall expect you, and if you fail to come, I shall think that this house, which has remained uninhabited for twenty years, must have some gloomy tradition or dreadful legend connected with it."

"I will come, M. le Comte,—I will be sure to come," said Villefort, eagerly.

"Thank you," said Monte Cristo; "now you must permit me to take my leave."

"You said before you were obliged to leave us, M. le Comte," said Madame de Villefort, "*must* you go?"

"Madame, you will think it odd," answered the Count, "but I am going to see a telegraph! I had often seen one at the end of a road on a hillock, and in the light of the sun its black arms, bending in every direction, reminded me of the claws of an immense beetle. I assure you it was never without emotion that I gazed on it, for I could not help thinking how wonderful it was that these various signs should be made to cleave the air with such precision as to convey to the distance of three hundred leagues the ideas and wishes of a man sitting at a table at one end of the line to another man similarly placed at the opposite extremity, and all this by the simple act of volition on the part of the individual communicating the intelligence. It never occurred to me to wish for a nearer inspection of these huge insects, but one day I learned that the mover of this telegraph was only a poor wretch, hired for twelve hundred francs a year, and employed all the day watching his fellow-insect, who was placed four or five leagues distant from him. At length I experienced a desire to study this living chrysalis, and to endeavour to understand the secret part played by those insect-actors simply by means of successively pulling different pieces of string."

" What telegraph do you intend visiting ? that of the Home department, or of the Observatoire ? "

" I shall visit one in the open country where I shall find a good-natured simpleton, who knows no more than the machine he is employed to work."

" You are a singular man," said Villefort.

" What line would you advise me to study ? "

" That which is most in use."

" The Spanish one, you mean, I suppose ! "

" Yes ; should you like a letter to the minister that they might explain to you——"

" No," said Monte Cristo ; " I do not wish to comprehend it. It is the insect with black claws which I wish to retain in my imagination in all its purity and significance."

" Go, then ; for in the course of two hours it will be dark, and you will not be able to see anything."

" Which is the nearest line ? Bayonne ? "

" Yes ! the road to Bayonne ! "

" Thank you. Good-bye. On Saturday I will tell you my impressions concerning the telegraph."

CHAPTER LXI

RIDDING A GARDENER OF DORMICE THAT ATE HIS PEACHES

NOT on the same night but next morning, the count of Monte Cristo went out by the barrier d'Enfer, taking the road to Orleans. Leaving the village of Linas, he reached the tower of Montlhéry, which is situated upon the highest point of the plain of that name. At the foot of the hill the count dismounted, and began to ascend by a winding path, but when he reached the summit his advance was blocked by a hedge.

Monte Cristo looked for the door of the enclosure, and was not long in finding it. It was a little wooden gate, worked on willow hinges, and fastened with a nail and string.

The count soon understood its mechanism, and the door opened. He then found himself in a little garden, about twenty feet long by twelve wide, bounded on one side by the hedge, in which was the door ; and on the other, by the old tower, covered with ivy and studded with wild flowers. Monte Cristo, after having closed the door and fastened the string to the nail, cast a look around.

" The man at the telegraph," said he, " must either engage a gardener or devote himself passionately to horticulture." Suddenly he stumbled against a man about fifty years old, who was plucking strawberries, which he was placing upon vine-leaves.

" You are gathering your crop, sir," said Monte Cristo, smiling.

" Excuse me, sir," replied the man, raising his hand to his cap ; " I am not on duty, I know, but I have only just come down."

" Calm yourself, my friend," said the count, with that smile which at his will became either terrible or benevolent, and which at present beamed only with kindness ; " I am not an inspector, but a traveller, conducted here by a curiosity he half repents of, since he causes you to lose your time."

" Ah ! my time is not valuable," replied the man with a melancholy smile. " Still it belongs to Government, and I ought not to waste it : but having received the signal that I might rest for an hour " (here he glanced at the sundial, for there was everything in the enclosure of Montlhéry, even a sundial), " and having still ten minutes before me, and my strawberries being ripe, when a day longer—— By-the-by, sir, do you think dormice eat them ? "

" Indeed, I should think not," replied Monte Cristo ; " dormice are bad neighbours for us who do not eat them preserved as the Romans did."

" Really ! They can't be nice, though they do say, ' as fat as a dormouse.' Listen ; last year I had four apricots, they stole one. I had one nectarine, only one ; well, sir, they ate half of it on the wall—a splendid nectarine ; I never ate a better."

" You ate it."

" That is to say, the half that was left. But this year I took care it should not happen, even if I sat up the whole night to watch when the strawberries are ripe."

Monte Cristo had heard enough. Every man has a devouring passion in his heart ; that of the man of the telegraph was horticulture. The Count began gathering the vine leaves which screened the sun from the grapes, and won the heart of the gardener. " Did you come here, sir, to see the telegraph ? "

" Yes ! if it be not contrary to the rules."

" Sir," said the gardener, glancing at the sundial, " the ten minutes are nearly expired, I must return to my post. Will you go up with me ? "

Monte Cristo entered the tower, which was divided into three stages ; the lowest contained gardening implements ; the second was the dwelling, or rather sleeping-place of the man ; it contained a few poor articles of household furniture and some dry herbs.

" Does it require much study to learn the art of telegraphing, sir ? " asked Monte Cristo.

" The study does not take long ; it was acting as a supernumerary that was so tiresome."

" And what is the pay ? "

" A thousand francs, sir."

" It is nothing."

" No ; but then we are lodged, as you perceive."

They passed on to the third stage ; it was the room of the telegraph. Monte Cristo looked in turns at the two iron handles by which the machine was worked. " It is very interesting," he said, " but it must be very tedious for a lifetime."

" Yes ! at first my neck was cramped with looking at it, but we have our hours of recreation and our holidays."

" Holidays ! "

" When we have a fog."

" How long have you been here ? "

" Ten years, and five as a supernumerary, make fifteen."

" You are——"

" Fifty-five years old."

" How long must you have served to claim the penson ? "

" Twenty-five years."

" And how much is the pension ? "

" A hundred crowns."

" And you understand these signals ? "

" Not at all."

" But have you never tried to understand them ? "

" Never ! why should I ? "

" There are some signals only addressed to you."

" Certainly."

" And they mean——"

" ' *Nothing new* ': or, ' *You have an hour* ': or, ' *To-morrow.* ' "

" This is simple enough," said the count ; " but look, is not your correspondent putting himself in motion ? "

" Ah, yes ; thank you, sir ! "

" And what is he saying—anything you understand ? "

" Yes ; he asks if I am ready."

" And you reply ? "

" By the same sign, which at the same time tells my righthand correspondent that I am ready, while it gives notice to my lefthand correspondent to prepare in his turn."

" It is very ingenious," said the count.

" You will see," said the man proudly ; " in five minutes he will speak."

" You are fond of gardening ? "

" Passionately."

" And you would be pleased to have, instead of this terrace of twenty feet, an enclosure of two acres ? "

" Sir, I should make an earthly paradise of it."

" You live badly on your thousand francs ? "

" Badly enough ; but yet I do live."

" Tell me, should you have the misfortune to turn your head while your righthand correspondent was telegraphing——"

" I could not repeat the signals."

" And then ? "

" Not having repeated them, through negligence, I should be fined."

" How much ? "

" A hundred francs."

" Well, suppose you were to alter a signal, and substitute another ? "

" Ah, that is another case ; I should be turned off, and lose my pension. So I am not likely to do any of these things."

" Not even for fifteen years' wages ? Come, it is worth thinking about ? "

" For fifteen thousand francs ! "

" Just so : fifteen thousand francs, do you understand ? "

" Sir, let me see my righthand correspondent ! "

" On the contrary, do not look at him, but on these."

" Bank-notes ! "

" Exactly ; fifteen of them."

" And whose are they ? "

" Yours, if you like."

" Mine ! " exclaimed the man, half suffocated.

" Yes ; yours—your own property."

"Sir, my righthand correspondent redoubles his signals; he is impatient."

"Never mind—take these;" and the count placed the packet in the hands of the man. "Now this is not all," he said; "you cannot live upon your fifteen thousand francs."

"I shall still have my place."

"No! you will lose it, for you are going to alter the sign of your correspondent."

"Sir, unless you force me—— "

"I think I can force you!" and Monte Cristo drew another packet from his pocket. "Here are ten thousand more francs. With five thousand you can buy a pretty little house with two acres of land; the remaining twenty thousand will bring you in a thousand francs a year."

"What am I to do?"

"Nothing very difficult."

"But what is it?"

"To repeat these signs." Monte Cristo took a paper from his pocket, upon which were drawn three signs, with numbers to indicate the order in which they were to be worked.

"There, you see it will not take long."

The mark was hit; red with fever, while the large drops fell from his brow, the man executed, one after the other, the three signs given by the count; notwithstanding the frightful contortions of the righthand correspondent, who, not understanding the change, began to think the gardener had become mad. As to the lefthand one, he conscientiously repeated the same signals, which were definitely carried to the Minister of the Interior. "Now you are rich," said Monte Cristo.

"Yes," replied the man, "but at what a price!"

"Listen, friend," said Monte Cristo. "I do not wish to cause you any remorse; believe me, then, when I swear to you that you have wronged no man, but on the contrary have benefited mankind." The man looked at the bank-notes, felt them, counted them; he turned pale, then red; then rushed into his room to drink a glass of water, but he had not time to reach the water jug, and fainted in the midst of his dried herbs. Five minutes afterwards, the new telegraph message reached the minister; Debray had the horses put to his carriage, and drove to Madame Danglars.

"Has your husband any Spanish bonds?" he asked of the baroness.

"He has six millions' worth."

" He must sell at any price."

" Why ? "

" Because Don Carlos has fled from Bourges, and has returned to Spain."

The baroness did not wait for a repetition ; she ran to her husband, who immediately hastened to his agent, and ordered him to sell at any price. When it was seen that Danglars sold, the Spanish funds fell directly. Danglars lost five hundred thousand francs ; but he rid himself of all his Spanish shares. The same evening the following was read in *Le Messager* :—" Don Carlos has escaped the vigilance exercised over him at Bourges, and returned to Spain by the Catalonian frontier. Barcelona has risen in his favour."

Next morning the *Moniteur* contained the following :—" It was without any foundation that ' *Le Messager* ' yesterday announced the flight of Don Carlos and the revolt of Barcelona. Don Carlos has not left Bourges, and the Peninsula is in the enjoyment of profound peace. A telegraphic signal, improperly interpreted, owing to the fog, was the cause of this error."

The funds rose one per cent. higher than the figure at which they stood before they fell. This made the difference of a million to Danglars.

" Good ! " said Monte Cristo to Morrel, who was at his house when the news arrived of Danglars' strange reverse of fortune. " I have just made a discovery for twenty-five thousand francs, for which I would have paid a hundred thousand."

" What have you discovered ? "

" How to rid a gardener of the dormice that ate his peaches."

CHAPTER LXII

THE PHANTOMS

AT first sight the exterior of the house at Auteuil presented nothing splendid as the destined residence of the count of Monte Cristo ; but this simplicity was according to the will of its master, who ordered nothing to be altered outside. The count had positively forbidden the garden to be touched. Bertuccio made amends, however, by loading the antechambers, staircases, and chimneys with flowers. What especially proved the capacity of the steward and his master's knowledge was that this house, which appeared only the night before so sad and gloomy, impregnated with that sickly smell one can almost fancy to be the smell of time had, in one day, acquired the aspect of life, was scented with its owner's favourite perfumes, and had the very light regulated according to his wish. When the count should come he would find at hand his books and arms; his eyes should rest upon his favourite pictures; his dogs, whose caresses he loved, should welcome him; the birds, whose songs delighted him, should cheer him with their music.

One chamber alone had been respected by Bertuccio. Past this room, to which one ascended by the grand, and left by the back staircase, the servants went with curiosity, and the steward with terror. At five o'clock precisely, the count arrived, followed by Ali. Bertuccio awaited him with mingled impatience and uneasiness. Monte Cristo descended into the court-yard, walked all over the house, without giving any sign of approbation or displeasure, until he entered his bedroom, situated on the opposite side of the closed room. When he approached a piece of furniture, made of rosewood, " That will at least serve to put my gloves in," he said.

"If your Excellency will deign to open it," said the delighted Bertuccio, " you will find gloves in it."

At precisely six o'clock the clatter of horses' hoofs was heard at the entrance-door: it was the captain of Spahis on Medea.

"I am sure I am the first," cried Morrel; " I came to have you a minute to myself. Julie and Emanuel have a thousand things to tell you. But, count, will your people take care of my horse?"

"Do not alarm yourself, my dear Maximilian—they understand."

"Because he wants petting. If you had seen at what a pace he came; like the wind!"

"I should think so,—a horse that cost 5,000 francs!" said Monte Cristo.

"Do you regret them?" asked Morrel, with his open laugh.

"I? Certainly not!" replied the count. "No; I should only regret if the horse had not proved good."

"It is so good, that I have distanced M. de Château-Renaud, one of the best riders in France, and M. Debray, who both mount the minister's Arabs; and close at their heels are the horses of Madame Danglars, which always go at six leagues an hour."

"Then they follow you?" asked Monte Cristo.

"See, they are here!" The carriage stopped at the steps, followed by the horsemen.

The instant Debray had touched the ground, he was at the

carriage-door. He offered his hand to the baroness, who, descending, took it with a peculiarity of manner imperceptible to everyone but Monte Cristo. But nothing escaped the count's notice; and he observed a little note slipped from the hand of Madame Danglars to that of the minister's secretary. After his wife the banker descended, pale, as though he had issued from his tomb, instead of his carriage. Madame Danglars ascended the steps, saying to Morrel, " Sir, if you were a friend of mine I should ask if you would sell your horse."

Morrel, with a wry face, turned to Monte Cristo, as if to ask him to extricate him from his embarrassment.

"Unfortunately," said the count, "I am witness that M. Morrel cannot give up his horse, his honour being engaged in keeping it."

"How so?"

"He laid a wager he would tame Medea in six months. If he were to get rid of it before that time, people would say he was afraid of it; and a captain of Spahis cannot risk this, even to gratify a pretty woman."

"You see my position, madame," said Morrel, bestowing a grateful smile on Monte Cristo.

Monte Cristo showed her two immense porcelain jars, of extraordinary size and delicacy, covered with marine plants.

The baroness was astonished. "How are such enormous jars manufactured?"

"I do not know; I have heard that an emperor of China had an oven built expressly for them, and that in this oven twelve jars like these were successively baked. Two broke, from the heat of the fire; the other ten were sunk three hundred fathoms deep into the sea. The emperor only left the documents proving the manufacture of the jars and their consignment to the deep. At the end of two hundred years the documents were found. Then divers descended into the bay where the jars had been thrown; but of ten three only remained, the rest having been broken by the waves."

Meanwhile Danglars, who cared little for curiosities, was mechanically tearing off the blossoms of a splendid orange tree, one after another.

"Sir," said Monte Cristo to him, "I do not recommend my pictures to you, who possess such splendid paintings; but, nevertheless, here are two by Hobbema, a Paul Potter, a Mieris, two Gerard Douws, a Raphael, a Vandyke, a Zurbaran, and two or three by Murillo, worth looking at."

"Stay!" said Debray; "I recognize this Hobbema; it was proposed for the Museum."

"Which, I believe, does not contain one?" said Monte Cristo.

"Yet they refused to buy it."

"Why?" said Château-Renaud.

"You pretend not to know,—because Government was not rich enough."

"Major Bartolomeo Cavalcanti and count Andrea Cavalcanti!" announced Baptistin.

A black satin stock, fresh from the maker's hands, grey moustaches, a bold eye, a major's uniform, ornamented with three medals and five crosses, and the thorough bearing of an old soldier —such was the appearance of Major Bartolomeo Cavalcanti. Close to him, dressed in new clothes, advanced smilingly count Andrea Cavalcanti, his dutiful son.

"Cavalcanti!" said Debray.

"A fine name," said Morrel.

"Yes," said Château-Renaud, "those Italians are well named and badly dressed."

"You are fastidious, Château-Renaud," replied Debray; "these clothes are well cut and quite new."

"That is just what I find fault with. That gentleman appears to be well-dressed for the first time in his life."

"Who are those gentlemen?" asked Danglars of Monte Cristo.

"You heard—Cavalcanti."

"That tells me their name, and nothing else."

"Ah! true. You do not know the Italian nobility; the Cavalcanti are all descended from princes."

"Have they any fortune?"

"An enormous one."

"What do they do?"

"Try to spend it all. They do business with you, I think. I will introduce you to them. The son has made up his mind to take a wife from Paris."

"A fine idea!" said Danglars shrugging his shoulders.

Madame Danglars looked at her husband with an expression which, at any other time, would have indicated a storm, but controlled herself.

"M. and Madame de Villefort!" cried Baptistin.

They entered. M. de Villefort, notwithstanding his self-control, was visibly affected, and when Monte Cristo touched his hand, he felt it tremble.

Presently the count saw Bertuccio, who, until then, had been occupied on the other side of the house, glide into an adjoining room. He went to him. " What do you want, M. Bertuccio ? " said he.

" Your Excellency has not stated the number of guests."

" Count for yourself."

" Is everyone here, your Excellency ? "

" Yes."

Bertuccio glanced through the door, which was ajar. The count watched him.

" Good Heavens ! " he exclaimed.

" What is the matter ? " said the count.

" That woman ! that woman ! "

" Which ? "

" The one with a white dress and so many diamonds—the fair one."

" Madame Danglars ? "

" I do not know her name—but it is she, sir, it is she ! "

" Whom do you mean ? "

" The woman of the garden !—she that was with child—she who was walking while she waited for—— "

" Waiting for whom ? "

" Him !—M. de Villefort, the *procureur du roi !* Then I did not kill him ! "

" No ; you see plainly he is not dead ; instead of striking between the sixth and seventh left rib, as your countrymen do, you must have struck higher or lower. There is no truth in anything you told me—is it not so ? It was a flight of the imagination—a dream of your fancy. Come, calm yourself, and reckon : M. and Madame de Villefort, two ; M. and Madame Danglars, four ; M. de Château-Renaud, M. Debray, M. Morrel seven ; Major Bartolomeo Cavalcanti, eight."

" Eight ! " repeated Bertuccio.

" You are in a shocking hurry—you forget one of my guests. Stay ! look at M. Andrea Cavalcanti—that young man in a black coat, looking at Murillo's ' Madonna ' ; now he is turning."

Bertuccio would have uttered an exclamation had not a look from Monte Cristo silenced him.

" Benedetto ! " he muttered ; " fatality ! "

Five minutes afterwards the doors of the drawing-room were thrown open, and Bertuccio appearing, said, with a violent effort, " The dinner waits."

The count of Monte Cristo offered his arm to Madame de Villefort. " M. de Villefort, will you conduct the Baroness Danglars ? "

CHAPTER LXIII

THE DINNER

ONE sentiment pervaded the whole of the guests on entering the dining-room. Each asked himself what strange influence had conducted them to this house; and yet astonished, uneasy as they were, they felt they would not like to be absent. Stimulated by an invincible curiosity, there was none present, even including Cavalcanti and his son, notwithstanding the stiffness of the one and the carelessness of the other, who was not thoughtful, on finding himself assembled at the house of this incomprehensible man. M. de Villefort had on the right hand Madame Danglars, on his left Morrel. The count was seated between Madame de Villefort and Danglars; the other seats were filled by Debray, who was placed between the two Cavalcanti, and by Château-Renaud, seated between Madame de Villefort and Morrel.

The repast was magnificent; Monte Cristo had endeavoured completely to overturn the Parisian ideas, and to feed the curiosity as much as the appetite of his guests. It was an Oriental feast, such as Arabian fairies might be supposed to prepare.

Monte Cristo noticed the general astonishment, and began laughing and joking about it. " Gentlemen," he said, " you will admit that, when one arrives at a certain degree of fortune, only the superfluities of life are desired; and the ladies will allow that, after having attained to a certain eminence, the ideal alone can be more exalted. Now, to follow out this reasoning : what is the marvellous ?—that which we do not understand. What is it that we really desire ?—that which we cannot obtain. Now, to see things which I cannot understand, to procure impossibilities, these are the study of my life. I gratify my wishes by two means—my will and my money. For example, you see these two fishes; one brought fifty leagues beyond St. Petersburg, the other, five leagues from Naples. Is it not curious to see both on the same table ? "

" What are they ? " asked Danglars.

" This one is, I think, a sterlet," said Château-Renaud. " Sterlets are only found in the Volga."

" And," said Cavalcanti, " I know that Lake Fusaro alone supplies lampreys of that size."

" Exactly ; one comes from the Volga, and the other from Lake Fusaro."

"Impossible!" cried all the guests simultaneously.

"Well, this is just what entertains me," said Monte Cristo. "This fish, which seems so exquisite to you, is very likely no better than perch or salmon; but it seemed impossible to procure it, and here it is."

"But how could you have these fishes brought to France?"

"Oh! nothing more easy. Each was brought in a cask, one filled with river herbs and weeds, the other with rushes and lake plants; they were placed in a waggon built on purpose; and thus the sterlet lived twelve days, the lamprey eight. You do not believe me, M. Danglars?"

"I cannot help doubting," answered Danglars, with his stupid smile.

"Baptistin," said the count, "have the other fish brought in—the sterlet and the lamprey which came in the other casks, and which are yet alive." Four servants carried in two casks covered with aquatic plants, and in each cask was breathing a fish similar to those on the table.

"But why have two of each sort?" asked Danglars.

"Merely because one might have died," carelessly answered Monte Cristo.

"You are certainly an extraordinary man," said Danglars; "and philosophers may well say it is a fine thing to be rich."

"And to have ideas," added Madame Danglars.

"True," said Monte Cristo; "but what would be the use of living 1,800 years after Lucullus, if we can do no better than he could?" The two Cavalcanti opened their enormous eyes, but had the good sense not to say anything.

"All this is very extraordinary," said Château-Renaud. "Is it not true that you only bought this house five or six days ago?"

"Not longer."

"Well! I am sure it is transformed since last week. If I remember rightly, it had another entrance, and the courtyard was paved and empty; to-day, we have a splendid lawn, bordered by trees which appear to be a hundred years old."

"Why not? I am fond of grass and shade," said Monte Cristo.

"In four days!" said Morrel; "it is extraordinary!"

"Indeed," said Château-Renaud, "it seems quite miraculous to make a new house out of an old one; for it was very old, and dull too. I recollect coming to look at it when M. de Saint Méran advertised it for sale two or three years ago."

"M. de Saint Méran!" said Madame de Villefort; "then this house belonged to M. de Saint Méran before you bought it?"

" It appears so," replied Monte Cristo.

" It is ten years since the house was occupied," said Château-Renaud ; " and it was quite melancholy to look at it, with the blinds closed, the doors locked, and the weeds in the court. Really, if the house had not belonged to the father-in-law of the *procureur du roi*, one might have thought it some accursed place where a horrible crime had been committed."

Villefort, who had hitherto not tasted the three or four glasses of rare wine which were placed before him, here took one and drank it off.

Monte Cristo allowed a short time to elapse, and then said, " It is singular, baron, but the same idea came across me the first time I entered it ; it looked so gloomy I should never have bought it if my steward had not acted for me. Perhaps the fellow had been bribed by the notary."

" It is probable," stammered out De Villefort ; " but believe me, I have nothing to do with this corruption. This house is part of the marriage-portion of Valentine, and M. de Saint Méran wished to sell it, for if it had remained another year or two uninhabited it would have fallen to ruin."

It was Morrel's turn to become pale.

" There was, above all, one room," continued Monte Cristo, " which, I know not why, appeared to me quite dramatic."

" Why so ? " said Danglars. " Why dramatic ? "

" Can we account for instinct ? " said Monte Cristo. " It is a chain of recollections ; an idea which carries you back to other times—to other places—which, very likely, have no connection with the present time and place. I will show the room to you, and then we will take coffee in the garden. After dinner the play."

Monte Cristo looked inquiringly at his guests ; Madame de Villefort rose, Monte Cristo did the same, and the rest followed their example. Villefort and Madame Danglars remained for a moment, as if rooted to their seats ; they interrogated each other with cold glazed eyes.

" Did you hear ? " said Madame Danglars.

" We must go," replied Villefort, offering his arm.

Everyone else was already scattered in different parts of the house, urged by curiosity. Monte Cristo waited for the two who remained ; then, when they had passed, he followed them with a smile, which, if they could have understood it, would have alarmed them much more than a visit to the room they were about to enter. At length they arrived at the famous room.

There was nothing particular about it, excepting that, although daylight had disappeared, it was not lighted, and everything in it remained antique while the rest of the rooms had been re-decorated. These two causes were enough to give it a gloomy tinge.

" Oh ! " cried Madame de Villefort, " it is really frightful."

Madame Danglars tried to utter a few words, but was not heard.

" Is it not so ? " asked Monte Cristo. " Look at that large clumsy bed, hung with such gloomy, blood-coloured drapery ! And those two crayon portraits, that have faded from the damp— they seem to say, with their pale lips and staring eyes, ' We have seen ! ' "

Villefort became livid ; Madame Danglars fell into a long seat placed near the chimney.

" Oh ! " said Madame de Villefort, smiling, " are you courageous enough to sit down upon the very seat upon which, perhaps, the crime was committed ? "

Madame Danglars rose suddenly.

" And then," said Monte Cristo, " this is not all."

" What ! is there more ? " said Debray, who had not failed to notice the agitation of Madame Danglars.

" There is this little staircase," said Monte Cristo, opening a door concealed by the drapery. " Tell me what you think of it."

" What a wicked-looking, crooked staircase ! " said Château-Renaud, smiling.

" Can you not imagine," said Monte Cristo, " some Othello or Abbé de Ganges, descending these stairs, step by step, carrying a load, which he wishes to hide from the sight of man, if not from God ? "

Madame Danglars half fainted on the arm of Villefort, who was obliged to support himself against the wall.

" Ah, madame," cried Debray, " what is the matter ? how pale you look ! "

" Nothing," she replied, with a violent effort. " I want air."

" Are you frightened, madame ? " said Monte Cristo.

" Oh, no, sir," said Madame Danglars ; " but you imagine scenes in a manner which gives them the appearance of reality."

" Ah, yes," said Monte Cristo, smiling ; " it is all a matter of the imagination. Why should we not imagine this the apartment of an honest house-mother ? And this bed with red hangings, a bed visited by the goddess Lucina ? And that mysterious staircase, the passage through which, not to disturb their sleep, the doctor and nurse pass, or even the father carrying the sleeping child ? "

Madame Danglars, instead of being calmed by the pleasing picture, uttered a groan and fainted.

"Madame Danglars is ill," said Villefort; "it would be better to take her to her carriage."

"Oh! and I have forgotten my smelling-bottle," said Monte Cristo.

"I have mine," said Madame de Villefort; and she passed over to Monte Cristo a bottle full of the same kind of red liquid whose good properties the count had tested on Edward.

"Ah!" said Monte Cristo, taking it from her hand.

"Yes," she said, "at your advice I have tried."

"And have you succeeded?"

"I think so."

Madame Danglars was carried into the adjoining room; Monte Cristo dropped a very small portion of the red liquid upon her lips; she returned to consciousness.

"Ah!" she cried, "what a frightful dream!"

Monte Cristo seemed in despair. He took the arm of Madame Danglars, and led her into the garden, where they found Danglars taking coffee between the Cavalcanti.

"Really, madame," he said, "did I alarm you much?"

"Oh, no, sir," she answered; "but you know things impress us differently, according to our mood."

"Well," said Monte Cristo, "my belief is that a crime has been committed in this house."

"Take care!" said Madame de Villefort, "the *procureur du roi* is here."

"Ah!" replied Monte Cristo, "since that is the case, I will take advantage of his presence to make my declaration."

"Oh, this is very interesting," said Debray; "if there has been a crime we will investigate it."

"There has been a crime," said Monte Cristo. "Come this way, gentlemen; come, M. de Villefort."

He then took de Villefort's arm, and, at the same time holding that of Madame Danglars under his own, dragged the *procureur* to the plantain tree, where the shade was thickest. The other guests followed.

"Stay," said Monte Cristo, "here in this very spot my man, digging, found a box, or rather the iron-work of a box, in the midst of which was the skeleton of a newly-born infant."

Monte Cristo felt the arm of Madame Danglars stiffen, while that of de Villefort trembled.

"A newly-born infant!" repeated Debray; "this affair becomes serious!"

" What is done to infanticides in this country ? " asked Major Cavalcanti, innocently.

" Oh, their heads are soon cut off," said Danglars.

" I think so : am I not right, M. de Villefort ? " asked Monte Cristo.

" Yes, count," replied de Villefort, in a voice now scarcely human.

Monte Cristo saw that the two persons for whom he had prepared this scene could scarcely bear it, so, not wishing to carry it too far, he said—" Come, gentlemen, some coffee, we seem to have forgotten it ; " and he conducted the guests to the table on the lawn.

" Indeed, count," said Madame Danglars, " your frightful stories have so upset me, that I must beg you to let me sit down."

Monte Cristo bowed and went to Madame de Villefort.   " I think Madame Danglars again requires your bottle," he said. But before Madame de Villefort could reach her friend, the *procureur* had found time to whisper to Madame Danglars, " I must speak to you."

" When ? "

" To-morrow."

" Where ? "

" In my office, or in the court, if you like, that is the surest place."

" I will come."

At this moment Madame de Villefort approached.

" Thanks, my dear friend," said Madame Danglars, trying to smile ; " it is over now and I am much better."

CHAPTER LXIV

THE BEGGAR

THE evening passed on ; Madame de Villefort expressed a desire to return to Paris, which Madame Danglars had not dared to do, notwithstanding her uneasiness. On his wife's request, M. de Villefort was the first to give the signal of departure. He offered a seat in his landau to Madame Danglars, that she might be under the care of his wife. As for M. Danglars, he paid no attention to anything that was passing. While Monte Cristo had begged the smelling-bottle of Madame de Villefort, he had remarked the approach of de Villefort to Madame Danglars, and soon guessed all that had passed between them. Without opposing their arrangements, he allowed Morrel, Château-Renaud, and Debray, to leave on horseback, and the ladies in M. de Villefort's carriage. Danglars, delighted with Major Cavalcanti, had offered him a seat in his carriage. Andrea Cavalcanti found his tilbury waiting at the door; the groom was standing on tiptoes holding a large iron-grey horse. He had been appropriated by Danglars, who, taking a rapid glance at the stiff-necked old major and his son, contemplated with unspeakable delight the large diamond which shone on the major's little finger; for the major, prudent man, in case of any accident to his bank notes, had converted them into articles of value. One thing above all the rest heightened the respect, nay, almost the veneration of Danglars for Cavalcanti. The latter had contented himself in proving his knowledge by saying in what lake the best lampreys were caught. Then he had eaten some without saying a word; Danglars, therefore, concluded that these luxuries were common at the table of the illustrious descendant of the Cavalcanti. Thus it was with much politeness of manner that he heard Cavalcanti pronounce these words,—" To-morrow, sir, I shall have the honour of waiting upon you on business."

" And I, sir," said Danglars, " shall be most happy to receive you." The major seated himself, therefore, by the side of Danglars, who was more and more charmed with the ideas of order and economy which ruled this man, who yet, being able to allow his son 50,000 francs a year, might be supposed to possess a fortune of 500,000 or 600,000 livres.

As for Andrea, he began, by way of showing off, to scold his groom. At that moment a hand touched his shoulder. The young man saw nothing but a strange face, sunburnt, and encircled by a beard, with eyes brilliant as carbuncles, and a smile upon the mouth which displayed a perfect set of white teeth, pointed and sharp as the wolf's or jackal's. A red handkerchief encircled his grey head; torn and filthy garments covered his large bony limbs, and the hand with which he leant upon the young man's shoulder and which was the first thing Andrea saw, seemed of a gigantic size. He shuddered and stepped back suddenly " What do you want of me ? " he asked.

" Pardon me, my friend, if I disturb you," said the man with the red handkerchief, " but I want to speak to you."

" Come," said Andrea, with sufficient nerve for his servant not to perceive his agitation, " What do you want ? Speak quickly, friend."

" Well, then, I want you to take me up in your fine carriage, and carry me back." Andrea turned pale, but said nothing.

" Yes ! " said the man, thrusting his hands into his pockets, and looking impudently at the youth ; " I have taken the whim into my head : do you understand, Master Benedetto ? "

At this name the young man reflected a little, and then went towards his groom, saying, " This man wishes to see me about a commission I gave him a fortnight ago. Take a cab at the barrier, that you may not be too late." The surprised groom retired.

" Don't think I want the honour of riding in your fine carriage," said the beggar ; " oh, no, it's only because I am tired and also because I have a little business to talk over with you."

" Come, step in," said the young man. Once out of Auteuil, Andrea looked around, in order to assure himself that he could neither be seen nor heard, and then, stopping the horse and crossing his arms before the man, asked, " Now ! tell me why you come to disturb my tranquillity ? "

" Let me ask you why you deceived me ? "

" How have I deceived you ? "

" How ! do you ask ? When we parted at the Pont du Far, you told me you were going to travel through Piedmont and Tuscany ; but instead of that you come to Paris."

" Does that annoy you ? "

" It does not ; on the contrary, I think it will answer my purpose."

" So," said Andrea, " you are speculating upon me ? "

" What fine words he uses ! "

" I warn you, Master Caderousse, that you are mistaken."

" I see you with a groom, a tilbury, and fine new clothes. You must have discovered a mine, or else become a stockbroker."

" So you are jealous ? "

" No, I am pleased ; so pleased, that I wished to congratulate you ; but as I am not properly dressed, I chose my opportunity, that I might not compromise you."

" Well," said Andrea, " what do you want ? "

" You do not speak affectionately to me, Benedetto, my old friend ; that is not right ; take care, or I may become troublesome."

This menace smothered the young man's passion. He trotted his horse on. " You should not speak so to an old friend like me ; you are old and obstinate, I am young and wilful. Between folk like us threats are out of place, everything should be amicably arranged. Is it my fault if Fortune, which has frowned on you, has been kind to me ? "

" You wrong me, my boy; now I have found you, nothing prevents my being as well-dressed as anyone, knowing, as I do, the goodness of your heart. If you have two coats you will give me one of them. I used to divide my soup and beans with you when you were hungry."

" True," said Andrea.

" How did you come to be dining with that prince ? "

" He is not a prince ; only a count ; but you had better not have anything to say to him, for he is not a very good-tempered gentleman."

" Oh ! I have no design upon your count ; you shall have him all to yourself. But," said Caderousse, " you must pay for it—you understand ? "

" Well, what do you want ? "

" I think that with a hundred francs per month——"

" Here are two hundred," said Andrea ; and he placed ten louis-d'or in the hand of Caderousse. " Apply to the steward on the first of every month, and you will receive a like sum."

" There now, again you degrade me."

" How so ? "

" By making me apply to the servants, when I want to transact business with you alone."

" Well ; be it so then : and so long as I receive my income, you shall be paid yours."

" Come, come ; I always said you were a fine fellow, and it is a blessing when good fortune happens to such as you. But tell me all about it."

" The fact is, I have found my father."

" What is his name ? "

" Major Cavalcanti."

" Who found this father for you ? "

" The count of Monte Cristo."

" I wish you would get me a situation with him as grandfather."

" I will mention you to him. Meanwhile, what are you going to do ? "

" I shall rent a room in some respectable house, wear a decent coat, shave every day, and go and read the papers in a café. Then, in the evening, I will go to the theatre : I shall look like some retired baker. This is my wish."

" And now that you have all you want, and we understand each other, jump down and make yourself scarce."

" Not at all, my good friend. Think for a moment ; with this red handkerchief on my head, with scarcely any shoes, no papers and ten gold louis in my pocket, I should be arrested at the barrier ! Inquiries follow ; it would be found that I left Toulon without giving due notice, and I should then be taken back to the shores of the Mediterranean. Then I should become simply No. 106, and good-bye to my dream of the retired baker ! No, no, my boy ; I prefer remaining in the capital."

Andrea scowled. His hand fell instantly into his pocket, where it began playing with a pistol. But, meanwhile, Caderousse, who had never taken his eyes off his companion, passed his hand behind his back, and unclasped a long Spanish knife, which he always carried with him, to be ready in case of need. The two friends, as we see, were worthy of and understood one another. Andrea's hand left his pocket inoffensively, and was carried up to the red moustachio, which it toyed with for some time.

" Good Caderousse," he said, " how happy you will be ! "

" I will do my best," said the innkeeper of the Pont du Gard, reclasping his knife.

" Well, then, we will go into Paris. But how will you pass through the barrier without exciting suspicion ? "

" Wait," said Caderousse, " and see."

He then put on the great-coat with the large collar, which the groom had left in the tilbury ; next he placed Cavalcanti's hat upon his own head ; and finally assumed the careless attitude of a servant whose master drives himself.

" But am I to remain bareheaded ? "

" Pooh ! " said Caderousse ; " it is so windy your hat was blown off."

They passed the barrier without accident. At the first cross street Andrea pulled up, and Caderousse leaped out, crying, as he went, " *Au revoir !* "

" Alas ! " said Andrea, sighing, " one cannot be completely happy in this world ! "

CHAPTER LXV

A CONJUGAL SCENE

At the Place Louis XV. the three young people separated. Most probably Morrel and Château-Renaud returned to their " domestic hearths "; but this was not the case with Debray, who arrived at M. Danglars' door at the same time as Villefort's landau stopped to leave the baroness at her own house. Debray threw his bridle into the hands of a footman, and returned to the door to conduct Madame Danglars to her apartments.

The gate once closed, Debray asked,—" What was the matter with you, Hermine ? and why were you so affected at that story, or rather fable, which the count related ? "

" Because I have been in such shocking spirits all the evening, my friend," said the baroness.

" No, Hermine," replied Debray, " someone has vexed you; I will allow no one to annoy you."

" You are deceived, Lucien, I assure you," replied Madame Danglars.

At the door of her apartment the baroness met Mademoiselle Cornélie, her confidential lady's-maid.

" What is my daughter doing ? " asked Madame Danglars.

" She practised all the evening, and then went to bed," replied Mademoiselle Cornélie.

" Well," said Madame Danglars, " come and undress me."

They entered the bedroom, Debray stretched himself upon a large couch, and Madame Danglars passed into her dressing-room with her maid.

" My dear M. Lucien," said Madame Danglars, through the door, " you are always complaining Eugénie will not address a word to you. I think this will pass off, and you will some day see her enter your study."

" Why so ? "

" To ask for an engagement at the Opera. Really, I never saw such an infatuation for music."

Debray smiled. " Well," said he, " let her come, with your consent and that of the baron, and we will try to give her an engagement, though we are very poor to pay such talent as hers."

" Go, Cornélie," said Madame Danglars, " I do not require you any longer."

Cornélie obeyed ; and the next minute Madame Danglars left her room in a charming loose dress, and sat down beside Debray. Then she began to caress the spaniel.

Lucien looked at her for a moment in silence. " Come, Hermine," he said, " something vexes you, is it not so ? "

" Nothing," answered the baroness.

Debray rose, smiling, when the door opened suddenly. M. Danglars appeared ; Debray reseated himself. At the sound Madame Danglars turned and looked upon her husband with an astonishment she took no trouble to conceal.

" Excuse me," said the banker, " but you will tire yourself, baroness, by such late hours, and M. Debray lives some distance from here."

" M. Lucien," said the baroness, " I assure you I have no desire to sleep, and have a thousand things to tell you, which you must listen to, even though you slept while hearing me."

" I am at your service, madame," replied Lucien, coldly.

" My dear M. Debray," said the banker, " do not kill yourself to-night listening to the follies of Madame Danglars, for you can hear them as well to-morrow ; but I claim to-night to talk over some serious matters with my wife."

This time the blow was so well-aimed that Lucien and the baroness were staggered and the irresistible will of the master of the house prevailed.

" Do not think I wish to turn you out, my dear Debray," continued Danglars ; " not at all. An unexpected occurrence compels me to have a little conversation with my wife ; it is so rarely I make such a request, I am sure you cannot grudge it."

Debray muttered something, bowed, and went out, knocking himself against the edge of the door, like Nathan in " Athalie."

Lucien having left, Danglars took his place on the sofa, closed the open book and, placing himself in a dreadfully dictatorial attitude, began playing with the dog ; but the animal, not liking him so well as Debray, and attempting to bite him, Danglars seized him by the skin of his neck and threw him to the other side of the room upon a couch.

" Do you know, sir," asked the baroness, " that you are improving ? Generally, you are only rude, but to-night you are brutal. Keep your ill-humour at home in your chests ; or since you have clerks whom you pay, vent it upon them."

" Not so," replied Danglars ; " your advice is wrong. My clerks are honest men, who earn my fortune, whom I pay much below their deserts, if I may value them according to what they bring in ; therefore I will not get into a passion with them : those with whom I will be in a passion are those who eat my dinners, mount my horses, and waste my fortune."

" And pray who are the persons who waste your fortune ? Explain yourself more clearly, I beg."

" You understand me perfectly," said Danglars ; " but, as you persist, I tell you I have just lost 700,000 francs upon the Spanish loan."

" Is it my fault you have lost 700,000 francs ? "

" Certainly it is not mine."

"Once for all, sir," replied the baroness, sharply, "I will not hear money named; I know only one thing I dislike more, and that is the sound of your voice."

"Well, this surprises me, for I thought you took the liveliest interest in my affairs!"

"I! What could put such an idea into your head?"

"Yourself."

"I should like to know upon what occasion?"

"Ah, that is very easily done! In March there was a question about a grant to a railway. Three companies presented themselves, each offering equal securities. You told me that your instinct led you to believe the grant would be given to the company called the Southern. I bought two-thirds of the shares of that company. As you had foreseen, the shares became of treble value, and I picked up a million francs, from which 250,000 francs were paid to you for pin-money. How have you spent this 250,000 francs? It is no business of mine."

"When are you coming to the point?" cried the baroness.

"Patience, madame, I am coming to it; you have this year received 500,000 livres."

"Well, sir, and what then?"

"Ah, yes, it was just after this that you spoiled everything!"

"Really, your manner of speaking——"

"It expresses my meaning, and that is all I want. Well, three days after that you talked politics with M. Debray, and you fancied from his words that Don Carlos had returned to Spain. Well, I sold my shares, the news was spread, and I no longer sold but gave them; next day I find the news was false, and by this false report I lost 700,000 francs."

"Well?"

"Well! since I gave you a fourth of my gains, I think you owe me a fourth of my losses: the fourth of 700,000 francs is 175,000 francs."

"What you say is absurd, and I cannot see why M. Debray's name should be mixed up in this affair."

"Because if you do not possess the 175,000 francs I reclaim, you must have lent them to your friends, and M. Debray is one of your friends."

"For shame!" exclaimed the baroness.

"Oh! let us have no gestures, no screams, no modern drama, or you will oblige me to tell you that I see Debray leave here, pocketing nearly the whole of the 500,000 livres; while he says to himself, with a smile, that he has found what the most skilful players have never discovered—a roulette, where he wins without playing and is no loser when he loses."

" Wretch ! " cried the baroness, " do you dare to tell me you did not know that with which you now reproach me ? "

" I do not say that I did know it, and I do not say that I did not know it. I merely tell you to look into my conduct during the last four years that we have ceased to be husband and wife, and see whether it has not always been consistent. You have taken a fancy to study diplomacy with the minister's secretary. You understand : it signifies nothing to me so long as you pay for your lessons out of your own cash-box. But to-day I find you are drawing on mine, and that your apprenticeship may cost me 700,000 francs per month. Stop there, madame ! for this cannot last. Either the diplomatist must give his lessons gratis, and I will tolerate him, or he must never set his foot again in my house ; —do you understand, madame ? "

" Oh, this is too much," cried Hermine, choking ; " you are worse than despicable."

" Besides, how do I know that this was not a political trick ; that the minister, enraged at seeing me in the Opposition, and jealous of the popular sympathy I excite, has not concerted with M. Debray to ruin me."

" A probable thing ! "

" Why not ? Who ever heard of such an occurrence as a false telegraphic despatch ? It is almost impossible for signals to have been made different from those of the two last telegrams. It was done to mislead me ; I am sure of it."

" Sir," said the baroness, " are you not aware that the employé was dismissed, and that the order for his arrest would have been put into execution if he had not taken to flight, which proved either madness or culpability ? It was a mistake."

" Yes, which has cost me 700,000 francs."

" But, sir," said Hermine, suddenly, " if all this is, as you say, caused by M. Debray, why, instead of going direct to him, do you come and tell me of it ? "

Danglars shrugged his shoulders. " Foolish creature," he exclaimed. " Women fancy they have talent because they have managed two or three intrigues without being the talk of Paris ! If you had hidden your irregularities from your husband, you would then have been but a faint imitation of most of your friends among the women of the world. But it has not been so with me,— not a step, not an action, not a fault, has escaped me ; thanks to my pretended ignorance, none of your friends, from M. de Villefort to M. Debray, but has trembled before me. I will allow you to make me hateful; but I will prevent you from rendering me ridiculous, and, above all, I forbid you to ruin me."

The baroness had been tolerably composed until the name of de Villefort was spoken; but then she became pale, and, rising, as if touched by a spring, stretched out her hands as though conjuring an apparition. Taking two or three steps towards her husband, as though to tear the secret from him, of which he was ignorant, or which he withheld from some odious calculation, as all his calculations were, she exclaimed, " M. de Villefort! What do you mean ? "

" I mean that M. de Nargonne, your first husband, being neither a philosopher nor a banker, or perhaps being both, and seeing there was nothing to be got out of a *procureur du roi*, died of grief or anger at finding, after an absence of nine months, that you had been *enceinte* six. Why did he kill himself instead of you ? Because he had no cash to save. My life belongs to my cash. M. Debray has made me lose 700,000 francs; let him bear his share of the loss, and we will go on as before; if not, let him become bankrupt for the 250,000 livres, and do as all bankrupts do—disappear. He is a charming fellow, I allow, when his news is correct; but when it is not, there are fifty others in the world who would do better than he."

Madame Danglars was rooted to the spot. Danglars did not even look at her, though she tried all she could to faint. He shut the bedroom door after him, without adding another word, and retired to his apartment.

CHAPTER LXVI

MATRIMONIAL PROJECTS

THE day following this scene, at the hour the banker usually chose to pay a visit to Madame Danglars, on his way to his office, his *coupé* did not appear in the court. At this time, that is, about half-past twelve, Madame Danglars ordered her carriage, and went out. Danglars, behind a curtain, watched the departure he had been waiting for. He gave orders that he should be informed directly Madame Danglars appeared; but at two o'clock she had not returned. He then called for his horses, and told the coachman to drive to the Avenue des Champs-Élysées, No. 30.

Monte Cristo was at home; only he was engaged with someone, and begged Danglars to wait in the drawing-room. While the banker was waiting, the door opened, and a man dressed as an abbé entered, and, passing on to the further apartments, disappeared. A minute afterwards the door by which the priest had entered re-opened, and Monte Cristo appeared. " Pardon me," said he, " my dear baron, but one of my friends, the Abbé Busoni, whom you perhaps noticed pass by, has arrived in Paris, and I had to see him."

" Nay," said Danglars, " it is my fault ; I have chosen my visit at a wrong time, and will retire."

" Not at all : but what is the matter with you ? For a capitalist to be sad, like the appearance of a comet, presages some misfortune to the world."

" Imagine a man who has transacted business with me for I do not know how long, to the amount of 800,000 or 900,000 francs during the year. Never a mistake or delay ; a fellow who paid like a prince. Well, I was a million in advance with him, and now my fine Jacopo Manfredi suspends payment ! "

" Really ? "

" It is an unheard-of fatality. I draw upon him for 600,000 francs, my bills are returned unpaid, and, more than that, I hold bills of exchange signed by him to the value of 400,000 francs, payable at his correspondent's in Paris at the end of this month. To-day is the 30th. I present them ; but my correspondent has disappeared. This, with my Spanish affairs, made a pretty end to the month."

"Why, how could you make such a mistake—such an old stager ?"

" Oh, it is all my wife's fault. She dreamed Don Carlos had returned to Spain ; she believes in dreams. On this conviction, I allow her to speculate ; she speculated and lost. It is true she speculates with her own money, not mine ; nevertheless, you can understand that when 700,000 francs leave the wife's pocket, the husband always finds it out. But do you mean to say you have not heard of this ?

" Yes, I heard it spoken of, but I did not know the details ; and no one can be more ignorant than I am of the affairs in the Bourse."

" Then you do not speculate ? "

" I ? I have no time for it. But touching these Spanish affairs, the papers said something about it, did they not ? I fancied that the honest *Messager* was an exception to the rule, and that it only announced telegraphic despatches."

" That is what puzzles me ; the news of the return of Don Carlos was brought by telegraph."

Q

" So that," said Monte Cristo, " you have lost nearly 1,700,000 francs this month."

" Not nearly, indeed ; that is exactly my loss."

" The result, then, of six more such months as this would be to reduce the house to despair."

" Oh ! " said Danglars, becoming pale, " how you are running on ! "

" Let us imagine seven such months," continued Monte Cristo, in the same tone. " Tell me, have you ever thought that seven times 1,700,000 francs make nearly twelve millions ? Well, out of the five or six millions, which form your real capital, you have just lost nearly two millions, which must, of course, in the same degree diminish your credit and fictitious fortune. Repeated three or four times, this will cause death—so pay attention to it, M. Danglars. Do you want money ? Do you wish me to lend you some ? "

" What a bad calculator you are ! " exclaimed Danglars, " I have made up for the loss of blood by nutrition. I lost a battle in Spain, I have been defeated in Trieste, but my naval army in India will have taken some galleons, and my Mexican pioneers will have discovered some mine."

" Very good ! But the wound remains, and will reopen at the first loss."

" No ! " replied Danglars, " to involve me, three Governments must crumble to dust."

" Recollect the seven fat and the seven lean kine."

" Or, that the sea should become dry, as in the days of Pharaoh ; and even then my vessels would become caravans."

" So much the better. I congratulate you, my dear M. Danglars," said Monte Cristo.

" While we are speaking of business," said Danglars, " tell me what I am to do for M. Cavalcanti ? "

" Give him money, if he is recommended to you, and the recommendation seems good."

" Excellent ! He presented himself this morning with a bond of 40,000 francs, payable at sight, on you, signed by Busoni, and returned by you to me, with your endorsement ; of course, I counted him over the forty bank-notes. But that is not all," continued Danglars ; " he has opened an account with my house for his son."

May I ask how much he allows the young man ? "

" Five thousand francs per month. But if he should want a few thousand more——"

" Do not advance it ; the father will never repay it ; you do not know these Ultramontane millionaires ; they are regular misers."

" Would you not trust the Cavalcanti ? "

" I ? Oh, I would advance six millions on his signature."

" By the way, I believe noblemen marry amongst themselves, do they not ? " asked Danglars, carelessly ; " they like to unite their fortunes."

" It is usual, certainly ; but Cavalcanti is an original, and does nothing like other people. I cannot help thinking he has brought his son to France to choose a wife."

" And you have heard his fortune mentioned ? "

" Nothing else was talked of ; some say he is worth millions, and others that he does not possess a farthing."

" And what is your opinion ? "

" My opinion is, that all these ancient *condottieri* have buried their millions in corners, the secret of which they have transmitted only to their eldest sons, who have done the same from generation to generation.

" Certainly," said Danglars, " and this is further supported by the fact of their not possessing an inch of land."

" I know of none which Cavalcanti possesses, excepting his palace in Lucca."

" Ah ; he has a palace ? " said Danglars, laughing ; " come, that is something."

" Yes ; and more than that, he lets it to the Minister of Finance, while he lives in a simple house. Oh ! as I told you before, I think the good man very close ! "

" Never mind ; accept my thanks for the client you have sent me ; it is a fine name to inscribe on my list, and my cashier was quite proud of it when I explained to him who the Cavalcanti were. By the by, when these kind of people marry their sons, do they give them any fortune ? "

" Oh, that depends upon circumstances. Should Andrea marry according to his father's views, he will, perhaps, give him one, two, or three millions. But if he dislikes his choice, the major takes the key, double-locks his coffer, and Master Andrea will be obliged to live like the son of a Parisian family, by shuffling cards or rattling the dice. But do you wish to marry Andrea, my dear M. Danglars, that you are asking so many questions ? "

" *Ma foi !* " said Danglars, " it would not be a bad speculation, I fancy, and you know I am a speculator."

" You are not thinking of Mademoiselle Danglars, I hope ;

you would not like poor Andrea to have his throat cut by Albert ? "

" I imagine Mademoiselle Danglars is as good as M. de Morcerf."

" But still, if Albert be not so rich as Mademoiselle Danglars," said the count, " you must allow he has a fine name."

" So he has ; but I like mine as well."

" Still, I should not think the Morcerfs would yield to the Cavalcanti ? "

" The Morcerfs ? Listen, my dear count ; M. de Morcerf has been my friend, or rather my acquaintance, during the last thirty years. When I was a clerk, Morcerf was a mere fisherman."

' And then he was called——"

" Fernando Mondego."

" Then, why did you think of giving your daughter to him ? "

" Because, Fernando and Danglars, being both *parvenus*, both having become noble, both rich, are about equal in worth, except- ing that there have been certain things mentioned of him that were never said of me."

" Ah, yes ! what you tell me recalls something about the name of Fernando Mondego. I have heard that name in Greece ! "

" In conjunction with the affairs of Ali Pasha ? "

" Exactly so."

" That is the mystery," said Danglars ; " I acknowledge I would give anything to find it out."

" Well, write to your correspondent in Janina, and ask him what part was played by a Frenchman named Fernando Mondego in the catastrophe of Ali Tebelen."

" I will."

" And if you should hear of anything very scandalous——"

" I will communicate it to you."

" You will oblige me."

Danglars rushed out of the room, and made but one leap into his *coupé*.

CHAPTER LXVII

THE OFFICE OF THE PROCUREUR DU ROI

MADAME DANGLARS, in her morning drive, directed her course towards the Faubourg Saint-Germain, went down the Rue de Seine, and stopped at the Passage du Pont Neuf. At the Rue Guénégaud she called a fiacre, and directed the driver to the Rue de Harlay. The driver was paid as the door opened, and stepping lightly up the stairs, Madame Danglars soon reached the hall des Pas-Perdus.

There was a great press of people in M. de Villefort's ante-chamber; but Madame Danglars had no occasion even to pronounce her name; the instant she appeared the doorkeeper rose, came to her, and asked whether she was not the person with whom the *procureur du roi* had made an appointment, and on an affirmative answer being given he conducted her by a private passage to M. de Villefort's office. The magistrate was seated in an armchair, writing, with his back towards the door.

"It is a long time, madame," said the *procureur du roi*, describing a half-circle with his chair, so as to place himself directly opposite to Madame Danglars—" it is a long time since I had the pleasure of speaking alone with you; and I regret that we have only now met to enter upon a painful conversation. It is true, then, that every step in our lives resembles the course of an insect on the sand—it leaves its track! Alas! to many the path is traced by etars."

" Sir," said Madame Danglars, " you can feel for my emotion, can you not? Spare me, then, I beseech you. The paths of which you were just speaking have been traced by all young men of ardent imaginations. Besides the pleasure there is always remorse, from the indulgence of our passions; and, after all, what have you men to fear; the world excuses and notoriety ennobles you! "'

" Madame," replied de Villefort, " you know that I am no hypocrite, or, at least, that I never deceive without a reason. If my brow be severe, it is because many misfortunes have clouded it; if my heart be petrified, it is that it might sustain the blows it has received. I am accustomed to brave difficulties, and, in the conflict, to crush those who, by their own free will, or by chance, voluntarily or involuntarily, interfere with me in my career. It is generally the case that what we most ardently desire is as ardently withheld from us by those who wish to obtain it, or from whom we attempt to snatch it. The means we might have used, which we in our blindness could not see, then seem simple and easy, and we say, ' Why did I not do this instead of that? ' Women, on the contrary, are rarely tormented with remorse; for the decision does not come from you, your misfortunes are generally imposed upon you, and your faults are the result of others' crimes."

" In any case, sir, you will allow," replied Madame Danglars,

" that even if the fault were alone mine, I last night received a severe punishment for it."

" Collect all your courage, for you have not yet heard all ! "

" Ah ! " exclaimed Madame Danglars, alarmed, " what more is there to hear ? "

" You only look back to the past ; and it is, indeed, bad enough. Well, picture to yourself, a future more gloomy still— certainly frightful—perhaps sanguinary ! How has this terrible past been recalled ? "

" Alas ! " said Hermine, " doubtless it is chance ! "

" Chance ! " replied Villefort ; " no, no, madame, there is no such a thing as chance ! "

" Oh, yes ; has not a fatal chance revealed all this ? Was it not by chance the count of Monte Cristo bought this house ? Was it not by chance he caused the earth to be dug ? Is it not by chance that the unfortunate child was disinterred under the trees ? That poor innocent offspring of mine, which I never even kissed, but for which I wept many, many tears. Ah ! my heart clung to the count when he mentioned the dear spoil found beneath the flowers."

" Well ! no ! madame ; this is the terrible news I have to tell you. M. de Monte Cristo, digging underneath these trees, found neither skeleton nor chest ; because neither was there."

" Neither there ! " repeated Madame Danglars, fixing upon him her eyes, which, by their fearful dilatation, indicated her alarm.

" No ! " said de Villefort, burying his face in his hands, " no ! But listen to me. You recollect that sad night, when you were half expiring on that bed in the red damask room, while I, scarcely less agitated than you, awaited your *accouchement.* The child was born—was given to me—without movement, without voice ; we thought it dead. I placed it in the chest which was to take the place of a coffin ; I descended to the garden ; I dug a hole, and then flung it down in haste. Scarcely had I covered it with mould, when the Corsican struck me. I fell lifeless, and fancied myself killed. Never shall I forget your sublime courage, when, having regained consciousness, I dragged myself to the foot of the stairs, where, at death's door yourself, you came to meet me. We were obliged to keep silent about the dreadful catastrophe. A duel was the pretext for my wound. I was ordered South. My recovery lasted six months. I never heard you mentioned, and I did not dare inquire for you. When I returned to Paris, I learned that, widow of M. de Nargonne, you had married M. Danglars.

"What had been the subject of my thoughts ever since consciousness had returned to me? Always the child's corpse, which, every night in my dreams, rising from the earth, fixed itself above the grave with a menacing look and gesture. I inquired immediately on my return to Paris; the house had just been let for nine years. I found the tenant. I pretended that I disliked the idea of a house belonging to my wife's father and mother passing into the hands of strangers; I offered to pay them for yielding up the lease; I made the tenant sign the cancelling deed; and galloped to Auteuil. No one had entered the house since I left it. It was five o'clock in the afternoon, I ascended into the red room, and waited for night. It was necessary, before everything else, and at all risks, that I should cause all traces of the past to disappear,—that I should destroy every material vestige. It was for this I had annulled the lease, —it was for this I had come. I allowed it to become quite dark. I was without a light in that room; when the wind shook all the doors, behind which I continually expected to see some spy, I trembled, I seemed everywhere to hear your moans behind me in the bed, and I dared not turn round. I consider myself as brave as most men; but when I opened the door, and saw the pale moon shedding a long stream of white light on the spiral staircase like a spectre, I leaned against the wall, and nearly shrieked. I reached the lower door. Outside this door a spade was placed against the wall; I took it, and advanced towards the thicket. I had provided myself with a dark lantern. In the middle of the lawn I stopped to light it, then I continued my path. I tied my lantern to a forked branch I had remarked a year before at the precise spot where I stopped to dig the hole. The hour for which I had been waiting during the last year had at length arrived. How I worked; how I hoped. I made a hole twice as large as the first. I thought I had been deceived, had mistaken the spot; I recollected that I was stabbed just as I was trampling the ground to fill up the hole; while doing so, I had leaned against a false ebony tree, behind me was an artificial rock, intended to serve as a resting-place for persons walking in the garden. On my right I saw the tree, behind me the rock. I stood in the same attitude, and threw myself down; I rose, and again began digging and enlarging the hole: still I found nothing—nothing—the chest was no longer there."

"Oh, Heaven!"

"When daylight dawned, I went down again. But I could find nothing,—absolutely nothing."

"Oh!" cried Madame Danglars, "it was enough to drive you mad."

"However, recovering my strength and my ideas, 'Why,' said I, 'should that man have carried away the corpse?'"

"But," replied Madame Danglars, "he would require it as a proof."

"Ah! no, madame, that could not be, dead bodies are not kept a year; they are shown to a magistrate, and the evidence is taken; now nothing of the kind has happened."

"What then?" asked Hermine, trembling violently.

"Something more terrible, more fatal, more alarming for us; the child was perhaps alive, and the assassin may have saved it."

Madame Danglars uttered a piercing cry; and, seizing de Villefort's hands, exclaimed, "My child was alive! you buried my child alive, sir! You were not certain my child was dead, and you buried it!"

"I know not; I merely suppose so, as I might suppose anything else," replied de Villefort.

"Ah, my child! my poor child!" cried the baroness, stifling her sobs in her handkerchief.

"You understand, then, that if it were so," said he, rising in his turn, and approaching the baroness, to speak to her in a lower tone, "we are lost; the child lives, and some one knows it lives; and since Monte Cristo speaks before us of a child disinterred, when that child could not be found, it is he who is in possession of our secret."

"But the child,—the child, sir!" repeated the agitated mother.

"How I have searched for him!" replied de Villefort, wringing his hands; "how I have called him in my long sleepless nights! At last, one day, when for the hundredth time, I took up my spade, I asked myself again and again what the Corsican could have done with the child; perhaps, on perceiving it alive, he had thrown it into the river."

"Impossible!" cried Madame Danglars; "a man would not deliberately drown a child."

"Perhaps," continued de Villefort, "he had put it in the foundling hospital?"

"Oh! yes, yes!" cried the baroness, "my child is there!"

"I ran to the hospital, and learned that a child had been brought there, wrapped in part of a fine linen napkin, purposely torn in half. This portion of the napkin was marked with half a baron's crown, and the letter H."

" Thank God ! my child was not dead."

" No, it was not dead."

" And you can tell me so without fearing to make me die of joy, sir ? Where is the child ? "

" Alas ! I know not. A woman, about six months later, came to claim it with the other half of the napkin. She gave all the requisite particulars, and it was entrusted to her. I feigned a criminal process, and employed all the most acute bloodhounds and skilful agents in search of her. They traced her to Châlons ; and there they lost her."

" And this is all," said she ; " and you stopped there ? "

" Oh, no," said de Villefort ; " I never ceased to search and to inquire. But now I will begin with more perseverance than ever, since fear urges me, not my conscience."

" But," replied Madame Danglars, " the count of Monte Cristo can know nothing or he would not seek our society as he does."

"Tell me," cried de Villefort, fixing his eyes more steadfastly on her than he had ever done before, " did you ever reveal to anyone our intimacy ? "

" Never, to anyone ! "

" Do you keep a journal ? "

" No ! my life has been passed in frivolity ; I wish to forget it myself."

" Do you talk in your sleep ? "

" I sleep soundly, like a child ; do you not remember ? " The colour mounted to the baroness's face.

" Well, I understand what I have to do," replied de Villefort. " In less than one week from this time I will ascertain who this M. de Monte Cristo is, and why he speaks in our presence of children that have been disinterred in a garden."

De Villefort pronounced these words with an accent which would have made the count shudder had he heard him. He then led Madame Danglars from the room, and she took a hackney coach back to her carriage, and found the coachman sleeping peacefully on the box.

CHAPTER LXVIII

A SUMMER BALL

THE same day, during the interview of Madame Danglars with the *procureur*, a travelling carriage entering the Rue du Helder, passed through the gateway of No. 27, and stopped in the yard. Madame de Morcerf alighted, leaning on her son's arm. Albert soon left her, ordered his horses, and having arranged his toilet, drove to the Champs Élysées, to the house of Monte Cristo. The count received him with his habitual smile.

"Here I am, dear count."

"Welcome home again."

"And I come directly to see you."

"That is extremely kind of you," said Monte Cristo, with a tone of perfect indifference.

"And what is the news?"

"M. Danglars dined with me."

"I know it; to avoid meeting him, my mother and I left town."

"But he met here M. Andrea Cavalcanti."

"Your Italian prince?"

"Not so fast; M. Andrea only calls himself count."

"What next? You said M. Danglars dined here."

"Yes, with Count Cavalcanti, the marquis his father, Madame Danglars, M. and Madame de Villefort, charming people, M. Debray, Maximilian Morrel, and M. de Château-Renaud."

"Did they speak of me?"

"Not a word."

"If they did not speak of me, I am sure they thought about me, and I am in despair."

"How will that affect you since Mademoiselle Danglars was not among the number who thought of you? Truly she might have thought of you at home."

"Listen!" said Morcerf. "If Mademoiselle Danglars were disposed to take pity on my supposed martyrdom on her account, and dispense with all matrimonial formalities, I am ready to agree to consent. In a word, Mademoiselle Danglars would make a charming mistress, but a wife,—*diable!*"

"And this," said Monte Cristo, "is your opinion of your intended spouse?"

"Yes; it is unkind, but it is true. To marry Mademoiselle Danglars would be awful."

"You are hard to please, viscount."

"One mode of release occurred to me," continued Albert. "Franz likes all that is eccentric; I tried to make him fall in love with Mademoiselle Danglars. But in spite of four letters in the most alluring style, he invariably answered—'My eccentricity may be great, but it will not make me break my promise.'"

"That is what I call devoted friendship, to recommend to another one whom you would not marry yourself."

Albert smiled. " *Apropos !* " continued he, " Franz is coming soon, but it will not interest you ; you dislike him, I think ? "

" I ! " said Monte Cristo ; " my dear viscount, how have you discovered that I do not like M. Franz ? I like everyone. I love everyone as God commands us to love our neighbour, as Christians, and I thoroughly hate but few. Let us return to M. Franz d'Épinay. Did you say he was coming ? "

" Yes ! summoned by M. de Villefort, who is apparently as anxious to get Mademoiselle Valentine married as M. Danglars is to see Mademoiselle Eugénie settled."

" But M. d'Épinay, unlike you, bears his misfortune patiently."

" Still more, he talks seriously about the matter, puts on a white cravat, and speaks of his family. He entertains a very high opinion of M. and Madame de Villefort."

" Pray take a cigar, and cease to struggle to escape marrying Mademoiselle Danglars. Let things take their course ; perhaps you may not have to retract."

" Bah ! " said Albert, staring.

" M. le Vicomte, you will not be taken by force ; but seriously, do you wish to break off your engagement ? "

" I would give a hundred thousand francs to be able to do so."

" Then make yourself quite happy ; M. Danglars would give double that sum to attain the same end."

" But has he any reason ? "

" Ah ! there is your proud and selfish nature. You would expose the self-love of another with a hatchet, but you shrink if your own is attacked with a needle."

" Thank you, I understand. But my mother,—no, not my mother, I mistake,—my father intends giving a ball. Will you take charge of our invitation to Messieurs Cavalcanti ? "

" When will it take place ? "

" On Saturday."

" M. Cavalcanti's father will be gone."

" But the son will be here ; will you invite young M. Cavalcanti ? "

" I do not know him, viscount."

" But you receive him at your house ? "

" That is another thing. Give him a direct invitation, but do not ask me to present him ; if he were afterwards to marry Mademoiselle Danglars you would accuse me of intrigue, and would be challenging me ; besides, I may not be there myself."

" Why should you not be there ? "

" Because you have not yet invited me."

"But I come expressly for that purpose. My mother begs you to come."

"The Countess de Morcerf?" said Monte Cristo, starting. "You have talked of me?"

"Yes, that is your privilege, being a living problem!"

"Then I am, also, a problem to your mother! I should have thought her too reasonable to be led by imagination."

"A problem, my dear count, for everyone—for my mother as well as others; much studied, but not solved, you still remain an enigma, do not fear. You will come on Saturday?"

"Yes, since Madame de Morcerf invites me. Will M. Danglars be there?"

"He has already been invited by my father. We shall try to persuade M. de Villefort to come, but have not much hope of seeing him."

Albert rose and took his hat; the count conducted him to the door.

"When do you expect M. d'Épinay?"

"In five or six days."

"And when is he to be married?"

"Immediately on the arrival of M. and Madame de St. Méran."

"Bring him to see me. Although you say I do not like him, I assure you I shall be happy to see him."

The count watched Albert, waving his hand to him. When he had mounted his phaeton, Monte Cristo turned, and seeing Bertuccio, "What news?" said he.

"She went to the Palais," replied the steward.

"Well, my dear Bertuccio," said the count, "I now advise you to go in quest of the little estate I spoke to you of in Normandy." Bertuccio started the same evening.

CHAPTER LXIX

THE INQUIRY

M. DE VILLEFORT kept the promise he had made to Madame Danglars to endeavour to find out how the count of Monte Cristo had discovered the history of the house at Auteuil. He wrote the same day to M. de Boville, who had now been promoted to a high office in the police, and the latter begged two days to ascertain who would be most likely to give him full particulars. At the end of the second day M. de Villefort received the following note:—

"The person called M. le comte de Monte Cristo is an intimate acquaintance of Lord Wilmore, a rich foreigner, who is sometimes seen in Paris, and who is there at this moment ; he is also known to the Abbé Busoni, a Sicilian priest, of high repute in the East, where he has done much good."

M. de Villefort replied by ordering the strictest inquiries to be made respecting these two persons ; his orders were executed, and the following evening he received these details :—

" The abbé, who is in Paris for a month, occupies a small house near St. Sulpice, consisting of a single storey and the ground-floor, two rooms are on each floor, and he is the only tenant. Lord Wilmore resides in Rue Fontaine Saint George. He is one of those English tourists who consume a large fortune in travelling. He hired the apartment in which he lives furnished, passes only a few hours in the day there, and rarely sleeps there. One of his peculiarities is never to speak French, which, however, he writes with great purity."

The day after these particulars had been furnished to the *procureur*, a man alighted from a carriage at the corner of the Rue Férou, and rapping at an olive-green door, asked if the Abbé Busoni were within. " No, he went out early this morning," replied the valet.

" Then, on his return give him that card and this sealed paper. Will he be at home at eight o'clock this evening ? "

" Doubtless, unless he is at work, which is the same as if he were out."

" I will come again at that time," replied the visitor, who then retired.

At the appointed hour the same man returned in the same carriage. From the signs of respect the valet paid him, he saw his note had produced a good effect.

" Is the abbé at home ? "

" Yes ; he is at work in his library, but he expects you, sir," replied the valet. The stranger ascended a rough staircase, and before a table, whose surface was illumined by a lamp, he perceived the abbé in a monk's dress, with a cowl on his head.

" Have I the honour of addressing the Abbé Busoni ? " asked the visitor.

" Yes, sir," replied the abbé ; " and you are the person whom M. de Boville sends to me from the prefect of police ? "

" Exactly, sir."

The abbé replaced the large spectacles, which covered not only his eyes, but his temples, and motioned to his visitor to a seat. " I am at your service, sir," said the abbé.

" The mission with which I am charged, sir," replied the visitor, speaking with hesitation, " is a confidential one on the part of him who fulfils it, and him by whom he is employed."

At this moment the abbé pressed down his side of the shade, which raised it on the other, and threw a bright light on the face of the stranger, while his own remained obscured.

"Excuse me, abbé," said the envoy of the prefect of police, " but the light tries my eyes very much." The abbé lowered the shade. " I will come at once to the point. Do you know the count of Monte Cristo ? "

" You mean M. Zaccone, I presume ? "

" Well, since M. de Monte Cristo and M. Zaccone are the same, I asked you if you knew him ? "

" Extremely well."

" Who is he ? "

" The son of a rich shipbuilder in Malta. I knew his father, M. Zaccone."

" But whence does he derive the title of count ? "

" You are aware that may be bought."

" And his immense riches, whence does he procure them ? "

" They may not be so very great."

" How much do you suppose he possesses ? "

" From one hundred and fifty to two hundred thousand livres per annum."

" That is reasonable," said the visitor ; " I have heard he had three or four millions per annum."

" That is not probable."

" Do you know his island of Monte Cristo ? "

" Certainly ; everyone who has returned from Palermo, from Naples, or from Rome to France, by sea, must know it, since he has passed close to it, and must have seen it."

" You have, doubtless, heard the adventures of M. Zaccone's youth ? "

" I know nothing certain ; at that period of his life, I lost sight of my young comrade."

" Did he go to war ? "

" I think he entered the service."

" Are you his confessor ? "

" No, sir ; I believe he is a Lutheran."

" We are not now inquiring into his creed, but his actions ; in the name of the prefect of police, I demand, what do you know of him ? "

" He passes for a very charitable man. The Pope has made

him a knight of Jesus Christ for the services he rendered to the Christians in the East; he has five or six rings from Eastern monarchs as testimonials of his services."

" Has he any friends ? "

" Yes, everyone who knows him is his friend."

" But has he any enemies ? "

" One only."

" What is his name ? "

" Lord Wilmore."

" Can he give me any particulars ? "

" Important ones; he was in India with Zaccone."

" Do you know his abode ? "

" It is in la Chaussée d'Antin."

" Do you think the count of Monte Cristo has ever been in France before he made this visit to Paris ? "

" No, sir, because he applied to me six months since for the particulars he required ; and as I knew not when I might again come to Paris, I recommended M. Cavalcanti to him."

" Do you know with what design M. de Monte Cristo purchased a house at Auteuil ? "

" To make a lunatic asylum of it similar to that founded by the count of Pisani at Palermo."

Having said this, the abbé bowed to imply he wished to pursue his studies.

The visitor rose and the abbé accompanied him to the door.

" You are a great almsgiver," said the visitor, " and, although you are said to be rich, I will venture to offer you something for your poor people ; will you accept my offering ? "

" I thank you, sir; I am only jealous of one thing, namely, that the relief I give should be entirely from my own resources."

The stranger bowed and took his leave, and the carriage conducted him straight to the house of M. de Villefort. An hour afterwards the carriage was ordered, to the Rue Fontaine Saint George, and stopped at No. 5, where Lord Wilmore lived. The stranger had written to Lord Wilmore, requesting an interview, which the latter had fixed for ten o'clock.

The visitor was introduced into the drawing-room. It was illuminated by lamps with ground-glass shades, which gave only a feeble light, as if out of consideration for the envoy's weak sight. As the clock struck ten, at the fifth stroke the door opened, and Lord Wilmore appeared. He was dressed with all the English peculiarity, namely, in a blue coat, with gilt buttons and high collar, in the fashion of 1811, a white kerseymere waistcoat, and nankeen pantaloons, three inches too short, which were prevented by straps from slipping up to the knee. His first remark on entering was :—" You know, sir, I do not speak French."

" And I," replied the visitor, changing his idiom, " know enough of English to keep up the conversation. Do not put yourself to the slightest inconvenience."

Then began the questions, which were similar to those which had been addressed to the Abbé Busoni. But as Lord Wilmore, in the character of the count's enemy, was less restrained in his answers, they were more numerous. He described the youth of Monte Cristo, who, he said had served in the Grecian ranks. While in that service he had discovered a silver mine in the mountains of Thessaly, but he had been careful to conceal it from everyone. After the battle of Navarino, when the Greek government was consolidated, he asked of King Otho a mining grant for that district, which was given him. Hence that immense fortune, which might, in Lord Wilmore's opinion, amount to one or two millions per annum, a precarious fortune, which would be lost by the failure of the mine.

" How much does he spend yearly ? " asked the prefect.

" He is a miser." Hatred evidently inspired the Englishman, who, having no other reproach to bring against the count, accused him of avarice.

" Do you know his house at Auteuil ? "

" Certainly. The count supposes there is in the neighbourhood of the house a mineral spring, equal to those at Bagnères, Luchon, and Cauterets. He is going to turn his house into a *badhaus*, as the Germans term it. He has already dug up all the garden two or three times to find the famous spring, and, being unsuccessful, he will soon purchase the adjoining houses."

" What was the cause of your enmity towards him ? "

" When in England he seduced the wife of one of my friends."

" Why do you not seek revenge ? "

" I have already fought three duels with him," said the Englishman ; " the first with the pistol, the second with the sword, and the third with the two-handed sword."

" And the result ? "

" The first time he broke my arm ; the second he wounded me in the breast ; and the third made this large wound." The Englishman turned down his shirt collar, and showed a scar, the redness of which proved it to be recent. " So that you see there is a deadly feud between us."

This was all the visitor wished to ascertain, or rather all the

Englishman appeared to know. The agent rose, and having bowed to Lord Wilmore, who returned his salutation with the stiff politeness of the English, he retired.

Lord Wilmore, having heard the door close after him, returned to his bedroom, where with one hand he pulled off his light hair, his red whiskers, his false jaw, and his wound, to resume his own black hair, the dark complexion, and the pearly teeth of the count of Monte Cristo.

CHAPTER LXX

THE BALL

IT was the warmest day of July, when, in due course the Saturday arrived upon which the ball of M. de Morcerf was to take place. The gardens were illuminated with coloured lanterns, according to the Italian custom, and, as usual in those countries where the luxuries of the table are well understood, the supper-table was loaded with wax-lights and flowers.

At the time the countess de Morcerf returned to the rooms, after giving her orders, many guests were arriving, more attracted by the charming hospitality of the countess than by the distinguished position of the count; for, owing to the good taste of Mercédès, one was sure of finding some arrangements at her fête worthy of relating, or even copying in case of need. Madame Danglars had hesitated in going to Madame de Morcerf, when during the morning her carriage happened to cross that of de Villefort. The latter made a sign, and, the carriages having drawn close together, he said, "You are going to Madame de Morcerf's, are you not? It is important that you should be seen there."

"In that case I will go." And the two carriages passed on towards their destinations. Madame Danglars therefore went, not only beautiful in person, but radiant with splendour; she entered by one door at the same time that Mercédès appeared at the other. The countess took Albert to meet Madame Danglars. He approached and offered his arm to conduct her to a seat. Albert looked around him. "You are looking for my daughter?" said the baroness, smiling.

"I confess it," replied Albert.

"Calm yourself. She has met Mademoiselle de Villefort, and has taken her arm; see, they are following us, both in white dresses, one with a bouquet of camellias, the other with myosotis. But tell me will not the count of Monte Cristo be here to-night?"

" Be satisfied, we shall have this ' lion ; ' we are among the privileged."

" Leave me here, and go and speak to Madame de Villefort, who is longing to engage your attention."

Albert bowed to Madame Danglars, and advanced towards Madame de Villefort, whose lips opened as he approached. " I wager anything," said Albert, interrupting her, " that you were going to ask me if the count of Monte Cristo were arrived."

" Not at all : I was going to ask you if you had received any news of M. Franz ? "

" Yes, yesterday."

" What did he tell you ? "

" That he was leaving at the same time as his letter."

" Well, now then, the count ? "

" The count will come, be satisfied."

" You know that he has another name besides Monte Cristo ? "

" I never heard it."

" Well, then, I am better informed than you ; his name is Zaccone."

" It is possible."

" The son of a shipowner."

" Really, you should relate all this aloud, you would have the greatest success."

" He served in India, discovered a mine in Thessaly, and comes to Paris to form an establishment of mineral waters at Auteuil."

" Well ! I am sure," said Morcerf ; " this is indeed news ! Am I allowed to repeat it ? "

" Yes, but cautiously ; tell one thing at a time, and do not say I told you."

Just then a handsome young man, with bright eyes, black hair, and glossy moustache, respectfully bowed to Madame de Villefort. Albert extended his hand. " Madame," said Albert, " allow me to present to you M. Maximilian Morrel, captain of Spahis, one of our best and bravest officers."

" I have already had the pleasure of meeting this gentleman at Auteuil, at the house of the count of Monte Cristo," replied Madame de Villefort, turning away with marked coldness. This answer, and, above all, the tone in which it was uttered, chilled poor Morrel ; but a recompense was in store for him ; turning round, he saw near the door a beautiful fair face, whose large blue eyes were fixed upon him, while the bouquet of myosotis was gently raised to her lips.

The salutation was so well understood, that Morrel, with the same expression in his eyes, placed his handkerchief to his mouth. They might have remained lost in one another, without anyone noticing their abstraction. The count of Monte Cristo had just entered, and attracted universal attention. Many men might have been handsomer ; but there could be none whose appearance was more *significant*, if the expression may be used.

The count advanced through the crowd of curious glances and exchange of salutations towards Madame de Morcerf, who, standing before a mantelpiece, ornamented with flowers, had seen his entrance in a looking-glass placed opposite the door, and was prepared to receive him. No doubt she fancied the count would speak to her, while on his side the count thought she was about to address him ; but both remained silent : and after a mere bow, Monte Cristo directed his steps to Albert, who received him cordially.

" Have you seen my mother ? "

" I have just had the pleasure," replied the count, " but I have not seen your father."

" He is there, talking politics with that little group of great geniuses."

"Indeed ! " said Monte Cristo : " and so those gentlemen are men of great talent. I should not have guessed it. For what kind of talent are they celebrated ? You know there are different sorts."

" That tall, harsh-looking man is very learned ; he discovered, in the neighbourhood of Rome, a kind of lizard with one vertebra more than usual, and he immediately laid his discovery before the Institute. The thing was discussed for a long time, but finally decided in his favour. I can assure you the vertebra made a great noise in the learned world ; and the gentleman, who was only a knight of the Legion of Honour, was made an officer."

" Come ! " said Monte Cristo, " this cross seems to me to be wisely awarded. I suppose, had he found another additional vertebra, they would have made him a commander."

Just then the count felt his arm pressed ; he turned round, it was Danglars.

" Ah ! Baron ! "

" Why do you call me baron ? " said Danglars ; you know that I care nothing for my title ; I am not like you, viscount ; you like your title, do you not ? "

" Certainly ; without my title I should be nothing, while you, sacrificing the baron, would still remain the millionaire."

" Unfortunately," said Monte Cristo," one's title to a millionaire does not last for life, like that of baron, peer of France, or Academician ; the millionaires Frank and Poulmann, of Frankfort, have just become bankrupts."

" Ah ! " exclaimed Danglars, " they have drawn on me for 200,000 francs."

" Well, you can guard against it ; their signature is worth five per cent."

" Yes ; but it is too late," said Danglars, " I have honoured their bills."

" Dear me ! " said Monte Cristo, " 200,000 francs gone after——"

" Hush ! Do not mention these things," said Danglars ; then approaching Monte Cristo, he added, " especially before young M. Cavalcanti ; " after which he smiled and turned towards the young man in question.

Albert had left the count to speak to his mother, Danglars had gone to converse with young Cavalcanti ; Monte Cristo was alone. Madame de Morcerf saw the Count took nothing, and noticed the movement with which he withdrew from refreshment.

" Albert," she asked, " have you noticed that the count will never accept an invitation to dine with us ? "

" Yes ; but he breakfasted with me."

" But your house is not M. de Morcerf's," murmured Mercédès, " and since he has been here I have watched him.   He has taken nothing yet.   The count is very temperate."   Mercédès smiled sadly.   " Insist upon his taking something."

Albert kissed his mother's hand, and drew near to the count. Another salver passed, loaded as the preceding ones ; Albert attempted to persuade the count, but he obstinately refused. Albert rejoined his mother ; she was very pale.   " Well," said she, " you see he refuses ? "

" Yes ; but why need this annoy you ? "

" Albert, women are singular creatures.   I should like to see the count take something in my house, if only a morsel of pomegranate.   Perhaps he cannot reconcile himself to the French style of living, and might prefer something else."

" Oh, no ! I have seen him eat of everything in Italy ; no doubt he does not feel disposed."

" And, besides," said the countess, " accustomed as he is to burning climates, possibly he does not feel the heat as we do."

" I do not think that, for he has complained of feeling almost suffocated, and asked why the Venetian blinds were not opened as well as the windows."   Mercédès left the room.   A minute afterwards the blinds were thrown open, and through the jessamine and clematis that overhung the window might be seen the garden, ornamented with lanterns, and the supper laid under the tent.

Mercédès reappeared and went straight to the group of which her husband formed the centre. Turning towards Monte Cristo, she said, " Count, will you oblige me with your arm ? " She leaned upon it, or rather just touched it with her hand, and together they descended the steps, lined with rhododendrons and camellias. Behind them, by another outlet, a group of about twenty persons rushed into the garden with loud exclamations of delight.

CHAPTER LXXI

BREAD AND SALT

MADAME DE MORCERF entered an archway of trees with her companion ; it was a grove of lindens, conducting to a conservatory.

" Do you know where I am leading you ? " said the countess.

" No, madame," replied Monte Cristo ; " but you see I make no resistance."

" We are going to the greenhouse at the end of this grove."

They reached the building, ornamented with magnificent fruits, which ripen even in July, in the artificial temperature which takes the place of the sun.

The countess left the arm of Monte Cristo, and gathered a bunch of Muscatel grapes. " See, count," she said, " our grapes are not to be compared with yours of Sicily and Cyprus, but you will make allowance for our climate."

The count bowed, and stepped back.

" Do you refuse ? " said Mercédès, in a tremulous voice.

" Pray excuse me, madame," replied Monte Cristo, " but I never eat Muscatel grapes."

" Take this peach, then," she said. The count again refused. What again ! " she exclaimed, in so plaintive an accent that it seemed but to stifle a sob ; " really, you pain me. There is a beautiful Arabian custom, which makes eternal friends of those who have together eaten bread and salt beneath the same roof."

" I know it, madame," replied the count ; " but we are in France, and not in Arabia ; and in France eternal friendships are as rare as the custom of dividing bread and salt with one another."

" But," said the countess, breathlessly, with her eyes fixed on Monte Cristo, whose arm she convulsively pressed with both hands, " we are friends, are we not ? "

"Certainly, we are friends," he replied; "why not?"

The answer was so little like the one Mercédès desired, that she uttered a sigh, which sounded more like a groan. "Thank you," she said. And they resumed walking. "Sir," suddenly exclaimed the countess, after their walk had lasted ten minutes in silence, "is it true that you have seen so much, travelled so far, and suffered so deeply?"

"I have suffered deeply, madame," answered Monte Cristo.

"But now you are happy?"

"Doubtless," replied the count, "since no one hears me complain."

"And your present happiness, has it softened your heart?"

"My present happiness equals my past misery," said the count.

"Are you not married?" asked the countess.

"I, married!" exclaimed Monte Cristo, shuddering; "who could have told you so?"

"No one told me you were; but you have been seen at the Opera with a young and lovely person."

"She is a slave whom I bought at Constantinople, madame, the daughter of a prince. I have adopted her as my daughter, having no one else to love in the world."

"You live alone, then?"

"I do."

"You have no sister—no son—no father?"

"I have no one."

"How can you exist thus, without anyone to attach you to life?"

"It is not my fault, madame. At Malta, I loved a young girl, was on the point of marrying her, when war came and carried me away. When I returned she was married. Perhaps my heart was weaker than those of the generality, and I suffered more than they would have done in my place; you know all."

The countess stopped for a moment, as if gasping for breath. "Yes," she said, "and you have still preserved this love in your heart—one can only love once—and did you ever see her again?"

"Never!"

"She is now at Malta?"

"I think so."

"And have you forgiven her for all she has made you suffer?"

"Yes, I have pardoned *her*."

"But only her; do you, then, still hate those who separated you?"

"I hate them! not at all,—why should I?"

Albert at this moment ran in. " Oh, mother ! " he exclaimed, " such a misfortune has happened ? "

" What ? what has happened ? "

" M. de Villefort is here."

" Well ? "

" He comes to fetch his wife and daughter."

" Why so ? "

" Because Madame de Saint Méran is just arrived in Paris, bringing the news of M. de Saint Méran's death, which took place on the first stage after he left Marseilles. Mademoiselle Valentine, at the first words, guessed the whole truth, notwithstanding all the precautions of her father ; the blow struck her like a thunderbolt, and she fell senseless."

" And how was M. de Saint Méran related to Mademoiselle de Villefort ? " said the count.

" He was her grandfather on the mother's side. He was coming here to hasten her marriage with Franz."

" Franz is delayed, then. Why is not M. de Saint Méran also grandfather to Mademoiselle Danglars ? "

" Albert ! Albert ! " said Madame de Morcerf, in a tone of mild reproof, " what are you saying ? Ah ! count, he esteems you so highly, tell him that he has spoken amiss." And she took two or three steps forward. Monte Cristo watched her with an air so thoughtful, and so full of affectionate admiration, that she returned, taking his hand, at the same time she grasped that of her son, and joined them together.

" We are friends ; are we not ? " she asked.

" Oh, madame, I do not presume to call myself your friend, but at all times I am your most respectful servant."

CHAPTER LXXII

MADAME DE SAINT MÉRAN

A GLOOMY scene had indeed just passed at the house of de Villefort. The *procureur du roi* had secluded himself, not to study, but to reflect ; and, with the door locked, and orders given that he should not be disturbed, excepting for important business, he sat down in his arm-chair, and began to ponder those events which had filled his mind with so many gloomy thoughts and bitter recollections. Then he opened the drawer of his desk, touched a spring, and drew out a parcel of notes, precious documents, amongst which he had arranged, in characters only known to himself, the names of all who, in his political career, in money matters, at the bar, or in his mysterious love affairs, had become his enemies. When he had run over all these names in his memory, again read and studied them, commenting meanwhile upon his lists, he shook his head.

" No ! " he murmured, " none of my enemies would have waited so patiently and laboriously for so long a space of time, that they might now come and crush me with this secret. The story has been told by the Corsican to some priest, who, in his turn, has also repeated it. M. de Monte Cristo may have heard it, and to enlighten himself—but why should he wish to enlighten himself upon the subject ? " asked de Villefort, after a moment's reflection. " In no period, in no case, in no circumstance, can there have been any contact between him and me."

But de Villefort uttered words which even he did not believe. He dreaded not the revelation so much, but what he was really anxious for, was to discover whose hand had traced it. While he was endeavouring to calm his fears, he heard the steps of an aged person ascending the stairs, followed by tears and lamentations. He unlocked his door, and an old lady entered, unannounced, carrying her shawl on her arm and her bonnet in her hand. " Oh, sir ! " she said ; " oh, sir, what a misfortune ! I shall die of it ; oh ! I shall die of it ! "

De Villefort ran towards his mother-in-law, for it was she. " Why, what can have happened ? " he exclaimed, " what has disturbed you ? Is M. de Saint Méran with you ? "

" M. de Saint Méran is dead ! " answered the marchioness ; she appeared stupefied. De Villefort drew back, and, clasping his hands together, exclaimed, " Dead ! so suddenly ? "

" A week ago." continued Madame de Saint Méran, " we went out together in the carriage after dinner. M. de Saint Méran had been unwell for some days ; still the idea of seeing our dear Valentine again inspired him with courage ; and, notwithstanding his illness, he would leave. At six leagues from Marseilles, he fell into such a deep sleep, that it appeared to me unnatural ; still I hesitated to wake him. I fancied his face became red, and that the veins in his temples throbbed more violently than usual. However, as it became dark, and I could no longer see, I fell asleep ; I was soon aroused by a piercing shriek. I stopped the postillion, I called to M. de Saint Méran, I applied my smelling-salts ; but all was over, and I arrived at Aix by the side of a corpse."

" And what did you do ? "

" M. de Saint Méran had always expressed a desire, in case of his death happening during his absence from Paris, that his body might be brought to the family vault. I had him put into a leaden coffin, and I am preceding him by a few days."

" Oh! my poor mother!" said de Villefort, " to have such duties at your age after such a blow!"

" God has supported me through all! Where is Valentine, sir? It is on her account I am here; I wish to see Valentine." De Villefort said that she had gone out with her stepmother, and that she should be fetched. " This instant, sir,—this instant, I beseech you!" said the old lady. De Villefort placed the arm of Madame de Saint Méran within his own, and conducted her to his apartment. " Rest yourself, mother," he said.

The marchioness raised her head at this word and, bursting into tears, fell on her knees before an armchair, in which she buried her venerable head. De Villefort left her to the care of the maids, and went himself to fetch his wife and daughter from Madame de Morcerf's. He was so pale when he appeared at the door of the ball-room, that Valentine ran to him, saying :—

" Oh! father! some misfortune has happened!"

" Your grandmamma has just arrived, Valentine," said M. de Villefort.

" And, grandpapa?" inquired the young girl, trembling with apprehension. M. de Villefort only replied by offering his arm to his daughter. Madame de Villefort instantly hastened to the carriage, saying, " What a singular event! Who could have thought it? Ah, yes, it is, indeed strange!" At the foot of the stairs, Valentine found Barrois awaiting her.

" M. Noirtier wishes to see you to-night," he said, in an under-tone.

" Tell him I will come when I leave my dear grandmamma," she replied. Valentine found her grandmother in bed; silent caresses, heart-wrung sobs, broken sighs, burning tears, were all that passed in this sad interview.

Valentine went up to M. Noirtier's room on leaving Madame de Saint Méran. She kissed the old man, who looked at her with such tenderness that her eyes again filled with tears, whose sources she thought must be exhausted. " Yes, yes," said Valentine, " you mean that I have yet a kind grandfather left, do you not?" The old man intimated that such was his meaning. " Happily I have," replied Valentine. " Without that what would become of me?"

The next morning she found her grandmother in bed. The

fever had not abated; on the contrary, her eyes glistened, and she appeared to be suffering from violent nervous irritability.

"Oh, dear grandmamma! are you worse?" exclaimed Valentine, perceiving all these signs of agitation.

"No, my child, no!" said Madame de Saint Méran, "but I was waiting for your arrival that I might send for your father."

Valentine durst not oppose her grandmother's wish, the cause of which she knew not; and an instant afterwards de Villefort entered.

"Sir," said Madame de Saint Méran, "you wrote to me about the marriage of this child?"

"Yes, madame," replied de Villefort; "it is not only projected but arranged."

"Your intended son-in-law is M. Franz d'Épinay?"

"Yes, madame!"

"Does he not dislike the idea of marrying the granddaughter of a Jacobin?"

"Our civil dissensions are now happily extinguished, mother," said de Villefort; "M. d'Épinay was quite a child when his father died. He knows very little of M. Noirtier, and will meet him if not with pleasure, at least with indifference."

"You approve of him?"

"He is one of the most distinguished young men I know." During the whole of this conversation Valentine had remained silent.

"Well, sir," said Madame de Saint Méran, after a few minutes' reflection, "I must hasten the marriage, for I have but a short time to live. I must hurry you, so that, having no mother, she may at least have a grandmother to bless her marriage. I am all that is left to her belonging to my poor Renée."

"It shall be as you wish, madame," said de Villefort; "more especially since your wishes coincide with mine; and as soon as M. d'Épinay arrives in Paris——"

"My dear grandmother," interrupted Valentine, "consider propriety. You would not have me marry under such sad auspices?"

"My child," exclaimed the old lady, sharply, "let us hear none of these conventional objections that deter weak minds from making their fortunes."

"Still that idea of death, madame!" said de Villefort.

"Still?—always! I tell you I am going to die—do you understand? Well, before dying, I wish to see my son-in-law. I will know him,—I will!" continued the old lady, with a fearful expression, " that I may rise from the depths of my grave to find him if he should not fulfil his duty."

" Madame," said de Villefort, " you must lay aside these ideas, which almost assume the appearance of madness."

" And I tell you, sir, that you are mistaken. This night I have had a fearful sleep. My eyes, which I tried to open, closed against my will ; and I saw with my eyes shut, issuing from that corner where there is a door leading into Madame de Villefort's dressing-room,—I saw, I tell you, silently enter a white figure." Valentine screamed.

" It was the fever that disturbed you, madame," said de Ville fort.

" Doubt, if you please, but I am sure of what I say. I saw a white figure. I heard my glass removed—the same which is there now on the table. I stretched my hand towards the bell : but when I did so, the shade disappeared ; my maid then entered with a light."

" But she saw no one ? "

" Phantoms are visible to those only who ought to see them. It was the soul of my husband ! Well, if my husband's soul can come to me, why should not my soul reappear to guard my grand-daughter ? The tie is even more direct. When does M. d'Épinay return ? "

" We expect him every moment."

" It is well ; as soon as he arrives inform me. We must be expeditious. I also wish to see a notary, that I may be assured that all our property returns to Valentine."

" Ah, grandmother ! " murmured Valentine. " How fever-ish you are ! We must not send for a notary, but for a doctor ! "

" A doctor ! " said she, shrugging her shoulders, " I am not ill ; I am thirsty—that is all."

" What are you drinking ? "

" The same as usual, my dear, my glass is on the table—give it me, Valentine." Valentine poured the orangeade into a glass, and gave it to her grandmother. The marchioness drained the glass at a single draught, and then turned on her pillow repeat-ing,—" The notary ! the notary ! "

M. de Villefort left the room, and Valentine seated herself at the bedside of her grandmother. Two hours passed thus : Madame de Saint Méran was in a feverish sleep, and the notary had arrived. Though announced in a very low tone, Madame de Saint Méran arose from her pillow. " The notary ! " she exclaimed ; " let him come in."

The notary, who was at the door, immediately entered. " Go, Valentine," said Madame de Saint Méran, " and leave me with this gentleman."

The young girl kissed her grandmother, and left with her handkerchief to her eyes ; at the door she found the valet who told her the doctor was waiting in the dining-room. The doctor was a friend of the family, one of the cleverest men of the day and very fond of Valentine, at whose birth he had been present.

" Oh," said Valentine, " we have been waiting for you with such impatience, dear M. d'Avrigny. But, first of all, how are Madeleine and Antoinette ? " Madeleine was the daughter of M. d'Avrigny, and Antoinette his niece. M. d'Avrigny smiled sadly. " Antoinette is very well," he said, " and Madeleine tolerably so. But you sent for me, my dear child. It is not your father or Madame de Villefort who is ill ? As for you, although we doctors cannot divest our patients of nerves, I fancy you have no further need of me than to recommend you not to allow your imagination to take too wide a field."

Valentine coloured. " No," she replied, " it is for my poor grandmother : you know the calamity that has happened to us, do you not ? "

" I know nothing," said M. d'Avrigny.

" Alas ! " said Valentine, restraining her tears, " my grandfather is dead."

" M. de Saint Méran ? "

" Yes ! and my poor grandmother fancies that her husband, whom she never left, has called her, and that she must go and join him. Oh, M. d'Avrigny, I beseech you do something for her ! "

" Where is she ? "

" In her room with the notary."

" What are your grandmother's symptoms ? "

" An extreme nervous excitement, and a strangely agitated sleep. She fancies that she saw a phantom enter her chamber, and even heard the noise it made on touching her glass."

" It is singular," said the doctor ; " I was not aware that Madame de Saint Méran was subject to such hallucinations. We will go and see. What you tell me seems very strange. "

The notary descended and Valentine was informed her grandmother was alone. " Go upstairs," she said to the doctor.

The doctor pressed Valentine's hand, and while he visited her grandmother, she went down the steps. She turned into the dark avenue which led to the bank ; then from the bank she went to the gate. As she advanced she fancied she heard a voice pronounce her name. She stopped astonished, then the voice reached her ear more distinctly, and she recognized it to be that of Maximilian.

CHAPTER LXXIII

THE PROMISE

It was indeed Maximilian Morrel, who had passed a wretched existence since the previous day. Valentine was ignorant of the cause of his sorrow and anxiety, and as it was not his accustomed hour for visiting her, pure chance, or rather a happy sympathy, had led her to that spot. " You here at this hour ? " said she.

" Yes, my poor girl," replied Morrel ; " I come to bring and to hear bad tidings. Listen, I entreat you ; what I am about to say is solemn. When are you to be married ? "

" I will tell you all," said Valentine ; " this morning the subject was introduced, and my dear grandmother not only declared herself favourable to it, but is so anxious for it, that they only await the arrival of M. d'Épinay, to sign the contract."

" Alas ! " replied he, " it is dreadful to hear my condemnation from your own lips. To-morrow you will be engaged to M. d'Épinay, for he came this morning to Paris."

Valentine uttered a cry.

" I was at the house of Monte Cristo an hour since," said Morrel ; " we were speaking, he of the sorrow your family had experienced, and I of your grief, when a carriage rolled into the courtyard. Albert de Morcerf entered first, and I began to hope my fears were groundless, when another young man advanced and the count exclaimed, ' Ah ! M. le Baron Franz d'Épinay ! " I summoned all my courage to my support, but five minutes later left without having heard one word that had passed."

" Poor Maximilian ! "

" Valentine, the time has arrived when you must answer me. What do you intend doing ? "

Valentine held down her head ; she was overwhelmed.

" Listen ! " said Morrel ; " it is not the first time you have contemplated our present position, which is a serious and urgent one. Do you intend to struggle against our ill-fortune ? Tell me, Valentine, for it is that I came to know."

Valentine trembled and looked at him with amazement. The idea of resisting her father, her grandmother, and all the family had never occurred to her. " What do you say, Maximilian ? " asked Valentine. " What do you term a struggle ? Oh ! it would be a sacrilege. To grieve my father—to disturb my grandmother's last moments—never ! "

" You are right," said Morrel calmly.

" In what a tone you speak ! " cried Valentine.

" I speak as one who admires you, mademoiselle."

" But, tell me, how can I do otherwise ? "

" Do not appeal to me, mademoiselle, I shall be a bad judge in such a case ; my selfishness will blind me," replied Morrel, whose low voice and clenched hands announced his growing desperation.

" What do you advise ? "

" I am free," replied Maximilian, " and rich enough to support you. I will take you to my sister, who is worthy also to be yours. We will get married and embark for Algiers, for England, for America, or, if you prefer it, retire to the country, and only return to Paris when our friends have reconciled your family." Valentine shook her head.

" You will then submit to what fate decrees for you without even attempting to contend with it ? "

" Yes,—if I die ! "

" Well, Valentine," resumed Maximilian, " I again repeat, you are right. Truly it is I who am mad ; and you prove to me that passion blinds the most correct minds. To-morrow you will be irrevocably promised to M. Franz d'Épinay, not only by the signature of the contract, but by your own will."

" Again you drive me to despair, Maximilian," said Valentine, " again you plunge the dagger in the wound ! What would you do, tell me, if your sister listened to such a proposition ? "

" Mademoiselle," replied Morrel, with a bitter smile, " I think only that I have known you now a whole year. One day you acknowledged that you loved me ; and since that day my hope of future happiness has rested on winning you ; for to gain you would be life to me. Now, I think no more ; I say only that fortune has turned against me—I had thought to gain heaven, and now I have lost it."

Morrel pronounced these words with perfect calmness ; Valentine looked at him with her large eyes, endeavouring not to let Morrel discover the grief which struggled in her heart. " But in a word, what are you going to do ? " she asked.

" I am going to have the honour of taking my leave of you, mademoiselle, assuring you that I wish your life may be so happy and so fully occupied, that there may be no place for me even in your memory."

" Oh ! " murmured Valentine.

" Adieu, Valentine, adieu ! " said Morrel, bowing.

" Where are you going ? " cried the young girl. " Before you leave me, tell me what you are going to do, Maximilian." The young man smiled sorrowfully.

" Oh ! fear not," said Maximilian, stopping at a short distance, " I do not intend to render another man responsible for the rigorous fate reserved for me. Another might threaten to seek M. Franz, to provoke him, and to fight with him ; all that would be folly. I have no enmity against M. Franz, and promise you the punishment shall not fall on him."

" On whom, then ?—on me ? "

" On you, Valentine ! Heaven forbid ! Woman is sacred, the woman one loves is holy."

" On yourself then, unhappy man ; on yourself ? "

" I am the only guilty person, am I not ? "

" Maximilian ! " said Valentine, " Maximilian, return, I entreat you ! " He drew near, with his sweet smile, and, but for his paleness, one might have thought him in his usual happy frame.

" Listen, my dear, my adored Valentine," said he, " in losing you, I lose my life. The moment you leave me, Valentine, I am alone in the world. This is what I will do ; I will wait until the last moment, and when my misery is certain and irremediable, I will put an end to my existence, as surely as I am the son of the most honest man who ever lived in France."

Valentine fell on her knees and pressed her almost bursting heart. " Maximilian ! " said she, " I entreat you, do as I do, live in suffering ; perhaps we may one day be united."

" Adieu, Valentine," repeated Morrel.

" My God," said Valentine, raising both her hands to heaven with a sublime expression, " I have done my utmost to remain a submissive daughter. I am resolved not to die of remorse, but rather of shame. Live, Maximilian, and I will be yours. Say when shall it be ? Speak, command, I will obey." Morrel, who had already gone some few steps away, again returned, and, pale with joy, extended both hands towards Valentine through the opening.

" Valentine," said he, " you must not speak thus. Why should I obtain you by violence, if our love is mutual ? Is it from mere humanity you bid me live ? I would rather die ! "

" Truly," murmured Valentine, " you are right ; Maximilian,

I will follow you, I will leave the paternal home, I will give up all. Oh! ungrateful girl that I am," cried Valentine, sobbing, " I will give up all, even my dear old grandfather, whom I had nearly forgotten."

" No," said Maximilian, " you shall not leave him. As soon as we are married, he shall come and live with us; instead of one child, he shall have two. I promise you solemnly, that instead of despair, it is happiness that awaits us."

" Oh! see, Maximilian, see the power you have over me, you almost make me believe you; and yet, what you tell me is madness, for my father will curse me—he is inflexible—he will never pardon me. Now listen to me, Maximilian; if by any means I can delay this marriage, will you wait?"

" Yes, I promise you, as faithfully as you have promised me that this marriage shall not take place, and if you are dragged before a magistrate or a priest, you will refuse."

" I promise you by all that is most sacred to me in the world, namely, by my mother."

" I rely on you, Valentine," said Morrel; " all you do will be well done; only if they disregard your prayers, if your father and Madame de Saint Méran insist that M. d'Épinay should be called to-morrow, to sign the contract——"

" I will rejoin you, and we will fly; but from this moment until then, let us not tempt Providence, Morrel; if we were surprised, if it were known that we met thus, we should have no further resource."

" You are right, Valentine, but how shall I ascertain?"

" From the notary, M. Deschamps. And for myself—I will write to you, depend on me. I dread this marriage, Maximilian, as much as you."

" Thank you, my adored Valentine, thank you; that is enough. When once I know the hour, I will hasten to this spot, you can easily get over this fence with my assistance, a carriage will await us at the gate, in which you will accompany me to my sister's. There living, retired or mingling in society as you wish, we shall be enabled to resist oppression."

" Adieu, then, till we meet again," said Valentine, tearing herself away.

" Thanks, thanks, dear love, adieu!" The sound of a kiss was heard, and Valentine fled through the avenue. The young man returned home and waited all the evening and all the next day without hearing anything. As he was starting to call on M. Deschamps, the notary, he received from the postman a brief letter, which he knew to be from Valentine. It was to this effect :—

" Tears, entreaties, prayers, have availed me nothing. Heaven is as inflexible as man, and the signature of the contract is fixed for this evening at nine o'clock. I have but one promise and but one heart to give. That promise is pledged to you, that heart is also yours. This evening, then, at a quarter past nine, at the gate.

"Your betrothed,
"VALENTINE DE VILLEFORT."

" P.S.—My poor grandmother gets worse and worse. You will be very kind to me, will you not, Morrel, to make me forget my sorrow in leaving her thus ? I think it is kept a secret from grandpapa Noirtier, that the contract is to be signed this evening."

Morrel went also to the notary, who confirmed his account of the proposed signature. Then he went to call on Monte Cristo, and heard still more. Franz had been to announce the solemnity, and Madame de Villefort had also written to beg the count to excuse her not inviting him. The day before, Franz had been presented to Madame de Saint Méran, who had left her bed to receive him, but had been obliged to return to it immediately afterwards.

It is easy to suppose that Morrel's agitation would not escape the count's penetrating eye. Monte Cristo was more affectionate than ever,—indeed, his manner was so kind, that several times Morrel was on the point of telling him all. But he recalled the promise he had made to Valentine, and kept his secret.

Morrel longed intensely for the moment when he should hear Valentine say, " Here I am, Maximilian ; come and help me." He had arranged everything for her escape. When the afternoon arrived, and he felt the hour was drawing near, his agitation was extreme. He entered the clover-field while the clock of Saint Philippe du Roule was striking eight. The night gradually drew on and the foliage in the garden assumed a deeper hue. The house, which was discernible through the trees, remained in darkness, and gave no indication that so important an event as the signature of a marriage contract was going on. He tremblingly fixed his ladder, and not to lose a moment, placed his foot on the first step. Amidst all these alternations of hope and fear, the clock struck ten. " It is impossible," said Maximilian, " that the signing of a contract should occupy so long a time without

R

unexpected interruptions. I have weighed all the chances, calculated the time required for all the forms ; something must have happened."

The idea that her strength had failed her in attempting to escape, and that she had fainted in one of the paths. most impressed him. " In that case," said he, " I should lose her, and by my own fault." At last the half-hour struck, it was impossible to wait longer. He passed one leg over the wall and in a moment leaped down on the other side. He followed a short distance close under the wall, then crossed a path and entered a clump of trees. In a moment he had passed through them, and could see the house distinctly. A light moved rapidly from time to time past three windows of the first floor. These three windows were in Madame de Saint Méran's room. Almost mad with grief, and determined to venture everything in order to see Valentine once more, and be certain of the misfortune he feared, Morrel gained the edge of the clump of trees, when the sound of a voice, still at some distance, reached him. At this sound, he stepped back and concealed himself completely, remaining perfectly motionless. The moon had just then escaped from behind the cloud which had concealed it, and Morrel saw de Villefort come out upon the steps, followed by a gentleman in black ; they advanced towards the clump of trees, and Morrel recognized the other gentleman as Doctor d'Avrigny.

The young man, seeing them approach, drew back mechanically, until he found himself stopped by a sycamore tree in the centre of the clump ; there he was compelled to remain. Soon the two gentlemen stopped also. " Ah, my dear doctor ! " said the *procureur*, " Heaven declares itself against my house ! What a dreadful death ! She is dead !—she is dead ! "

" My dear M. de Villefort," replied the doctor, in a tone which redoubled the terror of the young man, " I have not led you here to console you ; on the contrary——"

" What can you mean ? "

" I mean, that behind the misfortune which has just happened, there is another, perhaps still greater."

" Can it be possible ? " murmured de Villefort, clasping his hands.

" I have a terrible secret to communicate to you," said the doctor. " Let us sit down." De Villefort fell rather than seated himself. The doctor stood before him, with one hand placed on his shoulder. Morrel, horrified, supported his head with one hand, and with the other, pressed his heart, lest its beatings

should be heard. " Dead ! dead ! " he repeated within himself ;
and he felt as if he were also dying.

" Speak, doctor, I am listening," said de Villefort ; " strike, I
am prepared for everything ! "

" Were you present during the last struggle ? " asked M.
d'Avrigny.

" I was," replied the *procureur* ; " you begged me not to
leave."

" Did you notice the symptoms of the disease to which Madame
de Saint Méran has fallen a victim ? "

" I did. It was only when I saw her raise herself in the bed,
and her limbs and neck appear stiffened, that I became really
alarmed. Then I understood from your countenance there was
more to fear than I had thought. You held her hand, you were
feeling her pulse, and the second fit came on before you had
turned towards me. This was more terrible than the first ; the
same nervous movements were repeated, and the mouth contracted
and turned purple."

" And at the third she expired."

" At the end of the first attack I discovered symptoms of
tetanus ; you confirmed my opinion."

" Yes, before others," replied the doctor ; " but now we are
alone——"

" What are you going to say ? Oh, spare me ! "

" That the symptoms of tetanus and poisoning by vegetable
substances are the same."

M. de Villefort started from his seat, then fell back again,
silent and motionless. Morrel knew not if he were dreaming or
awake. " Do you speak to me as a magistrate or as a friend ? "
asked de Villefort.

" As a friend, and only as a friend at this moment. And to
that friend I say, ' During the three-quarters of an hour that the
struggle continued, I watched the convulsions and the death of
Madame de Saint Méran, and am convinced that not only did her
death proceed from poison, but I could also specify the poison.
Madame de Saint Méran has sunk under a violent dose of brucine
or strychnine, which, possibly by mistake, has been given to her."

" Have pity on me, doctor ! So many dreadful things have
happened to me lately that I am on the verge of madness."

" Indeed, my dear friend," said M. d'Avrigny, " I would not
accuse anyone ; but whether accident or mistake, the fact is
there ; it speaks to my conscience, and compels me to speak
aloud to you. Make inquiry."

" Of whom ?—how ?—of what ? "

" May not Barrois, the old servant, have made a mistake, and have given Madame de Saint Méran a dose prepared for his master ? "

" But how could a dose prepared for M. Noirtier poison Madame de Saint Méran ? "

" Nothing is more simple. Having tried every other remedy to restore movement and speech to M. Noirtier, for three months I have been giving him brucine ; so that in the last dose I ordered for him there were six grains. This quantity, which it is perfectly safe to administer to the paralysed frame of M. Noirtier, which has become gradually accustomed to it, would be sufficient to kill another person."

" My dear doctor, there is no communication between M. Noirtier's apartment and that of Madame de Saint Méran, and Barrois never entered my mother-in-law's room. In short, although I know you to be the most conscientious man in the world, I want, notwithstanding, to believe this axiom, *errare humanum est.*"

" Is there one of my brethren in whom you have equal confidence with myself ? "

" Why do you ask me that ? What do you wish ? "

" Send for him ; I will tell him what I have seen, and we will consult together, and examine the body."

" And you will find traces of poison ? "

" No, I did not say of poison, but we can prove what was the state of the body ; we shall discover the cause of her sudden death, and we shall say, ' Dear de Villefort, if this thing has been caused by negligence, watch over your servants ; if by hatred, watch your enemies.' "

" What do you propose to me, d'Avrigny ? You know a man does not arrive at the post I occupy—one has not been *procureur du roi* twenty-five years without having made a tolerable number of enemies. Let this affair be talked of ; it will be a triumph for them, and cover me with shame. Doctor, pray recall your words ; you have said nothing, have you ? "

" My dear M. de Villefort," replied the doctor, " my first duty is humanity. I would have saved Madame de Saint Méran, if science could have done it ; but she is dead, my duty regards the living. Meanwhile, sir, watch always—watch carefully, for, perhaps, the evil may not stop here. And when you have found the culprit, if you find him, I will say to you, ' You are a magistrate, do as you will ! ' "

" I thank you, doctor," said de Villefort, with indescribable joy ;
" I never had a better friend than you." And, as if he feared
Doctor d'Avrigny would recall his promise, he hurried him towards
the house.

When they were gone, Morrel ventured out from under the trees,
and the moon shone upon his face, which was so pale it might
have been taken for a phantom. " I am protected in the most
wonderful, but most terrible manner," said he ; " but Valentine,
poor girl ! how will she bear so much sorrow ? "

At the extremity of the building he saw one of the three windows
open. A wax-light placed on the mantelpiece threw some of its
pale rays without, and a shadow was seen for one moment on
the balcony. Morrel shuddered ; he thought he heard a
sob.

Although it was impossible Valentine could see him, hidden
as he was, he thought he heard the shadow at the window call
him ; his disturbed mind told him so. This double error became
an irresistible reality, and by one of those incomprehensible trans-
ports of youth, he bounded from his hiding-place, and having
passed the rows of orange-trees which extended in front of the
house, he reached the step, ran quickly up, and pushed the door,
which opened without offering any resistance. Morrel found the
staircase, which, being carpeted, prevented his approach from being
heard ; and he had regained that degree of confidence that the
presence of M. de Villefort even would not have alarmed him.
Happily he did not meet anyone.

Now, especially, did he find the description Valentine had
often given of the interior of the house useful to him ; he arrived
at the top of the staircase and, while feeling his way, a sob indicated
the direction he was to take ; a door partly opened enabled him
to see his road, and to hear the sorrowing voice. He pushed
it open and entered. At the other end of the room, under a
white sheet which covered it, lay the corpse, still more alarming
to Morrel since the account he had so unexpectedly overheard.
By the side, on her knees, and her head buried in the cushion of
an easy-chair, was Valentine, trembling and sobbing, her hands
extended above her head, clasped and stiff. He sighed, and
whispered a name, and the head bathed in tears and pressed on the
velvet cushion of the chair, was raised and turned towards him.
Valentine perceived him without betraying the least surprise.
Neither dared for some time to speak in that room. At length
Valentine ventured.

" My friend," said she, " how came you here ? Alas ! I would say you are welcome, had not death opened the way for you into this house."

"Valentine," said Morrel, with a trembling voice, "I had waited since half-past eight, and did not see you come; I became uneasy, leaped the wall, found my way through the garden, when voices conversing about the fatal event——"

"But it was risking the failure of our plan to come up here, love."

"Forgive me," replied Morrel; "I will go away."

"No," said Valentine, "you might meet someone; stay."

"But what has become of M. d'Épinay?" replied Morrel.

"M. Franz arrived to sign the contract just as my dear grandmother was dying."

"Alas!" said Morrel, with a feeling of selfish joy, for he thought this death would cause the wedding to be postponed indefinitely.

"But what redoubles my sorrow is that the poor old lady, on her death-bed, requested the marriage might take place as soon as possible; she, thinking to protect me, was acting against me."

"Hark!" said Morrel.

"It is my father, who has just left his study."

"To accompany the doctor to the door," added Morrel.

Valentine looked at the young man; they heard the street-door close; then M. de Villefort locked the garden-door, and returned upstairs.

"Now," said Valentine, "you can neither go out by the front door nor by the garden."

Morrel looked at her with astonishment.

"There is but one way left you that is safe," said she; "it is through my grandfather's room."

"Can you mean it, Valentine?"

"I have long wished it; he is my only remaining friend, and we both need his help,—come."

She then crossed the corridor, and led the way down a narrow staircase to M. Noirtier's room; Morrel followed her on tiptoe; at the door they found the old servant.

"Barrois," said Valentine, "shut the door, and let no one come in." She passed first. "Dear grandfather," said she, hurriedly, "you know poor grandmamma died an hour since, and now I have no friend in the world but you."

The paralytic motioned "Yes."

Valentine took Maximilian's hand. "Look attentively, then, at this gentleman." It is M. Maximilian Morrel," said she;

" the son of that good merchant of Marseilles, whom you doubtless recollect."

The old man signified that he recollected him.

" Well, grandpapa," said Valentine, kneeling before him, and pointing to Maximilian, " I love him, and will be only his ; were I compelled to marry another, I would destroy myself."

The eyes of the paralytic expressed a multitude of tumultuous thoughts.

" And you will protect us, your children, against the will of my father ? "

Noirtier looked at Morrel, as if to say, " Perhaps I may."

Maximilian understood him. " Mademoiselle," said he, " you have a sacred vigil to keep in your deceased grandmother's room ; will you allow me the honour of a few minutes' conversation with M. Noirtier ? "

Valentine rose, placed a chair for Morrel, requested Barrois not to admit anyone, and went away. To prove to Noirtier that he was in Valentine's confidence and knew all their secrets, Morrel took the dictionary, a pen, and some paper, and placed them all on a table, where there was a light.

It was an impressive sight to witness this old man, apparently a sheer hulk, becoming the sole protector, support, and adviser of the lovers, who were both young, beautiful, and strong. His noble and austere expression struck Morrel, who told him of his birth, position, fortune ; and more than once, when he consulted the look of the paralytic, that look answered, " That is good, proceed."

" And now," said Morrel, when he had finished the first part of his recital, " now I have told you of my love and my hopes, may I inform you of my intentions ? "

" Yes," signified the old man.

" This was our resolution : I intended to carry off Valentine to my sister's house, to marry her, and to wait respectfully M. de Villefort's pardon."

" No."

-" There is another way," said Morrel. " I will seek M. Franz d'Épinay, and will conduct myself towards him so as to compel him to challenge me. I will tell him of the ties which bind me to Valentine ; if he be a sensible man, he will prove it by renouncing the hand of his betrothed, and will secure my friendship and love until death ; if he refuse, I will fight with him, give him every advantage, and I shall kill him, or he will kill me ; if I am victorious, he will not marry Valentine, and if I die, I am sure Valentine will not marry him."

Noirtier, when Morrel had finished, shut his eyes several times, which was his manner of saying " No."

" Then, what should be done ? " asked Morrell. " Madame de Saint Méran's last request was, that the marriage might not be delayed ; must I let things take their course ? "

Noirtier did not move.

" I understand," said Morrel ; " I am to wait."

" Yes."

" But delay may ruin our plan, sir," replied the young man. " Believe me, there are only the two plans I have proposed to you ; forgive my vanity, and tell me which you prefer. Do you authorize Valentine to entrust herself to my honour ? "

" No."

" Do you prefer I should seek M. d'Epinay ? "

" No."

" Whence then will come the help we need—from you ? "

" Yes." There was so much firmness in the look which gave this answer, no one could doubt his will, if they did his power.

" Then I must wait ? " asked the young man.

" Yes."

" But the contract ! Will you assure me it shall not be signed ? "

" Yes," said Noirtier.

" The contract shall not be signed ! " cried Morrel. " Will they not sign it ? "

" No," said the invalid.

" What do you wish, sir ? " asked Morrel ; " that I should renew my promise of remaining tranquil ? " Noirtier's eye remained fixed and firm, as if to imply that a promise did not suffice.

" I swear to you, on my honour," said he, " to await your decision respecting the course I am to pursue with M. d'Epinay."

" That is right," said the old man.

" Now," said Morrel, " do you wish me to retire ? "

" Yes."

The young man pressed his lips on the old man's forehead and retired. He soon found the spot where he had entered the house ; he gained the top of the wall, and by his ladder was, in an instant, in the clover-field, where his cabriolet was still waiting for him. He got in it, and arrived about midnight in the Rue Meslay, threw himself on his bed, and slept soundly.

CHAPTER LXXIV

THE VILLEFORT FAMILY VAULT

Two days later, a considerable crowd was assembled, towards ten o'clock in the morning, round the door of M. de Villefort's house, and a file of mourning coaches and private carriages extended along the Faubourg Saint-Honoré and the Rue de la Pépinière. Among them was a kind of covered waggon, painted black. It was ascertained that, by a strange coincidence, this carriage contained the corpse of the Marquis de Saint Méran, and that those who had come, thinking to attend one funeral, would follow two. Their number was great. The Marquis de Saint Méran, one of the most zealous and most faithful dignitaries of Louis XVIII and Charles X, had a great number of friends, and these, added to the persons on whom the usages of society gave de Villefort a claim, formed a considerable body.

Due information was given to the authorities, and permission obtained that the two funerals should take place at the same time. The two bodies were to be interred in the Villefort family vault in the cemetery of Père-Lachaise. The remains of poor Renée, whom, after ten years of separation, her father and mother had now rejoined, already lay there. The Parisians, always affected by funeral display, looked on with solemn silence, while the splendid procession accompanied to their last abode two of the members of the old aristocracy.

In one of the mourning coaches, Albert, Beauchamp, Debray, and Château-Renaud were talking of the death of the marchioness. "I saw Madame de Saint-Méran last year at Marseilles. How old was she?"

"Franz assured me," replied Albert, "that she was seventy."

"Of what disease did she die?" asked Debray.

"It is said to have been congestion of the brain, or apoplexy."

"It is difficult to believe it was apoplexy," said Beauchamp.

"At any rate," said Albert, "whatever disease or doctor may have killed her, M. de Villefort, or Mademoiselle Valentine, or rather our friend Franz, will inherit a magnificent fortune, amounting, I believe, to 80,000 livres per annum."

"Which will be doubled at the death of the old Jacobin Noirtier."

"That is a tenacious old grandfather," said Beauchamp. "*Tenacem propositi virum.* I think he must have made an agreement with Death to outlive all his heirs, and he appears likely to succeed. But where is Franz?"

"In the first carriage, with M. de Villefort, who considers him already as one of the family."

Such was the conversation in almost all the carriages. Among the groups which flocked towards the family vault, Château-Renaud recognized Morrel, who had come alone in a cabriolet, and walked silently along the path bordered with yew-trees. "You here!" said Château-Renaud, passing his arm through the young captain's; "are you a friend of de Villefort's? How is it I have never met you at his house?"

"I am no acquaintance of M. de Villefort's," answered Morrel, "but I was of Madame de Saint Méran." Albert came up with Franz at this moment.

"The time and place are but ill suited for an introduction," said Albert; "but we are not superstitious. M. Morrel, allow me to present to you M. Franz d'Épinay. My dear Franz, M. Maximilian Morrel, an excellent friend I have acquired in your absence." Morrel hesitated for a moment; he struggled to conceal his emotion, and bowed to Franz.

"Mademoiselle de Villefort is in deep sorrow, is she not?" said Debray to Franz.

"Extremely," replied he; "she looked so pale this morning, I scarcely knew her." These apparently simple words pierced Morrel to the heart. This man had seen Valentine, and spoken to her! He turned towards the vault, where the attendants had already placed the two coffins.

"This is a magnificent habitation," said Beauchamp, "you will, in turn, enter it, my dear d'Épinay, for you will soon be numbered as one of the family."

"Politics have made you laugh at everything, and political men have made you disbelieve everything."

"I am prejudiced against Beauchamp," said Albert, drawing Franz away. The Villefort vault formed a square of white stones, about twenty feet high; an interior partition separated the two families, and each compartment had its entrance-door. All that was visible within the bronze gates was a gloomy-looking room, separated by a wall from the vault itself. The doors were in the middle of this wall, and enclosed the de Villefort and Saint Méran coffins.

The two coffins were placed on trestles previously prepared for their reception in the righthand division belonging to the Saint Méran family. De Villefort, Franz, and a few near relatives alone entered the sanctuary.

As the religious ceremonies had been performed at the door,

and there was no address given, most of the party separated. Franz remained with M. de Villefort : at the gate of the cemetery Morrel made an excuse to wait ; he saw Franz and M. de Villefort get into the same mourning coach, and thought this *tête-à-tête* forboded evil.

De Villefort and Franz returned to the Faubourg Saint-Honoré. The *procureur*, without going to see either his wife or his daughter, passed rapidly to his study, and, offering the young man a chair, " M. d'Épinay," said he, " allow me to remind you of the wish expressed by Madame de Saint Méran on her deathbed, that Valentine's wedding might not be deferred."

" Sir," replied M. d'Épinay, " it is not, perhaps, the moment for Mademoiselle Valentine, who is in deep distress, to think of a husband ; indeed, I fear——"

" Valentine will have no greater pleasure than that of fulfilling her grandmamma's last injunctions ; there will be no objection from that quarter."

" In that case," replied Franz, " as I will raise none, you may make arrangements when you please."

" Then," said de Villefort, " nothing further is required ; the contract was to have been signed three days since ; we shall find it all ready, and can sign it to-day. Mademoiselle de Villefort may return during the prescribed three months to her estate of Saint Méran ; I say hers, for she inherits it to-day. There, after a few days, if you like, the civil marriage shall be celebrated without pomp or ceremony."

" As you please, sir," said Franz.

" Then," replied M. de Villefort, " have the kindness to wait half an hour ; Valentine will come down into the drawing-room. I will send for M. Deschamps ; we will read and sign the contract before we separate, and this evening Madame de Villefort shall accompany Valentine to her estate, where we shall rejoin them in a week."

" Sir," said Franz, " I have one request to make. I wish Albert de Morcerf and Raoul de Château-Renaud to be present at this signature ; they are my witnesses."

" Half an hour will apprise them ; will you go for them yourself, or will you send ? "

" I prefer going, sir."

" I shall expect you, then, in half an hour, baron ; and Valentine will be ready." Franz bowed and left the room. Scarcely had the door closed, when M. de Villefort sent to tell Valentine to be ready. Valentine was thunderstruck. She looked round for help, and would have gone to her grandfather's room, but meeting M. de Villefort on the stairs, he took her arm, and led her into the drawing-room. One moment later, Madame de Villefort entered the drawing-room with her son. She sat down, took Edward on her knees, and, from time to time, pressed almost convulsively to her bosom this child, on whom her affections appeared centred. Two carriages were soon heard to enter the courtyard. In a moment the whole party was assembled.

The notary, after having, according to the customary method, arranged the papers on the table, turned towards Franz :—" Are you M. Franz de Quesnel, baron d'Épinay ? "

" Yes, sir," replied Franz.

The notary bowed. " I have, then, to inform you, sir, at the request of M. de Villefort, that your projected marriage with Mademoiselle de Villefort has changed the feeling of M. Noirtier towards his grandchild ; and that he disinherits her entirely of the fortune he would have left her. Let me hasten to add," continued he, " that the testator, having only the right to alienate a part of his fortune, and having alienated it all, the will will not bear scrutiny, and is declared null and void."

" Yes," said de Villefort ; " but I warn M. d'Épinay, that during my lifetime my father's will shall never be scrutinized, my position forbidding any doubt to be entertained."

" Sir," said Franz, " I regret such a question has been raised in the presence of Mademoiselle Valentine. My family has sought consideration in this alliance with M. de Villefort ; all I seek is happiness." Valentine imperceptibly thanked him, while two tears rolled down her cheeks.

" Besides, sir," said de Villefort, addressing himself to his future son-in-law, " excepting the loss of a portion of your hopes, this unexpected will need not wound you ; M. Noirtier's weakness of mind explains it. It is not because Mademoiselle Valentine is going to marry you that he is angry, but because she will marry ; a union with any other would have caused him the same sorrow. I am convinced that at the present time, although he knows his granddaughter is going to be married, M. Noirtier has even forgotten the name of his intended grandson." M. de Villefort had scarcely said this, when the door opened and Barrois appeared.

" Gentlemen," said he, in a tone strangely firm for a servant speaking to his masters in such solemn circumstances, " gentlemen, M. Noirtier de Villefort wishes to speak immediately to M. Franz de Quesnel, baron d'Épinay."

De Villefort started, Madame de Villefort let her son slip

from her knees. " It is impossible," said the *procureur du roi.*
" M. d'Épinay cannot leave the drawing-room at present."

" It is at this moment," replied Barrois, " that M. Noirtier,
my master, wishes to speak to M. Franz d'Épinay."

" Pray go, Valentine," said M. de Villefort, " and see what this
new fancy of your grandfather's is." Valentine rose quickly,
and was hastening joyfully towards the door, when M. de Villefort
changed his mind.

" Stop ! " said he ; " I will go with you."

" Excuse me, sir," said Franz, " since M. Noirtier sent for me,
I am ready to attend to his wish. I would not lose this opportunity of proving how wrong it would be of him to encourage
feelings of dislike to me, which I am determined to conquer by
my devotedness." So saying he followed Valentine and M de
Villefort went almost immediately after them.

CHAPTER LXXV

PROCÈS-VERBAL

NOIRTIER was prepared to receive them, dressed in black, and
installed in his armchair. When the three persons he expected
had entered, he looked at the door, which his valet immediately
closed.

" Here is M. Franz d'Épinay," said de Villefort to his father ;
" you requested to see him. We have all wished for this interview, and I trust it will convince you how ill-formed are your
objections to Valentine's marriage."

Noirtier answered by a look which made de Villefort's blood run
cold. He motioned to Valentine to approach, then fixed his eye
on the drawer of a small chest between the windows. She opened
the drawer and found a key ; understanding that was what
he wanted, she watched his eyes, which turned towards an old
secrétaire, long since forgotten, and supposed to contain none
but useless documents.

Valentine opened the middle drawer and drew out a bundle of
papers. " Is that what you wish for ? "

" No."

She took all the other papers out till the drawer was empty.
Noirtier's eye was fixed on the dictionary. " I understand."

She pointed to each letter of the alphabet. At the letter S
the old man stopped her and, in the usual way, she found the
word " secret."

" Ah ! a secret spring ! " said Valentine.

" Yes," said Noirtier.

" Who knows it ? " Noirtier looked at the door where the servant had gone out. " Barrois ? " said she.

" Yes."

Valentine went to the door and called Barrois.

" Barrois," said Valentine to the old valet, " my grandfather has told me to open that drawer in the secrétaire, but there is a secret spring in it, which you know—will you open it ? "

Barrois looked at the old man. " Obey," said Noirtier. Barrois touched a spring, the false bottom came out, and revealed a bundle of papers tied with a black string.

" Is that what you wish ? "

" Yes."

" Shall I give these papers to M. de Villefort ? "

" No."

" To Mademoiselle Valentine ? "

" No."

" To M. Franz d'Épinay ? "

" Yes."

Franz took them from Barrois, and, casting his eye on the cover, read :—" To be given, after my death, to General Durand, who shall bequeath the packet to his son, with an injunction to preserve it as containing an important document."

" Do you wish him to read it ? " said Valentine.

" Yes," replied the old man.

" You understand, baron, my grandfather wishes you to read this paper," said Valentine.

Franz untied it, and in the midst of profound silence, read :—

" *Extract of the Procès-verbal of a meeting of the Bonapartist Club in the Rue Saint Jacques, held February 5th, 1815.*"

Franz. stopped. " February 5th, 1815 ! " said he ; " it is the day my father was murdered." Presently he resumed :—

" The undersigned Louis Jacques Beaurepaire, lieutenant-colonel of artillery, Étienne Duchampy, general of brigade, and Claude Lecharpal, keeper of woods and forests, Declare, that on the 4th of February a letter arrived from the Isle of Elba, recommending to the kindness and the confidence of the Bonapartist Club General Flavien de Quesnel, who, having served the Emperor from 1804 to 1814, was supposed to be devoted to the interests of the Napoleon dynasty, notwithstanding the title of baron, which Louis XVIII had just granted to him with his estate of Épinay.

" A note was, in consequence, addressed to General de Quesnel, begging him to be present at the meeting next day, the 5th, and announcing to the General that someone would call for him if he would be ready at nine o'clock. At nine o'clock the President of the club presented himself ; the General was ready ; the President informed him one of the conditions of his introduction was that he should be eternally ignorant of the place of meeting, and that he would allow his eyes to be bandaged, swearing that he would not endeavour to take off the bandage. The General accepted the condition, but was refused the use of his own carriage, since the driver could not be blindfolded. The President said his own carriage was at hand. ' Our coachman is a member of the club ; we shall be driven by a State Councillor.' ' Then we run another risk,' said the General, laughing, ' that of being upset.' We insert this joke to prove that the General was not compelled to attend this meeting, but came willingly. The carriage stopped at a passage leading to the Rue Saint Jacques. The General alighted, leaning on the arm of the President ; they crossed the passage, mounted to the first storey, and entered the meeting-room.

" When in the middle of the room the General was invited to remove his bandage. He did so immediately, and was surprised to see so many well-known faces in a society of whose existence he had till then been ignorant. They questioned him as to his sentiments, but he contented himself with answering that the letters from the Isle of Elba ought to have informed them——"

Franz interpolated the remark—" My father was a Royalist ; they need not have asked his sentiments, which were well known."

" And hence," said de Villefort, " arose my affection for him, my dear M. Franz. A similarity of opinion soon binds."

Franz continued :—

" The General was then informed of the contents of the letter from Elba, in which he was recommended to the club as a man who would be likely to advance the interests of their party. One paragraph alluded to the return of Bonaparte, and promised another letter and further details on the arrival of the *Pharaon*, whose captain was devoted to the cause. During all this time, the General manifested signs of discontent and repugnance.

" ' Well,' asked the President, ' what do you say to this letter, General ? '

' I say that it is too soon after declaring myself for Louis XVIII to break my vow in behalf of the ex-Emperor.' ' Sir,' said the President, rising, with gravity, ' be careful what you say ;

your words clearly show us that they are deceived concerning you in the Isle of Elba, and have misled us! We will not constrain you to help us; we enrol no one against his conscience, but we will compel you to act generously, even if you are not disposed to do so.' 'You would call it acting generously, if, knowing your conspiracy, I refrained from informing against you; that is what I should call becoming your accomplice. You see, I am more candid than you.'

" ' Sir,' said the President, ' you have been invited to join this assembly—you were not forced here; it was proposed to you to come blindfolded—you accepted. It would be conceding too much to allow you to put on a mask to aid you in the discovery of our secret, and then to remove it that you may ruin those who have confided in you. No; you must first say, if you declare yourself for the king of a day who now reigns, or for his majesty the Emperor.' ' I am a Royalist,' replied the General. These words were followed by a murmur. The President again rose and, having imposed silence, said, ' Sir, you are too sensible a man not to understand the consequences of our present situation, and your candour has already dictated to us the conditions to offer you.' The General, putting his hand on his sword, exclaimed, ' If you talk of honour, do not begin by disavowing its laws, and impose nothing by violence.' ' And you, sir,' continued the President, with a calmness still more terrible than the General's anger, ' do not touch your sword, I advise you.' The General looked around him with some uneasiness; however, he did not yield, but recalling all his strength, said, ' I will not swear.' ' Then you must die,' replied the President. ' Think well of it and restore to us our secret.' After a pause the General said, ' I have a son and ought to think of him, finding myself among assassins.' ' One man may insult fifty,' remarked the President, ' it is the privilege of weakness; but he should not abuse it. Take my advice, swear and do not insult.' The General daunted by the superiority of the chief, hesitated a moment; then advancing to the President's desk, ' What is the form ? " said he.

" ' It is this :—" I swear by my honour not to reveal to anyone what I have seen and heard on the 5th of February 1815; and I plead guilty of death should I ever violate this oath." ' The General pronounced the required oath, but in so low a tone as to be scarcely audible to the majority of the members, who insisted on his repeating it clearly and distinctly, which he did.

" ' Now am I at liberty to retire ? ' said the General. The

President rose, appointed three members to accompany him, and got into the carriage with the General, after bandaging his eyes. ' Where do you wish to be taken ? ' asked the President. ' Anywhere out of your presence,' replied M. d'Épinay. The President stopped the coach. They were at that part of the Quai des Ormes where the steps lead down to the river. ' Why do you stop here ? ' asked d'Épinay. ' Because, sir,' said the President, ' you have insulted a man, and that man will not go one step farther without demanding honourable reparation. You are alone, one alone shall answer you ; you have a sword by your side, I have one in my cane ; you have no witness, one of these gentlemen will serve you. Now, if you please, remove your bandage.' The General tore the handkerchief from his eyes. ' At last,' said he, ' I shall know with whom I have to do.' They opened the door, the four men alighted.

" It was, as we said, the 5th of February. For three days there had been five or six degrees of frost. The ground from the steps to the river was covered with snow and hoar frost, the water looked black and deep. One of the seconds went for a lantern in a coal-barge near, and by its light they examined the arms. The President's sword was five inches shorter than the General's, and had no guard. The lantern was placed on the ground and the duel began. The light made the two swords appear like flashes of lightning ; as for the men, they were scarce perceptible, the darkness was so great. M. le Général d'Épinay passed for one of the best swordsmen in the army, but he was pressed so closely in the onset that he missed his aim and fell. His adversary helped him to rise, but this courtesy only irritated the General who, rushing on his foe, once more dropped to the ground. They thought he had slipped, and the witnesses, seeing he did not move, endeavoured to raise him, but the one who passed his arm round the body found it was moistened with blood. The General, who had almost fainted, revived. ' Ah ! ' said he, ' they have sent some fencing-master to fight with me.' He died five minutes later.

" The President, who had received two wounds on his right arm and one in his side, had hardly reached the top of the steps when he heard a splash in the water ; it was the General's body which the witnesses had just thrown into the river after ascertaining he was dead. The General fell in a loyal duel, and not in ambush, as it might have been reported. In proof of this we have signed this paper to establish the truth of the facts, lest the moment should arrive when either of the actors in this terrible scene should be accused of premeditated murder or of infringement of the laws of honour.

"Signed,
" BEAUREPAIRE, DUCHAMPY, AND LECHARPAL."

When Franz had finished reading this account, so dreadful for a son—when Valentine, pale with emotion, had wiped away a tear—when de Villefort, trembling and crouched in a corner, had endeavoured to lessen the storm by supplicating glances at the implacable old man,—

" Sir," said d'Épinay to Noirtier, " since you are well acquainted with all these details, which are attested by honourable signatures, tell me the name of the President of the club, that I may at least know who killed my father."

De Villefort mechanically felt for the handle of the door; Valentine, who understood sooner than anyone her grandfather's answer, and who had often seen two scars upon his right arm, drew back a few steps.

" Oh, mademoiselle !—mademoiselle ! " cried Franz, " help me !—lend me your assistance ! "

Noirtier looked at the dictionary. Franz took it with a nervous trembling, and repeated the letters of the alphabet successively, until he came to M. At that letter the old man signified " Yes."

At length Franz arrived at the word—" myself."

" You ! " cried Franz, whose hair stood on end ; " you, M. Noirtier !—you killed my father ? "

" Yes ! " replied M. Noirtier, fixing a majestic look on the young man.

Franz dropped helpless on a chair ; de Villefort opened the door and escaped, for the idea had entered his mind to stifle what little life remained in the old man's heart.

CHAPTER LXXVI

PROGRESS OF M. CAVALCANTI THE YOUNGER

MEANWHILE M. Cavalcanti the elder had returned to his service at the gaming-table of the baths of Lucca, of which he was one of the most assiduous courtiers. M. Andrea inherited all the papers, which proved that he had the honour of being the son of the Marquis Bartolomeo and the Marchioness Oliva Corsinari. Within a fortnight he had attained a very fair position. He was entitled M. le Comte; he was said to possess 50,000 livres per annum ; and his father's immense riches, buried in the quarries of Saravezza, were a constant theme of talk.

Such was the state of affairs when Monte Cristo went one evening to pay M. Danglars a visit. M. Danglars was out, but the count was asked to see the baroness, and he accepted the invitation. When Monte Cristo entered the boudoir, the baroness was examining some drawings which her daughter passed to her after having inspected them with M. Cavalcanti. The count's presence soon produced its usual effect. The baroness received him with smiles, although she had been a little disconcerted at the announcement of his name. Monte Cristo embraced the whole scene at a glance.

The baroness was partially reclining on a settee, Eugénie sat near her, and Cavalcanti was standing. Eugénie bowed coldly to the count, and availed herself of the first moment when the conversation became earnest to escape to her study, whence two cheerful and noisy voices, associated with the piano, assured Monte Cristo that she preferred the company of her singing mistress to that of himself and M. Cavalcanti.

" Have not the ladies invited you to join them at the piano ? " said Danglars, who had returned, to Andrea.

" Alas ! no, sir," replied Andrea, with a sigh.

Danglars immediately advanced to the study door and opened it. The two young ladies were seen seated on the same chair, at the piano, playing each with one hand, a fancy to which they had accustomed themselves, and performing admirably. Monte Cristo cast one rapid and curious glance round the sanctum ; it was the first time he had ever seen Mademoiselle d'Armilly, of whom he had heard much.

" Well ! " said the banker to his daughter, " are we all to be shut out ? " He led the young man into the study, and, either by chance or design, the door was partially closed after Andrea, so that from where they sat neither the count nor the baroness could see anything ; but as the banker had accompanied Andrea, Madame Danglars appeared to take no notice of it.

The count soon heard Andrea's voice, singing a Corsican song, accompanied on the piano. While the count smiled at hearing this song, which made him lose sight of Andrea in the recollection of Benedetto, Madame Danglars was boasting to Monte Cristo of her husband's strength of mind, who that very morning had lost three or four hundred thousand francs by a failure at Milan. " Hem ! " thought Monte Cristo, " he begins to conceal his losses ; a month since he boasted of them." Then he said aloud, " Oh, madame,

M. Danglars is so skilful, he will soon regain at the Bourse what he loses elsewhere."

"I see, like many more, you are under an erroneous impression."

"What is it?" said Monte Cristo.

"That M. Danglars gambles, whereas he never plays."

"Truly, madame, I recollect M. Debray told me it was you who sacrificed to the demon of the card-table. I have heard of a lucky hit that was made yesterday on the Neapolitan bonds."

"I have none, but we have talked long enough of money, count. We are like two stockbrokers; have you heard how fate is persecuting the poor Villeforts? They were going to marry their daughter——"

"To M. Franz d'Épinay. Is it broken off?"

"Yesterday morning, it appears, Franz declined the honour."

"How extraordinary! And how does M. de Villefort bear it?"

"Like a philosopher." Danglars returned at this moment.

"Well!" said the baroness, "do you leave M. Cavalcanti with your daughter?"

"And Mademoiselle d'Armilly," said the banker; "do you consider her no one?" Then, turning to Monte Cristo, he said, "Prince Cavalcanti is a charming young man, is he not? But is he really a prince?"

"I will not answer for it," said Monte Cristo. "His father was introduced to me as a marquis, so he ought to be a count; but I do not know that he is a prince."

"Why," said the banker, "if he is a prince he is wrong not to maintain his rank; I do not like anyone to deny his origin."

"Oh! you are a pure democrat," said Monte Cristo, smiling. "But do you see to what you are exposing yourself? If, perchance, M. de Morcerf should come, and find that young man with your daughter, he might be displeased."

"He! you are mistaken; M. Albert would not do us the honour to be jealous; he does not like Eugénie sufficiently. Besides, I care not for his displeasure."

The valet announced M. le Vicomte Albert de Morcerf. The baroness rose hastily, and was going into the study, when Danglars stopped her.

Albert entered, looking very handsome and in high spirits. He bowed politely to the baroness, familiarly to Danglars, and affectionately to Monte Cristo. Then, turning to the baroness: "May I ask how Mademoiselle Danglars is?" said he.

"She is quite well," replied Danglars, quickly; "she is at the piano with M. Cavalcanti." Albert preserved his calm and indifferent manner; he might feel, perhaps, annoyed, but he knew Monte Cristo's eye was on him.

" The prince and my daughter were universally admired yesterday. You were not of the party, M. de Morcerf ? "

" Pardon me," said Albert, " I was not aware he was a prince." This was followed by an awkward silence.

" May I also be allowed," said Morcerf, " to pay my respects to Mademoiselle Danglars ? "

" Wait a moment," said the banker, stopping the young man ; " do you hear that delightful cavatina ? Ta, ta, ta, ti, ta, ti, ta ; it is charming ; let them finish—one moment. Bravo ! bravi ! brava ! "

" Indeed," said Albert, " it is exquisite ; it is impossible to understand the music of his country better than Prince Cavalcanti does. Ask them to sing one more song ; it is so delightful to hear music in the distance, when the musicians are unrestrained by observation."

Danglars was quite annoyed by the young man's indifference. He took Monte Cristo aside. " What do you think of our lover ? " said he.

" He appears cool ! But, then, your word is given."

" Yes, doubtless, I have promised to give my daughter to a man who loves her, but not to one who does not. Even if Albert had Cavalcanti's fortune, he is so proud, I would not care to see him marry her."

" Oh ! " said Monte Cristo, " my fondness may blind me, but, I assure you, I consider Morcerf far preferable."

" Come, count, you don't do the prince justice."

" Well, I acknowledge it annoys me, knowing your relations to the Morcerf family, to see him throw himself in the way."

Danglars burst out laughing. " What a Puritan you are ! " said he ; " that happens every day."

" But you cannot break it off thus ; the Morcerfs are depending on this union."

' Then let them explain themselves. You should give the father a hint, you are so intimate with the family."

" Willingly, if you wish it."

" But let it be done explicitly. If he demands my daughter, let him fix the day—declare his conditions : in short, let us either understand each other, or quarrel—no more delay. A banker must, you know, be a slave to his promise."

" Bravo ! " cried Morcerf, as the duet ended. Danglars began to look suspiciously at Albert, when someone came and whispered a few words to him. "I shall soon return," said the banker to Monte Cristo.

The baroness took advantage of her husband's absence to push open the door of her daughter's study, and M. Andrea, who was sitting before the piano with Mademoiselle Eugénie, started up, rather embarrassed. Then Albert launched out in praise of Mademoiselle Danglars' voice, and regretted that, after what he had just heard, he had been unable to be present the previous evening.

"Now," said Madame Danglars, "leave music and compliments, and let us take tea."

"Come, Louise," said Mademoiselle Danglars to her friend. They passed into the next drawing-room, where tea was prepared. Just as they were beginning, in the English fashion, to leave the spoon in their cups, the door again opened, and Danglars entered, visibly agitated. Monte Cristo observed it particularly, and, by a look, asked the banker for an explanation. "I have just received my courier from Greece," said Danglars.

Albert advanced towards Eugénie, smiling. Meanwhile, Danglars, stooping to Monte Cristo's ear, "Your advice was excellent," said he : "there is a whole history connected with the names Fernando and Janina."

"Indeed ! " said Monte Cristo.

"Yes, I will tell you all ; but take away the young man ; I cannot endure his presence."

"He is going with me. Shall I send the father to you ? "

"Immediately." The count made a sign to Albert ; they bowed to the ladies and took their leave ; Albert perfectly indifferent to Mademoiselle Danglars' contempt, Monte Cristo reiterating his advice to Madame Danglars on the prudence a banker's wife should exercise in providing for the future. M. Cavalcanti remained master of the field.

CHAPTER LXXVII

HAIDÉE

SCARCELY had the count's horses cleared the angle of the boulevard when Albert, turning towards the count, burst into a fit of laughter much too loud to be natural. "Well," said he, "I will ask you the question which Charles IX. put to Catherine de' Medici, after the massacre of Saint Bartholomew ' How have I played my little part ? '

"Ah! no joking, viscount, if you please; I do not patronise M. Andrea—at least, not as concerns M. Danglars."

"You would be to blame for not assisting him, if the young man needed your help in that quarter; but, happily for me, he can dispense with it."

"What! do you think he is paying his addresses?"

"I am certain of it."

"What does that signify, so long as they favour your suit?"

"But it is not the case, my dear count; on the contrary, I am repulsed on all sides."

"But the father has the greatest regard possible for you," said Monte Cristo. I am commissioned to induce M. le comte de Morcerf to make some definite arrangement with the baron."

"Oh!" said Albert, with all the cajolery of which he was capable. "You surely will not do that, my dear count?"

"Certainly I shall, Albert, as I have promised to do it. But à propos of Debray, how is it that I have not seen him lately at the baron's house?"

"There has been a misunderstanding."

"With the baroness?"

"No, with the baron."

"Do you think he suspects?" said Monte Cristo, with a charming naïveté.

"Oh! my dear count, husbands are pretty much the same everywhere."

"But, then, what can have led to the quarrel between Danglars and Debray?"

"When M. Andrea Cavalcanti has become one of the family you can ask him that question."

The carriage stopped. "Here we are," said Monte Cristo; "it is only half-past ten o'clock, come in. My carriage will take you back."

"No, thank you; I gave orders for my coupé to follow me."

"There it is, then," said Monte Cristo, as he stepped out of the carriage. They both went into the house. "You will make tea for us, Baptistin," said the count. Baptistin in two seconds reappeared, bringing on a waiter all that his master had ordered, ready prepared.

"Really, my dear count, what I admire is your being served, without any question, in a moment; it is as if they guessed what you wanted by your manner of ringing, and made a point of keeping everything in readiness."

"What you say is perhaps true: they know my habits. You

shall see; how do you wish to occupy yourself during tea-
time ? "

" *Ma foi!* I should like to smoke." Monte Cristo took the
gong and struck it once. A private door opened at once, and
Ali appeared, bringing two chibouques filled with excellent
latakia. " It is quite wonderful ! " said Albert.

" Oh, no, it is as simple as possible," replied Monte Cristo.
" Ali knows I generally smoke whilst I am taking my tea or coffee ;
he has heard that I ordered tea, and he also knows that I brought
you home with me ; when I summoned him he naturally guessed
the reason of my doing so, and as he comes from a country where
hospitality is especially manifested through the medium of
smoking, he naturally concludes that we shall smoke in company,
and therefore brings two chibouques instead of one, and now
the mystery is solved."

" Ah ! but what do I hear ! " and Morcerf inclined his head
towards the door, through which sounds issued resembling those
of a guitar.

" *Ma foi!* my dear viscount, you are fated to hear music this
evening ; you have only escaped from the piano of Mademoiselle
Danglars to be attacked by the guzla of Haidée."

" Haidée ! what an adorable name ! "

" Silence ! " said the count, " Haidée may hear you."

" And she would be angry ? "

" No, certainly not," said the count, with a haughty expression.

" She is very amiable, then, is she not ? " said Albert.

" It is not to be called amiability, it is her duty ; a slave does
not dictate to a master."

" Really, count, you do nothing, and have nothing, like other
people. The slave of M. le comte de Monte Cristo ! why, it is a
rank of itself in France : and from the way in which you lavish
money, it is a place that must be worth a hundred thousand
francs a year."

" A hundred thousand francs ! the poor girl originally possessed
much more than that."

" She must be a princess ? "

" You are right ; one of the greatest in her country, too ! "

" And is her name a secret ? "

" From most people, but not from you, my dear viscount,
who are one of my most intimate friends, and on whose silence I
may rely, if it be necessary to enjoin it ; may I not do so ? "

" On my word of honour."

" You know the history of the pasha of Janina, do you not ? "

" Well ! what is Haidée to Ali Tebelen ? "

" Merely his daughter."

" And your slave ? "

" I bought her in the market at Constantinople.'

" My dear count, will you present me to your princess ? "

" On two conditions."

" I accept them at once."

" The first is, that you will never tell anyone that I have granted the interview."

" Very well," said Albert, extending his hand ; " I swear I will not."

" The second is, that you will not tell her that your father ever served hers."

" I give you my oath that I will not."

Albert followed the count, the latter having previously resumed his hat and gloves. Ali was stationed as a kind of advanced guard, and the door was kept by the three French maids, commanded by Myrtho. Haidée received her visitors in the first room of her suite of apartments, which was the drawing-room. Her large eyes were dilated with surprise and expectation, for it was the first time that any man, except Monte Cristo, had been introduced into her presence. On perceiving the count, she rose and welcomed him with a smile peculiar to herself, expressive at once of the most implicit obedience and also of the deepest love. Monte Cristo advanced towards her and extended his hand, which she, as usual, raised to her lips.

Albert had proceeded no farther than the door, where he remained rooted to the spot, being completely fascinated by the sight of such surpassing beauty, which he beheld for the first time, and of which an inhabitant of Northern climates could form no adequate idea.

" Whom do you bring ? " asked the young girl, in Romaic, of Monte Cristo.

" A friend," said Monte Cristo, in the same language.

" What is his name ? "

" Count Albert ; it is the man I rescued from the banditti at Rome."

" Then," said Haidée, " I will speak either in French or Italian, if my lord so wills it."

Monte Cristo reflected one instant. " You will speak in Italian," said he. Then, turning towards Albert, " It is a pity you do not understand either ancient or modern Greek, both of which Haidée speaks fluently : the poor child will be obliged to talk to you in Italian, which will give you but a very false idea of her powers of conversation." The count made a sign to Haidée to address his visitor. " Sir," said she to Morcerf, " you are most welcome as the friend of my lord and master."

Monte Cristo and Morcerf drew their seats towards a small table, on which were arranged music, drawings, and vases of flowers. Ali then brought coffee and chibouques.

The cups of coffee were prepared with the addition of a sugar-glass, which had been brought for Albert. At this moment two women entered, bearing salvers filled with ices and sherbet, which they placed on two small tables appropriated to that purpose. " My dear host, and you, signora," said Albert, in Italian, " excuse my apparent stupidity. I am bewildered, and it is natural that it should be so. Here I am in the heart of Paris; and now I feel as if I were suddenly transported to the East. Oh! signora, if I could but speak Greek, your conversation, added to the fairy scene which surrounds me, would furnish an evening of such delight as it would be impossible for me ever to forget."

" I speak sufficient Italian to enable me to converse with you, sir," said Haidée, quietly; " and if you like what is Eastern, I will do my best to secure the gratification of your tastes while you are here."

" On what subject shall I converse with her ? " said Albert, in a low tone to Monte Cristo ; "let me speak to her of the East."

" Do so, then, for of all themes which you could choose that will be the most agreeable to her." Albert turned towards Haidée.

" At what age did you leave Greece, signora ? " asked he.

" I left it when I was but five years old."

" And how far back do your recollections extend ? "

" I could scarcely walk when my mother, who was called Vasiliki, which means royal," said the young girl, tossing her head proudly, " took me by the hand, and we went out, both covered with veils, to solicit alms for the prisoners, saying, ' He who giveth to the poor lendeth to the Lord.' Then when our purse was full, it was divided amongst the prisoners."

" And how old were you at that time ? "

" I was three years old."

" Count," said Albert to Monte Cristo, " do allow the signora to tell me something of her history."

Monte Cristo turned to Haidée, " Tell us the fate of your father ; but neither the name of the traitor nor the treason." Haidée sighed deeply.

" What are you saying to her ? " said Morcerf, in an undertone.

" I again reminded her that you were a friend, and that she need not conceal anything from you."

" Then," said Albert, " this pious pilgrimage in behalf of the prisoners was your first remembrance ; what is the next ? "

" Oh ! then I remember, as if it were but yesterday, sitting on the borders of a lake, in the waters of which the trembling foliage was reflected as in a mirror. Under the oldest and thickest of the trees, reclining on cushions, sat my father ; my mother was at his feet, and I, child-like, amused myself by playing with his long white beard, which descended to his waist, and with the diamond hilt of the scimitar attached to his girdle. Then from time to time there came to him an Albanian, who said something, to which I paid no attention, but which he always answered in the same tone of voice, angrily,—' Kill or pardon.' "

" So young ; is it possible you can have known what suffering is except by name ? "

" Nothing is ever so firmly impressed on the mind as the memory of our early childhood, and with the exception of the two scenes I have just described to you, all my earliest reminiscences are fraught with deepest sadness."

" Speak, signora," said Albert, " I am listening with the most intense interest."

Haidée answered his remark with a melancholy smile. " You wish me, to relate the history of my past sorrows ? Well ! I was but four years old, when one night I was awakened by my mother. We were in the palace of Janina, she snatched me from the cushions on which I was sleeping, and on opening my eyes I saw hers were filled with tears. She bore me rapidly away. I saw then that we were descending a large staircase ; around us were all my mother's servants carrying trunks, bags, ornaments, jewels, purses of gold, and the like, with which they were hurrying away in the greatest distraction. Behind the women came a guard of twenty men armed with long guns and pistols, and dressed in the costume which the Greeks have assumed since they have again become a nation. Here and there, on the walls of the staircase, were reflected gigantic shadows, which trembled in the flickering light of the pine-torches till they seemed to reach to the vaulted roof above.

" ' Quick ! ' said a voice at the end of the gallery. This voice made everyone bow before it, resembling in its effect the wind passing over a field of corn, by its superior strength forcing every ear to yield obeisance. As for me, it made me tremble. This voice was that of my father. He was," said Haidée, raising her head, "that illustrious man known in Europe under the name of Ali Tebelen, pasha of Janina, before whom Turkey trembled."

Albert, without knowing why, started on hearing these words pronounced with such a haughty and dignified accent. "Soon," said Haidée, "we halted on our march, and found ourselves on the borders of a lake. Four marble steps led down to the water's edge, and below them was a boat floating on the tide. From where we stood I could see, in the middle of the lake, a large black mass ; it was the kiosk, to which we were going. Besides the rowers, the boat contained only the women, my father, mother, Selim, and myself. The Palicares had remained on the shore of the lake, ready to cover our retreat ; they were kneeling on the lowest of the marble steps, and in that manner intended making a rampart of the three others, in case of pursuit. Our barque flew before the wind. ' Why does the boat go so fast ? ' asked I of my mother.

" ' Silence, child ! Hush ! we are flying.' I did not understand. Why should my father fly ?—he, the all-powerful—he, before whom others were accustomed to fly,—he who had taken for his device—' They hate me, then they fear me ! '

" It was, indeed, a flight which my father was trying to effect. I have been told since, that the garrison of the castle of Janina, fatigued with long service, had treated with the Seraskier Kourchid, who had been sent by the Sultan to gain possession of the person of my father. It was then that Ali Tebelen took the resolution of retiring, after having sent to the Sultan a French officer in whom he reposed great confidence, to the asylum which he had long before prepared himself, and which he called *kataphygion*, or the refuge."

" And this officer, do you remember his name, signora ? "

Monte Cristo, unperceived by Albert, exchanged a rapid glance with the young girl. "No," said she, "I do not remember it at the moment. It was towards the kiosk that we were rowing. A ground-floor ornamented with arabesques, bathing its terraces in the water, and another floor, looking on the lake, was all which was visible to the eye. But beneath the ground-floor, stretching out into the island, was a large subterranean cavern, to which my mother, myself, and the women, were conducted. In this place were 60,000 purses and 200 barrels ; the purses contained 25,000,000 of coins in gold, and the barrels were filled with 30,000 pounds of gunpowder.

" Near these barrels stood Selim, my father's favourite. It was his duty to watch day and night with a lance, at the end of which was a lighted match, and he had orders to blow up all—kiosk, guards, women, gold, and Ali Tebelen himself, at the first signal given by my father. I cannot tell you how long we remained in this state. My father was endeavouring to pierce with his eager looks the remotest verge of the horizon, examining attentively every black speck which appeared on the lake, whilst my mother, reclining by his side, rested her head on his shoulder, and I played at his feet. The heights of Pindus towered above us; the castle of Janina rose white and angular from the blue waters of the lake, and the immense masses of black vegetation which, viewed in the distance, gave the idea of lichens clinging to the rocks, were, in reality, gigantic fir-trees and myrtles.

" One morning, my father sent for us; my mother had been crying all the night, and was very wretched; we found the pasha calm, but paler than usual. ' Take courage, Vasiliki,' said he: ' to-day arrives the firman of the master, and my fate will be decided. If my pardon be complete, we shall return triumphant to Janina; if the news be inauspicious, we must fly this night.' ' But supposing our enemy will not allow us to do so ? ' said my mother. ' Oh! make yourself easy on that head,' said Ali, smiling; ' Selim and his flaming lance will settle that matter. They would be glad to see me dead, but they would not like themselves to die with me.'

" Presently he made such a sudden movement that I was paralysed with fear. Then, without taking his eyes from the object which had first attracted his attention, he asked for his telescope. My mother gave it him; and, as she did so, looked whiter than the marble against which she leaned. I saw my father's hand tremble. ' A boat!—two!—three ! ' murmured my father ;— ' four ! ' He then rose, seizing his arms and priming his pistols. ' Vasiliki,' said he to my mother, trembling perceptibly, ' the instant approaches which will decide everything. In the space of half an hour we shall know the emperor's answer. Go into the cavern with Haidée.' ' Adieu, my lord,' murmured my mother, determining quietly to await the approach of death. ' Take away Vasiliki ! ' said my father to his Palicares.

" As for me, I had been forgotten in the confusion; I ran towards Ali Tebelen; he saw me hold out my arms to him, and he stooped down and pressed my forehead with his lips. Oh! how distinctly I remember that kiss! It was the last he ever gave me, and I feel as if it were still warm on my forehead. On descending, we distinguished through the lattice-work several boats which were becoming more distinct to our view. During this time, in the kiosk, at the feet of my father, were seated twenty Palicares, concealed from view by an angle of the wall, and watching with eager eyes the arrival of the boats. My father looked at his watch, and paced up and down with a countenance expressive of the greatest anguish. My mother and I traversed the gloomy passage leading to the cavern. We fetched our cushions from the other end of the cavern, and sat down by Selim. Young as I was, I understood that danger was hanging over our heads."

Albert had often heard the description of the last moments of the vizier of Janina ; but this history seemed to borrow new life from the voice and expression of the young girl. As to Haidée, these terrible reminiscences seemed to have overpowered her for the moment, for she ceased speaking, her head leaning on her hand like a beautiful flower bowing beneath the violence of the storm. Monte Cristo looked at her with an indescribable expression of interest and pity.

" Go on," said the count, in the Romaic language.

Haidée looked up abruptly, and resumed her narrative. " It was about four o'clock in the afternoon ; and although the day was brilliant out of doors, we were enveloped in the gloomy darkness of the cavern. My mother was a Christian, and she prayed. Selim repeated from time to time these sacred words :—' God is great ! ' However, my mother had still some hope. As she was coming down, she thought she recognized the French officer who had been sent to Constantinople, and in whom my father placed so much confidence, for he knew that all the soldiers of the French emperor were naturally noble and generous. She advanced some steps towards the staircase, and listened. ' They are approaching,' said she ; ' perhaps they bring us peace and liberty ! ' ' What do you fear, Vasiliki ? ' said Selim, in a voice at once so gentle and yet so proud : ' if they do not bring us peace we will give them war ; if they do not bring life we will give them death.' " ' Mamma, mamma,' I cried, ' are we really to be killed ? ' At the sound of my voice the slaves redoubled their prayers and lamentations. ' My child,' said Vasiliki, ' may God preserve you from ever wishing for that death which to-day you so much dread ! ' Then, whispering to Selim, she asked what were his master's orders. ' If he send me his poniard, it will signify that the emperor's intentions are not favourable, and I am to set fire to the powder ; if, on the contrary, he sends me his ring, it will be a sign that the emperor pardons him, and I extinguish the match and leave the magazine untouched.' ' My friend,' said my mother, ' when your master's order arrives, if it is the poniard which he sends, instead of despatching us by that horrible death which we both so much dread, you will mercifully kill us with this same poniard, will you not ? '—' Yes, Vasiliki,' replied Selim tranquilly.

" Suddenly we heard loud cries ; we listened : they were cries of joy ; the name of the French officer who had been sent to Constantinople resounded on all sides amongst our Palicares ; it was evident that he brought the answer of the emperor, and that it was favourable.

" The noise increased, steps were heard approaching nearer and nearer. Soon a figure appeared in the grey twilight at the entrance of the cave, formed by the reflection of the few rays of daylight which had found their way into this gloomy retreat. ' Who are you ? ' cried Selim. ' But whoever you may be, I charge you not to advance another step.' ' Long live the emperor ! ' said the figure. ' He grants a full pardon to the Vizier Ali ; and not only gives him his life, but restores to him his fortune and his possessions.' My mother uttered a cry of joy, and clasped me to her bosom. ' Stop ! ' said Selim, seeing that she was about to go out ; ' you see I have not yet received the ring.' ' True,' said my mother. And she fell on her knees at the same time, holding me up towards heaven, as if she desired, whilst praying to God in my behalf, to raise me actually to His presence."

Haidée stopped, overcome by such violent emotion that the perspiration stood upon her pale brow. She dried her eyes, and continued :—" By this time our eyes, habituated to the darkness, had recognized the messenger of the pasha,—it was a friend. Selim had also recognized him. ' In whose name do you come ? ' said he to him. ' I come in the name of our master, Ali Tebelen, and I bring you his ring.' At these words he raised his hand above his head to show the token, but it was too far off, and there was not light enough to enable Selim, where he was standing, to recognize the object presented to his view. ' I do not see what you have in your hand,' said Selim, ' place the object in the ray of light which shines there, and retire whilst I examine it.' ' Be it so,' said the envoy ; and he retired after having first deposited the token agreed on in the place pointed out to him by Selim.

" Selim, still holding in his hand the lighted match, walked towards the opening in the cavern, and aided by the faint light which streamed in through the mouth of the cave picked up the token. " ' It is well ! ' said he, kissing it ; ' it is my master's ring ! ' And throwing the match on the ground, he extinguished it. The messenger uttered a cry of joy, and clapped his hands. At this signal four soldiers of the Seraskier Kourchid suddenly appeared,

and Selim fell, pierced by blows. At this moment my mother
seized me in her arms, and bounding along numerous windings,
known only to ourselves, she arrived at a private staircase of the
kiosk, where was a scene of tumult and confusion. The lower
rooms were filled with our enemies. Just as my mother was on
the point of pushing open a small door, we heard the voice of the
pasha speaking in a loud and threatening tone. ' What do you
want ? ' said my father, to some people who were holding a paper
inscribed with characters of gold. ' What we want,' replied one
of them, ' is to communicate to you the will of his highness. Do
you see this firman ? ' ' I do,' said my father. ' Well, read it ;
he demands your head.'

" My father answered with a loud laugh, which was more frightful than even threats would have been, and he had not ceased
when two reports of a pistol were heard ; he had fired them himself and had killed two men. The Palicares at my father's feet
now sprang up and fired ; and the room was filled with fire and
smoke. Presently in a commanding voice my revered father
cried out, ' Selim, guardian of the fire, do your duty ! ' ' Selim
is dead ! ' replied a voice which seemed to come from the depths
of the earth, ' and you are lost, Ali ! ' At the same moment an
explosion was heard, and the flooring of the room in which my
father was sitting was torn up and shivered to atoms ; the enemy
were firing underneath ; three or four Palicares fell with their
bodies literally ploughed with wounds.

" My father plunged his fingers into the holes the balls had
made, and tore up one of the planks. But immediately
through this opening twenty more shots were fired, and the flame,
rushing up like fire from the crater of a volcano, soon gained the
tapestry, which it quickly devoured. In the midst of all this
tumult two reports followed by two shrieks more heartrending
than all froze me with terror ; these two shots had mortally
wounded my father, and it was he who had given utterance to
these frightful cries. At this crisis the whole flooring suddenly
gave way ; my father fell on one knee, and at the same moment
twenty hands were thrust forth, armed with sabres, pistols, and
poniards ; twenty blows were instantaneously directed against one
man, and my father disappeared in a whirlwind of fire and smoke
kindled by these demons. I felt myself fall to the ground ; my
mother had fainted." Haidée groaned as she said this.

" Calm yourself, my dear child," said Monte Cristo, " and
remember God will punish traitors."

" It is a frightful story, count," said Albert, terrified at the paleness of Haidée's countenance, " and I reproach myself for having preferred so thoughtless a request."

Presently Haidée resumed her story. "When my mother recovered her senses we were before the Seraskier. ' Kill me.' said she, ' but spare the honour of the widow of Ali.' ' It is not me to whom you must address yourself,' said Kourchid. ' To whom then ? ' ' To your new master,' pointing out one who had more than any contributed to the death of my father," said Haidée, in a tone of chastened anger.

" Then," said Albert, " you became the property of this man ? "

" No," replied Haidée, " he did not dare to keep us, so we were sold to some slave merchants who were going to Constantinople. We traversed Greece, and arrived, half dead, at the imperial gates. Suddenly, my mother having directed her eye to the object which was attracting their attention, uttered a piercing cry and fell to the ground, pointing, as she did so, to a head over the gates, and beneath it these words,—' This is the head of Ali Tebelen, Pasha of Janina.'

" I cried bitterly, and tried to raise my mother from the earth, but she was dead ! I was taken to the slave-market, and was purchased by a rich Armenian. He caused me to be instructed, gave me masters, and when I was thirteen years of age he sold me to the Sultan Mahmoud."

" Of whom I bought her," said Monte Cristo. " Come ! finish your cup of coffee : the history is ended."

CHAPTER LXXVIII

JANINA

COULD Valentine have seen the trembling step and agitated countenance of Franz when he quitted the chamber of M. Noirtier she would have been constrained to pity him. De Villefort had only given utterance to a few incoherent sentences, and then retired to his study, where he received about two hours afterwards the following letter :—

" After the disclosures which were made this morning M. Noirtier de Villefort must see the utter impossibility of any alliance between his family and that of M. Franz d'Épinay. M. d'Épinay must say that he is shocked and astonished that M. de Villefort, who appeared to be aware of all the circumstances, should not have anticipated him in this announcement."

S

This harsh letter, coming as it did from a man generally so polite and respectful, struck a mortal blow at the pride of Villefort. Hardly had he read it, when his wife entered.

M. de Villefort told her that an interchange of views had taken place between M. Noirtier, M. d'Épinay, and himself, and that the marriage between Valentine and Franz would be broken off. This was an awkward thing to have to report to those who were awaiting her return in the chamber of her father-in-law. She therefore contented herself by saying that M. Noirtier having, at the beginning of the discussion, been attacked by a sort of apoplectic fit, the affair would necessarily be deferred for some days longer. Valentine asked leave to retire to her own room, in order to recover her composure. Noirtier looked the permission which she solicited. But instead of going to her own room, Valentine entered the gallery and opening a small door at the end of it, found herself at once in the garden. It was high time she did so, for Maximilian had long awaited her coming. He had half guessed what was going on when he saw Franz quit the cemetery with M. de Villefort. He followed M. d'Épinay, saw him enter, afterwards go out, and then re-enter with Albert and Château-Renaud. He had no longer any doubts as to the nature of the conference : he therefore quickly resumed his original position, certain that Valentine would hasten to him the first moment she should be set at liberty. The first words she pronounced made his heart bound with delight.

" We are saved ! " said Valentine.

" Saved ! " repeated Morrel.

" By my grandfather. Oh, Morrel ! pray love him for all his goodness to us ! "

" But tell me, Valentine, how has it all been effected ? "

Valentine was on the point of relating all that had passed, but she remembered that in doing so she must reveal a terrible secret which concerned others as well as her grandfather, and she said, " I will tell you all about it some day."

" But when will that be ? "

" When I am your wife."

This was a topic so pleasing to Morrel that he was ready to accede to anything Valentine thought fit to propose. However, he would not leave without the promise of seeing her again next night. Valentine promised all that Morrel required of her, and it was less difficult now for her to believe that she should marry Maximilian than it was an hour ago to assure herself that she should not marry Franz. During the interview in the garden Madame de Villefort had gone to visit M. Noirtier. The old man looked at her with the stern and forbidding expression with which he was accustomed to receive her.

" Sir," said she, " it is superfluous for me to tell you that Valentine's marriage is broken off, since it was here that the affair was concluded. Now that this marriage, which I know you so much disliked, is done away with, I come to you on an errand which neither M. de Villefort nor Valentine could consistently undertake." Noirtier's eyes demanded the nature of her mission. " I come to entreat you, sir," continued Madame de Villefort, " to restore, not your love, for that she has always possessed, but your fortune to your granddaughter."

There was a dubious expression in Noirtier's eyes; he was trying to discover the motive of this proceeding, and could not succeed in doing so. " May I hope, sir, that your intentions accord with my request ? " Noirtier made a sign that they did. " In that case, sir," rejoined Madame de Villefort, " I will leave you, overwhelmed with gratitude and happiness at your acquiescence in my wishes." She then bowed to M. Noirtier and retired. The next day M. Noirtier sent for the notary; the first will was torn up and a second made, in which he left the whole of his fortune to Valentine, on condition that she should never be separated from him. It was then generally reported that Mademoiselle de Villefort, the heiress of the Marquis and Marchioness de Saint Méran, had regained the good graces of her grandfather, and that she would ultimately be in possession of an income of 900,000 livres. Whilst all the proceedings relating to the dissolution of the marriage-contract were being carried on at the house of M. de Villefort Monte Cristo had paid his visit to the count de Morcerf, who, in order to lose no time in responding to M. Danglars' wishes, donned his uniform of lieutenant-general, ordered his finest horses and drove to the Rue de la Chaussée d'Antin. Danglars was balancing his monthly accounts, and it was, perhaps, not the most favourable moment for finding him in his best humour. Morcerf, usually so stiff and formal, accosted the banker in an affable and smiling manner, and went at once straight to the point.

" Well, baron," said he, " here I am at last; some time has elapsed since our plans were formed, and they are not yet executed."

" To what do you allude, M. le Comte ? " said Danglars; as if he were trying in vain to guess at the meaning of the general's words.

Morcerf, with a forced smile, rose and, making a low bow to M. Danglars, said,—" M. le Baron, I have the honour of asking of you the hand of Mademoiselle Eugénie Danglars for my son, Viscount Albert de Morcerf."

But Danglars, instead of receiving this address in the favourable manner which Morcerf had expected, knit his brow and, without inviting the count, who was still standing, to take a seat, said,—
" M. le Comte, it will be necessary to reflect before I give you an answer. Things are constantly occurring in the world to induce us to lay aside our most established opinions, or to remodel them according to the change of circumstances, which may place affairs in a totally different light from that in which we at first viewed them."

" I do not understand you, M. le Baron," said Morcerf.

" What I mean is this, sir : during the last fortnight unforeseen circumstances have occurred——"

" You have seen M. de Monte Cristo, have you not ? "

" I see him very often," said Danglars, drawing himself up ; " he is a particular friend of mine."

" Well in a recent conversation with him you said I appeared to be forgetful and irresolute concerning this marriage ; did you not ? "

" I did say so."

" Well, here I am, proving at once that I am neither the one nor the other, by entreating you to keep your promise on that score."

Danglars did not answer. " Have you so soon changed your mind," added Morcerf, " or have you only provoked my request that you may have the pleasure of seeing me humbled ? "

" No, sir," said Danglars ; " I merely suspend my decision."

" And do you flatter yourself that I shall yield to all your caprices, and humbly await the time of again being received into your good graces ? "

" Then, M. le Comte, if you will not wait, we must look upon these projects as if they had never been entertained."

" My dear Danglars," said Morcerf, " we have been acquainted for many years, and ought to make some allowances for each other's failings. You owe me an explanation, and it is but fair that I should know what circumstance has deprived my son of your favour."

" It is from no personal ill-feeling towards the viscount, that is all I can say, sir," replied Danglars.

" Towards whom do you bear this personal ill-feeling, then ? " said Morcerf, turning pale with anger. The expression of the count's face had not remained unperceived by the banker; he fixed on him a look of greater assurance than before, and said, " Perhaps we had better not go into details, Count ? "

A trembling, caused by suppressed rage, shook the whole frame of the count, and making a violent effort over himself, he said,—" I have a right to insist on your giving me an explanation."

" Do not seek to discover the reason. I am ashamed to have been the cause of your undergoing such severe self-examination ; let us drop the subject, and adopt the middle course, namely, delay, which implies neither a rupture nor an engagement. Whilst we wait time will be progressing, events will succeed each other ; things which in the evening look dark and obscure appear but too clearly in the light of morning, and sometimes the utterance of one word, or the lapse of a single day, will reveal the most cruel calumnies."

" Calumnies, did you say, sir ? " cried Morcerf, turning livid. " Does anyone dare to slander me ? "

" M. le Comte, I told you I considered it best to avoid explanation."

" Enough, sir," said Morcerf, " we will speak no more on the subject." And clenching his gloves with passion he left the apartment.

That evening there was a long conference between several friends, and M. Cavalcanti, who had remained in the drawing-room with the ladies, was the last to leave the house of the banker.

Next morning, directly he awoke, Danglars asked for *L'Impartial*, the paper of which Beauchamp was the chief editor. He tore off the cover, opened the journal with nervous precipitation, and arriving at the miscellaneous intelligence, stopped, with a malicious smile, at a paragraph headed " JANINA." " Very good ! " observed Danglars, after having read the paragraph ; " here is a little article on Colonel Fernando, which, if I am not mistaken, would render the explanation which the Count de Morcerf required of me perfectly unnecessary."

At the same moment Albert de Morcerf might have been seen walking in the direction of Monte Cristo's house in the Champs Elysées. When he presented himself at the gate the porter informed him that the count had gone out about half an hour before. " Did he take Baptistin with him ? "

" No, M. le Vicomte."

" Call him, then ; I wish to speak to him." The concierge went to seek the valet, and returned with him in an instant.

" My good friend," said Albert, " I beg pardon for my intrusion ; but I was anxious to know from your own mouth if your master was really out or not."

" He is really out, sir."

" Out, even to me ? "

" I know how happy my master always is to receive M. le Vicomte," said Baptistin ; " and I should therefore never think of including him in any general order."

" You are right ; and now I wish to see him on an affair of great importance ; do you think it will be long before he comes in ? "

" No, I think not ; for he ordered his breakfast at ten o'clock."

" Well, I will take a stroll in the Champs Élysées, and return at ten."

As he was passing the Allée des Veuves Albert thought he saw the count's horses standing at Gossett's shooting-gallery ; he recognized the coachman. " Is M. le Comte shooting ? "

" Yes, sir," replied the coachman. Whilst he was speaking, Albert heard the report of pistol-shots. He entered, and on his way met the waiter. " Excuse me, M. le Vicomte," said the lad ; " but will you have the kindness to wait a moment ? "

" What for, Philip ? " asked Albert, who being a constant visitor, did not understand this opposition to his admittance.

" Because the person now in the gallery prefers being alone, and never practises before anyone."

" The very man I am looking for ; he is a friend of mine."

" Oh, that is quite another thing. I will inform him of your arrival." And Philip, urged by his own curiosity, entered the gallery ; a second afterwards Monte Cristo appeared on the threshold. " I ask your pardon, my dear count, " said Albert, " for following you here. I was walking about in order to pass the time till ten o'clock, when I saw your carriage and horses."

" What you have just said induces me to hope that you intend breakfasting with me."

" No, thank you, I am thinking of other things besides breakfast ; but we may take that meal at a later hour and in worse company."

" What on earth are you talking of ? "

" I am to fight to-day, and am come to beg you to be my second."

" That is a serious matter, and we will not discuss it here ; let us speak of nothing till we get home. Ali, bring me some water."

" Come in here, M. le Vicomte, and I will show you something droll." Morcerf entered, and instead of the usual mark, he perceived some playing-cards fixed against the wall. " Ah ! " said Albert, " I see you were preparing for a game of cards."

" No," said the count, " I was making a suit of cards."

" How ? " said Albert.

" Those are really aces and twos which you see, but my balls have turned them into threes, fives, sevens, eights, nines, and tens."

" *Diable !* " said Morcerf.

" What would you have, my dear viscount ? " said Monte Cristo. " But come, I am waiting for you." Both then entered Monte Cristo's chariot, which in the course of a few minutes deposited them safely at No. 30. Monte Cristo took Albert into his study, and pointing to a seat, placed another for himself.

" With whom are you going to fight ? "

" With Beauchamp."

" What has he done to you ? "

" There appeared in his journal last night—but wait, and read for yourself."

Albert handed over the paper to the count, who read as follows :—" A correspondent at Janina informs us of a fact of which until now we had remained in ignorance. The castle which formed the protection of the town was given up to the Turks by a French officer named Fernando, in whom the Grand Vizier, Ali Tebelen, had reposed the greatest confidence."

" Well ! " said Monte Cristo, " what do you see in that to annoy you ? "

" It signifies my father, the count of Morcerf, whose Christian name is Fernando ! "

" Did your father serve Ali Pasha ? "

" Yes ; that is to say, he fought for the independence of the Greeks, and hence arises the calumny."

" Who would know that this Fernando and the Count de Morcerf are one and the same person ? and who cares now about Janina, which was taken as long ago as 1822 ? "

" That just proves the blackness of the perfidy : they have allowed all this time to elapse, and then, all of a sudden, rake up events which have been forgotten, to furnish materials for scandal, in order to tarnish the lustre of our high position. I am going to Beauchamp, in whose journal this paragraph appears, and I will insist on his retracting the assertion before two witnesses."

" Beauchamp will never retract."

" Then he must fight."

" No, he will not, for he will tell you, what is very true, that perhaps there were fifty officers in the Greek army bearing the same name."

" We will fight, nevertheless."

" Oh, well, he will insert, ' We are warranted in believing that this Fernando is not the illustrious count de Morcerf, who also bears the same Christian name.'"

" I will not be content with anything short of an entire retractation."

" You do wrong."

" Which means, I suppose, that you refuse the service which I asked of you."

" You know my theory regarding duels ; I told you my opinion on that subject, if you remember, when we were at Rome."

" Nevertheless, my dear count, I found you this morning engaged in an occupation but little consistent with the notions you profess to entertain."

" Because, my dear fellow, one must never be eccentric."

" You admit that you would fight, then ? Well, if so, why do you object to my doing so ? "

" I do not say that you ought not to fight, I only say that a duel is a serious thing, and ought not to be undertaken without due reflection."

" Did he reflect before he insulted my father ? "

" Supposing the assertion to be true ? "

" A son ought not to submit to such a stain on his father's honour."

" Are you impervious to good advice ? "

" Not when it comes from a friend."

" Well, then, before going to Beauchamp with your witnesses, seek further information on the subject."

" From whom ? "

" From Haidée. She may be able to assert that your father had no hand in the defeat and death of the vizier ; or if by chance he had, indeed, the misfortunte to—— "

" I have already told you, my dear count, that I would not for one moment admit of such a supposition."

" You reject this means of information, then ? "

" Most decidedly."

" Then let me offer one more word of advice."

" But let it be the last."

" You do not wish to hear it, perhaps ? "

" On the contrary, I request it."

" Do not take any witnesses when you go to Beauchamp—visit him alone."

" Explain yourself."

" I will do so. If Beauchamp be disposed to retract, you ought at least to give him the opportunity of doing it of his own free will ; if, on the contrary, he refuses to do so, it will then be quite time enough to admit two strangers into your secret."

" Then I will go alone."

" Go ; but you would do better still by not going at all."

" But if, in spite of all my precautions, I am at last obliged to fight, will you not be my second ? "

" My dear viscount," said Monte Cristo gravely, "you must have seen before to-day that at all times and in all places I have been at your disposal, but the service you have demanded of me is one it is out of my power to render you."

" We will say no more about it, then. Good-bye, count." Morcerf took his hat, and left the room. He drove at once to Beauchamp's house. Beauchamp was in his office. The servant announced M. Albert de Morcerf. Beauchamp uttered an exclamation of surprise on seeing his friend leap over and trample under foot all the newspapers which were strewed about the room.

" Here ! here ! my dear Albert ! " said he, holding out his hand to the young man. " Are you out of your senses, or do you come peaceably to take breakfast with me ? "

" Beauchamp," said Albert, " it is of your journal that I come to speak."

" Indeed ! what do you wish to say about it ? "

" I desire that a statement contained in it should be rectified."

" Will you have the kindness to explain the nature of the statement which has displeased you ? "

" An announcement has been made which implicates the honour of a member of my family."

" What is it ? " said Beauchamp, much surprised ; " surely you must be mistaken."

" It is an article headed 'Janina.' "

Beauchamp read in an undertone the article to which Albert pointed.

" You see it is a serious annoyance," said Morcerf, when Beauchamp had finished the perusal. " Your paper has insulted a member of my family, and I insist on a retractation being made."

" You insist ? Permit me to remind you that you are not in the Chambre, my dear viscount."

" Nor do I wish to be there," replied the young man, rising ; " I repeat that I am determined to have the announcement contradicted. You have been my friend, and therefore sufficiently intimate with me to be aware that I am likely to maintain my resolution on this point."

" If I have been your friend, Morcerf, your present manner of speaking would almost lead me to forget that I ever bore that relation. You are irritated ; tell me how this Fernando is related to you."

" He is merely my father," said Albert ; " M. Fernando Mondego, count de Morcerf, whose honourable scars they would denounce as badges of disgrace."

" Is it your father ? " said Beauchamp ; " that is another thing. But the paper nowhere identifies this Fernando with your father."

" No, but the connection will be seen by others, and therefore I will have the article contradicted. You will retract this assertion, will you not, Beauchamp ? " said Albert, with increased though stifled anger.

" Yes," replied Beauchamp, " when I am convinced that the statement is false."

" But what is there to investigate, sir ? " said Albert, now enraged beyond measure. " If you do not believe it is my father, say so immediately : and if, on the contrary, you believe it to be him, state your reasons for doing so."

" Sir," replied Beauchamp, " if you came to me with the idea of demanding satisfaction, you should have gone at once to the point, and not have entertained me with the idle conversation to which I have been patiently listening for the last half-hour. Am I to put this construction on your visit ? "

" Yes, if you refuse to retract that infamous calumny."

" Wait a moment—no threats, if you please, M. Fernando Mondego, vicomte de Morcerf. You insist on my contradicting the article relating to General Fernando, an article in which, I assure you on my word of honour, I have not taken the slightest share ? "

" Yes, I insist on it ! " said Albert.

" Well," said Beauchamp, " here is my answer, my dear sir. The article was not inserted by me—I was not even aware of it ; but it will remain until it shall be either contradicted or confirmed by someone who has a right to do so."

" Sir," said Albert, rising, " I will do myself the honour of sending my seconds to you, and you will be kind enough to arrange with them the place of meeting and the arms which we are to use ; do you understand me ? "

" Certainly, my dear sir."

" And this evening, if you please, or to-morrow at the latest, we will meet."

" No ! no ! I will be on the ground at the proper time, but in my opinion the time ought not to be yet. Now I am going to put a question to you. Do you insist on this retractation so far as to kill me if I do not make it, although I was ignorant of the thing with which you charge me, and although I still declare that it is impossible for anyone but you to recognize the Count de Morcerf under the name of Fernando ? "

" I maintain my original resolution."

" Very well, my dear sir ; then I consent to cut throats with you, but I require three weeks' preparation : at the end of that time I shall come and say to you, ' The assertion is false, and I retract it,' or, ' The assertion is true,' when I shall immediately draw the sword from its sheath, or the pistols from the case, whichever you please."

" Well, let it be three weeks," said Morcerf ; " but remember, at the expiration of that time, no delay or subterfuge will justify you in——"

" M. Albert de Morcerf," said Beauchamp, rising in his turn, " to-day is the 29th of August, the 21st of September will therefore be the conclusion of the term agreed on, and till then we will refrain from growling and barking like two dogs chained within sight of each other." When he had concluded this speech, Beauchamp bowed coldly to Albert, turned his back upon him, and retired to his printing-office. Albert departed, not, however, without walking several times to the door of the printing-office, as if he had half a mind to enter it. Whilst Albert was lashing his chariot he perceived Morrel, walking with a quick step and a bright eye. " Ah ! " he said, " there goes a happy man ! "

CHAPTER LXXIX

THE LEMONADE

MORREL was, in fact, very happy. M. Noirtier had just sent for him, and he was hastening with rapid strides in the direction of the Faubourg Saint-Honoré. He advanced with a firm, manly tread, and poor Barrois followed him as he best might. On arriving at the house, Morrel was not even out of breath, for love lends wings to our desires ; but Barrois, who had long forgotten what it was to love, was sorely fatigued by the expedition.

The old servant introduced Morrel by a private entrance, closed the door of the study, and soon the rustling of a dress announced the arrival of Valentine. She looked marvellously beautiful in her deep mourning, and Morrel experienced such intense delight in gazing upon her that he felt as if he could almost have dispensed with the conversation of her grandfather. But the easy-chair of the old man was heard rolling along the floor, and he soon made his appearance in the room. Morrel cast on the invalid an inquiring look as to the new favour which he designed to bestow on him.

" Am I to say what you told me ? " asked Valentine. Noirtier made a sign that she was to do so.

" M. Morrel, my grandfather, M. Noirtier, had a thousand things to say, which he told me three days ago ; and since he has chosen me as his interpreter, I will be faithful to the trust, and will not alter a word of his intentions."

" Oh, I am listening with the greatest impatience," replied the young man ; " speak, I beg of you."

" My grandfather intends leaving this house," said she, " and Barrois is looking out suitable apartments for him in another."

" But you, Mademoiselle de Villefort, you, who are necessary to M. Noirtier's happiness—— "

" Me ? " interrupted Valentine ; " I will not leave my grandfather. My apartment will be close to his. Now, M. de Villefort must either give his consent to this plan or his refusal ; in the first case, I shall leave directly ; and in the second, I shall await my majority, which will be completed in about ten months. Then I shall be free, I shall have an independent fortune, and with my grandfather's consent I shall fulfil the promise which I have made you."

" Have I not explained your wishes, grandpapa ? " said Valentine, addressing Noirtier.

" Yes," looked the old man.

" Once under my grandfather's roof, M. Morrel can visit me in the presence of my good and worthy protector, if we still feel that the union we contemplated will be likely to ensure our future comfort and happiness ; in that case I shall expect M. Morrel to come and claim me at my own hands."

" Oh ! " cried Morrel, " what have I ever done in my life to merit such unbounded happiness ! "

" Until that time," continued the young girl, calm and self-possessed, " we will wait."

" I swear to make all the sacrifices which this word imposes, sir," said Morrel, " not only with resignation, but with cheerfulness." Noirtier regarded the lovers with a look of ineffable tenderness, whilst Barrois, who had remained in the room in the character of a man privileged to know everything that passed, smiled on the youthful couple as he wiped the perspiration from his bald forehead.

" Come, Barrois," said the young girl, " take some lemonade ; I see you long for a draught of it."

" The fact is, mademoiselle," said Barrois," I am dying of thirst, and since you are so kind, I cannot say I should object to drinking your health in a glass of it."

" Take some, then, and come back immediately." Barrois took away the waiter, and hardly was he outside the room when they saw him throw back his head and empty to the very dregs the glass Valentine had filled. Valentine and Morrel were exchanging their adieux in the presence of Noirtier when a ring was heard at the doorbell. It was the signal of a visit. Valentine looked at her watch.

" It is past noon," said she, " and to-day is Saturday : I daresay it is the doctor, grandpapa." Noirtier looked his conviction that she was right in her supposition. " He will come in here, and M. Morrel had better go : do you not think so, grandpapa ? "

" Yes," signed the old man.

" Barrois ! " called Valentine. " Barrois ! "

" I am coming, mademoiselle," replied he. " Barrois will open the door for you," said Valentine, addressing Morrel.

At this moment Barrois entered. " Who rang ? " asked Valentine.

" Doctor d'Avrigny," said Barrois, staggering as if he would fall.

" What is the matter, Barrois ? " said Valentine. The trembling which had attacked Barrois gradually increased, the features of the face became quite altered, and the convulsive movement of the muscles appeared to indicate the approach of a most serious nervous disorder.

" Ah, sir ! " said he, " tell me what is the matter with me. I am suffering—I cannot see. Ah ! don't touch me, pray don't." Valentine uttered a cry of horror. Barrois turned round and, with a great effort, stumbled a few steps, then fell at the feet of Noirtier, and resting his hand on the knee of the invalid, exclaimed, " My master ! my good master ! "

At this moment M. de Villefort, attracted by the noise, appeared on the threshold. Morrel relaxed his hold of Valentine, and retreating to a corner of the room, remained half hidden behind a curtain.

Noirtier, burning with impatience and terror, was in despair at his utter inability to help his old domestic, whom he regarded more in the light of a friend than a servant.

De Villefort seemed stupefied with astonishment, and stood gazing intently on the scene before him, without uttering a word. He had not seen Morrel. After a moment of dumb contemplation, he sprang towards the door, crying out, " Doctor ! come instantly ; pray come ! "

" Madame ! " cried Valentine, calling her stepmother, and running upstairs to meet her ; " come quickly, and bring your smelling-salts with you."

" What is the matter ? " said Madame de Villefort, in a harsh and constrained tone.

" But where is the doctor ? " exclaimed de Villefort ; " where is he ? "

Madame de Villefort now deliberately descended the staircase. In one hand she held her handkerchief, and in the other a bottle of English smelling-salts. She turned pale, and her eye passed quickly from the servant, and rested on the master.

" In the name of heaven, madame," said de Villefort, " where is the doctor ? He was with you just now. You see this is a fit of apoplexy and he might be saved, if he could but be bled ! "

" Has he eaten anything lately ? " asked Madame de Villefort, eluding her husband's question.

" Madame," replied Valentine, " he has not even breakfasted. He took nothing but a glass of lemonade."

" Ah ! "said Madame de Villefort ; " why did he not take wine ? Lemonade was a very bad thing for him."

" Grandpapa's bottle of lemonade was standing just by his side ; poor Barrois was thankful to drink anything he could find." Madame de Villefort started. Noirtier looked at her with a glance of the most profound scrutiny. " He has such a short neck," said she.

" Madame," said de Villefort, " I ask where is M. d'Avrigny ? In God's name answer me ! "

" He is with Edward."

De Villefort rushed upstairs to fetch him. " Take this," said Madame de Villefort, giving her smelling-bottle to Valentine. " They will, no doubt, bleed him ; therefore I will retire, for I cannot endure the sight of blood;" and she followed her husband upstairs.

Morrel now emerged from his hiding-place. "Go away as fast as you can, Maximilian," said Valentine, "and stay till I send for you. Go."

The young man pressed Valentine's hand to his lips, and left the house by a back staircase. As he quitted the room, de Villefort and the doctor entered by an opposite entrance. Barrois was now showing signs of returning consciousness; the crisis seemed passed; a low moaning was heard, and he raised himself on one knee. D'Avrigny and de Villefort laid him on a couch. "What do you prescribe, doctor?" demanded the latter.

"Send for some oil of turpentine and tartar emetic."

De Villefort immediately despatched a messenger. "And now let everyone retire."

Valentine looked at M. d'Avrigny with astonishment, kissed her grandfather on the forehead, and left the room. The doctor closed the door after her with a gloomy air. "Look! look! doctor," said de Villefort, "he is coming round; I do not think it is anything of consequence, after all."

M. d'Avrigny answered by a melancholy smile. "How do you feel yourself, Barrois?" asked he.

"A little better, sir."

"Will you drink some of this ether and water?" Barrois took the glass, and raising it to his purple lips, took about half of the liquid offered him. "Where do you suffer?" asked the doctor.

"Everywhere; I feel cramp over my whole body."

"Did you feel nothing of it yesterday or the day before?"

"Nothing."

"What have you eaten to-day?"

"I have eaten nothing; I only drank a glass of my master's lemonade—that's all."

"Where is this lemonade?" asked the doctor, eagerly.

"Downstairs, in the decanter."

"Shall I go and fetch it, doctor?" inquired de Villefort.

"No, stay here, and try to make Barrois drink the rest of this ether and water. I will fetch the lemonade." D'Avrigny bounded towards the door, flew down the back staircase, and in his haste, almost knocked down Madame de Villefort, who was herself going down to the kitchen. D'Avrigny paid no attention to her; possessed with but one idea, he cleared the last four steps with a bound, and rushed into the kitchen, where he seized the decanter about three parts empty still standing on the waiter, where it had been left. Panting with loss of breath, he returned to the room. Madame de Villefort was slowly ascending the steps which led to her room. " Is this the decanter you spoke of ? " asked d'Avrigny.

" Yes, doctor."

The doctor poured some drops of the lemonade into the palm of his hand, put his lips to it, and after having rinsed his mouth as a man does when he is tasting wine, he spat the liquor into the fireplace.

" It is the same," said he ; " did you drink any M. Noirtier ? "

" Yes."

" And did you notice a bitter taste ? "

" Yes."

" Oh ! doctor," cried Barrois, " the fit is coming on again. Oh ! have pity on me." The doctor flew to his patient. " That emetic, de Villefort ; see if it is coming." De Villefort sprang into the passage, exclaiming, " The emetic ! is it come yet ? " No one answered. The most profound terror reigned throughout the house. " Oh, sir," cried Barrois, " are you going to let me die without help ? Oh ! I am dying ! Oh ! save me ! "

This second attack was much more violent than the first, and he had slipped from the couch to the ground, where he was writhing in agony. The doctor left him in this paroxysm, knowing that he could do nothing to alleviate it, and going up to Noirtier, said abruptly, " How do you find yourself ?—well ? "

" Yes."

" Have you any weight on the chest ; or does your stomach feel light and comfortable—eh ? "

" Yes."

" Did Barrois make your lemonade ? "

" Yes."

" Was it you who asked him to drink some of it ? "

" It was your granddaughter, then, was it not ? "

" Yes."

A groan from Barrois, accompanied by a yawn which seemed to crack the very jawbones, attracted the attention of M. d'Avrigny ; he left M. Noirtier, and returned to the sick man. " Barrois," said the doctor, " who made the lemonade ? "

" I did."

" Who brought it into this room ? "

" Mademoiselle Valentine." D'Avrigny struck his forehead with his hand. " Gracious Heaven ! " exclaimed he.

" Doctor ! doctor ! " cried Barrois, who felt another fit coming.

" Will they never bring that emetic ? " asked the doctor.

" Here is a glass with one already prepared," said de Villefort, entering the room. " Drink it," said the doctor to Barrois. " Impossible, doctor, it is too late ; my throat is closing up. I am choking ! Oh ! my heart ! my head ! Oh ! what agony !— shall I suffer like this long ? "

" No, no, friend," replied the doctor, " you will soon cease to suffer."

" Ah ! I understand you," said the unhappy man. " My God, have mercy upon me ! " and, uttering a fearful cry, Barrois fell back as if he had been struck by lightning. D'Avrigny put his hand to his heart, and placed a glass before his lips.

" Well ? " said de Villefort.

" Go to the kitchen, and get me some syrup of violets."

" Do not be alarmed, M. Noirtier," said d'Avrigny, " I am going to take my patient into the next room to bleed him ; this sort of attack is very frightful to witness."

Taking Barrois under the arms, he dragged him into an adjoining room ; but almost immediately he returned to fetch the remainder of the lemonade. Noirtier closed his right eye. " You want Valentine, do you not ? I will tell them to send her to you." De Villefort returned, and d'Avrigny met him in the passage. " Well ! how is he now ? " asked he.

" Come in here," said d'Avrigny ; and he took him into the chamber where the sick man lay.

" Is he still in a fit ? " said the *procureur du roi.*

" He is dead."

De Villefort drew back a few steps, and clasping his hands, exclaimed, with real amazement and sympathy. " Dead ! and so soon too ! "

" Yes, it is very soon ! " said the doctor, " but that ought not to astonish you ; Monsieur and Madame de Saint Méran died as soon. People die very suddenly in your house, M. de Villefort."

" What ! " cried the magistrate, with an accent of horror and consternation, " are you still harping on that terrible idea ? "

" Still, sir ; I will always do so," replied d'Avrigny. " Listen well to what I am going to say, M. de Villefort." The magistrate trembled convulsively.

" There is a poison which destroys life almost without leaving any perceptible traces. I recognized the presence of this poison in the case of poor Barrois as well as in that of Madame de Saint Méran. Here is in this cup some syrup of violets, and this decanter contains the remainder of the lemonade of which M. Noirtier and Barrois partook.   If the lemonade be pure and inoffensive, the syrup will not colour; if, on the contrary, the lemonade be drugged with poison, the syrup will become green.   Look well at it!"

The doctor then slowly poured some drops of the lemonade from the decanter into the cup, and, in an instant, a kind of light cloudy sediment began to form at the bottom of the cup; this sediment first took a blue shade, then from the colour of sapphire it passed to that of opal, and from opal to emerald.

"Barrois has been poisoned," said d'Avrigny; "and I will maintain this assertion before God and man!"   De Villefort clasped his hands, opened his haggard eyes, and, overcome with emotion, sank into a chair.

CHAPTER LXXX

THE ACCUSATION

M. D'AVRIGNY soon restored the magistrate to consciousness. "Oh! death is in my house!" cried de Villefort.

"Say, rather, crime!" replied the doctor.

"Oh! speak, doctor, speak; I shall have courage."

"Well, sir, you have in your establishment, or in your family, perhaps, one of those frightful phenomena of which each century produces only one.   Locusta and Agrippina, Brunehault and Frédégonde—the same flower of innocence had flourished, or was still flourishing, on their brow, that is seen on the brow of the culprit in your house."   De Villefort shrieked, clasped his hands, and looked at the doctor with a supplicating air.   But the latter pursued without pity.

"'Seek whom the crime would profit,' says an axiom of jurisprudence."

"Doctor," cried de Villefort, "alas! how often has man's justice been deceived by those fatal words!   I know not why, but I feel that this crime——"

"You acknowledge, then, the existence of the crime?"

"Yes, I see too plainly that it does exist.   But it seems that it is intended to affect me personally.   I fear an attack myself, after all these disasters."

"Oh, man!" murmured d'Avrigny, "an ant cursing God from the top of a blade of grass!   And have those who have lost their lives lost nothing?   M. de Saint Méran, Madame de Saint Méran, M. Noirtier——"

" How ! M. Noirtier ? "

" Yes ; think you it was the poor servant's life was coveted ?
It was Noirtier the lemonade was intended for, and although
Barrois is dead, it was Noirtier whose death was wished for."

" But why did it not kill my father ? "

" Because his system is accustomed to that very poison ; and
the dose was trifling for him, which would be fatal to another."

" Pity, pity ! " murmured de Villefort, wringing his hands.

" Follow the culprit's steps ; he first kills M. de Saint Méran,
then Madame de Saint Méran—a double fortune to inherit."
De Villefort wiped the perspiration from his forehead.

" M. Noirtier," resumed M. d'Avrigny, in the same pitiless
tone,—" M. Noirtier had once made a will against you. But he
has no sooner destroyed his first will and made a second, than,
for fear he should make a third, he is struck down ; the will was
made the day before yesterday, I believe ; you see there has been
no time lost."

" Oh, mercy, M. d'Avrigny ! Have mercy on my child, sir ! "

" You see it is yourself who have first named her—you, her
father."

" Have pity on Valentine ! Listen ! it is impossible. I
would as willingly accuse myself ! Valentine, whose heart is
pure as a diamond or a lily."

" Pity ! There is no room for pity ; the crime is flagrant.
Mademoiselle herself packed all the medicines which were sent to
M. de Saint Méran, and M. de Saint Méran is dead ; Mademoiselle
de Villefort prepared all the cooling draughts which Madame de
Saint Méran took, and Madame de Saint Méran is dead. Mademoiselle de Villefort took from the hands of Barrois, who was sent
out, the lemonade which M. Noirtier has every morning, and he
has escaped only by a miracle. Mademoiselle de Villefort is the
culprit ! She is the poisoner ! I denounce Mademoiselle de
Villefort ; do your duty."

" Doctor, I resist no longer ; I can no longer defend myself :
I believe you ; but for pity's sake, spare my life, my honour ! "

"M. de Villefort," replied the doctor, with increasing vehemence,
" there are occasions when I dispense with all foolish human circumspection. Your daughter has seen three deaths,—has contemplated three murdered persons,—has knelt by three corpses !
To the scaffold with the poisoner ! to the scaffold ! Do you talk
of your honour ? Do what I tell you, and immortality awaits
you ! "

De Villefort fell on his knees. " Listen," said he ; " I have not the strength of mind you have, or rather which you would not have, if instead of my daughter Valentine your daughter Madeleine were concerned." The doctor turned pale. " Doctor, every son of woman is born to suffer and to die ; I am content to suffer and to await death."

" Beware," said M. d'Avrigny ; " it may come slowly ; you will see it approach after having struck your father, your wife, perhaps your son."

De Villefort, suffocating, pressed the doctor's arm. " Listen ! " cried he ; " pity me—help me ! No, my daughter is not guilty. I tell you I will not drag my daughter before a tribunal, and give her up to the executioner ! The bare idea would kill me,—would drive me like a madman to dig my heart out with my finger nails ! And, if you were mistaken, although I am a Christian, M. d'Avrigny, I should kill myself."

" Well," said the doctor, after a moment's silence : " I will wait. Only, if any one falls ill in your house, if you feel yourself attacked, do not send for me, for I will come no more."

" I entreat you, doctor ! "

" All the horrors that disturb my thoughts make your house odious and fatal. Adieu, sir."

" One word—one single word more, doctor ! What will be reported of the sudden death of this poor old servant ? "

" True," said M. d'Avrigny ; " we will return." The doctor went out first, followed by M. de Villefort ; the terrified servants were on the stairs and in the passage where the doctor would pass. " Sir," said d'Avrigny to de Villefort, so loud that all might hear, " poor Barrois has led too sedentary a life. The monotonous walk round that armchair has killed him ; he was stout, had a short thick neck, he was attacked with apoplexy, and I was called in too late. A propos," added he, in a low tone, " take care to throw that cup of syrup of violets in the ashes."

The doctor, without shaking hands with de Villefort, went out amid the tears and lamentations of the whole household. The same evening all the servants came to tell Madame de Villefort they wished to leave. No entreaty, no proposition of increased wages, could induce them to remain ; to every argument they replied, " We must go, for death is in this house." They all left, in spite of prayers and entreaties, testifying their regret at leaving so good a master and mistress, and especially Mademoiselle Valentine, so good, so kind, and so gentle. De Villefort looked at Valentine as they said this. She was in tears ; and, strange as it was, in spite of the emotions he felt at the sight of these tears, he looked also at Madame de Villefort, and it appeared to him as if a slight gloomy smile had passed over her thin lips, like those meteors which are seen passing inauspiciously between two clouds in a stormy sky.

CHAPTER LXXXI

THE ROOM OF THE RETIRED BAKER

THE evening of the day on which the Count de Morcerf had left Danglars' house with feelings of shame and anger, M. Andrea Cavalcanti had entered the courtyard of the banker's house in La Chaussée d'Antin. He had not been more than ten minutes in the drawing-room before he drew Danglars aside into the recess of a bow window ; he acknowledged the extreme kindness which had been shown him by the banker's family, in which he had been received as a son, and where, besides, his warmest affections had found an object on which to centre in Mademoiselle Danglars. Danglars listened with the most profound attention. He would not, however, yield immediately to the young man's request, but made a few conscientious scruples. " Are you not rather young, M. Andrea, to think of marrying ? "

" I think not, sir," replied M. Cavalcanti.

" Well, sir," said Danglars, " in case your proposals, which do me honour, are accepted by my wife and daughter, by whom shall the preliminary arrangements be settled ? "

" Sir, my father is a man of great foresight and prudence. Imagining I might wish to settle in France, he left me at his departure, a letter promising, if he approved of my choice, 150,000 livres per annum from the day I was married. So far as I can judge, I suppose this to be a quarter of my father's revenue."

" I," said Danglars, " have always intended giving my daughter 500,000 francs as her dowry ; she is, besides, my sole heiress."

" All, then, would be easily arranged if the baroness and her daughter are willing. Supposing, also, I should persuade the marquis to give me my capital, we would place these two or three millions in your hands, whose talent might make it realize ten per cent."

" I never give more than four per cent., and generally only three-and-a-half ; but to my son-in-law I would give five, and we would share the profit. But there is a part of your fortune your father could not refuse you ? "

"Which ? " asked the young man.

"What you inherit from your mother. How much is it ? "

"Indeed, sir," said Andrea, "I have never given the subject a thought ; but I suppose it must have been at least two millions."

Danglars felt overcome with joy.

"Well, sir," said Andrea, bowing respectfully, "may I hope ? "

"You may not only hope," said Danglars, "but consider it settled, if no obstacle arise on your part."

"I am rejoiced," said Andrea.

"But," said Danglars, thoughtfully, "how is it that your patron, M. de Monte Cristo, did not make this proposal for you ? "

Andrea blushed imperceptibly. "I have just left the count, sir ; if he will do nothing officially, he will answer any questions you propose to him. And now," continued he, with one of his most charming smiles, "having finished talking to the father-in-law, I must address myself to the banker."

"And what may you have to say to him ? " said Danglars, laughing.

"That to-morrow I shall have to draw upon you."

"Very well, at ten o'clock ; you are still at the Hôtel des Princes ? "

"Yes."

Scarcely had Andrea stepped out of his carriage, when the porter met him with a parcel in his hand. "Sir," said he, "the man has been."

"Oh ! " said Andrea, "my father's old servant. Well, you gave him the two hundred francs I had left for him ? "

"Yes, your Excellency." Andrea had expressed a wish to be thus addressed. "But," continued the porter, "he would not take them and gave me this letter, which he had brought with him already sealed."

Andrea read it :—" You know where I live ; I expect you to-morrow morning at nine o'clock."

"Very well," said he. "Poor man ! he is a worthy creature."

He left the porter to ponder these words, and the man knew not which most to admire, the master or the servant. "Take out the horses quickly, and come up to me," said Andrea to his groom. In two seconds the young man had reached his room and burnt Caderousse's letter. The servant entered as he had finished. "You are about my height, Peter," said he.

"I have that honour, your Excellency."

"I have an engagement with a little girl this evening, and do not wish to be known ; lend me your livery till to-morrow." Peter obeyed. Five minutes later, Andrea left the hotel, completely disguised, took a cabriolet, and ordered the driver to the Cheval Rouge, at Picpus. The next morning he left that inn, as he had left the Hôtel des Princes, and stopping at the door of the third house on the left, looked for someone of whom to make inquiry in the porter's absence. "For whom are you looking, my fine fellow ?" asked the fruiteress on the opposite side.

"M. Pailletin, if you please, my good woman," replied Andrea.

"He lives at the end of the yard, on the left, on the third storey." Andrea rang, and Caderousse's face appeared in the grating of the door. "Ah ! you are punctual," said he, as he unbolted the door.

"Confound you and your punctuality !" said Andrea.

"Come, come, my little fellow, don't be angry. See, I have thought about you—look at the good breakfast we are going to have ; nothing but what you are fond of." In an adjoining room, Andrea saw a tolerably clean table laid for two, two bottles of wine sealed, the one with green, the other with yellow, a considerable quantity of brandy in a decanter, and a measure of fruit in a cabbage-leaf, cleverly arranged on an earthenware plate.

"What do you think of it, my little fellow ?" said Caderousse "Ay ! that smells good !"

"But," said Andrea, ill-temperedly, "*pardieu !* if you disturbed me only to breakfast with you, I wish the devil had taken you."

"My boy," said Caderousse, sententiously, "one can talk while eating. And then, you ungrateful being ! are you not pleased to see an old friend ? I am weeping with joy." He was truly crying, but it would have been difficult to say whether joy or the onions produced the greater effect on the lachrymal glands of the old innkeeper of the Pont-du-Gard.

"Hold your tongue, hypocrite !" said Andrea ; "*you* love me !"

"Ah !" said Caderousse, wiping his large knife on his apron, "if I did not like you, do you think I should endure the wretched life you lead me ?"

"Well !" said Andrea, "admitting your love, why do you want me to breakfast with you ?"

"That I may have the pleasure of seeing you, my little fellow."

"What is the use of seeing me after we have made all our arrangements ?"

"Eh ! dear friend," said Caderousse, "are wills never made

without codicils ? But you first came to breakfast, did you not ? Ah ! yes ; you look at my room, my four straw chairs, my images, three francs each. But what do you expect ? This is not the Hôtel des Princes."

" Come ! you are growing discontented, you are no longer happy ; you who only wish to appear a retired baker."

Caderousse shrugged his shoulders. " It is humiliating," said he, " to receive money given grudgingly ; an uncertain supply which may soon fail. I know your prosperity is great, rascal ; you are to marry the daughter of Danglars."

" What ! of Danglars ! "

" Yes, to be sure ! must I say Baron Danglars ? I have dined many times with him and the count de Morcerf ; so you see I have some high connections, and were I to cultivate them a little, we might meet in the same drawing-rooms. Perhaps I may one day put on my best coat and introduce myself. Meanwhile, let us eat." Caderousse set the example, and attacked the breakfast with good appetite, praising each dish he set before his visitor.

" You wished to speak to me ? "

" An idea had struck me." Andrea shuddered ; he always did at Caderousse's ideas. " It is miserable—do you see ?— always to wait till the end of the month."

" Oh ! " said Andrea, philosophically, " does not life pass in waiting ? "

" I was going to say, if I were in your place—— "

" Well ? "

" I would ask for six months' allowance in advance, under pretence of being able to purchase a farm, then I would decamp."

" That is not a bad notion ! "

" My dear friend," said Caderousse, " eat of my bread, and take my advice, you will be none the worse off, physically or morally."

" But," said Andrea, " why do you not act on the advice you give me ? "

" But how the devil would you have me retire on twelve hundred francs ? "

" Ah ! Caderousse," said Andrea, " how coveteous you are ! two months since you were dying of hunger."

" In eating the appetite grows," said Caderousse, grinning and showing his teeth, like a monkey laughing or a tiger growling. " And," added he, " I have formed a plan. Can you, without expending one sou, put me in the way of getting thirty thousand francs ? "

" No," replied Andrea, drily, " I cannot."

" I do not think you understand me," replied Caderousse, calmly ; " I said without your laying out a sou."

" Well ! I will see ! I will recollect you ! " said Andrea.

" Meanwhile you will raise my allowance to five hundred francs, my little fellow ? I mean to get a housekeeper."

" Well ! you shall have your five hundred francs," said Andrea ; " but it is very hard for me, my poor Caderousse—you take advantage—— "

" Bah ! when you have access to countless stores."

" Are you my friend, Caderousse ? "

" Yes, in life or death."

"Well ! I will tell you a secret."

" What is it ? "

" I think I have discovered my father."

" And that father is—— "

" Well ! Caderousse, it is Monte Cristo."

" Bah ! "

" Yes, you understand, that explains all. He cannot acknowledge me openly, it appears, but he does it through M. Cavalcanti, and gives him fifty thousand francs for it."

" Fifty thousand francs for being your father ! I would have done it for half that, for twenty thousand, for fifteen thousand ; why did you not think of me, ungrateful man ? "

" Did I know anything about it, when it was all done when I was down there ? "

" Ah ! truly ! And by his will—— "

" He leaves me five hundred thousand livres."

" Oh ! the good father ! the brave father ! the very honest father ! " said Caderousse, twirling a plate in the air between his two hands.

" Now, say if I conceal anything from you ! "

" No, and your confidence makes you honourable in my opinion ; and your princely father, is he rich, very rich ? "

" Yes, in truth ; he does not himself know the amount of his fortune."

" And you go into his house ? " cried he, briskly.

" When I like."

" And does he not live in the Champs Élysées ? "

" Yes, No. 30."

" Ah ! " said Caderousse, " No. 30."

" A fine house standing alone, between a courtyard and a garden ; you must know it."

" Possibly ; but it is not the exterior I care for, it is the interior ; what beautiful furniture there must be in it ! Try, at least, to give me an idea of what it is."

" *Ma foi !* I require pen, ink, and paper to make a plan."

" They are all here," said Caderousse, briskly. He fetched from an old secrétaire a sheet of white paper, and pen and ink. " Here," said Caderousse, " trace me all that on the paper, my boy." Andrea took the pen with an imperceptible smile, and began.

" The house, as I said, is between the court and the garden ; in this way, do you see ? " Andrea traced the garden, the court, and the house.

" High walls ? "

" Not more than eight or ten feet."

" That is not prudent," said Caderousse.

" In the court are orange-trees in pots, turf, and clumps of flowers."

" The stables ? "

" Are on either side of the gate, which you see there." And Andrea continued his plan.

" Let us see the ground-floor," said Caderousse.

" On the ground-floor, dining-room, two drawing-rooms, billiard-room, staircase in the hall, and little back staircase."

" Windows ? "

" Magnificent windows, so beautiful, so large, that I believe a man of your size could pass through each frame."

" Why the devil have they any stairs with such windows ? "

" Luxury has everything."

" But shutters ? "

" They are never used. That Count of Monte Cristo is an original, who loves to look at the sky even at night."

" And where do the servants sleep ? "

" Oh ! they have a house to themselves. Picture to yourself a pretty coach-house at the righthand side where the ladders are kept. Well ! over that coach-house are the servants' rooms, with bells corresponding with the different apartments."

" Ah, *diable !* bells did you say ? "

" What do you mean ? "

" Oh, nothing ! I only say they cost a load of money to hang ; and what is the use of them, I should like to know ? "

" There used to be a dog let loose in the yard at night ; but it has been taken to the house at Auteuil, the one you went to, you know."

" Yes."

" I was saying to him only yesterday, ' You are imprudent, M. le Comte ; for when you go to Auteuil, and take your servants, the house is left unprotected.' ' Well,' said he, ' what next ? ' ' Well, next, some day you will be robbed.' "

" What did he answer ? "

" He quietly said, ' What do I care if I am ? ' "

" Andrea, he has some secrétaire with a spring, which catches the thief in a trap, and plays a tune. I was told there were such at the last Exhibition."

" He has simply a mahogany secrétaire, in which the key is always kept."

" There ought to be some money in that secrétaire ? "

" There may be. No one knows what there is."

" And where is it ? "

" On the first floor."

" Sketch me the plan of that floor, as you have done of the ground-floor, my boy."

" That is very simple." Andrea took the pen. " On the first storey, do you see, there is the ante-room and drawing-room ; to the right of the drawing-room, a library and a study ; to the left a bedroom and a dressing-room. The famous secrétaire is in the dressing-room."

" Is there a window in the dressing-room ? "

" Two, one here and one there." Andrea sketched two windows in the room. Caderousse became thoughtful. " Does he often go to Auteuil ? "

" Two or three times a week. To-morrow, for instance, he is going to spend the day and night there."

Andrea drew a cigar-case from his pocket, took a Havannah, quietly lit it, and began smoking. " When do you want your five hundred francs ? " he said to Caderousse.

" Now, if you have them." Andrea took five-and-twenty louis from his pocket.

" Yellows boys ? " said Caderousse : " no, I thank you. Silver for me ! "

" But do you suppose I carry five hundred francs about with me ? I should want a porter."

" Well, leave them with your porter ; he is to be trusted ; I will call for them."

" Well, to-morrow I will leave them when I go to Auteuil."

" I am going to give you another piece of good advice."

" What is it ? "

" To leave behind you the diamond you have on your finger.

We shall both get into trouble. You will ruin yourself and me by your folly."

" How so ? " said Andrea.

" How ! You put on livery ; you disguise yourself as a servant, and yet keep a diamond on your finger worth four or five thousand francs."

" You guess well."

" I know something of diamonds ; I have had some."

" You do well to boast of it," said Andrea, who, without becoming angry, as Caderousse feared, at this new extortion, quietly resigned the ring. Caderousse looked so closely at it that Andrea well knew that he was examining if all the edges were perfect.

" It is a false diamond," said Caderousse.

" You are joking now," replied Andrea.

" Do not be angry ; we can try it," Caderousse went to the window, touched the glass with it, and found it would cut.

"*Confiteor !*" said Caderousse, putting the diamond on his little finger ; " I was mistaken ; but those thieves of jewellers imitate so well that it is no longer worth while to rob a jeweller's shop—it is another branch of industry paralysed."

" Have you finished now ? " said Andrea, " do you want anything more ? will you have my waistcoat or my certificate ? Make free now you have begun."

" No ; you are, after all, a good companion ; I will not detain you, and will try to cure myself of my ambition. But I hope you will make me a handsome wedding-present the day you marry Mademoiselle Danglars."

" I have already told you it is a fancy you have taken in your head."

" What fortune has she ? "

" But I tell you—— "

" A million ? " Andrea shrugged his shoulders.

" Oh, I wish it you with all my heart ! " added Caderousse, with his hoarse laugh. " *Au revoir !* "

They parted. Caderousse remained on the landing until he had not only seen Andrea go down the three storeys but also cross the court. Then he returned hastily, shut his door carefully, and began to study the plan Andrea had left for him.

CHAPTER LXXXII

THE BURGLARY

THE day following that on which the conversation we have related took place the count of Monte Cristo set out for Auteuil,
accompanied by Ali and several attendants, and also taking
with him some horses whose qualities he was desirous of ascertaining. He was induced to undertake this journey by the arrival
of Bertuccio from Normandy, with intelligence respecting the
house and sloop. The house was ready, and the sloop, which
had arrived a week before, lay at anchor in a small creek, with her
crew of six men, who, after having observed all the requisite
formalities, were ready again to put to sea. The count praised
Bertuccio's zeal, and ordered him to prepare for a speedy departure, as his stay in France would not be prolonged more than a
month. "Now," said he, " I may require to go in one night from
Paris to Tréport ; let eight fresh horses be in readiness on the
road, which will enable me to go fifty leagues in ten hours. I
remain here a day or two, arrange accordingly." As Bertuccio
was leaving the room to give the requisite orders, Baptistin opened
the door : he held a letter on a silver waiter.

Baptistin approached the count, and presented the letter.
" Important and urgent," said he. The count opened the letter,
and read :—

" M. de Monte Cristo is apprised that this night a man will enter
his house in the Champs Élysées with the intention of carrying
off some papers supposed to be in the secrétaire in the dressing-
room. The count's well-known courage will render unnecessary
the aid of the police, whose interference might seriously affect
him who sends this advice. The count, by any opening from
the bedroom, or by concealing himself in the dressing-room,
would be able to defend his property himself. Many attendants
or apparent precautions would prevent the villain from the
attempt, and M. de Monte Cristo would lose the opportunity of
discovering an enemy whom chance has revealed to him who
now sends this warning to the count,—a warning he might not
be able to send another time, if this first attempt should fail
and another be made."

The count's first idea was that this was an artifice—a gross
deception to draw his attention from a minor danger in order
to expose him to a greater. He was on the point of sending
the letter to the commissaire de police, notwithstanding the

advice of his anonymous friend, or, perhaps, because of that advice, when suddenly the idea occurred to him that it might be some personal enemy, whom he alone should recognize ; and over whom, if such were the case, he alone could gain any advantage.

"They do not want my papers," said Monte Cristo, "they want to kill me." The count recalled Baptistin, who had left the room after delivering the letter. "Return to Paris," said he ; "assemble the servants who remain there. I want all my household at Auteuil."

"But will no one remain in the house, my lord ? " asked Baptistin.

"Yes, the porter."

"My lord will remember that the lodge is at a distance from the house."

"Well ? "

"The house might be stripped without his hearing the least noise."

"You are a fool, M. Baptistin ; thieves might strip the house— it would annoy me less than to be disobeyed." Baptistin bowed.

"You understand me ? " said the count, " bring your comrades here, one and all ; but let everything remain as usual, only close the shutters of the ground-floor."

"And those of the first floor ? "

"You know they are never closed. Go ! "

The count signified his intention of dining alone, and that no one but Ali should attend him. Having dined, the count, with a signal to Ali to follow him, went out by the side gate and on reaching the Bois de Boulogne, turned, apparently without design, towards Paris, and at twilight found himself opposite his house in the Champs Élysées. Monte Cristo leant against a tree, and, with that eye which was so rarely deceived, searched the double avenue, examined the passers-by, and carefully looked down the neighbouring streets, to see that no one was concealed. He hastened to the side door with Ali, entered precipitately, and gained his bedroom without opening or disarranging a single curtain, without even the porter having the slightest suspicion that the house contained its chief occupant.

Arrived in his bedroom, the count motioned to Ali to stop ; then he passed into the dressing-room, which he examined.

He doubly locked the secrétaire, took the key, returned to the bedroom door, removed the double staple of the bolt, and went in. With the arms Ali brought to him—a short carbine and a pair of double-barrelled pistols—the count held the life of five men in his hands. It was about half-past nine. Monte Cristo slipped aside one of the movable panels, which enabled him to see into the adjoining room. Two hours passed thus. It was intensely dark ; still Ali, thanks to his wild nature, and the count, thanks to his long confinement, could distinguish in the darkness the slightest movement of the trees. In Monte Cristo's idea, the villains sought his life, not his money. It would be his bedroom they would attack, and they must reach it by the back staircase, or by the window in the dressing-room. The clock of the Invalides struck a quarter to twelve. As the last stroke died away, the count heard a slight noise in the dressing-room. A well-practised hand was engaged in cutting the four sides of a pane of glass with a diamond. However, Monte Cristo only made a sign to apprise Ali, who, understand ing that danger was approaching from the other side, drew nearer to his master. Monte Cristo was eager to ascertain the strength and number of his enemies.

The window whence the noise proceeded was opposite the opening by which the count could see into the dressing-room. He fixed his eyes on that window, he distinguished a shadow in the darkness ; then one of the panes became quite opaque, as if a sheet of paper were stuck on the outside, then the square cracked without falling. Through the opening an arm was passed to find the fastening, then a second ; the window turned on its hinges, and a man entered. He was alone.

"That's a daring rascal ! " thought the count.

At that moment Ali touched him slightly on the shoulder ; he turned. Ali pointed to the window of the room in which they were, facing the street. " Good ! " said he, "there are two of them ; one acts while the other watches." He made a sign to Ali not to lose sight of the man in the street, and returned to the one in the dressing-room.

The glass-cutter had entered, and appeared to have made himself familiar with all parts. There were two doors ; he bolted them both.

When he drew near to that of the bedroom, Monte Cristo expected he was coming in, and raised one of his pistols ; but he simply heard the sound of the bolts sliding in their copper rings. It was only a precaution. The nocturnal visitor, ignorant of the count's having removed the staples, might now think himself at home, and pursue his purpose with full security. Alone and uncontrolled, the man then drew from his pocket something which the count could not discern, placed it on a stand, then went straight to the secrétaire, felt the lock, and, contrary to his expectation, found that the key was missing. The count soon heard the rattling of a bunch of shapeless keys such as the locksmith brings when called to force a lock. " Ah ! ah ! " whispered Monte Cristo, with a smile of disappointment, " he is only a thief ! "

But in the dark the man could not find the right key. He reached the instrument he had placed on the stand, touched a spring, and immediately a pale light was reflected on the hands and countenance of the man.

" Hold ! " exclaimed Monte Cristo, starting back, " it is——"

Ali raised his hatchet. " Don't," whispered Monte Cristo, " and put down your hatchet ; we shall require no arms." Then he added some words in a low tone ; immediately Ali went away noiselessly, and returned, bearing a black dress and a three-cornered hat. Meanwhile Monte Cristo had rapidly taken off his great coat, waistcoat, and shirt, and one might distinguish that he wore one of those pliant tunics of steel mail, of which the last in France was worn by Louis XVI, who feared the dagger at his breast, and whose head was cleft with a hatchet. This tunic soon disappeared under a long cassock, as did his hair under a priest's wig ; the three-cornered hat over this effectually transformed the count into an abbé.

The man, hearing nothing more, had advanced straight to the secrétaire, whose lock was beginning to crack under his implement. " Well done ! " whispered the count, who depended on the secret spring, which was unknown to the picklock, clever as he might be, " well done !—you have a few minutes' work there." He advanced to the window. The man whom he had seen seated on a fence had got down, and his attention was engrossed on what was passing at the count's ; his only aim appeared to be to discern every movement in the dressing-room.

Monte Cristo suddenly struck his finger on his forehead, and a smile passed over his lips. Then drawing near to Ali, he whispered :—

" Remain here, concealed in the dark, and whatever noise you hear, whatever passes, only come in or show yourself if I call you." Ali bowed in token of strict obedience. Monte Cristo then drew a lighted taper from a closet, and when the thief was deeply engaged with his lock, silently opened the door, taking care that the light should shine directly on his face.

" Good evening, dear M. Caderousse ! " said Monte Cristo ; " what are you doing here at such an hour ? "

"The Abbé Busoni" exclaimed Caderousse. The count placed himself between Caderousse and the window, thus cutting off the only chance of retreat.

"L'abbé! l'abbé!" murmured he, clenching his fists and his teeth chattering.

"So you would rob the Count of Monte Cristo?" continued the false abbé. "A pane of glass out, a dark lantern, a bunch of false keys, a secrétaire half forced; it is tolerably evident——"

Caderousse was choking; he looked round for some corner to hide in—some way of escape. "Come, come," continued the count, "I see you are still the same—an assassin."

"M. l'Abbé, I am impelled——"

"Every criminal says the same thing."

"Poverty——"

"Pshaw!" said Busoni, disdainfully. "And when the jeweller Joannes had paid you 45,000 francs for the diamond I had given you, and you killed him to get the diamond and the money both, was that also poverty?"

"Are you alone, M. l'Abbé, M. l'Abbé, or have you soldiers ready to seize me?"

"I am alone," said the abbé, "and I will again have pity on you and will let you escape, at the risk of the fresh miseries my weakness may lead to, if you tell me the truth. You mean to say you have been freed from confinement?"

"Yes, in truth, M. l'Abbé."

"Who was your liberator?"

"Lord Wilmore."

"Was this Englishman protecting you?"

"No, not me, but a young Corsican, my companion."

"What was this young Corsican's name?"

"Benedetto."

"This young man escaped with you?"

"In the hour of rest, between noon and one o'clock——"

"Galley-slaves having a nap after dinner! We may well pity the poor fellows!" said the abbé.

"While the rest slept, then, we severed our fetters with a file the Englishman had given us, and swam away."

"What became of this Benedetto?"

"I don't know."

"You ought to know."

"No, in truth; we parted at Hyères." To give more weight to his protestation, Caderousse advanced another step towards the abbé, who remained motionless in his place, as calm as ever,

T

pursuing his interrogation. "You lie!" said the Abbé Busoni, with a tone of irresistible authority.

"Oh, Monsieur l'Abbé!"

"Since you left Toulon what have you lived on? Answer me!"

"On what I could get."

"You lie!" repeated the abbé, in a still more imperative tone. Caderousse, terrified, looked at the count. "You have lived on the money he has given you."

"True!" said Caderousse; "Benedetto has become the son of a great lord."

"And what is that great lord's name?"

"The count of Monte Cristo, the very same in whose house we are."

"Benedetto the count's son!" replied Monte Cristo, astonished in his turn, "and what name does the young man bear meanwhile?"

"Andrea Cavalcanti."

"The youug man whom my friend the count of Monte Cristo has received into his house, and who is going to marry Mademoiselle Danglars?"

"Exactly."

"And you suffer that, you wretch!—you who know his life and his crime?"

"Why should I stand in a comrade's way?" said Caderousse.

"I will expose all."

"To whom?"

"To M. Danglars."

"By Heaven!" cried Caderousse, drawing from his waistcoat an open knife, and striking the count in the breast, "you shall disclose nothing, M. l'Abbé!" To Caderousse's great astonishment, the knife, instead of piercing the count's breast, flew back blunted. At the same moment the count seized with his left hand the assassin's wrist, and wrung it with such strength that his arm being dislocated, he fell first on his knees, then flat on the floor. The count placed his foot on his head, saying,— "I know not what restrains me from crushing your skull!"

"Ah, mercy—mercy!" cried Caderousse.

The count withdrew his foot. "Rise!"

"What a wrist you have, M. l'Abbé!" said Caderousse, rising and stroking his arm, all bruised by the fleshly pincers which had held it, "what a wrist!"

"Silence! God gives me strength to overcome a wild beast like you; in the name of that God I act—remember that, wretch! And to spare thee at this moment is still serving Him. Take this pen and paper and write what I dictate."

Caderousse, awed by the abbé, sat down and wrote:—

"Sir,—The man whom you are receiving at your house, and to whom you intend to marry your daughter, is a felon who escaped with me from confinement at Toulon. He was No. 59, and I No. 58. He was called Benedetto; but he is ignorant of his real name, having never known his parents."

"Sign it!" continued the count.

Caderousse signed it. "The address:—À Monsieur le Baron Danglars, banker, Rue de la Chaussée d'Antin." Caderousse wrote the address. The abbé took the note. "Now," said he, "that suffices—begone!"

"What do you intend doing with me?"

"I ask you what can I do? I have tried to make you a happy man, and you have turned out a murderer."

"M. l'Abbé," said Caderousse, "make one more attempt—try me once more!"

"I will," said the count. "Listen! you know if I may be relied on."

"Yes," said Caderousse.

"If you reach your home safely leave Paris, leave France; and wherever you may be, so long as you conduct yourself well, I will send you a small annuity. Now, begone!" said the count, pointing to the window.

Caderousse put his legs out of the window and stood on the ladder. "Now go down," said the abbé, folding his arms. Understanding he had nothing more to fear from him, Caderousse began to go down.

Monte Cristo returned to his bedroom, and, glancing rapidly from the garden to the street, saw Caderousse, who, after walking to the end of the garden, fixed his ladder against the wall at a different part from that at which he came in. The count then looking over into the street, saw the man who appeared to be waiting run in the same direction, and place himself against the angle of the wall where Caderousse would descend. Caderousse sat astride the coping, and, drawing up his ladder, passed it over the wall, and began to descend, or rather to slide down by the two stanchions, which he did with the ease of an old hand. But, once started, he could not stop. A man started from the shade as he touched the ground and, ere he could defend himself, struck him so violently in the back that he let go the ladder, crying,

" Help ! "   A second blow struck him almost in the side, and he fell, calling " Help ! Murder ! "   Then, as he rolled on the ground his adversary seized him by the hair, and struck him a third blow in the chest.   Caderousse endeavoured to call again, but only uttered a groan, and shuddered as the blood flowed from his three wounds.   The murderer, supposing him dead, let fall his head and disappeared.   Then Caderousse cried with great effort, " Murder ! I am dying !   Help, M. l'Abbé—help ! "

This mournful appeal pierced the darkness.   The door of the back-staircase opened, then the side gate of the garden, and Ali and his master were on the spot with lights.

CHAPTER LXXXIII

THE HAND OF GOD

CADEROUSSE continued to call piteously, " M. l'Abbé, help ! help ! "

" We are here ; take courage ! "

" Ah, it's all over !   You are come too late ; you are come to see me die.   What blows ! what blood ! "   He fainted.   Ali and his master conveyed the wounded man into a room.   Monte Cristo motioned to Ali to undress him, and he then examined his dreadful wounds.

Ali looked at his master for further instructions.

" Fetch the *procureur du roi*, M. de Villefort, who lives in the Faubourg St. Honoré.   As you pass the lodge, wake the porter and send him for a surgeon."

By and by Caderousse came to and asked for a surgeon.

" I have sent for one," replied the abbé.

" He cannot save me, but may strengthen me to give evidence."

" Against whom ? "

" Against my murderer."

" Did you recognize him ? "

" Yes—it was Benedetto."

" The young Corsican ? "

" Yes.   After giving me the plan of this house, doubtless hoping I should kill the count and he thus become his heir, or that the count would kill me and I should be out of his way, he waylaid me, and has murdered me."

" I have also sent for the *procureur du roi*."

" He will not come in time ; I feel my life fast ebbing."

" Stop ! " said Monte Cristo. He left the room and returned in five minutes with a phial.

" Hasten, M. l'Abbé !—hasten ! I shall faint again ! " Monte Cristo approached, and dropped on his purple lips three or four drops of the contents of the phial. Caderousse drew a deep breath.

" Oh, send for someone to whom I can denounce the wretch ! "

" Let me write your deposition. You can sign it."

Monte Cristo wrote :—

" I die murdered by the Corsican Benedetto, my comrade in the galleys at Toulon, No. 59."

" Quick, quick ! " said Caderousse, " or I shall be unable to sign it."

Monte Cristo gave the pen to Caderousse, who signed it, and fell back on the bed, saying, " You will tell all I have said : will you not, M. l'Abbé ? "

" Yes ; and much more. I will say that he had apprised the count, by a note, of your intention ; that he watched you the whole time, and that when he saw you leave the house, he ran to the angle of the wall to conceal himself."

" Did you see all that ? "

" I told you that if you reached home safely, I should believe God had forgiven you, and I would forgive you also."

" And you did not warn me ! " cried Caderousse, raising himself on his elbows.

" No, for I saw God's justice placed in the hands of Benedetto, and should have thought it sacrilege to oppose the designs of Providence."

" God's justice ! Speak not of it, M. l'Abbé. If God were just, you know many would be punished who now escape."

" Listen," said the abbé, extending his hand over the wounded man, as if to command him to believe ; " this is what the God in Whom, on your death-bed, you refuse to believe, has done for you : He gave you health, strength, regular employment, even friends—a life, in fact, which a man might enjoy with a calm conscience. When you had betrayed your friend God began not to strike, but to warn you : poverty overtook you ; you had already passed half your life in coveting what you might have honourably acquired, and already you contemplated crime under the excuse of want, when God worked a miracle in your behalf, sending you, by my hands, a fortune. But this unheard-of fortune sufficed you no longer when once you possessed it ; you wished to double it; and how? by murder! You succeeded, and then God snatched it from you, and brought you to justice."

Caderousse turned uneasily.

"God showed mercy to the galley-slave, for an Englishman visiting Toulon, who had vowed to rescue two men from infamy, chose you and your companion, and money and tranquillity—a second fortune—were restored to you. Then you tempted God a third time and the Almighty has punished you."

Caderousse was fast sinking. "Give me drink," said he; "I thirst—I burn!" Monte Cristo gave him a glass of water. "And yet that villain, Benedetto, will escape!"

"No one will escape; Benedetto will be punished."

"Then you, too, will be punished, for you did not do your duty as a priest—you should have prevented Benedetto from killing me."

"I?" said the count, with a smile which petrified the dying man, "when you had just broken your knife against the coat of mail which protected my breast! Yet if I had found you penitent, I might have prevented Benedetto from killing you; but you were vengeful, and I left you in the hands of God."

"I do not believe there is a God!" howled Caderousse; "you do not believe it; you lie—you lie!"

"Silence!" said the abbé; "you will force the last drop of blood from your veins. What! you do not believe in God when He is striking you dead? you will not believe in Him, who requires but a prayer, a word, a tear, and He will forgive? Reflect, wretched man, and repent."

"And who are you?" asked Caderousse, fixing his dying eyes on the count.

"Look well at me!" said Monte Cristo, putting the light near his face.

"Well! the abbé—the Abbé Busoni." Monte Cristo took off the wig which disfigured him, and let fall his black hair, which added so much to the beauty of his pallid features. "Oh!" said Caderousse, thunder-struck, "but for that black hair, I should say you were the Englishman, Lord Wilmore."

"I am neither the Abbé Busoni nor Lord Wilmore," said Monte Cristo; "think again, do you not recollect me?" There was a magic effect in the count's words which once more revived the exhausted powers of the miserable man. "Yes, indeed," said he, "I think I have seen you and known you formerly."

"Yes, Caderousse, you have seen me, you knew me once."

"Who, then, are you?"

The count watched the approach of death. He drew near to the dying man, and leaning over him whispered,—" I am—I am——" And his almost closed lips uttered a name so low that the count himself appeared afraid to hear it. Caderousse, clasping his hands and raising them with a desperate effort,—" Oh ! my God ! my God!" said he, "pardon me for having denied Thee. Pardon me, my God ; receive me, O my Lord !" Caderousse sighed deeply and fell back dead with a groan.

"*One !*" said the count, mysteriously, his eyes fixed on the corpse, disfigured by so awful a death.

CHAPTER LXXXIV

BEAUCHAMP

THE daring attempt to rob the count was the topic of conversation throughout Paris for the next fortnight : the dying man had signed a deposition declaring Benedetto to be the assassin. The count told everyone this adventure had happened during his absence at Auteuil, and that he only knew what was related by the Abbé Busoni. Bertuccio alone turned pale whenever Benedetto's name was mentioned in his presence. De Villefort, being called on to prove the crime, was preparing the brief with the same ardour as he was accustomed to exercise when called on to speak in criminal cases.

But three weeks had already passed, and the attempted robbery and the murder of the robber by his comrade were almost forgotten in anticipation of the marriage of Mademoiselle Danglars to the count Andrea Cavalcanti. Letters had been despatched to M. Cavalcanti, the count's father, who highly approved of the union and promised a wedding gift of a hundred and fifty thousand livres. It was agreed that the three millions should be entrusted to Danglars to improve. The baron adored count Andrea Cavalcanti ; not so Mademoiselle Eugénie Danglars. The baron may have perceived it, but attributing it to caprice, feigned ignorance.

The delay demanded by Beauchamp had nearly expired. Morcerf appreciated the advice of Monte Cristo, to let things die away of their own accord, for no one had identified his father with the traitor at Janina. Albert, however, felt no less insulted. He cherished the thought of the duel, hoping to conceal its true cause even from his seconds. Beauchamp had not been seen since the day he visited Albert. Where he was, no one knew. One morning Albert was awakened by his valet, who announced Beauchamp. Albert found Beauchamp pacing the smoking-room into which he had been shown; on perceiving him Beauchamp stopped.

"Albert," said Beauchamp, with a look of sorrow which stupefied the young man, "let us sit down and talk."

"But," asked Morcerf, impatiently, "what does this mean?"

"It means that I have just returned from Janina."

"You have been to Janina!"

"Albert, had you been a stranger, a foreigner, a simple lord, like that Englishman who came to demand satisfaction three or four months since, and whom I killed to get rid of, I should not have taken this trouble; but I thought this mark of consideration due to you. I took a week to go, another to return, four days of quarantine, and forty-eight hours of stay there; that makes three weeks. I returned last night; and here I am."

"You fear to acknowledge that your correspondent has deceived you? Oh! no self-love, Beauchamp. Acknowledge it, Beauchamp; your courage cannot be doubted."

"My friend," replied the journalist, "I would gladly apologize, but—the paragraph was true!"

"What! that French officer——"

"Yes."

"The traitor who surrendered the castle of the man in whose service he was——"

"Pardon me, my friend, that man was your father!" Albert advanced furiously towards Beauchamp; but the latter restrained him more by a mild look than by his extended hand. "Albert," said he, "here is the proof!"

Albert opened the paper; it was an attestation of four notable inhabitants of Janina, proving that Colonel Fernando Mondego, in the service of Ali Tebelen, had surrendered the castle for two million crowns. Albert tottered and fell, overpowered, in a chair. Beauchamp, who had watched with sincere pity the young man's grief, approached him. "Now, Albert," said he, "you understand me, do you not? I wished to see all, hoping the explanation would be in your father's favour, and that I might do him justice. But, on the contrary, the particulars prove that Fernando Mondego is no other than count Fernando de Morcerf; then, recollecting the honour you had done me, in admitting me to your friendship, I hastened to you to tell you, Albert, in this changing age, the faults of a father cannot be charged upon his children. Do you wish this frightful secret to remain with us? Confided to me, it shall never escape my lips; say, Albert, my friend, do you wish it?"

Albert threw himself on Beauchamp's neck. "Ah! noble fellow!" cried he.

"Take these," said Beauchamp, presenting the papers to Albert.

Albert seized them with a convulsive hand, tore them in pieces; and, trembling lest the least vestige should escape and one day appear to confront him, he approached the wax light, always kept burning for cigars, and consumed every fragment. "Dear, excellent friend!" murmured Albert, still burning the papers.

But the young man's joy was soon turned to mourning.

"Well," said Beauchamp, "what grieves you, my friend?"

"I am broken-hearted," said Albert. "Listen, Beauchamp! I cannot thus, in a moment, relinquish the respect, the confidence, the pride with which a father's untarnished name inspires a son. Oh! Beauchamp, how shall I now approach mine! Ah! my mother, my poor mother!" said Albert, gazing through his tears at his mother's portrait; "if you know this, how much must you suffer?"

"Come," said Beauchamp, taking both his hands, "take courage, my friend."

"But how came the note to be inserted? Some unknown enemy has done this thing."

"The greater reason, therefore, to bear yourself bravely and reserve your strength for the crash should it come."

"You think, then, all is not over yet?" said Albert, horror-stricken.

"I think nothing, my friend; but all things are possible. *À propos*——"

"What?" said Albert, seeing Beauchamp hesitated.

"Are you going to marry Mademoiselle Danglars?"

"How?" said Albert, whose brow reddened: "you think, M. Danglars——"

"I ask you only how your engagement stands? Pray put no construction on my words I do not mean they should convey, and give them no undue weight."

"No," said Albert, "the engagement is broken off."

"Well!" said Beauchamp, "let us call on Monte Cristo; he will revive your spirits, because he never interrogates; and those who ask no questions are the best comforters."

"Gladly," said Albert; "I love him: let us call."

CHAPTER LXXXV

THE JOURNEY

MONTE CRISTO uttered a joyful exclamation on seeing the young people together. "Ah!" said he, "I hope all is over, explained and settled."

"Yes," said Beauchamp; "so let us speak no more of it."

"Albert will tell you," replied the count, "that I gave him the same advice. Look," added he, "I am finishing the most execrable morning's work."

"What is it?" said Albert; "arranging your papers, apparently."

"My papers, thank God, no! my papers are in capital order, because I have none; but M. Cavalcanti's."

"Who," said Albert, with a forced smile, "is to marry Mademoiselle Danglars instead of me, which grieves me cruelly."

"And you, count, have made this match?" asked Beauchamp

"I? I make a match! No, you do not know me; I have done all in my power to oppose it. I have warned M. Danglars of it till I am tired, but he is fascinated with his Lucquois. I have even informed him of a circumstance I consider very serious; the young man was either changed by his nurse, stolen by gipsies, or lost by his tutor, I scarcely know which. Well, all that was useless. They have commissioned me to write to the major to demand papers; and here they are. I send them, but will have nothing more to do with the matter. But what is the matter, Albert? Are you, after all, in love with Mademoiselle Eugénie?"

"I am not aware of it," said Albert, smiling sorrowfully. Beauchamp turned to look at some paintings. "But," continued Monte Cristo, "you are not in your usual spirits?"

"I have a dreadful headache."

"Well! my dear viscount," said Monte Cristo, "I have an infallible remedy to propose to you."

"What is that?"

"A change."

"Indeed!" said Albert.

"Yes, and as I am just now excessively annoyed, I shall go from home. Shall we go together?"

"But what annoys you?"

"My amiable assassin—some former galley-slave, apparently."

"True," said Beauchamp; "I saw it in the paper. Who is this Caderousse?"

"Some provincial, it appears. M. de Villefort heard of him at Marseilles, and M. Danglars recollects having seen him. Consequently, the *procureur* is very active in the affair, and the prefect of police very much interested! and, thanks to that interest, for which I am very grateful, they send me all the robbers of Paris and the neighbourhood, under pretence of their being Caderousse's murderers; so that in three months, if this continue, every robber and assassin in France will have the plan of my house at his fingers' ends. I am resolved to go to some remote corner of the earth, and shall be happy if you will accompany me, viscount. I love the sea."

"Let us go, count."

"Well, viscount, there will be in my courtyard this evening a good travelling britska, in which one may rest as in a bed; M. Beauchamp, it holds four, will you accompany us?"

"Thank you, I have just returned from sea."

"What! have you been to sea?"

"Yes, I have just made a little excursion to the Borromées islands."

"What of that? come with us," said Albert.

"No, dear Morcerf, you know I only refuse when the thing is impossible. Besides, it is important," added he, in a low tone, "that I should remain in Paris just now to watch the paper."

"Ah! you are a good and an excellent friend."

Albert and Beauchamp parted; the pressure of their hands expressed what their tongues could not say before a stranger.

"Beauchamp is a worthy fellow," said Monte Cristo.

"Yes, and a sincere friend; I love him devotedly. But where are we going?"

"Into Normandy, if you like."

"Delightful; shall we be quite retired? have no society, no neighbours?"

"Our companions will be riding-horses, dogs to hunt with, and a fishing-boat."

"Exactly what I wished for; I will apprise my mother of my intention, and return to you."

"But shall you be allowed to go into Normandy? to accompany the mysterious Monte Cristo?"

"You forget, count, that I have often told you of the deep interest my mother takes in you."

"Indeed!" said Monte Cristo, sighing.

" So you see," said Albert, " that instead of opposing, she will encourage me."

" Adieu, then, until five o'clock ; be punctual, and we shall arrive at twelve or one."

" At Tréport ? "

" Yes ; or the vicinity. Meanwhile, viscount, since we cannot perform the journey in less than seven or eight hours, do not keep me waiting."

" Do not fear, I have little to prepare." Monte Cristo smiled as he nodded to Albert, and, after a few minutes' deep meditation, rang the bell twice and Bertuccio entered.

" Bertuccio," said he," I intend going this evening to Normandy; you will have sufficient time before five o'clock ; despatch a messenger to apprise the grooms at the first station. M. de Morcerf will accompany me." Bertuccio obeyed, and in six hours all the horses stationed on the road were ready. Before his departure, the count went to Haidée's apartments, told her his intentions, and resigned everything to her care.

Albert was punctual. The journey became interesting from its rapidity, of which Morcerf had formed no previous idea.

The count put his head out of the window and whistled. Ali, smiling, repeated the sound, grasped the reins with a firm hand, and spurred his horses, whose beautiful manes floated in the breeze. " I never knew till now the delight of speed," said Morcerf, " but where the devil do you get such horses ? are they made to order ? "

" Precisely," said the count ; " six years since I bought a horse in Hungary remarkable for its swiftness. The thirty-two that we shall use to-night are its progeny ; they are all entirely black, with the exception of a star upon the forehead."

" That is perfectly admirable ; but what do you do, count, with all these horses ? "

" When I no longer require them, Bertuccio will sell them to some Eastern vizier, who will empty his coffers to purchase them and refill them by applying the bastinado to his subjects."

" Count, may I suggest one idea ? "

" Certainly."

" It is that, next to you, Bertuccio must be the richest gentleman in Europe."

" You are mistaken, viscount ; I believe he has not a franc in his possession. M. Bertuccio is alone in the world, he uses my property without accounting for the use he makes of it ; he is sure never to leave my service."

" Why ? "

" He is the best servant over whom you have the power of life and death."

" Do you possess that right over Bertuccio ? "

" Yes." There are words which close a conversation as if with an iron door ; such was the count's " yes."

At midnight they arrived at the gate of a beautiful park. The porter was in attendance, he had been apprised by the groom of the last stage of the count's approach. At half-past two in the morning Morcerf was conducted to his apartments, where a bath and supper were prepared. Albert bathed, took his supper, and went to bed. On rising, he went to his window, which opened on a terrace, having the sea in front, and at the back, a pretty park bounded by a small forest. In a creek lay a little sloop, with a narrow keel and high masts, bearing on its flag the Monte Cristo arms, which were a mountain *or*, on a sea *azure*, with a cross *gules* on the shield. Around the schooner lay a number of small fishing-boats belonging to the fishermen of the neighbouring village, as humble subjects awaiting orders from their queen. There, as in every spot where Monte Cristo stopped, life became easy.

Towards the evening of the third day Albert was sleeping in an armchair near the window, when the sound of a horse at full speed on the high road made him look up. He was disagreeably surprised to see his own valet.

" Florentin here ! " cried he, starting up ; " is my mother ill ? " And he hastened to the door. Monte Cristo watched him, he saw him approach the valet, who drew a small sealed parcel from his pocket, containing a newspaper and a letter. " From whom is this ? " said Albert, eagerly.

" From M. Beauchamp," replied Florentin.

" Did he send you ? "

" Yes, sir ; I have come in fifteen hours."

Albert opened the letter with fear, uttered a shriek on reading the first line, and seized the paper.

" Poor young man ! " said Monte Cristo, with a low voice ; " it is true, then, that the sin of the father shall fall on the children to the third and fourth generation." Meanwhile Albert had revived, and continuing to read, he threw back his hair, saying, " Florentin, is your horse fit to return immediately ? "

" It is a poor lame post-horse."

" In what state was the house when you left ? "

" All was quiet ; but on returning from M. Beauchamp's I

found madame in tears. After a moment's reflection, she said, 'Go, Florentin, and fetch him.'"

"Yes, my mother," said Albert, "I will return, and woe to the infamous wretch! But, first, I must——"

He returned, completely changed, to the room where he had left Monte Cristo. "Count," said he, "I thank you for your hospitality, which I would gladly have enjoyed longer; but I must return to Paris."

"My stables are at your command, viscount; but you will kill yourself by riding on horseback; take a postchaise or a carriage."

"No, it would delay me, and fatigue will do me good." Albert reeled as if shot with a cannon-ball, and fell on a chair near the door. Monte Cristo did not see this second weakness; he was at the window, calling, "Ali, a horse for M. Morcerf! quick!" These words restored Albert; he darted from the room, followed by the count. "Thank you!" cried he, throwing himself on his horse. "Read this when I am gone, that you may not be witness of my anger."

The count watched him with a feeling of compassion, and when he had disappeared, read as follows:—

"The French officer in the service of Ali, Pasha of Janina, alluded to three weeks since in the *Impartial*, who not only surrendered the castle of Janina, but sold his benefactor to the Turks, styled himself truly at that time Fernando, as our honourable brother states; but he has since added to his Christian name a title of nobility and a family name. He now calls himself the Count of Morcerf and ranks among the peers."

Thus this terrible secret, which Beauchamp had so generously destroyed, appeared again as an armed phantom.

CHAPTER LXXXVI

THE TRIAL

AT eight o'clock in the morning Albert arrived at Beauchamp's. "Here I am," said Albert.

"Well, my poor friend," replied Beauchamp, "I expected you."

"I need not say, I think you are too faithful and too kind to have spoken of that painful circumstance. Have you the slightest idea whence this terrible blow proceeds?"

"I think I have a clue."

"But first tell me all the particulars of this shameful plot."

Beauchamp related to the young man the following facts :— Two days previously an article had appeared in another paper besides the *Impartial*. Beauchamp hastened to the publisher's office. The editor was reading, with apparent delight, a leading article in the same paper on beet-root sugar, probably a composition of his own.

" Ah ! *pardieu !* " said Beauchamp, " with the paper in your hand, my friend, I need not tell you the cause of my visit."

" What is it ? "

" The article relative to Morcerf."

" Indeed ! Is it not a curious affair ? "

" So curious that I think you are running a great risk of a prosecution for defamation of character."

" Not at all ; we have received with the information all the requisite proofs."

" Who has informed you ? "

" Oh ! that is very simple ; the news was brought to us. A man from Janina brought the formidable bundle of evidence."

Beauchamp left the office to despatch a courier to Morcerf. But he had been unable to send to Albert the following particulars, which he now proceeded to relate ; namely, that the same day a great agitation was manifest in the House of Peers among the usually calm groups of the noble assembly. The count was no favourite with his colleagues. The old nobility laughed at him, the talented repelled him, and the honourable instinctively despised him.

The count de Morcerf alone was ignorant of the news. He arrived at his usual hour, with a proud look and insolent demeanour ; he alighted, passed through the corridors, and entered the house without observing the hesitation of the doorkeepers or the coolness of his colleagues. At length an honourable peer, Morcerf's acknowledged enemy, ascended the tribune with that solemnity which announced the expected moment had arrived. The count did not notice the reference to the article, but at the names Janina and Colonel Fernando, he turned so pale that every member shuddered and fixed his eyes upon him.

The article having been read in painful silence the orator resumed. He stated his scruples and the difficulties of the case and concluded by calling for an examination, which might confound the calumnious report before it had time to spread, and restore M. de Morcerf to the position he had long held in public opinion. Morcerf was so overwhelmed by this unexpected calamity that he could scarcely stammer a few words as he looked round on the assembly. The President put it to the vote, and it was decided the examination should take place. The count was asked what time he required to prepare his defence. "My lords," answered he, "it is not by time I could repel the attack made on me by enemies unknown to me, and, doubtless, hidden in obscurity; it is immediately, and by a thunderbolt, I must repel the flash of lightning which, for a moment, startled me. Oh! that I could, instead of taking up this defence, shed my last drop of blood to prove to my noble colleagues that I am their equal in worth." These words made a favourable impression. "I demand that the examination shall take place as soon as possible, and I will furnish the House with all necessary information."

"What day do you fix?" asked the president.

"To-day I am at your service," replied the count.

A committee of twelve members was chosen to examine the proofs brought forward by Morcerf. The examination would begin at eight o'clock that evening in the committee-room. Morcerf asked leave to retire; he had to collect the documents he had long been preparing against the storm which his sagacity had foreseen.

Albert listened; he knew his father was guilty; and he asked himself how, since he was guilty, he could prove his innocence.

"What next?" asked Albert.

"The evening arrived," Beauchamp continued, "all Paris was in expectation. A young peer of my acquaintance called for me at seven, and, before anyone had arrived, asked a doorkeeper to place me in a box. At eight o'clock all were in their places, and M. de Morcerf entered at the last stroke. His presence produced a good effect. His committee was composed of Liberals, several of whom came forward to shake hands with him.

"At this moment one of the doorkeepers brought in a letter for the President. 'You are at liberty to speak, M. de Morcerf,' said the President, as he unsealed the letter; and the count began his defence, I assure you, Albert, in an eloquent and most skilful manner. He produced the ring, his mark of authority, with which Ali Pasha generally sealed his letters, and which the latter had given him that he might, on his return at any hour of the day or night, or even in his harem, gain access to him. Unfortunately, the negotiation failed, and when he returned to defend his benefactor, he was dead. 'But,' said the count, 'so great was Ali Pasha's confidence, that, on his deathbed, he resigned his favourite mistress and her daughter to my care.'" Albert started on hearing these words; the history of Haidée recurred to him, and he remembered what she had said of that message and the ring, and the manner in which she had been sold and made a slave.

"Meanwhile, the President carelessly opened the letter which had been brought to him; but the first lines aroused his attention: 'M. le Comte,' said he, 'you have said the vizier of Janina had confided his wife and daughter to your care? Have you any idea what is become of them?' 'Yes, sir, I heard they had fallen victims to their sorrow, and, perhaps, to their poverty. I could not seek them, to my great regret.' The President frowned imperceptibly. 'Gentlemen,' said he, 'you have heard M. le Comte de Morcerf's defence. Can you, M. le Comte, produce any witnesses to the truth of what you have asserted?' 'Alas! sir,' replied the count, 'all who surrounded the vizier, or who knew me at his court, are either dead or scattered. I have only the letters of Ali Tebelen, which I have placed before you; the ring, a token of his goodwill, which is here; and, lastly, the most convincing proof I can offer, namely, after an anonymous attack, the absence of all witness against my veracity and the purity of my military life.' The President resumed: 'Gentlemen, and you, M. le Comte, you will not be displeased, I presume, to listen to a letter I have just received on the subject; shall it be read, or shall it be passed over?' The committee decided to hear the letter. The President read:—

"'Mr. President,—I can furnish the committee of inquiry into the conduct of the Lieutenant-General Count de Morcerf in Epirus and in Macedonia with important particulars. I was on the spot at the death of Ali Pasha; I was present during his last moments; I know what is become of Vasiliki and Haidée; I am at the command of the committee, and even claim the honour of being heard. I shall be in the lobby when this note is delivered to you.'

"The doorkeeper was called. 'Is there anyone in the lobby?' said the President. 'Yes, sir.' 'Who is it?' 'A woman, accompanied by a servant.' 'Introduce her,' said the President. Five minutes afterwards the doorkeeper again appeared. Behind the doorkeeper walked a woman enveloped in a large veil, which completely concealed her. The President requested her to throw aside her veil, and it was then seen she was dressed in the Grecian costume, and was remarkably beautiful."

"Ah!" said Albert, "it was she."

"Who?"

"Haidée. But go on, Beauchamp."

"M. de Morcerf," continued Beauchamp, "looked at this female with surprise and terror. The President himself advanced to place a seat for the young lady ; but she declined it. As for the count, he had fallen on his chair, it was evident his legs refused to support him.

" ' Madame,' said the President, ' you have engaged to furnish the committee with some particulars respecting the affair at Janina, and you have stated that you were an eye-witness of the events.' ' I was indeed ! said the stranger. ' In what manner could those events concern you ? ' ' On them depended my father's life,' replied she. ' I am Haidée, the daughter of Ali Tebelen, pasha of Janina, and of Vasiliki, his beloved wife.'

" The count could not have been more overwhelmed if a thunderbolt had fallen at his feet and opened before him a yawning gulf. ' Madame,' replied the President, bowing with profound respect, ' allow me to ask one question, it shall be the last : ' Can you prove the authenticity of what you have now stated ? ' ' I can, sir,' said Haidée, drawing from under her veil a satin satchel highly perfumed ; ' for here is the register of my birth, signed by my father and his principal officers ; that of my baptism, for I was to be brought up in my mother's faith ; and lastly, the record of the sale of my person and that of my mother to the Armenian merchant, El-Kobbir, by the French officer, who, in his infamous bargain with the Porte, had reserved as his part of the booty, the wife and daughter of his benefactor, whom he sold for the sum of four hundred thousand francs." A greenish paleness spread over the count's cheeks, and his eyes became bloodshot at these terrible imputations. Haidée, still calm, handed to the President the record of her sale, registered in Arabic. One of the noble peers, who was familiar with the Arabian language, followed with his eye, as the translator read aloud :—

" ' I, El-Kobbir, a slave-merchant, and furnisher of the harem of his Highness, acknowledge having received for transmission to the Sublime Emperor, from the French lord, count of Monte Cristo, an emerald valued at eight hundred thousand francs, as the ransom of a young Christian slave of eleven years of age, named Haidée, the acknowledged daughter of the late Lord Ali Tebelen, pasha of Janina, and of Vasiliki, his favourite ; she having been sold to me by a French colonel in the service of the vizier Ali Tebelen, named Fernando Mondego.

" ' Given at Constantinople by authority of his Highness in the year 1247 of the Hegira.

" ' Signed EL-KOBBIR.'

" A dreadful silence succeeded the reading of this paper.

'Madame,' said the President, 'may reference be made to the count of Monte Cristo, who is now, I believe, in Paris?' 'Sir,' replied Haidée, 'the count of Monte Cristo, my other father, has been in Normandy the last three days.'

"'Who, then, has counselled you to take this step?' 'Sir,' replied Haidée. 'Since I set my foot in France, and knew the traitor lived in Paris, I have watched carefully. M. le Comte de Monte Cristo surrounds me with every paternal care, and I am ignorant of nothing which passes in the world. I learned what had happened this morning in the House of Peers, and what was to take place this evening—then, I wrote.' 'Then,' remarked the President, 'the count of Monte Cristo knows nothing of your present proceedings?' 'He is unaware of them; but it is a glorious day for me, this on which I find at last an opportunity of avenging my father.'

"The count had not uttered one word the whole of this time; his condition was depicted by sinister lines on his countenance. 'M. de Morcerf,' said the President, 'do you recognize this lady as the daughter of Ali Tebelen, Pasha of Janina?' 'No,' said Morcerf, attempting to rise. Haidée, turned hastily and, seeing the count standing, shrieked. 'You do not know me?' said she; 'well, I recognize you! You are Fernando Mondego, the French officer, who led the troops of my noble father. It is you who surrendered the castle of Janina! It is you who, sent by him to Constantinople, to treat with the emperor for the life or death of your benefactor, brought back a false mandate granting full pardon! It is you who, with that mandate obtained the Pasha's ring, which gave you authority over Selim, the fire-keeper! It is you who stabbed Selim! It is you who sold us, my mother and me, to the merchant, El-Kobbir! Assassin! assassin! assassin! you have still on your brow your master's blood? Look, gentlemen, all!'

"These words had been pronounced with such enthusiasm and evident truth that every eye was fixed on the count's forehead, and he himself passed his hand across it, as if he felt Ali's blood still moist upon it. 'You positively recognize M. de Morcerf as the officer, Fernando Mondego?' 'I do!' cried Haidée. 'My mother had said "Look well at that man, it is he who raised your father's head on the point of a spear; it is he who sold us, it is he who forsook us! Look well at his right hand, on which he has a large wound ⨉ if you forgot his features, you would know him by that hand into which fell one by one the golden pieces of the merchant El-Kobbir!"' 'I know him! Ah! let him say now if he does not recognize me!' Every word fell like a dagger on Morcerf, and as she uttered the last, he hid hastily in his bosom his hand, which had indeed been mutilated by a wound, and fell back on his chair, overwhelmed by wretchedness and despair. This scene completely changed the opinion of the Assembly respecting the accused count.

" 'M. le Comte de Morcerf,' said the President, ' do not allow yourself to be depressed ; answer : the justice of the court is supreme and impartial as that of God ; it will not suffer you to be trampled on by your enemies without giving you an opportunity of defending yourself. Shall further inquiries be made ? Shall two members of the House be sent to Janina ? What is your decision ? '

" 'I have no reply to make,' said the count in a low tone.

" 'Has the daughter of Ali Tebelen spoken the truth ? ' said the President. ' Is she the witness to whose charge you dare not plead " Not guilty ? " ' Have you committed the crimes of which you are accused ? ' The count looked round him with an expression which might have softened tigers, but which could not disarm his judges. Then, with a hasty movement, he tore open his coat, which seemed to stifle him, and flew from the room like a madman ; his footstep was heard one moment in the corridor, then the rattling of his carriage wheels, as he was driven rapidly away. ' Gentlemen,' said the President, when silence was restored, ' is M. le Comte de Morcerf convicted of felony, treason, and outrage ? ' ' Yes,' replied all the members of the committee of inquiry with a unanimous voice.

" Haidée remained until the close of the meeting ; then, drawing her veil over her face, she bowed majestically to the councillors, and left."

CHAPTER LXXXVII

THE CHALLENGE

" Then," continued Beauchamp, " I took advantage of the silence and the darkness to leave the house without being seen. I left with mingled feelings of sorrow and delight. Excuse me, Albert, sorrow on your account, and delight with that noble girl, thus pursuing paternal vengeance."

Albert held his head between his hands ; he raised his face, red with shame and bathed in tears, and seizing Beauchamp's arm,—" My friend," said he, " my life is ended ; I must discover

who pursues me with his hatred ; and when I have found him I
will kill him, or he will kill me. I rely on your friendship to assist
me, Beauchamp, if contempt has not banished it from your
heart."

"Contempt, my friend ! how does this misfortune affect you !
No, that prejudice is forgotten which made the son responsible
for the father's actions. No, Albert, take my advice ; you are
young and rich ; leave Paris, you will return after three or four
years with a Russian princess for a bride, and no one will think
more of what occurred yesterday than if it had happened sixteen
years ago."

"Thank you, my dear Beauchamp, thank you for the excellent
feeling which prompts your advice ; but it cannot be thus. If
you are still the friend you profess to be, help me to discover the
hand that struck the blow."

"Be it so," said Beauchamp ; "if you will seek your enemy, I
will assist you, and I will engage to find him, my honour being
almost as deeply interested as yours."

"Well, then you understand, Beauchamp, that we begin our
research immediately. The calumniator is not yet punished ;
and he may hope he will not be ; but if he thinks so, he deceives
himself."

"I will tell you what I did not like to mention on my return
from Janina. I went, of course, to the chief banker of the town
to make inquiries. At the first word, before I had even mentioned your father's name, 'Ah !' said he, 'I guess what brings
you here.' 'How, and why ?' 'Because a fortnight since I was
questioned on the same subject.' 'By whom ?' 'By a banker
of Paris, my correspondent.' 'Whose name is——' 'Danglars.'"

"If this be true," cried the young man ; "he shall pay me all I
have suffered."

"I do not condemn you, Albert ; I only restrain you. Act
prudently. Do you wish to see M. Danglars ? Let us go immediately."

They sent for a cabriolet. On entering the banker's mansion
they perceived the phaeton and servant of M. Andrea Cavalcanti.

"Ah ! *parbleu !* that's good," said Albert, in a gloomy tone ;
"if M. Danglars will not fight with me, I will kill his son-in-law :
Cavalcanti will fight."

The servant announced the young man ; but the banker, recollecting what had happened the day before, did not wish him
admitted. It was, however, too late ; Albert had followed the

footman, and hearing the order given, forced the door open, and followed by Beauchamp, entered the banker's cabinet.

" Sir," cried the latter, " am I no longer at liberty to receive whom I choose in my house ?   What is your errand with me ? "

" I mean," said Albert, " to propose a meeting in some retired corner where two men having met, one of them will remain on the ground." Danglars turned pale ; Cavalcanti moved a step forward, and Albert turned towards him.

" And you, too," said he, " come if you like, M. le Comte ; you have a claim, being almost one of the family, and I will give as many rendezvous of that kind as I can find persons willing to accept them." Cavalcanti looked at Danglars with a stupefied air ; and the latter, making an effort, advanced between the two young men.

" Sir," said Danglars to Albert, " if you are come to quarrel with this gentleman because I have preferred him to you, I shall resign the case to the *procureur du roi*."

" You mistake, sir," said Morcerf, with a gloomy smile ; " I am not alluding in the least to matrimony, and I only addressed myself to M. Cavalcanti, because he appeared disposed to interfere between us. In one respect you are right, for I am ready to quarrel with everyone to-day ; but you have the first claim, M. Danglars."

" Sir," replied Danglars, pale with anger and fear, " I warn you when I have the misfortune to meet with a mad dog I kill it. Is it my fault that your father has dishonoured himself ? "

" Yes ; miserable wretch ! " cried Morcerf ; " you have not directly made this exposure and brought this sorrow on us, but you provoked it."

" I ? "

" Yes ; you ! How came it known ? "

" I suppose you read it in the paper in the account from Janina ? "

" Who wrote to Janina ? "

" I imagine anyone may write to Janina."

" But one person only wrote ! and that was you ! "

" I doubtless wrote. It appears to me that when about to marry your daughter to a young man it is right to make some inquiries respecting his family ; it is not only a right but a duty."

" You wrote, sir, knowing what answer you would receive."

" I, indeed ! I assure you," cried Danglars, " I solemnly declare to you that I should never have thought of writing to Janina, had I known anything of Ali Pasha's misfortunes."

" Who, then, urged you to write ? Tell me."

" *Pardieu !* it was the most simple thing in the world. I was speaking of your father's past history. The person to whom I addressed my scruples asked me where your father had acquired his property ? I answered, ' in Greece.' ' Then,' said he, ' write to Janina.' "

" And who thus advised you ? "

" Your friend Monte Cristo."

Albert and Beauchamp looked at each other. " Sir," said Beauchamp, who had not yet spoken, " you appear to accuse the count, who is absent from Paris at this moment, and cannot justify himself."

" I accuse no one, sir," said Danglars ; " I relate, and I will repeat before the count what I have said to you."

" Does the count know what answer you received ? "

" Yes ; I showed it to him."

" Did he know my father's Christian name was Fernando and his family name Mondego ? "

" Yes ; I told him that long since ; and I did nothing more than any other would have done in my circumstances, and perhaps less. When the day after the arrival of this answer, your father came, by the advice of Monte Cristo, to ask my daughter's hand for you, I decidedly refused him, but without any explanation or exposure. In short, why should I have any more to do with the affair ? How did the honour or disgrace of M. de Morcerf affect me ? It neither increased nor decreased my income."

Albert felt the colour mounting to his brow ; there was no doubt upon the subject. He felt that Danglars, base as he was, was speaking the truth, at least in part, though probably more from fear than conscience. Besides, what was Morcerf seeking ? It was not whether Danglars or Monte Cristo was more or less guilty ; it was a man who would answer for the offence, whether trifling or serious ; it was a man who would fight, and it was evident Danglars would not fight. And, in addition to this, everything forgotten or unperceived before, presented itself now to his recollection   Monte Cristo knew everything, as he had bought the daughter of Ali Pasha ; and knowing everything, he had advised Danglars to write to Janina. Lastly, he had taken Albert to Normandy when he knew the final blow would fall. There could be no doubt that all had been calculated and previously arranged ; Monte Cristo was in league with his father's enemies. Albert took Beauchamp aside, and communicated these ideas to him.

"You are right," said the latter; "M. Danglars has only been a secondary agent in this business; and it is of M. de Monte Cristo that you must demand an explanation." Albert turned and went out with Beauchamp without appearing to notice Cavalcanti. Danglars accompanied him to the door, where he again assured Albert no motive of personal hatred influenced him against the count de Morcerf.

CHAPTER LXXXVIII

THE INSULT

AT the banker's door Beauchamp stopped Morcerf. "I told you it was of M. de Monte Cristo you must demand an explanation."

"We are going to his house."

"Reflect, Morcerf, one moment before you go."

"On what shall I reflect?"

"On the importance of the step you are taking."

"I only fear one thing, namely, that I shall not find a man who will fight."

"Do not be alarmed," said Beauchamp, "he will meet you. My only fear is that he will be too strong for you."

"My friend," said Morcerf, with a sweet smile, "that is what I wish; the happiest thing would be to die in my father's stead; that would save us all."

They ordered the driver to take them to No. 30, Champs Élysées. Beauchamp wished to go in alone; but Albert observed, as this was an unusual circumstance, he might be allowed to depart from the etiquette of duels. Beauchamp yielded and contented himself with following Morcerf. The count had just arrived, but he was bathing, and had forbidden that anyone should be admitted. "But after his bath?" asked Morcerf.

"My master will go to dinner."

"And after dinner?"

"He will sleep an hour."

"Then?"

"He is going to the opera."

"Are you sure of it?"

"My master has ordered his horses at eight o'clock."

"Very good," replied Albert; "that is all I wished to know." Then, turning towards Beauchamp, he said, "I depend on your accompanying me to the opera; and, if you can, bring Château-Renaud with you."

Beauchamp promised to call for Albert at a quarter before eight. On his return home the latter expressed his wish to Franz, Debray, and Morrel to see them at the opera that evening. Then he went to see his mother, who, since the events of the day before, had refused to see anyone, and had kept her room. He found her in bed, overwhelmed with grief at this public humiliation.

" My dear mother," said he, " do you know if M. de Morcerf has any enemy ? " Mercédès started.

" My son, persons in the count's situation have many secret enemies. Those who are known are not the most dangerous."

" I know it, and appeal to your penetration. You noticed, on the evening of the ball, M. de Monte Cristo would eat nothing in our house." Mercédès raised herself on her feverish arm.

" M. de Monte Cristo ! " she exclaimed ; " and how is he connected with the question you asked me ? "

" M. de Monte Cristo is almost an Oriental, and it is customary with them to secure full liberty of revenge by not eating or drinking in the house of their enemies."

" Do you say M. de Monte Cristo is our enemy ? " replied Mercédès, becoming paler than the sheet which covered her. " Who told you so ? Oh ! I entreat you, my son ; even more, my prayer is, retain his friendship. What has the count done ? Three days since you were with him in Normandy ; only three days since we looked on him as our best friend."

An ironical smile passed over Albert's lips, Mercédès saw it, and, with her double instinct of a woman and a mother, she guessed all ; but, prudent and strong-minded, she concealed both her sorrows and her fears. Albert was silent ; an instant later the countess resumed. " You came to inquire after my health ; I am not well. You should instal yourself here and cheer my solitude. I do not wish to be left alone."

" My mother," said the young man, " you know how gladly I would obey your wish ; but an urgent and important affair obliges me to leave you the whole evening."

Scarcely had he shut the door when Mercédès called a confidential servant, and ordered him to follow Albert wherever he should go that evening, and to come and tell her immediately what he observed. Then she rang for her lady's maid, and, weak as she was, she dressed in order to be ready for whatever might happen. The footman's mission was an easy one. Albert went to his room and dressed with unusual care. At ten minutes to eight Beauchamp arrived ; he had seen Château-Renaud, who had promised to be in the orchestra before the curtain was raised.

Both got into Albert's *coupé*, who, having no reason to conceal where he was calling, called aloud, "To the Opera." In his impatience, he had arrived before the beginning of the performance.

The bell summoned him to his seat, and he entered the orchestra with Château-Renaud and Beauchamp. At last, at the beginning of the second act, the door opened, and Monte Cristo entered. Morrel followed him, and looked for his sister and brother-in-law; he soon discovered them in another box, and kissed his hand to them.

The count, although not noticing Albert, did not lose sight of him; and when the curtain fell at the end of the second act he saw him leave the orchestra with his two friends. He was at the moment conversing cheerfully with Morrel, but he was well prepared for what might happen. The door opened, and Monte Cristo, turning round, saw Albert, pale and trembling, followed by Beauchamp and Château-Renaud.

"Well," cried he, "my cavalier has attained his object? Good."

"We are not come here, sir, to exchange hypocritical expressions of politeness, or false professions of friendship," said Albert, "but to demand an explanation, count."

"An explanation at the Opera?" said the count. "Little acquainted as I am with the habits of Parisians, I should not have thought this the place for such a demand."

"Still, if people will shut themselves up," said Albert, "and cannot be seen, we must avail ourselves of the opportunity whenever they are to be seen."

"I am not difficult of access, sir; for yesterday, if my memory does not deceive me, you were at my house,"

"Yesterday I was at your house, sir," said the young man; "because then I knew not who you were." In pronouncing these words Albert had raised his voice so as to be heard by those in the adjoining boxes and in the lobby.

"I do not understand you, sir," replied Monte Cristo; "and if I did, your tone is too high. I am at home here, and I alone have a right to raise my voice above another's. Leave the box, sir!" Monte Cristo pointed towards the door with the most commanding dignity.

"Ah! I shall know how to make you leave your home!" replied Albert, clasping in his convulsed grasp a glove, which Monte Cristo did not lose sight of.

"Well, well!" said Monte Cristo, quietly, "I see you wish to quarrel with me; but I would give you one counsel, and do not forget it; it is a bad habit to make a display of a challenge.

Display is not becoming to everyone, M. de Morcerf." At this name a murmur of astonishment passed round the group of spectators of this scene. Albert understood the allusion in a moment, and was about to throw his glove at the count, when Morrel seized his hand, while Beauchamp and Château-Renaud, fearing the scene would surpass the limits of a challenge, held him back. But Monte Cristo merely extended his hand, and taking the damp, crushed glove from the clenched hand of the young man,—" Sir," said he, in a solemn tone, " I consider your glove thrown, and will return it you round a bullet. Now leave me, or I will summon my servants to throw you out."

Albert stepped back, and Morrel closed the door. Monte Cristo took up his glass again as if nothing had happened. Morrel whispered. " What have you done to him ? "

" I ? Nothing—at least personally," said Monte Cristo.

" But there must be some cause for this strange scene."

" The count de Morcerf's adventure exasperates the young man "

" 'Have you anything to do with it ? "

" It was by Haidée the House was informed of his father's treason."

" Then," said Morrel, " I understand it all, and this scene was premeditated. Albert wrote to request me to come to the opera, doubtless that I might be a witness to the insult he meant to offer you. But what will you do with him ? "

" What will I do with Albert ? As certainly, Maximilian, as I now press your hand, I will kill him before ten o'clock to-morrow morning." Morrel, in his turn, took Monte Cristo's hand in both of his, and he shuddered to feel how cold and steady it was.

" Ah ! count," said he, " his father loves him so much ! "

" Do not speak to me of that ! " said Monte Cristo, with the first movement of anger he had betrayed ; " I will make him suffer."

Morrel, amazed, let fall Monte Cristo's hand. " Count ! count ! " said he.

" Dear Maximilian," interrupted the count, " listen how adorably Duprez is singing."

Morrel felt it was useless to say more. The curtain, which had been drawn up during the scene with Albert, again fell, and a rap was heard at the door.

" Come in ! " said Monte Cristo, without betraying the least emotion, and Beauchamp appeared.

" Sir, said he, " Albert was wrong, I acknowledge, to betray so much anger, and I come on my own account to apologize for him. I believe you too gentlemanly to refuse giving him some explanation concerning your connexion with Janina. Then I will add two words about the young Greek girl." Monte Cristo motioned him to be silent.

"Say no more, I entreat you. I do what I please, M. Beauchamp, and it is always well done."

"Sir," replied the young man, "honest men are not to be paid in such coin. I require honourable guarantees."

"I am, sir, a living guarantee," replied Monte Cristo, motionless, but with a threatening look; "we have both blood in our veins which we wish to shed—that is our mutual guarantee. Tell the viscount so, and that to-morrow, before ten o'clock, I shall see what colour his is."

"Then, I have only to make arrangements for the duel," said Beauchamp.

"It is quite immaterial to me," said Monte Cristo. "Tell your man that although I am the insulted party, I leave him the choice of arms, as I am sure to gain."

"Sure to gain!" repeated Beauchamp, looking with amazement at the count.

"Certainly," said Monte Cristo, slightly shrugging his shoulders, "otherwise I would not fight with M. de Morcerf. I shall kill him: I cannot help it. By a single line this evening at my house let me know the arms and the hour : I do not like to be kept waiting."

"Pistols, then, at eight o'clock, in the Bois de Vincennes," said Beauchamp, not knowing whether he were dealing with an arrogant braggadocio or a supernatural being.

"Very well, sir," said Monte Cristo. Beauchamp left the box, perfectly amazed.

"Now," said Monte Cristo, turning towards Morrel, "I may depend upon you, may I not ? "

"Certainly," said Morrel, "I am at your service, count; still——"

"What ? "

"It is desirable I should know the real cause."

"The young man himself is acting blindfolded, and knows not the true cause, which is known only to God and to me; but I give you my word, Morrel, that God Who does know it will be on our side."

"Enough," said Morrel, "who is your second witness ? "

"Do you think Emanuel would oblige me ? "

"I will answer for him, count."

"Hush! the curtain is rising. Listen! I never lose a note of this opera if I can avoid it; the music of ' William Tell ' is so sweet."

CHAPTER LXXXIX

THE NIGHT

M. DE MONTE CRISTO waited, according to his usual custom, until Duprez had sung his famous " Suivez-moi ; " then he rose, and went out. Then he stepped into his *coupé*, calm and smiling, and was at home in five minutes. No one who knew the count could mistake his expression, when, on entering, he said, " Ali, bring me my pistols with the ivory cross."

Ali brought the box to his master. These were particular pistols, which Monte Cristo had had made to shoot at a target in his room. He was just taking one in his hand, when the door opened, and Baptistin entered. Before he had spoken a word the count perceived in the next room a woman, veiled, who had followed closely after Baptistin and rushed in.

" Who are you, madame ? "

The stranger cast one look around her, then joining her hands, she said with an accent of despair, " Edmond, you will not kill my son ? "

The count retreated a step, uttered a slight exclamation, and let fall the pistol he held.

" What name did you pronounce then, Madame de Morcerf ? " said he.

" Yours ! " cried she, throwing back her veil, " yours, which I alone, perhaps, have not forgotten. Edmond, it is net Madame de Morcerf who is come to you, it is Mercédès."

" Mercédès is dead, madame, " said Monte Cristo ; " I know no one of that name."

" Mercédès lives, sir, she remembers, and she needs not to inquire what hand has dealt the blow at M. de Morcerf."

" Fernando, do you mean ? " replied Monte Cristo, with bitter irony ; " since we are recalling names, let us remember them all." Monte Cristo pronounced the name of Fernando with such hatred that Mercédès felt a thrill of terror run through every vein.

" You see, Edmond, I am not mistaken, and have cause to say, ' Spare my son ! ' "

" And who told you, madame, I have any hostile intentions against your son ? "

"A mother has a twofold sight. I guessed all; I followed him this evening to the Opera, and have seen all."

"If you have seen all, madame, you know that the son of Fernando has publicly insulted me," said Monte Cristo, with awful calmness.

"Oh! for pity's sake."

"You have seen that he would have thrown his glove in my face if Morrel, one of my friends, had not stopped him."

"Listen to me; my son has also guessed who you are; he attributes his father's misfortunes to you."

"Madame, you are mistaken, they are not misfortunes—it is a punishment. If I have sworn to revenge myself, it is not on the French captain, nor on the count de Morcerf, but on the fisherman Fernando, the husband of the Catalan Mercédès."

"Ah! sir," cried the countess, "how terrible a vengeance for a fault which fatality made me commit! For I am the only culprit, Edmond; and if you owe revenge to anyone, it is to me, who had not courage to bear your absence and my solitude."

"But," exclaimed Monte Cristo, "why was I absent? And why were you alone?"

"Because you had been arrested, Edmond, and were a prisoner."

"And why was I arrested? Why was I a prisoner?"

"I do not know," said Mercédès.

"You do not, madame; at least, I hope not. But I will tell you. I was arrested and became a prisoner, because under the arbour of La Réserve, the day before I was to marry you, a man named Danglars wrote this letter which the fisherman Fernando himself posted." Monte Cristo went to a secrétaire, opened a drawer by a spring, from which he took a paper which had lost its original colour, and the ink of which had become a rusty hue; this he placed in the hands of Mercédès. Mercédès read with terror the following lines:—

"Monsieur the Procureur de Roi is warned by a friend to the throne and religion that one Edmond Dantès, mate of the vessel *Pharaon*, which arrived in port this morning from Smyrna, after having touched at Naples and Porto Ferrajo, has been commissioned by Murat with a letter for the Usurper, and by the Usurper, with a letter for the Bonapartist Committee at Paris. Proof of this crime will be obtained on arresting him, for the letter will be found either on his person, or in his father's house, or in his cabin on board the *Pharaon*."

"How dreadful!" said Mercédès. "And the result of that letter——"

"You well know, madame, was my arrest; but you do not know how long that arrest lasted. You do not know that I remained for fourteen years within a quarter of a league of you, in a dungeon in the Château d'If. You do not know that each day of those fourteen years I renewed the vow of vengeance which I had made the first day; and yet I knew not you had married Fernando, my calumniator, and that my father had died of hunger!"

"Can it be?" cried Mercédès, shuddering.

"That is what I heard on leaving my prison, and that is why, on account of the living Mercédès and my deceased father, I have sworn to revenge myself on Fernando; and—I have revenged myself."

"And you are sure the unhappy Fernando did that?"

"I am satisfied, madame, he did what I have told you; besides that is not much more odious than a Frenchman, by adoption, passing over to the English; a Spaniard by birth, fighting against the Spaniards; a stipendiary of Ali, betraying and murdering Ali. Well! the French did not avenge themselves on the traitor; the Spaniards did not shoot the traitor; Ali, in his tomb, left the traitor unpunished; but I, betrayed, sacrificed, buried, have risen from my tomb, by the grace of God, to punish that man. He sends me for that purpose, and here I am."

The poor woman's legs bent under her; and she fell on her knees. "Forgive, Edmond, forgive for my sake, who love you still!"

The dignity of the wife stopped the enthusiasm of the lover and the mother. Her forehead almost touched the carpet, when the count sprang forward and raised her. Then, seated on a chair, she looked at the manly countenance of Monte Cristo, on which grief and hatred still disclosed a threatening expression. "Not crush that accursed race!" murmured he; "abandon my purpose at the moment of its accomplishment! Impossible, madame, impossible!"

"Edmond," said the poor mother, "when I call you Edmond, why do you not call me Mercédès?"

"Mercédès!" repeated Monte Cristo; "Mercédès! Well! yes, you are right, that name has still its charms. O Mercédès! I have uttered your name with the sigh of melancholy, with the groan of sorrow, with the last effort of despair. Mercédès! I must revenge myself, for I suffered fourteen years."

"Revenge yourself, then, Edmond," cried the poor mother; "but let your vengeance fall on the culprits; on him, on me, but not on my son ! " Monte Cristo groaned, and seized his hair with both hands.

"Edmond," continued Mercédès, her arms extended towards the count, "since I first knew you I have adored your name, have respected your memory. Edmond, if you knew all the prayers I have addressed to God for you while I thought you were living and since I have thought you must be dead ! What could I do for you, Edmond, besides pray and weep ? Listen ; during ten years I dreamed each night the same dream. I had been told you had endeavoured to escape ; that you had taken the place of another prisoner ; that you had slipped into the winding sheet of a dead body ; that you had been precipitated alive from the top of the Château d'If ; and the cry you uttered as you dashed upon the rocks first revealed to your gaolers that they were your murderers. Well, Edmond, I swear to you by the head of that son for whom I entreat your pity—Edmond, during ten years I have seen every night men balancing something shapeless and unknown at the top of a rock ; during ten years I have heard each night a terrible cry which has awoke me, shuddering and cold. And I, too, Edmond—oh ! believe me—guilty as I was—oh ! yes, I, too, have suffered much ! "

"Have you felt your father die in your absence ? " cried Monte Cristo ; " have you seen the woman you loved giving her hand to your rival while you were perishing at the bottom of a dungeon ? "

"No," interrupted Mercédès, " but I have seen him whom I loved on the point of murdering my son." Mercédès pronounced these words with an accent of such despair, that Monte Cristo could not restrain a sob. The lion was daunted ; the avenger was conquered.

"What do you ask of me ? " said he. "Your son's life ? Well, he shall live ! "

Mercédès uttered a cry which made the tears start from Monte Cristo's eyes ; but these tears disappeared almost instantaneously, for God had sent an angel to collect them ; far more precious were they in His eyes than the richest pearls of Guzerat and Ophir.

"Oh ! " said she, seizing the count's hand, and raising it to her lips, "now you are what I dreamt you were, such as I always loved you. Oh, now I may say so."

"So much the better," replied Monte Cristo, "as that poor Edmond will not have long to be loved by you. Death is about to return to the tomb, the phantom to retire in darkness."

"What do you say, Edmond ? "

"I say, since you command me, Mercédès, I must die."

" But the duel will not take place, Edmond, since you forgive ? "

" It will take place," said Monte Cristo, in a most solemn tone, " but instead of your son's blood, mine will flow." Mercédès shrieked, and sprang towards Monte Cristo, but suddenly stopping :

" Edmond," said she, and her eyes were wet with tears, " how noble it is of you, how great the action you have just performed ; how sublime to have taken pity on a poor woman who offered herself to you with every chance against her ! Alas ! I am grown old with grief more than with years, and cannot now remind my Edmond by a smile, or by a look, of that Mercédès with whom he once spent so many happy hours. Ah ! believe me, Edmond, I told you I too had suffered much ; I repeat it, it is melancholy to pass one's life without having one joy to recall, without preserving a single hope ; but that proves that all is not yet over. No ! it is not finished, I feel it by what remains in my heart. Oh ! I repeat it, Edmond ; what you have just done is beautiful,—it is sublime."

" You say so now, Mercédès, yet what would you say if you knew the extent of the sacrifice I make to you ? But, no, no, you cannot imagine what I lose in sacrificing my life."

" Edmond," said Mercédès, " I have but one word more to say to you." The count smiled bitterly. " Edmond," continued she, " I have seen you again—and have found you as noble and as great as formerly you were. Adieu, Edmond, adieu, and thank you."

But the count did not answer. Mercédès opened the door of the room and disappeared before he had recovered from the profound reverie into which his thwarted vengeance had plunged him. The clock of the Invalides struck one when the carriage which conveyed Madame de Morcerf away rolled on the pavement of the Champs Élysées, and made Monte Cristo raise his head. " What a fool I was," said he, " not to tear my heart out on the day when I resolved to revenge myself ! "

CHAPTER XC

THE MEETING

AFTER Mercédès had left Monte Cristo a gloomy shadow seemed to overspread everything. " What ! " said he to himself, " what ! this edifice which I have been so long preparing,—which I have reared with so much care and toil, is to crumble at a single touch, a word, even a slight breath ! What is death but one step

U

more towards repose ? No, it is not existence that I regret, but the ruin of my projects, so slowly carried out, so laboriously framed. Oh ! shall I, whom fourteen years of despair and ten of hope had rendered a believer in Providence, shall I once more become a fatalist ? And all because my heart, which I thought dead, was only sleeping ; because it has awakened and has beaten again ; because I have yielded to the pain of the emotion excited in my breast by a woman's voice. Yet," continued the count, "it is impossible that so noble-minded a woman should thus, through selfishness, consent to my death when in the prime of life and strength. No, she must have conceived some pathetic scene ; she will come and throw herself between us, and what would be sublime here will appear there ridiculous. I ridiculous ! No, I would rather die."

By thus exaggerating to his own mind the anticipated ill fortune of the next day, to which he had condemned himself by promising Mercédès to spare her son, the count at last exclaimed—" Folly ! folly ! folly ! to carry generosity so far as to place myself as a mark for that young man to aim at. He will never believe my death was a suicide ; and yet it is important the world should know that I have consented, by my free will, to stop my arm, already raised to strike, and that with that arm, so powerful against others, I have struck myself. It must be, it shall be."

Seizing a pen, he drew a paper from a secret drawer in his bureau, and at the bottom of that paper, which was no other than his will, made since his arrival in Paris, wrote a codicil, clearly explaining the nature of his death.

While thus agitated, the first rays of dawn pierced his windows, and shone upon the pale blue paper on which he had drawn up his justification. It was five o'clock in the morning, when a slight noise, which appeared like a stifled sigh, reached his ear. He arose, and quietly opening the door of the drawing-room, saw Haidée, who had fallen on a chair with her arms hanging down, and her beautiful head thrown back. The noise of the door did not awaken her, and Monte Cristo gazed at her with affectionate regret. "Mercédès remembered she had a son, and I forgot I had a daughter. Poor Haidée ! she wished to see me to speak to me. I cannot die without confiding her to someone." He resumed his seat and wrote under the other lines,—

"I bequeath to Maximilian Morrel, captain, and son of my former patron, Pierre Morrel, shipowner at Marseilles, the sum of twenty millions, a part of which may be offered to his sister Julie and brother-in-law Emanuel, if he does not fear this increase of fortune may mar their happiness. If his heart is free, and he will marry Haidée, the daughter of Ali, Pasha of Janina, he will thus accomplish my last wish. This will has already constituted Haidée heiress of the rest of my fortune, which, without the twenty millions, and the legacies to my servants, may still amount to sixty millions."

He was finishing the last line when a cry behind him made him start, and the pen fell from his hand. "Haidée," said he, "did you read it?"

"Oh! my lord," said she, "why are you writing thus at such an hour? why are you bequeathing all your fortune to me? Are you going to leave me?'

"I am going on a journey, dear child," said Monte Cristo, with an expression of infinite tenderness and melancholy; "and if any misfortune should happen to me, I wish my daughter to be happy."

Haidée smiled sorrowfully, and shook her head. "Do you think of dying, my lord?"

"The wise man has said, 'It is good to think of death,' child."

"Well, if you die," said she, "bequeath your fortune to others; for, if you die I shall require nothing," and, taking the paper, she tore it in four pieces and fell fainting on the floor. The count raised her in his arms, and seeing that sweet pale face, the idea occurred to him for the first time, that perhaps she loved him otherwise than as a daughter loves a father.

"Alas!" murmured he, with intense suffering; "I might then have been happy yet." He carried Haidée to her room, resigned her to the care of her attendants, and returning to his room again copied the destroyed will.

As he was finishing, a cabriolet entered the yard. Monte Cristo approached the window, and saw Maximilian and Emanuel alight. "Good!" said he; "it was time," and he sealed his will with three seals. One moment afterwards he heard a noise in the drawing-room, and went to open the door himself. Morrel was there, he had come twenty minutes before the time appointed..

"I am, perhaps, come too soon, count," said he; "but I frankly acknowledge I have not closed my eyes all night, nor has anyone in my house slept. I required to see you strong in your courageous assurance, to recover myself."

"Ah!" cried the count, "it is a happy day to feel I am beloved by a man like you." Then he rang the bell and handing a document to Ali, who had come at once, bade him take it to his solicitor. " It is my will, Morrel, and when I am dead, you will examine it."

" Dead ! *you* dead ! "

" Must I not be prepared for everything, dear friend ? But tell me, what did you do yesterday after leaving me ? "

" I went to see Beauchamp and Château-Renaud to get an exchange of weapons, to substitute the sword for the pistol."

" Yes : and you failed ? "

" Your skill is too formidable. They refused pointblank."

" Morrel," said the count, " have you ever seen me fire a pistol ? "

" Never."

" Well, we have time ; look." Monte Cristo took the pistol he held in his hands when Mercédès entered, and, fixing an ace or clubs against the iron-plate, with three shots he successively shot off the three sides of the club. At each shot Morrel turned pale. " It is astonishing ! " said he, " look, Emanuel." Then turning towards Monte Cristo : " Count," said he, " in the name of all that is dear to you, I entreat you not to kill Albert ! The unhappy youth has a mother."

" You are right," said Monte Cristo ; " and I have none." These words were uttered in a tone which made Morrel shudder. " You are the offended party, count."

" Doubtless ; what does that imply ? "

" That you will fire first."

" I fire first ? "

" The only chance for Albert's safety, then, will arise from your emotion."

" I suffer from emotion ? " said Monte Cristo. " I will tell you, Morrel," said the count, " that I do not need entreating to spare the life of M. de Morcerf ; he shall be so well spared that he will return quietly with his two friends, while I——"

" And you ? "

" My dear Morrel, M. de Morcerf will kill me."

" But what has happened, then, since last evening, count ? "

" The same thing which happened to Brutus the night before the battle of Philippi ; I have seen a phantom."

" And that phantom——"

" Told me, Morrel, I had lived long enough." Monte Cristo drew out his watch. " Let us go," said he, " it is five minutes past seven, and the appointment was for eight o'clock." A carriage was in readiness at the door. As the clock struck eight, they drove up to the place of meeting.

" We are the first," said Morrel, looking out of the window.

" Excuse me, sir," said Baptistin, who had followed his master with indescribable terror, " but I see a carriage under the trees."

Monte Cristo drew Morrel a step or two behind his brother-in-law. " Maximilian," said he, " are your affections free ? " Morrel looked at Monte Cristo with astonishment. " I do not seek your confidence, my dear friend. I only ask you a simple question : answer it—that is all I require."

" I love a young girl, count ! "

" Do you love her much ? "

" More than my life ! "

" Another hope defeated ! " said the count. Then, with a sigh, " Poor Haidée ! " murmured he.

" In truth, count, if I knew less of you, I should think you were less brave than you are."

" Because I sigh when thinking of someone I am leaving ? Come, Morrel, it is not like a soldier to be so bad a judge of courage. Do I regret life ? I know the world is a drawing-room, from which we must retreat politely and honestly ; that is, with a bow, and all debts of honour paid."

Morrel advanced towards Beauchamp and Château-Renaud, who, seeing his intention, came to meet him. The three young people bowed to each other courteously.

" Excuse me, gentlemen," said Morrel, " but I do not see M. de Morcerf."

" He sent us word this morning," replied Château-Renaud, " that he would meet us on the ground."

" There is a carriage coming," said Château-Renaud. It advanced rapidly along one of the avenues leading towards the open space where they were assembled. " You are doubtless provided with pistols, gentlemen ? M. de Monte Cristo yields his right of using his."

" We had anticipated this kindness on the part of the count," said Beauchamp, " and I have brought some arms which I bought eight or ten days since, thinking to want them on a similar occasion."

" Gentlemen," said Château-Renaud, " it is not Morcerf coming in that carriage. Ma foi ! it is Franz and Debray ! " The two young men he announced approached. " What chance brings you here ? " said Château-Renaud, shaking hands with each.

" Because," said Debray, " Albert sent this morning to request us to come.

" But, after all these arrangements, he does not come himself," said Château-Renaud ; " Albert is ten minutes after time."

" There he comes ! " said Beauchamp : " on horseback, at full gallop, followed by a servant."

" How imprudent ! " said Château-Renaud; " to come on horseback to fight with the pistol, after all the instructions I gave him."

Meanwhile Albert had arrived within ten paces of the group formed by the five young men. He jumped from his horse, threw the bridle on his servant's arm, and joined them. He was pale, and his eyes were red and swollen ; it was evident he had not slept. " I thank you, gentlemen," said he, " for having complied with my request ; I feel extremely grateful for this mark of friendship."

" M. Morrel," said Château-Renaud, " will you apprise the count of Monte Cristo that M. de Morcerf is arrived, and we are at his command ? " Morrel was preparing to fulfil his commission.

" Stop, gentlemen ! " said Albert ; " I have two words to say to the count of Monte Cristo."

" In private ? " asked Morrel.

" No, sir ; before all who are here."

Morrel, rejoiced at this unexpected incident, went to fetch the count, who was walking in a retired path with Emanuel.

The count advanced, accompanied by Maximilian and Emanuel; his serene look formed a singular contrast to Albert's grief-stricken face.

When at three paces distant Albert and the count stopped.

" Approach, gentlemen," said Albert ; " I wish you not to lose one word of what I am about to have the honour of saying to the count of Monte Cristo ; for it must be repeated by you to all who will listen to it, strange as it may appear to you."

" Proceed, sir," said the count.

" Sir," said Albert, at first with a tremulous voice, which gradually became firmer. " It is not Fernando Mondego's treachery towards Ali Pasha which induces me so readily to excuse you, but the treachery of the fisherman Fernando towards you, and the unheard-of miseries which were its consequences ; and I say, and proclaim it publicly, that you were justified in revenging yourself on my father ; and I, his son, thank you for not using greater severity."

It was as though a thunderbolt had fallen in the midst of the small company. The Count raised his eyes to Heaven with a look of infinite gratitude. He recognized the influence of Mercédès.

" Now, sir," said Albert, " if you think my apology sufficient, pray give me your hand. Next to the merit of infallibility which you appear to possess, I rank that of candidly acknowledging a fault. But this confession concerns me only. I acted well as a man, but you have acted better than man. An angel alone could have saved one of us from death—that angel came from heaven, if not to make us friends (which, alas! fatality renders impossible), at least to make us esteem each other."

Monte Cristo, with moistened eye, heaving breast, and lips half open, extended to Albert a hand, which the latter pressed with a sentiment resembling respectful fear. "Gentlemen," said he, "M. de Monte Cristo receives my apology; I had acted hastily towards him."

"What has happened during the night?" asked Beauchamp of Château-Renaud; "we appear to cut sorry figures here."

As for Monte Cristo, his head hung down, his arms were powerless; bowing under the weight of twenty-four years' reminiscences, he thought not of Albert, of Beauchamp, of Château-Renaud, or of any of that group, but of that courageous woman who had come to plead for her son's life, to whom he had offered his, and who had now saved it by the revelation of a dreadful family secret, capable of destroying for ever, in that young man's heart, every feeling of filial piety.

"Providence still!" murmured he; "now only am I fully convinced of being the emissary of God!"

CHAPTER XCI

THE MOTHER AND SON

THE count of Monte Cristo bowed to the young men with a melancholy and dignified smile, and got into his carriage with Maximilian and Emanuel. Albert looked at his two friends as if to ask their opinion of what he had done.

"My dear friend," said Beauchamp, who had either the most feeling or the least dissimulation, "allow me to congratulate you: this is a very unhoped-for conclusion of a very disagreeable affair. It is magnificent to be able to exercise so much self-control!"

"Assuredly; as for me, I should have been incapable of it," said Château-Renaud, with significant coolness.

"Gentlemen," interrupted Albert, "I think you did not understand that something very serious had passed between M. de Monte Cristo and myself."

"Possibly," said Beauchamp immediately; "but every simpleton would not be able to understand your heroism. May I give you a friendly counsel ? Set out for Naples, the Hague, or Saint Petersburg. Seek quietude and oblivion, so that you may return peaceably to France after a few years. Am I not right, M. de Château-Renaud ? "

" That is my opinion," said the gentleman ; " nothing induces serious duels so much as a fruitless one."

" Thank you, gentlemen," replied Albert, with a smile of indifference ; " I shall follow your advice not so much because you give it, as because I had already intended to quit France."

" Farewell, Albert," said Beauchamp suddenly. " Farewell," said Château-Renaud in his turn. Albert's lips scarcely whispered, " Farewell ! " but his look was more explicit ; it embraced a whole poem of restrained anger, proud disdain, and generous indignation. Presently, releasing his horse from the tree to which his servant had fastened it, he galloped off towards Paris. In a quarter of an hour he was entering the hotel of the Rue du Helder. As he alighted, he thought he saw behind the curtain of the count's bedroom his father's pale face ; Albert turned away his head with a sigh, and went to his own apartments. Then he took away his mother's portrait, with its oaken frame, leaving the gilt frame, from which he removed it, black and empty. He arranged all his beautiful Turkish arms, his fine English guns, his Japanese china, his cups mounted in silver, his artistic bronzes ; threw into a drawer of his secrétaire, which he left open, all the pocket money he had about him ; made an exact inventory of all, and placed it in the most conspicuous part of the table.

At the beginning of this work his servant, notwithstanding his prohibition, came to his room.

" Pardon me, sir," replied the valet ; " you had forbidden me to disturb you, but the count of Morcerf had called me ; and since he has sent for me, it is doubtless to question me on what has happened. What must I answer ? "

" You will say I apologized to the count of Monte Cristo."

The valet bowed and retired ; and Albert returned to his inventory. As he was finishing this work, the wheels of a carriage shaking his window, attracted his attention ; he approached the window, and saw his father get into it, and it drove away. The door was scarcely closed when Albert bent his steps to his mother's room ; and no one being there to announce him, he advanced to her bedroom, and, distressed by what he saw and guessed, stopped for one moment at the door. As if the same soul had animated these two beings, Mercédès was doing the same in her apartments as he had just done. Everything was in order : laces, dresses, jewels, linen, money, all were arranged in the drawers, and the countess was carefully collecting the keys.

" Oh, my mother," exclaimed Albert, so overcome he could scarcely speak ; " you cannot have made the same resolution that I have, for I am come to bid adieu to your house, and—and to you."

" I also," replied Mercédès, " am going, and I acknowledge I had depended on your accompanying me ; have I deceived myself ? "

" My mother," said Albert, with firmness, " I cannot make you share the fate I have planned for myself. I will ask Franz to lend me the small sum I shall require to supply my present wants."

" You, my poor child, suffer poverty and hunger ! Oh ! say not so, it will break my resolution."

" But not mine, mother," replied Albert. " I am young, I believe I am courageous, and since yesterday I have learned the power of will. No, my mother, from this moment I have done with the past, and accept nothing from it ; not even a name, because your son cannot bear the name of a man who ought to blush before another."

" Albert, my child," said Mercédès, " if I had a stronger heart that is the counsel I would have given you ! A pure heart like yours wants a spotless name, take my father's ; it was Herrera, I am sure, my Albert, whatever may be your career, you will soon render that name illustrious. Then, my friend, return to the world still more brilliant from the reflection of your former sorrows ; and if I am wrong, let me cherish these hopes, for I have no future to look forward to ; for me the grave opens when I pass the threshold of this house."

" I will fulfil all your wishes, my dear mother. But since our resolution is formed, let us act promptly. M. de Morcerf went out about half an hour since ; the opportunity is favourable to avoid an explanation."

" I am ready, my son," said Mercédès. Albert ran to fetch a hackney-coach ; he recollected there was a small furnished house to let in the Rue des Saints-Pères, where his mother would find a humble but decent lodging ; and thither he intended conducting the countess. As the hackney-coach stopped at the door, and Albert was alighting, a man approached, and gave him a letter. Albert recognized the bearer. " From the count," said Bertuccio. Albert took the letter, opened it, and read it ; then looked round for Bertuccio, but he was gone. He returned to Mercédès, and, without uttering a word, he gave her the letter. Mercédès read :—

" ALBERT,—While showing you that I have discovered your plans, I hope also to convince you of my delicacy. You are free, you leave the count's hotel, and you take your mother to your home : but reflect, Albert, you owe her more than your poor noble heart can pay her. Keep the struggle for yourself, bear all the suffering, but spare her the trial of poverty which must accompany your first efforts ; for she deserves not even the shadow of the misfortune which has this day fallen on her, and Providence wills not the innocent should suffer for the guilty. I know you are going to leave the Rue du Helder without taking anything with you. Now, listen, Albert. Twenty-four years ago I returned, proud and joyful, to my country. I had a betrothed, Albert, a lovely girl whom I adored, and I was bringing to my betrothed a hundred and fifty louis, painfully amassed by ceaseless toil. This money was for her, I destined it for her, and, knowing the treachery of the sea, I buried our treasure in the little garden of the house my father lived in at Marseilles, on the Allées de Meillan. Your mother, Albert, knows that poor house well. A short time since I passed through Marseilles, and went to see the old house, which revived so many painful recollections, and in the evening I took a spade and dug in the corner of the garden where I had concealed my treasure. The iron box was there, no one had touched it ; it was under a beautiful fig-tree my father had planted the day I was born, which overshadowed the spot. Well, Albert, this money, which was formerly designed to promote the comfort and tranquillity of the woman I adored, may now, from a strange and painful circumstance, be devoted to the same purpose. Oh ! feel for me, who could offer millions to that poor woman, but who return her only the piece of black bread, forgotten under my poor roof since the day I was torn from her I loved. You are a generous man, Albert, but, perhaps, you may be blinded by pride or resentment ; if you refuse me, if you ask another for what I have a right to offer you, I will say it is ungenerous of you to refuse the life of your mother at the hands of a man whose father was allowed to die in all the horrors of poverty and despair by your father."

Albert stood pale and motionless to hear what his mother would decide after she had finished reading this letter. Mercédès turned her eyes with an effable look towards heaven. " I accept it," said she ; " he has a right to pay the dowry, which I shall take with me to some convent ! " Putting the letter in her bosom, she took her son's arm, and with a firmer step than she herself expected, she went downstairs.

CHAPTER XCII

THE SUICIDE

MEANWHILE Monte Cristo had also returned to town with Emanuel and Maximilian. Their return was cheerful. Morrel, in a corner of the carriage, allowed his brother-in-law's gaiety to expend itself in words, while he felt equal inward joy, which, however, betrayed itself only by his look. At the Barrière du Trône they met Bertuccio. Monte Cristo put his head out of the window, exchanged a few words with him, and the steward disappeared. " M. le Comte," said Emanuel, when they were at the end of the Place Royale, " put me down at my door, that my wife may not have a single moment of needless anxiety on my account or yours."

The door was closed, and the carriage proceeded. " See what good fortune I brought you ! " said Morrel, when he was alone with the count. " Have you not thought so ? "

" Yes," said Monte Cristo, " for that reason I wished to keep you near me."

" It is miraculous ! " continued Morrel, answering his own thoughts.

" Yes," said the count, " you are right—it is miraculous."

" It is well for Albert he is not in the army," said Morrel.

" Why ? "

" An apology on the ground ! " said the young captain, shaking his head.

" Come," said the count, mildly, " do not entertain the prejudices of ordinary men, Morrel ! Acknowledge, if Albert is brave, he cannot be a coward. You will breakfast with me, will you not ? " he added, to turn the conversation.

" No, I must leave you at ten."

" Your engagement was for breakfast, then ? " said the count. Morrel smiled and shook his head.

" Oh ! " said the count, " I only know two things which destroy the appetite—grief, and as I am happy to see you very cheerful, it is not that; and love. Now, after what you told me this morning of your heart, I may believe——"

" Well, count," replied Morrel, gaily, " I will not dispute it."

" But you will not make me your confidant, Maximilian ? " said the count, in a tone which proved how gladly he would have been admitted to the secret."

" I showed you this morning I had a heart ; did I not, count ? " Monte Cristo only answered by extending his hand to the young man. " Well ! " continued the latter, " since that heart is no longer with you in the Bois de Vincennes, it is elsewhere, and I must go and find it."

" Go," said the count, deliberately, " go, dear friend, but promise me, if you meet with any obstacle, to remember that I have some power in this world ; that I am happy to use that power in the behalf of those I love ; and that I love you, Morrel."

" Well, I rely upon your promise."

Morrel sprang out on the pavement ; Bertuccio was waiting on the steps. Morrel disappeared through the avenue of Marigny, and Monte Cristo joined Bertuccio.

" Well ? " asked he.

" She is going to leave her house," said the steward.

" And her son ? "

" Florentin, his valet, thinks he is going to do the same."

" Come this way." Monte Cristo took Bertuccio into his cabinet, wrote the letter we have seen, and gave it to the steward. " Go," said he, quickly. " *Apropos*, let Haidée be informed I am returned."

" Here I am," said the young girl. Every transport of a daughter finding a father, all the delight of a mistress seeing an adored lover, were felt by Haidée during the first moments of this meeting, which she had so eagerly expected. Doubtless, although less evident, Monte Cristo's joy was not less intense.

Monte Cristo, elate with happiness, was reading eagerly the moistened gaze of Haidée, when suddenly the door opened. The count knit his brow.

" M. de Morcerf ! " said Baptistin.

" The viscount or the count ? "

" The count."

" Oh ! " exclaimed Haidée, " is it not yet over ? "

" I know not if it is finished, my beloved child, but I do know you have nothing more to fear."

Monte Cristo pressed on that pure beautiful forehead a kiss which made two hearts throb, the one violently, the other secretly. " Oh ! " murmured the count, " shall I then be permitted to love again ? Ask M. de Morcerf into the drawing-room," said he to Baptistin.

We must explain this visit, which, although Monte Cristo expected it, is unexpected to our readers. While Mercédès was making a similar inventory of her property to Albert's, she did not perceive a pale and sinister face at a glass door in the passage, from which everything could be seen and heard. He who was thus looking, without being heard or seen, probably heard and saw all that passed in Madame de Morcerf's apartments. From the glass door the pale-faced man went to his bedroom, where he remained ten minutes, motionless and dumb, listening to the beating of his heart. It was then that Albert returned from his rendezvous, perceived his father watching for his arrival behind a curtain, and turned aside. The count's eye expanded; he knew Albert had insulted Monte Cristo dreadfully, and that such an insult would lead to a deadly duel. Albert returned safely—then he, the count, was revenged.

He easily understood why his son did not come to see him before he went to avenge his father's honour; but when that was done, why did not his son come and throw himself into his arms?

Ten minutes afterwards General Morcerf's carriage drove up. The valet threw into it his military cloak, in which two swords were wrapped; and, shutting the door, took his seat by the side of the coachman.

"To the Champs Élysées," said the general; "the count of Monte Cristo's. Quickly!" The horses bounded beneath the whip, and in five minutes they stopped before the count's door.

A moment afterwards Baptistin announced the count de Morcerf to M. de Monte Cristo. The general was pacing the drawing-room the third time, when, in turning, he perceived Monte Cristo at the door.

"To what do I owe the pleasure of seeing M. de Morcerf so early?"

"Had you not a meeting with my son this morning?" asked the general.

"Yes sir, but you see, he has not killed me, and did not even fight."

"But to what do you attribute this conduct?"

"To the conviction, probably, that there was one more guilty than me."

"And who was that?"

"His father."

"A man who holds a sword in his hand, and sees a mortal enemy within reach of that sword, and does not fight, is a coward! Why is he not here, that I may tell him so?"

"Sir," replied Monte Cristo, coldly, "I did not expect you had come here to relate your family affairs. Tell Albert that, and he may know what to answer you."

"Oh, no, no!" said the general, smiling faintly, "I did not come for that purpose; you are right! I came to tell you that I also look upon you as my enemy. In short, since the young people of the present day will not fight, it remains for us to do it. Do you think so, sir ? "

" Yes, sir."

" Let us start, then ; we need no witnesses."

" Truly," said Monte Cristo, " we know each other so well ! "

" On the contrary," said the count, " we know so little of each other."

" Indeed ! " said Monte Cristo, " let us see. Are you not the soldier Fernando who deserted on the eve of the Battle of Waterloo ? Are you not the Lieutenant Fernando who served as guide and spy to the French army in Spain ? Are you not the Captain Fernando who betrayed, sold, and murdered his benefactor, Ali ? And have not all these Fernandos united, made the Lieutenant-General count de Morcerf peer of France ? "

" Oh ! " cried the general, as if branded with a hot iron, " wretch ! to reproach me with my shame ! I am aware you know me ; but I know you not, adventurer, sewn up in gold and jewellery. You have called yourself, in Paris, the count of Monte Cristo ; in Italy, Sindbad the Sailor ; in Malta, I forget what. But it is your real name I want to know, that I may pronounce it when we meet to fight, at the moment when I plunge my sword into your heart."

The count of Monte Cristo turned pale, his eye seemed to burn with a devouring fire ; he bounded towards a dressing-room, and tearing off his cravat, his coat, and waistcoat, put on a sailor's jacket and hat, from beneath which rolled his long black hair. He returned thus, formidable and implacable, with his arms crossed on his breast. " Fernando," cried he, " of my many names I need only tell you one, to overwhelm you ! But you guess it now ; do you not ?—or, rather, you remember it ? "

The general, with fixed gaze, looked silently at this dreadful apparition ; then seeking the wall to support him, glided along close to it until he reached the door, through which he went out backwards, uttering the single distressing cry,—Edmond Dantès! " Then he dragged himself to the door, and falling into the arms of his valet, said, in a voice scarcely intelligible,—" Home ! home ! "

The door of the house was wide open, a hackney-coach was standing in the middle of the yard—a strange sight before so noble a mansion ; the count looked at it with terror ; but without daring to ask, he rushed towards his apartment. Two persons were coming down the stairs : he had only time to creep into a room to avoid them It was Mercédès leaning on her son's arm and leaving the house. They passed close by the unhappy being, who, concealed behind the damask door, almost felt Mercédès dress brush against him, and his son's warm breath pronouncing these words. "Courage, my mother? This is no longer our home!" The general drew himself up, clinging to the door; he uttered the most dreadful sob which ever escaped from the bosom of a father abandoned at the same time by his wife and son. He soon heard the clatter of the iron step of the hackney-coach, then the coachman's voice, and then the rolling of the heavy vehicle shook the windows. At the very moment that the wheels of the coach crossed the gateway a report was heard, and a thick smoke escaped through one of the panes of the window, which was broken by the explosion.

CHAPTER XCIII

VALENTINE

WE may easily conceive where Morrel's appointment was. Noirtier and Valentine had given him leave to call twice a week, and he was now availing himself of that permission. He arrived; Valentine was expecting him. Uneasy, she seized his hand and led him to her grandfather. This uneasiness arose from the report Morcerf's adventure had made in the world; the affair at the opera was generally known. We may easily understand how eagerly the particulars were asked for, given, and received; and Morrel could read an indescribable joy in the eyes of his beloved, when she knew that the termination of this affair was as happy as it was unexpected.

"Now," said Valentine, "let us talk about our own affairs. You know, Maximilian, grandpapa once thought of leaving this house and taking an apartment away from M. de Villefort's. But do you know why?"

"Oh!" answered Morrel, "I believe he had a good reason."

"An excellent one," said Valentine. "The air of the Faubourg St. Honoré is not good for me."

"Do you suffer any pain?" asked Morrel quickly.

"Oh, it must not be called suffering; I feel a general out-of-sortness, that is all." Noirtier did not lose a word of what Valentine said.

"And what treatment do you adopt?"

"Every morning I take a spoonful of the mixture prepared for my grandfather. When I say one spoonful, I began by one—now I take four. Grandpapa says it is a panacea."

Maximilian, in his devotedness, gazed silently at her. From Valentine the young man looked towards Noirtier.

"But," said Morrel, "I thought this mixture, of which you now take four spoonfuls, was prepared for M. Noirtier ? "

" I know it is very bitter," said Valentine ; " Just now before I came down, I drank a glass of *eau sucrée ;* I left half, because it seemed so bitter."

Noirtier turned pale, and made a sign that he wished to speak. Valentine rose to fetch the dictionary ; Noirtier watched her with evident anguish. In fact, the blood was rushing to the young girl's head already, her cheeks were becoming red. " Oh ! " cried she, without losing any of her cheerfulness, " this is singular ! A dimness. Did the sun shine in my eyes ? "

" The sun is not shining," said Morrel. The young girl smiled. " Comfort yourself ! " said she to Noirtier. " Do not be alarmed, Maximilian ; it is nothing, and has already passed away. But listen ! Do I not hear a carriage in the courtyard ? Yes," said she, " it is Madame Danglars and her daughter, who are come to call on us. Stay with grandpapa, Maximilian ; I promise you not to persuade them to stay."

Morrel watched her as she left the room. As soon as she was gone Noirtier signed to Morrel to take the dictionary. Morrel obeyed. It was slow work, however, and ten minutes elapsed before the thought of the old man was translated by these words, " Fetch the glass of water and the decanter from Valentine's room." Morrel rang immediately for the servant who had taken Barrois' situation. The decanter and the glass were empty. Noirtier made a sign that he wished to speak. " Why are the glass and decanter empty ? " asked he. The translation of this new question occupied another five minutes. " I do not know," said the servant, " but the housemaid is in Mademoiselle Valentine's room."

" Ask her," said Morrel. The servant went out, but returned almost immediately. " Mademoiselle Valentine passed through the room to go to Madame de Villefort's," said he ; " and in passing, as she was thirsty, she drank what remained in the glass." Noirtier raised his eyes to heaven as a gambler does who stakes his all on one stroke. From that moment the old man's eyes were fixed on the door, and did not quit it.

It was Madame Danglars and her daughter whom Valentine had seen. The two ladies entered the drawing-room with that kind of conventional bearing that precedes a communication. Valentine entered at this moment, and the formalities were resumed. "My dear friend," said the baroness, while the two girls were shaking hands, "I and Eugénie are come to announce the marriage of my daughter with Prince Cavalcanti."

"Allow me to present you my sincere congratulations," replied Madame de Villefort. "M. le Prince Cavalcanti appears a young man of rare qualities."

"Listen," said the baroness, smiling; "speaking to you as a friend, I would say the prince does not yet appear all he will be, but M. Danglars assures me his fortune is majestic—that is his term."

"Moreover," said Eugénie, while turning over the leaves of Madame de Villefort's album, "you have taken a great fancy to the young man."

"And," said Madame de Villefort, "I need not ask you if you share that fancy."

"Not a bit," replied Eugénie candidly, "I don't wish to be any man's wife. My taste is for the life of the artist. But since I am to be married, whether I will or not, I ought to be thankful to Providence for having released me from my engagement with M. Albert de Morcerf, or I should this day have been the wife of a dishonoured man."

"It is true," said the baroness, "that had not the Morcerfs hesitated, my daughter would have married M. Albert."

"But," said Valentine, timidly, "does all the father's shame descend to the son? M. Albert appears to me innocent of the treason charged against the general."

"Excuse me," said the implacable Eugénie, "M. Albert deserves his share. After challenging M. de Monte Cristo at the Opera yesterday he apologized on the ground to-day."

Valentine also knew the truth, but she did not answer. She remembered that Morrel was expecting her in M. Noirtier's room, and lapsed into a brown study. Suddenly Madame Danglars' hand pressed on her arm aroused her from her lethargy.

"What is it?" said she, starting at Madame Danglars' touch as she would have done at an electric shock.

"You do not look well," cried the baroness.

"Indeed," cried Eugénie, "you are very pale!"

"Oh, do not be alarmed! I have been so for some days." Artless as she was, the young girl knew this was an opportunity to leave; besides, Madame de Villefort came to her assistance. "Retire, Valentine," said she; "you are really suffering, and these ladies will excuse you; drink a glass of pure water, it will restore you." Valentine kissed Eugénie, bowed to Madame Danglars, and went out. She had crossed Edward's room without noticing some trick of the child's, and had reached the staircase to M. Noirtier's room. She was at the bottom excepting three steps : she already heard Morrel's voice, when suddenly a cloud passed over her eyes, and, falling against the wall, she rolled down these three steps rather than walked. Morrel bounded to the door, opened it, and found Valentine on the floor. He raised her in his arms and placed her in a chair. Valentine opened her eyes.

" You have hurt yourself ? " said Morrel. " Another giddiness ! Oh ! attend to it, Valentine, I entreat you."

" But," said Valentine, " it is all past, and it was nothing. Now, let me tell you some news : Eugénie is to be married in a week, and in three days there is to be a grand feast, a sort of betrothing festival. We are all invited, my father, Madame de Villefort,—and I—at least I understood it so."

" When will it be our turn to think of these things ? Valentine, you have so much influence over your grandpapa, try to make him answer,—' Soon.' "

" And do *you*," said Valentine, " depend on me to stimulate grandpapa's interest ? " She burst into a forced and melancholy laugh, her arms stiffened and twisted, her head fell back on her chair, and she remained motionless. The cry of terror which was stopped on Noirtier's lips seemed to start from his eyes. Morrel rang the bell violently. Madame Danglars and Eugénie were just leaving ; they heard the cause of the disturbance.

" I told you so ! " cried Madame de Villefort. " Poor child ! "

CHAPTER XCIV

THE CONFESSION

AT the same moment M. de Villefort's voice was heard calling from his study, " What is the matter ? " Morrel consulted Noirtier's look and concealed himself in a cupboard. He had only time to get his hat and throw himself into the cupboard when the *procureur's* footstep was heard in the passage. De Villefort sprang into the room, ran to Valentine, and took her in his arms. " A physician ! a physician ! M. d'Avrigny ! " cried Villefort ; " I will go for him myself." He flew from the apartment, and Morrel darted out at the other door. He had been struck to the heart by a frightful recollection—the conversation he had heard between the doctor and de Villefort. At the same time Monte Cristo's voice seemed to resound in his ear, who had said only two hours before, " Whatever you want, Morrel, come to me, I have great power." More rapidly than thought he darted down the Rue Matignon, and thence to the Avenue des Champs Élysées.

Meanwhile M. de Villefort arrived in a cabriolet at M. d'Avrigny's. " Ah ! " said the doctor, " is it you ? "

" Yes," said de Villefort, closing the door after him. " Doctor, my house is accursed ! "

" What, ! " said the latter, " have you another invalid ? "

" Yes, doctor," cried Villefort ? "

D'Avrigny's look implied, " I told you so." Then he slowly uttered these words, " Who is now dying in your house ? What new victim is going to accuse you of weakness before God ? " A mournful sob burst from de Villefort's heart, as he answered, " it is Valentine's turn ! "

" Your daughter ! " cried d'Avrigny, with grief and surprise.

" Oh, ! this time, doctor, you shall not have to reproach me with weakness. This time I will track the assassin to his doom."

" Let us try first to save the victim before we think of avenging her," said d'Avrigny. " Come." The cabriolet which had brought de Villefort took them back at full speed, at the moment Morrel rapped at Monte Cristo's door. The count sprang to meet him. " What is the matter, Maximilian ? "

" I have just left a house where death has entered, to run to you."

" Have you come from M. de Morcerf's ? " asked Monte Cristo.

" No," said Morrel ; " is some one dead in his house ? "

" The general has just blown his brains out," replied Monte Cristo, with great coolness.

" Oh ! " said Morrel, " I know not, indeed, if I may reveal my secret to mortal ears ; but fatality impels me, necessity constrains me, count——"

" I am at your service."

" Oh ! I cannot live if she is not better."

" Shall I ring for Baptistin ? "

" No, I will go and speak to him myself." Morrel went out, called Baptistin, and whispered a few words to him.

" Well, have you sent ? " asked Monte Cristo, on Morrel's return.

" Yes, and now I shall be more calm."

" You know I am waiting," said Monte Cristo, smiling.

" Ah, then I will tell you. One evening I was in a garden. Two persons passed near me : I was so interested in what they said that I did not lose a single word. Someone had just died in the house to which that garden belonged. One of these persons was the master of the house; the other, the physician. The former was confiding to the latter his grief and fear; for it was the second time within a month that death had entered suddenly that house, which was apparently destined to destruction by some exterminating angel, as an object of God's anger. The doctor declared that the death was not a natural one, and must be attributed to poison."

"Indeed!" said Monte Cristo, "indeed, Maximilian, did you hear that?"

"Yes, my dear count, I heard it; and the doctor added, that if another death occurred in a similar way he must appeal to justice." Monte Cristo listened, or appeared to do so, with the greatest calmness. "Well!" said Maximilian, "death came a third time. Death is now, perhaps, striking a fourth blow. Count, what am I bound to do, being in possession of this secret?"

"My dear friend," said Monte Cristo, "you appear to be relating an adventure which we all know by heart. You say an exterminating angel appears to have devoted that house to God's anger, —well! who says your supposition is not reality? If it is God's justice, instead of His anger, which is walking through that house, Maximilian, turn away your face, and let His justice accomplish its purpose." Morrel shuddered. There was something mournful, solemn, and terrible in the count's manner. "Besides," continued he, "who says that it will begin again?"

"It has returned, count!" exclaimed Morrel; "that is why I hastened to you."

"Well! what do you wish me to do? Do you wish me to give information to the *procureur du roi*?"

Morrel, starting up, cried out, "You know of whom I speak, count?"

"Perfectly well, my good friend; and I will prove it to you by naming the persons. You were walking one evening in M. de Villefort's garden. You heard M. de Villefort talking to M. d'Avrigny about the death of M. de Saint Méran, and that, no less surprising, of the countess. M. d'Avrigny said he believed they both proceeded from poison; and you, honest man, have ever since been asking your heart, and sounding your conscience, to know whether you ought to expose or conceal this secret. Remain in peace, who have no remorse to disturb you." Deep grief was depicted on Morrel's features; he seized Monte Cristo's hand. "But it is beginning again, I say!"

"Well!" said the count, astonished at his perseverance, which he could not understand, and looking still more earnestly at

Maximilian, " let it begin again. Three months since, it was M. de Saint Méran ; Madame de Saint Méran two months since ; the other day it was Barrois ; to-day the old Noirtier or young Valentine."

" You knew it ? " cried Morrel, in such a paroxysm of terror that Monte Cristo started ; " you knew it, and said nothing ? "

" And what is it to me ? " replied Monte Cristo, shrugging his shoulders.

" But," cried Morrel, groaning with sorrow, " I love her ! "

" You love !—whom ? " cried Monte Cristo, starting on his feet, and seizing the two hands which Morrel was raising towards heaven.

" I love most fondly—I love madly—I love Valentine de Ville-fort, and I ask God and you how I can save her ? "

Monte Cristo uttered a cry : " Unhappy man ! " he said, wringing his hands in his turn ; " you love Valentine, that daughter of an accursed race ! " Never had Morrel witnessed such an expression on the count's face. He drew back terrified.

Monte Cristo, after this ebullition, closed his eyes, as if dazzled by internal light. This silence, self-control and struggle lasted about twenty seconds, then the count raised his pallid face. " See," said he, " my dear friend, how God punishes the most thoughtless and unfeeling for their indifference, by presenting dreadful scenes to their view. I, who was looking on, an eager and curious spectator, am, in my turn, bitten by the serpent whose tortuous course I was watching, and bitten to the heart ! "

Morrel groaned. " Come, come," continued the count. " I tell you to hope. Do you understand me ? Remember that I never uttered a falsehood, and am never deceived. Listen, Morrel !—it is noon, if Valentine is not now dead, she will not die."

" How so ? " cried Morrel, " when I left her dying ? "

Monte Cristo pressed his hand to his forehead. What was passing in that brain so loaded with dreadful secrets ? The count raised his head once more ; and this time he was calm as a child awaking from sleep. " Maximilian, return home ; I com-mand you not to stir, to attempt nothing, not to let your counte-nance betray a thought, and I will send you tidings. Go ! "

" Oh ! count, you overwhelm me with that coolness. Are you superhuman ? Are you an angel ? " Morrel, subdued by the extraordinary ascendency Monte Cristo exercised over every-body around him, pressed the count's hand and left.

Meanwhile de Villefort and d'Avrigny had made all possible haste. Valentine had not revived from her fit on their arrival, and the doctor examined the invalid, with an interest which the knowledge of the secret doubled. At last d'Avrigny slowly uttered these words :—" She is still alive ! "

" But is she safe ? " asked the father.

" Yes, since she lives." At that moment d'Avrigny's glance met Noirtier's eye. It glistened with such extraordinary joy, rich and full of thought, that the physician was struck. " Sir," said d'Avrigny to de Villefort, " call Mademoiselle Valentine's maid, if you please." De Villefort went to fetch her, and d'Avrigny approached Noirtier. " Have you something to tell me ? " asked he. The old man winked his eye expressively.

" Privately ? "

" Yes," said Noirtier.

" Well, I will remain with you." At this moment de Villefort returned, followed by the lady's maid ; and after her came Madame de Villefort.

" What is the matter, then, with this dear child ? she left me and complained of feeling unwell ; but I did not think seriously of it." D'Avrigny continued to look at Noirtier ; he saw the eyes of the old man dilate and become round. " Ah ! " said he, following Noirtier's eyes, which were fixed on Madame de Ville-fort, who repeated,—" This poor child would be better in bed. Come, Fanny, we will put her in bed." M. d'Avrigny, who saw that would be a means of his remaining alone with Noirtier, expressed his opinion that it was the best thing to do, but forbade anything to be given her excepting what he prescribed.

They carried Valentine away ; she had revived, but could scarcely move or speak, so shaken was she by the attack. D'Avrigny followed the invalid, wrote a prescription, ordered de Villefort to take a cabriolet, go in person to a chemist's to get the medicine, bring it himself, and wait for him in his daughter's room. Then, he went down again to Noirtier and shut the doors carefully. From long friendship the doctor knew how to converse with the invalid. " Do you," said he, " know anything of this young lady's illness ? "

' Yes," said the old man.

" Did you anticipate the accident which has happened to your granddaughter ? "

" Yes."

" Did you see poor Barrois die ? " Noirtier raised his eyes to heaven.

" Do you know of what he died ? " asked d'Avrigny.

" Yes," replied the old man.

" You believe Barrois was poisoned ? "

" Yes."

" Do you think the same hand which unintentionally struck Barrois has now attacked Valentine ? "

" Yes."

" Then, will she die, too ? " asked d'Avrigny.

" No ! "

" Then you hope the poison will take no effect on Valentine ? "

" Yes."

" Why do you think she will escape ? "

Noirtier gazed steadily at a certain spot. D'Avrigny followed the direction, and saw his eyes were fixed on a bottle containing the mixture which he took every morning.

" Ah ! " said d'Avrigny, struck with a sudden thought, " has it occurred to you to prepare her system to resist poison ? "

" Yes."

" By accustoming her to it by degrees."

" You have endeavoured to neutralize the effect of a similar poison ? You have succeeded," exclaimed d'Avrigny. " Valentine will not die."

At this moment de Villefort returned. " Here, doctor," said he, " is what you sent me for."

" Was this prepared in your presence ? "

" Yes," replied the *procureur du roi.*

" Well," said he, " let us go to Valentine ; I will give instructions to everyone, and you, M. de Villefort, will yourself see that no one departs from them."

As d'Avrigny was returning to Valentine's room, an Italian priest hired the house adjoining that of M. de Villefort. No one knew why the three former tenants of that house left it. Its foundation was said to be unsafe ; but the report did not prevent the new occupant from establishing himself with his modest furniture the same day at five o'clock. The tenant was called Signor Giacomo Busoni. Workmen were immediately called in, and the same night the passengers at the end of the Faubourg saw with surprise carpenters and masons occupied in repairing the lower part of the tumbledown house.

CHAPTER XCV

THE FATHER AND DAUGHTER

WE beg our readers to transport themselves into the beautifully gilded saloon which was the pride of its owner, the Baron

Danglars. In this room, at about ten o'clock in the morning, the banker had been walking some minutes, watching each door and listening to every sound. When his patience was exhausted, he called his valet. " Stephen," said he, " see why Mademoiselle Eugénie has asked me to meet her in the drawing-room, and why she makes me wait so long."

Mademoiselle Danglars had that morning requested an interview with her father in the drawing-room. Stephen soon returned from his errand. " Mademoiselle's lady's-maid says, sir, that mademoiselle is finishing her toilette, and will be here shortly."

Danglars nodded and Stephen retired. " Why the devil does she not come into my own room ? and why does she want to speak to me at all ? "

He was revolving this thought in his brain for the twentieth time, when Eugénie appeared. " Why, Eugénie, what is it you want ? and why in this solemn drawing-room when the study is so comfortable ? "

" I have chosen the drawing-room, sir, in order to avoid the disagreeable atmosphere of a banker's study. Private ledgers and piles of bank bills are apt, even unconsciously, to influence a father's mind, but in this brighter room one feels the sense of humanity. I rely much on external impressions ; perhaps, with regard to you, they are immaterial ; but I should be no artist if I had not some fancies."

" Very well," replied M. Danglars.

" You ask why I have requested this interview ; I will tell you in few words, sir ; I will not marry M. le Comte Andrea Cavalcanti."

Danglars bounded from his chair.

" Yes, indeed, sir," continued Eugénie, quite calmly ; " you are astonished, I see ; for since this little affair began, I have not manifested the slightest opposition. This passiveness proceeded from a wish to practise obedience."

" Well ? " asked Danglars.

" Well, sir," replied Eugénie, " I have tried to the very last ; and now the moment has come, in spite of all my efforts, I feel it is impossible."

" But," said Danglars, " what is your reason for this refusal, Engénie ? "

" My reason ? " replied the young girl. " Well ! it is not that the man is more ugly, more foolish, or more disagreeable than any other ; no, M. Andrea Cavalcanti may appear to those who look at men's faces and figures a very good model. I actually love no one, sir; you know it, do you not? I do not, then, see why, without real necessity, I should encumber my life with a perpetual companion. Well, my dear father, in the shipwreck of life—for life is an eternal shipwreck of our hopes—I cast into the sea my useless encumbrance, that is all; and I remain with my own will, disposed to live perfectly alone, and, consequently, perfectly free."

" Unhappy girl! " murmured Danglars, turning pale, for he knew, from long experience, the solidity of the obstacle he so suddenly encountered.

" Unhappy girl! " replied Eugénie, "do you say? No, indeed, the exclamation appears theatrical and affected. Happy, on the contrary; for what am I in want of? Why do you call me unhappy? "

Danglars knew the necessity for circumspection and placed a strong check on his utterance. " My daughter, you have perfectly explained to me the sentiments which influence a girl like you who is determined she will not marry; now it remains for me to tell you the motives of a father like me who have decided his daughter shall marry." Eugénie bowed, not as a submissive daughter, but as an adversary prepared for a discussion.

" My child," continued Danglars, " when a father asks his daughter to choose a husband, he has always some reason for wishing her to marry. I have proposed to you to marry, not for your sake, but because it suited me to marry you as soon as possible, on account of certain commercial speculations I am desirous of entering into." Eugénie became uneasy.

" It is just so, I assure you, and you must not be angry with me, for you have sought this disclosure. The credit of a banker is his physical and moral life; that credit sustains him as breath animates the body; and M. de Monte Cristo once gave me a lecture on that subject which I have never forgotten. As credit sinks the body becomes inert and lifeless; and this is what must happen very soon to the banker who is proud to own so good a logician as you for his daughter."

But, Eugénie, instead of stooping, drew herself up under the blow. " Ruined! " said she.

" Yes, ruined! Now it is revealed, this secret so full of horror, as the tragic poet says. Now, my daughter, learn from my lips how you may alleviate this misfortune, so far as it will affect you."

" Oh! " cried Eugénie, " you are a bad physiognomist, if you imagine I deplore, on my own account, the catastrophe you announce to me. I ruined? What will that signify to me?

Have I not my talent left ? And if I do not possess that talent, which your smile proves to me you doubt, should I not still have that furious love of independence which will be a substitute for all treasure, and which in my mind supersedes even the instinct of self-preservation ! Do you think I sorrow for Madame Danglars ? Undeceive yourself again; she has provided against the catastrophe which threatens you, and which will pass over without affecting her. Oh ! no, sir ; from my childhood I have been beloved by no one—so much the worse ; that has naturally led me to love no one—so much the better ; now you have my profession of faith."

" Then," said Danglars, pale with anger, which did not emanate from offended paternal love, " then, mademoiselle, you persist in your determination to accelerate my ruin ? "

" Your ruin ? I acccelerate your ruin ? What do you mean ! I do not understand you."

" So much the better, I have a ray of hope left ; listen."

" I am all attention," said Eugénie, looking so earnestly at her father that it cost him effort to bear her gaze.

" M. Cavalcanti," continued Danglars, " is about to marry you, and will place in my hands his fortune, amounting to three million livres."

" That is admirable ! " said Eugénie, with sovereign contempt, smoothing her gloves out.

" You think I shall deprive you of those millions," said Danglars ; " but do not fear it. They are destined to produce at least ten. I and a brother banker have obtained a grant of a railway. It is a deposit, belonging to a mortgage, which is an advance, as you see, since we gain at least ten, fifteen, twenty or a hundred livres' worth of iron in exchange for our money. Well, within a week I am to deposit four millions for my share ; these four millions, I promise you, will produce ten or twelve."

" But during my visit to you yesterday, sir," replied Eugénie, " I saw you lay up—is not that the term ?—five millions and a half ; you even pointed them out to me in two drafts on the Treasury, and you were astonished that so valuable a paper did not dazzle my eyes like lightning."

" Yes, but those five millions and a half are not mine, and are only a proof of the great confidence placed in me ; the deposit may be withdrawn at any moment, and to use it for another purpose would land me in a disgraceful bankruptcy. Now, if you marry M. Cavalcanti, my credit will be restored, and my fortune will revive. Do you understand me ? "

" Perfectly ; you pledge me for three millions, do you not ? "

" The greater the amount, the more flattering it is to you ; it gives you an idea of your value."

" Thank you. One word more, sir ; do you promise to make what use you can of the report of the fortune M. Cavalcanti will bring, without touching the sum ? This is no act of selfishness, but of delicacy. I am willing to help rebuild your fortune ; but I will not be an accomplice in the ruin of others."

" But since I tell you," cried Danglars, " that with these three millions——"

" Do you expect to recover your position, sir, without touching those three millions ? "

" I hope so, if the marriage should take place and confirm my credit."

" Shall you be able to pay M. Cavalcanti the five hundred thousand francs you promise for my dowry ? "

" He shall receive them on returning from the town-hall ? "

" Well ? I wish to know if, in demanding my signature, you leave me entirely free in my person ? "

" Absolutely."

" Then I am ready to marry M. Cavalcanti."

" But what are your projects ? "

" Ah ! that is my secret. What advantage should I have over you if, knowing your secret, I were to tell you mine ? " Danglars bit his lips.

" Then," said he, " you are ready to pay the official visits, which are absolutely indispensable ? "

" Yes," replied Eugénie.

" And to sign the contract in three days ? "

" Yes. Is the conference ended ? " asked Eugénie, rising.

Danglars indicated that he had nothing more to say. Five minutes afterwards the piano resounded to the touch of Mademoiselle d'Armilly's fingers, and Mademoiselle Danglars was singing Brabantio's malediction on Desdemona.

CHAPTER XCVI

THE CONTRACT

THREE days after the scene we have just described, as the count of Monte Cristo was preparing to go out, an elegant phaeton set down M. Andrea Cavalcanti at the door. He inquired for the count with his usual familiarity, and met him on the top of the stairs.

The count returned to a small drawing-room on the first floor, sat down, and, crossing his legs, motioned to the young man to take a seat also.

Andrea assumed his gayest manner. " You know, my dear count," said he, " the ceremony is to take place this evening. At nine o'clock the contract is to be signed at my father-in-law's."

" Well," said Monte Cristo, " you are fortunate, M. Cavalcanti! It is a most suitable alliance and Mademoiselle Danglars is a pretty girl."

" Yes, indeed she is," replied Cavalcanti, with a very modest tone.

" Above all, she is very rich,—at least I believe so," said Monte Cristo.

" Very rich, do you think ? " replied the young man.

" Doubtless ; it is said M. Danglars conceals at least half of his fortune."

" And he acknowledges fifteen or twenty millions," said Andrea, with a look sparkling with joy.

" Without reckoning," replied Monte Cristo, " that all his fortune will come to you, and justly too, since your own fortune, as your father assured me, is almost equal to that of your betrothed. But, enough of money matters. Do you know, M. Andrea, I think you have managed this affair rather skilfully ? "

" Not badly, by any means," said the young man ; " I was born for a diplomatist. But I must not forget one grand point."

" Which ? "

" That I have been singularly assisted by you."

" By me ? Not at all, prince," said Monte Cristo, laying a marked stress on the title ; " what have I done for you ? Are not your name, your social position, and your merit sufficient ? "

" No," said Andrea, " no ; it is useless for you to say so, count. I maintain that the position of a man like you has done more than my name, my social position, and my merit."

" You are completely mistaken, sir," said Monte Cristo, coldly. " It was your father's name, so well known in Italy and so highly honoured. Personally, I do not know you." This calm tone and perfect ease made Andrea feel he was, for the moment, restrained by a stronger hand than his own, and that the restraint could not be easily broken through.

" Oh ! then my father has really a very large fortune, count ? "

" It appears so, sir," replied Monte Cristo.

" Do you know if my promised dowry is come ? "

" I have been advised of it."

" But the three millions ? "

" The three millions are probably on the road."

" Then I shall really have them ? "

" Forsooth ! " said the count, " I do not think you have yet known the want of money."

" Well, I am come to ask you to take my father's part, and support me at the altar."

" Ah, my dear sir ! What ! after the numerous relations I have had the happiness to sustain towards you, you know me so little as to ask such a thing ! I preside at a wedding—never ! "

" But you introduced me to M. Danglars."

" By no means. You met him at a dinner-party in my house and introduced yourself at his. That is vastly different. Recollect what I told you when you asked me to propose you. 'I never make matches, my dear prince, it is my settled principle.' "

Andrea bit his lips.

" But you will sign the contract."

" I see no objection to that : my scruples do not go so far."

" Is my wife's fortune five hundred thousand livres ? "

" That is the sum M. Danglars himself announced."

" Must I receive it, or leave it in the hands of the notary ? "

" This is the way such affairs are generally arranged when it is wished to do them stylishly : The two solicitors appoint a meeting, after the contract is signed, for the next day or the following ; then they exchange the two portions, for which they each give a receipt ; then, when the marriage is celebrated, they place the amount at your disposal as chief of the community."

" Because," said Andrea, with ill-concealed uneasiness, " I thought I heard my father-in-law say he intended embarking our property in some famous railway."

" Well, it will be the means, everybody says, of trebling your fortune in twelve months. The Baron Danglars is a good father, and knows how to calculate."

" Come, then," said Andrea, " all is well, excepting your refusal, which quite grieves me."

" You must attribute it only to natural scruples."

" Well," said Andrea, " let it be as you wish : this evening, then, at nine o'clock."

" Adieu till then."

Andrea pressed the count's hand, jumped into his phaeton, and disappeared.

The four or five remaining hours Andrea employed in riding,

paying visits, dazzling those on whom he called with promises of feasts and other brilliant functions.

At half-past eight the grand saloon, the gallery adjoining, and the three other drawing-rooms on the same floor, were filled with a perfumed crowd. No one could dispute that the rooms were splendidly illuminated. Mademoiselle Eugénie was dressed with elegant simplicity : a figured white silk dress, a white rose half concealed in her jet black hair, were her only ornaments, unaccompanied by a single jewel. Her eyes, however, betrayed that perfect confidence which contradicted the girlish simplicity of this modest attire. Madame Danglars was chatting at a short distance with Debray, Beauchamp and Château Renaud. M. Danglars, surrounded by deputies and men connected with the revenue, was explaining a new theory of taxation which he intended to adopt when the course of events had compelled Government to call him into the Ministry. Andrea, on whose arm hung one of the most consummate dandies of the opera, was explaining his future projects, and the new luxuries he meant to introduce to Parisian fashions with his hundred and seventy-five thousand livres per annum. At the moment when the massive timepiece struck nine, the name of the count de Monte Cristo resounded in its turn, and, as if by an electric shock, all eyes turned towards the door. The count was dressed with his habitual simplicity. A circle was formed immediately round the door. The count perceived at one glance Madame Danglars at one end of the drawing-room, M. Danglars at the other, and Eugénie in front of him. He first advanced towards the baroness, who was chatting with Madame de Villefort, who had come alone, Valentine being still an invalid ; and without turning aside, so clear was the road left for him, he passed from the baroness to Eugénie, whom he complimented in such rapid and measured terms, that the proud artist was quite struck.

Having accomplished these social duties, Monte Cristo looked around him with that expression peculiar to a certain class, which seems to say, " I have done my duty, now let others do theirs." Andrea, who was in an adjoining room, had shared in the sensation caused by the arrival of Monte Cristo, and now came forward to pay his respects. He found him surrounded ; all were eager to speak to him, as is always the case with those whose words are few and weighty. The solicitors arrived at this moment, and arranged their scrawled papers on the velvet cloth embroidered with gold which covered the table prepared for the signature.

The contract was read during a profound silence. But as soon as it was finished, the buzz was redoubled. Andrea, complimented, flattered, beginning to believe in the reality of his dream, was almost bewildered. The notary solemnly took the pen, flourished it above his head and said, " Gentlemen, the contract is to be signed."

The baron was to sign first; then the representative of M. Cavalcanti, senior; then the baroness; afterwards the future couple, as they are styled on the ceremonious stamped papers. The baron took the pen, and signed, then the representative. The baroness approached, leaning on Madame de Villefort's arm. " My dear," said she, as she took the pen, " is it not vexatious ? An unexpected incident, in the affair of murder and theft at the count of Monte Cristo's, in which he nearly fell a victim, deprives us of the pleasure of seeing M. de Villefort."

" Indeed," said Monte Cristo, approaching, " I am much afraid I am the involuntary cause of that absence. But it is not my fault : as I shall endeavour to prove." Everyone listened eagerly : Monte Cristo, who so rarely opened his lips, was about to speak. " You remember," said the count, during the most profound silence, " that the unhappy wretch who came to rob me, died at my house ; it was supposed he was stabbed by his accomplice on attempting to leave it."

" Yes," said Danglars. " In order to examine his wounds, he was undressed, and his clothes were thrown into a corner, where officers of justice picked them up, with the exception of the waistcoat, which they overlooked."

Andrea turned pale and drew towards the door; he saw a cloud rising in the horizon.

" Well ! his waistcoat was discovered to-day, covered with blood, and with a hole over the heart. It was brought to me. My valet, in examining this dirty relic, felt a paper in the pocket and drew it out; it was a letter addressed to you, baron."

" But," asked Madame Danglars, looking at her husband with uneasiness, " how could that prevent M. de Villefort—— "

" In this simple way, madame," replied Monte Cristo ; " the waistcoat and the letter were both, what is termed, circumstantial evidence ! I therefore sent it all to the *procureur*." Andrea looked steadily at Monte Cristo, and disappeared into the second drawing-room.

" Possibly," said Danglars : " was not this murdered man an old galley-slave ? "

" Yes," replied the count; " a felon named Caderousse."

Danglars turned slightly pale, Andrea reached the anteroom beyond the little drawing-room.

"But go on signing," said Monte Cristo; "I perceive my story has caused a general emotion, and I beg to apologise to you, baroness, and to Mademoiselle Danglars." The baroness, who had signed, returned the pen to the notary.

"Prince Cavalcanti!" said the latter, "Prince Cavalcanti, where are you?"

"Andrea! Andrea!" repeated several young people, who were already on sufficiently intimate terms with him to call him by his Christian name.

"Call the prince; inform him it is his turn to sign!" cried Danglars to one of the doorkeepers.

At the same instant the crowd of guests rushed, terrified, into the principal salon. An officer was placing two soldiers at the door of each drawing-room, and was advancing towards Danglars, preceded by a commissary of police, girded with his scarf. Madame Danglars uttered a scream and fainted. Danglars, who thought himself threatened, appeared before his guests with a terrified countenance.

"What is the matter, sir?" asked Monte Cristo, advancing to meet the commissary.

"Which of you, gentlemen," asked the magistrate, without replying to the count, "answers to the name of Andrea Cavalcanti?"

"But who is Andrea Cavalcanti?" asked Danglars, in amazement.

"A galley-slave, escaped from confinement at Toulon."

"And what crime has he committed?"

"He is accused," said the commissary, "of having assassinated a man named Caderousse, his former companion in prison, at the moment he was making his escape from the house of the count of Monte Cristo." Monte Cristo cast a rapid glance around him. Andrea was gone.

CHAPTER XCVII

THE DEPARTURE FOR BELGIUM

A FEW minutes after the scene of confusion produced in the saloons of M. Danglars by the unexpected appearance of the brigade of soldiers, and by the disclosures which had followed, the large mansion was deserted. There remained in the house only Danglars, Madame Danglars, and Eugénie, who had retired to her room with her inseparable companion, Mademoiselle Louise d'Armilly. As for the numerous servants, venting on their employers their anger at what they termed the insult, they collected in groups, thinking very little of their duty, which was thus interrupted.

On reaching her room Eugénie locked her door, while Louise fell on a chair. " Ah, what a dreadful thing ! " said the young musician ; " who would have suspected it ? M. Andrea Cavalcanti a murderer—a galley-slave escaped—a convict ! " An ironical smile curled the lip of Eugénie. " In truth, I was fated," said she ; " I escaped the Morcerf only to fall into the Cavalcanti."

" What shall we do ? " asked Louise.

" Why, what we had intended doing three days since—set off."

" What ! although you are not now going to be married, you intend still—— "

" I hate this fashionable life and long to be free from it. This night's adventure will serve as my excuse. I did not seek for one. God sends it and I greet it gladly. Come, Louise, let us talk of our affairs. The post-chaise— "

" Was happily bought three days since."

" Our passport ? "

" Here it is."

Eugénie, with her usual precision, opened a printed paper, and read :—

" M. Léon d'Armilly, twenty years of age ; profession, artist ; hair black, eyes black ; travelling with his sister."

" Capital ! How did you get it ? "

" When I went to ask M. de Monte Cristo for letters for the directors of the theatres at Rome and at Naples, I expressed some doubts about travelling as a woman. He undertook to procure for me a man's passport, and two days later I received this, to which I have added with my own hand, 'travelling with his sister.' "

" Well," said Eugénie, cheerfully, " we have then only to pack up our trunks ; we shall start on the evening of the signature, instead of the evening of the wedding—that is all. How much have we, Louise ? "

" Twenty-three thousand francs," said she.

" And as much at least, in pearls, diamonds, and jewels," said Eugénie. " We are rich. But before six months—you with your music, and I with my voice—we shall double our capital. Now, the portmanteau ! let us make haste—the portmanteau ! "

And the two young girls began to heap into a trunk all the things they thought they should require. " There, now," said Eugénie, " while I change my costume do you lock the portmanteau." Louise pressed with all the strength of her little hands on the top of the portmanteau. " But I cannot," said she ; " I am not strong enough ; do you shut it."

" Ah, you are right ! " said Eugénie, laughing ; " I forgot I was Hercules." And the young girl, kneeling on the top, pressed the two parts of the portmanteau together, and Mademoiselle d'Armilly passed the bolt of the padlock through. When this was done, Eugénie opened a drawer, of which she kept the key, and took from it a wadded violet silk travelling cloak. " Here," said she, " you will see I have thought of everything : with this cloak you will not be cold."

" Will you dress here ? "

" Certainly. Come and help me."

From the same drawer she took a man's costume. Eugénie drew on the boots and pantaloons, tied her cravat, buttoned her waistcoat up to the throat, and put on a coat which admirably fitted her figure.

" Oh, that is very good !—indeed, it is very good ! " said Louise, looking at her with admiration ; " but that beautiful black hair, those magnificent braids, which made all the ladies sigh with envy, will they go under a man's hat."

" You shall see," said Eugénie. And seizing with her left hand the thick mass which her long fingers could scarcely grasp, she took with her right a pair of long scissors, and soon the steel met through the rich and splendid locks which fell entire at the feet of the young girl, who leaned back to keep it from her coat.

" Oh, the magnificent hair ! " said Louise, with regret. " Now where shall we go ? "

" To Brussels, if you like ; it is the nearest frontier. We can go to Brussels, Liège, Aix-la-Chapelle ; then up the Rhine to Strasburg. We will cross Switzerland, and go down into Italy by Mont St. Gothard. Will that do ? "

" Yes."

" What are you looking at ? "

" I am looking at you ; indeed, you are adorable, like that ! One would say you were carrying me off."

" And they would be right, *par Dieu !* "

" Oh ! I think you swore, Eugénie." And the two girls burst out laughing as they cleared away every trace of the disorder which had accompanied the preparations for flight. Then the two fugitives opened the door of a dressing-room which led, by a side staircase, down to the yard. The yard was empty : the clock was striking twelve. The porter was not yet gone to bed. Eugénie approached softly, and saw the old man sleeping soundly in an armchair in his lodge. She returned to Louise, took up the portmanteau, which she had placed on the ground, and they reached the archway under the shadow of the wall.

Eugénie concealed Louise in an angle of the gateway, so that if the porter chanced to awake he might see but one person. Then placing herself in the full light of the lamp which lit the yard,— " Gate ! " cried she, with her finest contralto voice, and rapping at the window.

The porter got up as Eugénie expected, and opened it immediately. Louise slid through the half-open gate like a snake, and bounded lightly forward. Eugénie went out in her turn. A porter was passing, they gave him the portmanteau ; then the two young girls, having told him to take it to No. 36, Rue de la Victoire, walked behind this man, whose presence comforted Louise. They arrived at the appointed spot. Eugénie ordered the porter to put down the portmanteau, gave him some money, and, having rapped at the shutter, sent him away. A laundress opened the door.

" Mademoiselle," said Eugénie, " let the porter get the post-chaise from the coach-house and fetch some post-horses from the hotel. Here are five francs for his trouble." The laundress looked on in astonishment, but, as she had been promised twenty louis, made no remark.

In a quarter of an hour the porter returned with a post-boy and horses. " Here is the passport," said the postillion ; " which way are we going, young gentleman ? "

" To Fontainebleau," replied Eugénie, with an almost masculine voice.

" What do you say ? " said Louise.

" I am giving the slip," said Eugénie ; " this woman to whom we have given twenty louis may betray us for forty ; we will soon alter our direction." And the young girl jumped into the britska, without scarcely touching the step.

A quarter of an hour afterwards the postillion, having been put in the right road, passed through the gateway of the Barrière Saint-Martin. " Ah ! " said Louise, breathing freely, " here we are out of Paris."

M. Danglars had lost his daughter.

CHAPTER XCVIII

THE HOTEL OF THE BELL AND BOTTLE

AND now let us return to poor Andrea Cavalcanti, so uncomfortably interrupted in his career of fortune. We have seen that, after crossing two or three rooms, he at last disappeared from all Danglars' house. But we have forgotten to mention that in one of the rooms the *trousseau* of the bride-elect was exposed to view, consisting of cases of diamonds, cashmere shawls, Valenciennes lace, English veils, and, in fact, all those tempting things the bare mention of which makes the hearts of young girls bound with joy. Now, in passing through this room, Andrea proved himself not only to be clever and intelligent, but also provident, for he helped himself to the most valuable of the ornaments before him. Furnished with this plunder, Andrea leaped with a lighter heart from the window, intending to slip through the hands of the gendarmes. Having passed through the Rue Mont Blanc, he found himself, with the instinct which thieves have in avoiding barriers, at the end of the Rue Lafayette. At this moment he perceived a cab at the top of the Faubourg Poissonnière.

" Ho, friend ! " said Benedetto.

" What do you want, sir ? " said the driver.

" Is your horse tired ? "

" He will go like the wind, only tell me which way to drive."

" Towards Louvres. I merely wish to overtake one of my friends. If you do not overtake him before he reaches Bourget you shall have twenty francs ; if not before Louvres, thirty."

" And if we do overtake him ? "

" Forty," said Andrea.

" That will do ? " said the man ; " get in, and we're off ! Prrrrouuu ! "

Andrea got into the cab, which passed rapidly through the Faubourg St. Denis, along the Faubourg St. Martin, crossed the barrier, and threaded its way through the interminable Villette. They never overtook the imaginary friend, yet Andrea frequently inquired of walking passers and at the inns which were not yet closed, for a green cabriolet and bay horse. Once the cab was passed by a calèche, rapidly whirled along by two post-horses. The calèche contained Mademoiselle Danglars and Mademoiselle d'Armilly. " Onwards ! onwards ! " said Andrea. " we must overtake him soon." And the poor horse

resumed the desperate gallop it had never slackened since leaving
the barrier, and arrived smoking at Louvres.

"Certainly," said Andrea, "I will not overtake my friend, but
we shall kill your horse if we don't stop. Here are thirty francs,
I will sleep at the Cheval Rouge, and secure a place in the first
coach. Good-night, friend!"

The coachman joyfully pocketed the sum, and turned back on
his road to Paris. Andrea pretended to go towards the hotel of
the Cheval Rouge, but after stopping an instant against the door,
he went on his road, and with a firm tread prepared for a walk of
two leagues. It would be impossible to make use of a diligence,
equally so to engage post-horses; to travel either way a passport
was necessary. It would also be impossible to remain in the
department of the Oise, one of the most open and most strictly
guarded in France. He sat down, buried his face in his hands
and reflected. Ten minutes afterwards he raised his head; his
resolution was made. He threw some dust over his paletot and,
proceeding to Chapelle-en-Serval, knocked loudly at the door of
the only inn in the place. The host opened it. "My friend,"
said Andrea. "I was coming from Montefontaine to Senlis,
when my horse, which is a troublesome creature, stumbled and
threw me. I must reach Compiègne to-night, or I shall cause deep
anxiety to my family. Could you let me hire a horse of you?"

The landlord told the stable-boy to saddle "Le Blanc"; then
ordered his son, a child of seven, to ride before the gentleman and
bring back the horse. Andrea gave the innkeeper twenty francs,
and in taking them from his pocket, dropped a visiting card. This
belonged to one of his friends at the Café de Paris, so that the innkeeper, picking it up after Andrea had left, was convinced he had
lent his horse to M. le comte de Mauléon, 25, Rue Saint-Dominique.
Four o'clock struck as Andrea reached Compiègne. Having dismissed the child and the horse, he knocked at the hotel of the
Bell and Bottle, with which he had been familiar during his
rides round Paris. The waiter duly opened the door.

"My friend," said Andrea, "I have lost my way, and have
been walking for the last four hours in the forest. Show me into
one of these pretty little rooms which overlook the court, and bring
me a cold fowl and a bottle of Bordeaux." While the waiter was
preparing his room the hostess rose; Andrea assumed his most
charming smile, and asked if he could have No. 3, which he had
occupied on his last stay at Compiègne. Unfortunately, No.
3 was engaged. Andrea appeared in despair, but consoled himself
when the hostess assured him that No. 7, prepared for him, was

situated precisely like No. 3, and he waited until they announced his room to be ready.

The fowl was fresh, the wine old, the fire clear and sparkling and Andrea was surprised to find himself eating with as good an appetite as though nothing had happened. Then he went to bed. Now here we are obliged to own that Andrea ought to have felt remorse, but he did not. Instead, he at once thought out a plan of safety. Before daybreak he would awake, leave the hotel after discharging his bill, and go to the forest, where, under pretence of making studies in painting, he would test the hospitality of some peasants, and procure the dress of a woodcutter and a hatchet, and become a woodman. Gradually, keeping to the different forests, he would reach the nearest frontier. Once past the frontier, Andrea proposed making money of his diamonds; he would then find himself possessor of about 50,000 livres, which he philosophically considered as no very deplorable condition, after all.

In order that he might wake early, he did not close the shutters, but contented himself with bolting the door and placing on the table an unclasped and long-pointed knife, whose temper he well knew, and which was never absent from him. About seven in the morning Andrea was awakened by a ray of sunlight, which, warm and brilliant, played upon his face. He had scarcely opened his eyes when instinct whispered that he had slept too long. He jumped out of bed and ran to the window. A gendarme was crossing the court.

"Why is that gendarme there?" asked Andrea of himself. "Bah!" he said, "there is nothing astonishing in seeing a gendarme at an inn; instead of being astonished, let me dress myself!" He dressed himself with remarkable rapidity, and, after he had put on his boots and cravat, stole gently to the window, and a second time lifted up the muslin curtain. Not only was the first gendarme still there, but the young man perceived a second at the foot of the staircase, while a third, on horseback, holding a musket in his fist, was posted as a sentinel at the great street-door, which alone afforded the means of egress.

"They seek me!" was the first thought of Andrea. "*Diable!*"

"I am lost!" was his second thought; and, indeed, for a man in Andrea's situation, an arrest comprehended the assizes, the trial, and death—death without mercy or delay. For a moment he convulsively pressed his head within his hands, and during that brief period he became nearly mad with terror; but soon a ray of hope glanced through the crowd of thoughts which bewildered his mind, and a faint smile played upon his white lips and pallid cheeks.   He looked round and saw the objects of his search upon the chimney-piece ; they were a pen, ink, and paper.   With forced composure he dipped the pen in the ink, and wrote upon a sheet of paper :—" I have no money to pay my bill, but I am not a dishonest man ; I leave behind me as a pledge this pin, worth ten times the amount.   I shall be excused for escaping at daybreak, for I was ashamed."

He then drew the pin from his cravat and placed it on the paper.   This done, instead of leaving the door fastened, he drew back the bolts, and even placed the door ajar, as though he had left the room, forgetting to close it, and, sliding up the chimney like a man accustomed to this sort of gymnastic exercise, having effaced the very marks of his feet upon the floor, he began climbing the hollow tunnel which afforded him the only means of escape left.   At this precise time the first gendarme Andrea had noticed walked upstairs, preceded by the commissary of police, and supported by the second gendarme who guarded the staircase, and was himself reinforced by the one stationed at the door.   Telegraphic despatches in all directions intimated the latest news of the murderer of Caderousse and his arrest was strenuously pressed forward.   Amongst other places Compiègne had received the tidings.   Then the arrival at the Bell and Bottle, the chief hotel, at the unusual hour of four in the morning, of a man on horseback with a little boy in front of him demanded investigation. The man had knocked at the door of the hotel, which was opened, and again closed after his entrance.   This late arrival had attracted much suspicion, and the man being no other than Andrea, the commissary and gendarme, who was a brigadier, directed their steps towards his room.   They found the door ajar.

" Oh ! oh ! " said the brigadier, who thoroughly understood the trick, " a bad sign to find the door open !   I would rather find it trebly bolted."   Indeed, the note and pin upon the table confirmed, or rather supported, the sad truth.   Andrea had fled. We say supported, because the brigadier was too experienced to yield to a single proof.   He glanced round, looked in the bed, shook the curtains, opened the closets, and finally stopped at the chimney.   The brigadier sent for some sticks and straw, and having filled the chimney with them, set a light to it.   The fire crackled, and the smoke ascended like the dull vapour from a volcano ; but still no prisoner fell down, as they expected.   The fact was, that Andrea had reached the roof and was crouching down against the chimney-pots.   At one time he thought he was saved, for he heard the brigadier exclaim, in a loud voice, to the two gendarmes, " He is not here ! "   But venturing to peep, he perceived that the latter, instead of retiring, were watching with increased attention.   If once discovered, he knew he would be lost, for a chase on the roofs afforded no chance of success ; he therefore resolved to descend, not through the same chimney by which he had mounted, but by a similar one conducting to another room.   He looked round for a chimney from which no smoke issued and, having reached one, disappeared through the orifice without being seen by any one.   The brigadier, calm and dignified as the law he represented, passed through the crowd, without answering the thousand questions addressed to him, and re-entered the hotel.

Suddenly a loud scream, accompanied by the violent ringing of a bell, resounded through the court of the hotel.   " Ah ! what is that ? " cried the brigadier.

" Some impatient customer," said the landlord.   " No. 3, waiter ! "

At this moment the screams and ringing were redoubled.

" The person who is ringing appears to want something more than a waiter ; we will attend upon him with a gendarme.   Who occupies number 3 ? "

" The little fellow who arrived last night in a post-chaise with his sister, and asked for a double-bedded room."   The bell rang a third time, with another shriek full of anguish.

" Wait an instant," cried the host, " No. 3 has an inner and an outer staircase."

" Good ! " said the brigadier, " I will take charge of the interior one," and he deputed the care of the other to a gendarme.

The brigadier, followed by the commissary, disappeared by the interior staircase.

Meanwhile how had it fared with Andrea ?   While cautiously descending the chimney his foot slipped and he dropped into the room with more speed and noise than he intended.   It would have signified little had the room been empty, but unfortunately it was occupied.   Two ladies, sleeping in one bed, were awakened by the noise, and fixing their eyes upon the spot whence the sound proceeded they saw a man.   One of these ladies, the fair one, uttered those terrible shrieks which resounded through the house ; while the other, rushing to the bell-rope, rang with all her strength.

" Andrea, the murderer ! " cried one of the ladies.

" Eugénie ! Mademoiselle Danglars ! " exclaimed Andrea, stupefied.

" Help ! help ! " cried Mademoiselle d'Armilly, taking the bell from her companion's hand, and ringing it yet more violently.

" Save me, I am pursued ! " said Andrea, clasping his hands. " For pity's, for mercy's sake, do not deliver me up ! "

The two ladies, pressing closely to one another, and drawing the bedclothes tightly round them, remained silent to this supplicating voice ; all their repugnance, all their fear inflamed their imaginations.

" Well ! be it so," at length said Eugénie, " return by the same road you came, and we will say nothing about you, unhappy wretch."

" Here he is ! here he is ! " cried a voice in the landing-place ; " here he is ! I see him ! " The brigadier had put his eye to the key-hole, and had perceived Andrea standing and entreating. A violent blow from the butt-end of the musket burst open the lock, two more blows forced out the bolts, and the door fell in. Andrea ran to the other door leading to the gallery, ready to rush out ; but he was stopped short ; and he stood with his body a little thrown back, pale, and with the useless knife in his clenched hands.

" Fly, then ! " cried Mademoiselle d'Armilly, whose pity returned as her fears diminished. " Or kill yourself ! " said Eugénie.

" Kill myself ! " he cried, throwing down his knife ; " why should I do so ? "

" Why," answered Mademoiselle Danglars, " you will be condemned to die like the worst criminals."

The brigadier advanced to him, sword in hand. " Come, come," said Andrea, " sheathe your sword, my fine fellow ; there is no occasion to make such a fuss, since I yield myself ;" and he held out his hands to be manacled.

" Have you any message for your father, Mademoiselle Danglars, for, in all probability, I shall return to Paris ? "

Eugénie covered her face with her hands.

" Oh ! oh ! " said Andrea, " you need not be ashamed, even though you did post after me. Was I not nearly your husband ? "

And with this raillery Andrea went out, leaving the two girls a prey to their own sufferings of shame, and to the comments of the crowd. An hour afterwards they stepped into their calèche, both dressed in female attire. The gate of the hotel had been closed to screen them from sight, but they were forced, when the door was opened, to pass through a throng of curious glances and whispering voices. Eugénie closed her eyes ; but though she could not see she could hear, and the sneers of the crowd reached

her in the carriage. " Oh ! why is not the world a wilderness ? "
she exclaimed.

Next day they stopped at the Hôtel de Flandres at Brussels.
The same evening Andrea was secured in the Conciergerie.

CHAPTER XCIX

THE LAW

MADAME DANGLARS, after remaining for a moment as if crushed
under the weight of the blow which had struck her, went to seek
her usual adviser, Lucien Debray. The baroness had looked forward to this marriage as a means of ridding her of a guardianship
which, over a girl of Eugénie's character, could not fail to be
troublesome ; for in those tacit understandings which maintain
the bond of family union the mother is only mistress of her
daughter so long as she presents herself to her as a model of
wisdom and type of perfection. Now, Madame Danglars feared
the penetration of Eugénie and the counsel of Mademoiselle
d'Armilly ; she had frequently observed the contempt with which
her daughter regarded Debray, a contempt which seemed to imply
that she understood all her mother's relations, pecuniary and
otherwise, with the secretary. Madame Danglars, therefore,
very much regretted that the marriage of Eugénie had not taken
place, not only because the match was good, and likely to ensure
the happiness of her child, but because it would also set her at
liberty. She went therefore to see Debray, who, after having, like
the rest of Paris, witnessed the contract scene and the scandal
attending it, had retired in haste to his club, where he was chatting with some friends upon the event. Although informed by
Debray's young man that his master was not at home, Madame
Danglars, discreetly disguised, insisted on remaining in the
secretary's apartments, in momentary expectation of his arrival.
She awaited him in a little green room, seated between two
baskets of flowers which she had that morning sent. But at
twenty minutes to twelve Madame Danglars, tired of waiting,
returned home.

The baroness returned to her apartment, which adjoined that
of Eugénie. She listened at Eugénie's door, then, hearing no
sound, tried to enter, but the bolts were drawn. She called her
maid and questioned her.

" Mademoiselle Eugénie," she said, " retired to her apartment
with Mademoiselle d'Armilly ; they then took tea together, after

which they desired me to leave, saying they required me no longer."
Madame Danglars, therefore, went to bed without a shadow of
suspicion, and mused over the past events. Then she remembered
that she had felt no pity for poor Mercédès, who had been afflicted
with as severe a blow through her husband.

"Eugénie," she said to herself, "is lost, and so are we. The
affair will cover us with shame ; for in society such as ours satire
inflicts an incurable wound. How fortunate that Eugénie is
possessed of that strange character which has so often made me
tremble ! "

Presently her thoughts, cleaving through space as a bird in the
air, rested on Cavalcanti. How could she extricate herself from
this labyrinth ? To whom could she apply to help her out of
this painful situation ? Debray could but give her advice ; she
must apply to some one more powerful than he. The baroness
then thought of M. de Villefort. It was M. de Villefort who had
caused Cavalcanti to be arrested. She would, therefore, see the
procureur next day, and if she could not make him relax his
duties as a magistrate, she would, at least, obtain all the indulgence he could grant.

At nine o'clock next morning she called a fiacre, and drove to
M. de Villefort's house. For the last month this wretched house
had presented the gloomy appearance of a lazaretto infected
with the plague. Madame Danglars, descending from the coach,
approached the door with trembling knees and rang the bell.
The concierge peeped through the door, which he opened just
wide enough to allow his words to be heard. He saw a fashionable, elegantly-dressed lady, and yet the door remained almost
closed.

"Do you intend opening the door ? " said the Baroness.

"First, madame, who are you ? "

"Who am I ? You know me well enough."

"Madame, these are my orders ; excuse me. Your name ? "

"The Baroness Danglars : you have seen me twenty times."

"Possibly, madame. And now, what do you want ? "

"Oh, how extraordinary ! I shall complain to M. de Villefort
of the impertinence of his servants."

"Madame, this is precaution, not impertinence ; no one enters
here without an order from M. d'Avrigny, or without speaking to
the *procureur*."

"But my business is with the *procureur*."

"Madame will await my return ? "

"Yes ; go." The concierge closed the door, leaving Madame

Danglars in the street. She had not long to wait; directly afterwards the door was opened wide enough to admit her, and when she had passed through, it was again shut. The valet appeared. "You will excuse this poor fellow, madame," he said, as he preceded the baroness; "but his orders are precise, and M. de Villefort begged me to tell you he could not have acted otherwise."

The baroness ascended the steps and was led to the study of the magistrate. "Forgive my servants," he said, "for a terror I cannot blame them for; from being suspected they have become suspicious."

"You, too, then, are unhappy?" she said.

"Yes, madame," replied the magistrate.

"Then you pity me?"

"Sincerely, madame."

"And you understand what brings me here?"

"You wish to speak to me about the circumstance which has just happened?"

"Yes, sir, a fearful misfortune."

"You mean a mischance."

"A mischance!" repeated the baroness.

"Alas! madame," said the *procureur du roi*, "I consider those alone misfortunes which are irreparable."

"And do you suppose this will be forgotten?"

"Everything will be forgotten, madame," said de Villefort; "your daughter will be married to-morrow, if not to-day; in a week, if not to-morrow. I do not think you can regret the intended husband of your daughter."

"Have I come to a friend?" she asked, in a tone full of mournful dignity.

"You know you have, madame," said de Villefort.

"Well, then, be more affectionate, my dear de Villefort," said the baroness.

"When I hear misfortunes named, madame," he said, "I have within the last few months contracted the bad habit of thinking of my own, and then I cannot help drawing up a selfish parallel in my mind. You were saying, madame——"

"I came to ask you, my friend," said the baroness, "what will be done with this impostor."

"Impostor!" repeated Villefort; "M. Andrea Cavalcanti, or, rather, M. Benedetto, is nothing more nor less than an assassin."

"Sir, I do not deny the justice of your correction; but the more severely you denounce that unfortunate, the more deeply will you strike our family. Come, forget him for a moment, and, instead of pursuing him, let him fly."

' You are too late, madame, the orders are issued."

" Yet, even if they should arrest him, he might be able to leave the prison ? "

The *procureur du roi* shook his head.

" At least keep him there till my daughter be married."

" Impossible, madame : justice has its formalities."

" What ! even for me ? " said the baroness, half jesting, half in earnest.

" For all, even for myself," replied de Villefort.

" Ah ! " exclaimed the baroness in a significant tone.

" Madame, you are thinking of those terrible rumours about this house and of the deaths which have kept me mourning, and of the danger from which Valentine has not yet recovered, and are saying to yourself, ' You who pursue crime so vindictively, answer now, why are there unpunished crimes in your dwelling ? ' " The baroness became pale. " You were saying this, were you not ? "

" Well, I own it."

" I will answer you."

Villefort drew his armchair nearer to Madame Danglars ; then, resting both hands upon his desk, he said, in a voice more hollow than usual,—" There are crimes which remain unpunished because the criminals are unknown, and we might strike the innocent instead of the guilty ; but when the culprits are discovered I swear to you by all I hold most sacred, that whoever they may be they shall die. Now, after the oath I have just taken, and which I will keep, madame, dare you ask for mercy for that wretch ? "

" And who is this wretch ? "

" Who can tell ?—a vagabond, a Corsican."

" Has no one owned him ? "

" No one ; his parents are unknown."

" But who was the man who brought him from Lucca ? "

" Another rascal like himself, perhaps his accomplice."

The baroness clasped her hands. " De Villefort ! " she exclaimed in her softest and most captivating manner.

" For Heaven's sake, madame," said de Villefort, with a firmness of expression not free from harshness, " for Heaven's sake, do not ask pardon of me for a guilty wretch. What am I ? The law. You will tell me that I am a living being and not a code ; a man, and not a volume. Woman ! siren that you are, do you persist in fixing on me that fascinating eye, which reminds me that

I ought to blush ? Well, be it so, let me blush for the faults you
know, and perhaps for even more than these ! But having
sinned myself, it may be more deeply than others, I never rest
till I have torn the disguises from my fellow-creatures, and found
out their weaknesses. Alas ! all the world is wicked, let us
therefore strike at wickedness ! "

De Villefort pronounced these last words with a feverish rage,
which gave a ferocious eloquence to his words.

" But," said Madame Danglars, resolving to make a last effort,
" this young man, though a murderer, is an orphan, abandoned
by everybody."

" So much the worse, or rather so much the better ; it has
been so ordained that he may have none to weep his fate."

" Oh, sir," exclaimed the baroness, " you are without pity for
others. Well, then, I tell you they will have no mercy on you ! "

" Be it so ! " said de Villefort, raising his arms to heaven.

" Sir," said the valet, entering the room, " a dragoon has brought
this despatch from the Minister of the Interior."

De Villefort hastily unsealed the letter. " Arrested ! " he
exclaimed ; " he was taken at Compiègne, and all is over."

Madame Danglars rose from her seat pale and cold, " Adieu,
sir ! " she said.

" Adieu, madame," replied the *procureur du roi*, as in an almost
joyful manner he conducted her to the door. Then, turning to
his desk, he said, striking the letter with his right hand, " Come ;
I had a forgery, three robberies, and two incendiaries ; I only
wanted a murder, and here it is : it will be a splendid session."

CHAPTER C

THE APPARITION

As the *procureur du roi* had told Madame Danglars, Valentine
was not yet recovered. During the daytime her perceptions
remained tolerably clear, owing to the constant presence of M.
Noirtier, who caused himself to be carried to his granddaughter's
room, and watched her with paternal tenderness ; De Villefort also
on his return from the Palais frequently passed an hour or two
with his father and his child. At six o'clock de Villefort retired
to his study, at eight M. d'Avrigny arrived himself, bringing the
night draught for the young girl, and then M. Noirtier was carried away. A nurse of the doctor's choice succeeded them, and

never left till about ten or eleven o'clock, when Valentine was asleep. Every morning Morrel called on Noirtier to receive news of Valentine, and, extraordinary as it seemed, each day found him less uneasy. Certainly, though Valentine still laboured under dreadful nervous excitement, she was better. This nervous excitement pursued her even in her sleep. First she fancied she saw her stepmother threatening her ; then Morrel stretched his arms towards her ; sometimes mere strangers, like the count of Monte Cristo, appeared to visit her. On the evening of the day on which Valentine had learnt of the flight of Eugénie and the arrest of Benedetto, de Villefort having retired as well as Noirtier and d'Avrigny, her thoughts wandered in a confused maze, alternately reviewing her own situation and the events she had just heard of.

Eleven o'clock had struck. Ten minutes had elapsed since the nurse had left, when suddenly Valentine thought she saw the door of her library, which was in the recess by the chimney-piece, open slowly, though she in vain listened for the sound of the hinges on which it turned. Her reason told her that all the visions she beheld were but the children of her imagination, and the conviction was strengthened by the fact that in the morning, no traces remained of the nocturnal phantoms, which disappeared with the daylight. The figure advanced towards the bed, and appeared to listen with profound attention. At this moment a ray of light glanced across the face of the midnight visitor.

"It is not he ! " she murmured ; and waited in the assurance of its being but a dream, for the man to disappear or assume some other form. Still she felt her pulse, and finding it throb violently, she remembered that the best method of dispelling such illusions was to drink, for a draught of the beverage prepared by the doctor to allay her fever seemed to cause a reaction of the brain, and, for a short time, she suffered less. Valentine therefore reached her hand towards the glass, but as soon as her trembling arm left the bed the apparition advanced more quickly towards her, and approached the young girl so closely, that she fancied she heard his breath, and felt the pressure of his hand. The pressure was evidently intended to arrest her arm, and she slowly withdrew it. Then the figure, took the glass and held it up to the nightlight, as if to test its transparency. The man then poured out about a spoonful and drank it. Valentine witnessed this scene with a sentiment of stupefaction. Every minute she had expected that it would vanish and give place to another vision ; but the man, instead of dissolving like a sha-

dow, again approached her, and said, in an agitated voice,—
"Now you may drink."

Valentine shuddered. It was the first time one of these
visions had ever addressed her in a living voice, and she was
about to utter an exclamation. The man placed his finger on
her lips. "The count of Monte Cristo!" she murmured.

"Do not call, do not be alarmed," said the count, "do not
let a shade of suspicion or uneasiness remain in your breast : the
man standing before you is nothing more than the tenderest
father and the most respectful friend you could dream of."

Valentine could not reply ; the voice which indicated the real
presence of a being in the room alarmed her so much that she
feared to utter a syllable.

"Listen to me," he said, "or rather look upon me ; look at
my face, paler even than usual, and my eyes, red with weariness
—for four days I have not closed them, for I have been constantly watching you, to protect and preserve you for Maximilian." The blood mounted rapidly to the cheeks of Valentine,
for the name just pronounced by the count dispelled all the fear
with which his presence had inspired her. "Maximilian!"
she exclaimed, and so sweet did the sound appear to her, that
she repeated it,—"Maximilian ! has he then owned all to you ? "

"Everything. He told me your life was his, and I have promised him you shall live."

"But, sir, you spoke of vigilance and protection. Are you a
doctor ? "

"Yes, the best you could have at the present time, believe me."

"But you say you have watched," said Valentine, uneasily ;
"where have you been ? I have not seen you."

The count extended his hand towards the library. "I was
hidden behind that door," he said, "which leads into the next
house, which I have rented."

Valentine turned her eyes away, and, with an indignant expression of pride and modest fear, exclaimed,—"Sir, I think you
have been guilty of an unparalleled intrusion, and what you call
protection more resembles an insult."

" Valentine," he answered, "during my long watch over you,
all I have observed has been what people visited you, what
nourishment was prepared, and what beverage was served ; then
when the latter appeared dangerous to me, I entered, as I have
now done, and substituted, in the place of the poison, a healthy
draught ; which, instead of producing the death intended, caused
life to circulate in your veins. But drink some of this ; "

and the count took a bottle from his pocket containing a red
liquid, of which he poured a few drops into the glass, " Drink
this and take nothing more to-night."

Valentine stretched out her hand ; but scarcely had she
touched the glass when she drew it back in fear. Monte Cristo
took the glass, and drank half its contents, and then presented
it to Valentine, who smiled and swallowed the rest. " Oh !
yes," she exclaimed, " I recognise the flavour of my nocturnal
beverage which refreshed me so much, and seemed to ease my
aching brain. Thank you, sir, thank you ! "

" This is how you have lived during the last four nights,
Valentine," said the count. " But, oh ! the torture I endured
when I saw the deadly poison poured into your glass, and how I
trembled lest you would drink it before I could throw it away ! "

" Sir," said Valentine at the height of her terror, " you say
you endured tortures when you saw the deadly poison poured
into my glass ; but if you saw this you must also have seen the
person who poured it ? "

" Yes."

Valentine raised herself in bed. " You saw the person ? "

" Yes ! " repeated the count.

" That which you tell me is horrible, sir. What ! an attempt to
murder me in my father's house ! Oh ! leave me, sir ; you are
tempting me ; you make me doubt the goodness of Providence ;
it is impossible, it cannot be ! "

" Are you the first that this hand has stricken ? Would not
M. Noirtier also have fallen a victim, had not the treatment
he has been pursuing for the last three years neutralized the effects
of the poison ? "

" Oh, heavens ! " said Valentine ; " is that why grandpapa
has made me share all his beverages during the last month ? "

" Then that explains all," said Monte Cristo. " Your grandfather knows that a poisoner lives here ; perhaps he even suspects the person. But even his precautions would have availed
little against a more deadly medium of death employed four days
ago, which is generally but too fatal."

" But who is this assassin—this murderer ? "

" You do not know who it is that attempts your life ? "

" No," said Valentine ; " who could desire my death ? "

" You shall know it now," said Monte Cristo, listening.

Midnight struck slowly and sadly ; every hour seemed to beat
with leaden weight upon the heart of the poor girl.

" Valentine," said the count, " summon up all your courage ;

still the beatings of your heart ; do not let a sound escape you, and feign to be asleep ; then you will see." Valentine seized the count's hand. " I think I hear a noise," she said ; " leave me."

" Good-bye for the present," replied the count : " not a movement—not a word ; let them think you asleep ; or, perhaps, you may be killed before I have the power of helping you." With this fearful injunction the count disappeared through the door.

CHAPTER CI

THE SERPENT

VALENTINE was alone ; two other clocks, slower than that of St. Philippe du Roule, struck the hour of midnight from different situations. One terrible idea pressed upon her mind, that some one existed in the world who had attempted to assassinate her, and who was about to endeavour to do so again. Supposing this person, wearied at the inefficacy of the poison, should have recourse to steel ! What if the count should have no time to run to her rescue ! What if her last moments were approaching, and she should never again see Morrel ! Twenty minutes, twenty tedious minutes, passed thus, then ten more, and at last the clock struck the half-hour. Just then the sound of fingernails slightly grating against the door of the library informed Valentine that the count was still watching, and warned her to do the same. On the opposite side, that is towards Edward's room, Valentine now fancied she heard the creaking of the floor ; the lock turned, and the door slowly opened.

Someone approached the bed and drew aside the curtains. Everything was still, excepting that Valentine heard the almost noiseless sound of some liquid being poured into the glass she had just emptied. Then she ventured to open her eyelid, and glance over her extended arm. She saw a female in a white dressing-gown pouring a liquor from a phial into her glass. During this short time Valentine must have moved in some slight degree, for the woman, disturbed, stopped and leaned over the bed, in order better to ascertain whether Valentine slept : it was Madame de Villefort.

On recognising her stepmother, Valentine could not repress a shudder, which caused a vibration in the bed. Madame de Villefort instantly stepped back close to the wall, and there, hidden by the bed-curtains, she silently and attentively watched the slightest movement of Valentine. Madame de Villefort, reassured by the silence, which was only disturbed by the regular breathing of Valentine, again extended her hand, and succeeded in emptying the contents of the phial into the glass. Then she retired so gently that Valentine did not know she had left the room.

The noiseless door again turned on its hinges and the count of Monte Cristo reappeared. "Well," said he, "have you seen?"

Valentine groaned. "Oh, yes!" she said, "I saw, but I cannot believe!"

"Would you rather die, then, and cause Maximilian's death?"

"But did you not say that my grandfather's precaution had neutralized the poison?"

"Yes, but not against a strong dose; the poison will be changed and the quantity increased." He took the glass and raised it to his lips. "It is already done," he said, "brucine is no longer employed, but a simple narcotic. If you had taken what Madame de Villefort has poured into this glass, Valentine, you would have been lost!"

"But," exclaimed the young girl, "why am I thus pursued?"

"You are rich, Valentine; you have 200,000 livres a year, and you prevent her son from enjoying that fortune."

"Edward? Poor child! have all these crimes been committed on his account?"

"Ah! now you understand?"

"And has this frightful combination of crimes been invented by a woman?"

"Do you recollect in the Hôtel des Postes, at Perugia, seeing a man in a brown cloak, whom your stepmother was questioning upon *aqua tofana?* Well, ever since then, the infernal project has been ripening in her brain."

"Ah, then, indeed, sir," said the sweet girl, bathed in tears, "I see that I am condemned to die!"

"No; for I have foreseen all their plots; you will live, Valentine, but to ensure this you must rely on me."

"Command me, sir—what am I to do?"

"You must blindly take what I give you. You must not confide in anyone—not even in your father."

"My father is not engaged in this fearful plot, is he, sir?" asked Valentine, clasping her hands.

"No; and yet he ought to have known that all these deaths have not happened naturally; it is he who should have watched over you, who should have risen against the assassin! Spectre against spectre ! " he murmured in a low voice, as he concluded his sentence.

"Well, sir, do as you will with me ; " and then she added, in a low voice, "Oh, heavens ! what will befall me ? "

"Whatever may happen, Valentine, do not be alarmed ; even though you should find yourself in a sepulchral vault or coffin. Even then, reassure yourself and reflect : 'At this moment a friend, a father, who lives for my happiness and that of Maximilian, watches over me ! ' "

"Alas ! alas ! what a fearful extremity ! "

"Valentine, would you rather denounce your stepmother ? "

"I would rather die a hundred times—oh, yes, die ! "

"No, you will not die ! but will you promise me, whatever happens, that you will not complain, but hope ? "

"I will think of Maximilian ! " and then she began to pray, gradually lapsing into a semi-unconscious state.

Monte Cristo gently laid his hand on the young girl's arm, drew the velvet coverlid close to her throat, and said with a paternal smile,—"My child, believe in my devotion to you as you believe in the goodness of Providence and the love of Maximilian."

Then he drew from his waistcoat pocket the little emerald box, raised the golden lid, and took from it a pastille, about the size of a pea, which he placed in her hand. She interrogated him by a look. "Yes," said he. Valentine carried the pastille to her mouth, and swallowed it. "And now, my dear child, adieu for the present. I will try to gain a little sleep, for you are saved."

"Go," said Valentine ; "whatever happen, I promise you not to fear."

As she yielded to the influence of the narcotic, Monte Cristo took the glass, emptied three parts of the contents in the fireplace, that it might be supposed Valentine had taken it, and replaced it on the table ; then he disappeared, after throwing a farewell glance on Valentine, who slept with the confidence and innocence of an angel.

CHAPTER CII

VALENTINE

THE nightlight continued to burn on the chimney-piece. All noise in the streets had ceased and the silence was profound, even appalling. Then the door of Edward's room opened, and Madame de Villefort stopped in the doorway, listened for a moment, and advanced to the table, to see if Valentine's glass were empty.

She emptied the contents into the ashes and replaced it on the table. If anyone could have looked into the room, he would have noticed the hesitancy with which Madame de Villefort approached the bed. At length she rallied, drew the curtain, and leaning over the pillow, gazed intently on Valentine. The young girl no longer breathed. Madame de Villefort raised the coverlet and pressed her hand upon Valentine's heart. It seemed to be motionless. One arm hung out of the bed, but the other appeared slightly distorted by convulsion. Madame de Villefort had no longer any doubt; all was over; she had consummated the last terrible work she had to accomplish. Just then the lamp flickered; the noise startled Madame de Villefort, who shuddered and dropped the curtain. Immediately afterwards the light expired, and the room was plunged in awful obscurity, while the clock at that minute struck half-past four. Overpowered with agitation, the poisoner groped her way to the door, and reached her room in an agony of fear. In two hours more the nurse's cough was heard on the stairs, and the woman entered the room with a cup in her hand.

"Good!" she exclaimed, approaching the table, "she has taken her draught."

Then she went to the fireplace and lit the fire, and although she had but just left her bed, threw herself into an armchair to snatch more rest. The clock striking eight awoke her. Astonished at the prolonged sleep of the patient, and alarmed to see that the arm was still hanging out of bed, she advanced towards Valentine, and for the first time noticed the white lips. She tried to replace the arm, but it moved with a stiffness which could not deceive a nurse. She screamed aloud, then running to the door, exclaimed, "Help! help!"

"What do you mean?" asked M. d'Avrigny, at the foot of the stairs, it being the hour he usually visited the patient.

"Call Madame de Villefort!—wake Madame de Villefort!" cried the *procureur du roi* from the door of his chamber, which it seemed he scarcely dared to leave. But instead of obeying him, the servants stood watching M. d'Avrigny, who ran to Valentine and lifted her in his arms.

"What! this one too!" he exclaimed. "Oh! when will this cease?" De Villefort rushed into the room.

"What are you saying, doctor?" he exclaimed, raising his hands to heaven.

"Valentine is dead," replied d'Avrigny, in a voice terrible in its solemn calmness.

M. de Villefort staggered and buried his head in the bed. On the exclamation of the doctor and the cry of the father, the servants all fled with muttered imprecations.   There was a rush into the court, and afterwards all was still ; they had, one and all, deserted the accursed house.

Meanwhile Madame de Villefort came on the scene and, while trying to conjure up some reluctant tears, was horrified to see M. d'Avrigny examining the glass, which she thought she had entirely emptied during the night.   It was a quarter full, just as it was when she threw the contents into the ashes.   It was, indeed, the same colour as the draught which she had poured into the glass, and which Valentine had drunk ; it was indeed the poison, which could not deceive M. d'Avrigny, which he now examined so closely ; it was doubtless a miracle from heaven, that, not-withstanding her precautions, there should be some trace, some proof remaining to reveal the crime.   While Madame de Villefort remained rooted to the spot like a statue of terror, d'Avrigny approached the window, and dipping the tip of his finger into the glass tasted its contents.

" Ah ! " he exclaimed, " it is not brucine ; let me see what it is."

Then he ran to one of the cupboards in Valentine's room, which had been transformed into a medicine closet, and taking from its silver case a small bottle of nitric acid, dropped a little into the liquor, which immediately changed to a blood-red colour.

" Ah ! " exclaimed d'Avrigny, in a voice in which the horror of a judge unveiling the truth was mixed with the delight of a student discovering a problem.   Madame de Villefort vanished silently from the room, and presently the sound, as of a heavy weight, was heard falling on the floor.   M. d'Avrigny, who had remarked her precipitate retreat, lifted up the drapery over the entrance to Edward's room, and, his eye reaching as far as Madame de Villefort's apartment, he beheld her extended on the floor.

" Go to the assistance of Madame de Villefort," he said to the nurse.   " Madame de Villefort is ill."

" But Mademoiselle de Villefort——" stammered the nurse.

" Mademoiselle de Villefort no longer requires help," said d'Avrigny; "she is dead."

" Dead ! dead ! " groaned forth de Villefort, in a paroxysm of grief, which was the more terrible from the novelty of the sensation in the iron heart of that man.

" Dead ! who said Valentine was dead ? "

The doctor and the *procureur* turned round, and saw Morrel

standing at the door, pale and terror-stricken. Morrel had presented himself at the usual time at the little door leading to Noirtier's room. The first thing he saw was the old man sitting in his armchair, in his usual place ; but his eyes expressed an internal fright, which was confirmed by the pallor which overspread his features.

"How are you, sir ? " asked Morrel, with a sickness of heart.

"Well ! " answered the old man, by closing his eyes. But his appearance manifested increasing uneasiness.

" You are thoughtful, sir," continued Morrel ; " you want something ; shall I call one of the servants ? "

" Yes," replied Noirtier.

Morrel pulled the bell, but, though he nearly broke the cord, no one answered.

" Oh ! " exclaimed Morrel. " What is the matter ? You alarm me. Valentine ? Valentine ? "

" Yes, yes," signed Noirtier.

Maximilian tried to speak, but he could articulate nothing ; he staggered, and supported himself against the wainscot. Then he pointed to the door. " Yes, yes, yes," continued the old man. Maximilian rushed up the little staircase, while Noirtier's eyes seemed to say, " Quicker ! quicker ! "

In a minute the young man darted through several rooms, till, at length, he reached Valentine's. A sob was the only sound he heard. He saw, as though in a mist, a black figure kneeling, buried in a confused mass of white drapery. A terrible fear transfixed him. It was then he heard a voice declare that Valentine was dead.

CHAPTER CIII

MAXIMILIAN

DE VILLEFORT rose, half ashamed of being surprised in such a paroxysm of grief. " Who are you, sir," he asked of Morrel, " that forget that this is not the manner to enter a house stricken with death ? " Go !—do you hear ? " said de Villefort, while d'Avrigny advanced to lead Morrel out. Maximilian went out, thrusting his hands through his hair in such a manner that de Villefort and d'Avrigny exchanged glances which seemed to convey,—" He is mad ! "

But, in less than five minutes, the staircase groaned beneath an extraordinary weight. Morrel was seen carrying, with superhuman strength, the armchair containing Noirtier, upstairs. When he reached the landing, he placed the armchair on the floor, and rapidly ran it into Valentine's room. The aged man's pale face and flaming glance appeared to de Villefort like a frightful apparition. Every time he had been brought into contact with his father something terrible had happened.

" Sir ! " cried Morrel, seizing M. Noirtier's moist hand, " they ask me who I am, and what right I have to be here ? " And the young man's voice was choked by sobs. As for the old man, his chest heaved with his panting respiration. One could have thought he was undergoing the agonies preceding death. At length, happier than the young man, who sobbed without weeping, tears glistened in the eyes of Noirtier. " Tell them," said Morrel, in a hoarse voice, " tell them I am her betrothed. Tell them she was my beloved, my noble girl, my only blessing in the world. Tell them—oh ! tell them, that corpse belongs to me." The young man fell heavily on his knees before the bed, which his fingers grasped with convulsive energy. D'Avrigny, unable to bear the sight of this emotion, turned away ; and de Villefort, without seeking any further explanation, extended his hand towards the young man. But Morrel saw nothing ; he had grasped the hand of Valentine, and, unable to weep, vented his agony in gnawing the sheets. At length de Villefort, the most composed of all, spoke : " Sir," said he to Maximilian, " you say you loved Valentine, that you were betrothed to her. But the angel you worshipped has left this earth—she has nothing more to do with the adoration of men. Take a last farewell, sir, of her sad remains ; Valentine now only requires the priest who will bless her."

" You are mistaken, sir," exclaimed Morrel, raising himself on one knee, his heart pierced by a more acute pang than any he had yet felt, " you are mistaken ; Valentine, dying as she has, not only requires a priest, but an avenger. *You*, M. de Villefort, send for the priest, *I* will be the avenger."

The eyes of Noirtier glistened, and d'Avrigny approached.

" Gentlemen," said Morrel, reading all that passed through their minds, " I know what I am saying, and you know as well as I do what I am about to say—Valentine has been assassinated ! Now, sir," continued Morrel, " in these days no one can disappear by violent means without some inquiries being made as to the cause of her disappearance, even were the person not a young, beautiful, and adorable creature like Valentine. M. le Procureur du Roi," said Morrel, with increasing vehemence, " no mercy is allowed ; I denounce the crime ; it is your place to seek the assassin."

" Sir," said de Villefort, " you are deceived, no one commits crime here. I am stricken by fate. It is horrible, but no one assassinates."

" And I say that murders *are* committed here," said Morrel, whose voice, though lower in tone, lost none of its terrible distinctness ; " I tell you that this is the fourth victim within the last four months. I tell you that you know these things as well as I do, since this gentleman has forewarned you, both as a doctor and a friend."

" You rave, sir," exclaimed de Villefort, in vain endeavouring to escape the net in which he was taken.

" I rave ? " said Morrel ; " well, then, I appeal to M. d'Avrigny himself. Ask him, sir, if he recollects some words he uttered in the garden of this hôtel on the night of Madame de Saint Méran's death." De Villefort and d'Avrigny exchanged looks. " Yes," continued Morrel ; " recall the scene, for the words you thought were only given to silence and solitude fell upon my ears. This fourth murder is apparent to all, and if thy father abandon thee, Valentine, I, and I swear it, will pursue the assassin." This time the words of Morrel were stifled in his throat ; his breast heaved ; and he threw himself, weeping, on his knees, by the side of the bed.

Then d'Avrigny spoke. " I too," he exclaimed in a low voice, " unite with M. Morrel, in demanding justice for crime ; my blood boils at the idea of having encouraged a murderer by my cowardly weakness ! "

" Oh, merciful Heaven ! " murmured de Villefort. Morrel raised his head, and reading the eyes of the old man, which gleamed with unnatural lustre, " Stay," he said, " M. Noirtier wishes to speak."

" Yes," indicated Noirtier, with an expression the more terrible, from all his faculties being centred in his glance.

" Do you know the assassin ? " asked Morrel.

" Yes," replied Noirtier.

" And will you direct us ? " exclaimed the young man. " Listen, M. d'Avrigny ! listen ! " Noirtier glanced towards the door.

" Do you wish me to leave ? " said Morrel, sadly.

" Yes, replied Noirtier.

" Must I go alone ? "

" No."

" Whom am I to take with me ? The doctor ? "

" Yes."

" You wish to remain alone with M. de Villefort ? "

" Yes."

D'Avrigny took the young man's arm and led him out of the room. At the end of a quarter of an hour a faltering footstep was heard, and de Villefort appeared at the door of the room where d'Avrigny and Morrel were waiting. " You can come," he said, and led them back to Noirtier. Morrel looked attentively on de Villefort. His face was livid, large drops rolled down his face : and in his fingers he held the fragments of a pen which he had torn to atoms. " Gentlemen," he said, in a hoarse voice, " give me your word of honour that this horrible secret shall for ever remain buried amongst ourselves ! " The two men drew back.

" Do not alarm yourself, justice will be done," said de Villefort. " My father thirsts for revenge as much as you do, yet even he conjures you as I do to keep this secret. Do you not, father ? "

" Yes," resolutely replied Nortier. Morrel suffered an exclamation of horror and surprise to escape him.

" Oh, sir ! " said de Villefort, arresting Maximilian by the arm. " Rest assured that within three days, in a less time than justice would demand, the revenge I shall have taken for the murder of my child will be such as to make the boldest heart tremble."

" Will this promise be fulfilled, M. Noirtier ? " asked Morrel, while d'Avrigny looked inquiringly.

" Yes," replied Noirtier, with an expression of sinister joy.

" Swear, then," said de Villefort, joining the hands of Morrel and d'Avrigny, " that you will spare the honour of my house, and leave me to avenge my child." D'Avrigny turned round and uttered a very feeble " Yes," but Morrel, disengaging his hand, rushed to the bed, and, after having pressed the cold lips of Valentine with his own, hurriedly left, uttering a long, deep groan of despair and anguish.

De Villefort retired to his study, and d'Avrigny went to summon the doctor of the mayoralty, whose office it was to examine bodies after decease, and who was expressively named " the doctor of the dead." M. Noirtier could not be persuaded to quit his grandchild. In a quarter of an hour M. d'Avrigny returned with his associate.

The two doctors entered the room alone. Noirtier was near the bed, pale, motionless, and silent as the corpse. The district doctor approached with the indifference of a man accustomed to spend half his time amongst the dead.

" Alas ! " said d'Avrigny, " she is indeed dead, poor child ! You can leave."

" Yes," answered the doctor, laconically, dropping the sheet he had raised. The " doctor of the dead " then laid his *procès-verbal* on the corner of the table, and, having executed his office, was conducted out by d'Avrigny. De Villefort met them at the door of his study; having in a few words thanked the district doctor, he returned to d'Avrigny, and said,—

"And now the priest."

"The nearest," said the district doctor, "is a good Italian abbé, who lives next door to you. Shall I call on him as I pass?"

"D'Avrigny," said de Villefort, "be so kind, I beseech you, as to accompany this gentleman. Here is the key of the door, so that you can go in and out as you please; bring the priest with you, and oblige me by introducing him into my child's room."

"Do you wish to see him?"

"I only wish to be alone. You will excuse me, will you not? A priest can understand a father's grief." And M. de Villefort, giving the key to d'Avrigny, again bade farewell to the strange doctor, and retired to his study, where he began to work. As the doctors entered the street, they saw a man in a cassock standing on the threshold of the next door. D'Avrigny accosted the priest. "Sir," he said, "are you disposed to confer a great obligation on an unhappy father who has just lost his daughter? I mean M. de Villefort, the *procureur du roi*."

"I had heard of your affliction. I was about to offer myself, sir," said the priest; "the servants said it was a young girl named Valentine. I have already prayed for her."

"Thank you, sir," said d'Avrigny; "come and watch by the dead, and all the family will be grateful to you."

"I do not hesitate to say that no prayers will be more fervent than mine." D'Avrigny led the priest to Valentine's room. On entering, Noirtier's eyes met those of the abbé, and no doubt he read some particular expression in them, for he remained in the room. In order that he might not be disturbed while fulfilling his sacred mission, the priest, as soon as d'Avrigny departed, rose, and not only bolted the door through which the doctor had just left, but also that leading to Madame de Villefort's room.

CHAPTER CIV

DANGLARS' SIGNATURE

THE morning of the funeral rose sad and cloudy. D'Avrigny called about eight o'clock; he met de Villefort on his way to Noirtier's room, and accompanied him to see how the old man was.

"See," said d'Avrigny to de Villefort, "nature knows how to

alleviate the deepest sorrow. No one can say M. Noirtier did not love his child, and yet he sleeps."

They both returned thoughtfully to the study of the *procureur du roi*. "I have not slept," said de Villefort, showing his undisturbed bed; "I have, however, been hard at work and have filled those papers, and made out the accusation against the assassin Benedetto. Oh, work! work! my passion, my joy, my delight! it is for thee to alleviate my sorrows!" and he convulsively grasped the hand of d'Avrigny.

"Do you require my services?" asked d'Avrigny.

"No," said de Villefort; "only return again at eleven o'clock; at twelve the—the—oh, Heaven! my poor, poor child!" and the *procureur du roi*, again becoming a man, lifted up his eyes and groaned.

"Shall you be present in the reception-room?"

"No, my cousin has undertaken this sad duty for me."

At the door d'Avrigny met the cousin whom de Villefort had mentioned, one of those beings devoted from their birth to make themselves useful to others. At twelve o'clock the mourning coaches rolled into the paved court, and the Rue du Faubourg St. Honoré was filled with a crowd of idlers, equally pleased to witness festivities or funerals. Gradually the reception-room was filled with the leading men of the day. The cousin standing at the door ushered in the guests. Those who were acquainted soon formed into little groups. One of these was composed of Debray, Château-Renaud, and Beauchamp.

"Poor girl!" said Debray, like the rest, paying an involuntary tribute to the sad event.

"Did you know her?"

"I spoke to her once or twice at Madame de Morcerf's amongst the rest; she appeared to me charming, though rather melancholy. Where is her stepmother? Do you know?"

"She is spending the day with the wife of the worthy gentleman who is receiving us."

"Have you mentioned this death in your paper?"

"It has been mentioned; but the article is not mine; indeed, I doubt if it will please M. de Villefort, for it says, that if four successive deaths had happened anywhere else than in the house of the *procureur du roi*, he would have interested himself somewhat more about it."

"Doctor d'Avrigny," said Château-Renaud, "who attends my mother, declares he is in despair about it. But whom are you seeking, Debray?"

" I am seeking the count of Monte Cristo."

" I met him going to his banker," said Beauchamp.

" That's Danglars, isn't it ? " asked Château-Renaud of Debray.

" I believe so," replied Debray, rather ill at ease. " But Monte Cristo is not the only one I miss here ; I do not see Morrel."

" Morrel ! Do they know him ? " asked Château-Renaud. " I think he had only been introduced to Madame de Villefort."

" Still he ought to have been here," said Debray.

Beauchamp told the truth when he said that on his way to the funeral he had met Monte Cristo, who was directing his steps towards the Rue de la Chaussée d'Antin to M. Danglars'. The banker saw the carriage of the count enter the court-yard, and advanced to meet him with a sad, though affable smile.

" Well ! " said he, extending his hand to Monte Cristo, " I suppose you have come to sympathize with me, for indeed misfortune has taken possession of my house. Do you know, count, that persons of our age have been very unfortunate this year ? For example, look at the *procureur du roi,* who has just lost his daughter, and in fact nearly all his family in so singular a manner ; Morcerf dishonoured and dead ; and then myself, covered with ridicule through the villainy of Benedetto ; besides, my daughter——"

" Mademoiselle Danglars ? "

" Eugénie has left us ! "

" Good heavens ! what are you telling me ? "

" The ʼtruth, my dear count. She could not endure the insult offered to us by that wretch, so she asked permission to travel."

" Still, baron," said Monte Cristo, " family griefs, or indeed any other afflictions which would crush a man whose child was his only treasure, are endurable to a millionaire. Philosophers may well say, and practical men will always support the opinion, that money mitigates many trials ; and if you admit the efficacy of this sovereign balm, you ought to be very easily consoled—you, the king of finance, who form the intersecting point of all the powers in Europe, nay, the world ! "

" That reminds me," Danglars said, " that when you entered, I was on the point of signing five little bonds ; I have already signed two, will you allow me to do the same to the others ? Stay," he added, " count, you who may be called the emperor, if I claim the title of king of finance, have you many pieces of paper of this size, each worth a million ? "

The count took the papers and read :—

" To the Governor of the Bank of France. Please to pay to my order, from the fund deposited by me, the sum of a million.

" BARON DANGLARS."

" It is a fine thing to have such credit. Five millions on five little scraps of paper ! It must be seen to be believed."

" You speak as if you doubted, but you shall be convinced; take my clerk to the bank, and you will see him leave it with an order on the Treasury for the same sum."

" No ! " said Monte Cristo, folding the five notes, " I will conduct the experiment myself. I am credited on you for six millions, I have drawn nine hundred thousand francs, you therefore still owe me five millions and a hundred thousand francs. I will take the five scraps of paper that I now hold, and here is a receipt in full for the six millions between us. I drew it up before I came, because I am pressed for money to-day." Monte Cristo placed the bonds in his pocket and tendered the receipt to Danglars. If a thunderbolt had fallen at the banker's feet he could not have shown greater terror.

" What ! " he stammered, " do you mean to take that money ? Excuse me, but I owe this money to the hospital, a deposit which I promised to pay this morning."

" Oh ! well, then," said Monte Cristo, " I am not particular about these five notes. Pay me in another form. Here are your notes," and he held the bonds towards Danglars, who seized them like a vulture extending its claws. Suddenly he rallied and a smile gradually widened the features of his disturbed countenance.

" Certainly," he said, " your receipt is money."

" Then I may keep this money ? "

" Yes," said Danglars, while the perspiration started from the roots of his hair. " Yes, keep it—keep it."

Monte Cristo replaced the notes in his pocket with that indescribable expression which seemed to say, " Come, reflect, if you repent there is still time."

" No," said Danglars, " no, decidedly no ; keep my signatures. But you know none is so formal as a banker in transacting business : I intended this money for the hospitals, and I seemed to be robbing them if I did not pay them with these precise bonds. How absurd ! as if one crown were not as good as another. But there is still a sum of one hundred thousand francs ? "

" Oh ! a bagatelle," said Monte Cristo. " The balance would come to about that sum ; but keep it, and we shall be quits."

" Count," said Danglars, " are you speaking seriously ? "

" I never joke with bankers," said Monte Cristo : and he turned to the door, just as the valet announced, " M. de Boville, receiver-general of the hospitals."

" *Ma foi !* " said Monte Cristo ; " I think I arrived just in time to obtain your signatures, or they would have been disputed with me."

Danglars again became pale, and hastened to conduct the count out. Monte Cristo exchanged a ceremonious bow with M. de Boville, who was standing in the waiting-room, and who was introduced into Danglars' room as soon as the count had left. The count smiled slightly as he noticed the portfolio the receiver-general held in his hand. At the door he found his carriage, and was immediately driven to the bank. Meanwhile Danglars advanced to meet the receiver-general, a smile of condescension upon his lips. " Good morning, creditor ! " said he ; " for I wager anything it is the creditor who visits me."

" You are right, baron," answered M. de Boville : " the hospitals present themselves to you through me ; the widows and orphans depute me to receive alms to the amount of five millions from you."

" Well, M. de Monte Cristo has just carried off their five millions."

" How so ? "

" The count had unlimited credit upon me ; a credit opened by Thomson and French, of Rome ; he came to demand five millions at once, which I paid him with cheques on the Bank ; my funds are deposited there ; and you can understand that if I draw out ten millions on the same day, it will appear rather strange to the Governor. Two days will be a different thing," said Danglars, smiling.

" Five millions ! "

" Here is his receipt. Believe your own eyes."

" The Count of Monte Cristo had five millions in your hands ! Why he must be a nabob ! "

" I do not know what he is ; he has three unlimited credits : one on me, one on Rothschild, one on Laffitte."

M. de Boville manifested signs of extraordinary admiration. " I must visit him," he said, " and obtain a donation from him."

" Oh ! you may make sure of him : his charities alone amount to 20,000 francs per month."

" It is magnificent ! I will set before him the example of Madame de Morcerf and her son."

" What example ? "

" They gave all their fortune to the hospitals."

" For what reason ? "

" Because they would not spend money so guiltily acquired."

" And what are they to live upon ? "

" The mother retires into the country, and the son enters the army."

" And how much did they possess ? "

" Oh, not much ! from twelve to thirteen hundred thousand francs. But to return to our millions."

" Certainly," said Danglars, in the most natural tone in the world. " Are you pressed for this money ? "

" Yes ; the examination of our cash will take place to-morrow at two o'clock."

" Send at twelve," said Danglars, smiling. M. de Boville said nothing, but nodded his head and took up the portfolio. " Now I think of it, you can do better," added Danglars, " this receipt of M. de Monte Cristo is as good as money ; take it to Rothschild's or Laffitte's, and they will take it of you directly ; it will only cost you a discount of 5,000 or 6,000 francs."

The receiver shook his head. " *Ma foi !* " he said, " I prefer waiting till to-morrow. What a proposition ! "

" Then it will be to-morrow ? "

" Yes ; but without fail."

" Send to-morrow at twelve, and the bank shall be informed."

" I will come myself."

" Better still, since it will afford me the pleasure of seeing you." They shook hands.

" By the way," said M. de Boville, " are you going to the funeral of poor Mademoiselle de Villefort, which I met on my road here ? "

" No," said the banker ; " I have appeared rather ridiculous since that affair of Benedetto, so I remain in the background."

" Bah ! you are wrong. Everybody pities you, sir ; and, above all, Mademoiselle Danglars ! "

" Poor Eugénie ! " said Danglars ; " do you know she is going to embrace a religious life ? "

" No."

" Alas ! it is unhappily but too true. The day after the event, she decided on leaving Paris with a nun of her acquaintance : they have gone to seek a very strict convent in Italy or Spain."

" Oh ! it is terrible ! " and M. de Boville retired with this exclamation, after expressing acute sympathy with the father. But he had scarcely left before Danglars exclaimed with tremendous energy, " Fool ! ! ! Come at twelve o'clock ; I shall then be far

away!" Then he placed Monte Cristo's receipt in his pocket-book, double-locked his door, emptied all his drawers, collected about fifty thousand francs in bank-notes, burned several papers, left others exposed to view, and began a letter which he addressed :—
"To Madame la Baronne Danglars."

"I will place it on her table myself to-night," he murmured. Then taking a passport from his drawer, he said,—" Good ! it is available for two months longer."

CHAPTER CV

THE CEMETERY OF PÈRE LACHAISE

M. DE BOVILLE had indeed met the funeral procession which conducted Valentine to her last home on earth. M. de Villefort, a true Parisian, considered the cemetery of Père Lachaise alone worthy of receiving the mortal remains of a Parisian family. He had therefore purchased a vault, which was quickly occupied by members of his family. The pompous procession, therefore, wended its way towards Père Lachaise from the Faubourg Saint-Honoré. Having crossed Paris, it passed through the Faubourg du Temple, then leaving the exterior Boulevards, it reached the cemetery. More than fifty private carriages followed the twenty mourning coaches, and behind them more than five hundred persons joined in the procession on foot.

These last consisted of young people, whom Valentine's death had struck like a thunderbolt. As they left Paris, an equipage with four horses, at full speed, was seen to draw up suddenly : it contained Monte Cristo. The count left the carriage and mingled in the crowd who followed on foot. Château-Renaud perceived him ; and immediately alighting from his *coupé*, joined him. " Where is Morrel ? " he asked.

" We have already asked that question," said Château-Renaud, " for none of us has seen him." The count was silent, but continued to gaze around him. At length they arrived at the cemetery. Monte Cristo glanced through clusters of bushes and trees, and was soon relieved from all anxiety, for he saw a shadow glide between the yew-trees, and recognised whom he sought. The shadow passed rapidly behind the tomb of Abelard and Héloïse, and placed itself close to the horses' heads belonging to the hearse, and, following the undertaker's men, arrived with them at the spot appointed for the burial. Monte Cristo saw nothing but the shadow which no one else heeded. Twice the count left the ranks to see whether the object of his interest had

Y

any concealed weapon beneath his clothes. When the procession stopped, this shadow was recognised as Morrel, who convulsively crushed his hat between his fingers, as he leant against a tree, situated on an elevation commanding the mausoleum, so that none of the funeral details might escape his observation. Everything was conducted in the usual manner. A few men, the least impressed by the scene, pronounced brief discourses, in which metaphor was exhausted, deploring this premature death or enlarging on the father's grief.

Monte Cristo only saw Morrel, whose calmness had a frightful effect on those who knew what was passing in his heart. " See ! " said Beauchamp, pointing out Morrel to Debray. " What is he doing up there ? "

" How pale he is ! " said Château-Renaud, shuddering.

" Bah ! " said Debray ; " he scarcely knew Mademoiselle de Villefort ; you said so yourself."

" True. Still I remember he danced three times with her at Madame de Morcerf's. Do you recollect that ball, count, where you produced such an effect ? "

" No, I do not," replied Monte Cristo. " The discourse is ended : farewell, gentlemen," said the count. And he disappeared without anyone seeing whither he went. The funeral being over, the guests returned to Paris.

Monte Cristo concealed himself behind a large tomb, and waited the arrival of Morrel, who, by degrees, approached the tomb, now abandoned by spectators and workmen. Morrel bent his head till it touched the stone, then clutching the grating with both hands, he murmured, " Oh ! Valentine ! " The count's heart was pierced by the utterance of these two words ; he stepped forward, and touching the young man's shoulders, said, " I was looking for you, my friend."

Morrel, turning round, said with calmness, " You see I was praying."

The count searched the young man from head to foot. He then seemed more easy. " Shall I drive you back to Paris ? " he asked.

" Leave me to pray." The count withdrew without opposition, but it was only to place himself in a situation where he could watch every movement of Morrel, who at length rose, and turned towards Paris, without once looking back. The count, dismissing his carriage, followed about a hundred paces behind. Maximilian crossed the canal and entered the Rue Meslay by the Boulevards. Five minutes after the door had been closed on Morrel's entrance, it was again opened for the count. Julie was at the entrance of the garden.

" Maximilian has just returned, has he not, madame ? " asked the count.

" Yes, I think I saw him pass : but pray, call Emanuel."

" Excuse me, madame, but I must go up to Maximilian's room this instant," replied Monte Cristo. " I have something of the greatest importance to tell him."

Monte Cristo soon ran up the staircase conducting from the ground floor to Maximilian's room ; when he reached the landing he listened attentively, but all was still. The door was panelled with glass, but one could not look into the room, because of the red curtain drawn behind the glass.

" What shall I do ? " he uttered, and reflected for a moment.

Presently he smashed one of the panes with his elbow ; then withdrawing the curtain, he saw Morrel, who had been writing at his desk, bound from his seat at the noise of the broken window.

" I beg a thousand pardons ! " said the count ; " there is nothing the matter, but I slipped and broke a panel of the door : do not disturb yourself—do not disturb yourself ! " And passing his hand through the broken glass, the count opened the door. " *Ma foi !* " said Monte Cristo, rubbing his elbow.

" Are you hurt, sir ? " coldly asked Morrel.

" I believe not. But what are you doing ? "

" Writing. I do sometimes, soldier though I am."

Monte Cristo advanced into the room ; Maximilian was obliged to let him pass, but he followed him.

" Your pistols are beside your desk," said Monte Cristo, pointing with his finger to the pistols on the table.

" I am on the point of starting on a journey," replied Morrel.

" My friend, my dear Maximilian, do not make a hasty resolution, I entreat you."

" I make a hasty resolution ? " said Morrel, shrugging his shoulders.

" Maximilian," said the count, " let us both lay aside the mask we have assumed. You no more deceive me with that false calmness than I impose upon you with my frivolous solicitude. Morrel, you are going to destroy yourself ! Here is the proof of what I say." Approaching the desk he removed the sheet of paper which Morrel had placed over the letter he had begun, and took the letter in his hands.

Morrel rushed forward to tear it from him. But Monte Cristo, perceiving his intention, seized his wrist with his iron grasp.

" You wish to destroy yourself," said the count, " you have written it."

" Well ! " said Morrel, " and if I do intend to turn this pistol against myself, who shall prevent me ? All my hopes are blighted, my heart is broken, my life a burden. When I tell you this with tears of heartfelt anguish, can you reply that I am wrong, can you prevent my putting an end to my miserable existence ? "

" Yes, Morrel," said Monte Cristo : " yes, I would do so."

" You ! " exclaimed Morrel, with increasing anger and reproach ; " you, who have deceived me with false hopes, who enact the part of a guardian angel upon earth, and could not find an antidote to a poison ! Ah ! sir, you would inspire me with pity, were you not hateful in my eyes."

" Morrel ! "

" Yes ; you tell me to lay aside the mask, and I will do so ! Since you abuse my confidence, since you have devised a new torture after I thought I had exhausted them all, then, count of Monte Cristo, the universal guardian, be satisfied you shall witness the death of your friend ; " and Morrel, with a maniacal laugh, rushed towards the pistols.

" Thou shalt not commit suicide."

" And who are you that arrogate to yourself this tyrannical right over free and rational beings ? "

" Who am I ? " repeated Monte Cristo. " Listen : I am the only man in the world having the right to say to you,—' Morrel, your father's son shall not die to-day. ' " The young man, involuntarily overcome by the command of this man, recoiled a step.

" Why do you mention my father ? " stammered he ; " why do you mingle a recollection of him with the affairs of to-day ? "

" Because I saved your father's life when he wished to destroy himself, as you do to-day,—because I am the man who sent the purse to your young sister, and the *Pharaon* to old Morrel,—because I am the Edmond Dantès who nursed you, a child, on my knees." Morrel made another step back, staggering, breathless, crushed ; then all his strength gave way, and he fell prostrate at the feet of Monte Cristo. Then his admirable nature underwent a complete and sudden revulsion ; he rose, bounded out of the room, and rushed to the stairs, exclaiming energetically, " Julie ! Julie ! Emanuel ! Emanuel ! "

Julie, Emanuel, and some of the servants ran up in alarm on hearing the cries of Maximilian. Morrel seized their hands, and opening the door, exclaimed in a voice choked with sobs,—" On your knees ! on your knees ! he is our benefactor ! the saviour of our father ! He is——"

He would have added "Edmond Dantès," but the count seized his arm and prevented him. Julie threw herself into the arms of the count, Emanuel embraced him as a guardian angel ; Morrel again fell on his knees and struck the ground with his forehead. Nothing was heard in the room but a succession of sobs, while incense from grateful hearts rose to heaven. Julie had scarcely recovered when she rushed out of the room, ran into the drawing-room and raised the glass shade which covered the purse given by the unknown of the Allées de Meillan. Meanwhile, Emanuel, in a broken voice, said to the count,—"Oh, count, how could you refrain from discovering yourself to us ? It was cruel to us, and—dare I say it ?—to you also."

"Listen, my friends," said the count ; "the discovery of this secret has been occasioned by a great event which you must never know. I wished to bury it during my whole life in my own bosom, but your brother, Maximilian, wrested it from me by a violence he repents of now, I am sure." Then, turning round and seeing Morrel, he added in a low voice, "Watch over him. I cannot explain myself ; but watch over him." Emanuel looked round the room and caught sight of the pistols. Emanuel went towards the pistols. "Leave them," said Monte Cristo. Then walking towards Morrel, he took his hand ; but the tumultuous agitation of the young man had given way to profound stupor. Julie returned, holding in her hands the silken purse, while tears of joy rolled down her cheeks.

"Here is the relic," she said ; "do not think it will be less dear to us now we are acquainted with our benefactor ! "

"My child," said Monte Cristo, colouring, "allow me to take back that purse ? Since you now know my face, I wish to be remembered through the affection I hope you will grant me."

"Oh ! " said Julie, pressing the purse to her heart ; "I beseech you, do not take it ; for some unhappy day you will leave us, will you not ? "

"You have guessed rightly, madame," replied Monte Cristo, smiling ; "in a week I shall have left this country." While announcing his departure, the count fixed his eyes on Morrel, and remarked that the words, "I shall have left this country," had failed to rouse him from his lethargy. He then saw that he must make another struggle against the grief of his friend, and, taking the hands of Emanuel and Julie, said, with the mild authority of a father, "My kind friends, leave me alone with Maximilian."

Julie saw the means offered of carrying off her precious relic, which Monte Cristo had forgotten.

"Let us leave them," she said to her husband.

The count was alone with Morrel, who remained motionless as a statue.

"Come," said Monte Cristo, touching his shoulder with his finger, "are you a man again, Maximilian?"

"Yes; for I begin to suffer again." The count frowned, apparently in gloomy hesitation.

"Maximilian," he said, "the ideas you yield to are unworthy of a Christian."

"O, do not fear, my friend," said Morrel, raising his head, and smiling with a sweet expression on the count. "I will not attempt my life. My grief will kill me."

"My friend," said Monte Cristo, "listen to me; one day, in a moment of despair like yours, since it led to a similar resolution, I, like you, wished to kill myself: one day, your father, equally desperate, wished to kill himself, too. If anyone had said to either of us then, ' Live ! the day will come when you will be happy, and will bless life ; " no matter whose voice had spoken, we should have heard him with the smile of doubt, or the anguish of incredulity ; and yet how many times has your father blessed life while embracing you ! how often have I myself——"

"Ah !" exclaimed Morrel, interrupting the count, "you had only lost your liberty, my father had only lost his fortune, but I have lost Valentine."

"Look at me," said Monte Cristo, "there are no tears in my eyes, nor is there fever in my veins, yet I see you suffer—you, Maximilian, whom I love as my own son. Well, does not this tell you that in grief, as in life, there is always something to look forward to beyond ? "

"Oh, heaven ! " said the young man ; " oh, heaven ! what are you saying, count ? Take care. But, perhaps, you have never loved ! "

"Child ! " replied the count.

"I mean, as I love. I reached the age of twenty-nine without loving; at twenty-nine I saw Valentine ; during the two years I have loved her, I have seen written in her heart as in a book all the virtues of a daughter and wife. Count, to possess Valentine would have been a happiness too perfect for this world, since it has been denied me ; but without Valentine the earth is desolate."

"I have told you to hope," said the count.

" My friend, my father," said Morrel, with excitement, " have a care, I again repeat, for the power you wield over me alarms me. Be cautious, or you will make me believe in supernatural agencies. I must obey you ; so in mercy be cautious."

" Hope, my friend," repeated the count.

" Ah ! " said Morrel, " you are playing with me. No, my friend, I was wrong to caution you ; do not fear, I will bury my grief so deep in my heart, I will disguise it so, that you shall not even care to sympathise with me. Adieu, my friend, adieu."

" On the contrary," said the count, " after this you must live with me—you must not leave me ; and in a week we shall have left France."

" Count, you render me sadder than before, if it be possible. You think the result of this blow has been to produce an ordinary grief, and you would cure it by an ordinary remedy—change of scene."

" Then," said the count, " your feeble spirit will not even grant me the trial I request ? Come ! do you know of what the count of Monte Cristo is capable ? Do you know that he holds terrestrial beings under his control ? Nay, that he can almost work a miracle ! Well ! wait for the miracle I hope to accomplish, or——"

" Or ? " repeated Morrel.

" Or, take care, Morrel, lest I call you ungrateful."

" Have pity on me, count ! "

" I feel so much pity towards you, Maximilian, that—listen to me attentively—if I do not cure you in a month, to the day, to the very hour, mark my words, Morrel, I will place loaded pistols before you, and a cup full of the deadliest Italian poison—a poison, more sure and more prompt than that which killed Valentine."

" Will you promise me ? "

" I not only promise, but swear it," said Monte Cristo, extending his hand.

" In a month, then, on your honour, if I am not consoled, you will let me take my life into my own hands, and whatever may happen, you will not call me ungrateful ? "

" In a month, to the day ; the very hour and the date is a sacred one, Maximilian. I do not know whether you remember that this is the 5th of September ; it is ten years to-day since I saved your father's life, who wished to die." Morrel seized the count's hand and kissed it, the count allowed him to pay the homage he felt due to him.

" And now," he said, " after to-day, you will come and live

with me : you can occupy Haidée's apartment, and my daughter will at least be replaced by my son."

" Haidée ? " said Morrel, " what has become of her ? "

" She departed last night."

" To leave you ? "

" To wait for me. Hold yourself ready, then, to join me at the Champs Élysées, and lead me out of this house without anyone seeing my departure."

Maximilian obeyed with childlike reverence.

CHAPTER CVI

THE DIVISION

THE first floor of the house in the Rue Saint Germain-des-Prés, chosen by Albert and Madame de Morcerf for their residence, consisting of one room, was let to a very mysterious person. This was a man whose face the concierge himself had never seen. Contrary to custom, this gentleman had not been watched, for as the report ran that he was a person of high rank and would allow no impertinent interference, his incognito was strictly respected. At half-past three in the winter the fire was lighted by the discreet servant, who had the superintendence of the apartment ; and in the summer ices were placed on the table at the same hour. At four o'clock the mysterious personage arrived. Twenty minutes afterwards a carriage stopped at the house, a lady alighted in a black or dark-blue dress, and always thickly veiled. Her face, like that of the gentleman, was perfectly unknown to the two concierges. We need not say she stopped at the first floor. Then she tapped at a door in a peculiar manner, which, after being opened to admit her, was again fastened. The same precautions were used in leaving as on entering the house.

The day after Monte Cristo had called upon Danglars, the mysterious lodger entered at ten o'clock in the morning instead of four in the afternoon. Almost directly afterwards, without the usual interval of time, a hackney coach arrived, and the veiled lady ran hastily upstairs. The door opened, but before it could be closed, the lady exclaimed : —" Oh, Lucien ! oh, my friend ! "

" Well, what is the matter, my dear ? " asked the gentleman whose name the lady's agitation revealed.

" Lucien ! a great event has happened ! " said the lady, glancing inquiringly at Lucien, " M. Danglars left last night ! "

" What do you mean ? Has he gone intending not to return ? "

" You had better read his letter," and the baroness took from her pocket a letter, which she gave to Debray, and which ran as follows :—

"Madame and most faithful wife——"

Debray mechanically stopped and looked at the baroness, whose face was suffused with blushes. "Read," she said.

Debray continued :—" When you receive this, you will no longer have a husband! I owe you some explanation of my conduct. Listen, then, I this morning received five millions, which I paid away; almost directly afterwards another demand for the same sum was presented to me; I postponed this creditor till to-morrow, and I intend leaving to-day, to escape that to-morrow, which would be rather too unpleasant to endure. You will understand this, because you are as conversant with my affairs as I am ; indeed, I think you understand them better, since I am ignorant of what has become of a considerable portion of my fortune, once very tolerable, while I am sure, madame, that you are perfectly acquainted with it. Have you admired the rapidity of my fall ? Have you been slightly dazzled at the sudden fusion of my ingots ? I confess I have seen nothing but the fire ; let us hope you have found some gold amongst the ashes. And here, madame, I must add another word of explanation. So long as I hoped you were working for the good of our house and for the fortune of our daughter, I philosophically closed my eyes ; but as you have transformed that house into a vast ruin, I will not be the foundation of another man's fortune. You were rich when I married you, but little respected. Excuse me for speaking so very candidly ; but as this is intended only for ourselves, I do not see why I should weigh my words. I have augmented our fortune, and it has continued to increase during the last fifteen years, till extraordinary and unexpected catastrophes have suddenly overturned it, without any fault of mine, I can honestly declare. You, madame, have only sought to increase your own, and I am convinced you have succeeded. I leave you, therefore, as I took you, rich, but little respected. Adieu! I also intend from this time to work on my own account. Accept my acknowledgments for the example you have set me, and which I intend following.

"Your very devoted husband,
"BARON DANGLARS."

The baroness watched Debray, saw him change colour once or twice. When he had ended he folded the letter, and resumed his pensive attitude. "Well ? " asked Madame Danglars, with an anxiety easy to be understood.

" Well, madame ? " unhesitatingly repeated Debray.

" With what ideas does that letter inspire you ? "

" Oh, it is simple enough, madame ; it inspires me with the idea that M. Danglars has left suspiciously."

" He is gone ! Gone, never to return ! "

" Oh, madame ! do not think that ! "

" I tell you he will never return ; I know his character, he is inflexible in any resolutions formed for his own interests. He has gone, and I am free for ever," added Madame Danglars, in the same supplicating tone. Debray, instead of answering, allowed her to remain in an attitude of nervous inquiry. " Well ? " she said at length, " do you not answer me ? "

" I have but one question to ask you,—what do you intend to do? "

" I was going to ask you," replied the baroness, with a beating heart.

" Ah ! then, you wish to ask advice of me ? "

" Yes ; I do wish to ask your advice," said Madame Danglars, with anxious expectation.

" Then, if you wish to take my advice," said the young man, coldly, " I would recommend you to travel."

" To travel ! " she murmured.

" Certainly ! As M. Danglars says, you are rich and free. The world will think you abandoned and poor ; for the wife of a bankrupt would never be forgiven, were she to keep up the appearance of opulence. You have only to remain in Paris for about a fortnight. Then you can quit your house, leaving your jewels, and giving up your jointure, and everyone's mouth will be filled with praises of your disinterestedness. They will know you are deserted, and think you also poor ; for I alone know your financial position, and am quite ready to give up my accounts as an honest partner."

" Deserted ! " she repeated : " ah, yes, I am, indeed, deserted ! you are right, sir, and no one can doubt my position." These were the only words uttered by the proud woman.

" But then you are rich—very rich indeed," continued Debray, taking out some papers from his pocket-book, which he spread upon the table. " Madame," Debray went on, " for nearly six months we have been associated. You furnished a principal of 100,000 francs. Our partnership began in the month of April, and we now find that our accounts, reckoning from the first day of partnership up to yesterday, when I closed them, showed a capital of 2,400,000 francs, that is, 1,200,000 for each of us. Now, madame," said Debray, delivering up his accounts in the methodical manner of a stockbroker, " there are still 80,000 francs, the interest of this money, in my hands. There are, then, 40,000 francs for your share, besides the 100,000 francs you furnished me to begin with, making, in all, 1,340,000 francs for your portion. Now, madame, I took the precaution of drawing out your money the day before yesterday. There is your money, half in bank-notes, the other half in cheques payable to the bearer. Now, madame, here are 800 notes of 1,000 francs each, resembling, as you see, a large book bound in iron ; to this I add a dividend of 25,000 francs ; then for the odd cash, making, I think, about 110,000 francs, here is a cheque upon my banker, who, not being M. Danglars, will pay you the amount, you may rest assured." Madame Danglars mechanically took the cheque, the dividend, and the heap of bank-notes, placed the bank-notes in her bag, put the dividend and cheque into her pocket-book, and then, standing pale and mute awaited one kind word of consolation. But she waited in vain.

" Now, madame," said Debray, " you have a splendid fortune. You will be able to indulge all your fancies ; besides, should you find your income insufficient, you can for the sake of the past, madame, make use of mine ; and I am ready to offer you all I possess, on loan."

" Thank you, sir—thank you," replied the baroness ; " you forget that what you have just paid me is much more than a poor woman requires, who intends, for some time, at least, to retire from the world."

Debray was for a moment surprised, but immediately recovering himself, he bowed.

Madame Danglars had, until then, perhaps, hoped for something ; but when she saw the careless bow of Debray, she raised her head, and without passion, or violence, or even hesitation, ran downstairs, disdaining to address a last farewell to one who could thus part from her.

" Bah ! " said Debray, when she had left. " She will remain at home, read novels, and speculate at cards, since she can no longer do so on the Bourse." Then, taking up his account-book, he cancelled, with the greatest care, all the amounts he had just paid away. " I have a million and 60,000 francs remaining," he said. " What a pity Mademoiselle de Villefort is dead ! She suited me in every respect, and I would have married her." And he calmly waited till twenty minutes had elapsed after Madame Danglars' departure before he left the house. During this time he occupied himself in making figures, with his watch by his side.

Asmodeus—that diabolical personage—who would have been created by every fertile imagination, if Le Sage had not acquired the priority in his *chef d'œuvre*—would have enjoyed a singular spectacle, if he had lifted up the roof of the little house in the Rue Saint-Germain-des-Prés, while Debray was casting up his figures. Above the room in which Debray had been dividing two millions and a half of francs with Madame Danglars was another, occupied by persons who have played too prominent a part in the incidents we have related for their appearance not to create some interest. Mercédès and Albert were in that room. Mercédès was much changed within the last few days; not that, even in her days of fortune, she had ever dressed with that magnificent display which makes us no longer able to recognise a woman when she appears in plain attire; nor, indeed, had she fallen into that state of depression where it is impossible to conceal the garb of misery; no, the change in Mercédès was, that her eye no longer sparkled, her lips no longer smiled, and there was now a hesitation in uttering the words which formerly fell so fluently from her ready wit. It was not poverty which had broken her spirit; it was not a want of courage which rendered her poverty burdensome. The beautiful Catalan and noble Countess had lost both her proud glance and charming smile, because she saw nothing but misery around her; the walls were hung with one of those grey papers which economical landlords choose as not likely to show the dirt; the floor was uncarpeted; the furniture was scanty; indeed, everything offended the eyes accustomed to refinement and elegance.

Madame de Morcerf had lived there since leaving her mansion; the continual silence of the spot oppressed her. Albert, too, was ill at ease; the remains of luxury had thus far prevented him from feeling the pinch of poverty, but in spite of all their economies, the time had come when he was obliged to tell his mother that they had no more money. Mercédès had never known misery; she had often, in her youth, spoken of poverty, but between want and necessity, though synonymous words, there is a wide difference. Amongst the Catalans, Mercédès wished for a thousand things, but still she never really wanted any. Upon the little she earned she lived as well as she could; now there were two to be supported, and nothing to live upon.

Winter approached. Mercédès had no fire in that cold and naked room; she, who was accustomed to stoves which heated the house from the hall to the boudoir.

" Mother ! " exclaimed Albert, just as Madame Danglars was

descending the stairs, " let us reckon our riches, if you please ; I want a capital to build my plans upon."

" Capital—nothing ! " replied Mercédès, with a mournful smile.

" No, mother,—capital 3,000 francs. And I have an idea of our leading a delightful life upon this 3,000 francs."

" You say this, my dear boy ; but do you think we ought to accept these 3,000 francs ? " said Mercédès, colouring.

" I think so," answered Albert, in a firm tone. " We will accept them the more readily, since we have them not here ; you know they are buried in the garden of the little house in the Allées de Meillan, at Marseilles. With 200 francs we can reach Marseilles."

Albert then took a pen, and wrote :—

	Frs.
"*Coupé*, thirty-five francs	35
From Châlons to Lyons you will go on by the steam-boat—six francs	6
From Lyons to Avignon (still by steamboat), sixteen francs	16
From Avignon to Marseilles, seven francs . .	7
Expenses on the road, about fifty francs. . .	50

"Total 114frs."

" Let us call it, 120," added Albert, smiling. " You see I am generous ; am I not, mother ? "

" But you, my poor child ? "

" I ! do you not see I reserve eighty francs for myself ? A young man does not require luxuries ; besides, I know what travelling is."

" With a post-chaise and valet ? "

" In any mode, mother."

" Well, be it so. But these 200 francs ? "

" Here they are, and 200 more besides. See, I have sold my watch for 100 francs, and the guard and seals for 300. Now we are rich, since, instead of the 114 francs we need for the journey, we find ourselves in possession of 250."

" But we owe something in this house ? "

" Thirty francs ; but I pay that out of my 150 francs ; that is understood. But that is not all. What do you say to this, mother ? "

Albert took out of a little pocketbook with golden clasps, a remnant of his old fancies, or perhaps a tender *souvenir* from one of those mysterious ladies who used to knock at his door, a note of 1,000 francs.

" What is this ? " asked Mercédès.

" A thousand francs."

" But how have you got it ? "

" Listen to me, mother, and do not yield to agitation." Albert, rising, kissed his mother on both cheeks, then stood looking at her. " You cannot imagine, mother, how beautiful I think you ! "

" Dear child ! " said Mercédès, endeavouring in vain to restrain a tear which glistened in the corner of her eye. " Indeed, you only want misfortune to change my love for you to admiration. I am not unhappy while I possess my son ! "

" Ah ! just so," said Albert ; " here begins the trial. Do you know the decision we have come to, mother ? "

" Have we come to any ? "

" Yes ; it is decided that you are to live at Marseilles, and that I am to leave for Africa, where I will earn the right to use the name I now bear, instead of the one I have thrown aside." Mercédès sighed. " Well, mother ! I yesterday engaged myself in the Spahis," added the young man. " I thought my body was my own, and that I might sell it. I yesterday took the place of another. I sold myself for more than I thought I was worth," he added, attempting to smile ; " I fetched 2,000 francs."

" These 1,000 francs——" said Mercédès, shuddering.

" Are half of the sum, mother ; the other will be paid in a year." Mercédès raised her eyes to heaven.

" The price of his blood ! " she murmured.

" Yes, if I am killed," said Albert, laughing.

" Merciful Heaven ! "

" Besides, mother, why should you make up your mind that I am to be killed ? Has Morrel, whom we know, been killed ? Think of your joy, mother, when you see me return with an embroidered uniform ! I declare, I expect to look magnificent in it, and chose that regiment only from vanity. Well ! now you understand, mother ! " continued Albert ; " here are more than 4,000 francs settled on you ; upon this you can live at least two years."

" Do you think so ? " said Mercédès.

" Yes, you will live ! "

" I shall live ! then you will not leave me, Albert ? "

" Mother, I must go," said Albert, in a firm, calm voice ; " you love me too well to wish me to remain useless and idle with you ; besides, I have signed."

" You will obey your own wish and the will of Heaven ! "

" Not my own wish, mother, but reason—necessity. Are we not two despairing creatures ? What is life to you ?—Nothing. What is life to me ?—Very little, without you, mother. Well, I will live, if you promise me still to hope. I will go to the governor of Algeria and tell him my gloomy story. I will beg him to turn his eyes now and then towards me ; and if he keep his word, and interest himself in me, in six months I shall be an officer or dead. If I am an officer, your fortune is certain, for I shall have money enough for both ; and, moreover, a name we shall both be proud of, since it will be our own. If I am killed—well, then, mother, you can also die, and there will be an end of our misfortunes."

" It is well," replied Mercédès, with her eloquent glance ; " you are right, my love ; let us prove to those who are watching our actions that we are worthy of compassion."

" And so our division is made, mother," said the young man, affecting ease of mind. " We can now part ; come, I shall take your place."

" And you, my dear boy ? "

" I shall stay here for a few days longer ; we must accustom ourselves to parting. I will join you again at Marseilles."

" Well, be it so ! Let us part," said Mercédès, folding round her shoulders the only shawl she had taken away, and which, accidentally, happened to be a valuable black cashmere. Albert gathered up his papers hastily, rang the bell to pay the thirty francs he owed to the landlord, and, offering his arm to his mother, they descended the stairs. Someone was walking down before them, and this person, hearing the rustling of a silk dress, turned round.

" Debray ! " muttered Albert.

" Morcerf ! " said Debray. Then, noticing, in the dim light, the still youthful and veiled figure of Madame de Morcerf—"Pardon me ! " he added, with a smile, " I leave you, Albert." Albert understood his thoughts. " Mother," he said, turning towards Mercédès, " this is M. Debray, secretary of the Minister for the Interior, once a friend of mine."

" How, once ! " stammered Debray ; " what do you mean ? "

" I say so, M. Debray, because I have no friends now, and I ought not to have any. I thank you for having recognised me, sir."

Debray stepped forward, and cordially pressed the hand of his interlocutor. " Believe me, dear Albert," he said, " I feel deeply for your misfortunes, and if in any way I can serve you, I am yours."

"Thank you, sir," said Albert, smiling. "In the midst of our misfortunes we are still rich enough not to require assistance from anyone. We are leaving Paris, and when our journey is paid, we shall have 5,000 francs left." The blood mounted to the temples of Debray, who held a million in his pocketbook, and, muttering a few words of general civility, he ran downstairs.

That day the minister's clerks and the subordinates had a great deal to put up with from his ill-humour. But the same night he found himself the possessor of a fine house, situated on the Boulevard de la Madeleine, and an income of 50,000 livres. The next day, just as Debray was signing the deed, Madame de Morcerf, after having affectionately embraced her son, entered the *coupé* of the diligence, which closed upon her.

A man was hidden in Laffitte's banking-house, behind one of the little arched windows : he saw Mercédès enter the diligence, and he also saw Albert withdraw. He passed his hand across his forehead. "Alas ! " he exclaimed, " how can I restore the happiness I have taken away from these poor innocent creatures ? God help me ! "

CHAPTER CVII

THE LION'S DEN

ONE division of La Force, in which the most dangerous and most desperate prisoners are confined, is called the court of Saint Bernard. The prisoners have named it the Lion's Den, probably because the captives possess teeth which frequently gnaw the bars, and sometimes the keepers also. The courtyard of this quarter is enclosed by enormous walls, over which the sun glances obliquely, when it deigns to penetrate into this gulf of moral and physical deformity. On this paved yard are to be seen, pacing from morning till night, pale, careworn, and haggard, like so many shadows, the men whom Justice holds beneath the steel she is sharpening. There, crouched against the side of the wall which attracts and retains the most heat, they may be seen sometimes talking to one another, but more frequently alone, watching the door, which sometimes opens to call forth one from the gloomy assemblage, or to throw in another outcast from society.

The court of Saint Bernard has its own particular parlour ; it is a long square, divided by two upright gratings, placed at a distance of three feet from one another, to prevent a visitor from shaking hands with or passing anything to the prisoners.

In the court, from which a damp vapour was rising, there might be seen walking with his hands in his pockets a young man who had excited much curiosity amongst the inhabitants of the Den. The cut of his clothes was elegant, but the clothes themselves had been torn to ribands. But his ingenuity had patched them up adroitly. He bestowed attention upon the cambric front of a shirt which had changed colour since his entrance into the prison ; and he polished his varnished boots with the corner of a handkerchief embroidered with initials surmounted by a coronet. Some of the inmates of the Lion's Den were watching the operations of the prisoner's toilet with considerable interest.

" See, the prince beautifies himself," said one of the thieves.

" He is naturally very handsome," said another, " and if he had only a comb and some pomatum, he would soon eclipse all the gentlemen in white kids."

" His coat looks nearly new, and his boots are brilliant. It is pleasant to have such well-dressed brethren ; and those gendarmes behaved shamefully. What jealousy ! to tear such clothes ! "

" He appears to be someone of consequence," said another ; " he dresses in firstrate style. And, then, to be here so young ! oh ! it is splendid ! "

Meanwhile the object of this hideous admiration approached the wicket, against which one of the keepers was leaning. " Come, sir," he said, " lend me twenty francs ; you will soon be paid ; you run no risks with me. Remember, I have relations who possess more millions than you have coppers." The keeper shrugged his shoulders.

" Come," said Andrea, " you are a man void of compassion ! I will cause you to lose your place." This made the keeper turn round, and he burst into a loud laugh. The prisoners then approached and formed a circle. " I tell you that with that wretched sum," continued Andrea, " I could obtain a coat, and a room in which to receive the illustrious visitor I am daily expecting."

" He is right ! he is right ! " said the prisoners ; " anyone can see he is a gentleman ! "

" Well, then, lend him the twenty francs," said the keeper, " surely you will not refuse a comrade ! "

" I am no comrade of these people," said the young man, proudly ; " you have no right to insult me."

" Do you hear him ? " said the keeper, with a disagreeable

smile ; " he rates you handsomely. Come, lend him the twenty francs—eh ! " The thieves looked at one another with low murmurs, and a storm gathered over the head of the aristocratic prisoner, raised less by his own words than by the manner of the keeper. They had already approached Andrea—some screaming, " *La savate ! La savate !* "—a cruel operation, which consists in flogging, not with an old shoe, but with an iron-heeled one, any comrade who may have fallen into disgrace. " Let us horsewhip the fine gentleman ! " said others.

But Andrea, turning towards them, winked his eyes, rolled his tongue round his cheeks, and smacked his lips in a manner equivalent to a hundred words among the bandits when forced to be silent. It was a masonic sign Caderousse had taught him. He was immediately recognised as one of them ; the iron-heeled shoe was replaced on the foot of the wretch to whom it belong and the mob retired.

The keeper was so stupefied at this scene, that he took Andrea by the hands, and began examining his person, attributing the sudden submission of the inmates of the Lion's Den to something more substantial than mere fascination. Andrea made no resistance, though he protested against it. Suddenly a voice was heard at the wicket.

" Benedetto ! " exclaimed an inspector. The keeper relaxed his hold.

" I am called," said Andrea.

" To the parlour ! " said the same voice.

" You see some one pays me a visit. Ah, my dear sir, you will see whether a Cavalcanti is to be treated like a common person ! " Andrea, gliding through the yard like a black shadow, rushed out through the wicket, leaving his comrades, and even the keeper, lost in wonder. A call to the parlour had scarcely astonished Andrea less than themselves ; for the wily youth, instead of making use of his privilege of waiting to be claimed on his entry into La Force, had maintained a rigid silence. " Everything," he said, " proves me to be under the protection of some powerful person The guardian hand which has been withdrawn for a while will be again stretched forth to save me, at the very moment when I shall think myself sinking into the abyss ! Why should I risk an imprudent step ? It might alienate my protector. He has two means of extricating me from this dilemma : the one by a mysterious escape, managed through bribery ; the other by buying off my judges with gold. I will say and do nothing until I am convinced that he has abandoned me ; and then——"

It was at this moment that the inspector summoned him to the visiting-room. Andrea felt his heart leap with joy. It was too soon for a visit from the *juge d'instruction*, and too late for one from the director of the prison, or the doctor : it must, then, be the visitor he hoped for. Behind the grating of the room into which Andrea had been led, he saw, while his eyes dilated with surprise, the dark and intelligent face of M. Bertuccio, who was also gazing with astonishment upon the iron bars, the bolted doors, and the shadow which moved behind the other grating.

" Ah ! " said Andrea, deeply affected.

" Do you not recognise me, unhappy child ? "

" Silence ! " said Andrea, who knew the delicate sense of hearing possessed by the walls ; " for Heaven's sake do not speak so loud ! "

" You wish to speak with me alone ? " said Bertuccio.

" Oh, yes ! "

" That is well ! " And Bertuccio, feeling in his pocket, signed to a keeper whom he saw through the window of the wicket.

" Read ! " he said.

" What is that ? " asked Andrea.

" An order to conduct you to a room, and leave you there to talk with me."

" Oh ! " cried Andrea, leaping with joy. Then he mentally added,—" Still my unknown protector ! I am not forgotten ! They wish for secrecy, since we are to converse in a private room. Bertuccio has been sent by my protector."

The keeper spoke for a moment with a superior, then opened the iron gates, and conducted Andrea to a room on the first floor. Bertuccio sat down upon the chair ; Andrea threw himself upon the bed ; the keeper retired.

" How did you know I was in prison ? "

" I recognised you, some time since, as the insolent dandy who used to ride in the Champs Élysées."

" Oh, the Champs Élysées ! Ah, we 'grow hot' as they say in some game. The Champs Élysées ! Come, let us talk about my father ! "

" Who, then, am I ? "

" You, sir !—you are my adopted father. Now, in the Champs Élysées there resides a very rich gentleman."

" At whose house you robbed and murdered, did you not ? "

" I believe I did."

" The count of Monte Cristo ? "

" You have named him. Well, am I to rush into his arms, and

strain him to my heart, crying, as they do in the dramas, ' My father ! my father ? ' "

" Do not let us jest," gravely replied Bertuccio ; " and dare not to utter that name again as you have pronounced it."

" Bah ! these are fine words."

" Do you think you are engaged with a pigmy like yourself ? " said Bertuccio, in so calm a tone, and with so steadfast a look, that Andrea was moved to the very soul. " Do not play with the thunderbolt."

" My father—I will know who my father is ! " said the obstinate youth ; " I will perish if I must, but I *will* know it. Come, who is my father ? "

" I came to tell you."

" Ah ! " cried Benedetto, his eyes sparkling with joy.

Just then the door opened, and the gaoler, addressing Bertuccio, said,—" Excuse me, sir, but the *juge d'instruction* is waiting for the prisoner."

" I will return to-morrow."

" Good ! Gendarmes, I am at your service. Ah, sir, do leave a few crowns for me at the gate, that I may have some things I am in need of ! "

" It shall be done," replied Bertuccio. Andrea extended his hand ; Bertuccio kept his own in his pocket, and merely jingled a few pieces of money.

" That's what I mean," said Andrea, endeavouring to smile. " Can I be deceived ? " he murmured, as he stepped into the oblong and grated vehicle which they call " the salad basket." " Never mind, we shall see ! Then, to-morrow ! " he added, turning towards Bertuccio.

" To-morrow ! " replied the steward.

CHAPTER CVIII

THE JUDGE

WE remember that the Abbé Busoni remained alone with Noirtier in the chamber of death, and that the old man and the priest were the sole guardians of the young girl's body. Perhaps it was the Christian exhortations of the abbé, perhaps his kind charity, perhaps his persuasive words, which had restored the courage of Noirtier; for ever since he had conversed with the priest his violent despair had yielded to a calm resignation which surprised all who knew his excessive affection for Valentine. The whole establishment had been changed ; another valet was engaged for the *procureur*, a new servant for Noirtier. The assizes, also, were about to begin ; and de Villefort, shut up in his room, exerted himself with feverish anxiety in drawing up the case against the murderer of Caderousse. The proofs were certainly not convincing, since they rested upon a few words written by an escaped galley-slave on his death-bed, who might have been actuated by hatred or revenge in accusing his companion. But the *procureur du roi* felt certain that Benedetto was guilty, and hoped by his skill in conducting this complicated case to flatter his self-love, which was about the only vulnerable point in his frozen heart.

The case was therefore fully prepared owing to the incessant labour of de Villefort, who wished it to be first on the list in the coming assizes. Once only had de Villefort seen his father ; it was the day after that upon which Bertuccio had paid his visit to Benedetto, when the latter was to learn his father's name. The magistrate, harassed and fatigued, had descended to the garden of his hôtel and, in a gloomy mood, began knocking off with his cane the long and dying branches of the rose trees, when he turned his eyes towards the house, where he heard his son playing noisily. While doing so, he observed M. Noirtier at an open window, where the old man had been placed that he might enjoy the last rays of the sun.

The eye of the old man was riveted on a spot which de Villefort could scarcely distinguish. His glance was so full of hate, ferocity, and savage impatience, that de Villefort turned aside to see at what person this dark look was directed. Then he saw beneath a clump of linden-trees, which were nearly divested of foliage, Madame de Villefort sitting with a book in her hand. De Villefort became pale ; he understood the old man's meaning. Noirtier continued to look at the same object, but suddenly his glance was diverted from the wife to the husband, and de Villefort himself had to submit to the searching investigation of those eyes, which, while changing their object and even their language, had lost none of their menacing expression.

De Villefort, drawn by an irresistible attraction, like that of the bird to the serpent, walked towards the house. As he approached it, Noirtier raised his eyes to heaven, as though to remind his son of a forgotten oath. " It is well, sir," replied de Villefort from below, have patience but one day longer ; what I have said I will do." Noirtier appeared calmed by these words, and turned his eyes with indifference to the other side. De Villefort violently unbuttoned his greatcoat, which seemed to strangle him, and passing his livid hand across his forehead, entered his study. The night was cold and still; the family had all retired to rest but de Villefort, who alone remained up, and worked till five o'clock in the morning, reviewing the last interrogatories made the night before by the *juge d'instruction*, compiling the depositions of the witnesses, and putting the finishing stroke to the deed of accusation, which was one of the most energetic and best conceived of any he had yet delivered.

The next day, Monday, was the first sitting of the assizes. The magistrate had slept a short time while the lamp gave forth its final struggles; its flickerings awoke him, and he opened the window; a bright yellow streak crossed the sky, and seemed to divide in half the poplars which stood out in black relief on the horizon. "To-day," he said with an effort, "to-day the man who holds the knife of justice must strike wherever there is guilt."

His head dropped upon his chest, and in this position he paced his study; then he threw himself, dressed as he was, upon a sofa, less to sleep than to rest his limbs. By degrees every one woke and the *procureur's* new valet brought him the papers and a cup of chocolate.

"What are you bringing me?"

"A cup of chocolate."

"I did not ask for it. Who has paid me this attention?"

"My mistress, sir. She said you would have to speak a great deal on the case of the murder, and that you should take something to keep up your strength;" and the valet placed the cup on the table nearest to the sofa, which was, like all the rest, covered with papers. The valet then left the room. De Villefort looked for an instant with a gloomy expression, then taking the cup up with a nervous motion, swallowed its contents at one draught. The breakfast-hour arrived, but M. de Villefort was not at table. The valet re-entered.

"Madame de Villefort wishes to remind you, sir," he said, "that eleven o'clock has just struck, and that the trial will begin at twelve."

"Well!" said de Villefort, "what then?"

"Madame de Villefort is dressed: she is quite ready, and wishes to know if she is to accompany you, sir?"

"Where to?"

"To the Palais."

"What to do?"

"My mistress wishes to be present at the trial."

"Ah!" said de Villefort, with a startling accent, "does she wish that?"

The servant drew back and said, " If you wish to go alone, sir, I will tell my mistress." De Villefort remained silent, and dented his cheeks with his nails. " Tell your mistress," he at length answered, " that I wish to speak to her, and I beg she will wait for me in her own room. Then come to dress and shave me."

" Directly, sir." The valet reappeared almost instantly, and having shaved his master, assisted him to dress entirely in black. When he had finished, he said, " My mistress said she should expect you, sir, as soon as you had finished dressing."

" I am going to her." De Villefort, with his papers under his arm, and, hat in hand, directed his steps towards the apartment of his wife. Madame de Villefort was sitting on an ottoman, impatiently turning over some newspapers and pamphlets which Edward, by way of amusing himself, was tearing in pieces before his mother could finish reading them.

" Ah ! here you are, sir," she said, in her naturally calm voice ; " but how pale you are ! Have you been working all night ? Why did you not come down to breakfast ? Well, will you take me, or shall I take Edward ? " Madame de Villefort had multiplied her questions in order to gain one answer, but to all her inquiries M. de Villefort remained mute and cold as a statue.

" Edward ! " said de Villefort, fixing an imperious glance on the child, " go and play in the drawing-room, my dear ; I wish to speak to your mamma." Edward looked at his mother, and then, finding that she did not confirm the order, began cutting off the heads of his leaden soldiers.

" Edward ! " cried M. de Villefort, so harshly that the child started on the carpet, " do you hear me ? Go ! " The child, unaccustomed to such treatment, rose, pale and trembling ; it would be difficult to say whether his emotion were caused by fear or passion. His father went up to him, took him in his arms, and kissed his forehead.

" Go," he said ; " go, my child." Edward ran out.

M. de Villefort went to the door, which he closed behind the child, and bolted. " Oh, heavens ! " said his wife, " what is the matter ? "

" Madame, where do you keep the poison you generally use ? " said the magistrate, without preface, placing himself between his wife and the door.

" Sir, I—I do not understand you."

" I asked," continued de Villefort, perfectly calm, " where you conceal the poison by the aid of which you have killed my father-in-law, M. de Saint Méran, my mother-in-law, Madame de Saint Méran, Barrois, and my daughter Valentine."

" Ah, sir ! " exclaimed Madame de Villefort, clasping her hands, " what do you say ? "

" It is not for you to interrogate, but to answer."

" Is it to the judge or to the husband ? " stammered Madame de Villefort.

" To the judge—to the judge ! "

" Ah, sir ! " she muttered, " ah, sir ! " and this was all.

" You do not answer, madame ! " exclaimed the terrible interrogator. " It is true, then : you do not deny it ! " She moved forward. " And you cannot deny it ! " added de Villefort. " You have accomplished these different crimes with a confidence which could only deceive those whose affection for you blinded them, and, as I told you just now, you no longer speak to the husband, but to the judge."

The young wife hid her face in her hands. " Oh, sir ! " she stammered, " I beseech you do not believe appearances."

" Are you a coward ? " cried de Villefort, in a contemptuous voice, " you who could count, one by one, the minutes of four death-agonies ?   Have *you*, then, who have calculated everything with such nicety, have you forgotten to calculate one thing—I mean where the revelation of your crimes will lead to ?   Ah ! it is impossible—you must have some surer, more subtle and deadlier poison than any other, that you might escape the punishment you deserve.   You have done this—I hope so, at least."   Madame de Villefort stretched out her hands, and fell on her knees.

" I understand," he said, " you confess ; but a confession made to the judges, a confession made at the last moment, extorted when the crime cannot be denied, diminishes not the punishment inflicted on the guilty ! "

" The punishment ! " exclaimed Madame de Villefort, " the punishment, sir ! "

" Certainly.   Did you think the punishment would be withheld because you are the wife of him who pronounces it ?   No ! madame, no ! the scaffold awaits the poisoner, whoever she may be, unless, as I just said, the poisoner has taken the precaution of keeping for herself a few drops of her deadliest poison."   Madame de Villefort uttered a wild cry, and a hideous and uncontrollable terror spread over her distorted features.

" Oh ! do not fear the scaffold, madame," said the magistrate, " I will not dishonour you, since that would be to dishonour myself : no ! if you have heard me distinctly you will understand that you are not to die on the scaffold."

" No, no,—oh, no ! "

" Well ! madame, it will be a laudable action on your part, and I will thank you for it ! "

" You will thank me—for what ? "

" For what you have just said."

" What did I say ? Oh, my brain whirls ; I no longer understand anything. Oh, heavens ! oh, heavens ! " She rose, her hair dishevelled and her lips foaming.

" Have you answered the question I put to you on entering the room : Where do you keep the poison you generally use, madame ? "

Madame de Villefort raised her arms to heaven, and convulsively struck one hand against the other. " No, no ! " she vociferated, " no, you cannot wish that ? "

" What I do wish, madame, is that you should not perish on the scaffold. Do you understand ? " asked de Villefort.

" Oh, mercy, mercy, sir ! "

" What I require is that justice be done. I am on the earth to punish, madame," he added, with a flaming glance ; " any other woman, were it the queen herself, I would send to the executioner ; but to you I will be merciful. To you I will say—Have you not, madame, put aside some of the surest, deadliest, most speedy poison ? "

" Oh, pardon me, sir ; let me live ! "

" You are a poisoner."

" In the name of heaven ! "

" No ! "

" In the name of the love you once bore me ! "

" No, no ! "

" In the name of our child ! Ah, for the sake of our child, let me live ! "

" No ! no ! no ! if I allow you to live, you will perhaps kill him as you have the others ! "

" I !—I kill my boy ! " cried the distracted mother, rushing towards de Villefort ; " I kill my son ! Ha, ha ! ha ! " and a demoniac laugh finished the sentence, which was lost in a hoarse rattle.

Madame de Villefort fell at her husband's feet. He approached her. " Think of it, madame," he said ; " if on my return justice has not been satisfied, I will denounce you with my own mouth, and arrest you with my own hands ! " She listened, panting, overwhelmed, crushed, her eye alone lived, and glared horribly. " Do you understand me ? " he said. " I am going to pronounce the sentence of death against a murderer. If I find you alive on my return, you shall sleep to-night in the Conciergerie."

Madame de Villefort sighed ; her nerves gave way, and she sank on the carpet. The *procureur du roi* seemed to experience a sensation of pity ; he looked upon her less severely, and bowing to her, said, slowly,—" Farewell, madame ! farewell ! " That farewell struck Madame de Villefort like the executioner's knife. She fainted. The *procureur du roi* went out, after having double-locked the door.

CHAPTER CIX

THE ASSIZES

THE Benedetto affair, as it was called in the Palais and by people in general, had produced a tremendous sensation. In the eyes of many, Benedetto appeared, if not a victim to, at least an instance of, the fallibility of the law. M. Cavalcanti, his father, had been seen in Paris, and it was expected he would reappear, to claim the illustrious outcast. Everyone, therefore, ran to the court ; some to witness the sight, others to comment upon it. From seven o'clock in the morning a crowd was stationed at the iron gates, and an hour before the trial began, the hall was full of the privileged.

Beauchamp, one of the kings of the press, and therefore claiming the right of a throne everywhere, was looking round on every side. He perceived Château-Renaud and Debray, who had just gained the good graces of a sergent-de-ville, and had persuaded the latter to let them stand before, instead of behind him, as he ought to have done. The worthy policeman, by way of paying extra attention to his noble neighbours, promised to keep their places while they paid a visit to Beauchamp.

" Well ! " said Beauchamp, " we shall see our friend ! "

" Yes, indeed ! " replied Debray. " That worthy prince. Deuce take those Italian princes ! "

" He will be condemned, will he not ? " asked Debray of Beauchamp.

" My dear fellow, I think we should ask you that question ; you know such news much better than we do. Did you see the president at the minister's last night ? "

" Yes."

" What did he say ? "

" Well ! he told me that Benedetto, who is considered a serpent of subtlety and a giant of cunning, is really but a very subordinate, silly rascal, and altogether unworthy of the experiments that will be made on his brain after his death."

" Bah ! " said Beauchamp ; " he played the prince very well. I assure you he passed quite readily with many people ; I saw him at the ministers' houses."

" Ah, yes ! " said Château-Renaud. " The idea of ministers understanding anything about princes ! "

" There is something in what you have just said," said Beauchamp, laughing.

" But ! " said Debray to Beauchamp, " if I spoke to the president, you must have been with the *procureur du roi.*"

" It was an impossibility ; for the last week M. de Villefort has secluded himself. It is natural enough ; this strange chain of domestic afflictions, followed by the no less strange death of his daughter——"

"Strange ! What do you mean, Beauchamp ? "

" Do you pretend that all this has been unobserved at the minister's ? " said Beauchamp, placing his eyeglass in his eye.

" Stay ! " said Beauchamp, " surely it is she."

" What is it ? "

" They said she had left."

" Mademoiselle Eugénie ? " said Château-Renaud : " has she returned ? "

" No ! but her mother."

" Madame Danglars ? Nonsense ! Impossible ? " said Château-Renaud.

Debray coloured slightly. " Come," he said, " it is only a veiled lady, some foreign princess. But you were speaking on a very interesting topic, Beauchamp."

" I ? "

" Yes ; you were telling us about the extraordinary death of Valentine."

" Ah, yes, so I was. But how is it that Madame de Villefort is not here ? "

" Poor dear woman ! " said Debray, " she is no doubt occupied in distilling balm for the hospitals, or making cosmetics for herself or friends. But I wonder she is not here. I should have been pleased to see her, for I like her very much. But to return to what you were saying, Beauchamp."

" Well ! do you know why people die so fast at M. de Villefort's house ? "

" Talking of that," said Debray, " Madame * * * was making

700 THE COUNT OF MONTE CRISTO

inquiries about that house, which for the last three months has been hung with black.

" Who is Madame * * * ? " asked Château-Renaud.

" The minister's wife, *pardieu !* "

" Oh, your pardon ! I never visit ministers ; I leave that to princes."

" Come, let us endeavour to hear the end of your story, Beauchamp : I told you Madame * * * made inquiries of me upon the subject ; enlighten me, and I will then communicate my information to her."

" Well, gentlemen, the reason people die so fast at M. de Villefort's is that there is an assassin in the house ! " The two young men shuddered.

" And who is the assassin ? " they asked together.

" Young Edward ! " A burst of laughter from the auditors did not in the least disconcert the speaker, who continued,

" Yes, gentlemen ; Edward, who is quite an adept in the art of killing. It appears the dear child has obtained possession of a bottle containing some drug, which he every now and then uses against those who have displeased him. First M. and Madame de Saint Méran incurred his displeasure, so he poured out three drops of his elixir,—three drops were sufficient ; then followed Barrois, the old servant of M. Noirtier, who sometimes rebuffed this little wretch ; he therefore received the same quantity of the elixir ; the same happened to Valentine, of whom he was jealous ; he gave her the same dose as the others, and all was over for her as well as the rest."

" It is absurd," said Debray.

" Ah ! " said Beauchamp, " you doubt me ? It was the talk of the house."

" And this elixir, where is it ? what is it ? "

" The child conceals it."

" But where did he find it ? "

" In his mother's laboratory."

" It is incredible ! "

" No, my dear fellow, it is not at all incredible ! You saw a child pass through the Rue Richelieu last year who amused himself with killing his brothers and sisters by sticking pins in their ears while they slept. The next generation will be very precocious ! "

" Come, Beauchamp," said Château-Renaud, " I will bet anything you do not believe a word of all you have been telling us ! "

" I do not see the count of Monte Cristo here ! "

" He is worn out," said Debray ; " besides, he could not

well appear in public, since he has been the dupe of the Cavalcanti, who cheated him out of 100,000 francs upon the hypothesis of this principality."

" Ah, now I think of it, the count of Monte Cristo cannot appear in the hall ! " said Beauchamp.

" Why not ? "

" Because he is an actor in the drama.''

" Has he assassinated anyone, then ? "

" No, on the contrary, they wished to assassinate him. You know that it was in leaving his house that Caderousse was murdered by Benedetto. You know that the famous waistcoat was found in his house, containing the letter which stopped the marriage contract. Do you see the waistcoat ? There it is, all blood-stained, on the desk, as a testimony of the crime."

" Hush, gentlemen ! here is the Court ; let us go back to our places."

A noise was heard in the hall ; the sergent-de-ville called his two *protégés*, with an energetic " Hem ! " and the doorkeeper appearing, called out, with that shrill voice peculiar to his order, even in the days of Beaumarchais, " The Court, gentlemen ! ''

CHAPTER CX

THE DEED OF ACCUSATION

THE judges took their places in the midst of the most profound silence ; the jury took their seats ; M. de Villefort, the object of unusual attention, and we had almost said of general admiration, sat in the armchair, and cast a tranquil glance around him.

" Gendarmes ! " said the president, " lead in the accused."

The door soon opened and Benedetto appeared. His features bore no signs of that deep emotion which stops the beating of the heart and blanches the cheek. His hands, gracefully placed, one upon his hat, the other in the opening of his white waistcoat, were not at all tremulous ; his eye was calm and even brilliant. Scarcely had he entered the hall when he glanced at the whole body of magistrates and assistants : his eye rested long on the president, and still longer on the *procureur du roi.* By the side of Andrea was placed the lawyer who was to conduct his defence and who had been chosen by the Court ; for Andrea disdained to pay any attention to those details, to which he appeared to attach no importance.

The president called for the deed of accusation, corrected, as we know, by the clever and implacable pen of de Villefort. The latter had never been so concise and eloquent : the crime was

represented under the liveliest colours; the previous life of the
prisoner and his transformation were set forth with all the talent
that a knowledge of human life could furnish to a mind like
that of the *procureur du roi*.

At length the deed was read.

" Accused," said the president, " your name and surname ? "

Andrea rose. " Excuse me, M. le Président," he said, in a clear
voice, " but I see you are going to adopt a course of questions
through which I cannot follow you. I have an idea, which I will
explain by-and-bye, of making an exception to the usual form of
accusation. Allow me, then, if you please, to answer in different
order, or I will not do so at all." The astonished president looked
at the jury, who themselves looked upon the *procureur du roi*.
The whole assembly manifested great surprise; but Andrea
appeared quite unmoved.

" Your age ? " said the president.

" I am twenty-one years old : or, rather, I shall be in a few
days, as I was born on the night of the 27th of September, 1817."
M. de Villefort, who was busy taking down some notes, raised
his head at the mention of this date.

" Where were you born ? " continued the president.

" At Auteuil, near Paris." M. de Villefort a second time raised
his head, looked at Benedetto, as if he had been gazing at the
head of Medusa, and became livid. As for Benedetto, he gracefully wiped his lips with a fine cambric pocket-handkerchief.
" Your profession ? "

" First I was a forger," answered Andrea, as calmly as possible ;
" then I became a thief ; and, lately, have become an assassin."
A murmur, or rather a storm, of indignation burst from all parts
of the assembly. M. de Villefort pressed his hand to his brow,
at first pale, now red and burning ; then rose, and looked around
as though he had lost his senses—he wanted air.

" Are you looking for anything, M. le Procureur du Roi ? "
asked Benedetto, with his most pleasing smile. M. de Villefort
answered nothing, but sat, or rather threw himself down again,
upon his chair. " And now, prisoner, will you consent to tell
your name ? " said the president. " The brutal affectation
with which you have enumerated and classified your crimes,
calls for a severe reprimand on the part of the court, both in the
name of morality, and out of the respect due to humanity. You
appear to consider this a point of honour, and it may be for this
reason you have delayed acknowledging your name. You wished
it to be preceded by all these titles."

"It is wonderful, M. le Président, how you have read my thoughts," said Benedetto, in his softest voice. "This is, indeed, the reason why I begged you to alter the order of the questions." There was no longer any deceit or bravado in the manner of the accused.

"Well!" said the president: "your name?"

"I cannot tell you my name, since I do not know it; but I know my father's and will pronounce it."

"Repeat your father's name," said the president.

"My father is the *procureur du roi*," replied Andrea, calmly.

"The *procureur du roi?*" said the president, stupefied, and without noticing the agitation which spread over the face of M. de Villefort; "the *procureur du roi?*"

"Yes; and if you wish to know his name, I will tell it,—he is named de Villefort." The explosion, which had been so long restrained, from a feeling of respect to the court of justice, now burst forth like thunder from the breasts of all present; the court itself did not seek to restrain the movement of the multitude. In the midst of this tumult the voice of the president was heard to exclaim,—"Are you playing with justice, accused, and do you dare set your fellow-citizens an example of disorder which in these times has never been equalled?"

Several persons hurried up to M. de Villefort, who was nearly buried in his chair, offering him consolation, encouragement, and protestations of zeal and sympathy. Order was re-established in the hall, with the exception of a few who still moved and whispered. A lady, it was said, had just fainted; they had supplied her with a smelling-bottle, and she had recovered. During the scene of tumult, Andrea had turned his smiling face towards the assembly :—" Gentlemen, I assure you I had no idea of insulting the court, or of making a useless disturbance in the presence of this honourable assembly. They ask me my age; I tell it. They ask where I was born; I answer. They ask my name; I cannot give it, since my parents abandoned me. But though I cannot give my own name, not possessing one, I can tell them my father's. Now I repeat, my father is M. de Villefort, and I will prove it."

The sincerity in the manner of the young man silenced the tumult. All eyes were turned towards the *procureur du roi*.

"But," said the irritated president, "you called yourself Benedetto, declared yourself an orphan, and claimed Corsica as your country."

"I said anything I pleased, in order that the solemn declaration I have just made should not be withheld, which otherwise would certainly have been the case. I now repeat that I was born at Auteuil on the night of the 27th September, 1817, and that I am the son of the *procureur du roi*, M. de Villefort. Do you wish for any further details ? I will give them. I was born in No. 28, Rue de la Fontaine, in a room hung with red damask : my father took me in his arms, telling my mother I was dead ; wrapped me in a napkin marked with H and N, and carried me into a garden, where he buried me alive."

A shudder ran through the assembly. " But how have you become acquainted with all these details ? "

" I will tell you, M. le Président. A man who had sworn vengeance against my father, and had long watched his opportunity to kill him, had introduced himself that night into the garden in which my father buried me. He was concealed in a thicket ; he saw my father bury something in the ground, and stabbed him in the midst of the operation ; then, thinking the deposit might contain some treasure, he turned up the ground, and found me still living. The man carried me to the foundling hospital, where I was entered, under the number 37. Some months afterwards a woman travelled from Rogliano to Paris to fetch me, and having claimed me as her son, carried me away. Thus, you see, though born in Paris, I was brought up in Corsica."

There was now a profound silence.

" Proceed ! " said the president.

" I might have lived happily amongst those good people, but my perverse disposition prevailed. I increased in wickedness till I committed crime. One day, when I cursed Providence for ordaining me to such a fate, my adopted father said to me, ' Do not blaspheme, unhappy child ! the crime is your father's, not yours ; your father's, who devoted you to death, or to a life of misery, in case, by a miracle, you should escape his doom.' Since then I ceased to blaspheme, but I cursed my father. This is why I have uttered the words for which you blame me. If I have committed an additional crime, punish me ; but if you will allow that ever since the day of my birth my fate has been sad, bitter, and lamentable, then pity me."

" But your mother ? " asked the president.

" My mother thought me dead ; she is not guilty. I did not even wish to know her name, nor do I know it." Just then a piercing cry, ending in a sob, burst from the centre of the crowd who encircled the lady who had before fainted, and who now fell into a violent fit of hysterics. She was carried out of the hall, and in doing so, the thick veil which concealed her face dropped off, and Madame Danglars was recognized. Notwithstanding his shattered nerves, the stunning sensation in his ears, and the species of madness which turned his brain, de Villefort rose as he perceived her.

"The proofs! the proofs!" said the president; "remember this tissue of horrors must be supported by the clearest proofs."

"Well, look at M. de Villefort, and then ask me for proofs."

Every one turned towards the *procureur du roi*, who, unable to bear the universal gaze now rivetted on him alone, advanced staggering into the midst of the tribunal, with his hair dishevelled and his face indented with the mark of his nails.

"Father!" said Benedetto, "I am asked for proofs, do you wish me to give them?"

"No, no, it is useless!" stammered M. de Villefort, "no, it is useless!"

"How useless?" cried the president, "what do you mean?"

"I mean that I feel it impossible to struggle against this deadly weight which crushes me. Gentlemen, I know I am in the hands of an avenging God! We need no proofs; everything relating to this young man is true."

A dull, gloomy silence, like that which precedes some awful phenomenon of nature, pervaded the assembly. "What! M. de Villefort," cried the president, "do you yield to a hallucination? This strange, unexpected, terrible accusation has disordered your reason. Come, recover."

The *procureur du roi* dropped his head.

"I am in possession of all my senses, sir," he said; "my body suffers, as you may suppose. I acknowledge myself guilty of all the young man has brought against me and hold myself under the authority of the *procureur du roi* who will succeed me."

The whole assembly was dumb with astonishment at the revelation and confession which had produced a catastrophe so different from that which had been anticipated.

"Well," said Beauchamp, "let them now say that drama is unnatural!"

"*Ma foi!*" said Château-Renaud, "I would rather end my career like M. de Morcerf; a pistol shot seems quite delightful compared with this catastrophe."

"And so he has committed murder," said Beauchamp.

"And I, who thought of marrying his daughter," said Debray. "She did well to die, poor girl!"

"The sitting is adjourned, gentlemen," said the president:

"fresh inquiries will be made, and the case will be tried next session by another magistrate." Andrea, calmer and more interesting than ever, left the hall, escorted by gendarmes, who involuntarily paid him some attention.

"Well, what do you think of this, my fine fellow ? " asked Debray of the sergent-de-ville, slipping a louis into his hand.

"There will be extenuating circumstances," he replied.

CHAPTER CXI

EXPIATION

NOTWITHSTANDING the density of the crowd, M. de Villefort saw it open before him. There is something so awe-inspiring in great afflictions, that the first emotion of a crowd generally is to sympathize with the sufferer. Thus de Villefort passed through the mass of spectators and officers of the Palais, and withdrew. Though he had acknowledged his guilt, he was protected by his grief. It would be difficult to describe the state of stupor in which he left the Palais. Habit alone guided him through the passage ; he threw aside his magisterial robe ; he could not bear the weight on his shoulders. Having staggered as far as the Rue Dauphiné, he perceived his carriage, awoke his sleeping coachman, by opening the door himself, threw himself on the cushions, and pointed towards the Faubourg Saint-Honoré ; the carriage drove on. All the weight of his fallen fortunes seemed suddenly to crush him ; he could not foresee the consequences ; he could not contemplate the future with the indifference of a cold murderer. The carriage rolled rapidly. De Villefort, while turning restlessly on the cushions, felt something press against him. He put out his hand to remove the object ; it was a fan which Madame de Villefort had left in the carriage ; this fan awakened a recollection which darted through his mind like lightning. He thought of his wife.

"Oh ! " he exclaimed, as though a red-hot iron were piercing his heart. His wife ! He had just acted the inexorable judge with her ; he had condemned her to death ; and she might at that very moment be preparing to die ! An hour had elapsed since her condemnation ; at that moment, doubtless, she was recalling all her crimes to her memory ; she was asking pardon for her sins ; perhaps she was even writing a letter imploring forgiveness from her virtuous husband—a forgiveness she was purchasing with her death ! De Villefort again groaned with anguish and despair. "Ah ! " he exclaimed, "that woman became criminal only from associating with me! I have dared to tell her—*I* have,—'Repent and die!' But no! she must not die; she shall live and follow me. We will flee from Paris, and go to the uttermost ends of the earth. Yes, we will fly: I will confess all to her,—I will tell her daily that I also have committed crime! She *must* live, that my infamy may diminish hers." And de Villefort threw open the window. "Faster! faster!" he cried, in a tone which electrified the coachman. The horses, impelled by fear, flew towards the house.

"Yes, yes!" repeated de Villefort, as he approached his home, "yes, that woman must live; she must repent and educate my son, the sole survivor, with the exception of the indestructible old man, of the wreck of my house. My wife and child shall escape from this gulf, carrying treasures with them; she will live and may yet be happy, since her child, in whom all her love is centred, will be with her. I shall have performed a good action, and my heart will be lighter." And the *procureur du roi* breathed more freely than he had done for some time.

The carriage stopped at the door of the mansion. De Villefort leaped out of the carriage, and saw his servants were surprised at his early return. As he passed by M. Noirtier's room, he perceived, through the half-open door, two figures; but he experienced no curiosity to know who was visiting his father; anxiety carried him no farther.

"Come," he said, as he ascended the stairs leading to his wife's room, "nothing is changed here." He then closed the door of the landing. "No one must disturb us," he said; "I must speak freely to her, accuse myself, and say"—he approached the door, touched the crystal handle, which yielded to his hand. With a single glance, de Villefort's eye ran through the room. "Not here," he said; "doubtless she is in her bedroom." He rushed towards the door; it was bolted: he stopped, shuddering. "Heloïse!" he cried. He fancied he heard the sound of a piece of furniture being removed. "Heloïse!" he repeated.

"Who is there?" answered the voice of her he sought. He thought that voice more feeble than usual.

"Open the door!" cried de Villefort; "open, it is I." But notwithstanding this request, notwithstanding the tone of anguish in which it was uttered, the door remained closed. Villefort burst it open with a violent blow. At the entrance of the room which led to her boudoir, Madame de Villefort was standing erect, pale, her features contracted, and her eyes glaring horribly "Heloïse! Heloïse!" he said, "what is the matter? Speak!";

The young woman extended her stiff white hand towards him.
" It is done, sir ! " she said, with a rattling which seemed to tear
her throat.   " What more do you want ? " and she fell on the
floor.

His wife was dead.   De Villefort, maddened with horror, stepped
back to the threshold of the door, fixing his eyes on the corpse.
" My son ! " he exclaimed suddenly, " where is my son ?—
Edward, Edward ! " and he rushed out of the room, still crying,
" Edward ! Edward ! "   The name was pronounced in such a tone
of anguish that the servants ran up.

" Where is my son ? " asked de Villefort ; " let him be removed from the house, that he may not see—— "

" Master Edward is not downstairs, sir," replied the valet.

" Then he must be playing in the garden ; go and see."

" No, sir ; Madame de Villefort sent for him half an hour ago ;
he went into her room, and has not been downstairs since."
A cold perspiration burst out on de Villefort's brow ; his legs
trembled, and his brain filled with a confused maze of ideas.
" In Madame de Villefort's room ? " he murmured, and slowly
returned, with one hand wiping his forehead, and with the other
supporting himself against the wall.   To enter the room, he must
again see the body of his unhappy wife.   To call Edward he must
re-awaken the echo of that room which now appeared like a
sepulchre ; to speak seemed like violating the silence of the
tomb.   His tongue cleaved to the roof of his mouth.

" Edward ! " he stammered—" Edward ! "   The child did
not answer.   Where, then, could he be, if he had entered his
mother's room, and not since returned ?   He stepped forward.
The corpse of Madame de Villefort was stretched across the doorway leading to the room in which Edward must be ; those glaring
eyes seemed to watch over the threshold, and the lips expressed
a terrible and mysterious irony.   Through the open door a portion of the boudoir was visible, containing an upright piano, and
a blue satin couch.   De Villefort stepped forward two or three
paces, and beheld his child lying—no doubt asleep on a sofa.
The unhappy man uttered an exclamation of joy ; a ray of light
seemed to penetrate the abyss of despair and darkness.   He had
only to step over the corpse, enter the boudoir, take the child in
his arms, and flee far, far away.

Villefort no longer presented a type of civilized man : he
more resembled a tiger wounded to death, whose teeth were
broken in his last agony.   He no longer feared realities, but
phantoms.   He leaped over the corpse as though it had been a

furnace. He took the child in his arms, pressed him, shook him, called him, but the child replied not. He pressed his burning lips to the cheeks, but they were icy cold and pale; he felt his stiffened limbs: he pressed his hand upon the heart, but it no longer beat: the child was dead. A folded paper fell from Edward's breast. Villefort, thunderstruck, fell upon his knees; the child dropped from his arms, and rolled on the floor by the side of its mother. He picked up the paper, and, recognizing his wife's writing, ran his eyes rapidly over it:—"You know that I was a good mother, since it was for my son's sake I became criminal. A good mother cannot depart without her son."

De Villefort could not believe his eyes: he dragged himself to the child's corpse, and examined it as a lioness contemplates its dead cub. Then a piercing cry escaped from his breast, and he cried, "Still the hand of God." He rose, his head bent beneath the weight of grief, and, shaking his damp hair, he who had never felt compassion for any one determined to seek his father, that he might have someone to whom he could relate his misfortunes,—someone by whose side he might weep. He entered Noirtier's room. The old man appeared to be listening as attentively as his infirmities would allow to the Abbé Busoni, who looked cold and calm, as usual. De Villefort, perceiving the abbé, passed his hand across his brow. He recollected the call he had made upon him after the dinner at Auteuil, and then the visit the abbé had himself paid to his house on the day of Valentine's death. "You here, sir!" he exclaimed; "do you, then, never appear but to act as an escort to death?"

Busoni turned round, and perceiving the excitement under which the magistrate laboured, he understood that the scene of the assizes had been accomplished; but beyond this he was ignorant.

"Why are you here now?"

"To tell you that you have sufficiently repaid your debt, and that I will pray to God to forgive you as I do."

"Good heavens!" exclaimed de Villefort, stepping back fearfully, "surely that is not the voice of the Abbé Busoni!"

"No!" the abbé threw off his false tonsure, shook his head, and his hair, no longer confined, fell in black masses around his face.

"It is the face of the count of Monte Cristo!" exclaimed the procureur du roi, with a haggard expression.

"You are not exactly right, M. le Procureur du Roi; you must go farther back."

" That voice ! that voice ! where did I first hear it ? "

" You heard it for the first time at Marseilles, twenty-three years ago, the day of your marriage with Mademoiselle de Saint Méran. Refer to your papers."

" You are not Busoni ? You are not Monte Cristo ? Oh, heavens ! you are, then, some implacable and mortal enemy ! I must have wronged you at Marseilles."

" You condemned me to a horrible, tedious death ; you killed my father ; you deprived me of liberty, of love, and happiness."

" Who are you, then ? Who are you ? "

" I am the spectre of a wretch you buried in the dungeons of the Château d'If. The form of the count of Monte Cristo was given to that spectre when he at length issued from his tomb, enriched with gold and diamonds, to lead him to you ! "

" Ah ! I recognize you ! I recognize you ! " exclaimed the *procureur du roi;* " you are—— "

" I am Edmond Dantès ! "

" You are Edmond Dantès ! " cried de Villefort, seizing the count by the wrist, " then come here ! " And he dragged Monte Cristo up the stairs.

" There ! Edmond Dantès ! " he said, pointing to the bodies of his wife and child. " See ! are you well avenged ? " Monte Cristo became pale at this horrible sight ; he felt he had passed beyond the bounds of vengeance, and that he could no longer say, " God is for and with me." With an expression of indescribable anguish he threw himself upon the body of the child, reopened its eyes, felt its pulse, and then rushed with it into Valentine's room, of which he double-locked the door.

" My child ! " cried de Villefort. " He carries away the body of my child ! Oh ! curses, woe, death to you ! " and he tried to follow Monte Cristo ; but, as though in a dream, he was transfixed to the spot ; his eyes glared as though they were starting through the sockets ; he gripped the flesh on his chest, until his nails were stained with blood : the veins of his temples swelled and boiled as though they would burst their narrow boundary, and deluge his brain with living fire. This lasted several minutes, until the frightful overturn of reason was accomplished ; then, uttering a loud cry, followed by a burst of laughter, he rushed down the stairs.

A quarter of an hour afterwards the door of Valentine's room opened, and Monte Cristo reappeared. In his arms he held the child, which no skill had been able to recall to life. Bending on one knee, he placed it reverently by the side of its mother, with its head upon her breast. Then rising, he went out, and meeting a servant on the stairs, he asked,—" Where is M. de Villefort ? "

The servant, instead of answering, pointed to the garden. Monte Cristo ran down the steps, and, advancing towards the spot designated, beheld de Villefort, encircled by his servants, with a spade in his hand, digging the earth with fury. " It is not here ! " he cried. " It is not here ! " And then he moved farther on and began digging anew.

Monte Cristo approached him, and said, in a low voice, with an expression almost humble, " Sir, you have indeed lost a son ; but—— "

De Villefort interrupted him ; he had neither listened nor heard. " Oh, I *will* find it ! " he cried ; " you may pretend he is not here, but I *will* find him, though I dig for ever ! " Monte Cristo drew back in horror. " He is mad ! " And as though he feared that the walls of the accursed house would crumble around him, he rushed into the street, for the first time doubting whether he had the right to do as he had done. " Oh ! enough of this,—enough of this," he cried, " let me save the last."

On entering his house he met Morrel, who wandered about like a ghost. " Prepare yourself, Maximilian," he said, with a smile ; " we shall leave Paris to-morrow."

" Have you nothing more to do here ? " asked Morrel.

" No," replied Monte Cristo, " God grant I may not have done too much already ! "

CHAPTER CXII

THE DEPARTURE

THE recent events formed the theme of conversation throughout all Paris. Emanuel and his wife conversed with natural astonishment in their apartment in the Rue Meslay upon the three successive catastrophes of Morcerf, Danglars, and de Villefort. Maximilian, who was paying them a visit, listened to their conversation, plunged in his accustomed apathy. " Indeed," said Julie, " might we not almost fancy, Emanuel, that those people, so rich, so happy but yesterday, had forgotten, in their prosperity, that an evil genius hovered over them, who appeared all at once to avenge himself for their fatal neglect ? "

" If the Supreme Being has directed the fatal blow," said Emanuel, " it must be that He in His great goodness has perceived nothing in the past lives of these people to merit mitigation of their awful punishment."

"That is a very rash judgment, Emanuel?" said Julie. "When my father, with a pistol in his hand, was on the point of committing suicide, had anyone then said, 'This man deserves his misery,' that person would have been entirely wrong.

"Yes, but your father was not allowed to fall; a being was commissioned to arrest the hand of Death."

Emanuel had scarcely uttered these words when the door of the room was opened, and the count of Monte Cristo appeared on the threshold. The young people uttered a cry of joy, while Maximilian raised his head, but let it fall again immediately. "Maximilian," said the count, without appearing to notice the impressions his presence had produced, "I come to seek you."

"I am ready to accompany you, sir," said Maximilian. "Adieu, my kind friends! Emanuel! Julie! Farewell!"

"How, farewell?" exclaimed Julie; "do you leave us thus, so suddenly, without any preparations for your journey?"

"Needless delays but increase the grief of parting," said Monte Cristo, "and Maximilian has provided himself with everything requisite; at least, I advised him to do so."

"And you quit us thus?" said Julie, "at a moment's warning; you do not give us a day—no, not even an hour, before your departure?"

"My carriage is at the door, madame; and I must be in Rome in five days."

"But does Maximilian go to Rome?" exclaimed Emanuel.

"I am going wherever it may please the count to lead me," said Morrel, with a smile full of grief; "I am devoted to him for the next month."

"Maximilian accompanies *me*," said the count, in his most persuasive manner; "therefore do not make yourself uneasy on his account."

"Once more, farewell, my dear sister; Emanuel, adieu!"

"His carelessness and indifference cut me to the heart," said Julie. "Oh! Maximilian, you are concealing something from us."

"We must leave you," said Monte Cristo.

"Before you go, count," said Julie, "will you permit us to express to you all that the other day—— "

"Madame," interrupted the count, taking her two hands in his, "all that you could say in words would never express that which I read in your eyes. On the eve of departure, I carry my egotism so far as to say, 'Do not forget me, my kind friends, for probably you will never see me again.'"

" Never see you again!" exclaimed Emanuel, whilst tears rolled down Julie's cheeks, " never behold you again! It is not a man, then, but some angel, that leaves us, and this angel is on the point of returning to heaven after having appeared on earth to do good."

" Say not so," quickly returned Monte Cristo, " say not so, my friends. No! Emanuel, I am but a man, and your admiration is as unmerited as your words are sacrilegious." And pressing his lips on the hand of Julie, who rushed into his arms, he extended his other hand to Emanuel; then he made a sign to Maximilian, who followed him with passive obedience.

" Restore my brother to peace and happiness," whispered Julie to Monte Cristo. The count pressed her hand in reply, as he had done eleven years before on the staircase leading to Morrel's study.

" You still confide, then, in Sindbad the Sailor?" asked he, smiling.

" Oh! yes," was the ready answer.

" Well, then, sleep in peace, and trust in the Lord."

The post-chaise was waiting; four powerful horses were pawing the ground with impatience, whilst at the foot of the steps, Ali, his face bathed in perspiration, and apparently just arrived from a long walk, was standing. " Well," asked the count in Arabic, " have you been to the old man's?" Ali made a sign in the affirmative.

"Have you placed the letter before him, as I ordered you to do?" The slave respectfully intimated that he had. " What did he say, or rather do?" Ali placed himself in the light, so that his master might see him distinctly, and then imitating in his intelligent manner the countenance of the old man, he closed his eyes, as Noirtier was in the custom of doing when saying " yes."

" Good! he accepts," said Monte Cristo; " now let us go."

These words had scarcely escaped him, when the carriage was on its road. Maximilian settled himself in his corner without uttering a word. Half an hour had fled when the carriage stopped suddenly; the count had just pulled the silken check-string, which was fastened to Ali's finger. The Nubian immediately descended, and opened the carriage-door It was a lovely starlight night—they had just reached the top of the hill Villejuif. The count remained alone, and on a sign from his hand, the carriage advanced some steps. He contemplated for some time, with his arms crossed, the vast city of Paris. " Great city!" murmured he, inclining his head and joining his hands as if in prayer, " less than six months have elapsed since first I entered thy gates. I believe that the spirit of God led my steps to thee, and that He also enables me to quit thee in triumph! The secret cause of my presence within thy walls I have confided alone to Him Who only has had the power to read my heart. God only knows that I retire from thee without pride or hatred, but not without many regrets ; He only knows that the power confided to me has never been made subservient to my personal good or to any useless cause. Oh! great city! it is in thy palpitating bosom that I have found that which I sought ; like a patient miner, I have dug deep into thy very entrails to root out evil thence ; now my work is accomplished, my mission is terminated, now thou canst afford me neither pain nor pleasure. Adieu, Paris! adieu! "

His look wandered over the vast plain like that of some genius of the night ; he passed his hand over his brow, and, getting into the carriage, it quickly disappeared on the other side of the hill.

CHAPTER CXIII

THE HOUSE IN THE ALLÉES DE MEILLAN

Ten leagues were passed in silence. Morrel was dreaming, and Monte Cristo was looking at the dreamer.

" Morrel," said the count to him at length, " do you repent having followed me ? "

" No, count ; but to leave Paris——"

" If I thought happiness might await you in Paris, Morrel, I would have left you there."

" Valentine reposes within the walls of Paris, and to leave Paris is like losing her a second time."

" Maximilian," said the count, " the friends we have lost do not repose in the bosom of the earth, but are buried deep in our hearts ; and it has been thus ordained, that we may always be accompanied by them. I have two friends, who in this way never depart from me ; the one who gave me being, and the other who conferred knowledge and intelligence on me. Their spirits live in me. I consult them when doubtful, and if I ever do any good, it is to their good counsels that I am indebted. Listen to the voice of your heart, Morrel, and ask it whether you ought to preserve this melancholy demeanour towards me."

" My friend," said Maximilian, " the voice of my heart is very sorrowful, and paints the future in most unhappy colours."

" It is ever thus that weakened minds see everything as through a black veil; the soul forms its own horizons; your soul is darkened, and consequently the future appears unpromising."

"That may be true," said Maximilian, subsiding into his thoughtful mood.

The journey was performed with that marvellous rapidity which the unlimited power of the count ever commanded. The following morning they arrived at Châlons, where the count's steamboat waited for them; the carriage was placed on board, and the two travellers embarked without delay. The boat was built for speed; her two paddle-wheels resembled two wings with which she skimmed the water like a bird. As the distance increased between the travellers and Paris, an almost superhuman serenity appeared to surround the count; he might have been taken for an exile about to revisit his native land. Ere long Marseilles came in view. Powerful memories were stirred within them by the sight of that round tower, that Fort Saint-Nicolas, and it was with one accord that they stopped on the Canebière. A vessel was setting sail for Algiers. The passengers and their relations crowded on the deck, friends taking a tender, but sorrowful, leave of each other.

"Here," said Morrel, leaning heavily on the arm of Monte Cristo, "here is the spot where my father stopped when the *Pharaon* entered the port; it was here that the good old man, whom you saved from death and dishonour, threw himself into my arms. I yet feel his warm tears on my face, and his were not the only tears shed, for many who witnessed our meeting wept also."

Monte Cristo gently smiled and said, "I was there," at the same time pointing to the corner of a street. In the very direction he indicated, a groan, expressive of bitter grief, was heard; and a woman was seen waving her hand to a passenger on board the vessel about to sail. Monte Cristo's emotion must have been remarked had not Morrel been watching the vessel.

"Oh! heavens!" exclaimed Morrel, "I do not deceive myself —that young man who is waving his hat is Albert de Morcerf!"

"Yes," said Monte Cristo, "I recognised him."

"How so?—you were looking the other way." The count smiled, and again turned his looks towards the veiled female, who soon disappeared at the corner of the street.

"Dear Maximilian," said the count, "have you anything to do in this land?"

"I have to weep over the grave of my father," replied Morrel, in a broken voice.

" Well, go,—wait for me there and I will soon join you."

" You leave me then ? "

" Yes ; I, also, have a pious visit to pay."

Monte Cristo remained on the spot until Maximilian was out of sight and then walked slowly towards the Allées de Meillan to seek out a small house with which our readers must have been familiar at the beginning of this story. It yet stood under the shade of a fine avenue of lime-trees, which formed one of the most frequented walks of the idlers of Marseilles. It was covered by an immense vine, which spread its aged and blackened branches over the stone front, burnt yellow by the ardent sun of the south. Two stone steps, worn away by the friction of the feet, led to the door, made of three planks, which, owing to their never having made acquaintance with paint or varnish, parted annually to reunite again when the damp season arrived. This house, with all its crumbled antiquity and apparent misery, was yet cheerful and picturesque, and was the same that old Dantès formerly inhabited—the only difference being that the old man occupied merely the garret, while the whole house was now placed at the disposal of Mercédès by the count.

The woman whom the count had seen leave the ship with so much regret entered this house and Monte Cristo followed her. On stepping into the house he heard a sigh, almost resembling a deep sob ; he looked in the direction whence it came, and there, under an arbour of Virginian jessamine, he perceived Mercédès seated, with bowed head and weeping bitterly. Monte Cristo advanced a few paces, which were heard on the gravel. Mercédès raised her head, and uttered a cry of terror on beholding a man before her.

" Madame," said the count, " it is no longer in my power to restore you to happiness, but I offer you consolation ; will you deign to accept it as coming from a friend ? "

" I am, indeed, most wretched," replied Mercédès. " Alone in the world, I had but my son, and he has left me ! "

" He possesses a noble heart, madame," replied the count, " and has acted rightly. Had he remained with you, his life must have become a burden, nor would he have participated in your griefs. Leave him to build up the future for you, and I venture to say, you will confide it to safe hands."

" Oh!" replied the wretched woman, shaking her head, "I pray God in His mercy to grant him prosperity, but I can never enjoy it. The bitter cup of adversity has been drained by me to the very dregs, and I feel that the grave is not far distant. You have acted kindly, count, in bringing me back to the place where

I enjoyed so much bliss. I ought to meet death where happiness was once all my own."

"Alas!" said Monte Cristo, "your words sear and embitter my heart, the more so as you have every reason to hate me; but why do you pity, instead of blaming me? You render me still more unhappy——"

"Hate you,—blame you,—you, Edmond! Hate—reproach the man that has spared my son's life! For was it not your intention to destroy that son of whom M. de Morcerf was so proud? Oh! look at me well, and discover, if you can, even the semblance of a reproach in me." The count looked up, and fixed his eyes on Mercédès, who, partly rising from her seat, extended both her hands towards him. "Oh! look at me," continued she, with a feeling of profound melancholy; "I neither reproach you nor hate you, my friend! Oh! no, Edmond! it is myself that I blame,—myself that I hate! Oh! miserable creature that I am!" cried she, clasping her hands, and raising her eyes to heaven. "I once possessed piety, innocence, and love,—the three attributes of the angels,—and now what am I?"

Monte Cristo approached her, and silently took her hand. "No," said she, withdrawing it gently, "no, my friend, touch me not. You have spared me, yet of all who have fallen under your vengeance I was the most guilty. Nay do not press my hand, Edmond! You are thinking of some kind expression, I am sure, to console me, but do not bestow it on me, for I am no longer worthy of kindness. See, misfortune has silvered my hair and my brow is wrinkled. You, Edmond, on the contrary,—you are still young, handsome, dignified; it is because you have never doubted the mercy of God, that He has supported and strengthened you in all your trials."

"Mercédès," said Monte Cristo, "you judge yourself with too much severity. You are a noble-minded woman, and it was your grief that disarmed me. Still I was but an agent, led on by an invisible and offended Deity, Who chose not to withhold the fatal blow that I was destined to hurl. I take that God to witness, at Whose feet I have prostrated myself daily for the last ten years, that I would have sacrificed my life for you, and, with my life, the projects that were indissolubly linked with it. But, and I say it with some pride, Mercédès, God required me and I lived. Examine the past and the present, and endeavour to dive into futurity, and then say whether I am not a Divine instrument. The most dreadful misfortunes, the most frightful sufferings, the abandonment of all those who loved me, the persecution of those who did not know me, formed the trials of my youth ; when suddenly, from captivity, solitude, misery, I was restored to light and liberty, and became the possessor of a fortune so brilliant, so unbounded, so unheard-of that I must have been blind not to be conscious that God had endowed me with it to work out His own great designs. From that time I viewed this fortune as confided to me for a particular purpose. Not a thought was given to a life which you once, Mercédès, had the power to render blissful, not one hour of peaceful calm was mine, but I felt myself driven on like an exterminating angel. I inured my body to the most violent exercises, my soul to the bitterest trials ; I taught my arm to slay, my eyes to behold excruciating sufferings, and my mouth to smile at the most horrid spectacles. From good-natured, confiding, and forgiving, I became immovable as fate. Then I launched out into the path that was opened to me ; I overcame every obstacle and reached the goal But woe to those who thwarted me in my career ! ''

" Enough," said Mercédès, " enough, Edmond ! Believe me that she who alone recognised you has been the only one to comprehend you. I tell you freely that the comparison I draw between you and other men will ever be one of my greatest tortures. No ! there is nothing in the world to resemble you in worth and goodness ! But we must say farewell, Edmond."

" Before I leave you, Mercédes, have you no request to make ? ''

" I desire but one thing, Edmond—the happiness of my son."

" Pray to the Almighty to spare his life, and I will take upon myself to promote his happiness. But have you no request to make for yourself ? ''

" For myself I want nothing. I live, as it were, between two graves. The one is that of Edmond Dantès—lost to me long, long since. He had my love ! The other is that of the man who met his death at the hand of Edmond Dantès. I approve of the deed, but I must pray for the dead."

" Yes, your son shall be happy, Mercédès," repeated the count.

" Then I shall enjoy as much happiness as this world can give."

" But what are your intentions ? ''

" To say that I shall live here, like the Mercédès of other times, gaining my bread by labour, would not be true, nor would you believe me. I have no longer the strength to do anything but to spend my days in prayer. However, I shall have no occasion to work, for the money buried by you, which I found in the place you mentioned, will maintain me. Rumour will doubtless be busy with me, my occupations, my manner of living : that will signify but little."

" Mercédès," said the count, " I do not say it to blame you, but you made an unnecessary sacrifice in relinquishing the whole of the fortune amassed by M. de Morcerf ; half of it, at least, by right belonged to you, in virtue of your management."

" I perceive what you are intending, but I cannot accept it, Edmond ; my son would not permit it."

" Nothing shall be done without the full approbation of Albert de Morcerf. But if he accept my offers, will you oppose them ? "

" You well know, Edmond, that I am no longer a reasoning creature. I live, because it is not ordained for me to die. If succour be sent to me I will accept it."

" Ah, madame," said Monte Cristo, " you should not talk thus ! It is not so we should evince our resignation to the will of heaven ; on the contrary, we are all free agents."

" Alas ! " exclaimed Mercédès, " if that were so, had I free will but lacked the power to render that will efficacious, it would drive me to despair."

Monte Cristo dropped his head and shrank from the vehemence of her grief. " Will you not even say you will see me again ? "

" On the contrary, we shall meet again," said Mercédès, pointing to heaven with solemnity. " I tell you so to prove to you that I still hope." And after pressing her own trembling hand upon that of the count, Mercédès rushed up the stairs and disappeared. Monte Cristo slowly left the house and turned towards the quay. But Mercédès saw not his departure. Her eyes were straining to see the ship which was carrying her son over the vast sea. But still her voice involuntarily murmured softly,—" Edmond ! Edmond ! Edmond ! "

CHAPTER CXIV

THE PAST

THE count departed with a sad heart from the house in which he had left Mercédès, probably never to behold her again. Since the death of little Edward a great change had taken place in Monte Cristo. Having reached the summit of his vengeance by a long and tortuous path, he saw an abyss of doubt on the other side of the mountain. More than this, his conversation with Mercédès had awakened so many recollections that he felt it necessary to combat them. He thought that he must have made an error in his calculations if he now found cause to blame himself.

" I cannot have deceived myself," he said ; " I must look upon the past in a false light. What ! " he continued, " can I have been tracing a false path ?—can the end which I propose be a mistaken end ? I cannot reconcile myself to this idea—it would madden me ! The reason I am dissatisfied is that I have not a clear appreciation of the past. Come, then, thou regenerate man, thou all-powerful visionary, thou invincible millionaire ! Once again review thy past life of starvation and wretchedness ; too much gold and splendour are now reflected by the mirror in which Monte Cristo seeks to behold Dantès. Bury thy gold, shroud thy splendour, exchange riches for poverty, liberty for a prison, a living body for a corpse ! " As he thus reasoned, Monte Cristo walked down the Rue de la Caisserie. It was the same through which, twenty-four years ago he had been conducted by the silent nocturnal guard ; the houses, to-day so smiling and animated, were on that night dark, mute, and closed. " And yet they were the same," murmured Monte Cristo, " it is the sun which brightens the place, and makes it appear so cheerful."

He proceeded towards the quay by the Rue Saint Laurent, and advanced to the Consigne ; it was the point where he had embarked. A pleasure-boat was passing, with its striped awning ; Monte Cristo called the owner, who immediately rowed up to him with the eagerness of a boatman hoping for a good fare. The weather was magnificent, and the excursion a treat.

But notwithstanding the golden light in which the whole scene was bathed, the count of Monte Cristo, wrapped in his cloak, could think only of that terrible voyage, the details of which were, one by one, recalled to his memory. The solitary light burning at the Catalans—that first sight of the Château d'If, which told him whither they were leading him, the struggle with the gendarmes when he wished to throw himself overboard, his despair when he found himself vanquished and the cold sensation of the end of the carbine touching his forehead,—all these were brought before him in vivid and frightful reality. Henceforth he no longer beheld the clear sky, the graceful boats, the golden light ; the sky appeared hung in black, and the gigantic structure of the Château d'If seemed like the phantom of a mortal enemy As they reached the shore, the count instinctively shrank to the extreme end of the boat, and the owner was obliged to call out in his sweetest tone of voice, " Sir, we have reached the shore."

Monte Cristo remembered that on that very spot, on the same rock, he had been violently dragged by the guards, who forced him to ascend the slope at the points of their bayonets. The journey had seemed very long to Dantès, but Monte Cristo found it short. Each stroke of the oar seemed to revive a new crowd of ideas, which sprang up with the froth of the sea.

No prisoners had been confined in the Château d'If since the revolution of July. A concierge waited at the door to exhibit this monument of curiosity to visitors, once a scene of terror. The count inquired whether any of the ancient gaolers were still there, but they had all been pensioned or had passed on to some other employment. The concierge who conducted him had only been there since 1830. He visited his own dungeon. He again beheld the dull light vainly endeavouring to penetrate the narrow opening. His eyes rested upon the spot where his bed, since then removed, had stood, and behind the bed, the new stones indicated where the breach made by the Abbé Faria had been. Monte Cristo felt his limbs tremble; he seated himself upon a log of wood.

"Are there any stories connected with this prison, besides the one relating to the poisoning of Mirabeau?" asked the count.

"Yes, sir; the gaoler Antoine told me one connected with this very dungeon."

Monte Cristo shuddered; Antoine had been his gaoler. The count turned round, and fancied he saw him in the corridor, rendered still darker by the torch carried by the concierge. "Would you like to hear the story, sir?"

"I should," said Monte Cristo, pressing his hand to his heart to still its violent beatings: he felt afraid of hearing his own history.

"This dungeon," said the concierge, "was occupied by a very dangerous prisoner, the more so since he was full of industry. Another person was confined in the Château at the same time, but he was not wicked, he was only a poor mad priest."

Monte Cristo raised his eyes, but he could not see the heavens; there was a stone veil between him and the firmament. "Could the prisoners see each other?" he asked.

"Oh, no, sir, it was expressly forbidden; but they eluded the vigilance of the guards, and made a passage from one dungeon to the other."

"Which of them made the passage?"

"The young man, certainly, for he was strong and industrious, while the abbé was aged and weak; besides, his mind was too vacillating to allow him to carry out an idea."

"Blind fools!" murmured the count.

"However, be that as it may, the young man made a passage,

how, or by what means no one knows ; but he made it, and there is the trace yet remaining.   You can see it," and the man held the torch to the wall.

" The result was, the two men were able to communicate. One day the old man fell ill and died.   Now guess what the young man did ? "

" Tell me."

" He carried off the corpse, which he placed in his own bed with its face to the wall ; then he entered the empty dungeon, closed the entrance, and slid himself into the sack which contained the dead body.   Did you ever hear of such a thing ? " Monte Cristo closed his eyes, and seemed again to experience all the sensations he had felt when the coarse canvas, yet moist with the cold dews of death, had touched his face.   The gaoler continued :—" Now this was his project ; he fancied they buried the dead at the Château d'If, and imagining they would not expend much labour on the grave of a prisoner, he calculated upon raising the earth with his shoulders ; but, unfortunately, their arrangements at the Château frustrated his plans : they never buried their dead ; they merely attached a heavy cannon ball to the feet, and then threw them into the sea.   This is what was done.   The young man was thrown from the top of the rock ; the corpse was found on the bed next day, and the whole truth was guessed : for the men who performed the office then mentioned what they had not dared to speak of before, namely, that at the moment the corpse was thrown into the deep, they heard a shriek, which was almost immediately stifled by the noise of the waves."   The count breathed with difficulty ; the cold drops ran down his forehead, and his heart was full of anguish.

" No," he muttered, " the doubt I felt was but the beginning of forgetfulness ; but here the wound reopens, and the heart again thirsts for vengeance.   And the prisoner," he continued aloud, " was he ever heard of afterwards ? "

" Oh ! no ; of course not.   You can understand that one of two things must have happened : he must either have fallen flat, in which case the blow, from a height of ninety feet, must have killed him instantly, or he must have fallen upright, and then the weight would have dragged him to the bottom, poor fellow."

" Then you pity him ? "

" *Ma foi !* yes ; though he was in his own element."

" What do you mean ? "

" He was a naval officer who had been confined for plotting with the Bonapartists."

" Was his name ever known ? "

" Oh ! yes ; but only as No. 34. Do you wish to see anything more, sir ? "

" Yes ; show me the poor abbé's room."

" Come, sir."

" Wait," said Monte Cristo, " I wish to take one final glance around this room."

" This is fortunate," said the guide ; " I have forgotten the other key."

" Go and fetch it."

" I will leave you the torch, sir."

" No, take it away ; I can see in the dark."

" Why, you are like No. 34. They said he was so accustomed to darkness, that he could see a pin in the darkest corner of his dungeon."

" He spent fourteen years learning that," muttered the count.

The guide carried away the torch. The count had spoken correctly. Scarcely had a few seconds elapsed when he saw everything distinctly. Then he looked around him and recognised his dungeon.

" Yes," he said, " there is the stone upon which I used to sit ; there is the impression made by my shoulders on the wall ; there is the mark of my blood made when I, one day, dashed my head against the wall." He saw in fancy the burial of his father, and the marriage of Mercédès. On the other side of the dungeon he perceived an inscription, the white letters of which were still visible on the green wall. " ' O God ! ' " he read, " ' preserve my memory ! ' " " Oh, yes ! " he cried, " that was my only prayer at last. O God ! Thou hast preserved my memory ; I thank Thee ! I thank Thee ! " At this moment the light of the torch was reflected on the wall ; the guide was advancing and Monte Cristo went to meet him.

" Follow me, sir ; " and without ascending the stairs, the guide conducted him by a subterranean passage to another entrance. The first thing that met his eye was the meridian drawn by the abbé on the wall, by which he calculated the time ; then he saw the remains of the bed on which the poor prisoner had died. The sight of this, instead of exciting the anguish experienced by the count in the dungeon, filled his heart with a soft and grateful sentiment, and tears fell from his eyes.

" This is where the mad abbé was kept, sir, and that is where the young man entered ; " and the guide pointed to the opening, which had remained unclosed.

Dantès took some louis from his pocket, and gave them to the man who had twice unconsciously pitied him. The guide took them, thinking them merely a few pieces of little value; but the light of the torch revealed, their true worth. " Sir," he said, " you have made a mistake; you have given me gold."

" I know it."

" Sir," he cried, scarcely able to believe his good fortune,— " sir, I cannot understand your generosity! "

" Oh! it is very simple, my good fellow; I have been a sailor, and your story touched me more than it would others."

" Then, sir, since you are so liberal, I ought to offer you something."

" What have you to offer to me, my friend? Shells? Strawwork? Thank you! "

" No, sir, neither of these; something connected with the story."

" Really! What is it? "

" Listen," said the guide; " I said to myself, ' Something is always left in a cell inhabited by one prisoner for fifteen years,' so I began to sound the wall and after some search I discovered a hollow sound against the head of the bed and under the hearth. I raised the stones, and found—"

" A rope-ladder and some tools? "

" How do you know that? " asked the guide, in astonishment.

" I do not know—I only guess it, because these sort of things are generally found in prisoners' cells."

" Yes, sir, a rope-ladder and tools. I sold them to visitors, who considered them great curiosities; but I have still something left."

" What is it? " asked the count, impatiently.

" A sort of book, written upon strips of cloth."

" Go and fetch it, my good fellow; and if it be what I hope, rest satisfied."

" I will run for it, sir; " and the guide went out. Then the count knelt down by the side of the bed, which death had converted into an altar. " Oh, second father! " he exclaimed,— " thou who hast given me liberty, knowledge, riches, thou who, like beings of a superior order to ourselves, couldst understand the science of good and evil; if in the depths of the tomb there still remain something within us which can respond to the voice of those who are left on earth; if after death the soul ever revisit the places where we have lived and suffered, then, noble heart; I conjure thee. by the paternal love thou didst bear me by the filial obedience I vowed to thee, grant me some sign, some revelation! Remove from me the remains of a doubt, which, if it change not to conviction, must become remorse!" The count bowed his head, and clasped his hands together.

"Here, sir," said a voice behind him.

Monte Cristo shuddered and rose. The concierge held out the strips of cloth upon which the Abbé Faria had spread the stores of his mind. The manuscript was the great work by the Abbé Faria upon the kingdoms of Italy. The count seized it hastily, and his eyes immediately fell upon the epigraph, and he read, "'Thou shalt tear out the dragons' teeth, and shalt trample the lions under foot,' saith the Lord."

"Ah!" he exclaimed, "here is my answer. Thanks, father, thanks!" And feeling in his pocket, he took thence a small pocketbook, which contained ten bank-notes, each of 1,000 francs.

"Here," he said, "take this pocketbook."

"Do you give it to me?"

"Yes; but only on condition that you will not open it till I am gone;" and placing the treasure he had just found in his breast, which was more valuable to him than the richest jewel, he rushed out of the passage, and reaching his boat, cried, "To Marseilles!" Then, as he departed, he fixed his eyes upon the gloomy prison. "Woe," he cried, "to those who confined me in that prison! and woe to those who forgot that I was there!" As he repassed the Catalans, the count turned round, and burying his head in his cloak, murmured the name of a woman. The name he pronounced, in a voice of tenderness, amounting almost to love, was that of Haidée.

On landing, the count turned towards the cemetery, where he felt sure of finding Morrel. Ten years ago Monte Cristo had returned to France with millions, but had been unable to find the grave of his father, who had perished from hunger. Morrel had, indeed, placed a cross over the spot, but it had fallen down, and the gravedigger had burnt it, as he did all the old wood in the churchyard. The worthy shipowner had been more fortunate. Dying in the arms of his children, he had been by them laid by the side of his wife, who had preceded him into eternity by two years. Two large slabs of marble, on which were inscribed their names, were placed on either side of a little enclosure, railed in, and shaded by four cypress trees. Morrel was leaning against one of these, mechanically fixing his eyes on the graves. His grief was so profound he was nearly unconscious.

"Maximilian," said the count, "you should not look on the graves, but there"; and he pointed upwards.

"The dead are everywhere," said Morrel; "did you not yourself tell me so as we left Paris?"

"Maximilian," said the count, "you asked me during the journey to allow you to remain some days at Marseilles. Do you still wish to do so?"

"I have no wishes, count: only I fancy I could pass the time less painfully here than anywhere else."

"So much the better, for I must leave you; but I carry your word with me, do I not?"

"Ah, count, I will not forget it."

"No, you will not forget it, because you are a man of honour, Morrel, because you have sworn, and are about to do so again."

"Oh, count! have pity upon me. I am so unhappy."

"I have known a man much more unfortunate than you, Morrel."

"Impossible!"

"Listen, Morrel, and pay attention to what I am about to tell you. I knew a man who, like you, had fixed all his hopes of happiness upon a woman. He was young, he had an old father whom he loved, a betrothed bride whom he adored. He was about to marry her, when one of those caprices of fate, deprived him of his mistress, of the future of which he had dreamed, and plunged him into a dungeon."

"Ah!" said Morrel, "one quits a dungeon in a week, a month, or a year."

"He remained there fourteen years, Morrel," said the count, placing his hand on the young man's shoulder. Maximilian shuddered.

"Fourteen years!" repeated the count. "During that time he had many moments of despair. He also, Morrel, like you, considered himself the unhappiest of men. But at the height of his despair God assisted him through human means. One day he miraculously left the prison, transformed, rich, powerful. His first cry was for his father, but that father was dead."

"My father, too, is dead," said Morrel.

"Yes, but your father died in your arms, happy, respected, rich, and full of years, his father died poor, despairing, almost doubtful of Providence; and when his son sought his grave ten years afterwards, his tomb had disappeared, and no one could say, 'There sleeps the father you loved so well.'"

"But then he still possessed the woman he loved?"

" You are deceived, Morrel. That woman——"

" She was dead ? "

" Worse than that ; she was faithless, and had married one of the persecutors of her betrothed. You see, then, Morrel, that he was a more unhappy lover than you."

" And does he ever expect to be happy ? "

" He hopes so, Maximilian." The young man's head fell on his breast.

" You have my promise," he said, after a minute's pause.

" On the 5th of October, Morrel, I shall expect you at the island of Monte Cristo. On the 4th a yacht will wait for you in the port of Bastia ; it will be called the *Eurus*. You will deliver your name to the captain, who will bring you to me. It is understood—is it not ? "

" But, count, do you remember that the 5th of October——"

" Child ! " replied the count, " not to know the value of a man's word ! Morrel, farewell ! I have business in Italy. I leave you alone with your misfortunes and with hope. Come with me to the harbour."

The steamer bearing Monte Cristo soon was scarcely distinguishable on the horizon amidst the fogs of the night.

CHAPTER CXV

PEPPINO

AT the same time that the steamer disappeared from Morrel's gaze, a man, travelling post on the road from Florence to Rome had just passed the town of Acquapendente. He was travelling fast enough to make a great deal of ground without becoming altogether suspicious. This man might be recognised, from the accent with which he spoke to the postillion, to be a Frenchman. Another proof that he was a native of the universal country was apparent in the fact of his knowing no other Italian words than the terms used in music. On reaching the point from whence Rome is first visible, the traveller evinced none of the enthusiastic curiosity which usually leads strangers to stand up and endeavour to catch sight of the dome of St. Peter's. He merely drew a pocketbook from his pocket, and took from it a paper folded in four, and, after having examined it in a manner almost reverential, he said,—" Good ! I have it still."

The carriage entered by the Porta del Popolo, turned to the left, and stopped at the Hôtel de Londres. Maître Pastrini, our old acquaintance, received the traveller at the door, hat in hand.

The traveller alighted, ordered a good dinner, and inquired the address of the house of Thomson and French, which was immediately given to him. It was situated in the Via dei Banchi, near St. Peter's. In Rome, as everywhere else, the arrival of a post-chaise is an event. Ten young descendants of Marius and the Gracchi, barefooted and out at elbows, with one hand resting on the hip, and the other arm gracefully curved above the head, stared at the traveller, the post-chaise, and the horses : to these were added about fifty little vagabonds from the States of his Holiness, who took up a collection for plunging into the Tiber at high water from the bridge of St. Angelo. Now, as these *gamins* of Rome, more fortunate than those of Paris, understand every language, more especially French, they heard the traveller order an apartment, a dinner, and finally inquire the way to the house of Thomson and French. The result was that when the new-comer left the hotel with the cicerone, a man detached himself from the rest of the idlers, and followed the stranger with as much skill as a Parisian agent of police would have used.

The Frenchman had been so impatient to reach the house of Thomson and French that he would not wait for the horses to be harnessed, but left word for the carriage to overtake him on the road, or to wait for him at the banker's door. The Frenchman entered, leaving his guide in the anteroom, and the man who had followed him entered, too. The Frenchman knocked at the inner door, and entered the first room ; his shadow did the same.

"Messrs. Thomson and French ? " inquired the stranger.

A footman rose at a sign from a confidential clerk belonging to the first desk. " Whom shall I announce ? " said the footman.

" The Baron Danglars."

" Follow me ! " said the man. A door opened, through which the footman and the baron disappeared. The man who had followed Danglars sat down on a bench. The clerk continued to write for the next five minutes. Then the pen of the clerk ceased to move over the paper ; he raised his head, and appearing to be perfectly sure of a *tête-à-tête*. " Ah ! " he said, " here you are, Peppino ! "

" Yes," was the laconic reply.

" You have found out that there is something worth having about this large gentleman ? "

" *Pardieu !* he has come to draw, but I don't know how much ! "

" You will know presently, my friend," said the clerk.

" Very well, only do not give me false information, as you did the other day."

" What do you mean, Peppino ? of whom do you speak ? Was it the Englishman who carried off 3,000 crowns from here the other day ? "

" No ; he really had 3,000 crowns, and we found them. I mean the Russian prince, who you said had 30,000 livres, and we only found 22,000."

" You must have searched badly."

" Luigi Vampa himself searched."

"Indeed! But you must let me make my observations, or the Frenchman will transact his business without my knowing the sum." Peppino nodded, and, taking a rosary from his pocket, began to mutter a few prayers, while the clerk disappeared through the same door by which Danglars and the footman had gone out. In ten minutes he returned, with a bright countenance.

" Well ? " asked Peppino of his friend.

" Joy, joy !—the sum is large."

" Five or six millions, is it not ? "

" Yes, you know the amount."

" On the receipt of the count of Monte Cristo ? "

" Why, how came you to be so well acquainted with all this ? "

" We were informed beforehand."

" Then why do you apply to me ? "

" That I may be sure I have the right man."

" Yes, it is indeed he ! Five millions—a pretty sum, eh, Peppino ? "

" Hush !—here is our man ! " The clerk seized his pen, and Peppino his beads. Danglars looked radiant with joy ; the banker accompanied him to the door.

Peppino followed Danglars.

According to arrangement, the carriage was waiting at the door. The guide held the door open. Guides are useful people, who will turn their hands to anything. Danglars leaped into the carriage like a young man of twenty. The cicerone closed the door, and sprang up by the side of the coachman. Peppino mounted the seat behind.

" Will your Excellency visit St. Peter's ? " asked the cicerone.

" I did not come to Rome to see," said Danglars, aloud : then ne added softly, with an avaricious smile, " I came to touch ! " and he tapped his pocketbook.

" Then your Excellency is going——"

" To the hotel."

" Casa Pastrini ! " said the cicerone to the coachman, and the carriage drove rapidly on. Ten minutes afterwards the baron entered his apartment, and Peppino stationed himself on the bench outside the door of the hotel, after having whispered something in the ear of one of the descendants of Marius and the Gracchi, who immediately ran down the road leading to the Capitol at his fullest speed. Danglars was tired and sleepy; he therefore went to bed, placing his pocketbook under his pillow. Peppino had a little spare time, so he had a game of *mora* with the facchina, lost three crowns, and then, to console himself, drank a bottle of Orvieto.

The next morning Danglars awoke late; he had not slept well for five or six nights, even if he had slept at all. He breakfasted heartily and, caring little, as he said, for the beauties of the Eternal City, ordered post-horses at noon. But Danglars had not reckoned upon the formalities of the police and the idleness of the posting-master. The horses only arrived at two o'clock, and the cicerone did not bring the passport till three.

"Which road?" asked the postillion in Italian. "The Ancona road," replied the baron. Maître Pastrini interpreted the question and answer, and the horses galloped off. Danglars intended travelling to Venice, where he would receive one part of his fortune, and then proceeding to Vienna, where he would find the rest; he meant to take up his residence in the latter town, which he had been told was a city of pleasure.

He had scarcely advanced three leagues out of Rome when daylight began to disappear. Danglars put his head out and asked the postillion how long it would be before they reached the next town. "*Non capisco*," was the reply. Danglars bent his head, which he meant to imply, "Very well." The carriage again moved on. "I will stop at the first posting-house," said Danglars, as he composed himself for sleep.

Now and then a jolt, more violent than the rest, caused him to open his eyes; then he felt that he was still carried with vast rapidity over the same country, thickly strewn with broken aqueducts. But the night was cold, dull, and rainy; and it was much more pleasant for a traveller to remain in the warm carriage than to put his head out of the window to make inquiries of a postillion whose only answer was, "*Non capisco*."

Danglars therefore continued to sleep, saying to himself that he would be sure to awake at the posting-house. When at last the carriage stopped, he fancied they had reached the long-desired point; he opened his eyes, looked through the window, expecting to find himself in the midst of some town, or at least village;

but he saw nothing but a ruin, whence three or four men went and came like shadows. Danglars waited for a moment, expecting the postillion to come and demand payment, having finished his stage. He intended taking advantage of the opportunity to make fresh inquiries of the new conductor; but the horses were unharnessed, and others put in their places, without anyone claiming money from the traveller. Danglars, astonished, opened the door; but a strong hand pushed him back, and the carriage rolled on. The baron was completely roused. " Eh ! " he said to the postillion, " eh, *mio caro ?* "

But *mio caro* replied not. Danglars then opened the window.

" Come, my friend," he said, thrusting his head through the opening, " where are we going ? "

" *Dentro la testa !* " answered a solemn and imperious voice, accompanied by a menacing gesture. Danglars thought *dentro la testa* meant " Put in your head ! " He was making rapid progress in Italian. He obeyed, not without some uneasiness, which, momentarily increasing, caused his mind, instead of being as unoccupied as it was when he began his journey, to fill with ideas which were very likely to keep a traveller awake, more especially one in such a situation as Danglars. Presently he observed a man in a cloak galloping on the right of the carriage.

" Some gendarme ! " he exclaimed. " Can I have been signalled by the French telegraphs to the pontifical authorities ? " He resolved to end his anxiety. " Where are you leading me ! " he asked. " *Dentro la testa,*" replied the same voice, with the same menacing accent.

Danglars turned to the left; another man on horseback was galloping on that side. " Decidedly ! " said Danglars, with the perspiration on his forehead, " I must be a prisoner." And he threw himself back in the *calèche,* not to sleep, but to think. Directly afterwards the moon rose. He then saw the great aqueducts he had before remarked, only then they were on the right hand, now they were on the left. He understood that they had described a circle, and were bringing him back to Rome. " How unfortunate ! " he cried. " They must have obtained my arrest ! " The carriage continued to roll on with frightful speed. At length he beheld a dark mass, which was no other than one of the ramparts encircling Rome.

" Oh ! oh ! " cried Danglars, " we are not returning to Rome; then it is not justice which is pursuing me ! Gracious heavens ! another idea presents itself : what if they should be robbers." Just then the carriage rolled on something harder than the gravelled road. Danglars hazarded a look on both sides of the road, and perceived monuments of a singular form; he felt sure he must be on the Appian Way. On the left, in a sort of valley, he perceived a circular excavation. It was Caracalla's circle. On a word from the man who rode at the side of the carriage, it stopped. At the same time the door was opened. "*Scendi!*" exclaimed a commanding voice. Danglars instantly descended. Four men surrounded him, besides the postillion.

"*Di quà*," said one of the men, going down a path leading out of the Appian Way. Danglars followed his guide and, after walking for about ten minutes, he found himself between a hillock and a clump of high weeds; three men, standing silent, formed a triangle, of which he was the centre. He wished to speak, but his tongue refused to move.

"*Avanti!*" said the same sharp and imperative voice.

This time Danglars had double reason to understand; for if the word and gesture had not explained the speaker's meaning, it was clearly expressed by the man walking behind him, who pushed him so rudely that he struck against the guide. This guide was our friend Peppino, who stopped before a pit overhung with thick hedges : the pit, half open, afforded a passage to the young man, who disappeared like the evil spirits in the fairy tales. The voice and gesture of the man who followed Danglars ordered him to do the same. Danglars acquitted himself like a man who is rendered brave by fear. Notwithstanding his large stomach, he slid down and, closing his eyes, landed on his feet. As he touched the ground, he opened his eyes. The path was wide, but dark. Peppino, who cared little for being recognised now he was in his own territories, lit a torch. Two other men descended after Danglars, forming the rearguard and pushing him whenever he happened to stop, and they arrived by a gentle declivity at the centre of a cross-road of sinister appearance. Indeed, the walls, hollowed out in sepulchres placed one above the other, seemed, in contrast with the white stones, to open their large dark eyes, like those which we see in a skull. A sentinel struck his carbine against his left hand. "Who goes there?" he cried.

"Friends!" said Peppino; "but where is the captain?"

"There!" said the sentinel, pointing over his shoulder to a sort of large hall, hollowed out of the rock, the lights from which shone into the passage through the large arched openings. "Fine spoil! captain, fine spoil!" said Peppino, in Italian; and taking Danglars by the collar of his coat, he dragged him to the hall, which the captain appeared to have made his dwelling-place.

" Is this the man ? " asked the captain, who was attentively reading Plutarch's " Life of Alexander."

" Himself, captain—himself."

" Very well, show him to me." At this rather impertinent order, Peppino raised his torch to Danglars' face, who hastily withdrew, that he might not have his eyelashes burnt. His agitated features presented the appearance of pale and hideous terror. " The man is tired," said the captain ; " conduct him to his bed."

" Oh ! " murmured Danglars, " that bed is probably one of the coffins hollowed in the wall, and the sleep I shall enjoy will be death from one of the poniards I see glistening in the shade."

From the depths of the hall were now seen to rise from their beds of dried leaves or goat's skin the companions of the man who had been studying the " Life of Alexander." The banker uttered a groan and followed his guide. At length, he found himself at the foot of a staircase ; a low door was opened before him, and bending his head to avoid striking his forehead, he entered a small room cut out of the rock. The cell was clean, though naked. Danglars, on beholding it, brightened, fancying it a type of safety.

" Oh ! God be praised ! " he said ; " it is a real bed ! "

" Ecco ! " said the guide, and pushing Danglars into the cell, he closed the door upon him.

A bolt grated ; Danglars was a prisoner ; besides, had there been no bolt, it would have been impossible for him to pass through the midst of the garrison who held the catacombs of St. Sebastian, encamped round Luigi Vampa. Danglars, too, had recognized the bandit, whose existence he would not believe when Albert de Morcerf mentioned him in Paris ; and not only did he recognize him, but also the cell in which Albert had been confined, and which was probably kept for the accommodation of strangers. These recollections were dwelt upon with some pleasure by Danglars, and restored him to some degree of tranquillity. Since the bandits had not despatched him at once, he felt that they would not kill him at all. They had arrested him for the purpose of robbery, and as he had only a few louis about him, he doubted not he would be ransomed. He remembered that Morcerf had been taxed at 4,000 crowns ; and as he considered himself of much greater importance than Morcerf, he fixed his own price at 8,000 crowns. This sum amounted to 48,000 livres : he would then have about 5,050,000 francs. With this amount he could manage to keep out of difficulties. Therefore, tolerably secure in being able to extricate himself from his position, he fell asleep with the tranquillity of the hero whose life Luigi Vampa was studying.

CHAPTER CXVI

LUIGI VAMPA'S BILL OF FARE

WE awake from every sleep except the one dreaded by Danglars. He awoke. " Yes, yes," he murmured, " I am in the hands of the brigands of whom Albert de Morcerf spoke." His first idea was to breathe, that he might know whether he was wounded.

" No," he cried, " they have not hurt me, but perhaps they have robbed me ! " and he thrust his hands into his pockets. They were untouched ; the hundred louis he had reserved for his journey from Rome to Venice were in his trousers pocket, and in that of his greatcoat he found the little note-case containing his letter of credit.

" Singular bandits ! " he exclaimed ; " they have left me my purse and my pocketbook. Let me see what time it is." Danglars' watch, one of Breguet's *chefs-d'œuvre*, struck half-past five. Should he demand an explanation from the bandits, or should he wait patiently for them to propose it ? The last alternative seemed the more prudent, so he waited until twelve o'clock. During all this time a sentinel, who had been relieved at eight o'clock, had been watching his door. Danglars suddenly felt a strong inclination to see the person who kept watch over him. He had remarked that a few rays from a lamp penetrated through the ill-joined planks of the door ; he approached it just as the brigand was refreshing himself with a mouthful of brandy, which, owing to the leather bottle containing it, sent forth an odour which was extremely unpleasant to Danglars. " Faugh ! " he exclaimed, retreating to the farthest corner of his cell.

At twelve, this man was replaced by another functionary, and Danglars, wishing to catch sight of his new guardian, approached the door again. He was an athletic, gigantic bandit, with large eyes, thick lips, and a flat nose ; his red hair fell in dishevelled masses like snakes around his shoulders. He took some black bread, cheese, and onions from his wallet, which he began devouring voraciously. " May I be hanged," said Danglars, " if I can understand how people can eat such filth ! "

But the secrets of nature are incomprehensible, and there are certain invitations contained in even the coarsest food which appeal very irresistibly to a fasting stomach. Danglars felt his own not to be very well supplied just then ; and gradually the man appeared less ugly, the bread less black, and the cheese more fresh, while those dreadful vulgar onions recalled to his mind certain sauces and side dishes which his cook prepared in a very superior manner whenever he said, " M. Deniseau, let me have a nice little fricassée to-day." He rose and knocked at the door ; the bandit raised his head. " *Che cosa* ? " asked the bandit. " Come, come," said Danglars, tapping his fingers against the door, " I think it is quite time to think of giving me something to eat ! " The giant, without answering, continued his dinner. Danglars felt his pride hurt, and not wishing to commit himself with the brute, threw himself down on his goat's skin bed, and did not breathe another word. Four hours passed by; the giant was replaced by another bandit. Danglars, who really began to feel sundry gnawings at the stomach, rose softly and, again applying his eye to the crack of the door, recognized the intelligent countenance of his guide. It was indeed Peppino, who was preparing to mount guard as comfortably as possible by seating himself opposite to the door, and placing between his legs an earthen pan, containing peas stewed with bacon. Near the pan he also placed a basket of grapes and a bottle of Orvieto. While witnessing these preparations Danglars' mouth watered. " Come," he said to himself, " let me try if he will be more tractable than the other ! " and he tapped gently at the door.

Danglars assumed his most agreeable manner, and said with a gracious smile, " Excuse me, sir, but are they not going to give me any dinner ? "

" Does your Excellency happen to be hungry ? "

" Happen to be hungry ! That's good, when I have not eaten for twenty-four hours ! " muttered Danglars. Then he added aloud, " Yes, sir, I am hungry—very hungry ! "

" What would your Excellency like ? " and Peppino placed his pan on the ground, so that the steam rose directly under the nostrils of Danglars. " Give your orders ! "

" Have you kitchens here ? "

" Kitchens ?—of course ! complete ones."

" And cooks ? "

" First rate ! "

" Well ! a fowl, fish, game, it signifies little, so that I eat."

" As your Excellency pleases ! You mentioned a fowl, I think ? "

" Yes, a fowl." Peppino, turning round, shouted, " A fowl for his Excellency ! " His voice yet echoed in the archway, when a

young man, handsome, graceful, and half naked, appeared, bearing
a fowl in a silver dish on his head, without the assistance of his
hands. " I could almost believe myself at the Café de Paris ! "
murmured Danglars.

" Here, your Excellency ! " said Peppino, taking the fowl from
the young bandit and placing it on the worm-eaten table, which,
with a stool and the goat's skin bed, formed the furniture of
the cell. Danglars asked for a knife and fork. " Here, Excellency," said Peppino, offering him a little blunt knife and a box-
wood fork. Danglars took the knife in one hand and the fork in
the other, and was about to cut up the fowl. " Pardon me,
Excellency," said Peppino, " people pay here before they eat.
They might not be satisfied, and——"

" Ah ! ah ! " thought Danglars, " this is no longer like Paris !
Never mind, I will carry it off well ! I should think a fowl is
worth about twelve sous at Rome."

" There," he said, throwing a louis down.

" Stay a moment, your Excellency," said Peppino, rising ;
" you still owe me something."

Resolving to resist the extortion, he said, " Come, how much
do I owe you for this fowl ? "

" Your Excellency has given me a louis on account."

" A louis on account for a fowl ? "

" Certainly ; and your Excellency now owes me 4,999 louis ! "
Danglars opened his enormous eyes on hearing this gigantic joke.

" Come, come, this is very droll—very amusing—I allow ;
but as I am very hungry, pray permit me to eat. Stay, here is
another louis for you."

" Then that will make only 4,998 louis," said Peppino, with
the same indifference. " I shall get them all in time."

" Oh ! as for that," said Danglars, angry at the fellow's per-
sistence in his joke, " you will never succeed. Go to the devil !
You do not know with whom you have to deal ! " Peppino made
a sign, and the youth hastily removed the fowl. Danglars threw
himself upon his goat's skin, and Peppino, shutting the door, again
began eating his peas and bacon. Though Danglars could not
see Peppino, the noise of his teeth allowed no doubt as to his occupation. He was certainly eating, and noisily too, like an ill-bred
man. " Brute ! " said Danglars. Peppino pretended not to
hear him, and without even turning his head, continued to eat
slowly. Danglars' stomach felt so empty, it seemed as though
it would be impossible ever to fill it again ; still, he had patience
for another half hour, which appeared to him like a century. He

again rose and went to the door. " Come, sir, do not keep me starving here any longer, but tell me what they want."

" Nay, your Excellency, it is you should tell us what you want. Give your orders, and we will execute them."

" Then open the door directly." Peppino obeyed. " *Pardieu!* I want something to eat ! Do you hear ? "

" What would your Excellency like to eat ? "

" A piece of dry bread, since the fowls are beyond all price in this accursed place."

" Bread ! Very well. Hallo, there ! Some bread ! " he exclaimed. The youth brought a small loaf.

" How much ? " asked Danglars.

" Four thousand nine hundred and ninety-eight louis," said Peppino. " You have paid two louis in advance."

" But you asked only 100,000 francs for a fowl ! "

" We have a fixed price for all our provisions. It signifies nothing whether you eat much or little—whether you have ten dishes or one,—it is always the same price."

" What ! still keeping up this silly jest ? My dear fellow, it is perfectly ridiculous—stupid ! You had better tell me at once that you intend starving me to death."

" Not at all, your Excellency, unless you intend to commit suicide. Pay and eat."

" And what am I to pay with, brute ? " said Danglars, enraged. " Do you suppose I carry 100,000 francs in my pocket ? "

" Your Excellency has 5,100,000 francs in your pocket ; that will be fifty-one fowls at 100,000 francs apiece."

Danglars shuddered. The bandage fell from his eyes, and he understood the joke, which he did not think quite so stupid as he had done just before. " Come," he said, " if I pay you the 100,000 francs, will you be satisfied, and allow me to eat at my ease ? "

" Certainly," said Peppino.

" But how can I pay them ? "

" Oh, nothing easier ; you have an account with Messrs. Thompson and French, Via dei Banchi, Rome. Give me a bill for 4,998 louis on these gentlemen, and our banker shall take it." Danglars thought it as well to comply with a good grace ; so he took the pen, ink, and paper Peppino offered him, wrote the bill, and signed it.

" Here," he said, " here is a bill at sight."

" And here is your fowl." Danglars sighed while he carved the fowl   it appeared very thin at the price. As for Peppino, he read the paper attentively, put it into his pocket, and continued eating his peas.

CHAPTER CXVII

THE PARDON

THE next day Danglars was again hungry; certainly the air of that dungeon was very appetising. Like an economical man he had concealed half of his fowl and a piece of the bread in the corner of his cell. But he had no sooner eaten than he felt thirst; he had forgotten that. He struggled against his thirst till his tongue stuck to the roof of his mouth : then no longer able to resist, he called out. The sentinel opened the door ; it was a new face. He sent for Peppino. " Here I am, your Excellency," said Peppino. " What do you want ? "

" Something to drink."

" Your Excellency knows that wine is beyond all price near Rome."

" Then give me water," cried Danglars, endeavouring to parry the blow. " Oh, water is even more scarce than wine, your Excellency, there has been such a drought ! "

" Come, my friend," said Danglars, " you will not refuse me a glass of wine ? "

" I have already told you that we do not sell retail."

" Well, then let me have a bottle of the least expensive."

" They are all the same price."

" And what is that ? "

" Twenty-five thousand francs the bottle."

" Tell me," cried Danglars, in a voice of extreme bitterness, " tell me that you wish to despoil me of all ; it will be sooner over than devouring me piecemeal."

" It is possible such may be the master's intention."

" Let me see him."

" Certainly."

Next moment Luigi Vampa appeared before Danglars.

" You sent for me," he said to the prisoner.

" How much do you require for my ransom ? "

" Only the 5,000,000 francs you have about you."

Danglars felt a dreadful spasm dart through his heart. " But that is all I have left in the world," he said, " out of an immense fortune. If you deprive me of that, take away my life also."

" We are forbidden to shed your blood."

" And by whom are you forbidden ? "

" By him we obey."

" You do, then, obey some one ?

" Yes, a chief."

" I thought you said you were the chief ? "

" So I am of these men ; but there is another over me."

" And did your superior tell you to treat me thus ? "

" Yes."

" Come," said Danglars, " will you take a million ? "

" No."

" Two millions ?—Three ?—Four ? Come—four ? I will give them to you on condition that you let me go."

" Why do you offer me 4,000,000 for what is worth 5,000,000 ? This is a kind of usury, banker, I do not understand."

" Take all, then ! Take all ! I tell you, and kill me ! "

" Come, come, calm yourself. You will excite your blood, and that would produce an appetite it would require a million a day to satisfy. Be more frugal ! "

" But when I have no more money left to pay you ? " asked the infuriated Danglars.

" Then you must suffer hunger."

" Suffer hunger ? " said Danglars, becoming pale.

" Most likely," replied Vampa, coolly.

" But you say you do not wish to kill me ? "

" No."

" And yet you will let me perish of hunger ? "

" Ah ! that is a different thing ! "

" Well, then, wretches ! " cried Danglars, " I will defy your infamous calculations ; I would rather die at once ; you may torture—torment—kill me,—but you shall not have my signature again."

" As your Excellency pleases," said Vampa, as he left the cell. Danglars, raving, threw himself on the goat's skin. Who was the invisible chief ? What could be his projects towards him ? And why, when everyone else was allowed to be ransomed, might he not also be ? A speedy, sudden death would be a fine means of cheating these remorseless enemies, who appeared to pursue him with such incomprehensible vengeance. But to die ! For the first time in his life Danglars contemplated death with a mixture of dread and desire.

Danglars resembled a timid animal excited in the chase ; first it flies, then despairs, and, at last, by the very force of despera-tion, succeeds in escaping. Danglars meditated an escape. But the walls were solid rock ; a man was sitting reading at the only outlet to the cell ; and behind that man figures armed with guns continually passed. His resolution not to sign lasted two days, after which he offered a million for some food. They sent him a magnificent supper and took his million.

From this time the prisoner resolved to suffer no longer, but to yield to all his exigencies. At the end of twelve days, after having made a splendid dinner, he reckoned his accounts, and found he had only 100,000 francs left. Then a strange reaction took place ; he who had just abandoned 5,000,000 endeavoured to save the 100,000 francs he had left ; and, sooner than give them up, he resolved to enter again upon his life of privation. He who for so long a time had forgotten God, began to think that miracles were possible ; that the accursed cave might be discovered by the officers of the Papal States, who would release him ; that then he would have 100,000 francs remaining, which would be sufficient to save him from starvation ; and, finally, he prayed that this sum might be preserved to him,—and, as he prayed, he wept. Three days passed thus, during which his prayers were frequent, if not heartfelt. Sometimes he was delirious, and fancied he saw an old man stretched on a pallet. He, also, was dying of hunger.

On the fourth, he was no longer a man, but a living corpse. He had picked up every crumb that had been left from his former meals, and was beginning to eat the matting which covered the floor of his cell. Then he entreated Peppino, as he would a guardian angel, to give him food ; he offered him 1,000 francs for a mouthful of bread. But Peppino did not answer. On the fifth day he dragged himself to the door of the cell.

"Are you not a Christian ? " he said, falling on his knees, " do you wish to assassinate a man who, in the eyes of heaven, is a brother ? Oh ! my former friends ! my former friends ! " he murmured, and fell with his face to the ground. Then rising with a species of despair, he exclaimed, " The chief ! the chief ! "

"Here I am ! " said Vampa, instantly appearing, " what do you want ? "

"Take my last gold," muttered Danglars, holding out his pocketbook, " and let me live here ; I ask no longer for liberty, I only ask to live."

"Then you suffer a great deal ? "

"Oh, yes ! yes ! cruelly."

"Still there have been men who suffered more than you."

"I do not think so."

"Yes ; those who have died of hunger."

Danglars thought of the old man whom in his hours of delirium he had seen groaning on his bed. He struck his forehead on the ground and groaned. "Yes," he said, "there have been some who have suffered more than I have, but then they must have been martyrs, at least."

"Do you repent?" asked a deep, solemn voice, which caused Danglars' hair to stand on end. His feeble eyes endeavoured to distinguish objects, and behind the bandit he saw a man enveloped in a cloak, half lost in the shadow of the stone column.

"Of what must I repent?" stammered Danglars.

"Of the evil you have done," said the voice.

"Oh, yes! oh, yes! I do indeed repent." And he struck his breast with his emaciated fist.

"Then I forgive you," said the man, dropping his cloak, and advancing to the light.

"The count of Monte Cristo!" said Danglars, more pale from terror than he had been from hunger and misery.

"You are mistaken—I am not the count of Monte Cristo!"

"Then who are you?'

"I am he whom you sold and dishonoured. I am he whose betrothed you prostituted. I am he upon whom you trampled that you might raise yourself to fortune. I am he whose father you condemned to die of hunger. I am he whom you also condemned to starvation, and who yet forgives you, because he hopes to be forgiven. I am Edmond Dantès!"

Danglars uttered a cry and fell prostrate. "Rise," said the count, "your life is safe; the same good fortune has not happened to your accomplices; one is mad, the other dead. Keep the 100,000 francs you have left. I give them to you. The 5,000,000 you robbed from the hospitals have been restored to them by an unknown hand. And now eat and drink; I will entertain you to-night. Vampa, when this man is satisfied, let him be free."

Danglars remained prostrate while the count withdrew; when he raised his head he saw nothing more than a shadow disappearing in the passage, before which the bandits bowed.

According to the count's directions, Danglars was waited on by Vampa, who brought him the best wine and fruits of Italy, then, having conducted him to the road, and pointed to his post-chaise, he left him leaning against a tree. Danglars remained there all night, not knowing where he was. When daylight dawned, he saw that he was near a stream; he was thirsty, and dragged himself towards it. As he stooped down to drink, he perceived that his hair had become quite white.

CHAPTER CXVIII

THE FIFTH OF OCTOBER

IT was about six o'clock in the evening; an opal-coloured light, through which an autumnal sun shed its golden rays, descended on the blue sea. The heat of the day had gradually decreased, and a light breeze arose, seeming like the respiration of nature on awakening from the burning siesta of the south; a delicious zephyr played along the coasts of the Mediterranean, and wafted from shore to shore the sweet perfume of plants, mingled with the fresh smell of the sea.

A light yacht, chaste and elegant in its form, was gliding along swiftly and gracefully, leaving behind it a glittering track. By degrees the sun disappeared behind the western horizon. The yacht moved rapidly onwards though there did not appear to be sufficient wind to ruffle the curls on the head of a girl. Standing on the prow was a tall man, of dark complexion, who saw with dilating eyes that they were approaching a dark mass of land in the shape of a cone, rising from the midst of the waves, like the hat of a Catalan. " Is that Monte Cristo ? " asked the traveller, in a melancholy voice.

" Yes, your Excellency," said the captain, " we have reached it ! "

" We have reached it ! " repeated the traveller, in an accent of indescribable sadness. Then he added, in a low tone, " Yes; that is the haven." A few minutes afterwards a flash of light, which was extinguished instantly, was seen on the land, and the sound of firearms reached the yacht.

" Your Excellency," said the captain, " that was the land signal, will you answer it yourself ? "

" What signal ? "

The captain pointed towards the island, up the side of which ascended a volume of smoke, increasing as it rose.

" Ah, yes," he said, as if awaking from a dream. " Give it to me."

The captain handed him a loaded carbine; the traveller slowly raised it, and fired in the air. Ten minutes afterwards, the sails were brailed, and they cast anchor about one hundred paces from the little harbour. The canoe was already in the sea, loaded with four rowers and the pilot. The traveller descended, and instead of sitting down at the stern of the boat, which had been decorated with a blue carpet for his accommodation, stood up with his arms crossed. "Proceed!" said the traveller. The eight oars fell into the sea simultaneously and the boat, yielding to the impulse, glided forward. Soon they found themselves in a little harbour, formed in a natural creek.

"Will your Excellency be so good as to mount the shoulders of two of our men, who will carry you ashore?" The young man answered this invitation with a gesture of indifference, and stepping out of the boat, the sea immediately rose to his waist.

"Ah!" said the captain, "you should not have done that. Our master will blame us.

After about thirty paces they landed; the young man stamped on the ground to shake off the wet, and looked round for some one to show him his road. As he turned, a hand rested on his shoulder, and a voice, which made him shudder, exclaimed "Good evening, Maximilian! you are punctual, thank you!"

"Ah! is it you, count?" said the young man, in an almost joyful accent, pressing Monte Cristo's hand with both his own.

"Yes; you see I am as exact as you are. But you are dripping, my dear fellow; you must change your clothes. Come, I have a habitation prepared for you, in which you will soon forget fatigue and cold."

Morrel was surprised that the men who had brought him had left without being paid or uttering a word.

"Oh," said the count, "you are looking for the sailors."

"Yes; I had not paid them."

"Never mind that, Maximilian," said Monte Cristo, smiling. "I have made an agreement with the navy, that the access to my island shall be free of all charge.

Morrel looked at the count with surprise. "Count," he said, "you are not the same here as in Paris."

"How so?"

"Here you laugh."

The count's brow became clouded. "You are right to recall me to myself, Maximilian," he said; "I was delighted to see you again, and forgot for the moment that all happiness is fleeting."

"Oh, no, no! count," cried Maximilian, seizing the count's hands, "pray laugh; be happy, and prove to me, by your indifference, that life is endurable to sufferers. Oh! how charitable, kind, and good you are; you affect this gaiety to inspire me with courage."

"You are wrong, Morrel; I was really happy."

"Then you forget me; so much the better."

" So you are not consoled ? " asked the count, surprised.

" Oh," exclaimed Morrel, with a glance, full of bitter reproach, " do you think I could be ? "

" When I ask you, if you are consoled, I speak to you as a man for whom the human heart has no secrets. Are you still actuated by the regret which drags the living to the pursuit of death, or are you only suffering from the prostration of fatigue and the weariness of ' hope deferred ? ' Oh ! my dear friend, if you can no longer weep, if you put all your trust in God, then, Maximillian, you are consoled—do not complain."

" Count," said Morrel, in a firm and at the same time soft voice, " listen to me. I come to die in the arms of a friend. There are people whom I love ; I love my sister, Julie,—I love her husband, Emanuel ; but I require a strong mind to smile on my last moments ; my sister would be bathed in tears and faint ; I could not bear to see her suffer ; Emanuel would tear the weapon from my hand, and alarm the house with his cries. You, count, who are more than mortal, will, I am sure, lead me to death by a pleasant path, will you not ? "

" My friend," said the count, " I have still one doubt,—are you weak enough to pride yourself upon your sufferings ? "

" No, indeed—I am calm," said Morrel, giving his hand to the count, " my pulse does not beat slower or faster than usual. No, I feel I have reached the goal, and I will go no farther. You told me to wait and hope ; do you know what you did, unfortunate adviser ? I waited a month, or rather I suffered for a month ! I did hope (man is a poor wretched creature), I did hope. What I cannot tell : something wonderful, an absurdity, a miracle, of what nature, He alone can tell Who has mingled with our reason that folly we call hope. Yes ; I did wait. I did hope, count, and during this quarter of an hour we have been talking together, you have unconsciously tortured my heart, for every word you have uttered proved that there was no hope for me. Oh ! count, I shall sleep calmly in the arms of death ! " Morrel pronounced these words with an energy which made the count shudder. " My friend," continued Morrel, " you named the fifth of October as the term of the delay you asked,—to-day is the fifth of October," he took out his watch ; " it is now nine o'clock —I have yet three hours to live."

" Be it so ! " said the count, " come."

Morrel mechanically followed the count, and they had entered the grotto before Maximilian perceived it. He felt a carpet under his feet, a door opened, perfumes surrounded him, and a brilliant light dazzled his eyes. Morrel hesitated to advance; he dreaded the enervating effect of all that he saw.

Monte Cristo drew him in gently. "Why should we not spend the last three hours remaining to us of life, like those ancient Romans, who when condemned by Nero, their emperor and heir, sat down at a table covered with flowers, and gently glided into death, through the perfume of heliotropes and roses?"

Morrel smiled. "As you please," he said; "death is always death—that is, forgetfulness, repose, exclusion from life, and therefore from grief." He sat down, and Monte Cristo placed himself opposite to him. They were in the dining-room, where the statues had baskets on their heads filled with fruits and flowers. Morrel had looked carelessly around, and had probably noticed nothing.

"Let us talk like men," he said, looking at the count.

"Proceed!"

"Count!" said Morrel, "you are the epitome of all human knowledge, and you seem to me a being descended from a wiser and more advanced world than ours."

"There is some truth in what you say," said the count. "I have descended from a planet, called Grief."

"I believe all you tell me without questioning its sense; in proof, you told me to live, and I did live; you told me to hope, and I almost did so. I am almost inclined to ask you, as though you had experienced death, 'Is it painful to die?'"

Monte Cristo looked upon Morrel with indescribable tenderness. "Yes," he said, "yes, doubtless it is painful; if you violently break the outer covering which obstinately begs for life, certainly you will suffer pain, and repent quitting life for a repose you have bought at so dear a price."

"Yes; I understand there is a secret of luxury and pain in death, as well as in life: the only thing is to understand it."

"You have spoken truly, Maximilian; according to the care we bestow upon it, death is either a friend who rocks us gently as a nurse, or an enemy who violently drags the soul from the body. Some day, when the world shall be much older, when mankind shall be master of all the destructive powers in nature—to serve for the general good of humanity—and shall have discovered the secrets of death, then that death will become as sweet as a slumber in the arms of your beloved."

"And if you wished to die, you would choose this death, count?"

"Yes."

Morrel extended his hand. "Now I understand," he said,

"why you brought me to this subterranean palace. It was
because you loved me well enough to give me one of those sweet
means of death of which we were speaking; a death without
agony, a death which allows me to fade away while pronouncing
Valentine's name and pressing your hand."

"Yes; you have guessed rightly, Morrel," said the count,
"that is what I intended."

"Thanks! the idea that to-morrow I shall no longer suffer is
sweet to my heart."

"Do you then regret nothing?"

"No," replied Morrel.

"Not even me?" asked the count, with deep emotion. Morrel's clear eye was for the moment clouded, then it shone with
unusual lustre, and a tear rolled down his cheek.

"What," said the count, "do you still regret anything in the
world, and yet seek to die?"

"Oh! I entreat you," exclaimed Morrel, in a low voice, "do
not speak another word, count, do not prolong my punishment."
The count fancied he was yielding, and this belief revived the
horrible doubt that had overwhelmed him at the Château
d'If. "I am endeavouring," he thought, "to make this man
happy. Now, supposing I am deceived, if this man has not been
unhappy enough to merit happiness, alas! what will become
of me, who can only atone for evil by doing good?" Then he
said aloud, "Listen, Morrel, I see your grief is great, but still you
do not like to risk your soul."

Morrel smiled sadly. "Count," he said, "I swear to you my
soul is no longer my own."

"Maximilian, you know I have no relation in the world. I
have accustomed myself to regard you as my son: well, then, to
save my son, I will sacrifice my life, nay, even my fortune."

"What do you mean?"

"I mean that you wish to quit life because you do not understand all the enjoyments which are the fruits of a large fortune.
Morrel, I possess nearly a hundred millions, I give them to you:
with such a fortune you can attain every wish. Are you ambitious? Every career is open to you. Overturn the world, change
its character, yield to mad ideas, be even criminal—but live."

"Count, I have your word," said Morrel, coldly, then taking out
his watch, he added, "it is half-past eleven."

"Morrel, can you intend it in my house, beneath my eyes?"

"Then let me go," said Maximilian. "or I shall think you did
not love me for my own sake, but for yours;" and he rose.

" It is well," said Monte Cristo, whose countenance brightened at these words ; " you wish it ; you are inflexible ; yes, as you said, you are indeed wretched, and a miracle alone can cure you ; sit down, Morrel, and wait."

Morrel obeyed ; the count rose, and unlocking a closet with a key suspended from his gold chain, took from it a silver casket, beautifully carved and chased. He placed the casket on the table ; then opening it, took out a little golden box, the top of which flew open when touched by a secret spring. This box contained an unctuous substance partly solid, of which it was impossible to discover the colour, owing to the reflection of the polished gold, sapphires, rubies, emeralds, which ornamented the box. It was a mixed mass of blue, red, and gold. The count took out a small quantity of this with a gilt spoon, and offered it to Morrel, fixing a long steadfast glance upon him. It was then observable that the substance was greenish.

" This is what you asked for," he said, " and what I promise to give you."

" I thank you from the depths of my heart," said the young man, taking the spoon from the hands of Monte Cristo. The count took another spoon, and again dipped it into the golden box. " What are you going to do, my friend ? " asked Morrel, arresting his hand.

" Ma foi ! Morrel, I was thinking that I, too, am weary of life, and since an opportunity presents itself——"

" Stay ! " said the young man. " You who love and are beloved ; you, who have faith and hope,—oh ! do not follow my example ; in your case it would be a crime. Adieu, my noble and generous friend, adieu ; I will go and tell Valentine what you have done for me." And slowly, though without any hesitation, he swallowed the mysterious substance offered by Monte Cristo. Then they were both silent. Ali, mute and attentive, brought the pipes and coffee, and disappeared. By degrees the lamps gradually faded in the hands of the marble statues which held them, and the perfumes appeared less powerful to Morrel. Seated opposite to him, Monte Cristo watched him in the shadow, and Morrel saw nothing but the bright eyes of the count. An overpowering sadness took possession of the young man ; his hands relaxed their hold ; the objects in the room gradually lost their form and colour ; and his disturbed vision seemed to perceive doors and curtains open in the wall.

" Friend," he cried, " I feel that I am dying ; thanks ! " He made a last effort to extend his hand, but it fell powerless beside him. Then it appeared to him that Monte Cristo smiled, not with that strange and fearful expression which had sometimes revealed to him the secrets of his heart, but with the benevolent kindness of a father for an infant. At the same time the count appeared to increase in stature : his form, nearly double its usual height, stood out in relief against the red tapestry, his black hair was thrown back, and he stood in the attitude of a menacing angel. Morrel, overpowered, turned round in the armchair ; a delicious torpor was insinuated into every vein ; a change of ideas presented themselves to his brain, like a new design in the kaleidoscope ; enervated, prostrate, and breathless he became unconscious of outward objects, he seemed to be entering that vague delirium preceding death. He wished once again to press the count's hand : but his own was immovable : he wished to articulate a last farewell, but his tongue lay powerless and heavy in his throat, like a stone at the mouth of a sepulchre. Involuntarily his languid eyes closed ; and still through his eyelashes a well-known form seemed to move amid the obscurity with which he thought himself enveloped.

The count had just opened a door. Immediately a brilliant light from the next room, or rather from the palace adjoining, shone upon the room in which he was gently gliding into his last sleep. Then he saw a woman of marvellous beauty appear on the threshold of the door separating the two rooms. " Is it heaven that opens before me ? " thought the dying man ; " that angel resembles the one I have lost." Monte Cristo pointed Morrel to the young woman, who advanced towards him with clasped hands and a smile upon her lips.

" Valentine ! Valentine ! " he mentally ejaculated, but his lips uttered no sound ; and as though all his strength were centred in that internal emotion, he sighed and closed his eyes. Valentine rushed towards him ; his lips again moved.

" He is calling you," said the count, " he to whom you have confided your destiny—he from whom death would have separated you, he calls you to him. Happily I vanquished death. Henceforth, Valentine, you will never again be separated on earth ; since he has rushed into death to find you. Without me you would both have died. May God accept my atonement of these two existences!"

Valentine seized the count's hand, and in her irresistible impulse of joy carried it to her lips.

" Oh ! thank me again ! " said the count, " tell me till you are weary, that I have restored you to happiness ; you do not know how much I require this assurance."

THE FIFTH OF OCTOBER

" Oh, yes, yes, I thank you with all my heart," said Valentine ; " and if you doubt the sincerity of my gratitude, oh, then, ask Haidée,—ask my beloved sister Haidée—who, ever since our departure from France, has caused me to wait patiently for this happy day, while talking to me of you."

" You love Haidée ? " asked Monte Cristo, with an emotion he in vain endeavoured to dissimulate.

" With all my soul."

" Well, listen, Valentine," said the count ; " I have a favour to ask of you."

" Of me ! Oh, am I happy enough for that ? "

" Yes ; you have called Haidée your sister ; let her become so indeed, Valentine ; render her all the gratitude you fancy you owe me ; protect her, for "—the count's voice was thick with emotion—" henceforth she will be alone in the world."

" Alone in the world ! " repeated a voice behind the count, " and why ? " Monte Cristo turned round. Haidée was standing pale, motionless, looking at the count with an expression of fearful amazement.

" Because to-morrow, Haidée, you will be free ; you will then assume your proper position in society, for I will not allow my destiny to overshadow yours. Daughter of a prince, I restore to you the riches and name of your father."

Haidée became pale, and lifting her transparent hands to heaven exclaimed in a voice hoarse with tears," Then you leave me, my lord?"

" Haidée, Haidée ! you are young and beautiful, forget even my name, and be happy ! "

" It is well," said Haidée, " your order shall be executed, my lord ; I will forget even your name, and be happy." And she stepped back to retire.

" Oh heavens ! " exclaimed Valentine, who was supporting the head of Morrel on her shoulder, " do you not see how pale she is ? Do you not see how she suffers ? "

Haidée answered with a heart-rending expression, " Why should he understand this, my sister ? He is my master, and I am his slave ; he has the right to notice nothing."

The count shuddered at the tones of a voice which penetrated the inmost recesses of his heart ; his eyes met those of the young girl, and he could not bear their brilliancy. " Oh, heavens ! " exclaimed Monte Cristo, " can my suspicions be correct ? Haidée, would it please you not to leave me ? "

" I am young," gently replied Haidée, " I love the life you have made so sweet to me, and should regret to die."

" You mean that if I leave you, Haidée—— "

" I should die ; yes, my lord."

" Do you love me ? "

" Oh, Valentine ! he asks whether I love him. Valentine, tell him whether you love Maximilian."

The count felt his heart dilate and throb ; he opened his arms, and Haidée, uttering a cry, sprang into them. " Oh, yes ! " she cried, " I do love you ! I love you as one loves a father, brother, husband ! I love you as my life, for you are the best, the noblest of created beings ! "

" Let it be, then, as you wish, sweet angel ; God has sustained me in my struggle with my enemies, and has given me this victory ; He will not let me end my triumph with this penance ; I wished to punish myself, but He has pardoned me ! Love me then, Haidée ! Who knows ? perhaps your love will make me forget all I wish not to remember."

" What do you mean, my lord ? "

" I mean that one word from you has enlightened me more than twenty years of slow experience ; I have but you in the world, Haidée ; through you I again connect myself with life, through you I shall suffer, through you rejoice."

" Do you hear him, Valentine ? " exclaimed Haidée ; " he says that through me he will suffer,—through *me*, who would yield my life for his."

The count withdrew for a moment. " Have I discovered the truth ? " he said ; " but whether it be for recompense or punishment, I accept my fate. Come, Haidée, come ! " and throwing his arm round the young girl's waist, he pressed the hand of Valentine and disappeared.

An hour had nearly passed, during which Valentine, breathless and motionless, watched steadfastly over Morrel. At length she felt his heart beat, a faint breath played upon his lips, a slight shudder, announcing the return of life, passed the young man's frame. At length his eyes opened, but they were at first fixed and expressionless ; then sight returned, and with it feeling and grief. " Oh ! " he cried, in an accent of despair, " the count has deceived me ; I am yet living," and extending his hand towards the table, he seized a knife.

" Dearest ! " exclaimed Valentine, with her adorable smile, " awake ! " Morrel uttered a loud exclamation and, dazzled as though by a celestial vision, fell upon his knees.

* * * * *

The next morning, at daybreak, Valentine and Morrel were

walking arm-in-arm on the sea-shore, Valentine relating how
Monte Cristo had appeared in her room ; how he had unveiled
everything ; how he had revealed the crime ; and, finally, how
he had saved her life by allowing her to seem dead. They had
found the door of the grotto opened, and went forth, the few remaining stars yet pressing through the morning light. Morrel
soon perceived a man standing amidst the group of rocks, who was
awaiting a sign from them to advance ; he pointed him out to
Valentine. " Ah, it is Jacopo," she said, " the captain of the
yacht ; " and she beckoned him towards them.

" Do you wish to speak to us ? " asked Morrel.

" I have a letter to give you from the count."

" From the count ! " murmured the two young people.

" Yes ; read it." Morrel opened the letter and read :—

" My dear Maximilian,

" There is a felucca for you at anchor. Jacopo will conduct
you to Leghorn, where M. Noirtier waits his granddaughter,
whom he wishes to bless before you lead her to the altar. All
that is in this grotto, my friend, my house in the Champs Élysées,
and my château at Tréport, are the marriage gifts bestowed by
Edmond Dantès upon the son of his old master, Morrel. Mademoiselle de Villefort will share them with you ; for I entreat her
to give to the poor the immense fortune reverting to her from her
father, now a madman, and her brother, who died last September,
with his mother. Tell the angel who will watch over your future
destiny, Morrel, to pray sometimes for a man, who like Satan,
thought himself for an instant, equal to God ; but who now
acknowledges, with Christian humility, that God alone possesses
supreme power and infinite wisdom. Perhaps those prayers may
soften the remorse he feels in his heart. As for you, Morrel, this
is the secret of my conduct towards you. There is neither happiness nor misery in the world ; there is only the comparison of one
state with another ; nothing more. He who has felt the deepest
grief is best able to experience supreme happiness. We must
have felt what it is to die, Morrel, that we may appreciate the
enjoyments of life.

" Live then, and be happy, beloved children of my heart ! and
never forget, that until the day when God will deign to reveal the
future to man, human wisdom is contained in these two words,—
' Wait and hope.'

" Your friend,
" EDMOND DANTÈS,
" Count of Monte Cristo."

During the perusal of this letter, which informed Valentine, for the first time, of the madness of her father and the death of her brother, she became pale, a heavy sigh escaped from her bosom, and tears, not the less painful because they were silent, ran down her cheeks ; her happiness cost her very dear.

Morrel looked round uneasily. " But," he said, " the count's generosity is too overwhelming ; Valentine will be satisfied with my humble fortune. Where is the count, friend ? Lead me to him." Jacopo pointed towards the horizon.

" What do you mean," asked Valentine. " Where is the count? —where is Haidée ? "—

" Look ! " said Jacopo.

The eyes of both were fixed upon the spot indicated by the sailor, and on the blue line separating the sky from the Mediterranean Sea, they perceived a large white sail.

" Gone ! " said Morrel : " Gone !—Adieu, my friend !—adieu, my father ! "

" Gone ! " murmured Valentine : " Adieu, my friend !—adieu, my sister ! "

" Who can say whether we shall ever see them again ? " said Morrel, with tearful eyes.

" My friend," replied Valentine, " has not the count just told us that all human wisdom is contained in these two words,— *Wait and hope ?* "

THE END.